P.D. JAMES

THREE COMPLETE NOVELS

P.D. JAMES

THREE COMPLETE NOVELS

Featuring Adam Dalgliesh of Scotland Yard

Cover Her Face

A Mind To Murder

Shroud For A Nightingale

AVENEL BOOKS
NEW YORK

This 1987 edition is published by Avenel Books, distributed by
Crown Publishers, Inc., 225 Park Avenue South, New York, New York 10003,
by arrangement with Scribner Book Company, Inc.

Manufactured in the United States of America

Library of Congress Cataloging-in-Publication Data
James, P. D.
Three Complete Novels
Contents: Cover her face—A mind to murder—
Shroud for a nightingale.
1. Dalgliesh, Adam (Fictitious character)—Fiction.
2. Detective and mystery stories, English. I. Title.
PR6060.A467A6 1987 823′.914 87-11566
ISBN 0-517-64111-9

h g f e d c b

INTRODUCTION

I HAVE a particular fondness for the three mystery novels included in this, my first, omnibus edition. *Cover Her Face* because it was my first novel and I retain for it that peculiarly defensive pride one has for a firstborn; *A Mind to Murder* because it proved to me that I wasn't a one-book writer (and none of us can be sure of this until the success of a second book); and *Shroud for a Nightingale* because, with this novel, I broke into a major world market. All of the stories feature my poet-detective Adam Dalgliesh of New Scotland Yard. In *Cover Her Face* he made his debut in a somewhat orthodox setting, the English country house. By *Shroud for a Nightingale* he and I were well established in that ambiguous and complicated partnership which exists between the writer and a continuing creation. He has reached the rank of commander, a rank, incidentally, which has nothing to do with the navy but is peculiar to the Metropolitan Police; there are no commanders in provincial forces. He has, therefore, risen high in his profession. How far he has developed as a human being is not perhaps for me to judge, but these three novels may give some early clues. I like him as a man. No writer, I suspect, continues to write about a character he or she despises or finds irritating. But I am not sure whether I would wish to serve under him. Dalgliesh is a complex human being, a hunter down of murderers who is also a poet. With his critical intelligence, essential self-sufficiency, his sensitivity, and low tolerance of fools, he could, I suspect, be an uncomfortable colleague. And I am quite sure that, were I a murderer, he is the last man I would wish to have allocated to my case.

And what about his private life, my readers frequently ask? Will he marry again, and, if so, will it be to Cordelia Gray, the young girl detective whose path so briefly crossed his in *An Unsuitable Job for a Woman*? Since how a character develops is largely outside his creator's understanding and may be outside her control, I confess myself at present as much in the dark on that point as are my readers. Dalgliesh is a man who likes women, including making love to them, but whether after the death of his wife and baby son he can ever again commit himself to a lasting relationship is, I think, highly doubtful. And in relation to this part of his life I rather incline to the view enshrined in English law that what consenting adults do in private is their own concern.

However much a fictional detective, once created, may go his own way, sometimes in spite of his author, a mystery writer embarking on a first book is faced with a number of important decisions. Is the detective to be male or female, young or old, married or single, a character in one novel or one on whom a series could be based, an amateur or a professional policeman? I suspect that, in the golden age of the thirties, the last question answered itself, particularly in England with our, some may think, exaggerated respect for amateurism. Here Sherlock Holmes set the pattern for a succession of amateur gentlemen sleuths of whom Lord Peter Wimsey is, perhaps, the second most notable example—independent, eccentric, brilliant, omniscient, in egregious contrast to the poorly paid, plodding, unimaginative and deferential police. Today the mystery novelist is more likely to choose, as I did, a professional police hero. This may have something to do with the search for greater social realism and the sophistication of modern readers who know that only a professional is likely to come constantly into contact with the crime of murder or have the authority, legal powers, and technical resources to solve it. There are, of course, a number of interesting new amateurs in the field and one should always be wary of making pronouncements about the future trend of mystery fiction, that most resilient and adaptable form of crime writing. But it does look as if the day of the brilliant and romanticized amateur sleuth is over, or at least as if the high noon of his popularity and success has finally passed. Increasingly the mystery novel is rooted in the realities of human existence, dealing perceptively with such universal absolutes as life and death, love and hate, treachery and failure, in which psychological truth is no longer sacrificed to the demands of the plot and the detection itself is closer to the realities, the ardors, the frustrations and the disappointments of real-life criminal investigation.

The old conventions may still be retained. There will be a violent death; a limited circle of suspects all with motives, means, and opportunity; false clues; and a tenable ending with a solution to the mystery which both author and reader hope will be a satisfying consummation of suspense and excitement but which the reader could himself arrive at by a process of logical deduction from revealed facts with the aid of no more luck or intuition than it is reasonable to permit to the detective himself.

There are problems as well as advantages in choosing a professional police hero. He may have all the technical resources of the force behind him, including a forensic pathology and forensic science service at his command and lowly detective constables and slightly less lowly detective sergeants to do the more boring investigation. But he has to work within the constraints of law and police powers and procedures, including in England the Judges' Rules which govern the way in which suspects can be questioned. But Adam Dalgliesh is, above all, a professional detective and I confess to a sense of satisfaction when senior police officers of my acquaintance acknowledge him to be a "good copper," even if a little too intellectual for their taste.

One of the most common questions any crime writer is asked is why did you choose to write mystery fiction? In my case it was because I had always enjoyed reading mysteries (Dorothy L. Sayers was a potent early influence); I thought I might be able to write a mystery rather well; I reasoned that such a popular genre might have the best chance of acceptance by a publisher; and I saw the writing of detective fiction with its challenging disciplines, its inner tensions between plot, character, and atmosphere, and its necessary reliance on structure and form, as the best possible apprenticeship for a serious novelist. Perhaps the chief reason why I am glad to have these three early books reissued in hardcover is that each was a landmark in my own gradual realization that, despite the constraints of this fascinating genre, a mystery writer can hope to call herself a serious novelist.

P. D. James

COVER HER FACE

Cover her face; mine eyes dazzle: she died young.
—The Duchess of Malfi

CHAPTER ONE

¶ 1

Exactly three months before the killing at Martingale Mrs. Maxie gave a dinner party. Years later, when the trial was a half-forgotten scandal and the headlines were yellowing on the newspaper lining of cupboard drawers, Eleanor Maxie looked back on that spring evening as the opening scene of tragedy. Memory, selective and perverse, invested what had been a perfectly ordinary dinner party with an aura of foreboding and unease. It became, in retrospect, a ritual gathering under one roof of victim and suspects, a staged preliminary to murder. In fact not all the suspects had been present. Felix Hearne, for one, was not at Martingale that week-end. Yet, in her memory, he too sat at Mrs. Maxie's table, watching with amused, sardonic eyes the opening antics of the players.

At the time, of course, the party was both ordinary and rather dull. Three of the guests, Dr. Epps, the vicar and Miss Liddell, Warden of St. Mary's Refuge for Girls, had dined together too often to expect either novelty or stimulation from each other's company. Catherine Bowers was unusually silent and Stephen Maxie and his sister, Deborah Riscoe, were obviously concealing with difficulty their irritation that Stephen's first free week-end from the hospital for over a month should have coincided with a dinner party.

Mrs. Maxie had just employed one of Miss Liddell's unmarried mothers as house-parlourmaid and the girl was waiting at table for the first time. But the air of constraint which burdened the meal could hardly have been caused by the occasional presence of Sally Jupp who placed the dishes in front of Mrs. Maxie and removed the plates with a dextrous efficiency which Miss Liddell noted with complacent approval.

It is probable that at least one of the guests was wholly happy. Bernard Hinks, the vicar of Chadfleet, was a bachelor, and any change from the nourishing but unpalatable meals produced by his housekeeping sister—who was never herself tempted away from the vicarage to dine—was a relief which left small room for the niceties of social intercourse. He was a gentle, sweet-faced man who looked older than his fifty-four years and who had a reputation for vagueness and timidity except on points of doctrine. Theology was his main, almost his sole, intellectual interest and if his parishioners could not always understand his sermons they were happy enough to accept this as sure evidence of their vicar's erudition. It was, however, accepted in the village that you could get both advice and help from the vicarage and that, if the former were sometimes a little muddled, the latter could generally be relied upon.

To Dr. Charles Epps the dinner meant a first-class meal, a couple of charming women to talk to and a restful interlude from the trivialities of a country practice. He was a widower who had lived in Chadfleet for thirty years and knew most of his patients well enough to predict with accuracy whether they would live or die. He believed that there was little any doctor could do to influence the decision, that there was wisdom in knowing when to die with the least inconvenience to others and distress to oneself and that much medical progress only prolonged life for a few uncomfortable months to the greater glory of the patient's doctor. For all that, he had less stupidity and more skill than Stephen Maxie gave him credit for and few of his patients faced the inevitable before their time. He had attended Mrs. Maxie at the births of both her children and was doctor and friend to her husband in so far as Simon Maxie's bemused brain could any longer know or appreciate friendship. Now he sat at the Maxie table and forked up chicken *soufflé* with the air of a man who has earned his dinner and has no intention of being infected by other people's moods.

"So you've taken Sally Jupp and her baby, Eleanor?" Dr. Epps was never inhibited from stating the obvious. "Nice young things both of them. Rather jolly for you to have a baby about the house again."

"Let us hope Martha agrees with you," said Mrs. Maxie dryly. "She needs help desperately, of course, but she's very conservative. She may feel the situation more than she says."

"She'll get over it. Moral scruples soon give way when it's a case of another pair of hands at the kitchen sink." Dr. Epps dismissed Martha Bultitaft's conscience with a wave of his podgy arm. "She'll be eating out of the baby's hand before long, anyway. Jimmy's an appealing child whoever his father was."

At this point Miss Liddell felt that the voice of experience should be heard.

"I don't think, Doctor, that we should talk about the problem of these children too lightly. Naturally we must show Christian charity"—here Miss Liddell gave a half bow in the direction of the vicar as if acknowledging the presence of another expert and apologizing for the intrusion into his field—"but I can't help feeling that society as a whole is getting too soft with these girls. The moral standards of the country will continue to fall if these children are to receive more consideration than those born in wedlock. And it's happening already! There's many a poor, respectable mother who doesn't get half the fussing and attention which is lavished on some of these girls."

She looked around the table, flushed and began eating again vigorously. Well, what if they did all look surprised? It had needed saying. It was her place to say it. She glanced at the vicar as if enlisting his support but Mr. Hinks, after his first puzzled glance at her, was concentrating on his dinner. Miss Liddell, baulked of an ally, thought irritably that the dear vicar really was just a little greedy over his food! Suddenly she heard Stephen Maxie speaking.

"These children are no different, surely, than any others except that we owe them more. I can't see that their mothers are so remarkable either. After all, how many people accept in practice the moral code which they despise these girls for breaking?"

"A great many, Dr. Maxie, I assure you." Miss Liddell, by nature of her job, was unaccustomed to opposition from the young. Stephen Maxie might be a rising young surgeon but that didn't make him an expert on delinquent girls. "I should be horrified if I thought that some of the behaviour I have to hear about in my work was really representative of modern youth."

"Well, as a representative of modern youth, you can take it from me that it's not so rare that we can afford to despise the ones who've been found out. This girl we have seems perfectly normal and respectable to me."

"She has a quiet and refined manner. She is quite well-educated too. A grammar-school girl! I should never have dreamed of recommending her to your mother if she weren't a most superior type of girl for St. Mary's. Actually, she's an orphan, brought up by an aunt. But I hope you won't let that play on your pity. Sally's job is to work hard and make the most of this opportunity. The past is over and is best forgotten."

"It must be difficult to forget the past when one has such a tangible memento of it," said Deborah Riscoe.

Dr. Epps, irked by a conversation which was provoking bad temper and, probably, worse digestion, hastened to contribute his placebo. Unfortunately, the result was to prolong the dissension.

"She's a good mother and a pretty girl. Probably she'll meet some chap and get married yet. Best thing too. I can't say I like this unmarried-mother-with-child relationship. They get too wrapped up in each other and sometimes end up in a mess psychologically. I sometimes think—terrible heresy I know, Miss Liddell—that the best thing would be to get these babies adopted into a good home from the start."

"The child is the mother's responsibility," pronounced Miss Liddell. "It is her duty to keep it and care for it."

"For sixteen years and without the help of the father?"

"Naturally we get an affiliation order, Dr. Maxie, whenever that is possible. Unfortunately Sally has been very obstinate and won't tell us the name of the father so we are unable to help."

"A few shillings don't go very far these days." Stephen Maxie seemed perversely determined to keep the subject alive. "And I suppose Sally doesn't even get the government children's allowance."

"This is a Christian country, my dear brother, and the wages of sin are supposed to be death, not eight bob of the taxpayers' money."

Deborah had spoken under her breath but Miss Liddell had heard and felt that she had been intended to hear. Mrs. Maxie apparently felt that the time had come to intervene. At least two of her guests thought that she might well have done so earlier. It was unlike Mrs. Maxie to let anything get out of hand. "As I want to ring for Sally," she said, "perhaps it would be as well if we changed the subject. I'm going to make myself thoroughly unpopular by asking about the church fête. I know it looks as if I've got you all here on false pretences but we really ought to be thinking about the possible dates." This was a subject on which all her guests could be safely voluble. By the time Sally came in the conversation was as dull, amicable and unembarrassing as even Catherine Bowers could wish.

Miss Liddell watched Sally Jupp as she moved about the table. It was as if the conversation at dinner had stimulated her to see the girl clearly for the first time. Sally was very thin. The heavy, red-gold hair piled under her cap seemed too heavy a weight for so slender a neck. Her childish arms were long, the elbows jutting under the reddened skin. Her wide mouth was disciplined now, her green eyes fixed demurely on her task. Suddenly Miss Liddell was visited by an irrational spasm of affection. Sally was really doing very nicely, very nicely indeed! She looked up to catch the girl's eye and to give her a smile of approval and encouragement. Suddenly their eyes met. For a full two seconds they looked at each other. Then Miss Liddell flushed and dropped her eyes. Surely she must have been mistaken! Surely Sally would never dare to look at her like that! Confused and horrified she tried to analyse the extraordinary effect of that brief contact. Even before her own features had assumed their proprietorial mask of commendation she had read in the girl's eyes, not the submissive gratitude which had characterized the Sally Jupp of St. Mary's Refuge, but amused contempt, a hint of conspiracy and a dislike which was almost frightening in its intensity. Then the green eyes had dropped again and Sally the enigma became once more Sally the submissive, the subdued, Miss Liddell's favourite and most favoured delinquent. But the moment left its legacy. Miss Liddell was suddenly sick with apprehension. She had recommended Sally without reserve. It was all, on the face of it, so very satisfactory. The girl was a most superior type. Too good for the job at Martingale really. The decision had been taken. It was too late to doubt its wisdom now. The worst that could happen would be Sally's ignominious return to St. Mary's. Miss Liddell was aware for the first time that the introduction of her favourite to Martingale might produce complications. She could not be expected to foresee the magnitude of those complications nor that they would end in violent death.

Catherine Bowers, who was staying at Martingale for the week-end, had said little during dinner. Being a naturally honest person she was a little horrified to find that her sympathies were with Miss Liddell. Of course, it was very generous and gallant of Stephen to champion Sally and her kind so vigorously, but Catherine felt as irritated as she did when her non-nursing friends talked about the nobility of her profession. It was all right to have romantic ideas but they were small compensation to those who worked among the bedpans or the delinquents. She was tempted to say as much, but the presence of Deborah across the table kept her silent. The dinner, like all unsuccessful social occasions, seemed to last three times its normal length. Catherine thought that never had a family lingered so long over their coffee, never had the men been so dilatory in putting in their appearance. But it was over at last. Miss Liddell had gone back to St. Mary's, hinting that she felt happier if Miss Pollack were not left too long in sole charge. Mr. Hinks murmured about the last touches for tomorrow's sermon and faded like a thin ghost into the spring air. The Maxies and Dr. Epps sat happily enjoying the wood fire in the drawing-room and talking about music. It was not the subject which Catherine would have chosen. Even the television would have been preferable, but the only set at Martingale was in Martha's sitting-room. If there had to be talk Catherine hoped that it would be confined to medicine. Dr. Epps might naturally say, "Of course you're a nurse, Miss Bowers, how nice for Stephen to have someone who shares his interests." Then the three of them would chat away while Deborah sat for a change in ineffectual silence and was made to realize that men do get tired of pretty, useless women, however well dressed, and that what Stephen needed was someone who understood his job, someone who could talk to his friends in a sensible and knowledgeable way. It was a pleasant dream and, like most dreams, it bore no relation to reality. Catherine sat holding her hands to the thin flames of the wood fire and tried to look at ease while the others talked about a composer called, unaccountably, Peter Warlock, of whom she had never heard except in some vague and forgotten historical sense. Certainly Deborah claimed not to understand him but she managed, as usual, to make her ignorance amusing. Her efforts to draw Catherine into the conversation by inquiring about Mrs. Bowers was evidence to Catherine of condescension, not of good manners. It was a relief when the new maid came in with a message for Dr. Epps. One of his patients on an outlying farm had begun her labour. The doctor heaved himself reluctantly out of his chair, shook himself like a shaggy dog and made his apologies. Catherine tried for the last time. "Interesting case, Doctor?" she asked brightly. "Lord no, Miss Bowers." Dr. Epps was looking around vaguely in search of his bag. "Got three already. Pleasant little woman though, and she likes to have me there. God knows why! She could deliver herself without turning a hair. Well, good-bye, Eleanor, and thank you for an excellent dinner.

I meant to go up to Simon before I left but I'll be in tomorrow if I may. You'll be needing a new prescription for the Sommeil I expect. I'll bring it with me." He nodded amiably to the company and shuffled out with Mrs. Maxie into the hall. Soon they could hear his car roaring away down the drive. He was an enthusiastic driver and loved small fast cars from which he could only extricate himself with difficulty, and in which he looked like a wicked old bear out on a spree.

"Well," said Deborah, when the sound of the exhaust had died away, "that's that. Now what about going down to the stables to see Bocock about the horses. That is, if Catherine would like a walk." Catherine was very anxious for a walk but not with Deborah. Really, she thought, it was extraordinary how Deborah couldn't or wouldn't see that she and Stephen wanted to be alone together. But if Stephen didn't make it plain she could hardly do so. The sooner he was married and away from all his female relations the better it would be for him. "They suck his blood" thought Catherine, who had met that type in her excursions into modern fiction. Deborah, happily unconscious of these vampire tendencies, led the way through the open window and across the lawn.

The stables which had once been Maxie stables and were now the property of Mr. Samuel Bocock were only two hundred yards from the house and the other side of the home meadow. Old Bocock was there, polishing harness by the light of a hurricane lamp and whistling through his teeth. He was a small brown man with a gnome-like face, slanting of eye and wide of mouth, whose pleasure at seeing Stephen was apparent. They all went to have a look at the three horses with which Bocock was attempting to establish his little business. "Really," thought Catherine, "it was ridiculous the fuss that Deborah made of them, nuzzling up to their faces with soft endearments as if they were human. Frustrated maternal instinct," she thought disagreeably. "Do her good to expend some of that energy on the children's ward. Not that she would be much use." She herself wished that they could go back to the house. The stable was scrupulously clean but there is no disguising the strong smell of horses after exercise and, for some reason, Catherine found it disturbing. At one time, Stephen's lean brown hand lay close to hers on the animal's neck. The urge to touch that hand, to stroke it, even to raise it to her lips was momentarily so strong that she had to close her eyes. And then, in the darkness, came other remembered pictures, shamefully pleasant, of that same hand half-circled around her breast, even browner against her whiteness, and moving slowly and lovingly, the harbinger of delight. She half-staggered out into the spring twilight and heard behind her the slow, hesitant speech of Bocock and the eager Maxie voices replying together. In that moment she knew again one of those devastating moments of panic which had descended upon her at intervals since she had loved Stephen. They came unheralded and all her common sense and will power were helpless against them. They were moments when everything seemed unreal and she could almost physically feel the sand shifting beneath her hopes. All her misery and uncertainty focused itself on Deborah. It was Deborah who was the enemy. Deborah who had been married, who had at least had her chance of happiness. Deborah who was pretty and selfish and useless. Listening to the voices behind her in the growing darkness Catherine felt sick with hate.

By the time they had returned to Martingale she had pulled herself together again and the black pall had lifted.

She was restored to her normal condition of confidence and assurance. She went early to bed and, in the conviction of her present mood, she could almost believe that he might come to her. She told herself that it would be impossible in his father's house, an act of folly on his part, an intolerable abuse of hospitality on hers. But she waited in the darkness. After a while she heard footsteps on the stairs—his footsteps and Deborah's. Brother and sister were laughing softly together. They did not even pause as they passed her door.

¶ 2

Upstairs in the low white-painted bedroom which had been his since childhood Stephen stretched himself on his bed.

"I'm tired," he said.

"Me too." Deborah yawned and sat down on the bed beside him. "It was rather a grim dinner-party. I wish Mummy wouldn't do it."

"They're all such hypocrites."

"They can't help it. They were brought up that way. Besides, I don't think that Eppy and Mr. Hinks have much wrong with them."

"I suppose I made rather a fool of myself," said Stephen.

"Well, you were rather vehement. Rather like Sir Galahad plunging to the defence of the wronged maiden, except that she was probably more sinning than sinned against."

"You don't like her, do you?" asked Stephen.

"My sweet, I haven't thought about it. She just works here. I know that sounds very reactionary to your enlightened notions but it isn't meant to be. It's just that I'm not interested in her one way or the other, nor she, I imagine, in me."

"I'm sorry for her." There was a trace of truculence in Stephen's voice.

"That was pretty obvious at dinner," said Deborah dryly.

"It was their blasted complacency that got me down. And that Liddell woman. It's ridiculous to put a spinster in charge of a Home like St. Mary's."

"I don't see why. She may be a little limited but she's kind and conscientious. Besides, I should have thought St. Mary's already suffered from a surfeit of sexual experience."

"Oh, for heaven's sake don't be facetious, Deborah!"

"Well, what do you expect me to be? We only see each other once a fortnight. It's a bit hard to be faced with one of Mummy's duty dinner-parties and have to watch Catherine and Miss Liddell sniggering together because they thought you'd lost your head over a pretty maid. That's the kind of vulgarity Liddell would particularly relish. The whole conversation will be over the village by tomorrow."

"If they thought that they must be mad. I've hardly seen the girl. I don't think I've spoken to her yet. The idea is ridiculous!"

"That's what I meant. For heaven's sake, darling, keep your crusading instincts under control while you're at home. I should have thought that you could have sublimated your social conscience at the hospital without bringing it home. It's uncomfortable to live with, especially for those of us who haven't got one."

"I'm a bit on edge today," said Stephen. "I'm not sure I know what to do."

It was typical of Deborah to know at once what he meant.

"She is rather dreary, isn't she? Why don't you close the whole affair gracefully? I'm assuming that there is an affair to close."

"You know damn well that there is—or was. But how?"

"I've never found it particularly difficult. The art lies in making the other person believe that he has done the chucking. After a few weeks I practically believe it myself."

"And if they won't play?"

" 'Men have died and worms have eaten them, but not for love.' "

Stephen would have liked to have asked when and if Felix Hearne would be persuaded that he had done the chucking. He reflected that in this, as in other matters, Deborah had a ruthlessness that he lacked.

"I suppose I'm a coward about these things," he said. "I never find it easy to shake people off, even party bores."

"No," replied his sister. "That's your trouble. Too weak and too susceptible. You ought to get married. Mummy would like it really. Someone with money if you can find her. Not stinking, of course, just beautifully rich."

"No doubt. But who?"

"Who indeed."

Suddenly Deborah seemed to lose interest in the subject. She swung herself up from the bed and went to lean against the window-ledge. Stephen watched her profile, so like his own yet so mysteriously different, outlined against the blackness of the night. The veins and arteries of the dying day were stretched across the horizon. From the garden below he could smell the whole rich infinitely sweet distillation of an English spring night. Lying there in the cool darkness he shut his eyes and gave himself up to the peace of Martingale. At moments like this he understood perfectly why his mother and Deborah schemed and planned to preserve his inheritance. He was the first Maxie to study medicine. He had done what he wanted and the family had accepted it. He might have chosen something even less lucrative although it was difficult to imagine what. In time, if he survived the grind, the hazards, the rat race of competition, he might become a consultant. He might even become sufficiently successful to support Martingale himself. In the meantime they would struggle on as best they could, making little housekeeping economies that would never intrude on his own comfort, cutting down the donations to charity, doing more of the gardening to save old Purvis's three shillings an hour, employing untrained girls to help Martha. None of it would inconvenience him very much, and it was all to ensure that he, Stephen Maxie, succeeded his father as Simon Maxie had succeeded his. If only he could have enjoyed Martingale for its beauty and its peace without being chained to it by this band of responsibility and guilt!

There was the sound of slow careful footsteps on the stairs and then a knock on the door. It was Martha with the nightly hot drinks. Back in his childhood old Nannie had decided that a hot milk drink last thing at night would help to banish the terrifying and inexplicable nightmares from which, for a brief period, he and Deborah had suffered. The nightmares had yielded in time to the more tangible fears of adolescence, but the hot drinks had become a family habit. Martha, like her sister before her, was convinced that they were the only effective talisman against the real or imagined dangers of the night. Now she set down her small tray cautiously. There was the blue Wedgwood mug that Deborah used and the old George V coronation mug which Grandfather Maxie had bought for Stephen. "I've brought your Ovaltine too, Miss Deborah," Martha said. "I thought I should find you here." She spoke in a low voice as if they shared a conspiracy. Stephen wondered whether she guessed that they had been discussing Catherine. This was rather like the old comfortable Nannie bringing in the night drinks and ready to stay and talk. But yet not really the same. The devotion of Martha was more voluble, more self-conscious and less acceptable. It was a counterfeit of an emotion that had been as simple and necessary to him as the air he breathed. Remembering this he thought also that Martha needed her occasional sop.

"That was a lovely dinner, Martha," he said.

Deborah had turned from the window and was wrapping her thin, red-nailed hands around the steaming mug.

"It's a pity the conversation wasn't worthy of the food. We had a lecture from Miss Liddell on the social consequences of illegitimacy. What do you think of Sally, Martha?"

Stephen knew that it was an unwise question. It was unlike Deborah to ask it.

"She seems quiet enough," Martha conceded, "but, of course, it is early days yet. Miss Liddell spoke very highly of her."

"According to Miss Liddell," said Deborah, "Sally is a model of all the virtues except one, and even that was a slip on the part of nature who couldn't recognize a high-school girl in the dark."

Stephen was shocked by the sudden bitterness in his sister's voice.

"I don't know that all this education is a good thing for a maid, Miss Deborah." Martha managed to convey that she had managed perfectly well without it. "I only hope that she knows how lucky she is. Madam has even lent her our cot, the one you both slept in."

"Well, we aren't sleeping in it now." Stephen tried to keep the irritation out of his voice. Surely there had been enough talk about Sally Jupp! But Martha was not to be cautioned. It was as if she personally and not merely the family cradle had been desecrated. "We've always looked after that cot, Dr. Stephen. It was to be kept for the grandchildren."

"Damn!" said Deborah. She wiped the spilt drink from her fingers and replaced the mug on the tray. "You shouldn't count your grandchildren before they're hatched. You can count me as a non-starter and Stephen isn't even engaged—nor thinking of it. He'll probably eventually settle for a buxom and efficient nurse who'll prefer to buy a new hygienic cot of her own from Oxford Street. Thank you for the drink, Martha dear." Despite the smile, it was a dismissal.

The last "good nights" were said and the same careful footsteps descended the stairs. When they had died away Stephen said, "Poor old Martha. We do rather take her for granted and this maid-of-all-work job is getting too much for her. I suppose we ought to be thinking of pensioning her off."

"On what?" Deborah stood again at the window.

"At least there's some help for her now," Stephen temporized.

"Provided Sally isn't more trouble than she is worth. Miss Liddell made out that the baby is extraordinarily good. But any baby's considered that who doesn't bawl for two nights out of three. And then there's the washing. Sally can hardly be much help to Martha if she has to spend half the morning rinsing out nappies."

"Presumably other mothers wash nappies," said Stephen, "and still find time for other work. I like this girl and I think she can be a help to Martha if only she's given a fair chance."

"At least she had a very vigorous champion in you,

Stephen. It's a pity you'll almost certainly be safely away at hospital when the trouble starts."

"What trouble, for God's sake? What's the matter with you all? Why on earth should you assume that the girl's going to make trouble?"

Deborah walked over to the door. "Because", she said, "she's making trouble already, isn't she? Good night."

CHAPTER TWO

¶ 1

Despite this inauspicious beginning Sally Jupp's first weeks at Martingale were a success. Whether she herself shared this view was not known. No one asked for her opinion. She had been pronounced by the whole village to be a very lucky girl. If, as so often happens with the recipients of favours, she was less grateful than she ought to be, she managed to conceal her feelings behind a front of meekness, respectfulness and willingness to learn, which most people were happy enough to take at its face value. It did not deceive Martha Bultitaft and it is probable that it would not have deceived the Maxies if they had bothered to think about it. But they were too preoccupied with their individual concerns and too relieved at the sudden lightening of the domestic load to meet trouble half-way.

Martha had to admit that the baby was at first very little trouble. She put this down to Miss Liddell's excellent training since it was beyond her comprehension that bad girls could be good mothers. James was a placid child who, for his first two months at Martingale, was content to be fed at his accustomed times without advertising his hunger too loudly and who slept between his feeds in milky contentment. This could not last indefinitely. With the advent of what Sally called "mixed feeding" Martha added several substantial grievances to her list. It seemed that the kitchen was never to be free of Sally and her demands. Jimmy was fast entering that stage of childhood in which meals become less a pleasant necessity than an opportunity for the exercise of power. Carefully pillowed in his high chair he would arch his sturdy back in an orgasm of resistance, bubbling milk and cereal through his pursed lips in ecstatic rejection before suddenly capitulating into charming and submissive innocence. Sally screamed with laughter at him, caught him to her in a whirl of endearments, loved and fondled him in contemptuous disregard of Martha's muttered disapproval. Sitting there with his tight curled mop of hair, his high beaked little nose almost hidden between plump cheeks as red and hard as apples, he seemed to dominate Martha's kitchen like a throned and imperious miniature Caesar. Sally was beginning to spend more time with her child and Martha would often see her during the mornings, her bright head bent over the pram where the sudden emergence of a chubby leg or arm showed that Jimmy's long periods of sleep were a thing of the past. No doubt his demands would increase. So far Sally had managed to keep up with the work allotted to her and to reconcile the demands of her son with those of Martha. If the strain was beginning to show, only Stephen on his fortnightly visits home noticed it with any compunction. Mrs. Maxie inquired of Sally at intervals whether she was finding the work too much and was glad to be satisfied with the reply she received. Deborah did not notice, or if she did, said nothing. It was, in any case, difficult to know whether Sally was overtired. Her naturally pale face under its shock of hair and her slim brittle-looking arms gave her an air of fragility which Martha, for one, thought highly deceiving. "Tough as a nut and cunning as a wagon-load of monkeys" was Martha's opinion.

Spring ripened slowly into summer. The beech trees burst their spearheads of bright green and spread a chequered pattern of shade over the drive. The vicar celebrated Easter to his own joy and with no more than the usual recriminations and unpleasantness among his flock over the church decorations. Miss Pollack, at St. Mary's Refuge, endured a spell of sleeplessness for which Dr. Epps prescribed special tablets, and two of the Home's inmates settled for marriage with the unprepossessing but apparently repentant fathers of their babies. Miss Liddell admitted two more peccant mothers in their place. Sam Bocock advertised his stables in Chadfleet New Town and was surprised at the number of youths and girls who, in new, ill-fitting jodhpurs and bright yellow gloves, were prepared to pay 7s. 6d. an hour to amble through the village under his tutelage. Simon Maxie lay in his narrow bed and was neither better nor worse. The evenings lengthened and the roses came. The garden at Martingale was heavy with their scent. As Deborah cut them for the house she had a feeling that the garden and Martingale, itself, were waiting for something. The house was always at its most beautiful in summer, but this year she sensed an atmosphere of expectancy, almost of foreboding, which was alien to its usual cool serenity. Carrying the roses into the house, Deborah shook herself out of this morbid fancy with the wry reflection that the most ominous event now hanging over Martingale was the annual church fête. When the words "waiting for a death" came suddenly into her mind she told herself firmly that her father was no worse, might even be considered a little better, and that the house could not possibly know. She recognized that her love for Martingale was not entirely rational. Sometimes she tried to discipline that love by talking of the time "when we have to sell" as if the very sound of the words could act both as a warning and a talisman.

St. Cedd's church fête had taken place in the grounds of Martingale every July since the days of Stephen's great-grandfather. It was organized by the fête committee, which consisted of the vicar, Mrs. Maxie, Dr. Epps and Miss Liddell. Their administrative duties were never arduous since the fête, like the church it helped to support, continued virtually unchanging from year to year, a symbol of immutability in the midst of chaos. But the committee took their responsibilities seriously and met frequently at Martingale during June and early July to drink tea in the garden and to pass resolutions which they passed the year before in identical words and in the same agreeable surroundings. The only member of the committee who occasionally felt genuinely uneasy about the fête was the vicar. In his gentle way he preferred to see the best in everyone and to impute worthy motives wherever possible. He included himself in this dispensation, having discovered early in his ministry that charity is a policy as well as a virtue. But once a year Mr. Hinks faced certain unpalatable facts about his church. He worried about its exclusiveness, its negative impact on the seething fringe of Chadfleet New Town, the suspicion that it was more of a social than a spiritual force in the village life. Once he had suggested that the fête should close as well as open with a prayer and a hymn, but the only committee member to support this startling innovation was Mrs. Maxie, whose chief quarrel with the fête was that it never seemed to end.

This year Mrs. Maxie felt that she was going to be glad of Sally's willing help. There were plenty of workers for the actual fête, even if some of them were out to extract the maximum of personal enjoyment with the minimum of work, but the responsibilities did not end with the successful organization of the day. Most of the committee would expect to be asked to dinner at Martingale and Catherine Bowers had written to say that the Saturday of the fête was one of her off-duty days and would it be too much of an imposition if she invited herself for what she described as "one of your perfect week-ends away from the noise and grime of this dreadful city". This letter was not the first of its kind. Catherine was always so much more anxious to see the children than the children were to see Catherine. In some circumstances that would be just as well. It would be an unsuitable match for Stephen in every way, much as poor Katie would like to see her only child eligibly married off. She herself had married, as they said, beneath her. Christian Bowers had been an artist with more talent than money and no pretensions to anything except genius. Mrs. Maxie had met him once and had disliked him but, unlike his wife, she did believe him to be an artist. She had bought one of his early canvases for Martingale, a reclining nude which now hung in her bedroom and gave her a satisfied joy which no amount of intermittent hospitality to his daughter could adequately repay. To Mrs. Maxie it was an object-lesson in the folly of an unwise marriage. But because the pleasure it gave her was still fresh and real, and because she had once been at school with Katie Bowers and placed some importance on the obligations of old and sentimental associations, she felt that Catherine should be welcome at Martingale as her own guest, if not as her children's.

There were other things that were slightly worrying. Mrs. Maxie did not believe in taking too much notice of what other people sometimes describe as "atmosphere". She retained her serenity by coping with shattering common sense with those difficulties which were too obvious to ignore and by ignoring the others.

But things were happening at Martingale which were

difficult to overlook. Some of them were to be expected, of course. Mrs. Maxie, for all her insensitivity, could not but realize that Martha and Sally were hardly compatible kitchen mates, and that Martha would be bound to find the situation difficult for a time. What she had not expected was that it should become progressively more difficult as the weeks wore on. After a succession of untrained and uneducated housemaids, who had come to Martingale because domesticity offered their only chance of employment, Sally seemed a paragon of intelligence, capability and refinement. Orders could be given in the confident assurance that they would be carried out where, before, even constant and painstaking reiteration had only resulted in the eventual realization that it was easier to do the job oneself.

An almost pre-war feeling of leisure would have returned to Martingale if it had not been for the heavier nursing which Simon Maxie now needed. Dr. Epps was already warning that they could not go on for long. Soon now it would be necessary to install a resident nurse or to move the patient to hospital. Mrs. Maxie rejected both alternatives. The former would be expensive, inconvenient and possibly indefinitely prolonged. The latter would mean that Simon Maxie would die in the hands of strangers instead of in his own house. The family could not afford a nursing home or a private ward. It would mean a bed in the local hospital for chronic cases, barrack-like, overcrowded and understaffed. Before this final stage of his illness had fallen upon him, Simon Maxie had whispered to her, "You won't let them take me away, Eleanor?" and she had replied, "Of course I won't." He had fallen asleep then, secure in a promise which both of them knew was no light assurance. It was a pity that Martha had apparently so short a memory for the overwork which had preceded

Sally's arrival. The new régime had given her time and energy to criticize what she had at first found surprisingly easy to accept. But so far she had not come into the open. There had been the veiled innuendoes but no definite complaint. Undoubtedly tension must be building up in the kitchen, thought Mrs. Maxie, and after the fête it would probably have to be coped with. But she was in no hurry; the fête was only a week away and the chief consideration was to get it successfully over.

¶ 2

On the Thursday preceding the fête Deborah spent the morning shopping in London, lunched with Felix Hearne at his club and went with him to see a Hitchcock revival at a Baker Street cinema in the afternoon. This agreeable programme was completed with afternoon tea at a Mayfair restaurant which holds unfashionable views on what constitutes an adequate afternoon meal. Replete with cucumber sandwiches and home-made chocolate éclairs Deborah reflected that the afternoon had really been very successful, even if a little low-brow for Felix's taste. But he had borne up under it well. There were advantages in not being lovers. If they had been having a love affair it would have seemed necessary to spend the afternoon together in his Greenwich house since the opportunity offered and an irregular union imposes conventions as rigid and compelling as those of marriage. And while the love-making would no doubt have been pleasant enough the easy undemanding companionship which they had enjoyed was more to her taste.

She did not want to fall in love again. Months of annihilating misery and despair had cured her of that particular folly. She had married young and Edward Riscoe had died of poliomyelitis less than a year later. But a marriage based on companionship, compatible tastes and the satisfactory exchange of sexual pleasure seemed to her a reasonable basis for life and one which could be achieved without too much disturbing emotion. Felix, she suspected, was enough in love with her to be interesting without being boring and she was only spasmodically tempted to consider seriously the expected offer of marriage. It was, nevertheless, beginning to be slightly odd that the offer was not made. It was not, she knew, that he disliked women. Certainly most of their friends considered him to be a natural bachelor, eccentric, slightly pedantic and perennially amusing. They might have been unkinder, but there was the inescapable fact of his war record to be explained away. A man cannot be either effeminate or a fool who holds both French and British decorations for his part in the Resistance Movement. He was one of those whose physical courage, that most respected and most glamorous of virtues, had been tried in the punishment cells of the Gestapo and could never again be challenged. It was less fashionable now to think of those things but they were not yet quite forgotten. What those months in France had done to Felix Hearne was anyone's guess, but he was allowed his eccentricities and presumably he enjoyed them. Deborah liked him because he was intelligent and amusing and the most diverting gossip she knew. He had a woman's interest in the small change of life and an intuitive concern for the minutiae of human relationships. Nothing was too trivial for him and he sat now listening with every appearance of amused sympathy to Deborah's report on Martingale.

"So you see, it's bliss to have some free time again, but I really can't see it lasting. Martha will have her out in time. And I don't really blame her. She doesn't like Sally and neither do I."

"Why? Is she chasing Stephen?"

"Don't be vulgar, Felix. You might give me the benefit of a more subtle reason than that. Actually, though, she does seem to have impressed him and I think it's deliberate. She asks his advice about the baby whenever he's at home, although I have tried to point out that he's supposed to be a surgeon not a paediatrician. And poor old Martha can't breathe a word of criticism without his rushing to Sally's defence. You'll see for yourself when you come on Saturday."

"Who else will be there apart from this intriguing Sally Jupp?"

"Stephen, of course. And Catherine Bowers. You met her the last time you were at Martingale."

"So I did. Rather poached-egg eyes but an agreeable figure and more intelligence than you or Stephen were willing to allow her."

"If she impressed you so much," retorted Deborah easily, "you can demonstrate your admiration this week-end and give Stephen a respite. He was rather taken with her once and now she sticks to him like a limpet and it bores him horribly."

"How incredibly ruthless pretty women are to plain ones! And by 'rather taken with her' I suppose you mean that Stephen seduced her. Well, that usually does lead to complications and he must find his own way out as better men have done before him. But I shall come. I love Martingale and I appreciate good cooking. Besides, I have a feeling that the week-end will be interesting. A house full of people all disliking each other is bound to be explosive."

"Oh, it isn't as bad as that!"

"Very nearly. Stephen dislikes me. He has never bothered

to hide it. You dislike Catherine Bowers. She dislikes you and will probably extend the emotion to me. Martha and you dislike Sally Jupp and she, poor girl, probably loathes you all. And that pathetic creature, Miss Liddell, will be there, and your mother dislikes her. It will be a perfect orgy of suppressed emotion."

"You needn't come. In fact, I think it would be better if you didn't."

"But, Deborah, your mother has already asked me and I've accepted. I wrote to her last week in my nice formal way, and I shall now make a note in my little black book to settle it beyond doubt." He bent his sleek fair head over his engagement diary. His face, with the pale skin which made the hair-line almost indistinguishable was turned away from her. She noticed how sparse were the eyebrows against that pallid forehead and the intricate folds and crinkles around his eyes. Deborah thought that he must once have had beautiful hands before the Gestapo played about with them. The nails had never fully grown again. She tried to picture those hands moving about the intricacies of a gun, curled into the cords of a parachute, clenched in defiance or endurance. But it was no good. There seemed no point of contact between that Felix who had apparently once known a cause worth suffering for and the facile, sophisticated, sardonic Felix Hearne of Hearne and Illingworth, publishers, just as there was none between the girl who had married Edward Riscoe and the woman she was today. Suddenly Deborah felt again the familiar *malaise* of nostalgia and regret. In this mood she watched Felix writing under Saturday's date in his cramped meticulous hand as if he were making a date with death.

¶ 3

After tea Deborah decided to visit Stephen, partly to avoid the rush-hour crowds but chiefly because she seldom came up to London without calling at St. Luke's Hospital. She invited Felix to accompany her but he excused himself on the grounds that the smell of disinfectant made him sick, and sent her off in a taxi with formal expressions of thanks for her company. He was punctilious about these matters. Deborah fought against the unflattering suspicion that he had tired of her conversation and was relieved to see her borne away in comfort and with speed, and concentrated on the pleasure of seeing Stephen. It was all the more disconcerting to find that he was not in the hospital. It was unusual too. Colley, the hall porter, explained that Mr. Maxie had had a telephone call and had gone out to meet someone saying that he wouldn't be long. Mr. Donwell was on duty for him. But Mr. Maxie would certainly not be long now. He had been gone nearly an hour. Perhaps Mrs. Riscoe would like to go up to the residents' sitting-room? Deborah stayed for a few minutes' chat with Colley whom she liked and then took the lift to the fourth floor. Mr. Donwell, a shy and spotty young registrar mumbled a greeting and made a speedy escape to the wards leaving Deborah in sole possession of four grubby armchairs, an untidy heap of medical periodicals and the half-cleared remnants of the residents' tea. It appeared that they had had Swiss roll again and, as usual, someone had used his saucer as an ash-tray. Deborah began to pile up the plates, but, realizing that this was a somewhat pointless activity since she did not know what to do with them, she took up one of the papers and moved to the window where she could divide her interest between waiting for Stephen and scanning the more intriguing or comprehensible of the medical articles. The window gave a view of the main hospital entrance farther along the street. In the distance she could discern the shining curve of the river and the towers of Westminster. The ceaseless rumbling of traffic was muted, an unobtrusive background to the occasional noises of the hospital, the clang of the lift gates, the ringing of telephone bells, the passing of brisk feet along the corridor. An old woman was being helped into an ambulance at the front door. From a height of four floors the figures below seemed curiously foreshortened. The ambulance door was shut without a sound and it slid away noiselessly. Suddenly she saw them. It was Stephen she noticed first, but the flaming red-gold head almost level with his shoulder was unmistakable. They paused at the corner of the building. They seemed to be talking. The black head was bent towards the gold. After a moment she saw him shake hands and then Sally turned in a flash of sunlight and walked swiftly away without a backward glance. Deborah missed nothing. Sally was wearing her grey suit. It was mass-produced and bought off the peg, but it fitted well and was a foil for the shining cascade of hair, released now from the restraint of cap and pins.

She was clever, thought Deborah. Clever to know that you had to dress simply if you wanted to wear your hair loose like that. Clever to avoid the greens for which most redheads had a predilection. Clever to have said "goodbye" outside the hospital and to have resisted the certain invitation to a hospital supper with its inevitable openings for embarrassment or regret. Afterwards Deborah was surprised that she should have noticed so keenly what Sally was wearing. It was as if she saw her for the first time through Stephen's eyes, and seeing her was afraid. It seemed a long time before she heard the drone of the lift and his quick footsteps along the corridor. Then he was by her side. She did not move away from the window so that he should know at once she had seen. She felt that she could not bear it if he did not tell her and it was easier that way. She did not know what she expected but when he spoke it was a surprise.

"Have you seen these before?" he asked.

In his outstretched palm was a rough bag made from a man's handkerchief tied together at the corners. He lifted one of the knots, gave a little jerk, and spilled out three or four of the tiny tablets. Their grey-brown colour was unmistakable.

"Aren't they some of Father's tablets?" It seemed as if he were accusing her of something. "Where did you get them?"

"Sally found them and brought them up to me. I expect you saw us from the window."

"What did she do with the baby?" The silly irrelevant question was out before she had time to think.

"The baby? Oh, Jimmy, I don't know. Sally left him with someone in the village I suppose or with Mother or Martha. She came up to bring me these and 'phoned from Liverpool Street to ask me to meet her. She found them in Father's bed."

"But how, in his bed?"

"Between the mattress cover and the mattress. Down the side. His draw-sheet was ruckled and she was smoothing it and pulling the macintosh tight when she noticed a little bulge in the corner of the mattress underneath the fitted cover. She found this. Father must have been saving them over several weeks, perhaps months. I can guess why."

"Does he know she found them?"

"Sally doesn't think so. He was lying on his side with his face away from her as she attended to the draw-sheet. She just put the handkerchief and the tablets in her pocket and went on as if nothing had happened. Of course they may have been there for a long time—he's been on Sommeil for eighteen months or more—and he may have forgotten about them. He may have lost the power to get at them and use them. We can't tell what goes on in his mind. The trouble is that we haven't bothered even to try. Except Sally."

"But Stephen, that isn't true. We do try. We sit with him and nurse him and try to make him feel that we're there. But he just lies, not moving, not speaking, not even seeming to notice people any more. He isn't really Father. There isn't any contact between us. I have tried, I swear I have, but it isn't any use. He can't really have meant to take those tablets. I can't think how he even managed to collect them, to plan it all."

"When it's your turn to give him his tablets, do you watch him while he swallows them?"

"No, not really. You know how he used to hate us to help him too much. Now I don't think he minds, but we still give him the tablets and then pour out the water and hold it up to his lips if he seems to want it. He must have secreted these away months ago. I can't believe he could manage it now, not without Martha knowing. She does most of the lifting and the heavier nursing."

"Well, apparently he managed to deceive Martha. But, by God, Deborah, I ought to have guessed, ought to have known. I call myself a doctor. This is the kind of thing which makes me feel like a specialized carpenter, good enough to carve patients up as long as I'm not expected to bother with them as people. At least Sally treated him as a human being."

Deborah was momentarily tempted to point out that she, her mother and Martha were at least managing to keep Simon Maxie comfortable, clean and fed at no small cost and that it was difficult to see where Sally had done more. But if Stephen wanted to indulge in remorse there was little to be gained by stopping him. He usually felt better afterwards, even if other people felt worse. She watched in silence as he rummaged about in the drawer of the desk, found a small bottle which had apparently once held aspirin, carefully counted the tablets—there were ten of them—into the bottle and labelled it with the name of the drug and the dose. They were the almost automatic actions of a man trained to keep medicines properly labelled. Deborah's mind was busy with questions she dared not ask. "Why did Sally come to you? Why not Mother? Did she really find those tablets or was it just a convenient ruse to see you alone? But she must have found them. No one could make up a story like that. Poor Father. What has Sally been saying? Why should I mind so much about this, about Sally? I hate her because she has a child and I haven't. Now I've said it, but admitting it doesn't make it any easier. That handkerchief bag. It must have taken him hours to tie it together. It looked like something made by a child. Poor Father. He was so tall when I was a child. Was I really rather afraid of him? Oh God, please help me to feel pity. I want to be sorry for him. What is Sally thinking now? What did Stephen say to her?"

He turned back from the desk and held out the bottle.

"I think you had better take this home. Put it in the medicine cupboard in his room. Don't say anything to Mother yet or to Dr. Epps. I think it would be wiser if we stopped the tablets for Father. I'll get you a prescription made up in the dispensary before you leave, the same kind of drug only in solution. Give him a tablespoonful at night in water. I should see to it yourself. Just tell Martha that I have stopped the tablets. When does Dr. Epps see him again?"

"He's coming in to see Mother with Miss Liddell after dinner. I suppose he may go up then. But I don't expect he'll ask about the tablets. They've been going on for so long now. We just say when the bottle is getting empty and he gives us a fresh prescription."

"Do you know how many tablets there are in the house now?"

"There's a new bottle with the seal unbroken. We were to start it tonight."

"Then leave it in the cupboard and give him the medicine. I shall be able to talk to Eppy about it when I see him on Saturday. I'll get down late tomorrow night. You had better come with me to the dispensary now and it would be wiser to get home straight away. I'll telephone Martha and ask her to keep you some dinner."

"Yes, Stephen." Deborah did not regret the loss of her meal. All the pleasure of the day had evaporated. It was time to be going home.

"And I would rather you said nothing to Sally about this."

"I hadn't the slightest intention of doing so. I only hope she's capable of a similar discretion. We don't want this story all over the village."

"That's an unfair thing to say, Deborah, and you don't even believe it. You couldn't have anyone safer than Sally. She was very sensible about it. And rather sweet."

"I'm sure she was."

"She was naturally worried about it. She's very devoted to Father."

"She seems to be extending her devotion to you."

"What on earth do you mean?"

"I was wondering why she didn't tell Mother about the tablets. Or me."

"You haven't done much to encourage her to confide in you, have you?"

"What on earth do you expect me to do? Hold her hand? I'm not particularly interested in her as long as she does her work efficiently. I don't like her and I don't expect her to like me."

"It's not true that you don't like her," said Stephen. "You hate her."

"Did she complain of the way she's been treated?"

"Of course she didn't. Do be sensible, Deb. This isn't like you."

"Isn't it," thought Deborah. "How do you know what's like me?" But she recognized in Stephen's last words a plea for peace and she held out her hand to him, saying, "I'm sorry. I don't know what's wrong with me lately. I'm sure Sally did what she thought best. It isn't worth quarrelling about anyway. Do you want me to wait up for you tomorrow night? Felix won't be able to get down until Saturday morning, but Catherine is expected for dinner."

"Don't bother. I may have to get the last bus. But I'll ride with you before breakfast if you like to call me."

The significance of this formal offer in place of the previously happily established routine did not escape Deborah. The chasm between them had only been precariously bridged. She felt that Stephen, too, was uneasily aware of the cracking ice beneath their feet. Never since the death of Edward Riscoe had she felt so alienated from Stephen; never since then had she been so in need of him.

¶ 4

It was nearly half past seven before Martha heard the sound she had been listening for, the squeak of pram wheels on the drive. Jimmy was whining softly and was obviously only persuaded from open bawling by the soothing motion of the pram and the soft reassurances of his mother. Soon Sally's head was seen to pass the kitchen window, the pram was wheeled into the scullery and, almost immediately, mother and child appeared through the kitchen door. There was an air of suppressed emotion about the girl. She seemed at once nervous and yet pleased with herself. Martha did not think that an afternoon wheeling Jimmy in the forest could altogether account for that look of secretive and triumphant pleasure.

"You're late," she said. "I should think the child is starving, poor mite."

"Well, he won't have to wait much longer, will you my pet? I suppose there isn't any milk boiled?"

"I'm not here to wait on you, Sally, please remember. If you want milk you must boil it yourself. You know well enough what time the child should be fed."

They did not speak again while Sally boiled the milk and tried, rather ineffectually, to cool it quickly whilst holding Jimmy on one arm. It was not until Sally was ready to take her child upstairs that Martha spoke.

"Sally," she said, "did you take anything from the master's bed when you made it this morning? Anything belonging to him? I want the truth now!"

"It's obvious from your tone that you know I did. Do you mean that you know that he had those tablets hidden? And you said nothing about them?"

"Of course I knew. I've looked after him now for five years haven't I? Who else would know what he does, what he's feeling? I suppose you thought he'd take them. Well, that needn't worry you. What business is it of yours anyway? If you had to lie there, year after year, perhaps you might like to know that you had something, a few little tablets maybe, that would end all the pain and the tiredness. Something that nobody else knew about, until a silly little bitch, no better than she should be, came ferreting them out. Very clever, weren't you? But he wouldn't have taken them! He's a gentleman. You wouldn't understand that either. But you can give me back those tablets. And if you mention a word of this to anyone or lay a hand on anything else belonging to the master, I'll have you out. You and that brat. I'll find a way, never fear!"

She held out her hand towards Sally. Never once had she raised her voice but her calm authority was more frightening than anger and the girl's voice was tinged with hysteria as she replied.

"I'm afraid you're unlucky. I haven't got the tablets. I took them to Stephen this afternoon. Yes, Stephen! And now I've heard your silly twaddle I'm glad I did. I'd like to see Stephen's face if I told him that you knew all the time! Dear, faithful old Martha! So devoted to the family! You don't care a damn for any of them, you old hypocrite, except for your precious master! Pity you can't see yourself! Washing him, stroking his face, cooing to him as if he were your baby. I could laugh sometimes if it weren't so pitiful. It's indecent! Lucky for him he's half gaga! Being mauled about by you would make any normal man sick!"

She swung the child on to her hip and Martha heard the door close behind her.

Martha lurched over to the sink and clutched it with shaking hands. She was seized with a physical revulsion that made her retch but her body found no relief in sickness. She put a hand to her forehead in a stock gesture of despair. Looking at her fingers she saw that they were wet with perspiration. As she fought for control the echo of that high, childish voice beat in her brain. "Being mauled about by you would make any normal man sick . . . being mauled about by you . . . mauled about." When her body stopped its shaking, nausea gave way to hate. Her mind solaced its misery with the sweet images of revenge. She indulged in phantasies of Sally disgraced, Sally and her child banished from Martingale, Sally found out for what she was, lying, wicked and evil. And, since all things are possible, Sally dead.

CHAPTER THREE

¶ I

The fickle summer weather which, for the last few weeks, had provided a sample of every climatic condition known to the country with the sole exception of snow, now settled into the warm grey normality for the time of the year. There was a chance that the fête would be held in dry weather if not in sun. Deborah, pulling on her jodhpurs for her morning ride with Stephen, could see the red and white marquee from her window, and scattered around the lawn, the skeletons of a dozen half-erected stalls awaiting their final embellishment of crêpe paper and Union Jacks. Away in the home field a course had already been ringed for the children's sports and the dancing display. An ancient car surmounted by a loudspeaker was parked under one of the elms at the end of the lawn and several lengths of wire coiled on the paths and slung between the trees bore witness to the efforts of the local wireless enthusiasts to provide a loudspeaker system for the music and the announcements. Deborah, after a good night's rest, was able to survey these preparations with stoicism. She knew from experience that a very different sight would meet her eyes by the time the fête was over. However careful people were—and many of them only began to enjoy themselves when they were surrounded by a familiar litter of cigarette packets and fruit peelings—it was at least a week's work before the garden lost its look of ravaged beauty. Already the rows of bunting stretched from side to side of the green walks gave the spinney an air of incongruous frivolity and the rooks seemed shocked into noisier than usual recriminations.

In Catherine's favourite day-dream of the Martingale fête she spent the afternoon helping Stephen with the horses, the centre of an interested, deferential and speculating group of the Chadfleet villagers. Catherine had picturesque if outdated notions of the place and importance of the Maxies in their community. This happy imagining faded in face of Mrs. Maxie's determination that both her guests should help where they were most needed. For Catherine this was plainly to be with Deborah on the white elephant stall. When the first disappointment had subsided it was surprising how pleasant the experience proved. The morning was spent in sorting, examining and pricing the miscellaneous hoard that had still to be dealt with. Deborah had an amazing knowledge, born of long experience, of the source of most of her wares, what each article was worth and who was likely to buy it. Sir Reynold Price had contributed a large shaggy coat with a detachable waterproof lining which was immediately placed on one side for the private consideration of Dr. Epps. It was just the thing he needed for winter visiting in his open car and, after all, no one noticed what you wore when you were driving. There was an old felt hat which belonged to the doctor himself and which his daily help tried to get rid of every year only to have it bought back by its irate owner. It was marked sixpence and prominently displayed. There were hand-knitted jumpers of startling style and hue, small objects in brass and china from the village mantelpieces, bundles of books and magazines and a fascinating collection of prints in heavy frames, appropriately named in spidery copperplate. There were "The First Love Letter", "Daddy's Darling", an ornate twin pair called "The Quarrel" and "Reconciliation" and several showing soldiers either kissing their wives farewell or enjoying the chaster pleasures of reunion. Deborah prophesied that the customers would love them and declared that the frames alone were worth half a crown.

By one o'clock the preparations were complete and the household had time for a hurried luncheon waited on by Sally. Catherine remembered that there had been some trouble that morning with Martha because the girl had overslept. Apparently she had had to rush to make up the lost time for she looked flushed and was, Catherine thought, concealing some excitement behind an outward air of docile efficiency. But the meal passed happily enough since the company was at present united in a common preoccupation and a shared activity. By two o'clock the bishop and his wife had arrived, the committee came out of the drawing-room windows to arrange themselves a little self-consciously on the circle of waiting chairs and the fête was formally opened. Although the bishop was old and retired he was not senile and his short speech was a model of simplicity and grace. As the lovely old voice came to her across the lawn, Catherine thought of the church for the first time with interest and affection. Here was the Norman font where she and Stephen would stand at the christening of their children. In these aisles were commemorated his ancestors. Here the kneeling figures of a sixteenth-century Stephen Maxie and Deborah, his wife, faced each other for ever petrified in stone, their thin hands curved in prayer. Here were the secular and ornate busts of the eighteenth-century Maxies and the plain tablets which told briefly of sons killed in Gallipoli and on the Marne. Catherine had often thought that it was as well the family obsequies had become progressively less extravagant since the Church of St. Cedd with St. Mary the Virgin, Chadfleet, was already less a public place of worship than a private repository for Maxie bones. But today, in a mood of confidence and exultation, she could think of all the family, dead and alive, without criticism and even a baroque reredos and Corinthian would have seemed no more than their due.

Deborah took her place with Catherine behind their stall and the customers began to approach and search warily for bargains. It was certainly one of the most popular attractions and business was brisk. Dr. Epps came early for his hat and was easily persuaded to buy Sir Reynold's coat for £1. The clothes and shoes were snapped up, usually by the very people Deborah had foretold would want them, and Catherine was kept busy handing out change and replenishing the stall from the large box of reinforcements which they kept under the counter. At the gate of the drive little groups of people continued to come in throughout the afternoon, the children's faces stretched into fixed unnatural smiles for the benefit of a photographer who had promised a prize for the "Happiest Looking Child" to enter the garden during the afternoon. The loudspeaker exceeded everyone's wildest hopes and poured forth a medley of Sousa marches and Strauss waltzes, announcements about teas and competitions, and occasional admonitions to use the rubbish baskets and keep the garden tidy. Miss Liddell and Miss Pollack, helped by the plainest, oldest and most reliable of their delinquent girls, bustled from St. Mary's to the fête and back again at the call of a conscience or duty. Their stall was by far the most expensive and the hand-made underclothes display suffered from an unhappy compromise between prettiness and respectability. The vicar, his soft white hair damped by exertion, beamed happily upon his flock, who were for once at peace with the world and each other. Sir Reynold arrived late, voluble, patronizing and generous. From the tea lawn came the sound of earnest admonitions as Mrs. Cope and Mrs. Nelson, with the help of the boys' class from the Sunday school, busied themselves with bridge tables, chairs from the village hall, and assorted table-cloths which would all have to find their eventual way back to their owners. Felix Hearne seemed to be enjoying himself as a free-lance. He did appear once or twice to help Deborah or Catherine but announced that he was having a much better time with Miss Liddell and Miss Pollack. Once Stephen came to inquire after business. For someone who habitually referred to the fête as "The Curse of the Maxies", he seemed happy enough. Soon after four o'clock Deborah went into the house to see if her father needed attention and Catherine was left in charge. Deborah returned after half an hour or so and suggested that they might go in search of tea. It was being served in the larger of the two tents and late arrivals, Deborah warned, were usually faced with a weak beverage and the less attractive cakes. Felix Hearne, who had stopped at the stall to chat and pass judgment on the remaining merchandise, was commandeered to take their places and Deborah and Catherine went into the house to wash. One or two people were usually found passing through the hall either because they thought it would be a short cut or because they were strangers to the village and thought their entrance fee included a free tour of the house. Deborah seemed unconcerned. "There's Bob Gittings, our local P.C., keeping an eye on things in the drawing-room," she pointed out. "And the dining-room's locked. This always happens. No one's ever taken anything yet. We'll go in the south door now and use the small bathroom. It'll be quicker." All the same it was disconcerting for them both when a man brushed past them on the back stairs with a hasty apology. They stopped and Deborah called after him. "Were you looking for someone? This is a private house." He turned and looked back at them, a nervous, lean man with greying hair swept back from a high forehead and a thin mouth which he drew back into a propitiatory smile. "Oh, I'm sorry. I didn't realize. Please excuse me. I was looking for the toilet." It was not an attractive voice. "If you mean the lavatory," said Deborah shortly, "there's one in the garden. It seemed adequately sign-posted to me." He flushed and mumbled some reply and then was gone. Deborah shrugged her shoulders. "What a scared rabbit! I don't suppose he was doing any harm. But I wish they'd keep out of the house." Catherine made a mental resolve that when she was mistress of Martingale arrangements would be made to see that they did.

The tea-tent was certainly crowded and the confused clatter of crockery, the babble of voices and the hissing of the tea-urn were heard against a background of the broadcast music which came muted through the canvas. The tables had been decorated by the Sunday school children as part of their competition for the best arrangements of wild flowers. Each table bore its labelled jam jar and the harvest of poppy, campion, sorrel and dog-rose, revived from the hours of clutching in hot hands, had a delicate and unselfconscious beauty, although the scent of the flowers was lost in the strong smell of trampled grass, hot canvas and food. The concentration of noise was so great that a sudden break in the clatter of voices seemed to Catherine as if a total silence had fallen. Only afterwards did she realize that not everybody had stopped talking, that not every head was turned to where Sally had come into the tent by the opposite entrance, Sally in a white dress with a low boat-shaped neckline and a skirt of swirling pleats, identical with the one Deborah was wearing, Sally with a green cummerbund which was a replica of the one round Deborah's waist, and with green ear-rings gleaming on each side of flushed cheeks. Catherine felt her own cheeks redden and could not help her quick inquiring glance at Deborah. She was not the only one. Faces were turning towards them from more and more of the tables. From the far end of the tent where some of Miss Liddell's girls were enjoying an early tea under Miss Pollack's supervision, there was a quickly suppressed giggling. Someone said softly, but not softly enough, "Good old Sal". Only Deborah appeared unconcerned. Without a second glance at Sally she walked up to the counter of trestle tables and asked equably for tea for two, a plate of bread and butter and one of cakes. Mrs. Pardy splashed tea from the urn into the cups with embarrassed haste, and Catherine followed Deborah to one of the vacant tables, clutching the plate of cakes and unhappily aware that she was the one who looked a fool.

"How dare she?" she muttered, bending her hot face over the cup. "It's a deliberate insult." Deborah gave a slight shrug of her shoulders. "Oh, I don't know. What does it matter? Presumably the poor little devil is getting a kick out of her gesture and it isn't hurting me."

"Where did she get the dress from?"

"The same place as I did, I imagine. The name's inside. It isn't a model or anything like that. Anyone could buy it who took the trouble to find it. Sally must have thought it worth the trouble."

"She couldn't have known you were going to wear it today."

"Any other occasion would have done as well, I expect. Must you go on about it?"

"I can't think why you take it so calmly. I wouldn't."

"What do you expect me to do? Go and tear it off her? There's a limit to the free entertainment the village can expect."

"I wonder what Stephen will say," said Catherine. Deborah looked surprised. "I doubt whether he will even notice, except to think how well it suits her. It's more her dress than mine. Are those cakes all right for you or would you rather forage for sandwiches?" Catherine, baulked of further discussion, went on with her tea.

¶ 2

The afternoon wore on. After the scene in the tea-tent the fun had gone out of the fête for Catherine and the rest of the jumble sale was little more than a laborious chore. They were sold out before five as Deborah had predicted, and Catherine was free to offer her help with the pony rides. She arrived in the home field to see Stephen lift Jimmy, screaming with delight, into the saddle in front of his mother. The sun, mellowing now at the ending of the day, shone through the child's hair and turned it into fire. Sally's shining hair swung forward as she leaned down to whisper to Stephen. Catherine heard his answering laugh. It was a moment of time that she was never to forget. She turned back to the lawns and tried to recapture some of the confidence and happiness with which she had started the day. But it was of no use. After wandering about in desultory search for something to occupy her mind, she decided to go up to her room and lie down before dinner. She did not see Mrs. Maxie or Martha on her way through the house. Presumably they were busy either with Simon Maxie or with preparations for the cold meal which was to end the day. Through her window she did see that Dr. Epps was still dozing beside his darts and treasure hunt, although the busiest part of the afternoon was over. The winners of the competitions would soon be announced, rewarded and acclaimed and a thin but steady stream of people was already passing out of the grounds to the bus terminus.

Apart from that moment in the home field Catherine had not seen Sally again, and when she had washed and changed and was on the way to the dining-room she met Martha on the stairs and heard from her that Sally and Jimmy were not yet in. The dining-room table had been set with cold meats, salads and bowls of fresh fruit, and all the party except Stephen were gathered there. Dr. Epps, voluble and cheerful as ever, was busying himself with the cider bottles. Felix Hearne was setting out the glasses. Miss Liddell was helping Deborah to finish laying the table. Her little squeals of dismay when she could not find what she wanted and her ineffectual jabbings at the table napkins were symptomatic of more than normal unease. Mrs. Maxie stood with her back to the others, looking into the glass above the chimneypiece. When she turned, Catherine was shocked by the lines and weariness of her face.

"Isn't Stephen with you?" she asked.

"No. I haven't seen him since he was with the horses. I've been in my room."

"He probably walked home with Bocock to help with the stabling. Or perhaps he's changing. I don't think we'll wait."

"Where's Sally?" asked Deborah.

"Not in apparently. Martha tells me that Jimmy is in his cot so she must have come in and gone out again." Mrs.

Maxie spoke calmly. If this was a domestic crisis she evidently regarded it as a comparatively minor one which warranted no further comment in front of her guests. Felix Hearne glanced at her and felt a familiar tingle of anticipation and foreboding which startled him. It seemed so extravagant a reaction for so ordinary an occasion. Looking across to Catherine Bowers he had a feeling that she shared his unease. The whole party was a little jaded. Except for Miss Liddell's inconsequential and maddening chatter they had little to say. There was the sense of anticlimax which follows most long-planned social functions. The affair was over and yet too much with them to permit relaxation. The bright sun of the day had given way to heaviness. There was no breeze now and the heat was greater than ever.

When Sally appeared at the door they turned to face her as if stung by a common urgency. She leaned back against the linen-fold panelling, the white pleats of her dress fanned out against its sombre darkness like a pigeon's wing. In this strange and stormy light her hair burned against the wood. Her face was very pale but she was smiling. Stephen was at her side.

Mrs. Maxie was aware of a curious moment in which each person present seemed separately aware of Sally and in which they yet moved quietly together as if tensed to face a common challenge. In an effort to restore normality she spoke casually. "I'm glad you're in, Stephen. Sally, you had better change back into your uniform and help Martha."

The girl's self-contained little smile cracked into laughter. It took her a second to gain sufficient control to reply in a voice which was almost obsequious in its derisive respectfulness.

"Would that be appropriate, madam, for the girl your son has asked to marry him?"

¶ 3

Simon Maxie had a night which was no worse and no better than any other. It is doubtful whether anyone else beneath his roof was as fortunate. His wife kept her vigil on the day bed in his dressing-room and heard the hours strike while the luminous hand on the clock beside her bed jerked forward towards the inevitable day. She lived through the scene in the drawing-room so many times that there now seemed no second of it which was not remembered with clarity, no nuance of voice or emotion which was lost. She could recall every word of Miss Liddell's hysterical attack, the spate of vicious and half-demented abuse which had provoked Sally's retort.

"Don't talk about what you've done for me. What have you ever cared about me, you sex-starved old hypocrite? Be thankful that I know how to keep my mouth shut. There are some things I could tell the village about you."

She had gone after that and the party had been left to enjoy their dinner with as much appetite as they could muster or simulate. Miss Liddell had made little effort. Once Mrs. Maxie noticed a tear on her cheek and she was touched with the thought that Miss Liddell was genuinely suffering, had cared to the limit of her capacity for Sally and had honestly taken pleasure in her progress and happiness. Dr. Epps had champed through his meal in an unwonted silence, a sure sign that jaw and mind were together exercised. Stephen had not followed Sally from the room but had taken his seat by his sister. In reply to his mother's quiet "Is this true, Stephen?" he had replied simply, "Of course". He had made no further mention of it and brother and sister had sat through the meal together, eating little but presenting a united front to Miss Liddell's distress and Felix Hearne's ironic glances. He, thought Mrs. Maxie, was the only member of the party who had enjoyed his dinner. She was not sure that the preliminaries had not sharpened his appetite. She knew that he had never liked Stephen and this engagement, if persisted in, was likely to afford him amusement as well as increasing his chances with Deborah. No one could suppose that Deborah would remain at Martingale once Stephen had married. Mrs. Maxie found that she could remember with uncomfortable vividness Catherine's bent face, flushed unbecomingly with grief or resentment and the calm way in which Felix Hearne had roused her to make at least a decent effort at concealment. He could be very amusing when he cared to exert himself and last night he had exerted himself to the full. Surprisingly, he had succeeded in producing laughter by the end of the meal. Was that really only seven hours ago?

The minutes ticked away sounding unnaturally loud in the quietness. It had rained heavily earlier in the night but had now stopped. At five o'clock she thought she heard her husband stirring and went to him, but he still lay in that rigid stupor which they called sleep. Stephen had changed his sleeping-drug. He had been given medicine instead of the usual tablet but the result appeared much the same. She went back to bed but not to sleep. At six o'clock she got up and put on her dressing-gown, then she filled and plugged in the electric kettle for her morning tea. The day with its problems had come at last.

It was a relief to her when there was a knock on the door and Catherine slipped in, still in her pyjamas and dressing-gown. Mrs. Maxie had a moment of acute fear that

Catherine had come to talk, that the affairs of the previous evening would have to be discussed, assessed, deprecated and re-lived. She had spent most of the night making plans that she could not share nor would wish to share with Catherine. But she found herself unaccountably glad to see another human being. She noticed that the girl looked pale. Obviously someone else had enjoyed little sleep. Catherine confessed that the rain had kept her awake and that she had woken early with a bad headache. She did not get them very often now but, when she did, they were bad. Had Mrs. Maxie any aspirin? She preferred the soluble kind but any would do. Mrs. Maxie reflected that the headache might be an excuse for a confidential chat on the Sally-Stephen situation but a longer look at the girl's heavy eyes decided her that the pain was genuine enough. Catherine was obviously in no state for planning anything. Mrs. Maxie invited her to help herself to the aspirin from the medicine cupboard and put out an extra cup of tea on the tray. Catherine was not the companion she would have chosen, but at least the girl seemed prepared to drink her tea in silence.

They were sitting together in front of the electric fire when Martha arrived, her bearing and tone demonstrating a nice compromise between indignation and anxiety.

"It's Sally, madam," she said. "She's overslept again I suppose. She didn't answer when I called her and, when I tried the door, I found that she's bolted it. I can't get in. I'm sure I don't know what she's playing at, madam." Mrs. Maxie replaced her cup in its saucer and noticed with clinical detachment and a kind of wonder that her hand was not shaking. The imminence of evil took hold of her and she had to pause for a second before she could trust her voice. But when the words came, neither Catherine nor Martha seemed aware of any change in her.

"Have you really knocked hard?" she inquired.

Martha hesitated. Mrs. Maxie knew what that meant. Martha had not chosen to knock very hard. It was suiting her purpose better to let Sally oversleep. Mrs. Maxie, after her broken night, found this pettiness almost too much to bear.

"You had better try again," she said shortly. "Sally had a busy day yesterday as we all did. People don't oversleep without reason."

Catherine opened her mouth as if to make some comment, thought better of it, and bent her head over her tea. Within two minutes Martha was back and, this time, there was no doubt of it. Anxiety had conquered irritation and there was something very like panic in her voice.

"I can't make her hear me. The baby's awake. He's whimpering in there. I can't make Sally hear!"

Mrs. Maxie had no memory of getting to the door of Sally's room. She was so certain, beyond any possible doubt, that the room must be open that she beat and tugged ineffectually at the door for several seconds before her mind accepted the truth. The door was bolted on the inside. The noise of the knocking had thoroughly woken Jimmy and his early morning whimpering was now rising into a crescendo of wailing fear. Mrs. Maxie could hear the rattling of his cot bars and could picture him, cocooned in his woollen sleeping-bag, pulling himself up to scream for his mother. She felt the cold sweat starting on her forehead. It was all she could do to prevent herself from beating in mad panic at the unyielding wood. Martha was moaning now and it was Catherine who laid a comforting and restraining hand on Mrs. Maxie's shoulder.

"Don't worry too much. I'll get your son." "Why doesn't she say 'Stephen'? " thought Mrs. Maxie irrelevantly. "Stephen is my son." In a moment he was with them. The knocking must have aroused him for Catherine could not have fetched him so quickly. Stephen spoke calmly.

"We'll have to get in by the window. The ladder in the outhouse will do. I'll get Hearne." He was gone and the little group of women waited in silence. The moments slowly passed.

"It's bound to take a little time," said Catherine reassuringly. "But they won't be long. I'm sure she's all right. She's probably still asleep."

Deborah gave her a long look. "With all this noise from Jimmy? My guess is that she won't be there. She's gone."

"But why should she?" asked Catherine. "And what about the locked door?"

"Knowing Sally, I presume that she wanted to do it the spectacular way and got out through the window. She seems to have a penchant for making scenes even when she can't be present to enjoy them. Here we are shivering with apprehension while Stephen and Felix lug ladders about, and the whole of the household is disorganized. Very satisfying to her imagination."

"She wouldn't leave the baby," said Catherine suddenly. "No mother would."

"This one apparently has," replied Deborah dryly. But her mother noticed that she made no move to leave the party.

Jimmy's yells had now reached a sustained climax which drowned any sound of the men's activities with the ladder or their entrance through the window. The next sound heard from the room was the quick scraping of the lock. Felix stood in the doorway. At the sight of his face Martha gave a scream, a high-pitched animal squeal of terror. Mrs. Maxie felt rather than heard the thud of her retreating footsteps, but no one followed her. The other women pushed past Felix's restraining arm and moved silently as if under some united compulsion to where Sally lay. The window was open and the pillow of the bed was blodged with rain. Over the pillow Sally's hair was spread like a web of gold. Her eyes were closed but she was not asleep. From the clenched corner of her mouth a thin trickle of blood had dried like a black slash. On each side of her neck was a bruise where her killer's hands had choked the life from her.

CHAPTER FOUR

¶ 1

"Nice-looking place, sir," said Detective-Sergeant Martin as the police car drew up in front of Martingale. "Bit of a change from our last job." He spoke with satisfaction for he was a countryman by birth and inclination and was often heard to complain of the proclivity of murderers to commit their crimes in overcrowded cities and unsalubrious tenements. He sniffed the air appreciatively and blessed whatever reasons of policy or prudence had led the local chief constable to call in the Yard. It had been rumoured that the chief constable personally knew the people concerned and, what with that and the still unsolved business on the fringe of the county, had thought it advisable to hand over this spot of trouble without delay. That suited Detective-Sergeant Martin all right. Work was work wherever you did it, but a man was entitled to his preferences.

Detective Chief-Inspector Adam Dalgleish did not reply but swung himself out of the car and stood back for a moment to look at the house. It was a typical Elizabethan manor house, simple but strongly formalized in design. The large, two-storeyed bays with their mullioned and transomed windows stood symmetrically on each side of the square central porch. Above the dripstone was a heavy carved coat of arms. The roof sloped to a small open stone balustrade also carved with symbols in relief and the six great Tudor chimneys stood up boldly against a summer sky. To the west curved the wall of a room which Dalgleish guessed had been added at a later date—probably during the last century. The french windows were of plated glass and led into the garden. For a moment he saw a face at one of them, but then it turned away. Someone was watching for his arrival. To the west a grey stone wall ran from the corner of the house in a wide sweep towards the gates and lost itself behind the shrubs and the tall beeches. The trees came very close to the house on this side. Above the wall and half-concealed behind a mosaic of leaves he could just see the top of a ladder placed against an oriel window. That presumably was the dead girl's room. Her mistress could hardly have chosen one more suitably placed for an illicit entry. Two vehicles were parked beside the porch, a police car with a uniformed man sitting impassive at the wheel and a mortuary van. Its driver, stretched back in his seat and with his peaked cap tilted forward, took no notice of Dalgleish's arrival while his mate merely looked up perfunctorily before returning to his Sunday newspaper.

The local superintendent was waiting in the hall. They knew each other slightly as was to be expected with two men both eminent in the same job, but neither had ever wished for a closer acquaintanceship. It was not an easy moment. Manning was finding it necessary to explain exactly why his chief had thought it advisable to call in the Yard. Dalgleish replied suitably. Two reporters were sitting just inside the door with the air of dogs who have been promised a bone if they behave and who have resigned themselves to patience. The house was very quiet and smelt faintly of roses. After the torrid heat of the car the air struck so cold that Dalgleish gave an involuntary shiver.

"The family are together in the drawing-room," said Manning. "I've left a sergeant with them. Do you want to see them now?"

"No, I'll see the body first. The living will keep."

Superintendent Manning led the way up the vast square staircase talking back at them as he went.

"I got a bit of ground covered before I knew they were calling in Central Office. They've probably given you the gist. Victim is the maid here. Unmarried mother aged twenty-two. Strangled. The body was discovered at about 7.15 a.m. this morning by the family. The girl's bedroom door was bolted. Exit, and probably entrance too, was via the window. You'll find evidence of that on the stack pipe and the wall. It looks as if he fell the last five feet or so. She was last seen alive at 10.30 p.m. last night carrying her late-night drink up to bed. She never finished it. The mug's on the bedside table. I thought it was almost certainly an outside job at first. They had a fête here yesterday and anyone could have got into the grounds. Into the house, too, for that matter. But there are one or two odd features."

"The drink, for example?" asked Dalgleish.

They had reached the landing now and were passing towards the west wing of the house. Manning looked at him curiously.

"Yes. The cocoa. It may have been doped. There's some stuff missing. Mr. Simon Maxie is an invalid. There's a bottle of sleeping dope missing from his medicine cupboard."

"Any evidence of doping on the body?"

"The police surgeon's with her now. I doubt it though. Looked a straightforward strangling to me. The P.M. will probably have the answer."

"She could have taken the stuff herself," said Dalgleish. "Is there any obvious motive?"

Manning paused.

"There could be. I haven't got any of the details but I've heard gossip."

"Ah. Gossip."

"A Miss Liddell came this morning to take away the girl's child. She was here to dinner last night. Quite a meal it must have been by her account. Apparently Stephen Maxie had proposed to Sally Jupp. You could call that a motive for the family, I suppose."

"In the circumstances I think I could," said Dalgleish.

The bedroom was white-walled and full of light. After the dimness of the hall and corridors bounded with oak linen-fold panelling, this room struck with the artificial brightness of a stage. The corpse was the most unreal of all, a second-rate actress trying unconvincingly to simulate death. Her eyes were almost closed, but her face held that look of faint surprise which he had often noticed on the faces of the dead. Two small and very white front teeth were clenched against the lower lip, giving a rabbit-look to a face which, in life, must, he felt, have been striking, perhaps even beautiful. An aureole of hair flamed over the pillow in incongruous defiance of death. It felt slightly damp to his hand. Almost he wondered that its brightness had not drained away with the life of her body. He stood very still looking down at her. He was never conscious of pity at moments like this and not even of anger, although that might come later and would have to be resisted. He liked to fix the sight of the murdered body firmly in his mind. This had been a habit since his first big case seven years ago when he had looked down at the battered corpse of a Soho prostitute in silent resolution and had thought, "This is it. This is my job."

The photographer had completed his work with the body before the police surgeon began his examination. He was now finishing with shots of the room and the window before packing up his equipment. The print man had likewise finished with Sally and intent on his private world of whorls and composites, was moving with unobtrusive efficiency from door-knob to lock, from cocoa-beaker to chest of drawers, from bed to window-ledge before heaving himself out on the ladder to work on the stack-pipe and on the ladder itself. Dr. Feltman, the police surgeon, balding, rotund and self-consciously cheerful, as if under a perpetual compulsion to demonstrate his professional imperturbability in the face of death, was replacing his instruments in a black case. Dalgleish had met him before and knew him for a first-class doctor who had never learned to appreciate where his job ended and the detective's began. He waited until Dalgleish had turned away from the body before speaking.

"We're ready to take her away now if that's all right by you. It looks simple enough medically speaking. Manual strangulation by a right-handed person standing in front of her. She died quickly, possibly by vagal inhibition. I'll be able to tell you more after the P.M. There's no sign of sexual interference but that doesn't mean that sex wasn't the motive. I imagine there's nothing like finding a dead body on your hands to take away the urge. When you pull him in you'll get the same old story, 'I put my hands round her neck to frighten her and she went all limp'. He got in by the window by the look of it. You might find fingerprints on that stack-pipe but I doubt whether the ground will be much help. It's a kind of courtyard underneath. No nice soft earth with a couple of handy sole marks. Anyway, it rained pretty hard last night which doesn't help matters. Well, I'll go and get the stretcher party if your man here has finished. Nasty business for a Sunday morning."

He went and Dalgleish inspected the room. It was large

and sparsely furnished, but the overall impression it gave was one of sunlight and comfort. He thought that it had probably previously been the family day nursery. The old-fashioned fireplace on the north wall was surrounded by a heavy meshed fireguard behind which an electric fire had been installed. On each side of the fireplace were deep recesses fitted with bookcases and low cupboards. There were two windows. The smaller oriel window against which the ladder stood was on the west wall and looked over the courtyard to the old stables. The larger window ran almost the whole length of the south wall, giving a panoramic view of the lawns and gardens. Here the glass was old and set with occasional medallions. Only the top mullioned windows could be opened.

The cream-painted single bed was set at right-angles to the smaller window and had a chair on one side and a bedside table with a lamp on the other. The child's cot was in the opposite corner half-hidden by a screen. It was the kind of screen which Dalgleish remembered from his own childhood, composed of dozens of coloured pictures and postcards stuck in a pattern and glazed over. There were a rug before the fireplace and a low nursing chair. Against the wall were a plain wardrobe and a chest of drawers.

There was a curious anonymity about the room. It had the intimate fecund atmosphere of almost any nursery compounded of the faint smell of talcum powder, baby-soap and warmly-aired clothes. But the girl herself had impressed little of her personality on her surroundings. There was none of the feminine clutter which he had half expected. Her few personal belongings were carefully arranged but they were uncommunicative. Primarily it was just a child's nursery with a plain bed for his mother. The few books on the shelves were popular works on baby care. The half-dozen magazines were those devoted to the interests of mothers and housewives rather than to the more romanticized and varied concerns of young working-women. He picked one from the shelf and flicked through it. From its pages dropped an envelope bearing a Venezuelan stamp. It was addressed to:

> D. Pullen, Esq.,
> Rose Cottage, Nessingford-road,
> Little Chadfleet, Essex, England.

On the reverse were three dates scribbled in pencil—Wednesday 18th, Monday 23rd, Monday 30th.

Prowling from the bookshelf to the chest of drawers, Dalgleish pulled out each drawer and systematically turned over its contents with practised fingers. They were in perfect order. The top drawer held only baby clothes. Most of them were hand-knitted, all were well washed and cared for. The second was full of the girl's own underclothes, arranged in neat piles. It was the third and bottom drawer which held the surprise.

"What do you make of this?" he called to Martin.

The sergeant moved to his chief's side with a silent swiftness which was disconcerting in one of his build. He lifted one of the garments in his massive fist.

"Hand-made by the look of it, sir. Must have embroidered it herself, I suppose. There's almost a drawer full. It looks like a trousseau to me."

"I think that's what it is all right. And not only clothes too. Table-cloths, hand towels, cushion covers." He turned them over as he spoke. "It's rather a pathetic little dowry, Martin. Months of devoted work pressed away in lavender bags and tissue paper. Poor little devil. Do you suppose this was for the delight of Stephen Maxie? I can hardly picture these coy tray-cloths being used at Martingale."

Martin picked one up and examined it appreciatively.

"She can't have had him in mind when she did this. He only proposed yesterday according to the Super and she must have been working on this for months. My mother used to do this kind of work. You buttonhole round the pattern and then cut out the middle bits. Richelieu or something they call it. Pretty effect it gives—if you like that sort of thing," he added in deference to his Chief's obvious lack of enthusiasm. He ruminated over the embroidery in nostalgic approval before yielding it up for replacement in the drawer.

Dalgleish moved over to the oriel window. The wide window-ledge was about three feet high. It was scattered now with the bright glass fragments of a collection of miniature animals. A penguin lay wingless on its side and a brittle dachshund had snapped in two. One Siamese cat, startingly blue of eye, was the sole survivor among the splintered holocaust.

The two largest and middle sections of the window opened outwards with a latch and the stack-pipe, skirting a similar window about six feet below, ran directly to the paved terrace beneath. It would hardly be a difficult descent for anyone reasonably agile. Even the climb up would be possible. He noticed again how safe from unwanted observation such an entry or exit would be. To his right the great brick wall, half hidden by overhanging beech boughs, curved away towards the drive. Immediately facing the window and about thirty yards away were the old stables with their attractive clock turret. From their open shelter the window could be watched, but from nowhere else. To the left only a small part of the lawn was visible. Someone seemed to have been messing about with it. There was a small patch ringed with cord where the grass had been hacked or cut. Even from the window Dalgleish could see the lifted sods and the rash of brown soil beneath. Superintendent Manning had come up behind him and answered his unspoken question.

"That's Doctor Epps's treasure hunt. He's had it in the same spot for the last twenty years. They had the church fête here yesterday. Most of the bunting's down—the vicar likes to get the place cleared up before Sunday—but it takes a day or two to erase all the evidence."

Dalgleish remembered that the Super was almost a local man. "Were you here?" he asked.

"Not this year. I've been on duty almost continuously for the last week. We've still got that killing on the county border to clear up. It won't be long now, but I've been pretty tied up with it. The wife and I used to come over here once a year for the fête but that was before the war. It was different then. I don't think we'd bother now. They still get a fair crowd though. Someone could have met the girl and found out from her where she slept. It's going to mean a lot of work checking on her movements during yesterday afternoon and evening." His tone implied that he was glad the job was not his.

Dalgleish did not theorize in advance of his facts. But the facts he had garnered so far did not support this comfortable thesis of an unknown casual intruder. There had been no sign of attempted sexual assault, no evidence of theft. He had a very open mind on the question of that bolted door. Admittedly, the Maxie family had all been on the right side of it at 7 a.m. that morning, but they were presumably as capable as anyone else of climbing down stack-pipes or descending ladders.

The body had been taken away, a white-sheeted lumpy shape stiff on the stretcher, destined for the pathologist's knife and the analyst's bottle. Manning had left them to telephone his office. Dalgleish and Martin continued their patient inspection of the house. Next to Sally's room was an old-fashioned bathroom, the deep bath boxed round with mahogany and the whole of one wall covered with an immense airing-cupboard, fitted with slatted shelves. The three remaining walls were papered in an elegant floral design faded with age and there was an old but still unworn fitted carpet on the floor. The room offered no possible hiding-place. From the landing outside a flight of drugget-covered stairs curved down to the panelled corridor which led on the one side to the kitchen quarters and on the other to the main hall. Just at the bottom of these stairs was the heavy south door. It was ajar, and Dalgleish and Martin passed out of the coolness of Martingale into the heavy heat of the day. Somewhere the bells of a church were ringing for Sunday matins. The sound came clearly and sweetly across the trees bringing to Martin a memory of boyhood's country Sundays and to Dalgleish a reminder that there was much to be done and little left of the morning.

"We'll have a look at that old stable block and the west wall beneath her window. After that I'm rather interested in the kitchen. And then we'll get on with the questioning. I've a feeling that the person we're after slept under this roof last night."

¶ 2

In the drawing-room the Maxies with their two guests and Martha Bultitaft waited to be questioned, unobtrusively watched over by a detective-sergeant who had stationed himself in a small chair by the door and who sat in apparently solid indifference, seeming far more at his ease than the owners of the house. His charges had their various reasons for wondering how long they would be kept waiting, but no one liked to reveal anxiety by asking. They had been told that Detective Chief-Inspector Dalgleish from Scotland Yard had arrived and would be with them shortly. How shortly no one was prepared to ask. Felix and Deborah were still in their riding-clothes. The others had dressed hurriedly. All had eaten little and now they sat and waited. Since it would have seemed heartless to read, shocking to play the piano, unwise to talk about the murder and unnatural to talk about anything else, they sat in almost unbroken silence. Felix Hearne and Deborah were together on the sofa but sitting a little apart and occasionally he leaned across to whisper something in her ear. Stephen Maxie had stationed himself at one of the windows and stood with his back to the room. It was a stance which, as Felix Hearne had noticed cynically, enabled him to keep his face hidden and to demonstrate an inarticulate sorrow with the back of his bent head. At least four of the watchers would have liked very much to know whether the sorrow was genuine. Eleanor Maxie sat calmly in a chair apart. She was either numbed by grief or thinking deeply. Her face was very pale but the brief panic which had caught her at Sally's door was over now. Her daughter noticed that she at least had taken trouble in her dressing and was presenting an almost normal appearance to her family and guests. Martha Bultitaft also sat a little apart, ill at ease on the edge of her chair and darting occasional furious looks at the sergeant whom she obviously held responsible for her embarrassment at having to sit with the family and in the drawing-room, too, while there was work to be done. She who had been the most upset and terrified at the morning's discovery now seemed to regard the whole thing as a personal insult, and she sat in sullen resentment. Catherine Bowers gave the greatest appearance of ease. She had taken a small notebook from her handbag and was writing in it at intervals as if refreshing her memory about the events of the morning. No one was deceived by this appearance of normality and efficiency, but they all envied her the opportunity of putting up so good a show. All of them sat in essential isolation and thought their own thoughts. Mrs. Maxie kept her eyes on the strong hands folded in her lap but her mind was on her son.

"He will get over it, the young always do. Thank God Simon will never know. It's going to be difficult to manage the nursing without Sally. One oughtn't to think about that I suppose. Poor child. There may be finger-prints on that lock. The police will have thought of that. Unless he wore gloves. We all know about gloves these days. I wonder how many people got through that window to her. I suppose I ought to have thought of it, but how could I? She had the child with her after all. What will they do with Jimmy? A mother murdered and a father he'll never know now. That was one secret she kept. One of many probably. One never knows people. What do I know about Felix? He could be dangerous. So could this chief inspector. Martha ought to be seeing to luncheon. That is, if anyone wants luncheon. Where will the police feed? Presumably they'll only want to use our rooms today. Nurse will be here at twelve so I'll have to go to Simon then. I suppose I could go now if I asked. Deborah is on edge. We all are. If only we can keep our heads."

Deborah thought "I ought to dislike her less now that she's dead, but I can't. She always did make trouble. She would enjoy watching us like this, sweating on the top line. Perhaps she can. I mustn't get morbid. I wish we could talk about it. We might have kept quiet about Stephen and Sally if Eppy and Miss Liddell hadn't been at dinner. And Catherine of course. There's always Catherine. She's going to enjoy this all right. Felix knows that

Sally was doped. Well, if she was, it was in my drinking mug. Let them make what they like of that."

Felix Hearne thought, "They can't be much longer. The thing is not to lose my temper. These will be English policemen, extremely polite English policemen asking questions in strict compliance with judges' rules. Fear is the devil to hide. I can imagine Dalgleish's face if I decided to explain. Excuse me, Inspector, if I appear to be terrified of you. The reaction is purely automatic, a trick of the nervous system. I have a dislike of formal questioning, and even more of the carefully staged informal session. I had some experience of it in France. I have recovered completely from the effects, you understand, except for this one slight legacy. I tend to lose my temper. It is only pure bloody funk. I am sure you will understand, Herr Inspector. Your questions are so very reasonable. It is unfortunate that I mistrust reasonable questions. We mustn't get this thing out of proportion of course. This is a minor disability. A comparatively small part of one's life is spent in being questioned by the police. I got off lightly. They even left me some of my finger-nails. I'm just trying to explain that I may find it difficult to give you the answers you want."

Stephen turned round.

"What about a lawyer?" he asked suddenly. "Oughtn't we to send for Jephson?"

His mother looked up from a silent contemplation of her folded hands. "Matthew Jephson is motoring somewhere on the Continent. Lionel is in London. We could get him if you feel it to be necessary."

Her voice held a note of interrogation. Deborah said impulsively, "Oh, Mummy! *Not* Lionel Jephson. He's the world's most pompous bore. Let's wait until we're arrested before we encourage him to come beetling down. Besides, he's not a criminal lawyer. He only knows about trusts and affidavits and documents. This would shock his respectable soul to the core. He couldn't help."

"What about you, Hearne?" asked Stephen.

"I'll cope unaided, thank you."

"We should apologize for mixing you up in this," said Stephen with stiff formality. "It's unpleasant for you and may be inconvenient. I don't know when you'll get back to London." Felix thought that this apology should more appropriately be made to Catherine Bowers. Stephen was apparently determined to ignore the girl. Did the arrogant young fool seriously believe that this death was merely a matter of unpleasantness and inconvenience? He looked across at Mrs. Maxie as he replied.

"I shall be very glad to stay—voluntarily or involuntarily—if I can be of use."

Catherine was adding her eager assurances to the same effect when the silent sergeant, galvanized into life, sprang to attention in a single movement. The door opened and three plain-clothes policemen came in. Superintendent Manning they already knew. Briefly he introduced his companions as Detective Chief-Inspector Adam Dalgleish and Detective-Sergeant George Martin. Five pairs of eyes swung simultaneously to the taller stranger in fear, appraisal or frank curiosity.

Catherine Bowers thought. "Tall, dark and handsome. Not what I expected. Quite an interesting face really."

Stephen Maxie thought, "Supercilious-looking devil. He's taken his time coming. I suppose the idea is to soften us up. Or else he's been snooping round the house. This is the end of privacy."

Felix Hearne thought, "Well, here it comes. Adam Dalgleish, I've heard of him. Ruthless, unorthodox, working always against time. I suppose he has his own private compulsions. At least they've thought us adversaries worthy of the best."

Eleanor Maxie thought, "Where have I seen that head before. Of course. That Dürer. In Munich was it? Portrait of an Unknown Man. Why does one always expect police officers to wear bowlers and raincoats."

Through the exchange of introductions and courtesies Deborah Riscoe stared at him as if she saw him through a web of red-gold hair.

When he spoke it was in a curiously deep voice, relaxed and unemphatic.

"I understand from Superintendent Manning that the small business room next door has been placed at my disposal. I hope it won't be necessary to monopolize either it or you for a very long time. I should like to see you separately please and in this order.

"See me in my study at nine, nine-five, nine-ten . . ." whispered Felix to Deborah. He was not sure whether he sought relief for himself or her, but there was no answering smile.

Dalgleish let his glance move briefly over the group. "Mr. Stephen Maxie, Miss Bowers, Mrs. Maxie, Mrs. Riscoe, Mr. Hearne and Mrs. Bultitaft. Will those who are waiting please stay here. If any of you need to leave this room there is a woman police officer and a constable outside in the hall who can go with you. This surveillance will be relaxed as soon as everyone has been interviewed. Would you come with me please, Mr. Maxie?"

¶ 3

Stephen Maxie took the initiative.

"I think I had better begin by letting you know that Miss Jupp and I were engaged to be married. I proposed to her yesterday evening. There's no secret about it. It can't have anything to do with her death and I might not have bothered to mention it except that she broke the news in front of the village's prize gossip, so you'd probably find out fairly soon."

Dalgleish, who had already found out and was by no means convinced that the proposal was nothing to do with the murder, thanked Mr. Maxie gravely for his frankness and expressed formal condolences on the death of his fiancée. The boy looked up at him with a sudden direct glance.

"I don't feel I've any right to accept condolences. I can't even feel bereaved. I suppose I shall when the shock of this has worn off a little. We were only engaged yesterday and now she's dead. It still isn't believable."

"Your mother was aware of this engagement?"

"Yes. All the family were except my father."

"Did Mrs. Maxie approve?"

"Hadn't you better ask her that yourself?"

"Perhaps I had. What were your relations with Miss Jupp before yesterday evening, Dr. Maxie?"

"If you are asking whether we were lovers the answer is 'no'. I was sorry for her, I admired her and I was attracted by her. I have no idea what she thought about me."

"Yet she accepted your offer of marriage?"

"Not specifically. She told my mother and her guests that I had proposed so I naturally assumed that she intended to accept me. Otherwise there would have been no point in breaking the news."

Dalgleish could think of several reasons why the girl should have broken the news, but he was not prepared to discuss them. Instead he invited his witness to give his own account of recent events from the time that the missing Sommeil tablets were first brought into the house.

"So you think she was drugged, Inspector? I told the Superintendent about the tablets when he arrived. They were certainly in my father's medicine chest early this morning. Miss Bowers noticed them when she went to the cupboard for aspirin. They aren't there now. The only Sommeil in the cupboard now is in a sealed packet. The bottle has gone."

"No doubt we shall find it, Dr. Maxie. The autopsy will discover whether or not Miss Jupp was drugged, and if so, how much of the stuff was taken. There is almost certainly something other than cocoa in that mug by the bed. She may, of course, have put the stuff in it herself."

"If she didn't, Inspector, who did? The stuff might not even have been meant for Sally. That was my sister's drinking-mug by the bed. We each have our own and they are all different. If the Sommeil was meant for Sally it must have been put in the drink after she had taken it up to her room."

"If the drinking-mugs are so distinctive it is curious that Miss Jupp should have taken the wrong one. That was an unlikely mistake surely?"

"It may not have been a mistake," said Stephen shortly.

Dalgleish did not ask him to explain but listened in silence as his witness described the visit of Sally to St. Luke's on the previous Thursday, the events of the church fête, the sudden impulse which had led him to propose marriage and the finding of his fiancée's body. The account he gave was factual, concise and almost unemotional. When he came to describe the scene in Sally's bedroom his voice was almost clinically detached. Either he had greater control than was good for him or he had anticipated this interview and had schooled himself in advance against every betrayal of fear or remorse.

"I went with Felix Hearne to get the ladder. He was dressed but I was still in my dressing-gown. I shed one of my bedroom slippers on the way to the outhouses opposite Sally's window so he reached them first and gripped the ladder. It's always kept there. Hearne had dragged it out by the time I caught up with him and was calling out to know which way to carry it. I pointed towards Sally's window. We carried the ladder between us although it's quite light. One person could manage it, although I'm not sure about a woman. We put it against the wall and Hearne went up first while I steadied it. I followed him at once. The window was open but the curtains were drawn across. As you saw, the bed is at right angles to the window with the head towards it. There's a wide window-ledge where the oriel window juts out and Sally apparently kept a collection of small glass animals there. I noticed that they had been scattered and most were broken. Hearne went over to the door and pulled back the lock. I stood looking at Sally. The bed-clothes were pulled up as far as her chin but I could see at once that she was dead. By this time the rest of the family were around the bed, and when I turned back the clothes we could see what had happened. She was lying on her back—we didn't disturb her—and she looked quite peaceful. But you know what she looked like. You saw her."

"I know what I saw," said Dalgleish. "I'm asking now what you saw."

The boy looked at him curiously and then closed his

eyes for a second before replying. He spoke in a flat expressionless voice as if repeating a lesson learnt by rote. "There was a trickle of blood at the corner of her mouth. Her eyes were almost closed. There was a fairly distinct thumb impression under the right lower jaw over the cornu of the thyroid and a less clear indication of fingermarks on the left side of the neck lying along the thyroid cartilage. It was an obvious case of manual strangulation with the right hand and from the front. Considerable force must have been used, but I thought that death was possibly due to vagal inhibition and may have been very sudden. There were few of the classic signs of asphyxia. But no doubt you will get the facts from the autopsy."

"I expect them to be in line with your own views. Did you form any idea of the time of death?"

"There were some rigor mortis in the jaw and neck muscles. I don't know whether it had spread any farther. I'm describing the signs that I noticed almost subconsciously. You will hardly expect a full post-mortem account in the circumstances."

Sergeant Martin, his head bent over his notebook, detected unerringly the first note of near hysteria and thought "Poor devil. The old man can be pretty brutal. He's stood up to it all right so far, though. Too well for a man who has just discovered the body of his girl. If she was his girl."

"I shall get the full post-mortem report in due course," said Dalgleish equably. "I was interested in your assessment of the time of death."

"It was a fairly warm night despite the rain. I should say not less than five hours nor more than eight."

"Did you kill Sally Jupp, Doctor?"

"No."

"Do you know who did?"

"No."

"What were your movements from the time that you finished dinner on Saturday night until Miss Bowers called you this morning with the news that Sally Jupp's door was bolted?"

"We had our coffee in the drawing-room. At about nine o'clock my mother suggested that we should start counting the money. It was in the safe here in the business room. I thought they might be happier without me and I was feeling restless, so I went out for a walk. I told my mother that I might be late and asked her to leave the south door open for me. I hadn't any particular idea in mind, but as soon as I'd left the house I felt I should like to see Sam Bocock. He lives alone in the cottage at the far end of the home meadow. I walked through the garden and over the meadow to his cottage and stayed there with him until pretty late. I can't exactly remember when I left, but he may be able to help. I think it was just after eleven. I walked back alone, entered the house through the south door, bolted it behind me and went to bed. That's all."

"Did you go straight home?"

The almost imperceptible hesitation was not lost on Dalgleish.

"Yes."

"That means you would have been back in the house by when?"

"It's only five minutes' walk from Bocock's cottage, but I didn't hurry. I suppose I was indoors and in bed by eleven-thirty."

"It's a pity that you can't be precise about the time, Dr. Maxie. It's also, surely, surprising in view of the fact that you have a small clock on your bedside table with a luminous dial."

"I may have. That doesn't mean that I always take a note of the times I sleep or get up."

"You spent about two hours with Mr. Bocock. What did you talk about?"

"Horses and music mainly. He has a rather fine record-player. We listened to his new record—Klemperer conducting the *Eroica* to be precise."

"Are you in the habit of visiting Mr. Bocock and spending the evening with him?"

"Habit? Bocock was groom to my grandfather. He's my friend. Don't you visit your friends when you feel like it, Inspector, or haven't you any?"

It was the first flash of temper. Dalgleish's face showed no emotion, not even satisfaction. He pushed a small square of paper across the table. On it were three minute splinters of glass.

"These were found in the outhouse opposite Miss Jupp's room, where you say that the ladder is normally kept. Do you know what they are?"

Stephen Maxie bent forward and studied this exhibit without apparent interest. "They're splinters of glass obviously. I can't tell you any more about them. They could be part of a broken watch-glass I suppose."

"Or part of one of the smashed glass animals from Miss Jupp's room."

"Presumably."

"I see you are wearing a small piece of plaster across your right knuckle. What's wrong?"

"I grazed myself slightly when I was coming home last night. I brushed my hand against the bark of a tree. At least, that's the most probable explanation. I can't remember it happening and only noticed the blood when I got to my room. I stuck this plaster on before I went to bed and I'd normally have taken it off by now. The graze wasn't really worth bothering about, but I have to look after my hands."

"May I see, please?"

Maxie came forward and placed his hand, palm down, on the desk. Dalgleish noted that it did not tremble. He picked at the corner of the plaster and ripped it off. Together they inspected the whitened knuckle underneath. Maxie still showed no sign of anxiety, but scrutinized his hand with the air of a connoisseur condescendingly inspecting an exhibit which was hardly worthy of his attention. He picked up the discarded plaster, folded it neatly and flicked it accurately into the waste-paper basket.

"That looks like a cut to me," said Dalgleish. "Or it could, of course, be a scratch from a finger-nail."

"It could, of course," agreed his suspect easily. "But if it were wouldn't you expect to find blood and skin under the nail which did the scratching? I'm sorry I can't remember how it happened." He looked at it again and added. "It certainly looks like a small cut but it's ridiculously small. In two days it won't be visible. Are you sure you don't want to photograph it?"

"No thank you," said Dalgleish. "We've had something rather more serious to photograph upstairs."

It gave him considerable satisfaction to watch the effect of his words. While he was in charge of this case none of his suspects need think that they could retreat into private worlds of detachment or cynicism from the horror of what had laid on the bed upstairs. He waited for a moment and then continued remorselessly.

"I want to be perfectly clear about this south door. It leads directly to the flight of stairs which go up to the old nursery. To that extent Miss Jupp slept in a part of the house which can be said to have its own entrance. Almost a self-contained flat in effect. Once the kitchen quarters were closed for the night she could let a visitor in through that door with little risk of discovery. If the door were left unbolted a visitor could gain entrance to her door with reasonable ease. Now you say that the south door was left unbolted for you from nine o'clock when you had finished dinner until shortly after 11 p.m. when you returned from Mr. Bocock's cottage. During that time is it true to say that anyone could have gained access to the house through the south door?"

"Yes. I suppose so."

"Surely you know definitely whether they could or not, Mr. Maxie?"

"Yes, they could. As you probably saw, the door has two heavy inside bolts and a mortice lock. We haven't used the lock for years. There are keys somewhere, I suppose. My mother might know. We normally keep the door closed during the day and bolt it at night. In the winter it is usually kept bolted all the time and is hardly used. There is another door into the kitchen quarters. We're rather slack about locking up, but we've never had any trouble here. Even if we did lock the doors carefully the house wouldn't be burglar-proof. Anyone could get in through the french windows in the drawing-room. We do lock them, but the glass could easily be broken. It has never seemed worth while worrying too much about security."

"And, in addition to this ever-open door, there was a convenient ladder in the old stable block?"

Stephen Maxie gave a slight shrug.

"It has to be kept somewhere. We don't lock up the ladders just in case someone gets the idea of using them to get through the windows."

"We have no evidence yet that anyone did. I am still interested in that door. Would you be prepared to swear that it was unbolted when you returned from Mr. Bocock's cottage?"

"Of course. Otherwise I couldn't have got in."

Dalgleish said quickly, "You realize the importance of determining at what time you finally bolted that door?"

"Of course."

"I'm going to ask you once more what time you bolted it and I advise you to think very carefully before you reply."

Stephen Maxie looked at him straight in the eye and said almost casually.

"It was thirty-three minutes past twelve by my watch. I wasn't able to get to sleep and at twelve-thirty I suddenly remembered that I hadn't locked up. So I got out of bed and did so. I didn't see anyone or hear anything and I went straight back to my room. It was no doubt very careless of me, but if there's a law against forgetting to lock up I should like to hear of it."

"So that at twelve-thirty-three you bolted the south door?"

"Yes," replied Stephen Maxie easily. "At thirty-three minutes past midnight."

¶ 4

In Catherine Bowers Dalgleish had a witness after every policeman's heart, composed, painstaking and confident. She had walked in with great self-possession, showing no signs of either nervousness or grief. Dalgleish did not like her. He knew that he was prone to these personal antipathies and he had long ago learned both to conceal and evaluate them. But he was right in supposing her to be an accurate observer. She had been quick to watch people's reactions as she had been to note the sequence of events. It was from Catherine Bowers that Dalgleish learned how shocked the Maxies had been at Sally's announcement, how triumphantly the girl had laughed out her news and what an unusual effect her remarks to Miss Liddell had produced on that lady. Miss Bowers was perfectly prepared, too, to discuss her own feelings.

"Naturally it was a terrible shock when Sally gave us her news, but I can quite see how it happened. No one is kinder than Dr. Maxie. He has too much social conscience as I am always telling him and the girl just took advantage of it. I know he couldn't have loved her really. He never mentioned it to me and he would have told me before anyone. If they had really loved each other he could have relied on me to understand and release him."

"Do you mean that there was an engagement between you?"

Dalgleish had difficulty in keeping the surprise out of his voice. It needed only one more fiancée to make the case fantastic.

"Not exactly an engagement, Inspector. No ring or anything like that. But we have been close friends for so long now that it was rather taken for granted . . . I suppose you might say we had an understanding. But there were no definite plans. Dr. Maxie has a long way to go before he can think of marriage. And there is his father's illness to consider."

"So that you were not, in fact, engaged to be married to him?"

Faced with this uncompromising question Catherine admitted as much, but with a little self-satisfied smile which conveyed that it could only be a matter of time.

"When you arrived at Martingale for this week-end, did anything strike you as unusual?"

"Well, I was rather late on Friday evening. I didn't arrive until just before dinner. Dr. Maxie didn't arrive until late that night and Mr. Hearne only came on Saturday morning, so there were only Mrs. Maxie, Deborah and me at dinner. I thought they seemed worried. I don't like having to say it, but I'm afraid Sally Jupp was a scheming little girl. She waited on us and I didn't like her attitude at all." Dalgleish questioned her further but the "attitude" as far as he could judge consisted of nothing more than a slight toss of the head when Deborah had spoken to her and a neglect to call Mrs. Maxie "Madam". But he did not discount Catherine's evidence as valueless. It was likely that neither Mrs. Maxie nor her daughter had been entirely oblivious to the danger in their midst.

He changed his tack and took her carefully over the events of Sunday morning. She described how she had woken with a headache after a poor night and had gone in search of aspirin. Mrs. Maxie had invited her to help herself. It was then that she had noticed the little bottle of Sommeil. At first she had mistaken the tablets for aspirin but had quickly realized that they were too small and were the wrong colour. Apart from that, the bottle was labelled. She had not noticed how many Sommeil tablets were in the bottle but she was absolutely certain that the bottle was in the drug cupboard at seven o'clock that morning and equally certain that it was no longer there when she and Stephen Maxie had looked for it after the finding of Sally Jupp's body. The only Sommeil in the cupboard then had been an unopened and sealed packet.

Dalgleish asked her to describe the finding of the body and was surprised at the vivid picture which she was able to give.

"When Martha came to tell Mrs. Maxie that Sally hadn't got up we thought at first that she'd just overslept again.

Then Martha came back to say that her door was locked and Jimmy crying so we went to see what was wrong. There's no doubt that the door was bolted. As you know, Dr. Maxie and Mr. Hearne got in through the window and I heard one of them drawing back the bolt. I think it must have been Mr. Hearne because he opened the door. Stephen was standing near the bed looking at Sally. Mr. Hearne said, 'I'm afraid she's dead.' Someone screamed. It was Martha, I think, but I didn't look round to see. I said, 'She can't be! She was all right last night!' We had moved over to the bed then and Stephen had drawn the sheet down from her face. Before that it had been up to her chin and folded quite neatly. I thought that it looked as if someone had tucked her up comfortably for the night. As soon as we saw the marks on her neck we knew what had happened. Mrs. Maxie closed her eyes for a moment. I thought that she was going to faint so I went over to her. But she managed to keep on her feet and stood at the bottom of the bed gripping the rail. She was shaking violently, so much that the whole bed was shaking. It is only a light single bed as you will have seen, and the shaking made the body bounce very gently up and down. Stephen said very loudly, 'Cover her face', but Mr. Hearne reminded him that we had better not touch anything more until the police came. Mr. Hearne was the calmest of us all, I thought, but I suppose that he is used to violent death. He looked more interested than shocked. He bent over Sally and lifted one of her eyelids. Stephen said roughly, 'I shouldn't worry, Hearne. She's dead all right.' Mr. Hearne replied, 'It isn't that. I'm wondering why she didn't struggle.' Then he dipped his little finger into the mug of cocoa on the bedside table. It was just over half full and a skin had formed on the top. The skin stuck to his finger and he scraped it off against the side of the mug before putting the finger in his mouth. We were all looking at him as if he were going to demonstrate something wonderful to us. I thought that Mrs. Maxie looked—well, rather hopeful. Rather like a child at a party. Stephen said, 'Well, what is it?' Mr. Hearne shrugged his shoulders and said, 'That's for the analyst to say. I think she's been doped.' Just then Deborah gave a kind of gasp and fumbled towards the door. She was deathly white and was obviously going to be sick. I tried to get to her, but Mr. Hearne said quite sharply, 'All right. Leave her to me.' He guided her out of the room, and I think they went into the maids' bathroom next door. I wasn't surprised. I would have expected Deborah to break down like that. That left Mrs. Maxie and Stephen in the room with me. I suggested that Mrs. Maxie should find a key so that the room could be locked and she replied, 'Of course. I believe that is usual. And oughtn't we to telephone the police? The extension in the dressing-room would be best.' I suppose she meant that it would be the most private. I remember thinking, 'If we 'phone from the dressing-room the maids won't overhear', forgetting that 'the maids' meant Sally and that Sally wouldn't be overhearing anything again."

"Do you mean that Miss Jupp was in the habit of listening to other people's conversation?" interrupted the inspector.

"I certainly always had that impression, Inspector. But I always thought she was sly. She never seemed the least grateful for all that the family had done for her. She hated Mrs. Riscoe, of course. Anyone could see that. I expect you've been told about the affair of the copied dress?"

Dalgleish expressed himself interested in this intriguing title and was rewarded with a graphic description of the incident and the reactions it had provoked.

"So you can see the type of girl she was. Mrs. Riscoe

pretended to take it calmly, but I could see what she was feeling. She could have killed Sally." Catherine Bowers pulled her skirt down over her knees with complacent mock modesty. She was either a very good actress or she was unconscious of her solecism. Dalgleish continued the questioning with a feeling that he might be facing a more complex personality than he had first recognized.

"Will you tell me please what happened when Mrs. Maxie, her son and you reached the dressing-room?"

"I was just coming to that, Inspector. I had picked up Jimmy from his cot and was still holding him in my arms. It seemed terrible to me that he should have been alone in that room with his dead mother. When we all burst in he stopped crying and I don't think any of us thought about him for a time. Then suddenly I noticed him. He had pulled himself up by the bars of his cot and was balancing there with his wet nappy hanging around his ankles and such an interested look on his face. Of course, he is too young to understand, thank God, and I expect he just wondered what we were all doing round his mother's bed. He had become perfectly quiet and he came to me quite willingly. I carried him with me into the dressing-room. When we got there Dr. Maxie went straight to the medicine cupboard. He said, 'It's gone!' I asked him what he meant and he told me about the missing Sommeil. That was the first time I heard about it. I was able to tell him that the bottle had been there when I went to the cupboard for aspirin that morning. While we were talking Mrs. Maxie had gone through to her husband's room. She was only there for a minute and when she got back she said, 'He's all right. He's sleeping. Have you got the police yet?' Stephen went across to the telephone and I said that I would take Jimmy with me while I dressed and then give him his breakfast. No one replied so I went to the door.

Just before I went out I turned round. Stephen had his hand on the receiver and suddenly his mother placed her hand over his and I heard her say, 'Wait. There's one thing I must know.' Stephen replied, 'You don't have to ask. I know nothing about it. I swear that.' Mrs. Maxie gave a little sigh and put her hand up to her eyes. Then Stephen picked up the receiver and I left the room."

She paused and looked up at Dalgleish as if expecting or inviting his comment. "Thank you," he said gravely, "Please go on."

"There isn't really much more to tell you, Inspector. I took Jimmy to my room, collecting a clean nappy from the small bathroom on my way. Mrs. Riscoe and Mr. Hearne were still there. She had been sick and he was helping to bathe her face. They didn't seem very pleased to see me. I said, 'When you feel better I daresay your mother would like some attention. I'm looking after Jimmy.' Neither of them replied. I found the nappies in the airing cupboard and went to my room and changed Jimmy. Then I let him play on my bed while I dressed. That only took about ten minutes. I took him to the kitchen and gave him a lightly boiled egg with bread and butter fingers and some warm milk. He was perfectly good the whole time. Martha was in the kitchen getting breakfast but we didn't speak. I was surprised to find Mr. Hearne there, too. He was making coffee. I suppose Mrs. Riscoe was with her mother. Mr. Hearne didn't seem inclined to talk either. I suppose he was annoyed with me for saying what I did to Mrs. Riscoe. She can do no wrong in his eyes as you've probably guessed. Well, as they didn't seem inclined to discuss what should be done next I decided to take matters into my own hands and I went into the hall with Jimmy and telephoned Miss Liddell. I told her what had happened and asked her to take back the baby until things had been sorted out. She came round by taxi within about fifteen minutes and, by then, Dr. Epps and the police had arrived. The rest you know."

"That has been a very clear and useful account, Miss Bowers. You have the advantage of being a trained observer, but not all trained observers can present their facts in logical sequence. I won't keep you very much longer. I just want to go back to the earlier part of the night. So far you have described very clearly for me the events of yesterday evening and this morning. What I want to establish now is the sequence of events from ten p.m. onwards. At that time I believe you were still in the business room with Mrs. Maxie, Dr. Epps and Miss Liddell. Could you please go on from there."

For the first time Dalgleish discerned a trace of hesitation in his suspect's response. Until now she had responded to his questioning with a ready fluency which had impressed him as being too spontaneous for guile. He could believe that, so far, Catherine Bowers had not found the interview unpleasant. It was difficult to reconcile such uninhibited outpourings with a guilty conscience. Now, however, he sensed the sudden withdrawal of confidence, the slight tensing to meet an unwelcome change of emphasis. She confirmed that Miss Liddell and Dr. Epps had left the business room to go home at about ten-thirty. Mrs. Maxie had seen them off and had then returned to Catherine. Together they had tidied the papers and locked the money in the safe. Mrs. Maxie had not mentioned seeing Sally. Neither of them had discussed her. After locking away the money they had gone to the kitchen. Martha had retired for the night, but had left a saucepan of milk on the top of the stove and a silver tray of beakers on the kitchen table. Catherine remembered noting that Mrs. Riscoe's Wedgwood beaker wasn't there and thought it strange that Mr. Hearne and Mrs. Riscoe could have come in from the garden without anyone knowing. It never occurred to her that Sally might have taken the beaker although, of course, one could see that it was just the sort of thing she might do. Dr. Maxie's mug had been there, together with a glass one in a holder which belonged to Mrs. Maxie and two large cups with saucers which had been put out for the guests. There were a bowl of sugar on the table and tins of two milk drinks. There was no cocoa. Mrs. Maxie and Catherine had collected their drinks and taken them up to Mr. Maxie's dressing-room where his wife was to spend the night. Catherine had helped her to make the invalid's bed and had then stopped to drink her Ovaltine before the dressing-room fire. She had offered to sit up with Mrs. Maxie for a time but the offer had not been accepted. After about half an hour Catherine had left to go to her own room. She was sleeping on the opposite side of the house from Sally. She had seen no one on the way to her room. After undressing she had visited the bathroom in her dressing-gown and had been back in her room by about a quarter past eleven. As she was closing the door she thought she heard Mrs. Riscoe and Mr. Hearne coming up the stairs but she couldn't be sure. She had seen or heard nothing of Sally up to that time. Here Catherine paused and Dalgleish waited patiently, but with a quickening of interest. In the corner Sergeant Martin turned over a page of his notebook in practised silence and cast a quick sidelong glance at his chief. Unless he was much mistaken the old man's thumbs were pricking now "Yes, Miss Bowers," prompted Dalgleish inexorably. His witness went bravely on. "I'm afraid this part you may find rather strange but it all seemed perfectly natural at the time. As you can understand the scene before dinner had been a great shock to me. I couldn't believe that Stephen and this girl were engaged. It wasn't he who had broken the news after all, and I don't think for one moment that he had really proposed to her. Dinner had been a terrible meal as you can imagine and, afterwards, everyone had gone on behaving as if nothing had happened. Of course, the Maxies never do show their feelings but Mrs. Riscoe went off with Mr. Hearne and I've no doubt they had a good talk about it and what could be done. But no one said anything to me although, in a sense, I was the one who was most concerned. I thought that Mrs. Maxie might have discussed it with me after the other two guests had left, but I could see that she didn't mean to. When I got to my room I realized that if I didn't do something no one would. I couldn't bear to lie there all night without knowing the worst. I felt I just had to find out the truth. The natural thing seemed to be to ask Sally. I thought that if she and I could only have a private talk together I might be able to get it all straightened out. I knew that it was late but it seemed the only chance. I had been lying there in the dark for some time but, when I had made up my mind, I put on the bedside lamp and looked at my watch. It said three minutes to midnight. That didn't seem so very late in the mood I was in. I put on my dressing-gown and took my pocket torch with me and went to Sally's room. Her door was locked but I could see that the light was on because it was shining through the keyhole. I knocked on the door and called her softly. The door is very strong as you know, but she must have heard me because the next thing I heard was the sound of the bolt being shot home and the light from the keyhole was suddenly obscured as she stood in front of it. I knocked and called once more but it was obvious that she wasn't going to let me in, so I turned and went back to my room. On the way there I suddenly thought I had to see Stephen. I couldn't face going back to bed in the same uncertainty. I thought that he might be wanting to confide in me, but not liking to come and see me. So I turned back from my own bedroom door and went to his. The light wasn't on so I knocked gently and went in. I felt that if only I could see him everything would be all right."

"And was it?" asked Dalgleish.

This time the air of cheerful competence had gone. There could be no mistaking the sudden pain in those unattractive eyes.

"He wasn't there, Inspector. The bed was turned down ready for the night but he wasn't there." She made a sudden effort to return to her former manner and gave him a smile which was almost pathetic in its artificiality. "Of course, I know now that Stephen had been to see Bocock, but it was very disappointing at the time."

"It must have been," agreed Dalgleish gravely.

¶ 5

Mrs. Maxie seated herself quietly and composedly, offered him whatever facilities he needed and only hoped that the investigation could be carried out without disturbing her husband who was gravely ill and incapable of realizing what had happened. Watching her across the desk Dalgleish could see what her daughter might become in thirty years' time. Her strong, capable, jewelled hands lay inertly in her lap. Even at that distance he could see how alike they were to the hands of her son. With greater interest he noticed that the nails, like the nails on the surgeon's fingers, were cut very short. He could detect no signs of nervousness. She seemed rather to personify the peaceful acceptance of an inevitable trial. It was not, he felt, that she had schooled herself to endurance. Here was a true serenity based on some kind of central stability which would take more than a murder investigation to disturb. She answered his questions with a deliberate thoughtfulness. It was as if she was setting her own value on every word. But there was nothing new that she could tell. She corroborated the evidence of Catherine Bowers about the discovery of the body and her account of the previous day agreed with the accounts already given. After the departure of Miss Liddell and Dr. Epps at about half past ten, she had locked up the house with the exception of the drawing-room window and the back door. Miss Bowers had been with her. Together they had collected their mugs of milk from the kitchen—only her son's then remained on the tray—and together they had gone up to bed. She had spent the night half sleeping and half watching her husband. She had heard and seen nothing unusual. No one had come near her until Miss Bowers had arrived early and had asked her for aspirin. She had known nothing of the tablets said to have been discovered in her husband's bed and found the story very difficult to believe. In her view it was impossible for him to have hidden anything in his mattress without Mrs. Bultitaft finding it. Her son had told her nothing of the incident, but had mentioned that he had substituted a medicine for the pills. She had not been surprised at this. She had thought that he was trying some new preparation from the hospital and was confident that he would have prescribed nothing without the approval of Dr. Epps.

Not until the patient probing questions on her son's engagement was her composure shaken. Even then it was irritation rather than fear which gave an edge to her voice. Dalgleish sensed that the smooth apologies with which he usually prefaced embarrassing questions would be out of place here, would be resented more than the questions themselves. He asked bluntly:

"What was your attitude, madam, to this engagement between Miss Jupp and your son?"

"It hardly lasted long enough to be dignified with that name surely. And I'm surprised that you bother to ask, Inspector. You must know that I would disapprove strongly."

"Well, that was frank enough," thought Dalgleish. "But what else could she say? We would scarcely believe that she liked it."

"Even though her affection for your son could have been genuine?"

"I am paying her the compliment of assuming that it was. What difference does that make? I would still have disapproved. They had nothing in common. He would have had to support another man's child. It would have hindered his career and they would have disliked each other within a year. These King Cophetua marriages seldom work out. How can they? No girl of spirit likes to think she's been condescended to and Sally had plenty of spirit even if she chose not to show it. Furthermore, I fail to see what they would have married on. Stephen has very little money of his own. Of course I disapproved of this so-called engagement. Would you wish for such a marriage for your son?"

For one unbelievable second Dalgleish thought that she knew. It was a commonplace, almost banal argument which any mother faced with her circumstances might casually have used. She could not possibly have realized its force. He wondered what she would say if he replied, "I have no son. My only child and his mother died three hours after he was born. I have no son to marry anyone—suitable or unsuitable." He could imagine her frown of well-bred distaste that he should embarrass her at such a time with a private grief at once so old, so intimate, so unrelated to the matter at hand. He replied briefly:

"No. I should not wish it either. I'm sorry to have taken up so much of your time with what must seem no one's business but your own. But you must see its importance."

"Naturally. From your point of view it provides a motive for several people, myself particularly. But one does not kill to avoid social inconvenience. I admit that I intended to do all I could to stop them marrying. I was going to have a talk with Stephen next day. I've no doubt we should have been able to do something for Sally without the necessity of welcoming her into the family. There must be a limit to what these people expect."

The sudden bitterness of her last sentence roused even Sergeant Martin from the routine automatism of his note-taking. But if Mrs. Maxie realized that she had said too much she did not aggravate her error by saying more. Watching her, Dalgleish thought how like a picture she was, an advertisement in water-colour for toilet water or soap. Even the low bowl of flowers on the desk between them emphasized her serene gentility as if placed there by the cunning hand of a commercial photographer. "Picture of an English lady at home," he thought, and wondered what the Chief Superintendent would make of her and, if it ever came to that, what a jury would make of her. Even his mind, accustomed to finding wickedness in strange as well as high places, could not easily reconcile Mrs. Maxie with murder. But her last words had been revealing.

He decided to leave the marriage question at present and concentrate on other aspects of the investigation. Again he went over the account of the preparation of the nightly hot drinks. There could be no confusion about the ownership of the different mugs. The Wedgwood blue one found at Sally's side belonged to Deborah Riscoe. The milk for the drinks was placed on top of the stove. It was a solid-fuel stove with heavy covers to each of the hot-plates. The saucepan of milk was left on top of one of these covers where there could be no danger of its boiling over. Any of the family wanting to boil the milk would transfer the saucepan to the hot-plate and replace it afterwards on top of the cover. Only the family's mugs and cups for their guests were placed on the tray. She could not say what Sally or Mrs. Bultitaft usually drank at night but, certainly, none of the family drank cocoa. They were not fond of chocolate.

"It comes to this, doesn't it," said Dalgleish. "If, as I am now assuming, the post-mortem shows that Miss Jupp was drugged and the analysis of the cocoa shows that the drug was in her last night drink, then we are faced with two possibilities. She could have taken the drug herself, perhaps for no worse reason than to get a good sleep after the excitement of the day. Or someone else drugged her for a reason which we must discover but which is not so difficult to guess. Miss Jupp, as far as is known, was a healthy young woman. If this crime was premeditated her murderer must have considered how he—or she—could get into that room and kill the girl with the least possible disturbance. To drug her is an obvious answer. That supposes that the murderer is familiar with the evening drink routine at Martingale and knew where the drugs were kept. I suppose a member of your household or a guest is familiar with your household routine?"

"Surely then he would know that the Wedgwood beaker belonged to my daughter. Are you satisfied, Inspector, that the drug was intended for Sally?"

"Not entirely. But I am satisfied that the killer did not mistake Miss Jupp's neck for Mrs. Riscoe's. Let us assume for the present that the drug was intended for Miss Jupp. It could have been put into the saucepan of milk, the Wedgwood beaker itself either before or after the drink was made, into the tin of cocoa, or into the sugar. You and Miss Bowers made your drinks from the milk in the same saucepan and sugared them from the bowl on the table without ill effects. I don't think that the drug was put in the empty beaker. It is brownish in colour and would be easily seen against the blue china. That leaves us with two possibilities. Either it was crumbled into the dry cocoa or it was dissolved in the hot drink some time after Miss Jupp made it but before she drank it."

"I don't think the latter is possible, Inspector. Mrs. Bultitaft always puts on the hot milk at ten. At about twenty-five minutes past we saw Sally carrying her mug up to her room."

"Who do you mean by 'we', Mrs. Maxie?"

"Dr. Epps, Miss Liddell and I myself saw her. I'd been upstairs with Miss Liddell to fetch her coat. When we came back into the hall Dr. Epps joined us from the business room. As we stood there together Sally came from the kitchen end of the house and went up the main staircase carrying the blue Wedgwood beaker on its saucer. She was wearing pyjamas and a dressing-gown. We all three saw her but no one spoke. Miss Liddell and Dr. Epps left at once."

"Was it usual for Miss Jupp to use that staircase?"

"No. The back one leads more directly from the kitchen to her room. I think she was trying to make some kind of gesture."

"Although she couldn't have known that she would meet anyone in the hall?"

"No. I don't see how she could have known that."

"You say that you noticed that Miss Jupp was carrying

Mrs. Riscoe's beaker. Did you mention this to either of your guests or remonstrate to Miss Jupp about it?"

Mrs. Maxie smiled faintly. For the second time the delicate claw was unsheathed.

"What old-fashioned ideas you have, Inspector! Did you expect me to tear it from her grasp to the embarrassment of my guests and the satisfaction of Sally herself? What an exciting and exhausting world yours must be."

Dalgleish pursued his question undeterred by this gentle irony. But he was interested to know that his witness could be provoked.

"What happened after Miss Liddell and Dr. Epps left?"

"I rejoined Miss Bowers in the business room where we tidied up the papers and locked away the bags of money in the safe. We then went to the kitchen and made our drinks. I had hot milk and Miss Bowers made Ovaltine. She likes it very sweet and added sugar from the bowl set ready. We carried our drinks to the dressing-room next to my husband's bedroom where I spend the nights when I am on duty nursing him. Miss Bowers helped me to re-make my husband's bed. I suppose we spent about twenty minutes together. Then she said 'good night' and left."

"Having had her Ovaltine?"

"Yes. It was too hot to drink at once but she sat down and finished it before she left me."

"Did she go to the drug cupboard while she was with you?"

"No. Neither of us did. My son had given his father something earlier to make him sleep and he appeared to be dozing. There was nothing to do for him except make his bed as comfortable as possible. I was glad of Miss Bowers's help. She is a trained nurse and, together, we were able to tidy the bed without disturbing him."

"What were Miss Bowers's relations with Dr. Maxie?"

"As far as I know Miss Bowers is a friend of both my children. That is the kind of question which it would be better to ask them and her."

"She and your son are not engaged to be married as far as you know?"

"I know nothing about their personal affairs. I should have thought it unlikely."

"Thank you," said Dalgleish. "I will see Mrs. Riscoe now if you will be good enough to send her in."

He rose to open the door for Mrs. Maxie but she did not move. She said, "I still believe that Sally took that drug herself. There's no reasonable alternative. But if someone else did administer it then I agree with you that it must have been put into the dry cocoa. Forgive me—but wouldn't you be able to tell that from an examination of the tin and its contents?"

"We might have been," replied Dalgleish gravely. "But the empty tin was found in the dustbin. It had been rinsed out. The inner paper lining isn't there. It was probably burnt in the kitchen stove. Someone was making assurance doubly sure."

"A very cool lady, sir," said Sergeant Martin when Mrs. Maxie had left them. He added with unaccustomed humour, "She sat there like a Liberal candidate waiting for the recount."

"Yes," agreed Dalgleish dryly. "But with every confidence in her Party organization. Well, let's hear what the rest of them have to tell us."

¶ 6

It was a very different room from last time, thought Felix, but that room, too, had been quiet and peaceful. There had been pictures and a heavy mahogany desk not unlike the one Dalgleish was sitting at now. There had been flowers, too, a small posy arranged in a bowl hardly larger than a teacup. Everything about that room had been homely and comfortable, even the man behind the desk with his plump white hands, his smiling eyes behind the thick spectacles. The room had retained that look. It was surprising how many procedures there were for the extracting of truth which did not shed blood, were calculatedly unmessy, did not require very much in the way of apparatus. He wrenched memory back and made himself look at the figure at the desk. The folded hands were leaner, the eyes dark and less kind. There was only one other person in the room and he, too, was an English policeman. This was Martingale. This was England.

So far it had not gone too badly. Deborah had been absent for half an hour. When she returned she walked to her seat without looking at him and he, just as silently, got up and followed the uniformed policeman into the business room. He was glad that he had resisted the desire to have a drink before his questioning and that he had refused Dalgleish's proffered cigarette. That was an old one! They couldn't catch him that way! He wasn't going to make them a present of his nervousness. If only he could keep his temper all would be well.

The patient man behind the desk looked at his notes.

"Thank you. That's clear so far. Now may we please go back a little? After coffee you went with Mrs. Riscoe to help wash up the dinner things. At about nine-thirty you both returned to this room where Mrs. Maxie, Miss Liddell, Miss Bowers and Dr. Epps were counting the money taken at the fête. You told them that you and Mrs. Riscoe were going out and you said 'Good night' to Miss Liddell and Dr. Epps, who would probably have left Martingale by the time you returned. Mrs. Maxie said that she would leave one of the french windows in the drawing-room open for you and asked you to lock it when you had come in. This arrangement was heard by everyone who was in the room at the time?"

"As far as I know it was. No one commented on it and, as they were busy counting money, I doubt whether they took it in."

"I find it surprising that the drawing-room window was left unlatched for you when the back door was also open. Isn't that a Stubbs on the wall behind you? This house has several very fine things which are easily portable."

Felix did not turn his head.

"The cultured cop! I thought they were peculiar to detective novels. Congratulations! But the Maxies don't advertise their possessions. There's no danger from the village. People have been wandering in and out of this house pretty freely for the last three hundred years. The locking-up here is rather haphazard except for the front door. That is ritually bolted and barred every night by Stephen Maxie or his sister almost as if it had some esoteric significance. Apart from that, they aren't thorough. In that, as in other matters, they appear to rely on our wonderful police."

"Right! You went out into the garden with Mrs. Riscoe at about nine-thirty p.m. and walked there together. What did you talk about, Mr. Hearne?"

"I asked Mrs. Riscoe to marry me. I am going out to our Canadian house in two months' time and I thought it might be pleasant to combine business with a honeymoon."

"And Mrs. Riscoe accepted?"

"It's charming of you to be interested, Inspector, but I'm afraid I must disappoint you. Inexplicable as it must seem to you, Mrs. Riscoe was not enthusiastic."

The memory flooded back in a wave of emotion. Darkness, the cloying scent of roses, the hard urgent kisses which were the expression of some compelling need in her but not, he felt, of passion. And afterwards the sick weariness in her voice. "Marriage, Felix? Hasn't there been enough talk of marriage in this family? God, how I wish she were dead!" He knew then that he had been betrayed into speaking too soon. The time and the place had both been wrong. Had the words been wrong too? What exactly was it that she wanted? Dalgleish's voice recalled him to the present.

"How long did you stay in the garden, sir?"

"It would be gallant to pretend that time ceased to exist. In the interest of your investigation, however, I will admit that we came in through the drawing-room window at ten-forty-five p.m. The chiming clock on the mantelpiece struck the three-quarters as I closed and bolted the window."

"That clock is kept five minutes fast, sir. Would you go on, please."

"Then we returned at ten-forty p.m. I did not look at my watch. Mrs. Riscoe offered me a whisky which I declined. I also declined a milk drink and she went to the kitchen to get her own. She came back in a few minutes and said that she'd changed her mind. She also said that, apparently, her brother was still out. We talked for a little time and arranged to meet to ride together at seven next morning. Then we went to bed. I had a reasonably good night. As far as I know Mrs. Riscoe had, too. I had dressed and was waiting for her in the hall when I heard Stephen Maxie calling down to me. He wanted my help with the ladder. The rest you know."

"Did you kill Sally Jupp, Mr. Hearne?"

"Not so far as I am aware."

"What do you mean by that?"

"Merely that I suppose I could have done it while in a state of amnesia, but that is hardly a practical supposition."

"I think we can dismiss that possibility. Miss Jupp was killed by someone who knew what he, or she, was doing. Have you any idea who?"

"Do you expect me to take that question seriously?"

"I expect you to take all my questions seriously. This young mother was murdered. I intend to find out who killed her without wasting too much of my own time or anyone else's and I expect you to co-operate with me."

"I have no idea who killed her and I doubt whether I should tell you if I had. I haven't your evident passion for abstract justice. However, I'm prepared to co-operate to the extent of pointing out some facts which, in your enthusiasm for lengthy interrogations of your suspects, you may possibly have overlooked. Someone had got through that girl's window. She kept glass animals on the ledge and they had been scattered. The window was open and her hair was damp. It rained last night from half-past twelve until three. I deduce that she was dead before twelve-thirty or she would have closed the window. The child did not awake until its normal time. Presumably then the visitor made little noise. It is unlikely that there was a violent quarrel. I imagine that Sally herself let in her visitor through the window. He probably used the ladder. She would know where it was kept. He probably came by appointment. Your guess is as good as mine as to why. I didn't know her but, somehow, she never struck me as being highly sexed or promiscuous. The man was probably in love with her and, when she told him about her intention to marry Stephen Maxie, he killed her in a sudden access of jealousy or anger. I can't believe that this was a premeditated crime. Sally had locked the door to secure their privacy and the man got out through the window without unlocking it. He may not have realized it was bolted. Had he done so he would probably have unbolted it and made his exit with more care. That bolted door must be a great disappointment to you, Inspector. Even you can hardly visualize any of the family pounding up and down a ladder to get in and out of their own house. I know how excited you must be about the Maxie–Jupp engagement but you don't need me to point out that, if we had to commit murder to get out of an unwelcome engagement, the mortality rate among women would be very high."

Even as he was speaking Felix knew that it was a mistake. Fear had trapped him into garrulity as well as anger. The police sergeant was looking at him with the resigned and slightly pitying look of a man who has seen too many men make fools of themselves to be surprised, but still rather wishes that they wouldn't do it. Dalgleish spoke mildly.

"I thought that you had a good night. Yet you noticed that it rained from half past twelve until three."

"It was a good night for me."

"You suffer from insomnia then? What do you take for it?"

"Whisky. But seldom in other people's houses."

"You described earlier how the body was discovered and how you went into the adjoining bathroom with Mrs. Riscoe while Dr. Maxie 'phoned the police. After a time

Mrs. Riscoe left you to go to her mother. What did you do after that?"

"I thought I had better see if Mrs. Bultitaft was all right. I didn't suppose that anyone would feel like breakfast, but it was obvious that we should need plenty of hot coffee, and that sandwiches would be a good idea. She seemed stunned and kept repeating that Sally must have killed herself. I pointed out as gently as I could that that was anatomically impossible and that seemed to upset her more. She gave me one curious look as if I were a stranger and then burst into loud sobbing. By the time I had managed to calm her Miss Bowers had arrived with the child and was being rather obviously capable with its breakfast. Martha took herself in hand and we got on with the coffee and with Mr. Maxie's breakfast. By that time the police had arrived and we were told to wait in the drawing-room."

"When Mrs. Bultitaft burst into tears, was that the first sign of grief that she had shown?"

"Grief?" The pause was almost imperceptible. "She was obviously very much shocked, as we all were."

"Thank you, sir. That has been very helpful. I will have your statement typed and later I will ask you to read it over and, if you agree with it, to sign it. If you have anything else you want to tell me there'll be plenty of opportunity. I shall be about the place. If you are going back to the drawing-room will you ask Mrs. Bultitaft if she will come in next."

It was a command not a request. As he reached the door Felix heard the quiet voice speaking again.

"You will scarcely be surprised to hear that your account of things tallies almost exactly with that of Mrs. Riscoe. With one exception. Mrs. Riscoe says that you spent almost the whole of last night in her room, not your own. She says, in fact, that you slept together."

Felix stood for a moment facing the door and then turned round and faced the man behind the desk.

"That was very sweet of Mrs. Riscoe, but it makes things difficult for me, doesn't it? I'm afraid you will have to make up your mind, Inspector, as to which of us is lying."

"Thank you," said Dalgleish. "I have already done so."

¶ 7

Dalgleish had met a number of Marthas in his time and had never supposed them to be complicated people. They were concerned with the comfort of the body, the cooking of food, the unending menial tasks which someone must carry out before the life of the mind can have any true validity. Their own undemanding emotional needs found fulfilment in service. They were loyal, hard-working and truthful and made good witnesses because they lacked both the imagination and the practice necessary for successful lying. They could be a nuisance if they decided to shield those who had gained their loyalty but this was an overt danger which could be anticipated. He expected no difficulty with Martha. It was with a sense of irritation that Dalgleish realized that someone had been talking to her. She would be correct, she would be respectful, but any information he extracted would be gained the hard way. Martha had been coached and it was not hard to guess by whom. He pressed patiently on.

"So you do the cooking and help with the nursing of Mr. Maxie. That must be a heavy load. Did you suggest to Mrs. Maxie that she should employ Miss Jupp?"

"No."

"Do you know who did?"

Martha was silent for several seconds as if wondering whether to chance an indiscretion.

"It may have been Miss Liddell. Madam may have thought of it herself. I don't know."

"But I presume that Mrs. Maxie talked it over with you before she employed the girl."

"She told me about Sally. It was for Madam to decide."

Dalgleish began to find this servility irritating but his voice did not change. He had never been known to lose his temper with a witness.

"Had Mrs. Maxie ever employed an unmarried mother before?"

"It would never have been thought of in the old days. All our girls came with excellent references."

"So that this was a new venture. Do you think it was a success? You had most to do with Miss Jupp. What sort of a girl was she?"

Martha did not reply.

"Were you satisfied with her work?"

"I was satisfied enough. At first, anyway."

"What caused you to change your mind? Was it her late rising?" The heavy-lidded, obstinate eyes slewed suddenly from side to side.

"There are worse things than lying abed."

"Such as?"

"She began to get cheeky."

"That must have been trying for you. I wonder what caused Miss Jupp to get cheeky."

"Girls are like that. They start quietly enough and then begin to act as if they are mistress in the house."

"Suppose Sally Jupp were beginning to think that she might be mistress here one day?"

"Then she was out of her mind."

"But Dr. Maxie did propose marriage to her on Saturday evening."

"I know nothing of that. Dr. Maxie couldn't have married Sally Jupp."

"Someone seems to have made that certain, don't they? Have you any idea who?"

Martha did not reply. There was, indeed, nothing to be said. If Sally Jupp really had been killed for that reason the circle of suspects was not large. Dalgleish began to take her with tedious thoroughness over the events of Saturday afternoon and evening. There was little she could say about the fête. She had apparently taken no part in it except to walk once round the garden before giving Mr. Maxie his evening meal and making him comfortable for the night. When she returned to the kitchen Sally had evidently given Jimmy his tea and taken him up for his bath because the pram was in the scullery and the child's plate and mug were in the sink. The girl did not appear and Martha had wasted no time in looking for her. The family had waited on themselves at dinner which was a cold meal and Mrs. Maxie had not rung for her. Afterwards Mrs. Riscoe and Mr. Hearne had come into the kitchen to help wash up. They hadn't asked whether Sally was back. No one had mentioned her. They had talked mostly about the fête. Mr. Hearne had laughed and joked with Mrs. Riscoe while they washed up. He was a very amusing gentleman. They hadn't helped to get the hot drinks ready. That was done later. The cocoa tin was in a cupboard with the other dry provisions and neither Mrs. Riscoe nor Mr. Hearne had been to the cupboard. She had stayed in the kitchen all the time that they were there.

After they left she turned on the television for half an hour. No, she hadn't worried about Sally. The girl would come in when she felt like it. At about five minutes to ten

Martha had put a saucepan of milk to heat slowly at the side of the stove. This was done most nights at Martingale so that she could get early to bed. She had put out the mugs on a tray. There were large cups and saucers put out for any guest who liked a hot drink at night. Sally knew very well that the blue beaker belonged to Mrs. Riscoe. Everyone at Martingale knew. After seeing to the hot milk Martha had gone to bed. She was in bed before half past ten and had heard nothing unusual all night. In the morning she had gone to wake up Sally and had found the door bolted. She had gone to tell Madam. The rest he knew.

It took over forty minutes to extract this unremarkable information but Dalgleish showed no sign of impatience. Now they came to the actual finding of the body. It was important to discover how far Martha's account agreed with that of Catherine Bowers. If it agreed, then at least one of his tentative theories might prove correct. The account did agree. Patiently he went on to inquire about the missing Sommeil. But here he was less successful. Martha Bultitaft did not believe that Sally had found any tablets in her master's bed.

"Sally liked to make out that she nursed the master. Maybe she took a turn at nights if Madam was extra tired. But he never liked anyone about him but me. I do all the heavy nursing. If there was anything hidden in the bed I should have found it."

It was the longest speech she had made. Dalgleish felt that it carried conviction. Finally he questioned her about the empty cocoa tin. Here, again, she spoke quietly but with unemphatic certainty. She had found the empty tin on the kitchen table when she came down to make the early morning tea. She had burned the inside paper, rinsed the tin and put it in the dustbin. Why had she rinsed it first? Because Madam disliked sticky or greasy tins being put in the dustbin. The cocoa tin hadn't been greasy, of course, but that didn't signify. All used tins were rinsed at Martingale. And why had she burned the inside wrapper? Well, she couldn't rinse the inside of the tin with the paper lining still there, could she? The tin was empty so she rinsed it out and threw it away. Her tone suggested that no reasonable person could have done otherwise.

For the life of him Dalgleish couldn't see how her story could be effectively countered. His heart sank at the thought of interrogating Mrs. Maxie on the usual method of disposal of the family's used tins. But, once again he suspected that Martha had been coached. He was seeing the beginning of a pattern. The infinite patience of the last hour had been well worth while.

CHAPTER FIVE

¶ I

St. Mary's Refuge was about a mile from the main part of the village, an ugly red-brick house with a multiplicity of gables and turrets which was set back from the main road behind a discreet shield of laurel bushes. The gravel drive led to a front door whose worn knocker gleamed with much polishing. The net curtains were snowy white at each of the windows. Shallow stone steps at the side of the house led down to a square lawn where several prams were clustered together. A maid in cap and apron admitted them, probably one of the mothers Dalgleish thought, and showed them into a small room at the left of the hall. She seemed uncertain what do to and could not catch Dalgleish's name although he repeated it twice. Large eyes stared at him uncomprehendingly through the steel-frame spectacles as she hovered miserably in the doorway. "Never mind," said Dalgleish kindly, "just let Miss Liddell know that there are two policemen to see her from Martingale. She'll know all about us."

"Please, I have to take the name. I'm being trained for a house parlourmaid." She hovered in desperate persistence, torn between fear of Miss Liddell's censure and embarrassment at being in the same room as two strange men, and both of them policemen at that. Dalgleish handed her his card. "Just give her this then. That will be even more proper and correct. And don't worry. You'll make a very nice house parlourmaid. Nowadays they're prized above rubies you know."

"Not saddled with an illegitimate kid, they aren't," said Sergeant Martin as the slight figure disappeared through the door with what might have been a whispered "Thank you".

"Funny to see a plain little thing like that here, sir. A bit missing by the way she acted. Someone took advantage of her I suppose."

"She's the kind of person who gets taken advantage of from the day she's born."

"Properly scared, too, wasn't she? I suppose this Miss Liddell treats the girls all right, sir?"

"Very well, I imagine, according to her own lights. It's easy to get sentimental over her job, but she has to deal with a pretty mixed bunch. What you want here is hope, faith and charity to an unlimited degree. In other words you want a saint and we can hardly expect Miss Liddell to measure up to that standard."

"Yes, sir," said Sergeant Martin. On second thoughts he felt that "No, sir" would have been more appropriate. Unconscious of having uttered any unorthodoxy Dalgleish moved slowly about the room. It was comfortable but unostentatious and was furnished, he thought, with many of Miss Liddell's personal possessions. All the wood glowed with polishing. The spinet and the rosewood table both looked as if they would have struck warm to the touch from the vigour and energy spent on them. The one large window which overlooked the lawn was curtained with flower-patterned cretonne now drawn against the sun. The carpet, although showing signs of age was not the kind provided by official bodies however voluntary and public spirited. The room was as much Miss Liddell's in spirit as if she had owned the house. Along the walls were photographs of babies. Babies lying naked on rugs, their heads reared towards the camera in helpless absurdity. Babies smiling toothlessly from prams and cradles. Woollen-clad babies held in their mothers' arms. There were even one or two lying lumpily in the arms of an embarrassed man. These presumably were the lucky ones, the ones who had achieved an official father at last. Above a small mahogany desk was the framed print of a woman at a spinning-wheel with a plaque attached to the base of the frame. "Presented by the Chadfleet and District Committee for Moral Welfare to Miss Alice Liddell in commemoration of twenty years' devoted service as Warden of St. Mary's Refuge." Dalgleish and Martin looked at it together. "I don't know that I'd call this place a refuge exactly," said the Sergeant. Dalgleish looked again at the furniture, the carefully tended legacies from Miss Liddell's childhood.

"It might well be to a single woman of Miss Liddell's age. She's made this place her home for over twenty years. She might do a great deal to prevent herself being driven out of it."

Sergeant Martin was prevented from replying by the entrance of the lady. Miss Liddell was always most at ease on her own ground. She shook hands composedly and apologized for keeping them waiting. Looking at her Dalgleish deduced she had spent the time in applying powder to her face and resolution to her mind. She was obviously determined to treat this as a social call as far as possible and she invited them to sit down with all the conscious charm of an inexperienced hostess. Dalgleish declined her offer of tea, carefully avoiding the reproachful eye of his sergeant. Martin was perspiring freely. His own view was that punctilio towards a possible suspect could be carried too far and that a nice cup of tea on a hot day had never yet obstructed justice.

"We shall try not to keep you too long, Miss Liddell. As I'm sure you have realized, I am investigating the death of Sally Jupp. I understand that you dined at Martingale yesterday evening. You were also at the fête during the afternoon and you did, of course, know Miss Jupp while she was with you here at St. Mary's. There are one or two matters which I am hoping you may be able to explain." Miss Liddell started at the use of his last word. As Sergeant Martin drew out his notebook with something akin to resignation, Dalgleish noted her quick moistening of her lips and the almost imperceptible tensing of her hands and knew that she was on her guard.

"Anything you care to ask, of course, Inspector. It is Inspector, isn't it? Of course I knew Sally very well and the whole thing is a dreadful shock to me. It is to us all. But I'm afraid I'm not likely to be of much help. I'm not very clever at noticing and remembering things, you know. It's rather a disadvantage sometimes, but we can't all be detectives can we?" The nervous laugh was a little too high to be natural. "We've got her scared all right," thought Sergeant Martin. "Might be something here after all."

"Perhaps we could begin with Sally Jupp herself," said Dalgleish gently. "I understand that she lived here during the last five months of her pregnancy and came back to you when she left the hospital after the birth. She stayed here until she started the job at Martingale which she did when her baby was four months old. Until that time she helped here with the household duties. You must have got to know her very well during this time. Did you like her, Miss Liddell?"

"Like her?" The woman laughed nervously. "Isn't that rather a funny question, Inspector?"

"Is it? In what way?"

She made an effort to conceal her embarrassment and to give the question the compliment of careful thought.

"I hardly know what to say. If you had asked me that question a week ago I should have had no hesitation in saying that Sally was an excellent little worker and a most deserving girl who was doing her best to atone for her mistake. But now, of course, I can't help wondering whether I was wrong about her, whether she was really genuine after all." She spoke with the sorrow of a connoisseur whose previously infallible judgment has at last been proved at fault. "I suppose now that we shall never know whether she was genuine or not."

"By genuine, I assume you mean whether she was sincere in her affection for Mr. Stephen Maxie."

Miss Liddell shook her head sadly. "The appearances were against it. I was never more shocked in my life, Inspector, never. Of course she had no right to accept him whatever she felt for him. She looked positively triumphant when she stood in that window and told us. He was horribly embarrassed of course, and went as white as a sheet. It was a dreadful moment for poor Mrs. Maxie. I'm afraid I shall always blame myself for what happened. I recommended Sally to Martingale, you know. It seemed such a wonderful chance for her in every way. And now this."

"You believe, then, that Sally Jupp's death is the direct result of her engagement to Mr. Maxie?"

"Well, it does look like that, doesn't it?"

"I agree that her death was highly convenient for anyone who had a reason to dislike the proposed marriage. The Maxie family for instance."

Miss Liddell's face flamed. "But that's ridiculous, Inspector. It's a terrible thing to say. Terrible. Of course, you don't know the family as we do, but you must take it from me that the whole suggestion is fantastic. You can't have thought I meant that! It's perfectly plain to me what happened. Sally had been playing fast and loose with some man we don't know about and when he heard of the engagement—well, he lost control of himself. He got through the window, didn't he? That's what Miss Bowers told me. Well, that proves it wasn't the family."

"The murderer probably got out of the room through the window. We have no knowledge as yet how he or she got in."

"You surely can't imagine Mrs. Maxie climbing down that wall. She couldn't do it!"

"I imagine nothing. There was a ladder in the customary place for anyone who cared to use it. It could have been put in place ready even if the murderer got in through the door."

"But Sally would have heard! Even if the ladder were placed there very gently. Or she might look out of her window and see it!"

"Perhaps. If she were awake."

"I don't understand you, Inspector. You seem determined to suspect the family. If only you knew what they've done for that girl."

"I should like to be told. And you must not misunderstand me. I suspect everyone who knew Miss Jupp and who has no alibi for the time she was killed. That is why I am here now."

"Well, you know about my movements presumably. I've no wish to make a secret of them. Dr. Epps brought me back here in his car. We left Martingale at about half past ten. I wrote in this room for a little while and then took a stroll in the garden. I went to bed at about eleven which is rather late for me. I heard about this dreadful thing while I was finishing my breakfast. Miss Bowers 'phoned and asked if I could take Jimmy back for a while until they knew what was to happen to him. Naturally I left my deputy, Miss Pollack, in charge of the girls and went round at once. I telephoned George Hopgood and told him to bring round his taxi."

"You said a little earlier that you thought the news of Miss Jupp's engagement to Mr. Maxie was the reason for her death. Was that news known outside the household? I was given to understand that Mr. Maxie only proposed on Saturday night so that no one who was not at Martingale after that time could have been told."

"Dr. Maxie may have proposed on Saturday, but no doubt the girl had made up her mind to have him before then. Something had been happening, I'm sure of it. I saw her at the fête and she was flushed with excitement all the afternoon. And were you told how she copied Mrs. Riscoe's dress?"

"You are hardly suggesting that that constituted another motive."

"It showed which way her mind was working. Make no mistake about it, Sally asked for what she got. I'm only desperately sorry that the Maxies should have been involved in all this trouble on her account."

"You have told me that you went to bed about eleven after a stroll in the gardens. Have you anyone to confirm that statement?"

"No one saw me as far as I know, Inspector. Miss Pollack and the girls are in bed by ten. I have my own key of course. It was an unusual thing for me to have gone out again like that but I was disturbed. I couldn't help thinking about Sally and Mr. Maxie and I knew I shouldn't get to sleep if I went to bed too early."

"Thank you. There are just two other questions. Where in the house do you keep your private papers? I mean documents referring to the administration of this Home. Letters from the committee for example."

Miss Liddell walked over to the rosewood desk.

"They are kept in this drawer, Inspector. Naturally I keep it locked although only the most trustworthy girls are allowed to look after this room. The key is kept in this little compartment at the top."

She lifted the desk lid as she spoke and indicated the place. Dalgleish reflected that only the dullest or least curious housemaid could have missed the hidden key if she had had sufficient nerve to look. Miss Liddell was obviously used to dealing with girls who had too fearful a respect for papers and official documents to tamper with them voluntarily. But Sally Jupp had been neither dull nor, he suspected, incurious. He suggested as much to Miss Liddell and, as expected, the image of Sally's picking fingers and amused ironic eyes roused her to even greater resentment than his earlier questions about the Maxies.

"You mean that Sally may have pried about among my things? I would never have believed that once, but you could be right. Oh, yes. I see it now. That was why she liked to work in here. All that docility, that politeness was so much pretence! And to think that I trusted her! I really thought that she cared for me, that I was helping her. She confided in me, you know. But I suppose all those stories were lies. She must have been laughing at me all the time. I suppose you think I'm a fool too. Well, I may be, but I've done nothing to be ashamed of. Nothing! They've told you about that scene in the Maxie dining-room no doubt. She couldn't frighten me. There may have been little difficulties here in the past. I'm not very clever with figures and accounts. I've never pretended to be. But I've done nothing wrong. You can ask any member of the committee. Sally Jupp could pry as much as she liked. A lot of good it's done her."

She was shaking with anger and made no attempt to hide the bitter satisfaction behind her last words. But Dalgleish was unprepared for the effect of his last question.

"One of my officers has been to see the Proctors, Sally Jupp's next-of-kin. Naturally we hoped that they might be able to give us some information about her life which might help us. Their young daughter was there and she volunteered some information. Can you tell me, Miss Liddell, why it was you telephoned Mr. Proctor early on Saturday morning—the morning of the fête? The child said she answered the telephone." The transformation from furious resentment to complete surprise was almost ludicrous. Miss Liddell gazed at him literally open-mouthed.

"Me? Telephoned Mr. Proctor? I don't know what you mean! I haven't been in touch with the Proctors since Sally first went to Martingale. They never took an interest in her. What on earth would I telephone Mr. Proctor about?"

"That", said Dalgleish, "was what I had been wondering."

"But it's ridiculous! If I had telephoned Mr. Proctor I should have no objection to admitting it. But I didn't. The child must be lying."

"Someone is lying, certainly."

"Well, it isn't me," reported Miss Liddell stoutly if ungrammatically. Dalgleish, on this point at least, was disposed to believe her. As she accompanied him to the door he asked casually:

"Did you tell anyone about the events at Martingale when you got home, Miss Liddell? If your deputy were still up no doubt it would be natural to mention Sally's engagement to her."

Miss Liddell hesitated then said defensively, "Well, the news was bound to get around, wasn't it? I mean, the Maxies could hardly expect to keep it secret. Actually, I did mention it to Miss Pollack. Mrs. Pullen was here, too. She came over from Rose Cottage to return some teaspoons which we'd lent for the fête teas. She was still here chatting to Miss Pollack when I got back from Martingale. So Mrs. Pullen knew and you're surely not suggesting that telling her had anything to do with Sally's death."

Dalgleish replied non-committally. He was not so sure.

¶ 2

By dinner-time the activity of the day at Martingale seemed to be slowing down. Dalgleish and the sergeant were still working in the business room from which the sergeant occasionally emerged to speak to the man on duty at the door. The police cars still mysteriously appeared, disgorged their uniformed or macintoshed passengers and, after a short wait, bore them away again. The Maxies and their guests watched these comings and goings from the windows, but no one had been sent for since the late afternoon and it looked as if the questioning was over for the day and that the party could think about dinner with some prospect of being able to eat undisturbed. The house had suddenly become very quiet and, when Martha nervously and half-heartedly sounded the gong at half past seven it boomed out like a vulgar intrusion into the silence of grief, sounding unnaturally loud to the family's heightened nerves. The meal itself passed almost in silence. The ghost of Sally moved from door to sideboard, and when Mrs.

Maxie rang and the door opened to admit Martha, no one looked up. Martha's own preoccupations were shown in the poverty of the meal. No one had any hunger and there was nothing to tempt hunger. Afterwards they all moved as if by unspoken but common summons into the drawing-room. It was a relief when they saw Mr. Hinks pass the window and Stephen went out to welcome him in. Here at least was a representative of the outside world. No one could accuse the vicar of murdering Sally Jupp. Presumably he had come to offer spiritual guidance and comfort. The only kind of comfort which would have been welcome to the Maxies was the assurance that Sally was not after all dead, that they had been living through a brief nightmare from which they could now awake, a little tired and distressed by the lack of sleep but raised into joy by the glorious realization that none of it was true. But if this could not be, it was at least reassuring to talk with someone who stood outside the shadow of suspicion and who could give this dreadful day the semblance of normality. They found that they had even been speaking in whispers and Stephen's call to the vicar rang out like a shout. Soon he was with them and, as he entered with Stephen behind him, four pairs of eyes looked up inquiringly as if anxious to know the verdict on them of the world outside.

"Poor girl," he said. "Poor little girl. And she was so happy yesterday evening."

"Did you speak to her after the fête then?" Stephen could not succeed in hiding the urgency in his voice.

"No, not after the fête. I get so muddled about times. Stupid of me. Now that you mention it I didn't speak to her at all yesterday, although, of course, I did see her about the gardens. Such a pretty white dress she was wearing. No, I spoke to her on Thursday evening. We walked up the road together and I asked about Jimmy. I think it was

Thursday. Yes, it must have been because I was at home all the evening on Friday. Thursday evening was the last time we spoke. She was so happy. She told me about her marriage and how Jimmy was to have a father. But you know all about that, I expect. It was a surprise to me, but, of course, I was glad for her. And now this. Have the police any news yet?"

He looked round in gentle inquiry seeming oblivious of the effect of his words. No one spoke for a moment and then Stephen said, "You may as well know, Vicar, that I had asked Sally to marry me. But she couldn't have told you about it on Thursday. She didn't know then. I never mentioned marriage to her until seven-forty p.m. on Saturday."

Catherine Bowers laughed shortly and then turned away in embarrassment as Deborah turned and looked at her. Mr. Hinks creased worried brows but his gentle old voice was firm.

"I do get times muddled I know, but it was certainly Thursday when we met. I was coming out of church after Compline and Sally was passing with Jimmy in his push-chair. But I couldn't be mistaken about the conversation. Not the exact words, but the general gist. Sally said that Jimmy was soon to have a father. She asked me not to tell anyone and I said I wouldn't, but that I was very glad for her. I asked whether I knew the bridegroom but she just laughed and said she would rather let it be a surprise. She was very excited and happy. We only walked a little way together as I left her at the vicarage and I suppose she came on here. I'm afraid I rather assumed that you knew all about it. Is it important?"

"Inspector Dalgleish will probably think so," said Deborah wearily. "I suppose you ought to go and tell him. There isn't much choice really. The man has an uncanny facility for extracting uncomfortable truths."

Mr. Hinks looked troubled, but was saved from the necessity of replying by a quick knock at the door and the appearance of Dalgleish. He held out his hand towards Stephen. Loosely wrapped in a man's white handkerchief was a small mud-caked bottle.

"Do you recognize this?" he asked.

Stephen went across and looked at it for a moment but did not try to touch it.

"Yes. It's the bottle of Sommeil from Father's drug cupboard."

"There are seven three-grain tablets left. Do you confirm that three tablets are missing since you put them in this bottle?"

"Naturally I do. I told you. There were ten three-grain tablets."

"Thank you," said Dalgleish and turned again to the door.

Deborah spoke just as his hand reached the door-knob:

"Are we permitted to ask where that bottle was found?" she asked.

Dalgleish looked at her as if the question really needed his serious consideration.

"Why not? It is probable that at least one of you would genuinely like to know. It was found by one of the men working with me, buried in that part of the lawn which was used for a treasure hunt. As you know, the turf has been cut about fairly intensively there, presumably by hopeful competitors. There are several sods still lying on the surface. The bottle had been placed in one of the holes and the turf pressed down over it. The person responsible had even been considerate enough to mark the place with one of the named wooden pegs which were lying about. Curiously enough it was yours, Mrs. Riscoe. Your mug with the drugged cocoa; your peg marking the hidden bottle."

"But why? Why?" said Deborah.

"If any of you can answer that question I shall be in the business room for an hour or two yet." He turned courteously to Mr. Hinks. "I think you must be Mr. Hinks, sir. I was hoping to see you. If it is convenient perhaps you could spare me a few minutes now."

The vicar looked around at the Maxies in puzzled pity. He paused and seemed about to speak. Then, without a word, he followed Dalgleish from the room.

¶ 3

It was not until ten o'clock that Dalgleish got round to interviewing Dr. Epps. The doctor had been out nearly all day seeing cases that might or might not have been urgent enough to warrant a Sunday visit, but which had certainly provided him with an excuse to postpone questioning. If he had anything to hide he had presumably decided on his tactics by now. He was not an obvious suspect. It was difficult, for one thing, to imagine a motive. But he was the Maxie family doctor and a close family friend. He would not willingly obstruct justice but he might have unorthodox ideas about what constituted justice and he would have the loop-hole of professional discretion if he wanted to avoid inconvenient questions. Dalgleish had had trouble with that kind of witness before. But he need not have worried. Dr. Epps, as if conceding some semi-medical recognition to the visit, invited him willingly enough into the red-brick surgery which had been misguidedly added to his pleasant Georgian house, and squeezed himself into a swivel-chair at his desk. Dalgleish was waved towards the patients' chair, a large Windsor of disconcerting lowness in which it was difficult to appear at ease or to take the initiative. He almost expected the doctor to begin on a string of personal and embarrassing questions. And, in fact, Dr. Epps had obviously decided to do most of the talking. This suited Dalgleish who knew very well when he might learn most by silence. The doctor lit a large and peculiarly shaped pipe.

"Won't offer you a smoke. Or a drink for that matter. Know you don't usually drink with suspects." He darted a sharp glance at Dalgleish to see his reaction but, receiving no comment, he established his pipe with a few vigorous sucks and began to talk.

"Won't waste your time saying what an appalling thing this is. Difficult to believe really. Still, someone killed her. Put his hand round her neck and throttled her. Terrible for Mrs. Maxie. For the girl, too, of course, but naturally I think of the living. Stephen called me in at about seven-thirty. No doubt the girl was dead, of course. Had been for seven hours as far as I could judge. The police surgeon knows more about that than me. Girl wasn't pregnant. I doctored her for the odd spot of trouble and I do know that. It'll be one in the eye for the village though. They do like to hear the worst. And it would have been a motive I suppose—for someone."

"If we're thinking about motive", replied Dalgleish, "we could start with this engagement to Mr. Stephen Maxie."

The doctor shifted uncomfortably in his chair.

"Lot of rot. The boy's a fool. He hasn't a bean except what he earns and God knows that's little enough. Of course, there will be something when his father dies, but these old families, living and keeping up property on capital, well, it's a wonder they haven't had to sell. The government's doing its best to tax them out of existence.

And that fellow Price surrounds himself with accountants and grows fat on untaxed expenses! Makes you wonder if we've all gone mad! Still, that's not your problem. You can take it from me, though, that Maxie isn't in a position to marry anyone at present. And where did he think Sally was going to live? Stay on at Martingale with her mother-in-law? Silly fool wants his head examined."

"All of which makes it plain", said Dalgleish, "that this projected match would have been calamitous for the Maxies. And that gives several people an interest in seeing that it didn't happen."

The doctor leaned across the desk at him challengingly.

"At the cost of killing the girl? By making that child motherless as well as fatherless? What sort of people do you think we are?"

Dalgleish did not reply. The facts were incontrovertible. Someone had killed Sally Jupp. Someone who had not even been deterred by the presence of her sleeping child. But he noted how the doctor's cry allied him with the Maxies. "What sort of people do you think we are?" There was no doubt where Dr. Epps's allegiance lay.

It was growing dark in the little room. Grunting with the slight effort, the doctor heaved himself across his desk and turned on a lamp. It was jointed and angled and he adjusted it carefully so that a pool of light fell on his hands but left his face in shadow. Dalgleish was beginning to feel weary but there was much to be done before his working day was over. He introduced the main object of his visit.

"Mr. Simon Maxie is your patient, I believe?"

"Of course. Always has been. Not much to be done for him now, of course. Just a matter of time and good nursing. Martha sees to that mostly. But, yes, he's my patient. Quite helpless. Advanced arteriosclerosis with other complications of one kind and another. If you're thinking that he crawled upstairs to do in the maid, well, you're wrong. I doubt if he knew she existed."

"I believe you've been prescribing some special sleeping tablets for him for the last year or so?"

"Wish you wouldn't keep on saying you believe this, that and the other. You know damn well I have. There's no secret about them. Can't see what they've got to do with this business though." He stiffened suddenly. "You don't mean she was doped first?"

"We haven't the post-mortem report yet, but it looks very like it."

The doctor did not pretend that he did not understand. "That's bad."

"It does rather narrow down the field. And there are other disquieting features."

Dalgleish then told the doctor about the missing Sommeil, where Sally was alleged to have found it, what Stephen did with the ten tablets and the finding of the bottle in the treasure-hunt plot. When he had finished there was a silence for a moment. The doctor was sagging back into the chair which had at first seemed too small to withstand his cheerful and comfortable rotundity. When he spoke the deep rumbling voice was suddenly an old and tired voice.

"Stephen never told me. Not much chance with the fête, of course. Might have changed his mind though. Probably thought I wouldn't be much help. I ought to have known, you see. He wouldn't overlook carelessness like that. His father . . . my patient. I've known Simon Maxie for thirty years. Brought his children into the world. You ought to know your patients, know when they want help. I just left the prescription week after week. Didn't even go up to him very often recently. Didn't seem much point in it.

Can't think what Martha was doing though. She nursed him, did everything. She must have known about those tablets. That is, if Sally was telling the truth."

"It's difficult to imagine her making the whole thing up. Besides, she had the tablets. I presume they can only be obtained by a doctor's prescription?"

"Yes. Can't just walk into a chemist's and buy them. Oh, it's true all right. Never doubted it really. I blame myself. Should have seen what was happening at Martingale. Not only to Simon Maxie. To all of them."

"So he thinks one of them did it," thought Dalgleish. "He can see clearly enough which way things are moving and he doesn't like it. Small blame to him. He knows this is a Martingale crime all right. The thing is, does he know for certain? And if so, which one?"

He asked about the Saturday evening at Martingale. Dr. Epps's account of Sally's appearance before dinner and the disclosure of Stephen's proposal was considerably less dramatic than that of Catherine Bowers or Miss Liddell, but the versions fundamentally agreed. He confirmed that neither he nor Miss Liddell had left the business room during the counting of the money and that he had seen Sally Jupp mounting the main staircase as he and his hostess were passing through the hall to the front door. He thought Sally was wearing a dressing-gown and carrying something, but he couldn't recall what. It might have been a cup and saucer or perhaps a beaker. He had not spoken to her. That was the last time he had seen her alive.

Dalgleish asked who else in the village had been prescribed Sommeil.

"I'll have to look up my records if you want accuracy. May take half an hour or so. It wasn't a common prescription. I can remember one or two patients who had it. May be others, of course. Sir Reynold Price and Miss Pollack at St. Mary's had it, I know. Mr. Maxie, of course. By the way, what's happening about his medicine now?"

"We're holding the Sommeil. I understand that Dr. Maxie has prescribed its equivalent. And now, Doctor, perhaps I might have a word with your housekeeper before I go."

It was a full minute before the doctor seemed to hear. Then he shuffled out of his chair with a muttered apology and led the way from the surgery into the house. There Dalgleish was able tactfully to confirm that the doctor had arrived home at 10.45 the evening before and had been called out to a confinement at 11.10. He hardly expected to hear otherwise. He would have to check with the patient's family, but no doubt they would provide an alibi for the doctor up to 3.30 in the morning when he had finally left Mrs. Baines of Nessingford in proud possession of her first-born son. Dr. Epps had been busy helping life into the world for most of Saturday night, not choking it out of Sally Jupp.

The doctor muttered something about a late visit and walked with Dalgleish to the gate, first protecting himself from the evening air by an opulent and voluminous coat at least a size too large for him. When they were at the gate the doctor, who had plunged his hands into his pockets, gave a little start of surprise and opened his right hand to reveal a small bottle. It was nearly full of small brown tablets. The two men looked at it in silence for a moment. Then Dr. Epps said, "Sommeil".

Dalgleish took a handkerchief, wrapped up the bottle and slipped it into his own pocket. He noted with interest the doctor's first instinctive gesture of resistance.

"That would be Sir Reynold's stuff, Inspector. Nothing to do with the family. This was Price's coat." His tone was defensive.

"When did the coat come into your possession, Doctor?" asked Dalgleish. Again there was a long pause. Then the doctor seemed to remember that there were facts which it was pointless to try to hide.

"I bought it on Saturday. At the church fête. I bought it rather as a joke between myself and . . . and the stall-holder."

"And that was . . . who?" asked Dalgleish inexorably.

Dr. Epps did not meet his eyes as he answered dully, "Mrs. Riscoe."

¶ 4

Sunday had been secularized and timeless, its legacy a week so out-of-joint that Monday dawned without any colour or individuality, a mere limbo of a day. The post was heavier than usual, a tribute to the efficiency both of the ubiquitous telephone and to those subtler and less scientific methods of country communications. Presumably tomorrow's post would be heavier still when the news of the Martingale murder reached those who depended on print for their information. Deborah had ordered half a dozen papers. Her mother wondered whether this extravagance was a gesture of defiance or a sop to genuine curiosity.

The police were still using the business room, although they had notified their intention of moving to the Moonraker's Arms later in the day. Mrs. Maxie privately wished them joy of the cooking. Sally's room was kept locked. Only Dalgleish held the key and he gave no explanation of his frequent visits there nor of what he had found or hoped to find.

Lionel Jephson had arrived early in the morning, fussy,

scandalized and ineffectual. The family only hoped that he was being as big a nuisance to the police as he was to them. As Deborah predicted he was at a loss in a situation so divorced from his normal concerns and experience. His obvious anxiety and reiterated admonitions suggested that he had either grave doubts of his clients' innocence or little faith in the efficiency of the police. It was a relief to the whole household when he scurried back to town before luncheon to consult with a colleague.

At twelve o'clock the telephone rang for the twentieth time.

Sir Reynold Price's voice boomed across the wire to Mrs. Maxie.

"But it's disgraceful, my dear lady. What are the police doing?"

"I think at the moment they're trying to trace the baby's father."

"Good God! Whatever for? I should think they'd do better to concentrate on finding who killed her."

"They seem to think there could be a connection."

"Damn silly ideas they would get. They've been here, you know. Wanted to know about some pills that Epps prescribed for me. Must have been months ago. Fancy him remembering after all that time. Now why do you suppose they worried about those? Most extraordinary thing. Not going to arrest me yet, Inspector, I said. You could see he was amused." Sir Reynold's hearty laughter crackled unpleasantly in Mrs. Maxie's ear.

"How very tiresome for you," said Mrs. Maxie. "I am afraid this sad business is causing a lot of trouble to everyone. Did you send them away happy?"

"The police? My dear lady, the police are never happy. I told them plainly that it's no use expecting to find anything in this house. Maids tidy up everything that isn't actually kept under lock and key. Fancy looking for a bottle of tablets which I had months ago. Damn silly idea. The inspector seemed to think I ought to remember just how many I took and what happened to the others. Well, I ask you! I told him that I was a busy man with something better to do with my time. They were asking, too, about that spot of bother we had at St. Mary's about two years ago. The inspector seemed very interested in it. Wanted to know why you had resigned from the committee and so on."

"I wonder how they got on to that?"

"Some fool's been talking too much, I suppose. Funny how people can't keep their mouths shut, especially to the police. That chap Dalgleish said to me that it was a funny thing you weren't on the St. Mary's committee when you ran practically everything else in the village. I told him you'd resigned two years ago when we had that spot of trouble and, naturally, he wanted to know what spot of trouble. Asked why we hadn't got rid of Liddell at the time. I said to him, 'My dear chap, you can't just chuck a woman out after twenty-five years' service. It's not as if there was actual dishonesty.' I take my stand on that, you know. Always have. Always will. Carelessness and general muddle with the accounts, maybe, but that's a far cry from deliberate dishonesty. I told the man that we'd had her before the committee—all very hushed up and tactful of course—and sent her a letter confirming the new financial arrangements so that there couldn't be any misunderstanding. Damn stiff letter, too, all things considered. I know you thought at the time that we should have turned over the Home to the diocesan welfare committee or one of the national associations for unmarried mothers, instead of keeping it on as a private charitable concern, and so I told the inspector."

"I thought it was time we handed over a difficult job to trained and experienced people, Sir Reynold." Even as she spoke Mrs. Maxie cursed the unwariness which had trapped her into this recapitulation of old history.

"That's what I mean. I told Dalgleish, 'Mrs. Maxie may well have been right. I'm not saying she wasn't. But Lady Price was keen on the Home—practically founded it, in fact—and naturally I wasn't keen to hand it over. Not enough of these small individual places left now. Personal touch is what counts. No doubt, though, that Miss Liddell had made a nonsense of the accounts. Too much worry for her. Figures not really woman's work.' He agreed of course. Had quite a laugh about it."

Mrs. Maxie could well believe it. The picture was not a pretty one. No doubt this facility for being all things to all men was a prerequisite of success as a detective. When the hearty man-to-man amusement had died down Mrs. Maxie had no doubt that Dalgleish's mind was busy with a new theory. Yet how was it possible? The mugs and cups for those last night drinks had certainly been placed ready by ten. After that time Miss Liddell had never been out of her hostess's sight. Together they had stood in the hall and watched that glowing triumphant figure carrying Deborah's beaker up to bed. Miss Liddell might possibly have a motive if Sally's taunt had any significance, but there was no evidence that she had the means, and certainly not that she had had the opportunity. Mrs. Maxie, who had never liked Miss Liddell, was still able to hope that the half-forgotten humiliations of two years ago could remain hidden and that Alice Liddell, not very efficient, not very intelligent, but fundamentally kind and well-meaning would be left in peace.

But Sir Reynold was still speaking.

"And by the way, I wouldn't take any notice of these extraordinary rumours that are going round the village. People are bound to talk you know, but it will all die down as soon as the police get their man. Let's hope they get a move on. Now don't forget, let me know if there's anything I can do. And mind you lock up carefully at night. It might be Deborah or yourself next. And there's another thing." Sir Reynold's voice became hoarsely conspiratorial and Mrs. Maxie had to strain to hear. "It's about the boy. Nice little fellow as far as I could see. Was watching him in his pram at the fête, you know. Thought this morning I'd like to do something there. Not much fun losing your mother. No real home. Someone ought to keep an eye on him. Where is he now? With you?"

"Jimmy's back at St. Mary's. It seemed best that way. I don't know what will be arranged for him. It's early yet, of course, and I don't know if anyone's given much thought to it."

"Time they did, dear lady. Time they did. Perhaps they'll put him up for adoption. Better get on the list, eh? Miss Liddell would be the person to ask, I suppose."

Mrs. Maxie was at a loss for an answer. She was more familiar with the laws of adoption than Sir Reynold and doubted whether he could be considered the most suitable applicant to have charge of a child. If Jimmy were to be adopted his situation would ensure that there were plenty of offers. She herself had already given thought to the child's future. She did not mention this, however, but contented herself by pointing out that Sally's relations might yet accept the boy and that nothing could be done until their views were known. It was possible, even, that the father would be traced. Sir Reynold dismissed this possibility with a hoot of derision but promised to do nothing in a hurry. With renewed warnings against homicidal maniacs he rang off. Mrs. Maxie wondered whether anyone could be as stupid as Sir Reynold appeared to be and what could have prompted his sudden concern for Jimmy.

She replaced the receiver with a sigh and turned to the day's letters. Half a dozen were from friends who, obviously in some social embarrassment, expressed their sympathy with the family and their confidence in Maxie innocence by invitations to dine. Mrs. Maxie found this demonstration of support more diverting than reassuring. The next three envelopes bore unfamiliar handwriting and she opened them reluctantly. Perhaps it would be better to destroy them unread but one never knew. Some information of value might be lost that way. Besides, it was more courageous to face unpleasantness and Eleanor Maxie had never lacked courage. But the first two letters were less objectionable than she had feared. One, indeed, was meant to be heartening. It contained three little printed texts with robins and roses in unseasonable proximity and an assurance that whosoever endured to the end would be saved. It asked for a contribution to enable this good news to be spread and suggested that the texts should be copied and distributed to those friends who were also in trouble. Most of Mrs. Maxie's friends were discreet about their troubles but, even so, she felt a tinge of guilt as she dropped the texts into the waste-paper basket. The next letter was in a mauve scented envelope from a lady who claimed psychic powers and was prepared, for a fee, to organize a séance at which Sally Jupp might be expected to appear and name her murderer. The assumption that Sally's disclosures would be completely acceptable to the Maxies did at least suggest that the writer gave them the benefit of the doubt. The last communication bore the local postmark and merely inquired, "Why weren't you content to work her to death, you dirty murderess?" Mrs. Maxie looked at the writing carefully but could not remember seeing it before. But the postmark was clear and she recognized a challenge. She decided to go down to the village and do some shopping.

The little village store was rather busier than usual and the buzz of talk which stopped as soon as she appeared left her in no doubt as to the subject of conversation. Mrs. Nelson was there, Miss Pollack, old Simon from the Weir cottage who was claimed as the oldest inhabitant and seemed to think that this absolved him from any effort at personal hygiene, and one or two of the women from the new agricultural cottages whose faces and personalities, if any, were still strange to her. There was a general murmur of "Good morning" in reply to her own greeting and Miss Pollack went so far as to say, "Lovely day again, isn't it?" before hurriedly consulting her shopping list and trying to conceal her red face behind the barricades of breakfast cereal. Mr. Wilson himself left the invoicing which was concerning him behind the scenes and came forward, quietly deferential as ever, to attend to Mrs. Maxie. He was a tall, lean, cadaverous-looking man with a face of such startling unhappiness that it was difficult to believe that he was not on the brink of bankruptcy instead of the owner of a flourishing little business. He heard more gossip than almost anyone in the village, but expressed an opinion himself so rarely that his pronouncements were listened to with great respect and commonly remembered. So far he had been uniformly silent on the subject of Sally Jupp, but it was not therefore supposed that he considered it an unsuitable subject for comment or was restrained by any reverence in the face of sudden death. Sooner or later, it was felt, Mr. Wilson would pronounce judgment, and the village would be very surprised if the judgment of the Law itself, given later and with more ceremony, were not substantially the same. He accepted Mrs. Maxie's order in silence and occupied himself with serving his most valued customer, while one by one the little group of women muttered their good-byes and crept or swept out of his shop.

When they had gone Mr. Wilson gave a conspiratorial glance around, cast his watery eyes upwards as if seeking guidance and then leaned across the counter towards Mrs. Maxie.

"Derek Pullen," he said. "That's who."

"I'm afraid I don't know what you mean, Mr. Wilson." Mrs. Maxie spoke the truth. She might have added that she had no particular desire to know.

"I'm saying nothing, mind you, madam. Let the police do their own work I say. But if they bother you at Martingale, ask them where Derek Pullen was going last Saturday night. Ask them that. He passed here at twelve or thereabouts. Saw him myself from the bedroom window."

Mr. Wilson drew himself up with the self-satisfied air of a man who has pronounced a final unanswerable argument and returned with a complete change of mood to the business of totalling Mrs. Maxie's bill. She felt that she ought to say that any evidence he possessed or thought that he possessed should be communicated to the police, but she could not bring herself to say words to this effect. She remembered Derek Pullen as she had last seen him, a small, rather spotty youth who wore over-cut city suits and cheap shoes. His mother was a member of the Women's Institute and his father worked for Sir Reynold on the larger of his two farms. It was too silly and unfair. If Wilson couldn't keep his mouth shut there would be the police at the Pullens' cottage before nightfall and it was anyone's guess what they would ferret out. The boy looked timid and would probably be scared out of the few wits he looked as if he possessed. Then Mrs. Maxie remembered that someone had been in Sally's room that night. It could have been Derek Pullen. If Martingale were to be saved any further suffering she must keep her allegiance clear. "If you have information, Mr. Wilson," she said, "I think you should give it to Inspector Dalgleish. In the meantime you might harm a great many innocent people by making accusations of that kind."

Mr. Wilson received this mild rebuke with the liveliest satisfaction as if it were the only confirmation needed of his own theories. He had obviously said all he intended to and the subject was now closed. "Four and five and ten and nine and one pound one shilling is one pound sixteen and two, if you please, madam," he intoned. Mrs. Maxie paid.

¶ 5

Meanwhile Johnnie Wilcox, a grubby and under-sized twelve-year-old, was being interviewed by Dalgleish in the business room. He had presented himself at Martingale with the announcement that the vicar had sent him to see the inspector and please it was important. Dalgleish received him with grave courtesy and invited him to sit down and tell his story in comfort. He told it clearly and well and it was the most intriguing piece of evidence that Dalgleish had heard for some time.

Apparently Johnnie had been detailed with other members of his Sunday school class to help with the teas and the washing-up. There had been some feeling over this arrangement which was generally felt by the boys to be domestic, degrading and, frankly, not much fun. True, there had been promises of feasting later with the left-overs but the teas were always popular and last year several helpers had arrived to lend a belated hand and to share the meagre spoils with those who had borne the heat of the day. Johnnie Wilcox had seen no advantage in lingering longer than necessary and as soon as enough children had arrived to make his absence less noticeable he had possessed himself of two fish sandwiches, three chocolate buns and a couple of jam tarts and had borne them off to Bocock's stable loft in the confidence that Bocock was safely occupied giving pony rides.

Johnnie had been sitting peacefully in the loft munching and reading his comic for some time—it was useless to expect him to estimate for how long but only one bun remained—when he had heard footsteps and voices. He had not been alone in a desire for privacy and two other people were coming into the stable. He did not wait to see whether they were also intending to climb the loft, but took the sensible precaution of removing himself and his bun to a corner where he hid behind a large bale of straw. This action did not seem unnecessarily timid. In Johnnie's world a great deal of unpleasantness from spankings to going to bed at an early hour was avoided by the simple expedient of knowing when not to be seen. This time his caution was again justified. The footsteps did come up into the hay loft and he heard the soft thud of the trap-door being replaced. After that he was forced to sit in silence and some boredom, nibbling quietly at his bun and trying to make it last out until the visitors should depart. There were only two of them, he was certain of that—and one of them was Sally Jupp. He had caught a brief glimpse of her hair as she came through the trap-door, but had been forced to dodge back before she was in full view. But there was no doubt about it. Johnnie knew Sally well enough to be quite certain that he had both seen and heard her in the hay loft on Saturday afternoon. But he had not seen nor recognized the man with her. Once Sally had entered the loft it would have been risky to peer round the bundle of hay since even the smallest movement caused an unexpectedly loud rustling, and Johnnie had employed all his energies in keeping perfectly, and most unnaturally still. Partly because the heavy hay bundle had muffled the voices and partly because he was used to finding the conversations of grown-up people both boring and incomprehensible, he made no effort to understand what was being said. All that Dalgleish could count on as reliable was that the two visitors had been arguing, but in low voices, that there was some mention of forty pounds, and that Sally Jupp had ended up by saying something about there being no risk if he kept his head and "watching for the light". Johnnie said that there had been a great deal of talk but most of it was spoken quietly and quickly. Only those few phrases remained in his memory. He could not say how long the three of them remained in the loft. It had seemed a dreadfully long time and he was stiff and thoroughly bored before he heard the sound of the trap-door being banged back and the girl and her companion left the loft. Sally had gone first and the man had followed. Johnnie had not felt safe in peering from his hiding-place until the sound of their footsteps was heard disappearing down the steps. Then he was in time to see a brown gloved hand replacing the trap-door. He had waited another few minutes himself then had run back to the fête where his absence had aroused very little interest. That, indeed, was the sum total of Johnnie Wilcox's Saturday afternoon adventure and it was irritating to consider how a few changes in circumstances might have added to its value. If Johnnie had been a little more adventurous he might have seen the man. If he had been a few years older or of a different sex he certainly would have considered this clandestine meeting in a more intriguing light than the mere interruption of a feast and would have certainly listened to and remembered as much of the conversation as possible. Now it was difficult to place any interpretation on the scraps he had overheard. He seemed an honest and reliable little boy, but ready enough to admit that he might have made a mistake. He thought that Sally had talked about "the light" but he might have imagined it. He hadn't really been listening and they were speaking quietly. On the other hand he had no doubt at all that it was Sally he had seen and was equally firm in his belief that it was not a friendly meeting. He couldn't be sure of the time when he left the stable. Teas began about half past three and lasted as long as people wanted them and the food held out. Johnnie thought it must have been about half past four when he first made his escape from Mrs. Cope. He couldn't remember how long he was hidden in the stable. It had seemed a very long time. With that Dalgleish had to be content. The whole thing was suspiciously like a case of blackmail and it seemed likely that another assignation had been made. But the fact that Johnnie had not recognized the man's voice seemed to prove conclusively that it could not have been either Stephen Maxie or a local man, most of whom would be well known to him. That at least supported the theory that there was another man to be considered. If Sally were blackmailing this stranger and he was actually at the church fête, then things looked brighter for the Maxies. As he thanked young Johnnie, warned him against talking to anyone else about his experience, and dismissed him to the comforting pleasure of revealing all that had passed to the vicar, Dalgleish's mind was already busy with new evidence.

CHAPTER SIX

¶ 1

The Inquest was fixed for three oclock on Tuesday and the Maxies found they were almost looking forward to it as at least one known obligation which might help to speed the slow, uncomfortable hours. There was a sense of constant unease like the tension of a thundery day when the storm is inevitable and yet will not break. The tacit assumption that no one at Martingale could be a murderer precluded any realistic discussion of Sally's death. They were all afraid of saying too much or of saying it to the wrong person. Sometimes Deborah wished that the household could get together and at least decide on some solid basis of strategy. But when Stephen hesitantly voiced the same wish she drew back in sudden panic. Stephen talking about Sally was not to be borne.

Felix Hearne was different. With him it was possible to discuss almost anything. He did not fear death for himself nor was he shy of it and he apparently saw no breach of good taste in discussing Sally Jupp's death dispassionately and even lightly. At first Deborah took part in these conversations in a spirit of bravado. Later she realized that humour was only a feeble attempt to denigrate fear. Now, before Tuesday luncheon, she paced between the roses at Felix's side while he poured out his spate of blessedly foolish chatter, provoking her to an equally dispassionate and diverting flow of theories.

"Seriously, though, Deborah. If I were writing a book I should make it one of the village boys. Derek Pullen, for example."

"But he didn't. Anyway, he hasn't a motive."

"Motive is the last thing to look for. You can always find a motive. Perhaps the corpse was blackmailing him. Perhaps she was pressing him to marry her and he wouldn't. She could tell him that there was another baby on the way. It isn't true, of course, but he wasn't to know that. You see, they had been having the usual passionate *affaire*. I should make him one of the quiet, intense kind. They're capable of anything. In fiction, anyway."

"But she didn't want him to marry her. She had Stephen to marry. She wouldn't want Derek Pullen if she could have Stephen."

"You speak, if I may say so, with the blind partiality of a sister. But have it your own way. Whom do you suggest?"

"Suppose we make it Father."

"You mean the elderly gentleman, tied to his bed?"

"Yes. Except that he wasn't. It could be one of those Grand Guignol plots. The elderly gentleman didn't want his son to marry the scheming hussy so he crawled upstairs step by step and strangled her with his old school tie."

Felix considered this effort and rejected it.

"Why not make it the mysterious visitor with a name like a cinema cat. Who is he? Where does he come from? Could he be the father of her child?"

"Oh, I don't think so."

"Well, he was. He had met the corpse when she was an innocent girl at her first job. I shall draw a veil over that painful episode but you can imagine his surprise and horror when he meets her again, the girl he has wronged, in the home of his fiancée. And with his child too!"

"Has he a fiancée?"

"Of course. An extremely attractive widow whom he is determined to snare. Anyway, the poor wronged girl threatens to tell all so he has to silence her. I should make him one of those cynical, unlikeable characters so that no one would worry when he got copped."

"You don't think that would be rather sordid? What about making it the Warden of St. Mary's. It could be one of those psychological thrillers with highbrow quotations at the beginning of the chapters and a lot of Freud."

"If it's Freud you fancy I'd put my money on the corpse's uncle. Now there would be a fine excuse for some deep psychological stuff. You see, he was a hard, narrow-minded man who had turned her out when he heard about the baby. But like all Puritans in fiction, he was just as bad himself. He had been carrying on with a simple little girl whom he met singing in the choir and she was in the same Home as the corpse having her baby. So the whole horrible truth came out and, of course, Sally was blackmailing him for thirty bob a week and nothing said. Obviously he couldn't risk exposure. He was far too respectable for that."

"What did Sally do with the thirty bob?"

"Opened a savings account in the baby's name of course. All that will come to light in due course."

"It would be nice if it did. But aren't you forgetting about the corpse's prospective sister-in-law? No difficulty about motive there."

Felix said easily, "But she wasn't a murderess."

"Oh, damn you, Felix! Must you be so blatantly tactful?"

"Since I know very well that you didn't kill Sally Jupp, do you expect me to go about registering embarrassment and suspicion just for the fun of it?"

"I did hate her, Felix. I really hated her."

"All right, my sweet. So you really hated her. That is bound to put you at a disadvantage with yourself. But don't be too anxious to confide your feelings to the police. They are worthy men, no doubt, and their manners are beautiful. They may, however, be limited in imagination. After all, their great strength is their common sense. That is the basis of all sound detective work. They have the method and the means so don't go handing them the motive. Let them do some work for the taxpayers' money."

"Do you think Dalgleish will find out who did it?" asked Deborah after a little pause.

"I think he may know now," replied Felix calmly. "Getting enough evidence to justify a charge is a different matter. We may find out this afternoon how far the police have got and how much they're prepared to tell. It may amuse Dalgleish to keep us in suspense but he's bound to show his hand sooner or later."

But the inquest was both a relief and a disappointment. The coroner sat without a jury. He was a mild-voiced man with the face of a depressed St. Bernard dog who gave the impression of having wandered into the proceedings by mistake. For all that, he knew what he wanted and he wasted no time. There were fewer villagers present than the Maxies had expected. Probably they were conserving time and energy for the better entertainment of the funeral. Certainly, those present were little wiser than they were before. The coroner made it all seem deceptively simple. Evidence of identification was given by a nervous, insignificant little woman who proved to be Sally's aunt. Stephen Maxie gave evidence and the factual details of finding the body were briefly elicited. The medical evidence showed that death was caused by vagal inhibition during manual strangulation and had been very sudden. There were about one and a half grains of barbiturate acid derivative in the stomach. The coroner asked no questions other than those necessary to establish these facts. The police asked for an adjournment and this was granted. It was all very informal, almost friendly. The witnesses crouched on the low chairs used by the Sunday school children while the coroner drooped over the proceedings from the superintendent's dais. There were jam jars of summer flowers on the window-sills and a flannelgraph on one wall showed the Christian's journey from baptism to burial in crayoned pictures. In these innocent and incongruous surroundings the law, with formality but without fuss, took note that Sarah Lillian Jupp had been feloniously done to death.

¶ 2

Now there was the funeral to face. Here, unlike the inquest, attendance was optional and the decision whether or not to appear was one which none but Mrs. Maxie found easy. She had no difficulty and made it clear that she had every intention of being present. Although she did not discuss the matter, her attitude was obvious. Sally Jupp had died in their house and in their employ. Her only relations had obviously no intentions of forgiving her for being as embarrassing and unorthodox in death as she had been in life. They would have no part in the funeral and it would take place from St. Mary's and at the expense of that institution. But, apart from the need for someone to be there, the Maxies had a responsibility. If people died in your house the least you could do was to attend the funeral. Mrs. Maxie did not express herself in these words, but her son and daughter were unmistakably given to understand that such attendance was mere courtesy and that those who extended to others the hospitality of their homes should, if it unfortunately proved necessary, extend that hospitality to seeing them safely into their graves. In all her private imaginings of what life at Martingale would be during a murder investigation Deborah had never considered the major part which comparatively minor matters of taste or etiquette would play. It was strange that the overriding anxiety for all their futures would be, temporarily at least, less urgent than the worry of whether or not the family should send a wreath to the funeral, and if so, what appropriate condolence should be written on the card. Here again the question did not worry Mrs. Maxie who merely inquired whether they wished to club together or whether Deborah would send a wreath of her own.

Stephen, it appeared, was exempt from these obsequies. The police had given him permission to return to hospital after the inquest and he would not be at Martingale again until the following Saturday night, except for fleeting visits. No one expected him to provide a chaste wreath for the delectation of the village gossips. He had every excuse for returning to London and carrying on with his job. Even Dalgleish could not expect him to hang about at Martingale indefinitely for the convenience of the police.

If Catherine had almost as valid an excuse for returning to London she did not avail herself of it. Apparently she had still seven days of her annual leave in hand and was willing and happy to stay on at Martingale. Matron had been approached and was sympathetic. There would be absolutely no difficulty if she could help Mrs. Maxie in any way. Undeniably she could. There was still the heavy nursing of Simon Maxie to be coped with, there was the continual interruption of household routine caused by Dalgleish's investigation, and there was the lack of Sally.

Once it was established that her mother intended to be at the funeral, Deborah set about subduing her natural abhorrence of the whole idea and announced abruptly that she would be there. She was not surprised when Catherine expressed a similar intention, but it was both unexpected and a relief to find that Felix meant to go with them.

"It's not in the least necessary," she told him angrily. "I can't think what all the fuss is about. Personally I find the whole idea morbid and distasteful, but if you want to come and be gaped at, well, it's a free show." She left the drawing-room quickly but returned a few minutes later to say with the disconcerting formality which he found so disarming in her: "I'm sorry I was so rude, Felix. Please do come if you will. It was sweet of you to think of it."

Felix felt suddenly angry with Stephen. It was true that the boy had every excuse for returning to work, but it was nevertheless typical and irritating that he should have so ready and simple an excuse for evading responsibility and unpleasantness. Neither Deborah nor her mother, of course, would see it that way and Catherine Bowers, poor besotted fool, was ready to forgive Stephen anything. None of the women would intrude their troubles or difficulties on Stephen. But, thought Felix, if that young man had disciplined his more quixotic impulses none of this need have happened. Felix prepared for the funeral in a mood of cold anger and fought resolutely against the suspicion that part of his resentment was frustration and part was envy.

It was another wonderful day. The crowd were dressed in summer dresses, some of the girls in clothes which would have been more suitable on a bathing-beach than in a cemetery. A large number had evidently been picnicking and had only heard of the better entertainment to be offered in the churchyard by chance. They were laden with the remains of their feasts and some were actually still engaged in finishing their sandwiches or oranges. They were perfectly well behaved once they got near to the grave. Death has an almost universally sobering effect and a few nervous giggles were soon repressed by the outraged glances of the more orthodox. It was not their behaviour that enraged Deborah, it was the fact that they should be there at all. She was filled with a cold contempt and an anger that was frightening in its intensity. Afterwards she was glad of this since it left no room for grief or for embarrassment.

The Maxies, Felix Hearne and Catherine Bowers stood together at the open graveside with Miss Liddell and a handful of girls from St. Mary's bunched behind them. Opposite them stood Dalgleish and Martin. Police and suspects faced each other across the open grave. A little way away another funeral was in progress taken by some alien clergyman from another parish. The little group of mourners were all in black and huddled so close to the grave in a tight circle that they seemed engaged in some secret and esoteric rite that was not for the eyes of others. No one took any notice of them and the voice of their priest could not be heard above the minor rustlings of Sally's crowd. Afterwards they went quietly away. They, thought Deborah, had at least buried their dead with some dignity. But now Mr. Hinks was speaking his few words. Wisely he did not mention the circumstances of the girl's death, but said gently that the ways of Providence were strange and mysterious, an assertion which few of his listeners were competent to disprove, even though the presence of the police suggested that some at least of this present mystery was the work of human agency.

Mrs. Maxie took an active interest in the whole ceremony, her audible "Amens" sounded emphatic agreement at the end of each petition, she found her way about the Book of Common Prayer with capable fingers and helped two of the St. Mary's girls to find the place when they were too overcome with grief or embarrassment to manage their books themselves. At the end of the service she stepped up to the grave and stood for a moment gazing down at the coffin. Deborah felt rather than heard her sigh. What it meant no one could have told from the composed face that turned itself again to confront the crowd. She pulled on her gloves and leaned down to read one of the mourning-cards before joining her daughter.

"What an appalling crowd. One would think people had something better to do. Still, if that poor child Sally were half the exhibitionist she seems to have been, this funeral would meet with her approval. What is that boy doing? Is this your mother? Well, surely your little boy knows that one doesn't jump about on graves. You must control him better if you want to bring him into the churchyard. This is consecrated ground, not the school playground. A funeral isn't suitable entertainment for a child anyway."

The mother and child gaped after them, two pale astounded faces with the same sharp noses, the same scrawny hair. Then the woman pulled her child away with a frightened backward glance. Already the bright splurge of colour was dispersing, the bicycles were being dragged from among the Michaelmas daisies by the churchyard wall, the photographers were packing up their cameras. One or two little groups still waited about, whispering together and watching an opportunity to snoop among the wreaths. The sexton was already picking up the legacy of orange peel and paper bags, muttering under his breath. Sally's grave was a sheet of colour. Reds, blues and gold spread over the piled turfs and wooden planks like a gaudy patchwork quilt and the scent of rich earth mixed with the scent of the flowers.

¶ 3

"Isn't that Sally's aunt?" asked Deborah. A thin, nervous-looking woman with hair which might once have been red was talking to Miss Liddell. They walked away together towards the churchyard gate. "Surely it's the same woman who identified Sally at the inquest. If it is the aunt perhaps we could drive her home. The buses are dreadfully infrequent at this time of day."

"It might be worth while having a word with her," said Felix consideringly. Deborah's suggestion had originally been prompted by simple kindness, the wish to save someone a long wait in the hot sun. But now the practical advantages of her proposal asserted themselves.

"Do get Miss Liddell to introduce you, Felix. I'll bring the car round. You might find out where Sally worked before she got pregnant, and who Jimmy's father is and whether Sally's uncle really liked her."

"In two or three moments of casual conversation? I hardly think so."

"We should have all the drive to pump her. Do try, Felix."

Deborah sped after her mother and Catherine with as much speed as decency permitted, leaving Felix to his task. The woman and Miss Liddell had reached the road now and were pausing for a last few words. From a distance the two figures seemed to be executing some kind of ceremonial dance. They moved together to shake hands, then bobbed apart. Then Miss Liddell, who had turned away, swung back with some fresh remark and the figures drew together again.

As Felix moved towards them they turned to watch him and he could see Miss Liddell's lips moving. He joined them and the inescapable introductions were made. A thin hand, gloved in cheap black rayon, held his hand timidly for a brief second and then dropped. Even in that apathetic and almost imperceptible contact he sensed that she was shaking. The anxious grey eyes looked away from his as he spoke.

"Mrs. Riscoe and I were wondering if we might drive you home," he said gently. "There will be a long wait for a bus and we should be very glad of the drive." That at least was the truth. She hesitated. Just as Miss Liddell had apparently decided that the offer, although unexpected, could not in decency be ignored and might even be safely accepted and had begun to urge this course, Deborah drew up beside them in Felix's Renault and the matter was settled. Sally's aunt was introduced to her as Mrs. Victor Proctor and was comfortably ensconced beside her in the front of the car before anyone had time for argument. Felix settled himself in the back, aware of some distaste for the enterprise but prepared to admire Deborah in action. "Painless extractions a speciality" he thought as the car swung away down the hill. He wondered how far they were going and whether Deborah had bothered to tell her mother how long they would be away. "I think I know roughly where you live," he heard her saying. "It's just outside Canningbury, isn't it? We go through it on our way to London. But I shall have to rely on you for the road. It's very sweet of you to let us drive you home. Funerals are so awful. It really is a relief to get away for a time." The result of this was unexpected. Suddenly Mrs. Proctor was crying, not noisily, hardly even without moving her face. Almost as if her tears were without any possibility of control she let them slide in a stream down her cheeks and fall on to her folded hands. When she spoke her voice was low but clear enough to be heard above the engine. And still the tears fell silently and without effort.

"I shouldn't have come really. Mr. Proctor wouldn't like it if he knew I'd come. He won't be back when I get home and Beryl is at school, so he won't know. But he wouldn't like it. She's made her own bed so let her lie on it. That's what he says and you can't blame him. Not after what he's done for her. There was never any difference made between Sally and Beryl. Never. I'll say that to the day I die. I don't know why it had to happen to us."

This perennial cry of the unfortunate struck Felix as unreasonable. He was not aware that the Proctors had accepted any responsibility for Sally since her pregnancy and they had certainly succeeded in dissociating themselves from her death. He leaned forward to hear more clearly. Deborah may have made some kind of encouraging sound, he could not be sure. But there was to be no question of pumping this witness. She had been keeping things to herself for too long. "We brought her up decently. No one can say we didn't. It hasn't always been easy. She did get the scholarship but we still had to feed her. She wasn't an easy child. I used to think it was the bombing but Mr. Proctor wouldn't have that. They were with us at the time, you know. We had a house in Stoke Newington then. There hadn't been many raids and somehow we felt safe with the Anderson shelter and everything. It was one of those VI rockets that did for Lil and George. I don't remember anything about it nor about being dug out. They never told me about Lil for a week afterwards. They got us all out but Lil was dead and George died in hospital. We were the lucky ones. At least I suppose we were. Mr. Proctor was really bad for a long time and, of course, he's got his disability. But they said we were the lucky ones."

"Like me," thought Felix bitterly. "One of the lucky ones."

"And then you took Sally and brought her up," prompted Deborah.

"There wasn't anyone else really. Mother couldn't have taken her. She wasn't fit for it. I tried to think that Lil would have liked it, but those sort of thoughts can't help you to love a child. She wasn't loving really. Not like Beryl. But then Sally was ten before Beryl arrived and I suppose it was hard on her after being the only one for so long. But we never made a difference. They always had the same, piano lessons and everything. And now this. The police came round after she died. They weren't in uniform or anything, but you could see who they were. Everyone knew about it. They asked who the man was but, of course, we couldn't say."

"The man who killed her?" Deborah sounded incredulous.

"Oh no. The father of the baby. I suppose they thought he might have done it. But we couldn't tell them anything."

"I suppose they asked a lot of questions about where you were on the night."

For the first time Mrs. Proctor seemed aware of her tears. She fumbled in her handbag and wiped them away. Interest in her story seemed to have assuaged whatever grief she was indulging. Felix thought that it was unlikely that she wept for Sally. Was it the resurrected memory of Lil, of George and of the helpless child they had left behind which had caused those tears, or was it just weariness and a sense of failure? Almost as if she sensed his question she said, "I don't know why I'm crying. Crying can't bring back the dead. I suppose it was the service. We had that hymn for Lil. 'The King of Love my Shepherd is'. It doesn't seem right for either of them really. You were asking about the police. I suppose you've had your share of them, too. They came to us all right. I told them I was at home with Beryl. They asked if we went to the fête at Chadfleet. I told them we didn't know anything about it. Not that we would have gone. We didn't see Sally ever and we didn't want to come nosing around where she worked. I could remember the day all right. It was funny really. Miss Liddell telephoned in the morning to talk to Mr. Proctor which she hadn't done since Sally took her new job. Beryl answered the 'phone and it made her feel quite queer. She thought something must have happened to Sally for Miss Liddell to 'phone. But it was only to say that Sally was doing all right. It was funny though. She knew we didn't want to hear."

It must have struck Deborah as strange, too, for she asked. "Had Miss Liddell telephoned before to tell you how Sally was getting on?"

"No. Not since Sally went to Martingale. She telephoned to tell us that. At least I think she did. She may have written to Mr. Proctor, but I can't be sure. I suppose she thought that we ought to know about Sally leaving the Home, Mr. Proctor being her guardian. At least he used to be, but now she's over twenty-one and on her own it's nothing to us where she goes. She never cared for us not for any of us, not even Beryl. I thought I'd better come today because it looks queer if no one from the family's there, whatever Mr. Proctor may say. But he was right really. You can't help the dead by being there and it's only upsetting. All those people, too. They ought to have something better to do."

"So Mr. Proctor hadn't seen Sally since she left your house?" pursued Deborah.

"Oh, no. There wouldn't be any point in it, would there?"

"I expect the police asked him where he was on the night she died. They always do. Of course it's only a formality."

If Deborah had been afraid of causing offence she was worrying unnecessarily.

"It's funny the way they go on. You'd have thought we knew something about it by the way they talked. Asking questions about Sally's life and whether she had any expectations and who her friends were. Anyone would think she was someone important. They had Beryl in to ask about the telephone call from Miss Liddell. They even asked Mr. Proctor what he was doing the night Sally died. Not that we were likely to forget that night. It was the one he had his cycle accident. He wasn't home till twelve and he was in a proper bad state with his lip all swollen and the cycle bent up. He lost his watch, too, which was upsetting as his father left it to him and it was real gold. Very valuable they always told us. We aren't likely to forget that night in a hurry I can tell you."

Mrs. Proctor had now recovered completely from the emotional effects of the funeral and was chatting away with the eagerness of someone who is more accustomed to listening than to getting a hearing. Deborah was making light work of the driving. Her hands lay gently on the wheel and her blue eyes gazed steadily on the road ahead, but Felix had little doubt that most of her mind was on other matters. She made sympathetic sounds in reply to Mrs. Proctor's story and replied, "What a horrid shock for you both! You must have been terribly worried when he was so late. How did it happen?"

"He came off at the bottom of a hill somewhere Finchworthy way. I don't know exactly where. He was coming down fast and someone had left broken glass in the road. Of course it ripped the front tyre and he lost control and went into the ditch. He might have been killed as I told him, or badly injured, and if he had, goodness knows what would have happened because those roads are very lonely. You could lie there for hours and no one come by. Mr. Proctor doesn't like the busy roads for cycling and I don't wonder. There's no peace if you don't get away by yourself."

"Is he fond of cycling?" asked Deborah.

"Cycling mad. Always has been. Of course he doesn't go in for the real road work now. Not since the war and being bombed. He did a lot of it when he was young though. But he still likes to get about and we don't usually see much of him on Saturday afternoons."

Mrs. Proctor's voice held a shade of relief which was not lost on either of her listeners. A bicycle and an accident can be a useful alibi, thought Felix, but he can't be a serious suspect if he was indoors by twelve. It would take him at least an hour to get home from Martingale even if the accident were faked, and he had the use of the bicycle all the way. It was difficult, too, to imagine an adequate motive since Proctor had obviously found no reason to murder his niece before her admission to St. Mary's and had apparently had no contact with her since. Felix's mind played with the possibility of a future inheritance for Sally which, at her death, would conveniently devolve upon Beryl Proctor. But in his heart he knew that he was looking not for the murderer of Sally Jupp but for someone with sufficient motive and opportunity to divert the police investigation from more likely suspects. It seemed a forlorn hope so far as the Proctors were concerned, but Deborah had obviously made up her mind that there was something to be discovered from them. The time factor was apparently worrying her, too.

"Did you wait up for your husband, Mrs. Proctor? You must have been getting pretty desperate by midnight unless he was usually late."

"Well, he was usually a bit late and he always said not to wait up so I didn't. I go to the pictures most Saturdays with Beryl. We've got the telly, of course, and we sometimes watch that, but it makes a change to get out of the house once a week."

"So you were in bed when your husband returned?" Deborah insisted gently.

"He had his own key, of course, so there wasn't any point in waiting up. If I'd known he was going to be so late it would have been different. I usually go up to bed about ten when Mr. Proctor's out. Mind you, there's not the same rush on a Sunday morning, but I was never one for late nights. That's what I told the police. 'I was never one for late nights', I said. They were asking about Mr. Proctor's accident, too. The inspector was very sympathetic. 'Not home until nearly twelve', I told them. They could see it had been a worrying night without Sally getting herself murdered like that."

"I expect Mr. Proctor woke you when he arrived home. It must have been terribly worrying to see him in that condition."

"Oh, it was! I heard him in the bathroom and when I called out he came in to me. His face looked awful, a terrible green colour streaked with blood, and he was shaking all over. I don't know how he got home. I got up to make him a cup of tea while he had a bath. I remember the time because he called down to me to ask me what it was. He'd lost his watch you see after the accident, and we'd only got the little kitchen clock and the one in the front room. That said ten minutes past midnight and the kitchen one said the same. It was a shock to me I can tell you. It must have been half past twelve before we were back in bed and I never thought he'd be fit to get up the next morning. But he did, the same as usual. He always goes down first and makes the tea. He thinks no one can make tea like him and he does bring up a good cup. But I never thought he'd get up early that Sunday, not after what he looked like the night before. He's still shaken up by it even now. That's why he didn't go to the inquest. And then to have the police arriving that morning to tell us about Sally. We shan't forget that night in a hurry."

¶ 4

They had reached Canningbury now and there was a long wait at the traffic lights which regulated the surge of traffic meeting at the High Road and the Broadway. It was obviously a popular shopping afternoon in this over-crowded suburb of east London. The pavements were spilling with housewives who every now and then, as if propelled by some primeval urge, streamed with maddening slowness across the path of the traffic. The shops on both sides of the road had once been a row of houses and their grandiose windows and frontages were in incongruous contrast to the modest roofs and windows above. The town hall, which looked as if it had been designed by a committee of morons in an excess of alcohol and civic pride, stood in isolated splendour bounded by two bombed sites where rebuilding had only just begun.

Closing his eyes against the heat and the noise Felix reminded himself sternly that Canningbury was one of the more enlightened suburbs with an enviable record of good public services and that not everyone wanted to live in a quiet Georgian house in Greenwich where the mist came up from the river in white fingers and only the most persistent friends found their way to his door. He was glad when the traffic lights changed and, under Mrs. Proctor's guidance, they moved forward in a series of gentle jerks and turned left away from the main road. Here was the backwash of the shopping centre, the women walking home with their laden baskets, the few smaller gown shops and hairdressers with pseudo-French names over the converted front-room windows. After a few minutes they turned again into a quiet street where a row of identical houses stretched as far as the eye could see. Although they were identical in structure, however, they were very different in appearance for hardly two of the small front gardens were alike. All were carefully sown and tended. A few householders had expressed their individuality with monkey-puzzle trees, coy stone gnomes fishing from basins or spurious rock gardens, but the majority had contented themselves by creating a little show of colour and fragrance which shamed the dull nonentity of the house behind. The curtains showed signs of careful if misguided choosing and of frequent washing, and were supplemented by additional half-curtains of draped lace or net which were carefully drawn against the curiosity of a vulgar world. Windermere Crescent had the respectable look of a street that is a cut above its neighbours and whose inhabitants are determined to maintain that superiority.

This then had been the home of Sally Jupp who had fallen so lamentably from its standards. The car drew in to the kerb at the gate of number 17 and Mrs. Proctor clutched her black shapeless handbag to her chest and began to fumble at the door. "Let me," said Deborah, and leaned across her to release the catch. Mrs. Proctor extricated herself and began her profuse thanks which Deborah cut short.

"Please don't. We were very glad to come. I wonder if I might bother you for a glass of water before we leave. It's silly, I know, but driving is so thirst-making in this heat. Really only water. I hardly ever drink anything else."

"Don't you, by God!" thought Felix as the two women disappeared into the house.

He wondered what Deborah was up to now and hoped that the wait wouldn't be too long. Mrs. Proctor had been offered no choice about inviting her benefactor into the house. She could hardly have brought a glass of water out to the car. Nevertheless Felix was certain that she had not welcomed the intrusion. She had glanced anxiously up the road before they went in and he guessed that the time was getting dangerously late and that she was desperately anxious that the car should be gone before her husband came home. Some of the anxiety she had shown when they first met her in the churchyard had returned. He felt a momentary spasm of irritation with Deborah. The exercise was unlikely to be useful and it was a shame to worry that pathetic little woman.

Deborah, untouched by such nice refinement of feeling, was being shown into the front room. A schoolgirl was arranging her music on the piano in evident preparation for her practice but was bundled out of the room with a hasty injunction to "Fetch a glass of water, dear" spoken in the falsely bright tone often used by parents in the presence of strangers. The child went out rather reluctantly Deborah thought and not without giving her a long and deliberate stare. She was a remarkably plain child, but the likeness to her dead cousin was unmistakable. Mrs. Proctor had not introduced her and Deborah wondered whether this was an oversight due to nervousness or a deliberate wish to keep the child in ignorance of her mother's afternoon's activities. If so, presumably some story would be concocted to explain the visit, although Mrs. Proctor had not struck her as possessing much inventive faculty.

They sat down in opposite armchairs, each with its embroidered chair-back of a crinolined and bonneted female gathering hollyhocks and its plump unsullied cushions. This was obviously the best room, used only for entertaining or for piano practice. It had the faint musty smell compounded of wax polish, new furniture and seldom-opened windows. On the piano were two photographs of young girls in ballet dresses, their graceless bodies bent into unnatural and angular poses and their faces set into determined smiles beneath the wreaths of artificial roses. One of them was the child who had just left the room. The other was Sally. It was strange how, even at that age, the same family colouring and similar bone structure should have produced in one an essential distinction and in the other a heavy plainness that held little promise for the future. Mrs. Proctor saw the direction of her glance.

"Yes," she said, "we did everything for her. Everything. There was never any difference made. She had piano lessons, too, the same as Beryl although she never had Beryl's gift. But we always treated them alike. It's a dreadful thing that it's all ended like this. That other photo is the group we had took after Beryl's christening. That's me and Mr. Proctor with the baby and Sally. She was a pretty little thing then, but it didn't last."

Deborah moved over to the photograph. The group had been stiffly posed in heavy carved chairs and against a contrived background of draped curtains which made the photograph look older than it was. Mrs. Proctor, younger and more buxom, held her child awkwardly and looked ill at ease in her new clothes.

Sally looked sulky. The husband was posed behind them, his gloved hands leaning proprietorially on the backs of the chairs. There was something unnatural in his stance, but his face gave nothing away. Deborah looked at him carefully. Somewhere she was certain that she had seen that face before, but the recognition was tenuous and unsatisfactory. It was, after all, an unremarkable face and the photograph was more than ten years old. She turned away from the photograph with a sense of disappointment. It had told her very little and she hardly knew what else she had expected to gain from it.

Beryl Proctor came back with the glass of water, one of the best glasses carried on a small papiermâché tray. No introductions were made and Deborah was conscious as she drank that both of them wished her away· Suddenly she wished nothing more herself than to be out of the house and free of them. Her coming in had been an incomprehensible impulse. It had been prompted partly by boredom, partly by hope and very largely by curiosity. Sally dead had become more interesting than Sally alive and she had wanted to see from what sort of home Sally had been rejected. That curiosity now seemed presumption and her entry into the house an intrusion which she did not want to prolong.

She said her "good-byes" and rejoined Felix. He took the wheel and they did not speak until the town was behind them and the car was shaking free of the suburban tentacles and climbing into the country.

"Well," said Felix at last, "was the exercise in detection worth while? Are you sure you want to go on with it?"

"Why not?"

"Only that you might discover facts which you would prefer not to know."

"Such as my family contains a murderer?"

"I didn't say that."

"You have been studiously careful not to say it, but I would prefer honesty to tact. That is what you think, isn't it?"

"Speaking as a murderer myself, I admit that it's a possibility."

"You're thinking of the Resistance. That wasn't murder. You didn't kill women."

"I killed two. I admit it was by shooting, not by strangulation, and it seemed at the time to be expedient."

"This killing was expedient all right—for someone," said Deborah.

"Then why not leave it to the police? Their greatest difficulty will be to get enough evidence to justify a charge. If we start interfering we may only hand them the evidence they want. The case is wide open. Stephen and I got through Sally's window. So could almost anyone else. Most people in the village must have known where that ladder was kept. The evidence of that locked door is incontrovertible. However her murderer got in he didn't go out through the door. There's only the Sommeil to connect this crime with Martingale and the two need not be related. Other people had access to the stuff even if they are."

"Aren't you relying too much on coincidence?" asked Deborah coldly.

"Coincidences happen every day. An average jury will be able to think up half a dozen instances in their own experience. The most likely interpretation of the facts so far is that someone known to Sally got in through her window and killed her. He may or may not have used the ladder. There are scratches on the walls as if he slid down by the stack pipe and lost his hold when he was nearly at the ground. The police must have noticed these, but I don't see how they can prove when the scratches were made. Sally may have been admitting callers that way on previous occasions."

"It seems a curious thing to say but somehow I can't believe that. It's not in character. I'd like to believe it for all our sakes, but I don't. I never liked Sally, but I don't believe that she was promiscuous. I don't want safety at the price of blackening the poor little devil's reputation further now that she isn't here to defend herself."

"I think you are right about her," said Felix. "But I don't advise you to make the inspector a present of your opinion. Let him make his own psychological assessment of Sally. The whole case may run into the sand if we keep our heads cool and our mouths shut. The Sommeil is the greatest danger. The hiding of that bottle makes the two things seem connected. Even so, the drug was put into your drinking-mug. It could have been put there by anyone."

"Even by me."

"Even by you. It could have been put there by Sally. She may have taken the mug to annoy you. I think she did. But she may have put the drug in her cocoa for no more sinister reason than the desire for a good night. It wasn't a lethal dose."

"In which case, why was the bottle hidden?"

"Let us say that it was hidden either by someone who erroneously believed that the drugging and the murder were connected and who wanted to conceal that fact, or by someone who knew that they weren't but who wanted to implicate the family. As your stake marked the hiding-place we may assume that such a person specifically wished to implicate you. That's a pleasant thought for you to be going on with."

They were cresting the hill above Little Chadfleet now. Below them lay the village and there was a glimpse of the tall grey chimneys of Martingale above the trees. With the return home the oppression and fear which the drive had only partially relieved fell like a black cloud.

"If they never solve this crime," said Deborah, "can you really imagine us living on happily at Martingale? Don't you ever feel that you must know the truth? Do you honestly never convince yourself that Stephen did it, or I?"

"You? Not with those hands and finger-nails. Didn't you notice that very considerable force was used and that her neck was bruised, but not scratched? Stephen is a possibility. So are Catherine and your mother and Martha. So am I. The superfluity of suspects is our greatest protection. Let Dalgleish take his pick. As for not living on at Martingale with an unsolved crime hanging over you—I imagine that the house has seen its share of violence in the past three hundred years. Not all your ancestors lived such well-regulated lives even if their deaths were with benefit of clergy. In two hundred years the death of Sally Jupp will be one of the legends told on All-Hallows to frighten your great grandchildren. And if you really can't stand Martingale there will always be Greenwich. I won't bore you with that again, but you know what I feel."

His voice was almost expressionless. His hands lay lightly on the wheel and his eyes still looked at the road ahead with easy and unstrained concentration. He must have known what she was thinking for he said:

"Don't let it worry you. I shan't complicate things more than I can help. I just don't want any of those beefy types you run around with to misunderstand my interest."

"Would you want me, Felix, if I were running away?"

"Isn't that being melodramatic? What else have most of us been doing for the last ten years? But if you want marriage as an escape from Martingale you may yet find the sacrifice unnecessary. As we left Canningbury we passed Dalgleish and one of his minions on the way in. My guess is that they were on the same errand. Your instinct about Proctor may not have been so far wrong after all."

They garaged the car in silence and passed into the coolness of the hall. Catherine Bowers was mounting the stairs. She was carrying a linen-covered tray and the white nylon overall which she usually wore when nursing Simon Maxie looked cool, efficient and not unbecoming. It is never agreeable to see another person competently and publicly performing duties which conscience suggests are one's own and Deborah was honest enough to recognize the reason for her spasm of irritation. She tried to hide it by an unusual burst of confidence.

"Wasn't the funeral awful, Catherine? I'm terribly sorry that Felix and I ran off like that. We drove Mrs. Proctor home. I had a sudden urge to fix the murder on the wicked uncle."

Catherine was unimpressed.

"I asked the inspector about the uncle when he questioned me for the second time. He said that the police are satisfied that Mr. Proctor couldn't have killed Sally. He didn't explain why. I should leave the job to him. Goodness knows there's enough work here."

She went on her way. Looking after her, Deborah said:

"I may be uncharitable, but if anyone at Martingale killed Sally I should prefer it to have been Catherine."

"It isn't likely, though, is it?" said Felix. "I can't see her capable of murder."

"And the rest of us are? Even Mother?"

"She particularly, I think, if she felt it were necessary."

"I don't believe it," said Deborah. "But even if it were true, can you see her saying nothing while police overrun Martingale and people like Miss Liddell and Derek Pullen are suspected?"

"No," replied Felix. "No, I can't see that."

CHAPTER SEVEN

¶ 1

Rose Cottage on the Nessingford Road was a late eighteenth century labourer's cottage with enough superficial charm and antiquity to tempt the passing motorist to an opinion that something could be made of it. In the Pullens' hands something had, a replica of a thousand urban council houses. A large plaster model of an Alsatian dog occupied all the window space in the front room. Behind it the lace curtains were elegantly draped and tied with blue ribbon. The front door opened straight into the living-room. Here the Pullens' enthusiasm for modern décor had outrun discretion and the result was curiously irritating and bizarre. One wall was papered with a design of pink stars against a blue background. The opposite wall was painted in matching pink. The chairs were covered with blue striped material obviously carefully chosen to tone with the paper. The haircord carpet was a pale pink and had suffered from the inevitable comings and goings of muddy feet. Nothing was clean, nothing made to last, nothing was simple or honest. Dalgleish found it all profoundly depressing.

Derek Pullen and his mother were at home. Mrs. Pullen showed none of the normal reactions to the arrival of police officers engaged in a murder investigation, but greeted them with a spate of welcoming miscellanea, as if she had stayed at home specially to receive them and had long awaited their arrival. The phrases tumbled against one another. Delighted to see them . . . her brother a police constable . . . perhaps they had heard of him . . . Joe Pullen over at Barkingway . . . always better to tell the truth to the police . . . not that they's anything to tell . . . poor Mrs. Maxie . . . couldn't hardly believe it when Miss Liddell told her . . . come home and told Derek and he didn't believe it neither . . . not the sort of girl a decent man would want . . . very proud the Maxies were . . . a girl like that asked for trouble. As she spoke the pale eyes wavered over Dalgleish's face but with little comprehension. In the background stood her son, braced to the inevitable.

So Pullen had known about the engagement late on Saturday night although, as the police had already ascertained, he had spent the evening at the Theatre Royal, Stratford, with a party from his office and had not been at the fête.

Dalgleish had difficulty in persuading the voluble Mrs. Pullen to retire to her kitchen and leave the boy to answer for himself but he was helped by Pullen's fretful insistence that she should leave them alone. He had obviously been expecting the visit. When Dalgleish and Martin were announced he had risen from his chair and faced them with the pathetic courage of a man whose meagre reserves have scarcely carried him through the waiting period. Dalgleish dealt with him gently. He might have been speaking to a son. Martin had seen this technique in use before. It was a cinch with the nervous, emotional types, especially if they were burdened with guilt. Guilt, thought Martin, was a funny thing. This boy, now, had probably done nothing worse than meet Sally Jupp for a bit of kiss and cuddle but he wouldn't feel at peace until he'd spilt the beans to someone. On the other hand he might be a murderer. If he were, then fear would keep his mouth shut for a little longer. But in the end he'd crack. Before long he would see in Dalgleish, patient, uncensorious and omnipotent, the father confessor whom his conscience craved. Then it would be difficult for the shorthand writer to catch up with the spate of self-accusation and guilt. It was a man's own mind which betrayed him in the end and Dalgleish knew that better than most. There were times when Sergeant Martin, not the most sensitive of men, felt that a detective's job was not a pretty one.

But, so far, Pullen was standing up well to the questioning. He admitted that he had walked past Martingale late on Saturday night. He was studying for an examination and liked to get some air before going to bed. He often went for a late walk. His mother could confirm that. He took the Venezuelan envelope found in Sally's room, pushed a pair of bent spectacles up on his forehead and peered short-sightedly at the scribbled dates. Quietly he admitted that the writing was his. The envelope had come from a pen friend in South America. He had used it to jot down the times when he could meet Sally Jupp. He couldn't remember when he had given it to her but the dates referred to their meetings last month.

"She used to lock her door and then come down the stack-pipe to you, didn't she?" asked Dalgleish. "You needn't be afraid of breaking her confidence. We found her palm-marks on the pipe. What did you do when you had those meetings?"

"We went for walks in the garden once or twice. Mostly we sat in the old stable block opposite her room and talked." He must have fancied that he saw incredulity in Dalgleish's face for he flushed and said defensively:

"We didn't make love if that's what you're thinking. I suppose all policemen have to cultivate dirty minds but she wasn't like that."

"What was she like?" asked Dalgleish gently. "What did you talk about?"

"Anything. Everything really. I think she was lonely for someone her own age. She wasn't happy when she was at St. Mary's but there were the other girls to have a laugh with. She was a wonderful mimic. I could almost hear Miss Liddell talking. She talked about her home too. Her parents were killed in the war. Everything would have been different for her if they had lived. Her father was a university don and she would have had a different kind of home from her aunt's. Cultured and . . . well, different."

Dalgleish thought that Sally Jupp had been a young woman who enjoyed exercising imagination and in Derek Pullen she had at least found a credulous listener. But there was more in these meetings than Pullen was choosing to say. The girl had been using him for something. But for what?

"You looked after her child for her, didn't you, when she went up to London on the Thursday before she died?"

It was a complete shot in the dark but Pullen did not even seem surprised that he knew.

"Yes, I did. I work in a local government office and I can take a day's leave now and then. Sally said that she wanted to go up to town and I didn't see why she shouldn't. I expect she wanted to see a flick or go shopping. Other mothers can."

"It seems strange that Sally didn't leave her child at Martingale if she wanted to go up to London. Mrs. Bultitaft would probably have been willing to look after him occasionally. All this secrecy was surely rather unnecessary."

"Sally liked it that way. She liked things to be secret. I think that was half the attraction of sneaking out at night. I had a feeling sometimes that she wasn't really enjoying it. She was worried about the baby or just plain sleepy. But she had to come. It made her pleased to know next day that she had done it and got away with it."

"Didn't you point out that it would make trouble for both of you if it were discovered?"

"I don't see how it could affect me," said Pullen sulkily.

"I think you're pretending to be a great deal more simple than you are, surely. I'm ready to believe that you and Miss Jupp weren't lovers because I like to think I know when people are telling the truth and because it fits in with what I know so far of both of you. But you can't honestly believe that other people would be so accommodating. The facts bear one obvious interpretation and that is the one most people would put on them, especially in the circumstances."

"That's right. Just because the kid had an illegitimate child then she must be a nymphomaniac." The boy used this last word self-consciously as if it were one he had only recently known and had not used before.

"You know, I doubt whether they'd understand what that word means. Perhaps people have rather nasty minds, but then it's surprising how often the nastiness is justified. I don't think Sally Jupp was being very fair to you when she used these stables as a retreat from Martingale. Surely you must have thought that, too?"

"Yes, I suppose so." The boy looked away unhappily and Dalgleish waited. He felt that there was still something to be explained but that Pullen was enmeshed in his own inarticulateness and frustrated with the difficulty of explaining the girl he had known, alive, gay and foolhardy, to two officers of police who had never even met her. The difficulty was easily understood. He had no doubt how Pullen's story would look to a jury and was glad that it would never be his job to convince twelve good men and true that Sally Jupp, young, pretty and already lapsed from grace, had been sneaking out of her bedroom at night and leaving her baby alone, however briefly, for the sole pleasure of intellectual discussion with Derek Pullen.

"Did Miss Jupp ever suggest to you that she was afraid of anyone or had an enemy?" he asked.

"No. She wasn't important enough to have enemies."

"Not until Saturday night, perhaps," thought Dalgleish.

"She never confided in you about her child, who the father was, for example?"

"No." The boy had mastered some of his terror and his voice was sullen.

"Did she tell you why she wanted to go to London last Thursday afternoon?"

"No. She asked me to look after Jimmy because she was sick of carting him around the forest and wanted to get away from the village. We arranged where she was to hand him over at Liverpool Street Station. She brought the folding pram and I took him to St. James's Park. In the evening I handed him back and we travelled home separately. We weren't going to give the village tabbies anything else to gossip about."

"You never thought she might be falling in love with you?"

"I knew damn well she wasn't." He gave Dalgleish one quick direct glance and then said, as if the confidence surprised him:

"She wouldn't even let me touch her."

Dalgleish waited for a moment and then said quietly,

"Those aren't your normal spectacles, are they? What happened to the ones you usually wear?"

The boy almost snatched them from his nose and closed his hands over the lenses in a gesture which was pathetic in its futility. Then, realizing the significance of that instinctive gesture, he dug in his pocket for a handkerchief and made a show of cleaning the lenses.

His hands shook as he pushed the spectacles back on his nose where they rested lopsidedly, his voice croaked with fright:

"I lost them. That is, I broke them. I'm having them mended."

"Did you break them at the same time as you got that bruise over your eye?"

"Yes. I knocked into a tree."

"Indeed. The trees around here seem curiously hazardous. Dr. Maxie grazed his knuckle on the bark of one, I'm told. Could it have been the same tree?"

"Dr. Maxie's troubles are nothing to do with me. I don't know what you mean."

"I think you do," said Dalgleish gently. "I'm going to ask you to think over what we've said and later I shall want you to make a statement and sign it. There isn't any tremendous hurry. We know where to find you if we want you. Talk it over with your father when he comes in. If either of you want to see me let me know. And remember this: someone killed Sally. If it wasn't you, then you've got nothing to fear. Either way, I hope you'll find the courage to tell us what you know." He waited for a moment but his eyes met only the glazed stare of fear and resolution. After a minute he turned away and beckoned Martin to follow.

Half an hour later the telephone rang at Martingale. Deborah, carrying her father's tray through the hall, paused, balanced it on her hip, and lifted the receiver. A minute later she put her head round the drawing-room door.

"It's for you, Stephen. The 'phone. Derek Pullen of all people."

Stephen, home unexpectedly for a few hours only, did not look up from his book but Deborah could see the sudden arrest of movement and the slight tensing of his back.

"Oh Lord, what does he want?"

"He wants you. He sounds pretty worried."

"Tell him I'm busy, Deb."

Deborah translated this message into the semblance of civility. The voice at the end of the line rose into incoherence. Holding the receiver away from her ear Deborah made soothing noises and felt the well of hysterical laughter which nowadays was never far submerged. She went back to the drawing-room.

"You'd better come, Stephen. He really is in a bad way. What on earth have you been up to? He says the police have been with him."

"Is that all? He's not the only one. Tell him they've been with me for about six hours all told. And they haven't finished yet. Tell him to keep his mouth shut and stop flapping."

"Hadn't you better tell him yourself?" suggested Deborah sweetly. "I'm not in your confidence and I'm certainly not in his."

Stephen swore softly and went to the telephone. Pausing in the hall to balance her tray, Deborah could hear his quick impatient expostulations.

"All right. All right. Tell them if you want to. I'm not stopping you. They're probably listening in to this conversation anyway. . . . No, as a matter of fact I didn't, but don't let that influence you . . . Quite the little gentleman, aren't you . . . . My dear man, I don't care a damn what you tell them, or when or how, only for God's sake don't be such a bore about it. Good-bye."

Moving out of earshot along the gallery, Deborah thought sadly, "Stephen and I have grown so far apart that I could ask him outright whether he killed Sally without being certain what answer I'd get."

¶ 2

Dalgleish and Martin sat in the small parlour of The Moonraker's Arms in that state of repletion without satisfaction which commonly follows a poor meal. They had been assured that Mrs. Piggott who, with her husband, kept the inn, was noted for her good plain cooking and plenty of it. The expression had struck ominously on the ears of men whose travels had inured them to most of the vagaries of good plain English fare. It is probable that Martin suffered most. His war service in France and Italy had given him a taste for continental food which he had been indulging ever since on holidays abroad. Most of his spare time and all of his spare money was spent in this way. He and his cheerful, enterprising wife were enthusiastic and unsophisticated travellers, confident of their ability to be understood, tolerated and well fed in almost any corner of Europe. So far, strangely enough, they had never been disappointed. Sitting in deep abdominal distress Martin let his mind rumble on *cassoulet de Toulouse* and remembered with yearning the *poularde en vessu* he had first eaten in a modest hotel in the Ardèche. Dalgleish's needs were at once simpler and more exacting. He merely craved simple English food properly cooked.

Mrs. Piggott was reputed to take trouble with her soups. This was true in so far as the packaged ingredients had been sufficiently well mixed to exclude lumps. She had even experimented with flavours and today's mixture of tomato (orange) and oxtail (reddish brown), thick enough to support the spoon unaided, was as startling to the palate as to the eye. Soup had been followed by a couple of mutton chops nestling artistically against a mound of potato and flanked with tinned peas larger and shinier than any peas which had ever seen pod. They tasted of soya flour. A green dye which bore little resemblance to the colour of any known vegetable seeped from them and mingled disagreeably with the gravy. An apple and black-currant pie had followed in which neither of the fruits had met each other nor the pastry until they had been arranged on the plate by Mrs. Piggott's careful hand and liberally blanketed with synthetic custard.

Martin wrenched his mind from a contemplation of these culinary horrors and fixed it on the matter in hand.

"It's curious, sir, that Dr. Maxie should have fetched Mr. Hearne to help with the ladder. It's one that a strong man can manage on his own. The quickest way to the old stable block would have been down the back stairs. Instead of that, Maxie goes to find Hearne. It looks as if he wanted a witness to the finding of the body."

"That's possible, of course. Even if he didn't kill the girl he may have wanted a witness to whatever was to be found in that room. Besides that, he was in pyjamas and dressing-gown. Hardly the most convenient garb for climbing up ladders and through windows."

"Sam Bocock confirmed Dr. Maxie's story to some extent. Not that it means much until the time of death is established. Still, it does prove he was telling the truth on one point."

"Sam Bocock would confirm anything the Maxies said. That man would be a gift to the defending counsel. Apart from his natural gift for saying little while creating an impression of absolute and incorruptible veracity he honestly believes that the Maxies are innocent. You heard him. 'They're good people up at the House.' A simple statement of truth. He would maintain it against the evidence of God Almighty at the Judgment Seat itself. The Old Bailey isn't likely to frighten him."

"I thought him an honest witness, sir."

"Of course you did, Martin. I would have liked him better if he hadn't looked at me with that curious expression, half amused, half pitying, which I've noticed before on the faces of old country people. You're a countryman yourself. No doubt you can explain it."

No doubt Martin could, but his was a nature in which discretion had long taken precedence of valour.

"He seemed a very musical old gentleman. That was a fine record-player he had. It looked funny seeing a hi-fi instrument in a cottage like that."

The player, with its surrounding racks of long-play records, had indeed struck an incongruous note in the cottage sitting-room where almost every other article was a legacy from the past. Bocock evidently shared the normal countryman's respect for fresh air. The two small windows were shut; showed, indeed, no signs of ever having been opened. The wallpaper bore the entwined and faded roses of another era. Hung in erratic profusion were the trophies and mementoes of the First World War, a posse of mounted cavalrymen, a small glass frame of medals, a luridly coloured reproduction of King George V and his Queen. There were the family photographs, relations whom no casual observer could hope to identify. Was the serious bewhiskered young man with his Edwardian bride Bocock's father or grandfather? Could he really have a personal memory of a family loyalty for these sepia groups of bowler-hatted countrymen in their Sunday best with their solid sloping-bosomed wives and daughters?

Above the mantelpiece were the newer photographs. Stephen Maxie, proud on his first shaggy pony with an unmistakable but younger Bocock by his side. A pigtailed Deborah Maxie bending from the saddle to receive her rosette. For all its conglomeration of old and new, the room bore evidence of an old soldier's disciplined care of his personal chattels.

Bocock had welcomed them in with an easy dignity. He had been having his tea. Although he lived alone he had the woman's habit of putting everything edible on the table at once, presumably to provide for any sudden whim of taste. There had been a loaf of crusty bread, a pot of jam supporting its spoon, an ornate glass jar of sliced beetroot and one of spring onions, and a cucumber stuck precariously in a small jug. In the middle of the table a bowl of lettuce disputed with a large and obviously home-baked cake for pride of place. Dalgleish had recalled that Bocock's daughter was married to a farmer in Nessingford and kept an eye on her father. The cake was probably a recent offering of filial duty. In addition to this bounty there was evidence by sight and smell that Bocock had just finished a meal of fried fish and chipped potatoes.

Dalgleish and Martin were ensconced in the heavy armchairs which flanked the fireplace—even on that warm July day there was a small fire burning, its faint incandescent flame hardly visible in a shaft of sunlight from the western window, and were offered cups of tea. This done, Bocock obviously felt that the obligations of hospitality had been met and that it was the duty of his guests to announce their business. He carried on with his tea, snapping off pieces of bread with lean brown hands and casting them almost absent-mindedly into his mouth where they were chewed and turned in silent concentration. He volunteered no remarks of his own, answered Dalgleish's questions with a deliberation which gave the impression of lack of interest rather than any unwillingness to co-operate and he regarded both policemen with that frank amused appraisal which Dalgleish, his thighs prickled by the horsehair and his face sweating with the heat, found a little disconcerting and more than a little irritating.

The slow catechism had produced nothing new, nothing unexpected. Stephen Maxie had been at the cottage the previous evening. He had arrived during the nine o'clock news. Bocock couldn't say when he had left. It had been latish. Mr. Stephen would know. Very late? "Aye. After eleven. Maybe later. Maybe a goodish bit later." Dalgleish remarked dryly that no doubt Mr. Bocock would remember more precisely when he had had time to think about it. Bocock admitted the force of this possibility. What had they talked about? "Listened to Beethoven mostly. Mr. Stephen wasn't much of a one for talking." Bocock spoke as if deploring his own volubility and the distressing garrulity of the world at large and of policemen in particular. Nothing else emerged. He had not noticed Sally at the fête except during the latish part of the afternoon when she gave the baby a ride in her arms on one of the horses, and about six o'clock when one of the Sunday school children's balloon had got caught in an elm and Mr. Stephen had fetched the ladder to get it down. Sally had been with him then with her child in the pram. Bocock remembered her holding the foot of the ladder. Apart from that he hadn't noticed her about. Yes, he had seen young Johnnie Wilcox. That was at ten to four or thereabouts. Sneaking away from the tea-tent he was with as suspicious-looking a bundle as Bocock had seen. No, he hadn't stopped the boy. Young Wilcox was a good enough lad. None of the boys liked helping with the teas. Bocock hadn't much cared for it in his young days. If Wilcox said he left the tent at four-thirty he was a bit out, that's all. That lad hadn't put in more than thirty minutes' work at the most. If the old man wondered why the police should be interested in Johnnie Wilcox and his peccadilloes he gave no sign. All Dalgleish's questions were answered with equal composure and apparent candour. He knew nothing of Mr. Maxie's engagement and had heard no talk of it in the village, either before or after the murder. "Some folks'll say anything. You've no call to mind village talk. They're good people up at the house." That had been his final word. No doubt, if and when he had talked to Stephen Maxie and knew what was wanted he would remember more clearly the time when Maxie had left him the previous night. At the moment he was wary. But his allegiance was clear. They had left him still eating, sitting in solitary and impressive state among his music and his memories.

"No," said Dalgleish. "We're not likely to get anything helpful about the Maxies out of Bocock. If young Maxie was looking for an ally he knew where to go. We've gained something though. If Bocock is right about times, and he's certainly more likely to be accurate than Johnnie Wilcox, the meeting in the loft probably took place before four-thirty. That would fit in with what we know of Jupp's subsequent movements, including the scene in the tea-tent when she appeared in a duplicate of Mrs. Riscoe's dress. Jupp hadn't been seen in it before four-forty-five p.m. so that she must have changed after the interview in the stable loft."

"It was a funny thing to do, sir. And why wait until then?"

"She may have bought the dress with the idea of wearing it publicly on some occasion or other. Perhaps something happened at that interview which freed her from any future dependence on Martingale. She could afford to make a last gesture. On the other hand, if she knew before last Saturday that she was going to marry Maxie, she was presumably free to make her gesture whenever the fancy took her. There's a curious conflict of evidence about that proposal of marriage. If we are to believe Mr. Hinks—and why not?—Sally Jupp certainly knew that she was to marry someone when she met him on the previous Thursday. I find it difficult to believe that she had two prospective bridegrooms and there isn't a surfeit of obvious candidates. And while we're considering young Maxie's love life here's something you haven't seen."

He handed over a thin sheet of official-looking writing-paper. It bore the name of a small coastal hotel.

Dear Sir,

Although I have my reputation to think of and am not particularly anxious to be mixed up in police matters, I think it my duty to inform you that a Mr. Maxie stayed at this hotel last May 24th with a lady he signed for as his wife. I have seen a photograph in the *Evening Clarion* of Dr. Maxie who is mixed up in the Chadfleet murder case and who the papers say is a bachelor and it is the same one. I have not seen any photographs of the dead girl so could not swear to her, but I thought it my duty to bring the above to your notice. Of course it may not mean anything and I do not wish to be mixed up in anything unpleasant so I would be grateful if my name could be kept out of this. Also the name of my hotel which has always catered for a very good class of people. Mr. Maxie only stayed for one night and they were a very quiet couple, but my husband thinks it is our duty to bring this information to your notice. It is, of course, entirely without prejudice.

Yours faithfully,

LILY BURWOOD (Mrs.)

"The lady seems curiously concerned with her duty," said Dalgleish, "and it is a little difficult to see what she can mean by 'without prejudice'. I feel that her husband has a great deal to do with this letter, including the phraseology, without quite managing to bring himself to signing it. Anyway, I sent that eager young fledgeling, Robson, down to investigage and I've no doubt he enjoyed himself hugely. He managed to convince them that the night in question has nothing to do with the murder and that the best interests of the hotel will be served by forgetting the whole thing. It isn't quite as simple as that, though. Robson took some photographs down with him, one or two of those taken at the fête, and they confirmed a rather interesting little theory. Any idea who young Maxie's partner in sin was?"

"Would it be Miss Bowers, sir?"

"It would. I hoped that might surprise you."

"Well, sir, if it had to be someone from here she was the only one. There isn't any evidence that Dr. Maxie and Sally Jupp had been carrying on. And that was nearly a year ago."

"So you aren't inclined to pay much attention to it?"

"Well, the young today don't seem to make so much of it as I was taught to."

"It's not that they sin less but that they bear their sins more lightly. But we have no evidence that Miss Bowers feels the same. She may easily have been very hurt by what happened. She doesn't strike me as an unconventional person and she is very much in love and not particularly clever at concealing the fact. I think she is desperately anxious to marry Dr. Maxie and her chances have, after all, increased since Saturday night. She was present at the scene in the drawing-room. She knew what she had to lose."

"Do you think it's still going on, sir?" Sergeant Martin could never bring himself to be more explicit about these sins of the flesh. He had seen and heard enough in thirty years of police work to have shattered most men's illusions, but he was of a tough yet gentle disposition and could never believe that men were either as wicked or as weak as the evidence consistently proved them to be.

"I should think it very unlikely. That week-end was probably the only excursion into passion. Perhaps it wasn't particularly successful. Perhaps it was, as you rather unkindly suggest, a mere bagatelle. It's a complication though. Love, that kind of love, is always a complication. Catherine Bowers is the sort of woman who tells her man that she will do anything for him, and sometimes does."

"Could she have known about the tablets though, sir?"

"No one admits to having told her and I think she was telling the truth when she said she knew nothing. Sally Jupp might have told her but they weren't on particularly good terms, in fact they weren't on any terms at all as far as I can see, and it seems unlikely. But that proves nothing. Miss Bowers must have known that there were sleeping-tablets of some kind in the house and where they were likely to be kept and the same thing applies to Hearne."

"It seems strange that he's able to stay around."

"That probably means that he thinks one of the family did it and wants to be on the spot to see that we don't get the same idea. He may actually know who did it. If so, he's not likely to slip up, I'm afraid. I got Robson on to him, too. His report, stripped of a lot of psychological jargon about everyone he interviewed, is much what I expected. Here we are. All the details on Felix Georges Mortimer Hearne. He has a fine war record, of course. God knows how he did it or what it did to him. Ever since 1945 he seems to have flitted around doing a little writing and not much else. He is a partner in Hearne and Illingworth the publishers. His great-grandfather was old Mortimer Hearne who founded the firm. His father married a French woman, Mlle Annette D'Apprius, in 1919. The marriage brought more money into the family. Felix was born in 1921. Educated in the usual and expensive places. Met Deborah Riscoe through her husband who was at school with him, although considerably his junior, and as far as Robson can tell, never saw Sally Jupp until he met her in this house. He has a very pleasant little house in Greenwich, still true to type you see, and an ex-batman to look after him. Gossip says that he and Mrs. Riscoe are lovers, but there's no evidence, and Robson says you would get nothing out of the manservant. I doubt whether there's anything to get. Mrs. Riscoe was certainly lying when she said they spent all Saturday night together. I suppose Felix Hearne might have murdered Sally Jupp to save Deborah Riscoe from embarrassment, but a jury wouldn't believe it and neither would I."

"There is no mention of his having the drug in his possession?"

"None at all. I don't think there's much doubt that the Sommeil used to drug Sally Jupp came from the bottle which was taken from Mr. Maxie's cupboard. Still, other people did have the stuff. The Martingale bottle could have been hidden in that melodramatic way as a blind. According to Dr. Epps he prescribed Sommeil for Mr. Maxie, Sir Reynold Price and Miss Pollack of St. Mary's. None of these insomniacs can account for the correct dose. I'm not surprised at that. People are very careless about medicines. Where's that report? Yes, here we are. Mr. Maxie we know all about. Sir Reynold Price. His Sommeil was prescribed in January of this year and dispensed by Goodliffes of the City on January 14th. He had twenty three-gr. tablets and says that he took about half and then forgot all the rest. Apparently his insomnia was quickly overcome. Taking the common-sense view his was the bottle of nine tablets left in his overcoat pocket and found by Dr. Epps. Sir Reynold is ready enough to claim them without being able to remember putting them in his pocket. It's not a very likely place to keep sleeping-tablets, but he spends nights away from home and says that he probably picked them up in a hurry. We know all about Sir Reynold Price, our local business man *cum* farmer, making a calculated loss on the second activity to compensate for his profits on the first. He fumes against what he calls the desecration of Chadfleet New Town from a Victorian pseudo-castle so ugly that I'm surprised someone hasn't formed a trust to preserve it. Sir Reynold is a philistine, no doubt, but not, I think, a murderer. Admittedly he has no alibi for last Saturday night and all we know from his staff is that he left home in his car at about ten p.m. and didn't return until early Sunday morning. Sir Reynold is being so guilty and embarrassed by this absence, is so patently trying to preserve a gentlemanly reticence, that I think we can take it that there's a 'little woman' in the case. When we really put on the pressure and he appreciates that there's a murder charge involved I think we shall get the lady's name. These one-night excursions are fairly regular with him and I don't think they had anything to do with Jupp. He would hardly make himself conspicuous by taking his Daimler on a surreptitious visit to Martingale.

"We know about Miss Pollack. She seems to have regarded the tablets as a cocaine addict ought to regard cocaine, but so seldom does. She wrestled long with the twin evils of temptation and insomnia and ended by trying to put the Sommeil down the w.c. Miss Liddell dissuades her and returns them to Dr. Epps. Dr. Epps, according again to Robson, thinks he may have had them back but isn't sure. There weren't enough to be a really dangerous dose and they were labelled. Shockingly careless of someone I suppose, but then people are careless. And Sommeil, of course, isn't on the D.D.A. Besides, it only took three tablets to drug Sally Jupp and, taking the common-sense view, those tablets came from the Martingale bottle."

"Which leads us back to the Maxies and their guests."

"Of course. And it's not such a stupid crime as it appears on the face of it. Unless we can find those tablets and get some evidence that one of the Maxies administered them, there's no hope of getting a conviction. You can see how it would go. Sally Jupp knew about the tablets. She might have taken them herself. They were put into Mrs. Riscoe's mug. No evidence to show they were meant for Sally Jupp. Anyone could have got into the house during the fête and lain in wait for the girl. No adequate motive. Other people had access to Sommeil. And as far as I know at present he might be right."

"But if the murderer had used more of the tablets and killed the girl that way there might have been no suspicion of murder."

"It couldn't be done. Those barbiturates are notoriously slow-acting if you want to kill. The girl might have been in a coma for days and then recovered. Any doctor would know that. On the other hand it would be difficult to smother a strong and healthy girl, or even to get into her bedroom unobserved, unless she were drugged. The combination was risky for the murderer, but not as risky as one method on its own. Besides, I doubt whether anyone would swallow a fatal dose without suspecting something. Sommeil is supposed to be less bitter than most of these sleeping-tablets, but it's not tasteless. That is probably why Sally Jupp left most of the cocoa. She could hardly have felt sleepy with so small a dose in her, and yet she still died without a struggle. That's the curious part of it. Whoever entered that bedroom must have been either expected by Jupp or at least not feared. And if that were so, why the drugging? They may be unconnected but it's really too much of a coincidence that someone should put a dangerous dose of barbiturate in her drink on the same night as someone else chooses to throttle her. Then there is the curious distribution of finger-prints. Someone went down that stack-pipe, but the only prints are those of Jupp herself and they're possibly not recent. The cocoa tin was found empty in the dustbin with the paper lining missing. The tin bore the prints of Jupp and Bultitaft. The lock of the bedroom has a print of Jupp only, although it's badly smudged. Hearne says that he protected the lock with his handkerchief when he opened the door which, considering the circumstances, shows some presence of mind. Perhaps too much presence of mind. Hearne of all these people is the one least likely to lose his head in an emergency or to overlook any essential points."

"Something had rattled him pretty badly by the time he came to be questioned, though."

"It had indeed, Sergeant. I might have reacted more positively to his offensiveness if I hadn't known it was only pure funk. It takes some people that way. The poor devil was almost pitiable. It was a surprising exhibition coming from him. Even Proctor put up a better show and heaven knows he was scared enough."

"We know Proctor couldn't have done it."

"So presumably does Proctor. Yet he was lying about a number of things and we shall break him when the time's right. I think he was telling the truth about that telephone call, though, or at least part of the truth. It was unlucky for him that his daughter took the call. If he had answered the 'phone I doubt whether we should have been told about it. He still maintains that the call was from Miss Liddell and Beryl Proctor confirms that the caller gave that name. First of all Proctor tells his wife and us that she was merely ringing to give him news of Sally. When we question him again and tell him that Liddell denies making the call he still persists that the call was either from her or from someone impersonating her, but admits that she told him that Sally was engaged to be married to Stephen Maxie. That would certainly be a more reasonable motive for the call than a general report on his niece's progress."

"It's interesting how many people claim to have known about this engagement before it actually took place."

"Or before Maxie admits that it took place. He still insists that he proposed as a result of an impulse when they met in the garden at about seven-forty p.m. on Saturday night and that he had never previously considered asking her to marry him. That doesn't mean that she hadn't considered it. She may even have expected it. But surely it was asking for trouble to spread the glad news in advance. And what possible motive had she for telling her uncle unless it was an understandable urge to gloat over him or disconcert him? Even so, why pretend to be Miss Liddell?"

"You're satisfied that Sally Jupp made that call then, sir?"

"Well—we've been told, haven't we, what a good mimic she was? I think we can be certain that Jupp made that call and it's significant that Proctor isn't yet willing to admit as much. Another minor mystery, which we'll very likely never solve, is where Sally Jupp spent the hours between putting her child to bed on Saturday night and her final appearance on the main staircase at Martingale. No one admits to having seen her."

"Doesn't that make it likely that she stayed in her room

with Jimmy and then went to get her last night drink when she knew that Martha would have gone to bed and the coast be clear?"

"It's certainly the likeliest explanation. She would hardly have been welcome either in the drawing-room or the kitchen. Perhaps she wanted to be alone. God knows, she must have had plenty to think about!"

They sat in silence for a moment. Dalgleish pondered on the curious diversity of the clues which he felt were salient in the case. There was Martha's significant reluctance to dwell on one of Sally's shortcomings. There was the bottle of Sommeil pressed hastily into the earth. There were an empty cocoa tin, a golden-haired girl laughing up at Stephen Maxie as he retrieved a child's balloon from a Martingale elm, an anonymous telephone call and a gloved hand briefly glimpsed as it closed the trap-door into Bocock's loft. And at the heart of the mystery, the clue which could make all plain, lay the complex personality of Sally Jupp.

CHAPTER EIGHT

¶ 1

The Thursday morning list at St. Luke's had been a heavy one and it was not until he sat down for lunch that Stephen Maxie remembered Sally. Then, as always, the remembrance came down like a knife severing appetite, cutting him off from the careless and undemanding pleasure of everyday life. The talk at table sounded false; a barrage of trivialities put up to cover his colleagues' embarrassment at his presence. The newspapers were too tidily folded away in case a chance headline should draw attention to the presence among them of a suspected murderer. They included him too carefully in their conversation. Not too much in case he should think they were sorry for him. Not too little in case he should think they were avoiding him. The meat on his plate was as tasteless as cardboard. He forced down a few more mouthfuls—it would never do if the suspect went right off his food—and made a show of despising the pudding. The need for action was upon him. If the police could not bring this thing to a head perhaps he could. With a murmured apology he left the residents to their speculation. And why not? Was it so very surprising that they wanted to ask him the one crucial question. His mother, her hand over his on the telephone, her ravaged face turned to him in desperate inquiry, had wanted to ask the same. And he had replied, "You don't have to ask. I know nothing about it. I swear it."

He had a free hour and he knew what he wanted to do. The secret of Sally's death must lie in her life, and probably in her life before she came to Martingale. Stephen had the conviction that the baby's father would hold the key if only he could be found. He did not analyse his motives, whether this urge to find an unknown man had its roots in logic, curiosity or jealousy. It was enough to find relief in action, however fruitless its results.

He remembered the name of Sally's uncle but not the full address and it took some time to hunt through the Proctors in search of a Canningbury number. A woman answered in the stilted, artificial voice of one unused to the telephone. When he announced himself there was a silence so long that he thought they must have been cut off. He sensed her distrust like a physical impulse along the wire and tried to propitiate it. When she still hesitated he suggested that she might prefer him to ring later and speak to her husband. The proposal was not meant as a threat. He had merely imagined that she was one of those women who are incapable of even the simplest independent action. But the result of his suggestion was surprising. She said quickly, "Oh, no! No! There wasn't any need for that. Mr. Proctor didn't want to talk about Sally. It wouldn't do to telephone Mr. Proctor. After all it couldn't do any harm to tell Mr. Maxie what he wanted to know. Only it would be better if Mr. Proctor didn't know that he had 'phoned." Then she gave the address Stephen wanted. When she became pregnant, Sally had been working for the Select Book Club, at Falconer's Yard in the City.

The Select Book Club had its offices in a courtyard near St. Paul's Cathedral. It was approached through a narrow passage, dark and difficult to find, but the courtyard itself was full of light and as quiet as a provincial cathedral close. The grinding crescendo of city traffic was muted to a faint moan like the far sound of the sea. The air was full of the river smell. There was no difficulty in finding the right house. On the sunlit side of the court a small bay window was dressed with the Select Book Club choices arranged with carefully contrived casualness against a draped back-cloth of purple velvet. The Club had been carefully named. Select Books catered for that class of reader which likes a good story without caring much who writes it, prefers to be spared the tedium of personal choice, and believes that a bookcase of volumes equal in size and bound in exactly the same colour gives tone to any room. Select Books preferred virtue to be rewarded and vice suitably punished. They eschewed salacity, avoided controversy and took no risks with unestablished writers. Not surprisingly they often had to look far back in the publishers' lists to produce a current choice. Stephen noticed that only a few of the selected volumes had originally borne the imprint of Hearne and Illingworth. He was surprised that there were any.

The front door steps were scrubbed white and the open door led into a small office obviously furnished for the convenience of those customers who preferred to collect their monthly book in person. As Stephen entered an elderly clergyman was suffering the prolonged and sprightly farewells of the woman in charge who was determined that he should not escape until the merits of the current choice, including details of the plot and the really astonishing surprise ending, had been explained in detail. This done, there were the members of his family to inquire for and his opinion of last month's choice to be solicited. Stephen waited in patience until this was concluded and the woman was free to turn her determinedly bright glance on him. A small framed card on the desk proclaimed her as Miss Titley.

"I'm so sorry to have kept you waiting. You're a new customer, aren't you? I don't think I've had the pleasure before? I get to know everyone in time and they all know me. That was Canon Tatlock. A very dear customer. But he won't be hurried, you know. He won't be hurried."

Stephen exerted all his charm and explained that he wanted to see whoever was in charge. The matter was personal and very important. He wasn't trying to sell anything and would honestly not take long. He was sorry that he couldn't be more explicit but it really was important. "To me, anyway", he added with a smile.

The smile was successful. It always had been. Miss Titley, flustered into normality by the unusual, retired to the back of her office and made a furtive telephone call. It was a little prolonged. She gave several glances at him during her conversation as if to reassure herself as to his respectability. Eventually she replaced the receiver and came back with the news that Miss Molpas was prepared to see him.

Miss Molpas had her office on the third floor. The drugget-covered stairs were steep and narrow and Stephen and Miss Titley had to stand aside on each of the landings while women clerks passed. There were no men to be seen. When he was finally shown into Miss Molpas's room he saw that she had chosen well. Three steep flights were a small price to pay for this view over city roofs, this glimpse of a silver ribbon threading down from Westminster. Miss Titley breathed an introduction which was as reverent as it was inarticulate and faded away. From behind her desk Miss Molpas rose stockily to her feet and waved him to a chair. She was a short, dark woman of remarkable plainness. Her face was round and large and her hair was cut in a thick straight fringe above her eyebrows. She wore horn-rimmed spectacles so large and heavy that they seemed an obvious aid to caricature. She was dressed in a short tweed skirt and man's white shirt with a yellow and green woven tie which reminded Stephen unpleasantly of a squashed cabbage caterpillar. But she had one of the pleasantest speaking voices he had ever heard in a woman and the hand which she held out to him was cool and firm.

"You're Stephen Maxie, aren't you? Saw your picture in the *Echo*. People are saying that you killed Sally Jupp. Did you?"

"No," said Stephen. "And neither did any member of my family. I haven't come to argue about that. People can believe what they like. I wanted to know something more about Sally. I thought you might be able to help. It's the child I'm really worrying about. Now that he hasn't a mother it seems important to try to find his father. No one's come forward, but it did strike me that the man may not know. Sally was very independent. If he doesn't know and would like to do something about Jimmy—well, I think he should be given the chance."

Miss Molpas pushed a packet of cigarettes across the table at him.

"D'you smoke? No? Well, I will. You're meddling a bit, aren't you? Better get your own motives straight. You can't believe the man didn't know. Why shouldn't he? He must know now anyway. There's been enough publicity. The police have been here on the same tack but I don't imagine they're interested in the child's welfare. More likely looking for a motive. They're very thorough. You'd do better to leave them to it."

So the police had been there. It was stupid and irrational to suppose otherwise, but he found the news depressing. They would always be one step ahead. It was presumptuous to suppose that there was anything significant to be discovered about Sally that the police, experienced, persevering and infinitely patient, would not already have found. The disappointment must have shown in his face for Miss Molpas gave a shout of laughter.

"Cheer up! You may beat them to it yet. Not that I can help you much. I told the police all I know and they wrote it down most conscientiously, but I could see it wasn't getting them anywhere."

"Except to fix the guilt more firmly where they already believe it rests—on someone in my family."

"Well, it certainly doesn't rest on anyone here. I can't even produce a possible father for the child. We haven't a man on the premises. She certainly got herself pregnant while she was working here, but don't ask me how."

"What was she really like, Miss Molpas?" asked Stephen. He forced out the question against his own realization of its absurdity. They were all asking the same thing. It was as if, in the heart of this maze of evidence and doubt, someone would at last be found who could say, "This was Sally".

Miss Molpas looked at him curiously.

"You should know what she was like. You were in love with her."

"If I were I should be the last person to know."

"But you weren't." It was a statement not an impertinent question and Stephen met it with a frankness which surprised him.

"I admired her and I wanted to go to bed with her. I suppose you wouldn't call that love. Never having felt more than that for any woman, I wouldn't know."

Miss Molpas looked away from him and out towards the river.

"I should settle for that. I doubt whether you'll ever

feel more. Your kind don't." She turned towards him again and spoke more briskly:

"But you were asking what I thought of her. So did the police. The answer's the same. Sally Jupp was pretty, intelligent, ambitious, sly and insecure."

"You seem to have known her very well," said Stephen quietly.

"Not really. She wasn't easy to know. She worked here for three years and I knew no more about her home circumstances when she left than I did the day I engaged her. Taking her on was an experiment. You've probably noticed that we haven't any youngsters here. They're difficult to get except at double the wages they're worth and they don't keep their minds on the job. I don't blame them. They've only a few years to find a husband and this isn't a promising hunting-ground. They can be cruel, too, if you put them to work with an older woman. Have you seen young hens pecking away at an injured bird? Well, we only employ old birds here. They may be a bit slow but they're methodical and reliable. The work doesn't call for much intelligence. Sally was too good for the job. I never understood why she stayed. She worked for a secretarial agency after finishing her training and came to us as a temporary relief when we were short of staff during a 'flu epidemic. She liked the job and asked to stay on. The Club was growing and the business justified another shorthand-typist. So I took her on. As I said, it was an experiment. She was the only member of the staff who was under forty-five."

"Staying in this job doesn't suggest ambition to me," said Stephen. "What made you think she was sly?"

"I watched her and listened to her. We're rather a collection of has-beens here and she must have known it. But she was clever, was our Sally. 'Yes, Miss Titley. Certainly,

Miss Croome. Can I get it for you, Miss Melling?' Demure as a nun and respectful as a Victorian parlourmaid. She had the poor fools eating out of her hand of course. They said how nice it was to have a young thing about the office. They bought her birthday and Christmas presents. They talked to her about her career. She even asked for advice about her clothes! As if she cared a damn what we wore or what we thought! I should have thought her a fool if she had. It was a very pretty piece of acting. It wasn't altogether surprising that, after a few months of Sally, we had an office atmosphere. That's probably not a phenomenon which you have experienced. You can take it from me that it isn't comfortable. There are tensions, whispered confidences, barbed remarks, unexplained feuds. Old allies no longer speak to each other. Incongruous friendships spring up. It all plays havoc with the work, of course, although some people seem to thrive on it. I don't. I could see what the trouble was here. She'd got them all in a tizzy of jealousy and the poor fools couldn't see it. They were really fond of her. I think Miss Melling loved her. If Sally confided in anyone about her pregnancy it would have been Beatrice Melling."

"Could I talk to Miss Melling?" asked Stephen.

"Not unless you're clairvoyant. Beatrice died following an uncomplicated operation for appendicitis the week after Sally left. Left, incidentally, without even saying 'goodbye' to her. Do you believe in death from a broken heart, Dr. Maxie? No, of course you don't."

"What happened when Sally became pregnant?"

"Nothing. No one knew. We're hardly the most likely community to spot that kind of trouble. And Sally! Meek, virtuous, quiet little Sally! I noticed that she looked wan and even thinner than usual for a few weeks. Then she was prettier than ever. There was a kind of radiance about her.

She must have been about four months' pregnant when she left. She gave in her week's notice to me and asked me to tell no one. She gave me no reasons and I asked for none. Frankly, it was a relief. I had no tangible excuse for getting rid of her, but I had known for some time that the experiment was a failure. She went home one Friday and, on Monday, I told the rest of the staff that she had left. They drew their own conclusions, but no one as far as I know drew the right one. We had one glorious row. Miss Croome accused Miss Melling of having driven the girl away by her over-possessiveness and unnatural affection. To do Miss Croome justice I don't think she meant anything more sinister than that Jupp felt obliged to eat her luncheon sandwiches in Melling's company when she would rather have visited the nearest Lyons with Croome."

"So you have no idea who the man was or where she could have met him?"

"None at all. Except that they met on Saturday mornings. I got that from the police. We work a five-day week here and the office is never open on Saturdays. Apparently Sally told her uncle and aunt that it was. She came up to town nearly every Saturday morning as if to work. It was a neat deception. They apparently took no interest in her job and, even had they tried to telephone her on a Saturday morning, the assumption would be that the line had been left unattended. She was a clever little liar was Sally."

The dislike in her voice was surely too bitter to be the result of anything but a personal hurt. Stephen wondered what else could have been told about Sally's office life.

"Were you surprised to hear of her death?" he asked.

"As surprised and shocked as one usually is when something as horrible and unreal as murder touches one's own world. When I thought about it I was less surprised. She seemed in some ways a natural murderee. What did astound me was the news that she was an unmarried mother. She struck me as too careful, too scheming for that kind of trouble. I would have said, too, that she was undersexed rather than the reverse. We had one curious incident when she had been here a few weeks. The packing was done in the basement then and we had a male packer. He was a quiet, middle-aged, undersized little man with about six children. We didn't see much of him, but Sally was sent down to the packing-room with a message. Apparently he made some kind of sexual advance to her. It can't have been serious. The man was genuinely surprised when he got the sack for it. He may only have tried to kiss her. I never did get the whole story. But from the fuss she made you'd have thought she was stripped naked and raped. It was all very estimable of her to be so shocked, but most girls today seem to be able to cope with that kind of situation without having hysterics. And she wasn't play-acting that time. It was real, all right. You can't mistake genuine fear and disgust. I felt rather sorry for Jelks. Luckily I have a brother with a business in Glasgow, which was the man's home town, and I was able to get him fixed up there. He's doing well and, no doubt, he's learnt his lesson. But, believe me, Sally Jupp was no nymphomaniac."

That much Stephen had known for himself. There seemed nothing more to be learnt from Miss Molpas. He had already been away from the hospital for over an hour and Standen would be getting impatient. He said his "good-byes" and made his own way back to the ground-floor office. Miss Titley was still in attendance and had just finished pacifying an aggrieved subscriber whose last three books had failed to satisfy. Stephen waited for a moment while they finished their conversation. The neat rows of maroon-backed volumes had touched a chord of memory. Someone he knew subscribed to Select Books Limited. It was no one at the hospital. Methodically he let his mind range over the bookcases of his friends and acquaintances and time brought the answer.

"I'm afraid I haven't much time for reading," he said to Miss Titley. "But the books look wonderful value. I think one of my friends is a member. Do you ever see Sir Reynold Price?"

Miss Titley did indeed see Sir Reynold. Sir Reynold was a dear member. He came in himself for his monthly books and they had such interesting talks together. A charming man in every way was Sir Reynold Price.

"I wonder if he ever met Miss Sally Jupp here?" Stephen asked his question diffidently. He expected it to provoke some surprise, but Miss Titley's reaction was unexpected. She was affronted. With infinite kindness but great firmness, she explained that Miss Jupp could not have met Sir Reynold at Select Books Limited. She, Miss Titley, was in charge of the public office. She had held that job for over ten years now. All the customers knew Miss Titley and Miss Titley knew them. Dealing personally with the members was a job requiring tact and experience. Miss Molpas had every confidence in Miss Titley and would never dream of putting anyone else in the public office. Miss Jupp, concluded Miss Titley, had only been the office junior. She was just an inexperienced girl.

And with this ironic parting shot Stephen had to be content.

It was nearly four when Stephen got back to the hospital. As he passed by the porter's room Colley called to him and leaned over his counter with the wariness of a conspirator. His kind old eyes were troubled. Stephen remembered that the police had been to the hospital. It was Colley they would have spoken to. He wondered how much harm the old man might have done by a too-loyal determination to give nothing away. And there was nothing to give away. Sally had only been to the hospital once. Colley could only have confirmed what the police already knew. But the porter was speaking:

"There's been a telephone call for you, sir. It was from Martingale. Miss Bowers said would you please ring as soon as you came in. It's urgent, sir."

Stephen fought down panic and made himself scan the letter-rack as if for an expected letter before replying.

"Did Miss Bowers leave a message, Colley?"

"No, sir. No message."

He decided to telephone from the public call box in the hall. There was a greater chance of privacy there even if it did mean that he was in full view of Colley. He counted out the necessary coins deliberately before entering the box. As usual there was a slight delay in getting the Chadfleet exchange but at Martingale Catherine must have been sitting by the telephone. She answered almost before the bell had rung.

"Stephen? Thank God you're back. Look, can you come home at once. Someone's tried to kill Deborah."

¶ 2

Meanwhile in the little front room of 17 Windermere Crescent, Inspector Dalgleish faced his man and moved relentlessly towards the moment of truth. Victor Proctor's face held the look of a trapped animal which knows that the last escape hole is barred but cannot even yet bring itself to turn and face the end. His dark little eyes moved restlessly from side to side. The propitiatory voice and smile had gone. Now there was nothing left but fear. In the last few minutes the lines from nose to mouth seemed to have deepened. In his red neck, scraggy as a chicken's, the Adam's apple moved convulsively.

Dalgleish pressed remorselessly on.

"So you admit that this return which you made to the 'Help Them Now Association' in which you claimed that your niece was a war orphan without means was untrue?"

"I suppose I should have mentioned about the £2,000, but that was capital not income."

"Capital which you had spent?"

"I had to bring her up. It may have been left to me in trust for her but I had to feed her, didn't I? We've never had much to come and go on. She got her scholarship but we still had her clothes. It hasn't been easy let me tell you."

"And you still say that Miss Jupp was unaware that her father had left this money?"

"She was only a baby at the time. Afterwards there didn't seem any point in telling her."

"Because, by then, the trust money had been converted to your own use?"

"I used it to help keep her, I tell you. I was entitled to use it. My wife and I were made trustees and we did our best for the girl. How long would it have lasted if she'd had it when she was twenty one? We fed her all those years without another penny."

"Except the three grants which the 'Help Them Now Association' gave."

"Well, she was a war orphan, wasn't she? They didn't give much. It helped with her school uniform, that's all."

"And you still deny having been in the grounds of Martingale House last Saturday?"

"I've told you. Why do you keep on badgering? I didn't go to the fête. Why should I?"

"You might have wanted to congratulate your niece on her engagement. You said that Miss Liddell telephoned early on the Saturday morning to tell you about it. Miss Liddell still denies that she did any such thing."

"I can't help that. If it wasn't the Liddell woman it was someone pretending to be her. How do I know who it was?"

"Are you quite sure that it wasn't your niece?"

"It was Miss Liddell I tell you."

"Did you, as a result of that telephone conversation, go to see Miss Jupp at Martingale?"

"No. No. I keep telling you. I was out cycling all day."

Deliberately Dalgleish took two photographs from his wallet and spread them out on the table. In each a bunch of children were seen entering the vast wrought-iron gates of Martingale, their faces contorted into wide grimaces in an effort to persuade the hidden photographer that there was the "Happiest-looking child to enter the fête". At their backs a few adults made their less spectacular entrances. The furtive, macintoshed figure turning hands in pockets towards the pay table was not very clearly in focus but was still unmistakable. Proctor half reached out his left hand as if to tear the photograph in two and then sank back in his chair.

"All right," he said. "I'd better tell you. I was there."

¶ 3

It had taken a little time to arrange for his work to be covered. Not for the first time Stephen envied those whose personal problems were not always secondary to the demands of their profession. By the time the arrangements were complete and he had borrowed a car he felt something like hatred for the hospital and every one of his demanding, insatiable patients. Things would have been easier if he could have spoken frankly of what had happened, but something held him back. They probably thought that the police had sent for him, that an arrest was imminent. Well, let them. Let them all bloody well think what they liked. God, he was glad to get away from a place where the living were perpetually sacrificed to keep the half-dead alive!

Afterwards he could remember nothing of the drive home. Catherine had said that Deborah was all right, that the attempt had failed, but Catherine was a fool. What were they all doing to have let it happen? Catherine had been perfectly calm on the telephone but the details she had given, although clear, had explained nothing. Someone had got into Deborah's room early this morning and had attempted to strangle her. She had shaken herself free and screamed for help. Martha had reached her first and Felix a second later. Deborah had recovered sufficiently by then to pretend that she had awoken from a nightmare. But she had obviously been terrified and had spent the rest of the night sitting by the fire in Martha's room, with the door and windows locked and her dressing-gown collar hugged high round her neck. She had come down to breakfast with a chiffon scarf at her throat but, apart from looking pale and tired, had been perfectly composed. It was Felix Hearne who, sitting next to Deborah at luncheon, had noticed the edge of the bruise above the scarf and who had subsequently got the truth from her. He had consulted Catherine. Deborah had implored them not to worry her mother and Felix had been willing to give in to this, but Catherine had insisted on sending for the police. Dalgleish was not in the village. One of the constables thought that he and Sergeant Martin were in Canningbury. Felix had left no message except to ask that Dalgleish should visit Martingale as soon as convenient. They had told Mrs. Maxie nothing. Mr. Maxie was too ill now to be left for long and they were hoping that the bruise on Deborah's neck would have faded before her mother became suspicious. Deborah, explained Catherine, seemed more terrified of upsetting her mother than of being attacked for a second time. They were waiting for Dalgleish now, but Catherine thought that Stephen ought to know what had happened. She hadn't consulted Felix before telephoning. Probably Felix wouldn't have approved of her sending for Stephen. But it was time someone took a firm line. Martha knew nothing. Deborah was terrified that she might refuse to stay at Martingale if the truth came out. Catherine had no sympathy with that attitude. With a murderer at large Martha had the right to protect herself. It was ridiculous of Deborah to think that the attack could be kept secret much longer. But she had threatened to deny everything if the police told Martha or her mother. So would Stephen please come at once and see what he could do. Catherine really couldn't take any more responsibility herself. Stephen was not surprised. Hearne and Catherine between them seemed to have taken too much responsibility already. Deborah must be mad to try and conceal a thing like that. Unless she had her own reasons. Unless even the fear of a second attempt was better than knowing the truth. While his feet and hands worked with automatic co-ordination at brakes and throttle, wheel and gear lever, his mind, sharpened by apprehension, posed its questions. How long had it been after Deborah's scream before Martha arrived —and Felix? Martha slept next door. It was natural that she should have woken first. But Felix? Why had he agreed to hush it up? It was madness to think that murder and attempted murder could be treated like one of his wartime escapades. They all knew that Felix was a bloody hero, but his brand of heroics wasn't wanted at Martingale. How much did they know about him anyway? Deborah had behaved strangely. It was unlike Deborah he knew to scream for help. Once she would have fought back with more fury than fear. But he remembered her stricken face when Sally's body was discovered, the sudden retching, the blind stumbling for the door. One couldn't guess how people would behave under stress. Catherine had behaved well, Deborah badly. But Catherine had more experience of violent death. And a better conscience?

The heavy front door of Martingale was open. The house was strangely quiet. He could hear only a murmur of voices from the drawing-room. As he entered four pairs of eyes looked up at him and he heard Catherine's quick sigh of relief. Deborah was sitting in one of the winged chairs before the fireplace. Catherine and Felix stood behind her, Felix upright and watchful, Catherine with her arms stretched over the back of the chair and her hands resting on Deborah's shoulders in an attitude which was half-protective, half-comforting. Deborah did not seem to resent it. Her head was thrown back. Her high-necked shirt was open and a yellow chiffon scarf dangled from her hand. Even from the door Stephen could see the purpling bruise above the thin shoulder-blades. Dalgleish was sitting opposite her, relaxed on the edge of his chair, but his eyes were watchful. He and Felix Hearne confronted each other like cats across a room. Somewhere in the background Stephen was conscious of the ubiquitous Sergeant Martin with his notebook. In the second before anyone spoke or moved the little gilded clock chimed the three-quarters, dropping each beautiful note into the silence like a crystal pebble. Stephen moved swiftly to his sister's side and bent his head to kiss her. The smooth cheek was icy cold against his lips. As he drew back her eyes met his with a look which was hard to interpret. Could it have been entreaty—or warning? He looked at Felix.

"What happened?" he asked. "Where's my mother?"

"Upstairs with Mr. Maxie. She spends most of the day with him now. We told her that Inspector Dalgleish was making a routine visit. There's no need to add to her worries. Or Martha's either. If Martha takes fright and decides to go it will mean importing another trained nurse and we can't cope with that just now. Even if we could find one who would be willing to come."

"Aren't you forgetting something," said Stephen roughly. "What about Deborah? Do we all sit back quietly and wait for another attempt?" He resented both Felix's calm assumption of responsibility for the family arrangements and the inference that someone had to cope with these matters while the son of the house put his professional responsibilities before his family. It was Dalgleish who answered:

"I am looking after Mrs. Riscoe's safety, Doctor. Would you please examine her throat and let me know what you think."

Stephen turned to him.

"I prefer not to. Dr. Epps treats my family. Why not call him?"

"I'm asking you to look at the throat, not to treat it. This isn't the time to indulge in spurious professional scruples. Do as I say, please."

Stephen bent his head again. After a moment he straightened up and said, "He grasped the neck with both hands just above and behind the shoulder-blades. There is fairly extensive bruising but no nail scratches and no thumb-marks. The grip could have been with the base of the thumbs in front and the fingers behind. The larynx is almost certainly untouched. I should expect the bruises to fade in a day or two. There's no real harm done." He added, "Physically at any rate."

"In other words", said Dalgleish, "it was rather an amateur effort?"

"If you care to put it like that."

"I do care. Doesn't it suggest to you that this assailant knew his job rather well? Knew where to apply pressure and how much to apply without causing harm? Are we expected to believe that the person who killed Miss Jupp with such expertise couldn't do better than this? What do you think, Mrs. Riscoe?"

Deborah was buttoning up her shirt. She shrugged herself free of Catherine's proprietary grasp and rewound the chiffon scarf round her neck.

"I'm sorry you're disappointed, Inspector. Perhaps next time he'll make a better job of it. He was quite expert enough for me, thank you."

"I must say you seem to be taking it very coolly," cried Catherine indignantly. "If Mrs. Riscoe hadn't managed to shake herself free and scream she wouldn't be alive now. Obviously he got the best grip he could in the dark but was scared off when she called out. And this may not have been the first attempt. Don't forget that the sleeping-drug was put into Deborah's mug."

"I haven't forgotten that, Miss Bowers. Nor that the missing bottle was found under her name stake. Where were you last night?"

"Helping to nurse Mr. Maxie. Mrs. Maxie and I were together for the whole of the night, except when we went to the bathroom. We were certainly together from midnight onwards."

"And Dr. Maxie was in London. This attack has certainly happened at a convenient time for you all. Did you see this mysterious strangler, Mrs. Riscoe? Or recognize him?"

"No. I wasn't sleeping very deeply. I think I was having

a nightmare. I woke up when I felt the first touch of his hands on my throat. I could feel his breath on my face but I couldn't recognize him. When I screamed and felt for the light switch he made off through the door. I put on the light and screamed. I was terrified. It wasn't a rational fear even. Somehow my dream and the attack had merged together. I couldn't tell where one horror ended and the other began."

"And yet when Mrs. Bultitaft arrived you said nothing?"

"I didn't want to frighten her. We all know there's a strangler about but we've got to get on with our jobs. It wouldn't help her to know."

"That shows a commendable concern for her peace of mind, but less for her safety. I must congratulate you all on your insouciance in the face of this homicidal maniac. For that is obviously what he is. Surely you are not trying to tell me that Miss Jupp was killed by mistake, that she was mistaken for Mrs. Riscoe?"

Felix spoke for the first time. "We're not trying to tell you anything. It's your job to tell us. We only know what happened. I agree with Miss Bowers that Mrs. Riscoe is in danger. Presumably you're prepared to offer her the protection she's entitled to."

Dalgleish looked at him.

"What time did you reach Mrs. Riscoe's room this morning?"

"About half a minute after Mrs. Bultitaft, I suppose. I got out of bed as soon as Mrs. Riscoe called out."

"And neither you nor Mrs. Bultitaft saw the intruder?"

"No. I presume he was down the stairs before we came out of our rooms. Naturally I made no search as I wasn't told until this afternoon what had happened. I've looked since, but there's no trace of anyone."

"Have you any idea how this person got in, Mrs. Riscoe?"

"It could have been through one of the drawing-room windows. We went into the garden last night and must have forgotten to lock it. Martha mentioned that she found it open this morning."

"By 'we' do you mean yourself and Mr. Hearne?"

"Yes."

"Were you wearing your dressing-gown by the time your maid arrived in your room?"

"Yes. I had just put it on."

"And Mrs. Bultitaft accepted your story of a nightmare and suggested that you should spend the remainder of the night by the electric fire in her room?"

"Yes. She didn't want to go back to bed herself, but I made her. First of all we had a pot of tea together by her fire."

"So it comes to this," said Dalgleish. "You and Mr. Hearne take an evening walk in the garden of a house where there has recently been a murder and leave a french window open when you come in. In the night some unspecified man comes to your room, makes an inexpert attempt at strangling you for no motive which you or anyone else can suggest and then vanishes, leaving no trace. Your throat is so little affected that you are able to scream with enough force to attract the people sleeping in near-by rooms yet, by the time they arrive in a matter of minutes, you have recovered from your fright sufficiently to lie about what has happened, a lie made more effective by the fact that you have taken the trouble to get out of bed and put on your dressing-gown with its concealing collar. Does that strike you as rational behaviour, Mrs. Riscoe?"

"Of course it doesn't," said Felix roughly. "Nothing

that has happened in this house since last Saturday has been rational. But even you can hardly suppose that Mrs. Riscoe tried to strangle herself. Those bruises can't have been self-inflicted, and if they weren't, who inflicted them? Do you really suppose that a jury wouldn't believe the two crimes to be related?"

"I don't think a jury will be asked to consider that possibility," said Dalgleish evenly. "I have nearly completed my investigation into Miss Jupp's death. What happened last night isn't likely to affect my conclusions. It has made one difference. I think it's time the matter was settled and I propose to take a short cut. If Mrs. Maxie has no objection I want to see you all together in this house at eight o'clock to night."

"Did you want something of me, Inspector?" They turned towards the door. Eleanor Maxie had come in so quietly that only Dalgleish had noticed her. She did not wait for his reply but moved swiftly to her son.

"I'm glad you're here, Stephen. Did Deborah telephone? I meant to myself if he didn't improve. It's difficult to tell, but I think there's a change. Could you get Mr. Hinks? And Charles, of course."

It was natural, Stephen thought, for her to ask for the priest before the doctor.

"I'll come up myself first," he said. "That is, if the inspector will excuse me. I don't think there is anything more we can usefully discuss."

"Not until eight o'clock tonight, Doctor."

Stung by his tone Stephen wanted, not for the first time, to point out that surgeons were addressed as "Mister". He was saved from this pedantic pettiness by a realization of its futility and of his mother's need. For days now he had hardly thought of his father. Now there were amends which he must make. For a second Dalgleish and his investigation, the whole horror of Sally's murder faded before this new and more immediate need. In this at least he could act like a son.

But suddenly Martha was blocking the door. She stood there, white and shaking, her mouth opening and shutting soundlessly. The tall young man behind her stepped past her into the room. With one terrified glance at her mistress and a stiff little gesture of her arm which was less one of ushering the stranger in than of abandoning him to the company, Martha gave an animal-like moan and disappeared. The man looked back at her with amusement and then turned to face them. He was very tall, over six feet, and his fair hair, cut short all over the head, was bleached by the sun. He was dressed in brown corduroy trousers with a leather jacket. From its open neck the throat rose sunburnt and thick, supporting a head which was arresting in its animal health and virility. He was long-legged, long-armed. Over one shoulder was slung a ruck-sack. In his right hand he carried an airline hold-all, pristine new with its golden wings. It looked as incongruous as a woman's toy in his great brown fist. Beside him Stephen's good looks paled into a commonplace elegance and all the weariness and futility which Felix had known for fifteen years seemed at once graven on his face. When he spoke his voice, confident with happiness, held no trace of diffidence. It was a soft voice slightly American in tone, and yet there could be no doubt of his Englishness.

"It seems I've given your maid a bit of a shock. I'm sorry to butt in like this but I guess Sally never told you about me. The name's James Ritchie. She'll be expecting me all right. I'm her husband." He turned to Mrs. Maxie. "She never told me exactly what sort of a job she's got here and I don't want to cause inconvenience, but I've come to take her away."

¶ 4

In the years that followed when Eleanor Maxie sat quietly in her drawing-room she would often see again in her mind's eye that gangling and confident ghost from the past confronting her from the doorway and could sense again the shocked silence which followed his words. That silence could only have lasted for seconds yet, in retrospect, it seemed as if minutes passed while he looked round at them in confident ease and they gazed back at him in incredulous horror. Mrs. Maxie had time to think how like a tableau it was, the very personification of surprise. She felt none herself. The last few days had drained her of so much emotion that this final revelation fell like a hammer on wool. There was nothing left to discover about Sally Jupp which had power to surprise any more. It was surprising that Sally was dead, surprising that she had been engaged to Stephen, surprising to learn that so many people were implicated in her life and death. To learn now that Sally had been a wife as well as a mother was interesting but not shocking. Detached from their common emotion she did not miss the quick glance that Felix Hearne gave Deborah. He was shaken all right but that swift appraisal held something, too, of amusement and triumph. Stephen looked merely dazed. Catherine Bowers had flushed deep red and was literally open-mouthed, the stock registration of surprise. Then she turned to Stephen as if throwing on him the burden of spokesman for them all. Finally Mrs. Maxie looked at Dalgleish and for a second their eyes held. In them she read a momentary but unmistakable compassion. She was conscious of thinking irrelevantly "Sally Ritchie. Jimmie Ritchie. That's why she called the child Jimmy after his father. I could never understand why it had to be Jimmy Jupp. Why are they staring at him like that? Someone ought to say something." Someone did. Deborah, white to her lips, spoke like someone in a dream:

"Sally's dead. Didn't they tell you? She's dead and buried. They say that one of us killed her." Then she began to shake uncontrollably and Catherine, getting to her before Stephen, caught her before she fell and supported her into a chair. The tableau broke. There was a sudden spate of words. Stephen and Dalgleish moved over to Ritchie. There was a murmur of "better in the business room" and the three of them were suddenly gone. Deborah lay back in her chair, her eyes closed. Mrs. Maxie could witness her distress without feeling more than a faint irritation and a passive curiosity as to what lay behind it all. Her own preoccupations were more compelling. She spoke to Catherine.

"I must go back to my husband now. Perhaps you would come to help. Mr. Hinks will be here soon and I don't expect Martha will be much use at present. This arrival seems to have unnerved her." Catherine might have replied that Martha was not the only one to be unnerved, but she murmured an acquiescence and came at once. Her real usefulness and genuine care of the invalid did not blind Mrs. Maxie to her guest's self-imposed role of the cheerful little helpmeet competent to cope with all emergencies. This last emergency might prove one too many but Catherine had plenty of stamina and the more Deborah weakened the more Catherine grew in strength. At the door Mrs. Maxie turned to Felix Hearne.

"When Stephen has finished talking to Ritchie I think he should come to his father. He's deeply unconscious, of course, but I think Stephen should be there. Deborah should come up, too, when she has recovered. Perhaps you would tell her." Answering his unspoken comment, she added, "There's no need to tell Dalgleish. His plans for tonight can stand. It will all be over before eight." Deborah was stretched back in her chair, her eyes closed. The chiffon scarf had loosened around her neck.

"What is the matter with Deborah's throat?" Mrs. Maxie sounded only vaguely interested.

"Some rather childish horseplay, I'm afraid," replied Felix. "It was as unsuccessful as it deserved to be."

Without another glance at her daughter, Eleanor Maxie left them together.

¶ 5

Half an hour later Simon Maxie died. The long years of half-life were over at last. Emotionally and intellectually he had been dead for three years. His last breath was the technicality which finally and officially severed him from a world which he had once known and loved. It was not within his capacity now to die with courage or with dignity but he died without fuss. His wife and children were with him and his parish priest said the prescribed prayers as though they could be heard and shared by that stiffened grotesque figure on the bed. Martha was not there. Afterwards the family were to say that there seemed no point in asking her. At the time they knew that her sentimental weeping would have been more than they could bear. This death-bed was only the culmination of a slow process of dying. Although they stood white-faced about the bed and tried to evoke some pietas of remembrance and grief their thoughts were with that other death and their minds reached towards eight o'clock.

Afterwards all of them met in the drawing-room, except Mrs. Maxie, who was either without curiosity about Sally's husband, or who had decided to detach herself momentarily from the murder and all its ramifications. She merely instructed the family not to let Dalgleish know that her husband was dead then walked with Mr. Hinks back to the vicarage.

In the drawing-room Stephen poured the drinks and told his story:

"It's simple enough really. Of course I had only time for the bare details. I wanted to get up to Father. Dalgleish stayed on with Ritchie after I left and I suppose he got all the information he wanted. They were married all right. They met while Sally was working in London and married there secretly about a month before he went to Venezuela on a building job."

"But why didn't she say?" asked Catherine. "Why all the mystery?"

"Apparently he wouldn't have got the job abroad if the firm had known. They wanted an unmarried man. The pay was good and it would have given them a chance to set up house. Sally was mad keen to get married before he went. Ritchie rather thinks she liked the idea of putting one over on her aunt and uncle. She was never happy with them. The idea was that she would have stayed with them and kept on with her job. She planned to save £50 before Ritchie came back. Then, when she found the baby was coming, she decided to stick to her side of the bargain. Heaven knows why. But that part didn't surprise Ritchie. He said that was just the kind of thing that Sally would do."

"It's a pity he didn't make sure that she wasn't pregnant before he left her," said Felix dryly.

"Perhaps he did," said Stephen shortly. "Perhaps he asked her and she lied. I didn't question him about his sexual relationship. What business is that of mine? I was faced by a husband who had returned to find his wife murdered in this house, leaving a child he never even knew existed. I don't want a half an hour like that again. It was hardly the time to suggest that he might have been more careful. So might we, by God!"

He gulped down his whisky. The hand which held the glass was shaking. Without waiting for them to speak he went on:

"Dalgleish was wonderful with him. I could like him after tonight if he were here in any other capacity. He's taken Ritchie with him. They're calling in at St. Mary's to see the child and then they hope to get a room for Richie at The Moonraker's Arms. Apparently he hasn't any family to go to." He paused to refill his glass. Then he went on:

"This explains a lot, of course. Sally's conversation with the vicar on Thursday, her telling him that Jimmy was going to have a father."

"But she was engaged to you!" cried Catherine. "She accepted you."

"She never actually said she'd marry me. Sally loved a mystery all right and this one was at my expense. I don't suppose she ever told anyone that she was engaged to me. We all assumed it. She was in love with Ritchie all the time. She knew he was soon coming home. He was pathetically anxious to let me know just how much in love they were. He kept crying and trying to force some of her letters on me. I didn't want to read them. Heaven knows I was hating myself enough without that. God, it was awful! But once I'd started reading I had to go on. He kept pulling them out of that bag he had and pushing them into my hand, the tears running down his face. They were pathetic, sentimental and naïve. But they were real, the emotion was genuine."

No wonder you're upset then, thought Felix. You never felt a genuine emotion in your life.

Catherine Bowers said reasonably, "You mustn't blame yourself. None of this would have happened if Sally had told the truth about her marriage. It's asking for trouble to pretend about a thing like that. I suppose he wrote to her through an intermediary."

"Yes. He wrote through Derek Pullen. The letters were sent in an envelope enclosed in one addressed to Pullen. He handed them over to Sally at pre-arranged meetings. She never told him they were from a husband. I don't know what story she concocted, but it must have been a good one. Pullen was pledged to secrecy and, as far as I know, he never gave her away. Sally knew how to choose her dupes."

"She liked amusing herself with people," said Felix. "They can be dangerous playthings. Obviously one of her dupes thought that the joke had gone far enough. It wasn't you by any chance, was it, Maxie?"

The tone was deliberately offensive and Stephen took a quick step towards him. But before he could answer they heard the clang of the front door-bell and the clock on the mantelpiece struck eight.

CHAPTER NINE

¶ 1

By common consent they met in the business room. Someone had arranged the chairs in a half circle around the heavy table, someone had filled the water carafe and placed it at Dalgleish's right hand. Sitting alone at the table with Martin behind him, Dalgleish watched his suspects as they came in. Eleanor Maxie was the most composed. She took a chair facing the light and sat, detached and at peace, looking out at the lawns and the far trees. It was as if her ordeal were already over. Stephen Maxie strode in, threw Dalgleish a glance of mingled contempt and defiance, and sat down by his mother. Felix Hearne and Deborah Riscoe came in together but did not look at each other and sat apart. Dalgleish felt that their relationship had subtly altered since the unsuccessful play-acting of the night before. He wondered that Hearne should have lent himself to so palpable a deceit. Looking at the darkening bruise on the girl's neck, only half hidden by the knotted scarf, he wondered more at the force which Hearne had apparently found it necessary to use. Catherine Bowers came in last. She flushed as she saw their eyes on her and scurried to the only vacant chair like an anxious probationer arriving late for a lecture. As Dalgleish opened his dossier he heard the first slow notes of the church bell. The bells had been ringing when he first arrived at Martingale. They had sounded often as a background to his investigation, the mood music of murder. Now they tolled like a funeral bell and he wondered irrelevantly who in the village had died; someone for whom the bells were tolling as they had not tolled for Sally.

He looked up from his papers and began to talk in his calm deep voice.

"One of the most unusual features of this crime was the contrast between the apparent premeditation and the actual execution. All the medical evidence pointed to a crime of impulse. This was not a slow strangulation. There were few of the classical signs of asphyxiation. Considerable force had been used and there was a fracture of the superior cornu of the thyroid at its base. Nevertheless, death was due to vagal inhibition and was very sudden. It may well have taken place even if the strangler had used considerably less force. The picture on the face of it was of a single unpremeditated attack. This is borne out, too, by the use of hands. If a murderer intends to kill by strangulation, it is usually done with a cord, or with a scarf, or stocking, perhaps. This isn't invariable, but you can see the reason for it. Few people can be confident of thcir ability to kill with the bare hands. There is one person in this room who might feel that confidence, but I don't think he would have used this method. There are more effective ways of killing without a weapon and he would have known them."

Felix Hearne murmured under his breath, "But that was in another country and besides, the wench is dead." If Dalgleish heard the quotation or sensed the slight tensing of muscles as his audience controlled the impulse to look at Hearne he made no sign but went on quietly:

"In contrast to this apparent impulse in the deed we were faced with the evidence of the attempted and partial drugging of the victim which certainly indicated an intention to render the girl insensible. This could have been with the object of getting into her bedroom more easily and without waking her or of murdering her in her sleep. I dismissed the theory of two separate and different attempts on her life in the same night. No one in this room had any reason to like Sally and some of you may even have had reason to hate her. But it was straining incredulity too far seriously to consider that two people chose the same night to attempt murder."

"If we did hate her," said Deborah quietly, "we weren't the only ones."

"There was that Pullen boy," said Catherine. "You can't tell me that there was nothing between them." She saw Deborah's wince at the solecism and went on belligerently.

"And what about Miss Liddell? It's all over the village how Sally had found out something discreditable about her and was threatening to tell. If she could blackmail one she could blackmail another."

Stephen Maxie said wearily:

"I can hardly see poor old Liddell climbing up stack-pipes, or sneaking in at the back door, to face Sally alone. She wouldn't have the nerve. And you can't imagine her seriously setting out to kill Sally with her bare hands."

"She might," said Catherine, "if she knew that Sally was drugged."

"But she couldn't have known," Deborah pointed out. "And she couldn't have put the drug in Sally's beaker, either. She and Eppy were leaving the house as Sally took the beaker up to bed. And it was my beaker she took, remember. Before that they were both in this room with Mummy."

"She took your beaker in the same way that she copied

your dress," said Catherine. "But the Sommeil must have been put in it later. No one could want to drug you."

"It couldn't have been put in later," said Deborah shortly. "What chance would there have been? I suppose one of us tiptoed in with Father's bottle of tablets, pretended to Sally that it was just a cosy social call, and then waited until she was bending over the baby and popped a tablet or two into her cocoa. It doesn't make sense."

Dalgleish's quiet voice broke in:

"None of it makes sense if the drugging and the strangling are connected. Yet, as I said, it was too great a coincidence that someone should have decided to strangle Sally Jupp on the same night as someone else set out to poison her. But there could be another explanation. What if this drugging were not an isolated incident? Suppose someone had regularly been doping Sally's evening drink. Someone who knew that only Sally drank cocoa so that the Sommeil could safely be put into the cocoa tin. Someone who knew where the drug was kept and was experienced enough to use the right amount. Someone who wanted Sally discredited and out of the house, and could complain if she persistently overslept. Someone who had probably suffered more from Sally than the rest of the household realized and was glad of any action, however apparently ineffective, which would give her a sense of power over the girl. In a sense, you see, it was a substitute for murder."

"Martha," said Catherine involuntarily. The Maxies sat silent. If they had known or guessed, none of them gave a sign. Eleanor Maxie thought with compunction of the woman she had left weeping in the kitchen for her dead master. Martha had stood up at her entrance, her thick coarse-grained hands folded over her apron. She had made no sign when Mrs. Maxie told her. The tears were the more distressing for their silence. When she spoke her voice had been perfectly controlled, although the tears still ran down her face and dripped over the quiet hands. With no fuss and without explanation she had given in her notice. She would like to leave at the end of the week. There was a friend in Herefordshire to whom she could go for a time. Mrs. Maxie had neither argued nor persuaded. That was not her way. But, bending now a courteous and attentive gaze on Dalgleish, her honest mind explored the motives which had prompted her to exclude Martha from the death-bed and interested itself in this revelation that a loyalty which the family had all taken for granted had been more complicated, less acquiescent than any of them had suspected and had at last been strained too far.

Catherine was speaking. She was apparently without apprehension and was following Dalgleish's explanation as if he were expounding an interesting and atypical case history:

"Martha could always get Sommeil of course. The family were appallingly careless over Mr. Maxie's drugs. But why should she want to dope Sally on that particular night? After the scene at dinner Mrs. Maxie had more to worry about than Sally's late rising. It was too late to get rid of her that way. And why did Martha hide the bottle under Deborah's name-peg? I always thought she was devoted to the family."

"So did the family," said Deborah dryly.

"She drugged the cocoa again that night because she didn't know about the supposed engagement," said Dalgleish. "She wasn't in the dining-room at the time and no one told her. She went to Mr. Maxie's room and took the Sommeil and hid it in a panic because she thought she had killed Sally with the drug. If you think back you will realize that Mrs. Bultitaft was the only member of the household who didn't actually enter Sally's room. While the rest of you stood around the bed her one thought was to hide the bottle. It wasn't a reasonable thing to do but she was beyond behaving reasonably. She ran into the garden with it and hid it in the first soft earth she found. It was meant, I think, to be a temporary hiding-place. That's why she hastily marked it with the nearest peg. It was by chance that it happened to be yours, Mrs. Riscoe. Then she went back to the kitchen, emptied the remaining cocoa powder and the lining-paper into the stove, washed out the tin and put it in the dustbin. She was the only person who had the opportunity to do these things. Then Mr. Hearne came into the kitchen to see if Mrs. Bultitaft was all right and to offer his help. This is what Mr. Hearne told me." Dalgleish turned a page of his dossier and read:

"She seemed stunned and kept repeating that Sally must have killed herself. I pointed out that that was anatomically impossible and that seemed to upset her more. She gave me one curious look . . . and burst into loud sobbing."

Dalgleish looked up at his audience. "I think we can take it," he said, "that Mrs. Bultitaft's emotion was the reaction of relief. I suspect, too, that before Miss Bowers arrived to feed the child Mr. Hearne had coached Mrs. Bultitaft for the inevitable police questioning. Mrs. Bultitaft tells me that she didn't admit to him or to any of you that she was responsible for drugging Sally. That may be true. It doesn't mean that Mr. Hearne didn't guess. He was quite ready, as he has been throughout the case, to leave well alone if it were likely to mislead the police. Towards the end of this investigation, with the faked attack on Mrs. Riscoe, he took a more positive line in attempting to deceive."

"That was my idea," said Deborah quietly. "I asked him. I made him do it."

Hearne ignored the interruption and merely said:

"I may have guessed about Martha. But she was perfectly truthful. She didn't tell me and I didn't ask. It wasn't my affair."

"No," said Dalgleish bitterly. "It wasn't your affair." His voice had lost its controlled neutrality and they looked up at him startled by his sudden vehemence.

"That has been your attitude throughout, hasn't it? Don't let's pry into each other's affairs. Don't let's be vulgarly interested. If we must have a murder let it be handled with taste. Even your efforts to hamper the police would have been more effective if you had bothered to find out a little more from each other. Mrs. Riscoe need not have persuaded Mr. Hearne to stage an attack on her while her brother was safely in London if that brother had confided in her that he had an alibi for the time of Sally Jupp's death. Derek Pullen need not have tortured himself wondering whether he ought to shield a murderer if Mr. Stephen Maxie had bothered to explain what he was doing with a ladder in the garden on Saturday night. We finally got the truth from Pullen, but it wasn't easy.

"Pullen wasn't interested in shielding me," said Stephen indifferently. "He just couldn't bear not to behave like a little gent! You should have heard him telephoning to explain just how old-school-tie he was going to be. Your secret is safe with me, Maxie, but why not do the decent thing? Damn his insolence!"

"I suppose there's no objection to us knowing what you were doing with a ladder," inquired Deborah.

"Why should there be? I was bringing it back from outside Bocock's cottage. We used it during the afternoon to retrieve one of the balloons which got caught up in his elm. You know what Bocock is. He would have dragged it up here first thing in the morning and it's too heavy for him.

I suppose I was in the mood for a little masochism so I slung it over my shoulder. I wasn't to know that I'd find Pullen lurking about in the old stables. Apparently he made a habit of it. I wasn't to know, either, that Sally would be murdered and that Pullen would use his great mind to put two and two together and assume that I'd used the ladder to climb into her room and kill her. Why climb in anyway? I could have got through the door. And I wasn't even carrying the ladder from the right direction."

"He probably thought that you were trying to cast suspicion on an outside person," suggested Deborah. "Himself, for instance."

Felix's lazy voice broke in:

"It didn't occur to you, Maxie, that the boy might be in genuine distress and indecision?"

Stephen moved uneasily in his chair.

"I didn't lose any sleep over him. He had no right on our property and I told him so. I don't know how long he'd been waiting there but he must have watched me while I put down the ladder. Then he stepped out of the shadows like an avenging fury and accused me of deceiving Sally. He seems to have curious ideas about class distinctions. Anyone would think I had been exercising *droit de seigneur*. I told him to mind his own business, only less politely, and he lunged out at me. I'd had about as much as I could stand by then so I struck out and caught him on the eye, knocking off his spectacles. It was all pretty vulgar and stupid. We were too near the house to be safe so we daren't make much noise. We stood there hissing insults at each other in whispers and grovelling around in the dust to find his glasses. He's pretty blind without them so I thought I'd better see him as far as the corner of Nessingford Road. He took it that I was escorting him off the premises, but his pride would have been hurt either way so it didn't matter much. By the time we came to say good night he had obviously persuaded himself into what he imagined was an appropriate frame of mind. He even wanted to shake hands! I didn't know whether to burst out laughing or to knock him down again. I'm sorry, Deb, but he's that sort of person."

Eleanor Maxie spoke for the first time:

"It is a pity that you didn't tell us about this earlier. That poor boy should certainly have been spared a great deal of worry."

They seemed to have forgotten the presence of Dalgleish, but now he spoke:

"Mr. Maxie had a reason for his silence. He realized that it was important for you all that the police should think that a ladder had been available within easy reach of Sally's window. He knew the approximate time of death and he wasn't anxious for the police to know that the ladder hadn't been returned to the old stable before twenty past twelve. With luck we should assume that it had been there all night. For much the same reason he was vague about the time he left Bocock's cottage and lied about the time he got to bed. If Sally was killed at midnight by someone under this roof he was anxious that there should be no lack of suspects. He realized that most crimes are solved by a process of elimination. On the other hand I think he was telling the truth about the time he locked the south door. That was at about twelve thirty-three and we know now that at twelve thirty-three Sally Jupp had been dead for over half an hour. She died before Mr. Maxie left Bocock's cottage and about the same time as Mr. Wilson of the village store got out of bed to shut a creaking window and saw Derek Pullen walking quickly past, head bent, towards Martingale. Pullen was hoping, perhaps, to see Sally and to hear her explanation. But he only reached the cover of the old stables before Mr. Maxie arrived, carrying the ladder. And by then Sally Jupp was dead.

"So it wasn't Pullen?" said Catherine.

"How could it have been," said Stephen roughly. "He certainly hadn't killed her when he spoke to me and he was in no condition to turn back and kill her after I had left him. He could hardly see his way to his own front gate."

"And if Sally was dead before Stephen got back from visiting Bocock, it couldn't have been him either," pointed out Catherine. It was, Dalgleish noticed, the first time that any of them had specifically referred to the possible guilt or innocence of a member of the family.

Stephen Maxie said:

"How do you know that she was dead then? She was alive at ten-thirty p.m. and dead by the morning. That's as much as anyone knows."

"Not really," replied Dalgleish. "Two people can put the time of death closer than that. One is the murderer, but there is someone else who can help too."

¶ 2

There was a knock on the door and Martha stood there, capped and aproned, stolid as always. Her hair was strained back beneath her curiously high old-fashioned cap, her ankles bulged above the barred black shoes. If the Maxies were seeing in their mind's eye a desperate woman, clutching to herself that incriminating bottle and homing to her familiar kitchen like a frightened animal they gave no sign. She looked as she had always looked and if she had become a stranger she was less alien than they now were to each other. She gave no explanation of her presence except to announce "Mr. Proctor for the Inspector". Then she was gone again and the shadowy figure behind her stepped forward into the light. Proctor was too angry to be disconcerted at being shown thus summarily into a roomful of people obviously occupied with their private concerns. He seemed to notice no one but Dalgleish and advanced towards him belligerently.

"Look here, Inspector, I've got to have protection. It isn't good enough. I've been trying to get you at the station. They wouldn't tell me where you were, if you please, but I wasn't going to be fobbed off with that station sergeant. I thought I'd find you here. Something's got to be done about it."

Dalgleish considered him in silence for a minute.

"What isn't good enough, Mr. Proctor?" he inquired.

"That young fellow. Sally's husband. He's been round home threatening me. He was drunk if you ask me. It's not my fault if she got herself murdered and I told him so. I won't have him upsetting my wife. And there are the neighbours. You could hear him shouting his insults right down the avenue. My daughter was there, too. It's not nice in front of a child. I'm innocent of this murder as you very well know, and I want protection."

He looked indeed as if he could have done with protection against more than James Ritchie. He was a scrawny red-faced little man with the look of an angry hen and a trick of jerking his head as he talked. He was neatly but cheaply dressed. The grey raincoat was clean and the trilby hat, held stiffly in his gloved hands, had recently acquired a new band. Catherine said suddenly, "You were in this house on the day of the murder, weren't you? We saw you on the stairs. You must have been coming from Sally's room."

Stephen glanced at his mother and said:

"You'd better come in and join the prayer meeting, Mr.

Proctor. Public confessions are said to be good for the soul. Actually you've timed your entrance rather well. You are, I assume, interested in hearing who killed your niece?"

"No!" said Hearne suddenly and violently. "Don't be a fool, Maxie. Keep him out of it."

His voice recalled Proctor to a sense of his surroundings. He focused his attention on Felix and seemed to dislike what he saw. "So I'm not to stay! Suppose I choose to stay. I've a right to know what's going on." He glared round at the watchful, unwelcoming faces. "You'd like it to be me, wouldn't you? All of you. Don't think I don't know. You'd like to pin it on me all right if you could. I'd have been in queer street if she'd been poisoned or knocked on the head. Pity one of you couldn't keep your hands off her, wasn't it? But there's one thing you can't pin on me and that's a strangling. And why? That's why!"

He gave a sudden convulsive movement, there was a click and a moment of sheer unbelievable comedy as his artificial right hand fell with a thud on the desk in front of Dalgleish. They gazed at it fascinated while it lay like some obscene relic, its rubber fingers curved in impotent supplication. Breathing heavily, Proctor hitched a chair beneath himself with a deft twist of his left hand and sat there triumphantly, while Catherine turned her pale eyes on him reproachfully as if he were a difficult patient who had behaved with more than customary petulance.

Dalgleish picked up the hand.

"We knew about this, of course, although I'm glad to say that my own attention was first brought to it less spectacularly. Mr. Proctor lost his right hand in a bombing incident. This ingenious substitute is made of moulded linen and glue. It's light and strong and has three articulated fingers with knuckle joints like a real hand. By flexing his left shoulder and slightly moving his arm away from his body, the wearer can tighten a control cord which runs from the shoulder to the thumb. This opens the thumb against the pressure of a spring. Once the tension on the shoulder is released the spring automatically closes the thumb against the firm fixed index finger. It is, as you can see, a clever contraption, and Mr. Proctor can do a great deal with it. He can get through his work, ride a bicycle and present an almost normal appearance to the world. But there's one thing he can't do, and that is to kill by manual strangulation."

"He could be left-handed."

"He could be, Miss Bowers, but he isn't, and the evidence shows that Sally was killed by a strong right-handed grip." He turned the hand over and pushed it across the table to Proctor.

"This, of course, was the hand which a certain small boy saw opening the trap-door of Bocock's stables. There could only be one person connected with this case who would be wearing leather gloves on a hot summer day and at a garden fête. This was one clue to his identity and there were others. Miss Bowers is quite right. Mr. Proctor was in Martingale that afternoon."

"What if I was? Sally asked me to come. She was my niece, wasn't she?"

"Oh, come now, Proctor," said Felix. "You aren't going to tell us that this was a dutiful social call, that you were just dropping in to inquire after the baby's health! How much was she asking?"

"Thirty pounds," said Proctor. "Thirty pounds she was after and much good they would do her now."

"And being in need of thirty pounds," went on Felix remorselessly, "she naturally turned to her next of kin who might be expected to help. It's a touching story."

Before Proctor could answer Dalgleish broke in:

"She was asking for thirty pounds because she wanted to have some money ready for the return of her husband. It had been arranged that she should go on working and save what she could. Sally meant to keep that bargain to the last pound, baby or no baby. She intended to get this money from her uncle by a not uncommon method. She told him that she was shortly to get married, she didn't say to whom, and that she and her husband would make his treatment of her public unless he bought her silence. She threatened to expose him to his employers and the respectable neighbours of Canningbury. She talked about being done out of her rights. On the other hand, if he chose to pay up, neither she nor her husband would ever see or worry the Proctors again."

"But that was blackmail," cried Catherine. "He should have told her to go ahead and say what she liked. No one would have believed her. She wouldn't have got a penny out of me!" Proctor sat silent. The others seemed to have forgotten his presence. Dalgleish continued.

"I think Mr. Proctor would have been very willing to take your advice, Miss Bowers, if his niece hadn't made use of one particular phrase. She talked about being done out of her rights. She probably meant no more than that a difference was made in the treatment of herself and her cousin, although Mrs. Proctor would deny that this was so. She may have known more than we realize. But for reasons which we needn't discuss here that phrase struck uncomfortably on her uncle's ear. His reaction must have been interesting and Sally was intelligent enough to take the clue. Mr. Proctor is no actor. He tried to find out how much his niece knew and the more he probed the more he gave away. By the time they parted Sally knew that those thirty pounds, and perhaps more, were well within her grasp."

Proctor's grating voice broke in:

"I said I'd want a receipt from her, mind you. I knew what she was up to. I said I was willing to help her this once as she was getting married and there was bound to be expense. But that would be the end. If she tried it on again I'd go to the police, and I'd have the receipt to prove it."

"She wouldn't have tried it on again," said Deborah quietly. The men's eyes swung round to her. "Not Sally. She was only playing with you, pulling the strings for the fun of watching you dance. If she could get thirty pounds as well as her fun so much the better, but the real attraction was seeing you sweat. But she wouldn't have bothered to go on with it. The entertainment palled after a time. Sally liked to eat her victims fresh."

"Oh no, no." Eleanor Maxie opened her hands in a little gesture of protest. "She wasn't really like that. We never really knew her." Proctor ignored her and suddenly and surprisingly smiled across at Deborah as if accepting an ally.

"That's true enough. You knew what she was like. I was on a string all right. She had it all worked out. I was to get the thirty pounds that night and bring it to her. She made me follow her into the house and up to her room. That was bad enough, the sneaking in and out. That's when I met you on the stairs. She showed me the back door and said that she would open it for me at midnight. I was to stay in the trees at the back of the lawn until she switched her bedroom light on and off. That was to be the signal."

Felix gave a shout of laughter.

"Poor Sally. What an exhibitionist! She had to have drama if it killed her."

"In the end it did," said Dalgleish. "If she hadn't played with people Sally would be alive today."

"She was in a funny mood that day," remembered

Deborah. "There was a kind of madness about her. I don't only mean copying my dress or pretending to accept Stephen. She was as full of mischief as a child. I suppose it could have been her kind of happiness."

"She went to bed happy," said Stephen. And suddenly they were all quiet, remembering. Somewhere a clock struck sweetly and clearly but there was no other sound except the thin rasp of paper as Dalgleish turned over a page. Outside, rising into coolness and silence, was the staircase up which Sally had carried that last bedtime drink. As they listened it was almost possible to imagine the sound of a soft footfall, the brush of wool against the stairs, the echo of a laugh. Outside in the darkness the edge of the lawn was a faint blur and the desk light reflected above it like a row of Chinese lanterns hung in the scented night. Was there the suspicion of a white dress floating between them, a swirl of hair? Somewhere above them was the nursery, empty now, white and aseptic as a morgue. Could any of them face that staircase and open that nursery door without the fear that the bed might not be empty? Deborah shivered and spoke for them all. "Please," she said. "Please tell us what happened!"

Dalgleish lifted his eyes and looked at her. Then the deep level voice went on.

¶ 3

"I think the killer went to Miss Jupp's room driven by an uncontrollable impulse to find out exactly what the girl felt, what she intended, the extent of the danger from her. Perhaps there was some idea of pleading with her—although I don't think that is very likely. It is more probable that the intention was to try to arrange some kind of a bargain. The visitor went to Sally's room and either walked in or knocked and was let in. It was a person, you see, from whom nothing was feared. Sally would be undressed and in bed. She must have been sleepy but she had only taken a little of the cocoa and was not drugged, only too tired to be bothered with finesse or rational argument. She didn't trouble to get up from her bed nor to put on her dressing-gown. You may think, in view of what we have learned about her character, that she would have done so had her visitor been a man. But that is hardly the kind of evidence which is worth very much.

"We don't know yet what happened between Sally and her visitor. We only know that, when that visitor left and closed the door, Sally was dead. If we assume that this was an unpremeditated killing we can make a guess at what happened. We know now that Sally was married, was in love with her husband, was waiting for him to come to fetch her, was even expecting him daily. We can guess from her attitude to Derek Pullen and from the careful way in which she kept her secret, that she enjoyed the feeling of power that this hidden knowledge gave her. Pullen has said, 'She liked things to be secret.' A woman I interviewed for whom Sally had worked said, 'She was a secretive little thing. She was with me for three years and I knew no more about her at the end of them than when she first came.' Sally Jupp kept the news of her marriage secret under very difficult circumstances. Her behaviour wasn't reasonable. Her husband was overseas and doing well. The firm would hardly have sent him home. The firm need not even have known. If Sally had told the truth someone could have been found to help her. I think she kept her secret partly because she wanted to prove her loyalty and trustworthiness and partly because she was the kind of person to whom secrecy made its appeal. It gave her an opportunity of hurting her uncle and aunt for whom she had no affection, and it provided her with considerable entertainment. It also gave her a free home for seven months. Her husband has told me, 'Sally always did say that the unmarried mothers had the best of it.' I don't suppose anyone here agrees with that, but Sally Ritchie obviously believed that we live in a society which salves its conscience more by helping the interestingly unfortunate than the dull deserving and was in the position to put her theory to the test. I think she enjoyed herself at St. Mary's Refuge. I think she sustained herself by the knowledge that she was different from the others. I imagine that she relished in advance the look on Miss Liddell's face when she knew the truth and the fun that she would have mimicking the inmates of St. Mary's to her husband. You know the sort of thing. 'Let Sal tell you about the time she was an unmarried mother.' I think, too, that she enjoyed the feeling of power which her hidden knowledge gave her. She enjoyed watching the consternation of the Maxies at a danger which only she knew had no reality."

Deborah moved uncomfortably in her chair.

"You seem to know a great deal about her. If she knew the engagement had no reality why did she consent to it. She would have saved everyone a great deal of trouble by telling Stephen the truth."

Dalgleish looked across at her.

"She would have saved her own life. But was it in character for her to tell? There was not much longer to wait. Her husband would be flying home, perhaps in the next day or two. Dr. Maxie's proposal was merely one additional complication, adding its own stimulus of excitement and amusement to the total situation. Remember, she never overtly accepted the proposal. No, I would have expected her to act as she did. She obviously disliked Mrs. Riscoe and was becoming more audacious in showing it as the time for her husband's return drew nearer. This proposal offered new chances of private amusement. I think that, when her visitor came to her, she was lying back on her bed in sleepy, happy, amused confidence, feeling perhaps, that she held the Maxie family, the whole situation, the world itself in the hollow of her hand. Not one of the dozens of people I have interviewed have described her as kind. I don't think she was kind to her visitor. She underestimated the force of the anger and desperation which were confronting her. Perhaps she laughed. And when she did that the strong fingers closed around her throat."

There was a silence. Felix Hearne broke it by saying roughly:

"You've mistaken your profession, Inspector. That dramatic histrionic was worthy of a larger audience."

"Don't be a fool, Hearne." Stephen Maxie lifted a face drained of colour and etched with weariness. "Can't you see that he's satisfied enough with the reactions we're providing." He turned to Dalgleish with a sudden spurt of anger. "Whose hands?" he demanded. "Why go on with this farce? Whose hands?"

Dalgleish ignored him.

"Our killer goes to the door and turns out the light. This is to be the moment of escape. And then, perhaps, there comes a doubt. It may be the need to make certain just once more that Sally Jupp is dead. It may be that the child turns in his sleep and there is the natural and human wish not to leave him crying and alone with his dead mother. It may be the more selfish concern that his cries will awaken the household before the killer can make good his escape. Whatever the reason, the light is momentarily switched on again. On and then off. Waiting at the edge of the lawn and in the shelter of the trees Sydney Proctor sees what he thinks is the awaited signal. He has no watch. He must depend on the flashing light. He makes his way along the edge of the lawn towards the back door still keeping in the shadow of the trees and the shrubs."

As Dalgleish paused his audience looked towards Proctor. He was more self-possessed now and seemed, indeed, to have lost both his earlier nervousness and his defensive truculence. He took up the story simply and calmly as if the recollection of that dreadful night and the intense and concentrated interest of his audience had released him from self-consciousness and guilt. Now that he was beyond noisy self-justification they found him easier to tolerate. Like them he had been in some sense a victim of Sally. Listening, they shared the desperation and fear which had driven him forward to her door.

"I thought I must have missed the first flash. She'd said two flashes so I waited for a bit and watched. Then I thought I'd better take a chance. There wasn't any sense in messing about. I'd come so far and I might as well go on with it. She'd see that I did, anyway. It hadn't been easy to raise the thirty quid. I'd got what I could from my Post Office account, but that was only ten. I hadn't much at home, only what I'd put by for the instalments on the telly. I took that and pawned my watch at a shop in Canningbury. The chap could see I was pretty desperate I suppose, and didn't give me what it was worth. Still, I had enough to keep her quiet. I'd written out a receipt for her to sign, too. I wasn't taking any chances with her after that scene in the stables. I thought I'd just hand over the cash, make her sign the receipt and get off home. If she tried any more funny business I could threaten to charge her with blackmail. The receipt would be useful if it came to that, but I didn't think it would. She just wanted the money and afterwards she'd leave me in peace. Well, there wouldn't be much sense in trying it on again, would there? I can't raise money to order and Sally knew that well enough. She was no fool was our Sally.

"The heavy outside door was open just as she said. I had my torch and it was easy to find the stairs and get up to her room. She'd shown me the way that afternoon. It was a piece of cake. The house was dead quiet. You'd have thought it was empty. Sally's door was shut and there was no light showing through the keyhole or under the door. That struck me as queer. I wondered whether to knock, but I wasn't keen on making a sound. The whole place was so quiet it was eerie. In the end I opened the door and called to her quietly. She didn't answer. I shone the light of the torch across the room and on to the bed. She was lying there. At first I thought she was asleep and—well, it was like a reprieve. I wondered whether I ought to leave the cash on her pillow and then I thought, 'Why the hell should I?' She had asked me to come. It was up to her to stay awake. Besides, I wanted to get out of the house. I don't know when I first realized that she wasn't asleep. I went up to the bed. It was then that I knew that she was dead. Funny how you can't mistake it. I knew that she wasn't ill or unconscious. Sally was dead. One eye was closed but the other was half open. It seemed to be looking at me, so I put out my left hand and drew down the lid. I don't know what made me touch her. Damn silly thing to do really. It was just that I had to close that staring eye. The sheet was folded down under her chin just as if someone had made her comfortable. I drew it down and then I saw the bruise on her neck. Until then I don't think the word 'murder' had come into my mind. When it did, well I suppose I lost my head. I ought to have known that it was a right-handed job and that no one could suspect me, but you don't think like that when you're frightened. I still held my torch and I was shaking so that it made little circles of light round her head. I couldn't hold it steady. I was trying to think straight, wondering what to do. Then it came over me that she was dead and I was in her room and with the money on me. You could see what people would think. I knew I'd got to get away. I don't remember reaching the door but I was too late. I could hear footsteps coming along the passage. They were only faint. I suppose I wouldn't have heard them in the ordinary way. But I was keyed up so that I could hear my own heart beating. In a second I drew the bolt across the door and leaned back against it, holding my breath. It was a woman on the other side of the door. She knocked very quietly and called out, 'Sally. Are you asleep, Sally?' She called quite softly. I don't see how she expected to be heard. Perhaps she didn't really care. I've thought about it a good deal since but, at the time, I didn't wait to see what she would do. She might have knocked louder and set the kid bawling or she might have realized that something was wrong and fetched the family. I had to get away. Luckily I keep myself fit and heights don't worry me. Not that there was much in it. I got out of the side window, the one sheltered by the trees, and the stack-pipe was handy enough. I couldn't hurt my hands and my soft cycling shoes gave me a grip. I fell the last few feet and turned my ankle, but I didn't feel it at the time. I ran into the shelter of the trees before I looked back. Sally's room was still in darkness and I began to feel safe.

"I'd hidden my cycle in the hedge at the side of the lane and I was glad to see it again, I can tell you. It wasn't until I got on that I realized about my foot. I couldn't grasp the pedal with it. Still, I got on all right. I was beginning to think out a plan, too. I had to have an alibi. When I got to Finchworthy I staged my accident. It wasn't difficult. It's a quiet road and a high wall runs on the left of it. I drove the cycle hard against it until the front wheel buckled. Then I slashed the front tyre with my pocket-knife. I didn't need to worry about myself. I looked the part all right. My ankle was swelling by now and I felt sick. It must have started raining some time in the night because I was wet and cold, although I don't remember the rain. It took some doing to drag myself and the bike into Canningbury and it was well after one before I got home. I had to be pretty quiet so I left the bike in the front garden and let myself in. It was important not to wake Mrs. Proctor before I had a chance to alter the two downstairs clocks. We haven't a clock or watch in the bedroom. I used to wind the gold one every night and keep it by the bed. If I could only get in without waking the wife I reckoned I should be all right. I thought I was going to be unlucky. She must have been awake and listening for the door because she came to the top of the stairs and called out. I'd had about as much as I could take by then, so I shouted at her to get back to bed and I'd be up. She did what she was told—she usually does—but I knew she'd be down before long. Still, it gave me my chance. By the time she'd got on her dressing-gown and come pussy-footing down I'd got the clocks put back to midnight. She fussed about getting me a cup of tea. I was in a sweat to get her back into bed before any of the town clocks struck two. It was the sort of thing she might notice. Anyway, I did get her back upstairs eventually and she went off to sleep quickly enough. It was different with me, I can tell you. My God, I never want to live through another night like that! You can say what you like about us and the way we treated Sally. She didn't do so badly out of us to my way of thinking. But if she felt hard done by, well, the little bitch got her own back that night."

He spat the shocking word at them and then, in the silence, muttered something which might have been an apology and covered his face with that grotesque right hand. No one spoke for a moment and then Catherine said:

"You didn't come to the inquest, did you? We wondered about that at the time, but there was some talk that you were ill. Was that because you were afraid of being recognized? But you must have known by then how Sally died and that no one could possibly suspect you."

Under the stress of emotion Proctor had told his story with unselfconscious fluency. Now the need for self-justification reasserted itself and brought a return of his former truculence.

"Why should I go? I wasn't in a fit state for it anyway. I knew how she had died all right. The police told us that when they sent someone round on Sunday morning. He didn't take long before he was asking when I'd last seen her, but I had my story ready. I suppose you all think that I ought to have told them what I knew. Well, I didn't! Sally had caused enough trouble while she was alive and she wasn't going to add to it now she was dead if I could help it. I didn't see why my private affairs should have to come out in court. It isn't easy to explain these things. People might get the wrong ideas."

"Worse still, they might understand only too well," said Felix dryly.

Proctor's thin face flushed. Getting to his feet he deliberately turned his back on Felix and spoke to Eleanor Maxie.

"If you'll excuse me now I'll be on my way. I didn't mean to intrude. It was just that I had to see the inspector. I'm sure I hope this all turns out satisfactorily, but you don't want me here."

"He talks as if we're about to give birth," thought Stephen. The wish to assert an independence of Dalgleish and to show that at least one of the family still considered himself a free agent made him ask:

"Can I drive you home? The last bus went at eight."

Proctor made a gesture of refusal but did not look at him.

"No. No thank you. I have my bicycle outside. They've made a good job of it, all things considered. Please don't bother to see me out."

He stood there, his gloved hands hanging loosely, an unlikeable and pathetic figure but not without dignity.

"At least," thought Felix. "He has the grace to know when he's not wanted." Suddenly, and with a stiff little gesture, Proctor held out his left hand to Eleanor Maxie and she took it.

Stephen went with him to the door. While he was away no one spoke. Felix felt the heightening of tension and his nostrils twitched at the remembered smell of fear. They must know now. They had been told everything except the actual name. But how far were they letting themselves recognize the truth? From under lowered eyelids he watched them. Deborah was curiously tranquil as if the end of lying and deceit had brought their own peace. He did not believe that Deborah knew what was coming. Eleanor Maxie's face was grey, but the folded hands lay relaxed in her lap. He could almost believe that her thoughts were elsewhere. Catherine Bowers sat stiffly, her lips pursed as if in disapproval. Earlier Felix had thought that she was enjoying herself. Now he was not so sure. He noticed with sardonic satisfaction the clenching of her hands, the nervous twitching at the corner of her eyes.

Suddenly Stephen was back with them and Felix spoke.

"Hasn't this gone on long enough? We've heard the

evidence. That back door was opened until Maxie locked it at twelve-thirty-three a.m. Some time before then someone got in and killed Sally. The police haven't found out who and they aren't likely to find out. It could have been anyone. I suggest that we none of us say anything more." He looked round at them. The warning was unmistakable. Dalgleish said mildly:

"You are suggesting that a perfect stranger entered the house, made no attempt to steal, went unerringly to Miss Jupp's room and strangled her while, with no attempt of raising the alarm, she lay back obligingly on the bed?"

"She could have invited him to come, whoever he was," said Catherine.

Dalgleish turned to her.

"But she was expecting Proctor. We can't imagine that she wanted to make a party of that little transaction. And whom would she invite? We have checked on everyonc who knew her."

"For God's sake stop discussing it," cried Felix. "Can't you see that's what he wants you to do! There's no proof!"

"Isn't there?" said Dalgleish softly. "I wonder."

"We know who didn't do it, anyway," said Catherine. "It wasn't Stephen or Derek Pullen because they've got alibis and it wasn't Mr. Proctor because of his hand. Sally couldn't have been killed by her uncle."

"No," said Dalgleish. "Nor by Martha Bultitaft who didn't know how the girl had died until Mr. Hearne told her. Nor by you, Miss Bowers, who knocked at her door and tried to speak to her after she was dead. Nor by Mrs. Riscoe, whose finger-nails would inevitably have left scratches. No one can grow nails that length overnight and the murderer didn't wear gloves. Nor by Mr. Hearne, whatever he might like me to think. Mr. Hearne didn't know which room Sally slept in. He had to ask Mr. Maxie where he should carry the ladder."

"Only a fool would have shown that he knew. I could have pretended."

"Only you weren't pretending," said Stephen roughly. "You can keep your bloody patronage to yourself. You were the last person to want Sally dead. Once Sally was installed here Deborah might have married you. Believe me, you wouldn't have got her on any other terms. She'll never marry you now and you know it."

Eleanor Maxie looked up and said quietly:

"I went to her room to talk to her. It seemed that the marriage might not be so bad a thing if she were really fond of my son. I wanted to find out what she felt. I was tired and I should have waited till the morning. She was lying there on her bed and singing to herself. It would have been all right if she hadn't done two things. She laughed at me. And she told me, Stephen, that she was going to have your child. It was so very quick. One second she was alive and laughing. The next she was a dead thing in my hands."

"Then it was you!" said Catherine in a whisper. "It was you."

"Of course," said Eleanor Maxie gently. "Think it out for yourself. Who else could it have been?"

¶ 4

The Maxies thought that going to prison must be rather like going to hospital, except that it was even more involuntary. Both were abnormal and rather frightening experiences to which the victim reacted with a clinical detachment and the onlookers with a determined cheerfulness which was intended to create confidence without giving the suspicion of callousness. Eleanor Maxie, accompanied by a calm and tactful woman police sergeant, went to enjoy the comfort of a last bath in her own house. She had insisted on this and, as with the final preparations for hospital, no one liked to point out that bathing was the first procedure inflicted on admission. Or was there, perhaps, a difference between prisoners in custody and those convicted? Felix might have known but no one cared to ask. The police car driver waited in the background, watchful and unobtrusive as an ambulance attendant. There were the last instructions, the messages for friends, the telephone calls and the hurried packing. Mr. Hinks arrived from the vicarage, breathless and unsurprised, steeling himself to give advice and comfort but looking so desperately in need of them himself that Felix took him firmly by the arm and walked with him back to the vicarage. From a window Deborah watched them talking together as they passed out of sight and wondered briefly what they were saying. As she was mounting the stairs to her mother Dalgleish was telephoning from the hall. Their eyes met and held. For a second she thought he was going to speak, but his head bent again to the receiver and she passed on her way, recognizing suddenly and without surprise that, had things been different, here was the man to whom she would have instinctively turned for reassurance and advice.

Stephen, left alone, recognized his misery for what it was, an overmastering pain which had nothing in common with the dissatisfaction and ennui which he had previously thought of as unhappiness. He had taken two drinks but realized in time that drinking wasn't helping. What he needed was someone to minister to his misery and assure him of its essential unfairness. He went in search of Catherine.

He found her kneeling before a small case in his mother's room wrapping jars and bottles in tissue paper. When she looked up at him he saw that she had been crying. He was shocked and irritated. There was no room in the house for a lesser grief. Catherine had never mastered the art of crying appealingly. Perhaps that was one reason why she had learnt early to be stoical in grief as in other things. Stephen decided to ignore this intrusion on his own misery.

"Cathy," he said. "Why on earth did she confess? Hearne was perfectly right. They would never have proved it if she'd only kept quiet."

He had only called her Cathy once before and then, too, he had wanted something from her. Even in the moment of physical love it had struck her as an affectation. She looked up at him. "You don't know her very well, do you? She was only waiting for your father to die before she confessed. She didn't want to leave him and she promised him that he wouldn't be sent away. That was the only reason why she kept silent. She told Mr. Hinks about Sally when she walked back to the vicarage with him earlier tonight."

"But she sat so calmly through all the disclosures!"

"I suppose she wanted to know just what happened. None of you told her anything. I think she worried most thinking that it was you who had visited Sally and locked the door."

"I know. She tried to ask me. I thought she was asking me if I was the murderer. They'll have to reduce the charge. It wasn't premeditated after all. Why doesn't Jephson hurry up and come. We've telephoned for him."

Catherine was sorting a few books she had taken from the bedside table, considering whether to pack them. Stephen went on:

"They'll send her to prison either way. Mother in prison! Cathy, I don't think I can bear it!"

And Catherine, who had grown to like and respect Eleanor Maxie very much, was not sure that she could bear it either and lost her patience.

"You can't bear it! I like that! You don't have to bear it. She does. And it's you that put her there, remember."

Catherine, once started, found it hard to stop and her irritation found a more personal expression.

"And there's another thing, Stephen. I don't know what you feel about us . . . about me if you like. I don't want to talk about this again so I'm just saying now that it's all over. Oh, for heaven's sake get your feet out of that tissue paper! I'm trying to pack."

She was crying in earnest now like an animal or a child. The words were thickened so that he could only just hear them.

"I was in love with you, but not any more. I don't know what you expect now, but it doesn't matter. It's all off."

And Stephen, who had never for one moment intended that it should be on, looked down on the blotched face, the swollen protuberant eyes and felt, irrationally, a spasm of chagrin and regret.

¶ 5

One month after Eleanor Maxie had been found guilty on the lesser charge of manslaughter Dalgleish, on one of his rare off-duty days, drove through Chadfleet on his way back to London from the Essex estuary where he had laid up his 30-foot sailing-boat. It was not much out of his way, but he did not choose to analyse too precisely the motives which had prompted him to these three additional miles of winding, tree-shadowed roads. He passed the Pullens' cottage. There was a light in the front room and the plaster Alsatian dog stood darkly outlined against the curtains. And now came St. Mary's Refuge. The house looked empty with only a lone pram at the front door steps to hint at the life inside. The village itself was deserted, somnolent in its tea-time five o'clock calm. As he was passing Wilson's General Stores the front door blinds were being drawn and the last customer was leaving. It was Deborah Riscoe. There was a heavy-looking shopping-basket on her arm and he stopped the car instinctively. There was no time for indecision or awkwardness and he had taken the basket from her and she had slid into the seat beside him before it had struck him to wonder at his boldness or her compliance. Stealing a quick glance at her calm uplifted profile, he saw that the look of strain had gone. She had lost none of her beauty but there was a serenity about her which reminded him of her mother.

As the car turned into the drive of Martingale he hesitated but she gave an almost imperceptible shake of the head and he drove on. The beeches were golden now but the twilight was draining them of colour. The first fallen leaves crackled into dust beneath the tyres. The house came into view as he had first seen it, but greyer now and slightly sinister in the fading light. In the hall Deborah slipped off her leather jacket and unwound her scarf.

"Thank you. I was glad of that. Stephen has the car in town this week and Wilson's can only deliver on Wednesdays. I'm always running out of things I've forgotten. Would you like a drink, or tea or something?" She gave him a quick mocking smile. "You aren't on duty now. Or are you?"

"No," he said. "I'm not on duty now. Just indulging myself."

She did not ask for an explanation and he followed her into the drawing-room. It was dustier than he remembered, and somehow more bare but his trained eye saw that there was no real change, only the naked look of a room from which the small personal change of living has been tidied away.

As if she guessed what he was thinking, she said:

"There's only me here most of the time. Martha has left and I've replaced her by a couple of dailies from the new town. At least, they call themselves dailies but I can never be sure they'll turn up. It adds spice to our relationship. Stephen is home most week-ends, of course, and that helps. There will be plenty of time for a good clean-up before mummy comes home. It's mostly paper work at present, Daddy's will and death duties and lawyers fussing."

"Ought you to be here alone?" asked Dalgleish.

"Oh, I don't mind. One of the family has to stay. Sir Reynold did offer me one of his dogs but they're a little too bite-happy for me. Besides, they aren't trained to exorcise ghosts."

Dalgleish took the drink she handed him and asked after Catherine Bowers. She seemed the safest person to mention. He had little interest in Stephen Maxie and too much interest in Felix Hearne. To ask after the child was to evoke that golden-haired wraith whose shadow was already between them.

"I see Catherine sometimes. Jimmy is still at St. Mary's for the present and Catherine comes down with his father quite often to take him out. She and James Ritchie will get married, I think."

"That's rather sudden, isn't it?"

She laughed.

"Oh, I don't think Ritchie knows it yet. It will be rather a good thing really. She loves the child, really cares about him, and I think Ritchie will be lucky. I don't think there's anyone else to tell you about. Mummy's very well really and not too unhappy. Felix Hearne is in Canada. My brother is at hospital most of the time and terribly busy. Everyone's been very kind though, he says."

"They would be," thought Dalgleish. His mother was serving her sentence and his sister was coping unaided with death duties, housework and the hostility or—and she would hate this worse—the sympathy of the village. But Stephen Maxie was back at hospital with everyone being very kind. Something of what he felt must have shown in his face for she said quickly:

"I'm glad he's busy. It was worse for him than for me."

They sat together in silence for a little time. Despite their apparent easy companionship Dalgleish was morbidly sensitive to every word. He longed to say something of comfort or reassurance but rejected each of the half formulated sentences before they reached his lips. "I'm sorry I had to do it." Only he wasn't sorry and she was intelligent and honest enough to know it. He had never yet apologized for his job and wouldn't insult her by pretending to now. "I know you must dislike me for what I had to do." Mawkish, sentimental, insincere and with an arrogant presumption that she could feel about him one way or the other. They walked to the door in silence and she stood to watch him out of sight. As he turned his head and saw the lonely figure, outlined momentarily against the light from the hall, he knew with sudden and heart-lifting certainty that they would meet again. And when that happened the right words would be found.

A MIND TO MURDER

For

EDWARD GORDON JAMES

Author's Note

There is only a small number of autonomous psychiatric out-patient clinics in London and it is obvious that these units, dealing as they do with the same medical specialty and organized within a unified National Health Service, must inevitably have some methods of treatment and administrative procedures in common. A number of these they share with the Steen Clinic. It is the more important to state clearly that the Steen is an imaginary clinic situated in an imaginary London square, that none of its patients or staff, medical or lay, represent living people, and that the deplorable events which took place in its basement have their origin only in that curious psychological phenomenon—the imagination of the crime novelist.

P. D. J.

Chapter One

Dr. Paul Steiner, consultant psychiatrist at the Steen Clinic, sat in the front ground floor consulting-room and listened to his patient's highly rationalized explanation of the failure of his third marriage. Mr. Burge lay in comfort on a couch the better to expound the complications of his psyche. Dr. Steiner sat at his head in a chair of the carefully documented type which the Hospital Management Committee had decreed for the use of consultants. It was functional and not unattractive but it gave no support to the back of the head. From time to time a sharp jerk of his neck muscles recalled Dr. Steiner from momentary oblivion to the realities of his Friday evening psychotheraphy clinic. The October day had been very warm. After a fortnight of sharp frosts during which the staff of the clinic had shivered and pleaded, the official date for starting the central heating had coincided with one of those perfect autumn days when the city square outside had brimmed with yellow light and the late dahlias in the railed garden, bright as a paintbox, had shone like the gauds of high summer. It was now nearly seven o'clock. Outside, the warmth of the day had long given way, first to mist and then to chilly darkness. But here, inside the clinic, the heat of noon was trapped, the air, heavy and still, seemed spent with the breath of too much talking.

Mr. Burge enlarged on the immaturity, coldness and insensitivity of his wives in a querulous falsetto. Dr. Steiner's clinical judgment, not uninfluenced by the late effects of a large lunch and the unwise choice of a cream doughnut with his afternoon tea, told him that the time was not yet ripe to point out that the one defect shared by the three mesdames Burge had been a singular lack of judgment in their choice of husband. Mr. Burge was not yet ready to face the truth of his own inadequacy.

Dr. Steiner felt no moral indignation about his patient's behaviour. It would indeed have been most unethical had any such improper emotion clouded his judgment. There were few things in life which aroused Dr. Steiner's moral indignation and most of them affected his own comfort. Many of them were, indeed, concerned with the Steen Clinic and its administration. He disapproved strongly of the administrative officer, Miss Bolam, whose preoccupation with the number of patients he saw in a session and the accuracy of his travelling expense form he saw as part of a systematic policy of persecution. He resented the fact that his Friday evening clinic coincided with Dr. James Baguley's electro-convulsive therapy session so that his psychotherapy patients, all of them of high intelligence and sensible of the privilege of being treated by him, had to sit in the waiting-room with the motley crowd of depressed suburban housewives and ill-educated psychotics that Baguley seemed to delight in collecting. Dr. Steiner had refused the use of one of the third-floor consulting-rooms. These had been formed by partitioning the large and elegant Georgian rooms and he despised them as badly proportioned and unpleasing cells, ill-suited either to his grade or to the importance of his work. Nor had he found it convenient to change the time of his session. Baguley, therefore, should change his. But Dr. Baguley had stood firm and in this, too, Dr. Steiner had seen the influence of Miss Bolam. His plea that the ground floor consulting-rooms should be sound-proofed had been turned down by the Hospital Management Committee on the grounds of expense. There had, however, been no demur over providing Baguley with a new and highly expensive contraption for shocking his patients out of the few wits they still possessed. The matter, had, of course, been considered by the Clinic Medical Committee, but Miss Bolam had made no secret of where her sympathies lay. In his diatribes against the administrative officer, Dr. Steiner found it convenient to forget that her influence over the Medical Committee was non-existent.

It was difficult to forget the irritations of the E.C.T. session. The clinic building had been put up when men built to last, but even the sturdy oak door of the consulting-room could not muffle the comings and goings of a Friday night. The front door was closed at 6 p.m. and patients at the evening clinics were booked in and out since the time, over five years ago, when a patient had entered unobserved, secreted herself in the basement lavatory and chosen that insalubrious place in which to kill herself. Dr. Steiner's psychotherapy sessions were punctuated by the ringing of the front-door bell, the passing of feet as patients came and went, the hearty voices of relatives and escorts exhorting the patient or calling good-byes to Sister Ambrose. Dr. Steiner wondered why relatives found it necessary to shout at the patients as if they were deaf as well as psychotic. But possibly after a session with Baguley and his diabolic machine they were. Worst of all was the clinic domestic assistant, Mrs. Shorthouse. One might imagine that Amy Shorthouse could do the cleaning early in the mornings as was surely the normal arrangement. That way there would be the minimum of disturbance to the clinic staff. But Mrs. Shorthouse maintained that she couldn't get through the work without an extra two hours in the evenings and Miss Bolam had agreed. Naturally, she would. It appeared to Dr. Steiner that very little domestic work was done on Friday evenings. Mrs. Shorthouse had a predilection for the E.C.T. patients—indeed, her own husband had once been treated by Dr. Baguley—and she was usually to be seen hanging around the hall and the ground floor general office while the session was being held. Dr. Steiner had mentioned it at the Medical Committee more than once and had been irritated by his colleagues' general uninterest in the problem. Mrs. Shorthouse should be kept out of sight and encouraged to get on with her work, not permitted to stand around gossiping with the patients. Miss Bolam, so unnecessarily strict with other members of the staff, showed no inclination to discipline Mrs. Shorthouse. Everyone knew that good domestic workers were hard to get but an administrative officer who knew her job would recruit them somehow. Weakness solved nothing. But Baguley could not be persuaded to complain about Mrs. Shorthouse and Bolam would never criticize Baguley. The poor woman was probably in love with him. It was up to Baguley to take a firm line instead of sloping around the clinic in that ridiculously long white coat which made him look like a second-rate dentist. Really, the man had no idea of the dignity with which a consultant clinic should be conducted.

Clump, clump went someone's boots along the passage. It was probably old Tippett, a chronic schizophrenic patient of Baguley's who, for the past nine years had regularly spent Friday evenings carving wood in the art therapy department. The thought of Tippett increased Dr. Steiner's petulance. The man was totally unsuitable for the Steen. If he were well enough to be out of hospital, which Dr. Steiner doubted, he ought to attend a Day Hospital or one of the County Council's sheltered workshops. It was patients like Tippett who gave the clinic a dubious reputation and obscured its real function as an analytically orientated centre of psychotherapy. Dr. Steiner felt positively embarrassed when one of his own carefully selected patients encountered Tippett creeping about the clinic on a Friday evening. Tippett wasn't even safe to be out. One day there would be an incident and Baguley would find himself in trouble.

Dr. Steiner's happy contemplation of his colleague in trouble was punctured by the ring of the front-door bell. Really, it was impossible! This time it was apparently a hospital car service driver calling for a patient. Mrs. Shorthouse went to the door to speed them away. Her eldritch screech echoed through the hall. "Cheerio, ducks. See you next week. If you can't be good be careful."

Dr. Steiner winced and shut his eyes. But his patient, happily engaged in his favourite hobby of talking about himself, seemed not to have heard. Mr. Burge's high whine had not, in fact, faltered for the past twenty minutes.

"I don't pretend I'm an easy person. I'm not, I'm a complicated devil. That's something which Theda and Sylvia have never understood. The roots of it go deep of course. You remember that session we had in June? Some pretty basic stuff came out then I thought."

His therapist did not recall the session in question but was unconcerned. With Mr. Burge pretty basic stuff was invariably near the surface and could be trusted to emerge. An unaccountable peace fell. Dr. Steiner doodled on his notepad, regarded his doodle with interest, and concern, looked at it again with the pad held upside down and became for a moment more preoccupied with his own subconscious than with that of his patient. Suddenly he became aware of another sound from outside, faint at first and then becoming louder. Somewhere a woman was screaming. It was a horrible noise, high, continuous, and completely animal. Its effect on Dr. Steiner was peculiarly unpleasant. He was naturally timid and highly strung. Although his job involved him in the occasional emotional crises he was more adept at circumventing than coping with an emergency. Fear gave vent to irritation and he sprang from his chair exclaiming.

"No! Really, this is too bad! What's Miss Bolam doing? Isn't anyone supposed to be in charge here?"

"What's up?" inquired Mr. Burge, sitting up like a jack-in-the-box and dropping his voice half an octave to its more normal tone.

"Nothing. Nothing. Some woman having an attack of hysteria that's all. Stay where you are. I'll be back," commanded Dr. Steiner.

Mr. Burge collapsed again but with eye and ear cocked for the door. Dr. Steiner found himself in the hall.

Immediately a little group swung round to face him. Jennifer Priddy, the junior typist, was clinging to one of the porters, Peter Nagle, who was patting her shoulder in embarrassed pity and looking puzzled. Mrs. Shorthouse was with them. The girl's screams were subsiding into whimpers but her whole body was shaking, and she was deathly pale.

"What's the matter?" asked Dr. Steiner sharply. "What's wrong with her?"

Before anyone had a chance to reply the door of the E.C.T. room opened and Dr. Baguley came out followed by Sister

Ambrose and his anaesthetist, Dr. Mary Ingram. The hall seemed suddenly full of people. "Calm down, that's a good girl," said Dr. Baguley mildly. "We're trying to run a clinic." He turned to Peter Nagle and asked in a low voice: "What's the matter anyway?"

Nagle seemed about to speak when, suddenly, Miss Priddy gained control. Breaking free of him she turned to Dr. Baguley and said with absolute clearness:

"It's Miss Bolam. She's dead. Someone's killed her. She's in the basement record room and she's murdered. I found her. Enid's been murdered!"

She clung to Nagle and began to cry again but more quietly. The dreadful shaking had ceased. Dr. Baguley said to the porter:

"Take her into the treatment-room. Make her lie down. Better give her something to drink. Here's the key. I'll be back."

He made for the basement stairs and the rest, abandoning the girl to Nagle's ministrations, followed in a jostling bunch. The basement at the Steen was well lit; all its rooms were used by the clinic which, like most psychiatric units, was chronically short of space. Here, below stairs, in addition to the boiler-room, the telephone equipment-room and the porters' quarters, was the art therapy department, a medical records storeroom and, at the front of the building, a treatment-room for the lysergic acid patients. As the little group reached the bottom of the stairs the door of this room opened and Nurse Bolam, Miss Bolam's cousin, looked out briefly—a shadowy wraith in her white uniform against the darkness of the room behind. Her gentle, puzzled voice floated to them down the corridor. "Is there anything wrong? I thought I heard a scream a few minutes ago."

Sister Ambrose said with brusque authority:

"There's nothing wrong, Nurse. Get back to your patient."

The white figure disappeared and the door was shut. Turning to Mrs. Shorthouse, Sister Ambrose went on:

"And there's nothing for you to do here, Mrs. Shorthouse. Please stay upstairs. Miss Priddy might like a cup of tea."

Mrs. Shorthouse was heard to mutter rebelliously but bea a reluctant retreat. The three doctors, with sister in tow, pressed on.

The medical record-room was on their right, between the porters' rest-room and the art therapy department. The door was ajar and the light was on.

Dr. Steiner, who had become unnaturally aware of every small detail, noticed the key was in the lock. No one was about. The steel racks, with their tight-packed rows of manilla folders, ran ceiling high and at right angles to the door forming a series of narrow aisles, each lit by a fluorescent light. The four high windows were barred and dissected by the racks; it was an airless little room rarely visited and seldom dusted. The little group pushed its way down the first passage and turned left to where there was a small windowless space clear of shelving and furnished with a table and chair where records could be sorted for filing or information copied from the notes without the need to take the file away. Here was chaos. The chair was overturned. The floor was littered with records. Some had their covers wrenched apart and their pages torn, others lay dumped in shifting layers beneath gaps on the shelves which looked too narrow to have held such a weight of paper. And in the middle of this confusion, like a plump and incongruous Ophelia afloat on a tide of paper, was the body of Enid Bolam. On her chest rested a heavy and grotesque image carved in wood, her hands folded about its base so that she looked, horribly, like a parody of motherhood with her creature ritually laid to her breast.

There could be no doubt that she was dead. Even in the midst of his fear and repugnance Dr. Steiner could not miss that final diagnosis. Staring at the wooden figure he cried:

"Tippett! That's his fetish! That's the carving he's so proud of. Where is he? Baguley, he's your patient! You'd better handle this!"

He looked round nervously as if expecting Tippett to materialize, arm raised to strike, the very personification of violence.

Dr. Baguley was kneeling by the body. He said quietly:

"Tippett isn't here this evening."

"But he's always here on Fridays! That's his fetish! That's the weapon!" Dr. Steiner wailed against such obtuseness.

Dr. Baguley gently lifted Miss Bolam's left eyelid with his thumb. Without looking up he said:

"We had a phone call from St. Luke's this morning. Tippett's been admitted with pneumonia. Last Monday, I think. Anyway, he wasn't here this evening." Suddenly he gave an exclamation. The two women bent closer to the body. Dr. Steiner, who could not bring himself to watch the examination, heard him say:

"She's been stabbed, too. Through the heart by the look of it and with a black-handled chisel. Isn't this one of Nagle's, Sister?" There was a pause and Dr. Steiner heard Sister's voice:

"It looks very like it, Doctor. All his tools have black handles. He keeps them in the porters' rest-room." She added defensively, "Anyone could get at them."

"It looks as if someone has." There was the sound of Dr. Baguley getting to his feet. Still keeping his eyes on the body he said: "Phone Cully on the door, will you, Sister. Don't alarm him, but tell him that no one is to be admitted or to leave the building. That includes the patients. Then get Dr. Etherege and ask him to come down. He'll be in his consulting-room I imagine."

"Oughtn't we to phone the police?" Dr. Ingram spoke nervously and her pink face, so ridiculously like that of an angora rabbit, flushed pinker. It was not only in moments of high drama that one was apt to overlook the presence of Dr. Ingram, and Dr. Baguley stared blankly at her as if he had momentarily forgotten her existence.

"We'll wait for the medical director," he said.

Sister Ambrose disappeared with a rustle of starched linen. The nearest telephone was just outside the record-room door but, insulated by tiers of paper from every outside noise, Dr. Steiner strained his ears in vain to hear the lift of the receiver or the murmur of Sister's voice. He forced himself to look once more at Miss Bolam's body. In life he had thought of her as graceless and unattractive, and death had lent her no dignity. She lay on her back, her knees raised and parted so that there was an expanse of pink woollen knicker clearly visible, looking far more indecent than naked flesh. Her round, heavy face was quite peaceful. The two thick plaits which she wore wound above her broad forehead were undisturbed. But then, nothing had ever been known to disturb Miss Bolam's archaic hair style. Dr. Steiner was reminded of his private fantasy that the thick, lifeless plaits exuded their own mysterious secretion and were fixed for ever, immutably, about that placid brow. Looking at her in the defenceless indignity of death, Dr. Steiner tried to feel pity and knew that he felt fear. But he was fully conscious only of repugnance. It was impossible to feel tenderly towards something so ridiculous, so shocking, so obscene. The ugly word spun unbidden to the surface of thought. Obscene! He felt a ridiculous urge to pull down her skirt, to cover that puffy, pathetic face, to replace the spectacles which had slipped from her nose and hung, askew, from her left ear. Her eyes were half closed, her small mouth pursed as if in disapproval of so undignified and unmerited an end. Dr. Steiner was not unfamiliar with that look; he had seen it on her face in life. He thought, "She looks as if she's just confronting me with my travelling expense form."

Suddenly he was seized with an intolerable need to giggle. Laughter welled up uncontrollably. He recognized that this horrible urge was the result of nervousness and shock but understanding did not bring control. Helplessly, he turned his back on his colleagues and fought for composure, grasping the edge of a filing rack and pressing his forehead for support against the cold metal, his mouth and nostrils choked with the musty smell of old records.

He was not aware of Sister Ambrose's return but, suddenly, he heard her speaking.

"Dr. Etherege is on his way down. Cully is on the door and I've told him that no one is to leave. Your patient is making rather a fuss, Dr. Steiner."

"Perhaps I'd better go up to him." Faced with the need for decision, Dr. Steiner regained control. He felt that it was somehow important that he should stay with the others and be there when the medical director arrived; that it would be wise to ensure that nothing important was said or done out of his hearing. On the other hand he was not anxious to stay with the body. The records-room, brightly lit as an operating theatre, claustrophobic and overheated, made him feel like a trapped animal. The heavy close-packed shelves seemed to press upon him, compelling his eyes again and again to that lumpen figure on its paper bier.

"I'll stay here," he decided. "Mr. Burge must wait like everyone else."

They stood together without speaking. Dr. Steiner saw that Sister Ambrose, white-faced but otherwise apparently unmoved, stood stockily calm with her hands loosely clasped over her apron. So must she have stood time without number in nearly forty years of nursing, waiting at the bedside of a patient, quietly deferential, for the doctor's orders. Dr. Baguley pulled out his cigarettes, looked at the packet for a moment as if surprised to find it in his hand, and replaced it in his pocket. Dr. Ingram seemed to be silently crying. Once Dr. Steiner thought he heard her murmur: "Poor woman. Poor woman!"

Soon they heard footsteps and the medical director was with them followed by the senior psychologist, Fredrica Saxon. Dr. Etherege knelt down beside the body. He did not touch it but put his face close to Miss Bolam's as if he were about to kiss her. Dr. Steiner's sharp little eyes did not miss the glance that Miss Saxon gave Dr. Baguley, that instinctive move towards each other and the quick withdrawal.

"What happened?" she whispered. "Is she dead?"

"Yes. Murdered apparently." Baguley's tone was flat. Miss Saxon made a sudden gesture. For one unbelievable moment Dr. Steiner thought that she was going to cross herself.

"Who did it? Not poor old Tippett? That's his fetish, surely."

"Yes, but he isn't here. He's in St. Luke's with pneumonia."

"Oh, my God! Then who?" This time she moved close to

Dr. Baguley and they did not draw apart. Dr. Etherege scrambled to this feet.

"You're right, of course. She's dead. Stunned first apparently and then stabbed through the heart. I'll go upstairs to phone the police and let the rest of the staff know. We'd better keep people together. Then we three had better search the building. Nothing must be touched of course."

Dr. Steiner dared not meet Dr. Baguley's eyes. Dr. Etherege in his role of the calm, authoritative administrator had always struck him as slightly ridiculous. He suspected that Baguley felt the same.

Suddenly they heard footsteps and the senior psychiatric social worker Miss Ruth Kettle appeared from behind the filing racks, peering at them short-sightedly.

"Ah, there are you, Director," said Miss Kettle, in her fluting, breathless voice. (She was the only staff member, thought Dr. Steiner, to give Dr. Etherege that ridiculous title and God only knew why. It made the place sound like a nature-cure clinic.)

"Cully told me you were down here. Not busy, I hope? I'm so distressed, I don't want to make trouble but it really is too bad! Miss Bolam has booked me a new patient for ten on Monday. I've just seen the appointment in my diary. No consultation with me of course. She knows I always see the Worrikers then. It's quite deliberate, I'm afraid. You know, Director, someone has really got to do something about Miss Bolam."

Dr. Baguley stood aside and said grimly: "Someone has."

At the other end of the square Superintendent Adam Dalgliesh of the Criminal Investigation Department was attending the ritual autumn sherry party given by his publishers which had coincided with the third reprint of his first book of verse. He didn't overestimate his talent or the success of his book. The poems, which reflected his detached, ironic and fundamentally restless spirit, had happened to catch a public mood. He did not believe that more than half a dozen would live even in his own affections. Meanwhile he found himself awash on the shallows of an unfamiliar sea in which agents, royalties and reviews were agreeable hazards. And now there was this party. He had thought of it without enthusiasm as something to be endured, but it had proved unexpectedly enjoyable. Messrs Hearne and Illingworth were as incapable of providing poor sherry as they were of publishing poor work; Dalgliesh estimated that his publishers' share of his own book's profits had been drunk in the first ten minutes. Old Sir Hubert Illingworth had made his brief appearance in the course of it, had shaken Dalgliesh sadly by the hand, and had shuffled off muttering under his breath as if deploring that yet another writer on the firm's list was exposing himself and his publisher to the doubtful gratifications of success. To him all writers were precocious children; creatures to be tolerated and encouraged but not overexcited in case they cried before bedtime.

There were less welcome diversions than the brief appearance of Sir Hubert. Few of the guests knew that Dalgliesh was a detective and not all of them expected him to talk about his job. But there were inevitably those who thought it inappropriate that a man who caught murderers should also write verse and who said so with varying degrees of tact. Presumably they wanted murderers caught however much they might argue about what should happen to them afterwards; but they displayed a typical ambivalence towards those who did the catching. Dalgliesh was used to this attitude and found it less offensive than the common assumption that there was a particular glamour in being a member of the murder squad. But if there had been the expected quota of furtive curiosity and the inanities common to all such parties, there had also been agreeable people saying agreeable things. No writer, however apparently detached about his talent, is immune to the subtle reassurrance of disinterested praise and Dalgliesh, fighting the suspicion that few of those who admired had actually read and fewer still had bought, found that he was quietly enjoying himself and was honest enough to admit why.

The first hour had been hectic but, soon after seven o'clock, he found himself standing alone glass in hand beside the ornate

James Wyatt chimney-piece. A thin wood fire was burning, filling the room with a faint country smell. It was one of those inexplicable moments when one is suddenly completely alone in the middle of a crowd, when the noise is muted and the pressing bodies seem to recede and become remote and mysterious as actors on some distant stage. Dalgliesh leaned the back of his head against the mantelpiece, savouring this momentary privacy and noting appreciatively the elegant proportions of the room. Suddenly he saw Deborah Riscoe. She must have come into the room very quietly. He wondered how long she had been there. Immediately his diffuse sense of peace and happiness gave way to a pleasure as keen and painful as that of a boy in love for the first time. She saw him at once and, glass in hand, edged her way across the room to him.

Her appearance was wholly unexpected and he did not deceive himself that she was there on his account. After their last encounter that would hardly be likely.

He said, "It's very pleasant to see you here."

"I should have come anyway," she replied. "But actually I work here, Felix Hearne got me the job after Mummy died. I'm quite useful. I'm the general dogsbody. Shorthand and typing, too. I took a course."

He smiled.

"You make it sound like a cure."

"Well, in a way it was."

He did not pretend not to understand. They were both silent. Dalgliesh knew that he was morbidly sensitive to any allusion to the case which nearly three years ago, had led to their first meeting. That sore could not stand even the gentlest of probes. He had seen the announcement of her mother's death in the paper about six months ago, but it had seemed impossible and impertinent then to send her a message or to speak the customary words of condolence. After all, he was partly responsible for her death. It was no easier now. Instead they talked of his verse and of her job. Taking his share of this casual undemanding small talk he wondered what she would say if he asked her to have dinner with him. If she didn't turn him down flat—and she probably would—it could be for him the beginning of involvement. He didn't deceive himself that he only wanted an agreeable meal with a woman he happened to think beautiful. He had no idea what she thought of him, but, ever since their last meeting, he had known himself to be on the brink of love. If she accepted—for this or for any evening—his solitary life would be threatened. He knew this with complete certainty and the knowledge frightened him. Ever since the death of his wife in childbirth he had insulated himself carefully against pain; sex little more than an exercise in skill; a love affair merely an emotional pavanne, formalized, danced according to the rules, committing one to nothing. But, of course, she wouldn't accept. He had absolutely no reason to think that she was interested in him. It was only this certainty that gave him the confidence to indulge his thoughts. But he was tempted to try his luck. As they talked he mentally rehearsed the words, wryly amused to recognize after so many years the uncertainties of adolescence.

The light tap on his shoulder took him by surprise. It was the chairman's secretary to say that he was wanted on the telephone. "It's the Yard, Mr. Dalgliesh," she said, with well-controlled interest as if Hearne and Illingworth's authors were accustomed to calls from the Yard.

He smiled his excuses at Deborah Riscoe and she gave a little resigned shrug of her shoulders.

"I won't be a moment," he said. But even as he threaded his way through the crush of chatterers he knew that he wouldn't be back.

He took the call in a small office next to the boardroom, struggling to the telephone through chairs heaped with manuscripts, rolled galley proofs and dusty files. Hearne and Illingworth fostered an air of old-fashioned leisureliness and general muddle which concealed—sometimes to their authors' discomfiture—a formidable efficiency and attention to detail.

The familiar voice boomed in his ear.

"That you, Adam? How's the party? Good. Sorry to break it up but I'd be grateful if you'd look in over the way. The Steen Clinic, Number 31. You know the place. Upper class neuroses catered for only. It seems that their secretary or administrative officer or what have you has got herself murdered. Bashed on the head in the basement and then stabbed expertly through the heart. The boys are on their way. I've sent you Martin, of course. He'll have your gear with him."

"Thank you, sir. When was it reported?"

"Three minutes ago. The medical director rang. He gave me a concise account of practically everyone's alibi for the supposed time of death and explained why it couldn't possibly be one of the patients. He was followed by a doctor called Steiner. He explained that we met about five years ago at a dinner party given by his late brother-in-law. Dr. Steiner explained why it couldn't have been him and favoured me with his interpretation of the psychological makeup of the killer. They've read all the best detective fiction. No one has touched the body, they're not letting anyone in or out of the building and they've all collected into onc room to keep an eye on each other. You'd better hurry over, Adam, or they'll solve the crime before you arrive."

"Who is the medical director?" asked Dalgliesh.

"Dr. Henry Etherege. You must have seen him on television. He's the establishment psychiatrist, dedicated to making the profession respectable. Distinguished looking, orthodox and earnest."

"I've seen him in court," said Dalgliesh.

"Of course. Remember him in the Routledge case? He practically had me weeping into my hankie and I knew Routledge better than most. Etherege is the natural choice of any defence counsel—if he can get him. You know their bleat. Find me a psychiatrist who looks respectable, speaks English and won't shock the jury or antagonize the judge. Answer. Etherege. Ah, well, good luck!"

The A.C. was optimistic in supposing that his message could break up the party. It had long reached the stage when the departure of a solitary guest disconcerted no one. Dalgliesh thanked his host, waved a casual good-bye to the few people who caught his eye and passed almost unnoticed out of the building. He did not see Deborah Riscoe again. And made no effort to find her. His mind was already on the job ahead and he felt that he had been saved, at best from a snub and, at worst, from folly. It had been a brief, tantalizing, inconclusive and unsettling encounter but, already, it was in the past.

Walking across the square to the tall Georgian building that housed the Steen Clinic, Dalgliesh recalled some of the scant items of information about the place that had come his way. It was a well-known witticism that you had to be exceptionally sane to be accepted for treatment at the Steen. Certainly it had a reputation—Dalgliesh thought probably undeserved—for selecting its patients with more regard to their intelligence and social class than their mental condition, subjecting them to diagnostic procedures designed to deter all but the most enthusiastic, and then placing them on a waiting list for treatment long enough to ensure that the curative effects of time could exert their maximum influence before the patient actually attended for his first psychotherapy session. The Steen, Dalgliesh remembered, had a Modigliani. It was not a well-known painting, nor did it represent the artist at his best, but it was, undeniably, a Modigliani. It hung in the first-floor boardroom, the gift of a former grateful patient, and it represented much that the clinic stood for in the public eye. Other National Health Service clinics brightened their walls with reproductions from the Red Cross picture library. The Steen staff made no secret that they preferred a second-rate original to a first-class reproduction any day. And they had a second-rate original to prove it.

The house itself was one of a Georgian terrace. It stood at the south corner of the square, comfortable, unpretentious and wholly pleasing. At the rear a narrow passage ran into Lincoln Square Mews. There was a railed basement; in front of the house the railings curved on each side of the broad steps which led to the door and supported two wrought-iron lamp standards. On the right of the door an unpretentious bronze plaque bore the name of the Hospital Management Committee which administered the unit and, underneath, the words, "The Steen Clinic". No other information was given. The Steen did not advertise its function to a vulgar world nor did it wish to invite an influx of the local psychotics seeking treatment or reassurance. There were four cars parked outside but no signs yet of the police. The house looked very quiet. The door was shut but a light shone from the elegant Adam fanlight above the door and between the folds of drawn curtains in the ground floor rooms.

The door was opened almost before he had taken his finger from the bell. They had been waiting for him. A stockily-built young man in porter's uniform opened the door and let him in without speaking. The hall blazed with light and struck very warm after the coolness of the autumn night. To the left of the door was a glass-panelled reception kiosk with a telephone switchboard. A second, and much older, porter sat at the board in an attitude of utter misery. He looked round and glanced briefly at Dalgliesh with rheumy eyes, then returned to his contemplation of the board as if the arrival of the superintendent was the last straw of an intolerable burden which, if ignored, might be lifted from him. In the main body of the hall the reception committee came forward, the medical director with outstretched hand as if welcoming a guest. "Superintendent Dalgliesh? We're very glad to see you. May I introduce my colleague, Dr. James Baguley, and the secretary of the Hospital Management Committee, Mr. Lauder."

"You got here very promptly, sir," said Dalgliesh to Lauder. The group secretary said:

"I didn't know about the murder until I arrived ten minutes ago. Miss Bolam telephoned me at lunchtime today and said she wanted to see me urgently. Something was going on at the clinic and she needed advice. I came as soon as I could and found that she'd been murdered. In the circumstances, I had more reasons than one for deciding to stay around. It looks as if she needed advice more than she knew."

"Whatever it was you've come too late, I'm afraid," said Dr. Etherege.

Dalgliesh saw that he was much shorter than his television appearances suggested. His large, high-domed head with its aureole of white hair soft and fine as a baby's, looked too weighty for the slight supporting body which seemed to have aged independently giving him an oddly disintegrated appearance. It was difficult to guess his age but Dalgliesh thought that he must be nearer seventy than sixty-five, the normal retiring age for a consultant. He had the face of an indestructible gnome, the cheeks mottled with high colour so that they looked painted, the eyebrows springing above eyes of a piercing blue. Dalgliesh felt that those eyes and the soft, persuasive voice were not the least of the medical director's professional assets.

In contrast, Dr. James Baguley was six feet tall, nearly as tall as Dalgliesh, and the immediate impression he gave was of intense weariness. He was wearing a long white coat which hung loosely from his bowed shoulders. Although he was much the younger man he had none of the medical director's vitality. His hair was straight and turning iron-grey. From time to time he swept it out of his eyes with long nicotine-stained fingers. His was a handsome, bony face, but the skin and eyes were dulled as if with permanent tiredness.

The medical director said:

"You will, of course, want to see the body straight away. I'll ask Peter Nagle, our second porter, to come down with us if you've no objection. His chisel was one of the weapons used—not that he could help that, poor fellow—and no doubt you will want to ask him questions."

"I shall want to question everyone here in due course," replied Dalgliesh.

It was apparent that the medical director had taken charge. Dr. Baguley, who had not yet spoken, seemed glad to accept that position. Lauder had apparently decided to adopt a watching brief. As they moved towards the basement stairs at the back of the hall he caught Dalgliesh's eye. The momentary glance was hard to analyse, but Dalgliesh thought he detected an amused gleam and a certain wry detachment.

They stood in silence as Dalgliesh knelt by the body. He did not touch it except to part the cardigan and blouse, both of which were unbuttoned, and expose the handle of the chisel. It had been driven in up to the hilt. There was very little bruising of the tissues and no blood. The woman's vest had been rolled up above her breasts to expose the flesh for that vicious, calculated thrust. Such deliberation suggested that the killer had a confident knowledge of anatomy. There were easier ways of killing than to pierce the heart with one thrust. But for those with the knowledge and the strength there were few ways so sure.

He got to his feet and turned to Peter Nagle.

"Is that your chisel?"

"Apparently. It looks like it and mine isn't in the box." Despite the omission of the usual "sir" the voice, educated and unemphatic, held no trace of insolence or resentment. Dalgliesh asked:

"Any idea how it got here?"

"None at all. But I'd hardly be likely to say if I had, would I?"

The medical director gave Nagle a quick frown of warning or admonition and placed his hand briefly on the porter's shoulder. Without consulting Dalgliesh he said gently:

"That will be all for the present, Nagle. Just wait outside, will you?"

Dalgliesh made no demur as the porter quietly detached himself from the group and left without another word.

"Poor boy! The use of his chisel has naturally shocked him. It looks unpleasantly like an attempt to implicate him. But you will find, Superintendent, that Nagle is one of the few members of the staff with a complete alibi for the presumed time of death." Dalgliesh did not point out that this was, in itself, highly suspicious.

"Did you make any estimate of the time of death?" he asked.

Dr. Etherege replied:

"I thought that it must have been very recent. That is Dr. Baguley's view too. The clinic is very warm today—we've just started our central heating—so that the body would cool very slowly. I didn't try for rigor. I am, of course, little more than a layman in such matters. Subsequently I knew that she must have died within the hour. Naturally we have been talking among ourselves while waiting for you and it appears that Sister Ambrose was the last person to see Miss Bolam alive. That was at twenty-past six. Cully, our senior porter, tells me that Miss Bolam rang him on the internal phone at about six-fifteen to say that she was going down to the basement and that Mr. Lauder should be directed to her office if he arrived. A few minutes later, as far as she can judge, Sister came out of the E.C.T. room on the ground floor and crossed the hall to the patients' waiting-room to let a husband know that his wife was ready to be taken home. Sister saw Miss Bolam going down the hall towards the basement stairs. No one saw her alive again after that."

"Except her murderer," said Dalgliesh.

Dr. Etherege looked surprised.

"Yes, that would be so, of course. I mean that none of us saw her alive again. I have asked Sister Ambrose about the time and Sister is quite sure . . ."

"I shall be seeing Sister Ambrose and the other porter."

"Of course. Naturally you will want to see everybody. We expect that. While waiting we telephoned our homes to say that we would be delayed tonight but gave no explanation. We had already searched the building and ascertained that the basement door and the ground floor rear entrance were both bolted. Nothing has been touched in here naturally. I arranged for the staff to stay together in the front consulting-room except for Sister and Nurse Bolam who are with the remaining patients in the waiting-room. No one but Mr. Lauder and you have been allowed in."

"You seem to have thought of everything, Doctor," said Dalgliesh. He got up from his knees and stood looking down at the body.

"Who found her?" he asked.

"One of our medical secretaries, Jennifer Priddy. Cully, the senior porter, has been complaining of stomach-ache most of the day and Miss Priddy went to find Miss Bolam to ask if he could go home early. Miss Priddy is very upset but she was able to tell me . . ."

"I think it would be better if I heard it from her direct. Was this door kept locked?"

His tone was perfectly courteous but he felt their surprise. The medical director's tone did not change as he replied:

"Usually it is. The key is kept on a board with other clinic keys in the porters' duty-room here in the basement. The chisel was kept there, too."

"And this fetish?"

"Taken from the basement art-therapy-room across the passage. It was carved by one of our patients."

It was still the medical director who replied. So far Dr. Baguley hadn't spoken a word. Suddenly he said:

"She was knocked out with the fetish and then stabbed through the heart by someone who was either knowledgeable or damned lucky. That much is obvious. What isn't obvious is why they had this free-for-all with the medical records. She's lying on them so it must have happened before the murder."

"The result of a struggle, perhaps," suggested Dr. Etherege.

"It doesn't look like it. They were pulled out of the shelves and deliberately chucked about. There must have been a reason. There wasn't anything impulsive about this murder."

It was then that Peter Nagle, who had apparently been standing outside the door, came into the room.

"There's been a ring at the door, sir. Would that be the rest of the police?"

Dalgliesh noted that the records-room was almost soundproof. The front-door bell was strident but he had not heard it.

"Right," he said. "We'll go up."

As they moved together towards the stairs Dr. Etherege said:

"I wonder, Superintendent, if you could see the patients fairly soon. We have only two still with us, a male psychotherapy patient of my colleague Dr. Steiner, and a woman who has been receiving lysergic acid treatment down here in the basement front treatment-room. Dr. Baguley will be able to explain the treatment to you—she is his patient—but you can be assured that she wasn't capable of leaving her bed until twenty minutes ago and certainly wouldn't know anything about the murder. These patients become quite disorientated during treatment. Nurse Bolam was with her all the evening."

"Nurse Bolam? She is a relation of the dead woman?"

"Her cousin," said Dr. Baguley briefly.

"And your disorientated patient, Doctor. Would she know if Nurse Bolam left her alone during treatment?"

Dr. Baguley said curtly:

"Nurse Bolam would not have left her."

They mounted the stairs together to meet the murmur of voices in the hall.

That ring at the door brought into the Steen Clinic the paraphernalia and skills of an alien world. Quietly and without fuss the experts in violent death got busy. Dalgliesh disappeared into the record-room with the police surgeon and photographer. The print man, small and plump-cheeked as a hamster, with tiny delicate hands, gave his attention to door handles, locks, the tool case and Tippett's fetish. Plain-clothes men, looking disconcertingly like television actors playing plain-clothes men, made their methodical search of every room and cupboard in the clinic verifying that there was indeed no unauthorized person on the premises and that the back doors both of the ground floor and the basement were securely locked from the inside. The clinic staff, excluded from these activities and congregated in the front ground-floor consulting-room, which had been hastily furnished with additional easy chairs from the patients' waiting-room, felt that their familiar ground had been taken over by strangers and that they were caught up in the inexorable machinery of justice and being ground forward to God knew what embarrassments and disasters. Only the group secretary appeared unperturbed. He had stationed himself in the hall like a watchdog and sat there patient and alone until his turn came to be interviewed.

Dalgliesh took Miss Bolam's office for his use. It was a small room on the ground floor situated between the large general office at the front of the building and the E.C.T. treatment-room and recovery-room at the rear. Opposite it was a suite of two consulting-rooms and the patients' waiting-room. The office had been formed by partitioning the end of a larger room so that it was oddly proportioned and unattractively narrow for its height. It was sparsely furnished and lacked all evidence of personal taste except for a large bowl of chrysanthemums set on one of the filing cabinets. There was an old-fashioned safe against one wall and the other was lined with green metal filing cabinets. The desk was unostentatious and held nothing but a stationery office desk calendar, a jotting pad, and a small stack of manilla folders. Dalgliesh looked through them and said. "This is odd. These are staff dossiers apparently, but only of the female staff. Her own isn't here incidentally. I wonder why she got these out?"

"Checking on people's annual leave entitlement or something like that perhaps," suggested Sergeant Martin.

"Could be, I suppose. But why only the women? Oh well, it's hardly of immediate importance. Let's have a look at that jotter."

Miss Bolam was apparently one of those administrators who prefer not to trust to memory. The top leaf of the jotter, headed with the date, was well filled with notes in a sloping, rather childish handwriting.

Medical Committee—speak M.D. re proposed Adolescent Dept.

Speak Nagle—broken sash cord Miss Kallinski's room.

Mrs. Shorthouse—? leave.

These notes were at least self-explanatory but the jottings below them—written it appeared in some hurry—were less explicit.

Woman. Here eight years. To arrive 1st Monday.

Dalgliesh said: "These look like the jottings of a telephone call. It could have been a private call, of course, and nothing to do with the clinic. It could have been a doctor trying to trace a patient, or vice versa. Something, or someone, is apparently expected to arrive on the first Monday or on Monday the first. There are a dozen possible interpretations and none of them relevant to the murder. Still, someone phoned recently about a woman and Miss Bolam was obviously examining the dossiers of every woman on the staff except herself. Why? To check which of them were here eight years ago? It's all pretty far-fetched. We'll leave the pleasures of conjecture for the moment and get down to seeing these people. I'd like that typist in first. The girl who found the body. Etherege said she was upset. Let's hope she's calmed down by now or we'll be here half the night."

But Jennifer Priddy was perfectly calm. She had obviously been drinking and her grief was overlaid with a barely suppressed excitement. Her face, still swollen from crying, was blotched with high colour and her eyes were unnaturally bright. But the drink had not fuddled her and she told her story well. She had been busy in the ground-floor general office for most of the evening and had last seen Miss Bolam at about five-forty-five when she had gone into the A.O.'s office with a query about a patient's appointment. Miss Bolam had seemed the same as usual to her. She had returned to the general office and had been joined by Peter Nagle at about six-ten. He was wearing his coat and had come to collect the outgoing post. Miss Priddy had registered the last few letters in the post book and handed them to him. At about quarter- or twenty-past six Mrs. Shorthouse had joined them. Mrs. Shorthouse had mentioned that she had just come from Miss Bolam's office where she had been settling a query about her annual leave entitlement. Peter Nagle had gone out with the post and she and Mrs. Shorthouse had stayed together until his return some ten minutes later. Nagle had then gone down to the basement porters' room to hang up his coat and feed Tigger, the office cat, and she had followed him down almost immediately. She had helped him feed Tigger and they had returned to the general office together. At about seven the senior porter, Cully, complained again about his stomach-ache which had been troubling him all day. Miss Priddy, Mrs. Bostock, the other medical secretary, and Peter Nagle had all had to take Cully's place at the switchboard from time to time because of his stomach-ache, but he had refused to go home. Now he was willing to go and Miss Priddy had gone to the A.O.'s office to ask Miss Bolam if he could leave early. Miss Bolam wasn't in her office so she had looked in the nurses' duty-room on the ground floor. Sister Ambrose told her that she had seen the A.O. passing down the hall towards the basement stairs about thirty minutes or so earlier, so Miss Priddy had looked in the basement. The record-room was usually kept locked but the key was in the lock and the door just ajar, so she had looked inside. The light was on. She had found the body—here Miss Priddy's voice faltered—and had rushed upstairs at once to get help. No, she hadn't touched anything. She didn't know why the medical records were strewn around. She didn't know how she had known that Miss Bolam was dead. It was just that Miss Bolam had looked so very dead. She didn't know why she had been so sure it was murder. She thought she had seen a bruise on Miss Bolam's head. And, then, there had been Tippett's fetish laying on the body. She was afraid that Tippett was hiding among the record racks and would jump out at her. Everyone said that he wasn't dangerous—at least everyone except Dr. Steiner—but he had been in a mental hospital and, after all, you couldn't be really sure, could you? No, she hadn't known that Tippett wasn't in the clinic. Peter Nagle had taken the call from the hospital and had told Miss Bolam but he hadn't told her. She hadn't seen the chisel in Miss Bolam's chest but Dr. Etherege had told the staff about the stabbing when they were gathered together in the front consulting-room waiting for the police. She thought that most of the staff knew where Peter Nagle kept his tools and also which key opened the door of the basement record room. It hung on hook number 12 and was shinier than the other keys, but it wasn't labelled. Dalgliesh said:

"I want you to think very hard and very carefully. When you went downstairs to help Mr. Nagle feed the cat was the record-room door ajar and the light on as it was when you went down later and found Miss Bolam?"

The girl pushed back her dank blonde hair and said with sudden weariness:

"I . . . I can't remember. I didn't go past that door you see. I went straight into the porters' room at the bottom of the stairs. Peter was there clearing up Tigger's plate. He hadn't eaten all of his last meal so we scraped it off his plate and washed it at the sink. We didn't go near the record-room."

"But you could see the door as you came down the stairs. Would you be likely to notice if the door were ajar? The room isn't often used, is it?"

"No, but anyone might go there if they wanted a record. I mean, if the door were open I wouldn't go to see who was there or anything like that. I think I would notice if the door was wide open so I suppose it wasn't, but I can't remember, honestly I can't."

Dalgliesh ended by asking her about Miss Bolam. It appeared that Miss Priddy knew her outside the clinic, that the Priddy family attended the same church and that Miss Bolam had encouraged her to take the job at the clinic.

"I shouldn't have got this job if it hadn't been for Enid. Of course, I never called her that inside the clinic. She wouldn't have liked it." Miss Priddy gave the impression that she had only reluctantly brought herself to use the Christian name outside the clinic. She went on: "I don't mean she actually appointed me. I had to be interviewed by Mr. Lauder and by Dr. Etherege, but I know she spoke up for me. My shorthand and typing weren't very good then—it was nearly two years ago when I came—and I was lucky to get here. I didn't see very much of Enid at the clinic but she was always very kind and keen for me to get on. She wanted me to take the Institute of Hospital Administration Diploma so that I needn't be a shorthand typist all my life."

This ambition for Miss Priddy's future career struck Dalgliesh as a little odd. The child gave no impression of being ambitious and she would surely marry in time. It hardly needed the Institute's diploma, whatever that might be, to save her from being a shorthand typist for life. He felt a little sorry for Miss Bolam who could scarcely have picked a less promising protégée. She was pretty, honest and naïve, but not, he thought, particularly intelligent. He had to remind himself that she had given her age as twenty-two not seventeen. She had a shapely and oddly mature body, but her thin face with its frame of long, straight hair, was the face of a child.

There was little she could tell him about the administrative officer. She hadn't noticed any change recently in Miss Bolam. She didn't know that the A.O. had sent for Mr. Lauder and had no idea what could be worrying Miss Bolam at the clinic. Everything was going on very much as usual. Miss Bolam had no enemies as far as she knew, certainly no one who would wish to kill her.

"She was happy here, then, as far as you know? I was wondering whether she had asked for a move. A psychiatric clinic can't be the easiest unit to administer."

"Oh, it isn't! I don't know how Enid carried on sometimes. But I'm sure she would never ask for a move. Someone must have given you the wrong impression. She was never one to give up. If she thought people wanted her to go she'd dig her toes in. The clinic was a kind of challenge to her."

It was probably the most illuminating thing she had said about Miss Bolam. As he thanked her and asked her to wait with the rest of the staff until his preliminary interviews were over, Dalgliesh pondered on the possible nuisance value of an administrator who regarded her job as a challenge, a battleground from which she would never willingly retreat. He asked next to see Peter Nagle.

If the junior porter was worried by the killer's choice of his chisel as a weapon he gave no sign. He answered Dalgliesh's questions calmly and politely, but so dispassionately that they might have been discussing some minor point of clinic procedure which was only doubtfully his concern. He gave his age as twenty-seven and an address in Pimlico and confirmed that he had been employed at the clinic for just over two years and was previously at a provincial art school. His voice was level and educated, his mud-brown eyes were large, almost expressionless. Dalgliesh noticed that he had unusually long arms which, held loosely from his short and powerful body, gave an impression of simian strength. His hair was black, coiling tightly over the scalp. It was an interesting face, withdrawn but intelligent. There could scarcely have been a greater contrast with poor old Cully, long since despatched home to nurse both his stomach-ache and his grievance at being kept late.

Nagle confirmed Miss Priddy's story. He again identified his chisel with no more emotion than a brief moue of distaste and said that he had last seen it at eight o'clock that morning when he had arrived on duty and—for no particular reason—

had made a check of his toolbox. Everything was in order then. Dalgliesh asked whether it was generally known where the box was kept. Nagle replied:

"I'd be a fool if I said no, wouldn't I?"

"You'd be a fool to say anything but the truth now or later."

"I suppose most of the staff knew. Those who didn't could find out easily enough. We don't keep the porters' room locked."

"Isn't that rather unwise? What about the patients?"

"They don't go down to the basement on their own. The lysergic acid patients are always escorted and the art therapy people usually have someone keeping an eye on them. The department hasn't been down there for long. The light's bad and it isn't really suitable. It's a temporary department."

"Where used it to be, then?"

"On the third floor. Then the clinic Medical Committee decided they wanted the large room there for the marital problems discussion groups, so Mrs. Baumgarten—she's the art therapist—lost it. She's been agitating to get it back, but the M.P.D. patients say it would be psychologically disturbing for them to meet in the basement."

"Who runs the M.P.D.?"

"Dr. Steiner and one of the psychiatric social workers, Miss Kallinski. It's a club where the divorced and the single tell the patients how to be happy though married. I don't see how it can concern the murder."

"Nor do I. I asked about it to satisfy my curiosity as to why the art therapy department was so unsuitably housed. When did you hear that Tippett wasn't attending today, by the way?"

"At about nine o'clock this morning. The old boy had been worrying St. Luke's Hospital to telephone and let us know what had happened. So they did. I told Miss Bolam and Sister."

"Anyone else?"

"I think I mentioned it to Cully when he came back on the board. He's had belly-ache for most of the day."

"So I'm told. What's wrong with him?"

"Cully? Miss Bolam made him go to hospital for an examination but nothing was found. He gets these belly-aches if anyone upsets him. They say here it's psychosomatic."

"What upset him this morning?"

"I did. He got here before me this morning and started sorting the post. That's my job. I told him to concentrate on his own work."

Dalgliesh took him patiently over the events of the evening. His story agreed with Miss Priddy's and, like her, he was unable to say whether the door of the basement record-room had been ajar when he returned from posting the letters. He admitted that he had passed the door when he went to ask Nurse Bolam if the laundry was sorted. It was usual for the door to be closed as the room was seldom visited and he thought he would have noticed had it been open. It was frustrating and maddening that this crucial point could not be cleared up, but Nagle stood firm. He hadn't noticed. He couldn't say. He hadn't noticed, either, whether the record-room key was on the board in the porters' rest-room. This was easier to understand. There were twenty-two hooks on the board and most of the keys were in use and missing. Dalgliesh said:

"You realize that Miss Bolam's body was almost certainly lying in the record-room when you and Miss Priddy were together feeding the cat? You realize how important it is to remember whether the door was open or shut?"

"It was ajar when Jenny Priddy went down later. That's what she says and she's no liar. If it was shut when I got back from the post someone must have opened it between six-twenty-five and seven. I don't see what's so impossible about that. It would be better for mc if I could remember about the door, but I can't. I hung up my coat in my locker, went straight to ask Nurse Bolam about the clean laundry, and then returned to the rest-room. Jenny met me at the bottom of the stairs."

He spoke without heat, almost unemotionally. It was as if he said. "That's what happened. Like it or not, it happened that way." He was too intelligent not to see that he was in some danger. Perhaps he was also intelligent enough to know that the danger was minimal to an innocent man who kept his head and told the truth.

Dalgliesh told him to let the police know at once if he remembered anything fresh and let him go.

Sister Ambrose was seen next. She strutted into the room, armour-plated in white linen, belligerent as a battleship. The bib of her apron, starched rigid as a board, curved against a formidable bosom on which she wore her nursing badges like medals of war. Grey hair spurted from each side of her cap which she wore low on her forehead above a face of uncompromising plainness. Her colour was high; Dalgliesh thought that she was finding it difficult to control her resentment and distrust. He dealt with her gently, but his questions were answered in an atmosphere of rigid disapproval. She confirmed briefly that she had last seen Miss Bolam walking through the hall towards the basement stairs at about twenty-past six. They had not spoken and the administrative officer had looked the same as usual. Sister Ambrose was back in the E.C.T. room before Miss Bolam was out of sight and had been there with Dr. Ingram until the body was found. In reply to Dalgliesh's question whether Dr. Baguley had also been with them for the whole of that time, Sister Ambrose suggested that he should ask the doctor direct. Dalgliesh replied mildly that this was his intention. He knew that the Sister could give him a great deal of useful information about the clinic if she chose but, apart from a few questions about Miss Bolam's personal relationships from which he gained nothing, he did not press her. He thought that she was probably more shocked by the murder, by the calculated violence of Miss Bolam's death, than anyone he had yet seen. As sometimes happens with unimaginative and inarticulate people, this shock gave vent to ill-temper. She was very cross; with Dalgliesh because his job gave him the right to ask impertinent and embarrassing questions; with herself because she could not conceal her feelings; with the victim, even, who had involved the clinic in this bizarre predicament. It was a reaction Dalgliesh had met before and no good came of trying to force co-operation on such a witness. Later on Sister Ambrose might be induced to talk more freely; at present, it was a waste of time to do more than elicit the facts which she was prepared to give. One fact at least was crucial. Miss Bolam was alive and making her way towards the basement stairs at about twenty-past six. At seven o'clock her body was discovered. Those forty minutes were vital and any member of the staff who could produce an alibi covering them could be eliminated from the enquiry. On the face of it the case presented little difficulty. Dalgliesh did not believe that an outsider had somehow gained access to the clinic and lain in wait for Miss Bolam. The killer was almost certainly still in the building. It was now a matter for careful questioning, for the methodical checking of alibis, for the seeking out of a motive. Dalgliesh decided to talk to the one man whose alibi appeared unassailable and who would have the detached, outsider's view of the clinic and its varied personalities. He thanked Sister Ambrose for her valuable co-operation—a flicker of the eyes behind the steel-rimmed spectacles suggested that the irony was not lost on her—and asked the constable at the door to send in Mr. Lauder.

Chapter Two

It was the first chance Dalgliesh had had to observe the group secretary closely. He saw a thick-set, chubby-featured man, mild-eyed behind the heavy square spectacles, who looked, in his well-cut tweeds, more like a country doctor or small-town solicitor than a bureaucrat. He was completely at ease and bore himself like a man confident of his powers, unwilling to be hurried, keeping always something in reserve, including, Dalgliesh thought, a keener intelligence than his appearance might suggest.

He seated himself opposite Dalgliesh, drew his chair comfortably forward and, without either apology or excuse, took a pipe from one pocket and sought in the other for his tobacco pouch. Nodding towards Martin and his open note book he said, in a slow voice with a trace of north-country accent:

"Reginald Iven Lauder. Date of birth, 21st April 1905. Address, 42 Makepeace Avenue, Chigwell, Essex. Occupation, Group Secretary, East Central Hospital Management Committee. And now, Superintendent, what do you want to know?"

"A great deal, I'm afraid," said Dalgliesh. And firstly, have you any idea at all who could have killed Miss Bolam?" The group secretary established his pipe and, leaning his elbows on the desk, regarded its glowing head with satisfaction.

"I wish I had. I'd have been in here to tell you before now, never fear. But, no. I've no help of that kind for you."

"Miss Bolam had no enemies as far as you were aware?"

"Enemies? Well now, Superintendent, that's a strong word!

She had people who didn't much like her, the same as I have. You, too, no doubt. But we don't go in fear of being murdered. No, I wouldn't have said she had enemies. Mind you, I know nothing of her private life. That's not my concern."

"Could you tell me something about the Steen and the position she held? I know something of the clinic's reputation, of course, but it would be helpful if I could have a clear picture of what goes on here."

"A clear picture of what goes on?" It might have been imagination, but Dalgliesh thought he saw the group secretary's mouth twitch.

"Well, the medical director could tell you more about that than I—on the medical side, that is. But I can give you a gist. The place was founded between the wars by the family of a Mr. Hyman Stein. The story goes that the old man suffered from impotence, got himself some psychotherapy and subsequently fathered five children. So far from impoverishing him they all did well and when papa died they put the clinic on a sound financial footing as a memorial to him. After all, they did owe the place something. The sons all changed their name to Steen—for the usual reason I suppose—and the clinic was given the anglicized name. I often wonder what old Hyman would have thought."

"Is it well endowed?"

"It was. The state got the endowments of course on the Appointed Day following the 1946 Act. A bit has come in since, but not much. People aren't so keen to will money to institutions run by the Government. But the place was quite well off before 1948 as these places go. They did themselves well in the way of equipment and facilities. The Hospital Management Committee's had quite a job providing for them in the way to which they'd become accustomed."

"Is the clinic difficult to administer? I imagine there may be personality problems."

"No more difficult than any other small unit. You get personality problems anywhere. I'd rather deal with a difficult psychiatrist than a difficult surgeon any day. They're the real *prima donnas*."

"Did you consider Miss Bolam a successful administrative officer?"

"Well . . . she was efficient. I hadn't really any complaints. She was a bit rigid, I suppose. After all, Ministry circulars haven't even the force of law, so there's no sense in treating them as if they are personally dictated by God Almighty. I doubt whether Miss Bolam would have got much further. Mind you, she was a competent, methodical and highly conscientious officer. I don't think she ever sent in an inaccurate return."

"Poor devil!" thought Dalgliesh, stung by the bleak anonymity of that official epitaph. He asked:

"Was she popular here? With the medical staff, for example?"

"Well, now, Superintendent, you'll have to ask them. I can't think of any reason why she shouldn't be."

"You were not then under any pressure from the medical committee to remove her from the clinic?"

The mild grey eyes grew suddenly blank. There was a momentary pause before the group secretary calmly replied:

"I have had no official request of that kind made to me."

"But unofficially?"

"There has been a feeling here from time to time, I believe, that a change of job might be helpful to Miss Bolam. Now that's not such a bad idea, Superintendent! Any officer in a small unit, particularly a psychiatric clinic, can benefit from a change of experience. But I don't transfer my staff at the whim of medical committees. Bless me, no! And, as I said, no official request was made. If Miss Bolam herself had asked for a transfer, that would have been a different matter. Even so, it wouldn't have been easy. She was a general administrative officer and we haven't many posts in that grade."

Dalgliesh then asked again about Miss Bolam's telephone call and Lauder confirmed that he had spoken to her at about ten to one. He remembered the time because he was just about to go for lunch. Miss Bolam had asked to speak to him personally and had been put through by his secretary. She had asked whether she could see him urgently.

"Can you remember the exact conversation?"

"More or less. She said: 'Can I have an appointment to see you as soon as possible? I think there may be something going on here that you ought to know about. I should like your advice. Something that started well before my time here.' I said that I couldn't see her this afternoon as I would be in the Finance and General Purposes Committee from two-thirty onwards and had a Joint Consultative Committee immediately afterwards. I asked whether she could give me any idea what it was all about and whether it couldn't wait until Monday. She hesitated, so, before she could reply, I said I'd drop in on my way home this evening. I knew they had a late clinic on Fridays. She said that she would arrange to be alone in her office from six-thirty onwards, thanked me, and rang off. The J.C.C. lasted longer than I expected—that Committee always does—and I got here just before seven-thirty. But you know that. I was still in Committee at the time they found the body, as no doubt you'll be checking in due course."

"Did you take Miss Bolam's message seriously? Was she the sort of woman who ran to you with trifles or would a request to see you really mean that something serious was wrong?"

The group secretary thought for a moment before replying: "I took it seriously. That's why I came round tonight."

"And you have no idea at all what it might be?"

"None, I'm afraid. It must have been something that she learned about since Wednesday. I saw Miss Bolam then at the House Committee meeting in the late afternoon and she told me afterwards that things were pretty quiet here at present. That is the last time I saw her incidentally. She was looking rather well I thought. Better than for some time."

Dalgliesh asked the group secretary what, if anything, he knew of Miss Bolam's private life.

"Very little. I believe she has no near relations and lives alone in a flat in Kensington. Nurse Bolam will be able to tell you more about her. They're cousins, and Nurse Bolam is probably the nearest living relative. I've got an idea that she had private means. All the official information about her career will be on her dossier. Knowing Miss Bolam, I expect her file will be as meticulously kept as any other staff dossier. It'll be here no doubt."

Without moving from his chair he leaned sideways, jerked open the top drawer of the filing cabinet and inserted a chubby hand between the manilla folders.

"Here we are. Bolam, Enid Constance. I see she came to us in October 1949 as a shorthand typist. She spent eighteen months in Group Headquarters, was transferred to one of our chest clinics on 19th April 1951 on Grade B and applied for the vacant post of administrative officer here on 14th May 1957. The post was then Grade D and she was lucky to get it. We hadn't a very strong field, I remember. All administrative and clerical jobs were regraded in 1958 following the Noel Hall report and, after some argument with the Regional Board we managed to get this one graded as general administrative. It's all down here. Date of birth, 12th December 1922. Address, 37a Ballantyne Mansions, S.W.8. Then come details about her tax code, national insurance number and incremental date. She's only had one week off sick since she came here and that was in 1959 when she had 'flu. There isn't much more here. Her original application form and letters of appointment will be on her main dossier at Group Headquarters."

He handed the file to Dalgliesh who looked through it and then said:

"This states that her previous employers were the Botley Research Establishment. Isn't that Sir Mark Etherege's show? They dabble in Aeronautical research. He's Dr. Etherege's brother, isn't he?

"I think Miss Bolam did mention to me when she was appointed to this post that she knew Dr. Etherege's brother slightly. Mind you now, it can't have been more than that. She was only a shorthand typist at Botley. It's a bit of a coincidence, I suppose, but then she had to come from somewhere. I seem to remember it was Sir Mark who gave her a reference when she applied to us. That will be on her Group dossier, of course."

"Would you mind telling me, Mr. Lauder, what arrangements you propose making here now that she's dead?"

The group secretary replaced the file in the cabinet.

"I don't see why not. I shall have to consult my Committee, of course, as the circumstances are unusual, but I shall recommend that the senior medical stenographer here, Mrs. Bostock, takes over in an acting capacity. If she can do the job—and I think she can—she'll be a strong candidate for the vacancy, but the post will be advertised in the usual way."

Dalgliesh did not comment but he was interested. Such a quick decision on Miss Bolam's successor could only mean that Lauder had earlier given some thought to it. The approaches of the medical staff may have been unofficial, but they had probably been more effective than the group secretary cared to admit. Dalgliesh returned to the telephone call which had brought Mr. Lauder to the clinic. He said:

"The words Miss Bolam used strike me as significant. She said that there may be something very serious going on here which you ought to know about and that it started before her time. That suggests, firstly that she wasn't yet certain but only suspicious, and secondly that she wasn't worried about a particular incident but about something of long standing. A systematic policy of thieving, for example, as opposed to one isolated theft."

"Well now, Superintendent, its odd you should mention theft. We have had a theft recently, but it was an isolated incident, the first we've had here for years, and I can't see how it could be connected with murder. It was just over a week ago, last Tuesday if I remember rightly. Cully and Nagle were the last to leave the clinic as usual and Cully asked Nagle to have a drink with him at the 'Queen's Head'. You know it, I expect. It's the pub on the far corner of Beefsteak Street. There are one or two odd things about this story and one of the strangest is that Cully should invite Nagle for a drink. They've never struck me as buddies. Anyway, Nagle accepted and they were in the 'Queen's Head' together from about seven. At about half-past, a pal of Cully's came in and said he was surprised to see Cully there as he had just passed the clinic and there was a faint light in one of the windows—as if someone was moving around with a torch, he said. Nagle and Cully went off to investigate and found one of the back basement windows broken, or rather, cut out. Quite a clever job it was. Cully didn't feel inclined to investigate further without reinforcements and I'm not sure that I blame him. He's sixty-five, remember, and not strong. After some whispering together, Nagle said that he'd go in and Cully had better telephone the police from the kiosk on the corner. Your people came pretty smartly but they didn't get the intruder. He gave Nagle the slip inside the building, and when Cully got back from telephoning he was just in time to see the man slip out of the mews."

"I'll check how far our people have got with the investigation," said Dalgliesh. "But I agree that a connection between the crimes seems unlikely on the face of it. Was much taken?"

"Fifteen pounds from a drawer in the psychiatric social worker's office. The door was locked but he wrenched it open. The money was in an envelope addressed in green ink to the administrative secretary of the clinic and had been received a week earlier. There was no letter with it, only a note to say that the money was from a grateful patient. The other contents of the drawer were torn and scattered but nothing else was stolen. Some attempt had been made to force open the cabinets of records in the general office and Miss Bolam's desk drawers had been forced but nothing taken."

Dalgliesh asked whether the fifteen pounds should have been placed in the wall safe.

"Well now, Superintendent, you're right, of course. It should have been. But there was a little difficulty about using the money. Miss Bolam phoned me about its arrival and said that she thought it should be paid immediately into the clinic's free money account to be used in due course on the authority of the House Committee. That was a very proper course of action, and so I told her. Shortly afterwards the medical director phoned me to ask if he could have authority to spend the money on some new flower vases for the patients' waiting-room. The vases were certainly needed and it seemed a correct use for non-Exchequer funds, so I rang the chairman of the House Committee and got his approval. Apparently Dr. Etherege wanted Miss Kettle to choose the vases and asked Miss Bolam to hand over the cash. I had already notified Miss Bolam of the decision so she did so, expecting that the vases would be bought at once. Something happened to change Miss Kettle's plans and, instead of returning the cash to the A.O. for safe custody, she locked it in her drawer."

"Do you know how many of the staff knew that it was there?"

"That's what the police asked. I suppose most people knew that the vases hadn't been bought or Miss Kettle would have shown them around. They probably guessed that, having been handed the cash, she wouldn't be likely to return it even temporarily. I don't know. The arrival of that fifteen pounds was mysterious. It caused nothing but trouble and its disappearance was equally mysterious. Anyway, Superintendent, no one here stole it. Cully only saw the thief for a second but he was certain that he didn't know the man. He did say, though, that he thought the chap looked like a gentleman. Don't ask me how he knew or what his criteria are. But that's what he said."

Dalgliesh thought that the whole incident was odd and would bear further investigation but he could see no apparent connection between the two crimes. It was not even certain that Miss Bolam's call to the group secretary for advice was related to her death, but here the presumption was much stronger. It was very important to discover, if possible, what she had suspected. He asked Mr. Lauder once more whether he could help.

"I told you, Superintendent, I haven't an idea what she meant. If I suspected that anything was wrong I shouldn't wait for Miss Bolam to phone me. We're not quite so remote from the units at group offices as some people think and I usually get to know anything I ought to know. If the murder is connected with that phone message something pretty serious must be happening here. After all, you don't kill just to prevent the group secretary knowing that you've fiddled your travelling claim or overspent your annual leave. Not that anyone has as far as I know."

"Exactly," said Dalgliesh. He watched the group secretary's face very closely and said, without emphasis:

"It suggests something that might ruin a man professionally. A sexual relationship with a patient perhaps—something as serious as that." Mr. Lauder's face did not change.

"I imagine every doctor knows the seriousness of that, particularly psychiatrists. They must have to be pretty careful with some of the neurotic women they treat. Frankly, I don't believe it. All the doctors here are eminent men, some of them with world-wide reputations. You don't get that sort of reputation if you're a fool and men of that eminence don't commit murder."

"And what about the rest of the staff? They may not be eminent, but presumably you consider them honest?"

Unruffled, the group secretary replied:

"Sister Ambrose has been here for nearly twenty years and Nurse Bolam for five. I would trust them both absolutely. All the clerical staff came with good references and so did the two porters, Cully and Nagle." He added wryly: "Admittedly I didn't check that they hadn't committed murder but none of them strike me as homicidal maniacs. Cully drinks a bit and is a pathetic old fool with only another four months' service to complete. I doubt whether he could kill a mouse without making a hash of it. Nagle is a cut above the usual hospital porter. I understand he's an art student and works here for pocket money. He's only been with us a couple of years so he wasn't here before Miss Bolam's time. Even if he's been seducing all the female staff, which seems unlikely, the worst that could happen to him would be the sack and that wouldn't worry him as things are today. Admittedly she was killed with his chisel but anyone could have got their hands on that."

"I'm afraid this was an inside job, you know," said Dalgliesh gently. "The murderer knew where Tippett's fetish and Nagle's chisel were kept, knew which key opened the old record-room, knew where that key was hung on the board in the porters' duty-room, probably wore one of the rubber aprons from the art therapy room as a protection, certainly had medical knowledge. Above all, of course, the murderer couldn't have left the clinic after the crime. The basement door was bolted and so was the ground floor back door. Cully was watching the front door."

"Cully had a belly-ache. He could have missed someone."

"Do you really believe that's possible?" asked Dalgliesh. And the group secretary did not reply.

At first sight Marion Bolam could be thought beautiful. She had the fair, classical good looks which, enhanced by her nurse's uniform, gave an immediate impression of serene loveliness. Her blonde hair, parted above a broad forehead and twisted into a high roll at the back of her head, was bound by the simple white cap. It was only at second glance that the illusion faded and beauty gave way to prettiness. The features, individually analysed, were unremarkable, the nose a little too long, the lips a little too thin. In ordinary clothes, hurrying home perhaps at the end of the day, she would be undistinguished. It was the combination of the starched formal linen with that fair skin and yellow hair which dazzled the eye. Only in the broad forehead and the sharpness of the nose could Dalgliesh detect any likeness to her dead cousin. But there was nothing ordinary about the large grey eyes which met his fully for a brief second before she lowered her glance and gazed fixedly at the clasped hands in her lap.

"I understand that you are Miss Bolam's next of kin. This must be a terrible shock for you."

"Yes. Oh, yes, it is! Enid was my cousin."

"You have the same name. Your fathers were brothers?"

"Yes, they were. Our mothers were sisters, too. Two brothers married two sisters so that we were doubly related."

"Had she no other relations living?"

"Only Mummy and me."

"I shall have to see Miss Bolam's solicitor, I expect," said Dalgliesh, "but it would be helpful if you would tell me as much as you know about her affairs. I'm afraid I have to ask these personal questions. Usually they have no bearing on the crime, but one must know as much as possible about everyone concerned. Had your cousin any income apart from her salary?"

"Oh, yes. Enid was quite well off. Uncle Sydney left her mother about £25,000 and it all came to Enid. I don't know how much was left, but I think she had about £1,000 a year coming in apart from her salary here. She kept on auntie's flat in Ballantyne Mansions and she . . . she was always very good to us."

"In what way, Miss Bolam? Did she make you an allowance?"

"Oh, no! Enid wouldn't want to do that. She gave us presents. Thirty pounds at Christmas and fifty in July for our summer holiday. Mummy has disseminated sclerosis and we couldn't go away to an ordinary hotel."

"And what happens to Miss Bolam's money now?"

The grey eyes lifted to meet his with no trace of embarrassment. She answered simply:

"It will come to Mummy and me. There wasn't anyone else to leave it to, was there? Enid always said it would come to us if she died first. But, of course, it wasn't likely that she would die first; not while Mummy was alive anyway."

It was indeed unlikely, in the ordinary course of events, that Mrs. Bolam would ever have benefited from that £20,000 or what was left of it, thought Dalgliesh. Here was the obvious motive, so understandable, so universal, so dear to any prosecuting counsel. Every juryman understood the lure of money. Could Nurse Bolam really be unaware of the significance of the information which she was handing him with such unembarrassed candour? Could innocence be so naïve or guilt so confident? He said suddenly:

"Was your cousin popular, Miss Bolam?"

"She hadn't many friends. I don't think she would have called herself popular. She wouldn't want that. She had her church activities and the Guides. She was a very quiet person really."

"But you know of no enemies?"

"Oh, no! None at all. Enid was very much respected."

The formal, old-fashioned epithet was almost inaudible.

Dalgliesh said:

"Then it looks as if this is a motiveless, unpremeditated crime. Normally that would suggest one of the patients. But it hardly seems possible and you are all insistent that it isn't likely."

"Oh, no! It couldn't be a patient! I'm quite sure none of our patients would do a thing like that. They aren't violent."

"Not even Mr. Tippett?"

"But it couldn't have been Tippett. He's in hospital."

"So I'm told. How many people here knew that Mr. Tippett wouldn't be coming to the clinic this Friday?"

"I don't know. Nagle knew because he took the message and he told Enid and Sister. Sister told me. You see, I usually try to keep an eye on Tippett when I'm specialling the LSD patients on Fridays. I can't leave my patient for more than a second, of course, but I do pop out occasionally to see if Tippett is all right. Tonight it wasn't necessary. Poor Tippett, he does love his art therapy! Mrs. Baumgarten has been away ill for six months now, but we couldn't stop Tippett from coming. He wouldn't hurt a fly. It's wicked to suggest that Tippett could have anything to do with it. Wicked!"

She spoke with sudden vehemence. Dalgliesh said mildly:

"But no one is suggesting anything of the sort. If Tippett is in hospital—and I haven't the least doubt we shall find that he is—then he couldn't have been here."

"But someone put his fetish on the body, didn't they? If Tippett had been here you would have suspected him straight away and he would have been so upset and confused. It was a wicked thing to do. Really wicked!"

Her voice broke and she was very near to tears. Dalgliesh watched the thin fingers twisting in her lap. He said gently:

"I don't think we need worry about Mr. Tippett. Now I want you to think carefully and tell me everything that you know happened in the clinic from the time you came on duty this evening. Never mind about other people, I just want to know what you did."

Nurse Bolam remembered very clearly what she had done and, after a second's hesitation, she gave a careful and logical account. It was her job on Friday evenings to "special" any patient undergoing treatment with lysergic acid. She explained that this was a method of releasing deep-seated inhibitions so that the patient was able to recall and recount the incidents which were being repressed in his subconscious and were responsible for his illness. As she spoke about the treatment Nurse Bolam lost her nervousness and seemed to forget that she was talking to a layman. But Dalgliesh did not interrupt.

"It's a remarkable drug and Dr. Baguley uses it quite a lot. It's name is lysergic acid diethylamide and I think it was discovered by a German in 1942. We administer it orally, and the usual dose is 0.25 mg. It's produced in ampoules of 1 mg. and mixed with from 15 to 30 c.c.'s of distilled water. The patients are told not to have any breakfast. The first effects are noticed after about half an hour and the more disturbing subjective experiences occur from one to one and a half hours after administration. That's when Dr. Baguley comes down to be with the patient. The effects can last for as long as four hours and the patient is flushed and restless and quite withdrawn from reality. They're never left alone, of course, and we use the basement room because it's secluded and quiet and other patients aren't distressed by the noise. We usually give LSD treatments on Friday afternoon and evening, and I always 'special' the patient."

"I suppose that, if any noise, such as a cry, were heard on Fridays in the basement most of the staff would assume that it was the LSD patient?"

Nurse Bolam looked doubtful.

"I suppose they might. Certainly these patients can be very noisy. My patient today was more disturbed than usual which was why I stayed close to her. Usually I spend a little time in the linen-room which adjoins the treatment-room sorting the clean laundry as soon as the patient is over the worst. I keep the door open between the rooms, of course, so that I can watch the patient from time to time."

Dalgliesh asked what exactly had happened during the evening.

"Well, the treatment began just after three-thirty and Dr. Baguley looked in shortly after four to see if all was well. I stayed with the patient until four-thirty when Mrs. Shorthouse came to tell me that tea was made. Sister came down while I went upstairs to the nurses' duty-room and drank tea. I came down again at quarter to five and rang for Dr. Baguley at five.

He was with the patient for about three-quarters of an hour. Then he left to return to his E.C.T. clinic. I stayed with the patient, and as she was so restless I decided to leave the laundry until later in the evening. At about twenty to seven Peter Nagle knocked on the door and asked for the laundry. I told him that it wasn't sorted and he looked a bit surprised but didn't say anything. A little time after that I thought I heard a scream. I didn't take any notice at first as it didn't seem very close and I thought it was children playing in the square. Then I thought I ought to make sure and I went to the door. I saw Dr. Baguley and Dr. Steiner coming into the basement with Sister and Dr. Ingram. Sister told me that nothing was wrong and to go back to my patient, so I did."

"Did you leave the treatment-room at all after Dr. Baguley left you at about quarter to six?"

"Oh, no! There wasn't any need. If I'd wanted to go to the cloakroom or anything like that (Nurse Bolam blushed faintly) I would have phoned for Sister to come and take my place."

"Did you make any telephone calls from the treatment-room at all during the evening?"

"Only the one to the E.C.T. room at five to call Dr. Baguley."

"Are you quite sure you didn't telephone Miss Bolam?"

"Enid? Oh, no! There wouldn't be any reason to call Enid. She . . . that is, we, didn't see very much of each other in the clinic. I am responsible to Sister Ambrose, you see, and Enid wasn't concerned with the nursing staff."

"But you saw quite a lot of her outside the clinic?"

"Oh, no! I didn't mean that. I went to her flat once or twice, to collect the cheque at Christmas and in the summer, but it isn't easy for me to leave Mummy. Besides, Enid had her own life to live. And then she's quite a lot older than me. I didn't really know her very well."

Her voice broke and Dalgliesh saw that she was crying. Fumbling under her apron for the pocket in her nurse's dress, she sobbed:

"It's so dreadful! Poor Enid! Putting that fetish on her body as if he was making fun of her, making it look as if she was nursing a baby!"

Dalgliesh hadn't realized that she had seen the body and said so.

"Oh, I didn't! Dr. Etherege and Sister wouldn't let me go in to her. But we were all told what had happened."

Miss Bolam had indeed looked as if she were nursing a baby. But he was surprised that someone who hadn't seen the body should say so. The medical director must have given a graphic description of the scene.

Suddenly Nurse Bolam found her handkerchief and drew it out of her pocket. With it came a pair of thin, surgical gloves. They fell at Dalgliesh's feet. Picking them up he asked:

"I didn't realize that you used surgical gloves here."

Nurse Bolam seemed unsurprised by his interest. Checking her sobs with surprising control she replied:

"We don't use them very often but we keep a few pairs. The whole Group's gone over to disposable gloves now, but there are a few of the old kind about. That's one of them. We use them for odd cleaning jobs."

"Thank you," said Dalgliesh. "I'll keep this pair if I may. And I don't think I need worry you any more at present."

With a murmured word which could have been "thank you", Nurse Bolam almost backed out of the room.

The minutes dragged heavily to the clinic staff waiting in the front consulting-room to be interviewed. Fredrica Saxon had fetched some papers from her room on the third floor and was scoring an intelligence test. There had been some discussion about whether she ought to go upstairs alone, but Miss Saxon had stated firmly that she didn't intend to sit there wasting time and biting her nails until the police chose to see her, that she hadn't the murderer hidden upstairs, nor was she proposing to destroy incriminating evidence and that she had no objection to any member of the staff accompanying her to satisfy themselves on this point. This distressing frankness had provoked a murmur of protests and reassurance, but Mrs. Bostock had announced abruptly that she would like to fetch a book from the medical library and the two women had left the room and returned together. Cully had been seen early, having established his right to be classed as a patient, and had been released to cosset his stomach-ache at home. The only remaining patient, Mrs. King, had been interviewed and allowed to depart with her husband in attendance. Mr. Burge had also left, protesting loudly at the interruption of his session and the trauma of the whole experience.

"Mind you, he's enjoying himself, you can see that," confided Mrs. Shorthouse to the assembled staff. "The Superintendent had a job getting rid of him, I can tell you."

There was a great deal which Mrs. Shorthouse seemed able to tell them. She had been given permission to make coffee and prepare sandwiches in her small ground-floor kitchen at the rear of the building, and this gave her an excuse for frequent trips up and down the hall. The sandwiches were brought in almost singly. Cups were taken individually to be washed. This coming and going gave her an opportunity of reporting the latest situation to the rest of the staff who awaited each instalment with an anxiety and eagerness which they could only imperfectly conceal. Mrs. Shorthouse was not the emissary they would have chosen but any news, however obtained and by whomever delivered, helped to lighten the weight of suspense and she was certainly unexpectedly knowledgeable about police procedure.

"There's several of them searching the building now and they've got their own chap on the door. They haven't found anyone, of course. Well, it stands to reason! We know he couldn't have got out of the building. Or in for that matter. I said to the sergeant: 'This clinic has had all the cleaning from me that it's getting today, so tell your chaps to mind where they plant their boots. . . .' '

"The police surgeon's seen the body. The fingerprint man is still downstairs and they're taking everyone's prints. I've seen the photographer. He went through the hall with a tripod and a big case, white on top and black at the bottom. . . .'

"Here's a funny thing now. They're looking for prints in the basement lift. Measuring it up, too."

Fredrica Saxon lifted her head, seemed about to say something, then went on with her work. The basement lift, which was about four feet square and operated by a rope pulley, had been used to transport food from the basement kitchen to the first-floor dining-room when the clinic was a private house. It had never been taken out. Occasionally medical records from the basement record-room were hoisted in it to the first- and second-floor consulting-rooms, but it was otherwise little used. No one commented on a possible reason why the police should test it for prints.

Mrs. Shorthouse departed with two cups to be washed. She was back within five minutes.

"Mr. Lauder's in the general office phoning the chairman. Telling him about the murder, I suppose. This'll give the H.M.C. something to natter about and no mistake. Sister is going through the linen inventory with one of the police. Seems there's a rubber apron from the art therapy-room missing. Oh, and another thing. They're letting the boiler out. Want to rake it through, I suppose. Nice for us, I must say. This place'll be bloody cold on Monday. . . ."

"The mortuary van's arrived. That's what they call it. The mortuary van. They don't use an ambulance, you see. Not when the victim's dead. You probably heard it arrive. I dare say if you draw the curtains back a bit you'll see her being took in."

But no one cared to draw back the curtains and, as the soft, careful feet of the stretcher-bearers shuffled past the door no one spoke. Fredrica Saxon laid down her pencil and bowed her head as if she were praying. When the front door closed their relief was heard in the soft hiss of breath released. There was a brief silence and then the van drove off. Mrs. Shorthouse was the only one to speak.

"Poor little blighter! Mind you I only gave her another six months here what with one thing and another, but I never thought she'd leave feet first."

Jennifer Priddy sat apart from the rest of the staff on the edge of the treatment couch. Her interview with the superintendent had been unexpectedly easy. She didn't know quite what she had expected but certainly it wasn't this quiet, gentle, deep-voiced man. He hadn't bothered to commiserate with her on the shock of finding the body. He hadn't smiled at her. He hadn't been paternal or understanding. He gave the impression that he was interested only in finding out the truth as quickly as possible and that he expected everyone else to feel the same. She thought that it would be difficult to tell him a lie and she hadn't tried. It had all been quite easy to remember, quite straightforward. The Superintendent had questioned her closely about the ten minutes or so she had spent in the basement with Peter. That was only to be expected. Naturally he was wondering whether Peter could have killed Miss Bolam after he returned from the post and before she joined him. Well, it wasn't possible. She had followed him downstairs almost immediately and Mrs. Shorthouse could confirm it. Probably it hadn't taken long to kill Enid—she tried not to think about that sudden, savage, calculated violence—but however quickly it was done, Peter hadn't time.

She thought about Peter. Thinking about him occupied most of her few solitary hours. Tonight, however, the familiar warm imaginings were needled with anxiety. Was he going to be cross about the way she had behaved? She remembered with shame her delayed scream of terror after finding the body, the way she had thrown herself into his arms. He had been very kind and considerate, of course, but then he always was considerate when he wasn't working and remembered she was there. She knew that he hated fuss and that any demonstration of affection irked him. She had learned to accept that their love, and she dared no longer doubt that it was love, must be taken on his terms. Since their brief time together in the nurses' duty-room after the finding of Miss Bolam she had scarcely spoken to him. She couldn't guess what he felt. She was only sure of one thing. She couldn't possibly pose for him tonight. It hadn't anything to do with shame or guilt; he had long since cut her free of those twin encumbrances. He would expect her to arrive at the studio as planned. After all, her alibi was fixed and her parents would accept that she was at her evening class. He would see no reasonable grounds for altering their arrangements and Peter was a great one for reason. But she couldn't do it! Not tonight. It wasn't so much the posing as what would follow. She wouldn't be able to refuse him. She wouldn't want to refuse him. And tonight, with Enid dead, she felt that she couldn't bear to be touched.

When she returned from her talk with the Superintendent, Dr. Steiner had come to sit beside her and had been very kind. But then Dr. Steiner was kind. It was easy enough to criticize his indolence or laugh at his odd patients. But he did care about people, whereas Dr. Baguley, who worked so hard and wore himself out with his heavy clinics, didn't really like people at all, but only wished that he did. Jenny wasn't sure how she knew this so clearly. She hadn't really thought about it before. Tonight, however, now that the first shock of finding the body had passed, her mind was unnaturally clear. And not only her mind. All her perceptions were sharpened. The tangible objects about her, the chintz covering on the couch, the red blanket folded at its foot, the bright varied greens and golds of the chrysanthemums on the desk, were clearer, brighter, more real to her than ever before. She saw the line of Miss Saxon's arm as it rested on the desk curved around the book she was reading and the way in which the small hairs on her forearm were tipped with light from the desk lamp. She wondered whether Peter always saw the life around him with this wonder and clarity as if one were born into an unfamiliar world with all the first bright hues of creation fresh upon it. Perhaps this was what it felt like to be a painter.

"I suppose it's the brandy," she thought, and giggled a little. She remembered hearing the muttered grumblings of Sister Ambrose half an hour earlier.

"What's Nagle been feeding to Priddy? That child's half drunk." But she wasn't drunk and she didn't really believe it was the brandy.

Dr. Steiner had drawn his chair close to her and had laid his hand briefly on her shoulder. Without thinking, Miss Priddy had said:

"She was kind to me and I didn't like her."

She no longer felt sad or guilty about it. It was a statement of fact.

"You mustn't worry about it," he said gently, and patted

her knee. She didn't resent the pat. Peter would have said: "Lecherous old goat! Tell him to keep his paws to himself." But Peter would have been wrong. Jenny knew that it was a gesture of kindliness. For a moment she was tempted to put her hand over his to show that she understood. He had small and very white hands for a man, so different from Peter's long, bony, paint-stained fingers. She saw how the hairs curled beneath his shirt cuffs, the stubble of black along the knuckles. On his little finger he wore a gold signet ring, heavy as a weapon.

"It's natural to feel as you do," he said. "When people die we always wish that we had been kinder to them, had liked them better. There is nothing to be done about it. We shouldn't pretend about our feelings. If we understand them we learn in time to accept them and to live with them."

But Jenny was no longer listening. For the door had opened quietly and Peter Nagle had come in.

Bored with sitting in the reception desk and exchanging commonplace remarks with the uncommunicative policeman on duty there, Nagle sought diversion in the front consulting-room. Although his formal interview was over he wasn't yet free to leave the clinic. The group secretary obviously expected him to stay until the building could be locked for the night and it would be his job to open it again on Monday morning. The way things were going it looked as if he would be stuck in the place for another couple of hours at least. That morning he had planned to get home early and work on the picture, but it was no use thinking of that now. It might well be after eleven o'clock before this business was settled and he was free to go home. But even if they could go to the Pimlico flat together Jenny wouldn't pose for him tonight. One glance at her face told him that. She did not come across to him as he entered the room and he was grateful for that amount of restraint at least. But she gave him her shy, elliptical glance, half conspiratorial and half pleading. It was her way of asking him to understand, of saying sorry. Well, he was sorry, too. He had hoped to put in a good three hours tonight and time was getting short. But if she was only trying to convey that she wasn't in the mood for making love, well, that suited him all right. It suited him most nights if she only knew. He wished that he could take her—since she was so tiresomely insistent on being taken—as simply and quickly as he took a meal, a means of satisfying an appetite that was nothing to be ashamed of but nothing to fuss about either. But that wasn't Jenny. He hadn't been as clever as he thought and Jenny was in love. She was hopelessly, passionately and insecurely in love, demanding a constant reassurance, facile tenderness and time-consuming technique which left him exhausted and barely satisfied. She was terrified of becoming pregnant so that the preliminaries to love-making were irritatingly clinical, the aftermath, more often than not, her wild sobbing in his arms. As a painter he was obsessed by her body. He couldn't think of changing his model now and he couldn't afford to change. But the price of Jenny was getting too high.

He was almost untouched by Miss Bolam's death. He suspected that she had always known just how little work he did for his money. The rest of the staff, deluded by comparing him with that poor fool, Cully, thought they had a paragon of industry and intelligence. But Bolam had been no fool. It was not that he was lazy. One could have an easy life at the Steen—and most people, including some psychiatrists, did—without risking that imputation. Everything required of him was well within his capabilities and he gave no more than was required. Enid Bolam knew that all right, but it worried neither of them. If he went she could only hope to replace him by a porter who did less and did it less efficiently. And he was educated, personable and polite. That had meant a great deal to Miss Bolam. He smiled as he remembered how much it had meant. No, Bolam had never bothered him. But he was less confident about her successor.

He glanced across the room to where Mrs. Bostock sat alone, gracefully relaxed in one of the more comfortable patients' chairs that he had brought in from the waiting-room. Her head was studiously bent over a book, but Nagle had little doubt that her mind was otherwise occupied. Probably working out her incremental date as A.O., he thought. This murder was a break for her all right. You couldn't miss compulsive ambition in a woman. They burnt with it. You could almost smell it sizzling their flesh. Underneath that air of calm unflappability she was as restless and nervous as a cat on heat. He sauntered across the room to her and lounged against the wall beside her chair, his arm just brushing her shoulder.

"Nicely timed for you, isn't it?" he said.

She kept her eyes on the page but he knew that she would have to answer. She could never resist defending herself even when defence only made her more vulnerable. She's like the rest of them, he thought. She can't keep her bloody mouth shut.

"I don't know what you mean, Nagle."

"Come off it. I've been admiring your performance for the last six months. Yes, Doctor. No, Doctor. Just as you like, Doctor. Of course, I'd like to help, Doctor, but there are certain complications here. . . . You bet there were! She wasn't giving up without a struggle. And now she's dead. Very nice for you. They won't have to look far for their new A.O."

"Don't be impertinent and ridiculous. And why aren't you helping Mrs. Shorthouse with the coffee?"

"Because I don't choose to. You're not the A.O. yet, remember."

"I've no doubt the police will be interested in knowing where you were this evening. After all, it was your chisel."

"I was out with the post and fetching my evening paper. Disappointing, isn't it? And I wonder where you were at six-twenty-two."

"How do you know she died at six-twenty-two?"

"I don't. But Sister saw her going down to the basement at six-twenty and there wasn't anything in the basement to keep her as far as I know. Not unless your dear Dr. Etherege was there, of course. But surely he wouldn't demean himself cuddling Miss Bolam. Not quite his type I'd have said. But you know his tastes in that direction better than I do, of course."

Suddenly she was out of her chair and, swinging her right arm, she slapped his cheek with a force that momentarily rocked him. The sharp crack of the blow echoed in the room. Everyone looked at them. Nagle heard Jennifer Priddy's gasp, saw Dr. Steiner's worried frown as he looked from one to the other in puzzled inquiry, saw Fredrica Saxon's contemptuous glance at them before her eyes fell again to her book. Mrs. Shorthouse, who was piling plates on to a tray at a side table, looked round a second too late. Her sharp little eyes darted from one to the other, frustrated at having missed something worth seeing. Mrs. Bostock, her colour heightened, sank back in her chair and picked up her book. Nagle, holding his hand to his cheek, gave a shout of laughter.

"Is anything the matter?" asked Dr. Steiner. "What happened?"

It was then that the door opened and a uniformed policeman put his head in and said:

"The superintendent would like to see Mrs. Shorthouse now, please."

Mrs. Amy Shorthouse had seen no reason why she should stay in her working clothes while waiting to be interviewed so that, when called in to Dalgliesh, she was dressed ready to go home. The metamorphosis was striking. Comfortable working slippers had been replaced by a modish pair of high-heeled court shoes, white overall by a fur coat, and head scarf by the latest idiocy in hats. The total effect was curiously old-fashioned. Mrs. Shorthouse looked like a relic of the gay twenties, an effect which was heightened by the shortness of her skirt and the careful curls of peroxided hair which lay cunningly arranged on forehead and cheeks. But there was nothing false about her voice and little, Dalgliesh suspected, about her personality. The little grey eyes were shrewd and amused. She was neither frightened nor distressed. He suspected that Amy Shorthouse craved more excitement than her life customarily afforded and was enjoying herself. She would not wish anyone violently dead but, since it had happened, one might as well make the most of it.

When the preliminaries were over and they got down to the events of the evening, Mrs. Shorthouse came out with her prize piece of information.

"No good saying I can tell you who did it because I can't.

Not that I haven't got my own ideas. But there's one thing I can tell you. I was the last person to talk to her, no doubt about that. No, scrub that out! I was the last person to talk to her, face to face. Excepting the murderer, of course."

"You mean that she subsequently spoke on the telephone? Hadn't you better tell me about it plainly? I've got enough mystery here for one evening."

"Smart, aren't you?" said Mrs. Shorthouse without rancour. "Well, it was in this room. I came in at about ten-past six to ask how much leave I'd got left on account of wanting a day off next week. Miss Bolam got out my dossier—leastwise it was already out come to think of it—and we fixed that up and had a bit of a chat about the work. I was on my way out really, just standing at the door for a few last words as you might say, when the phone rang."

"I want you to think very carefully, Mrs. Shorthouse," said Dalgliesh. "That call may be important. I wonder if you can remember what Miss Bolam said?"

"Think someone was enticing her down to her death, do you?" said Mrs. Shorthouse with alliterative relish. "Well, could be, come to think of it."

Dalgliesh thought that his witness was far from being a fool. He watched while she screwed up her face in a simulated agony of effort. He had no doubt that she remembered very well what had been said.

After a nicely judged pause for suspense, Mrs. Shorthouse said:

"Well, the phone rang like I said. That would be about six-fifteen, I suppose. Miss Bolam picked up the receiver and said, 'Administrative officer speaking.' She always answered like that. Very keen on her position she was. Peter Nagle used to say, 'Who the hell does she think we're expecting to hear? Khruschev?' Not that he said it to her. No fear! Anyway, that's what she said. Then there was a little pause and she looked up at me and said: 'Yes, I am.' Meaning, I suppose, that she was alone, not counting me. Then there was a longer pause while the chap at the other end spoke. Then she said: 'All right, stay where you are. I'll be down.' Then she asked me to show Mr.

Lauder into her office if I was about when he arrived, and I said I would and pushed off."

"You're quite sure about her conversation on the telephone?"

"Sure as I'm sitting here. That's what she said all right."

"You talked about the chap at the other end. How could you tell it was a man?"

"Never said I could. Just assumed it was a chap, I suppose. Mind you, if I'd been closer I might have known. You can sometimes get an idea who's speaking from the crackly noise the phone makes. But I was standing against the door."

"And you couldn't hear the other voice at all?"

"That's right. Suggests he was talking low."

"What happened then, Mrs. Shorthouse?"

"I said cheerio and toddled off to do a bit in the general office. Peter Nagle was there taking young Priddy's mind off her work as usual, and Cully was in the reception kiosk, so it wasn't them. Peter went out with the post as soon as I arrived. He always does at about a quarter-past six."

"Did you see Miss Bolam leaving her office?"

"No, I didn't. I told you. I was in with Nagle and Miss Priddy. Sister saw her, though. You ask her. Sister saw her going down the hall."

"So I understand. I have seen Sister Ambrose. I wondered whether Miss Bolam followed you out of the room."

"No, she didn't. Not at once anyway. Perhaps she thought it would do the chap good to be kept waiting."

"Perhaps," said Dalgliesh. "But she would have gone down promptly I expect if a doctor had phoned for her."

Mrs. Shorthouse gave a shriek of laughter.

"Maybe. Maybe not. You didn't know Miss Bolam."

"What was she like, Mrs. Shorthouse?"

"All right. We got on. She liked a good worker and I'm a good worker. Well—you can see how the place is kept."

"I can indeed."

"Her yea was yea and her nay, nay, I'll say that for her. Nothing unpleasant behind your back. Mind you, quite a bit of unpleasantness in front of your face sometimes if you didn't watch out. Still, I'd rather have it that way. She and me understood each other."

"Had she any enemies—anyone who bore her a grudge?"

"Must have had, mustn't she? That wasn't no playful tap on the head. Carrying a grudge a bit far, if you ask me." She planted her feet apart and leaned towards Dalgliesh confidentially.

"Look, ducks," she said. "Miss B put people's backs up. Some people do. You know how it is. They can't make no allowances. Right was right and wrong was wrong and nothing in between. Rigid. That's what she was. Rigid." Mrs. Shorthouse's tone and tightened mouth expressed the ultimate in virtuous inflexibility. "Take the little matter of the attendance book now. All the consultants are supposed to sign it so that Miss Bolam could make her monthly return to the Board. All very right and proper. Well, the book used to be kept on a table in the doctors' cloakroom and no trouble to anyone. Then Miss B gets to noticing that Dr. Steiner and Dr. McBain are coming in late, so she moves the book to her office and they all have to go in there to sign. Mind you, as often as not Dr. Steiner won't do it. 'She knows I'm here,' he says. 'And I'm a consultant not a factory hand. If she wants her stupid book signed she can put it back in the medical cloakroom.' The doctors have been trying to get rid of her for a year or more, I do know that."

"How do you know, Mrs. Shorthouse?"

"Let's just say that I know. Dr. Steiner couldn't stand her. He goes in for psychotherapy. Intensive psychotherapy. Ever heard of it?"

Dalgliesh admitted that he had. Mrs. Shorthouse gave him a look in which disbelief fought with suspicion. Then she leaned forward conspiratorially as if about to divulge one of Dr. Steiner's less reputable idiosyncrasies.

"He's analytically orientated, that's what he is. Analytically orientated. Know what that means?"

"I've some idea."

"Then you know that he doesn't see many patients. Two a session, three if you're lucky, and a new patient once every eight weeks. That doesn't push up the figures."

"The figures?"

"The attendance figures. They go to the Hospital Management Committee and the Regional Board every quarter. Miss Bolam was a great one for pushing up the figures."

"Then she must have approved thoroughly of Dr. Baguley. I understand that his E.C.T. sessions are usually very busy."

"She approved all right. Not about his divorce, though."

"How could that affect the figures?" asked Dalgliesh, innocently obtuse. Mrs. Shorthouse looked at him pityingly.

"Who said anything about the figures? We were talking about the Baguleys. Getting a divorce, they were, on account of Dr. Baguley having an affair with Miss Saxon. It was in all the papers, too. Psychiatrist's wife cites psychologist. Then suddenly Mrs. Baguley withdrew the case. Never said why. No one said why. Didn't make any difference here, though. Dr. B and Miss Saxon went on working together easy as you please. Still do."

"And Dr. Baguley and his wife were reconciled?"

"Who said anything about reconciled? They stay married. That's all I know. Miss Bolam couldn't say a good word for Miss Saxon after that. Not that she ever talked about it; she wasn't one for gossip I'll give her that. But she let Miss Saxon see what she felt. She was against that sort of thing Miss Bolam was. No carrying on with her, I can tell you!"

Dalgliesh inquired whether anyone had tried. It was a question he usually put with the maximum of tact, but he felt that subtlety would be lost on Mrs. Shorthouse. She gave a scream of laughter.

"What do you think? She wasn't one for the men. Not as far as I know, anyway. Mind you, some of the cases they have here would put you off sex for life. Miss Bolam went to the medical director once to complain about some of the reports Miss Priddy was given to type. Said they weren't decent. Of course, she was always a bit odd about Priddy. Tried to fuss round the kid too much if you ask me. Priddy used to be in Miss Bolam's Guide Company or something when she was young, and I suppose Bolam wanted to keep an eye on her in case she forgot what captain had taught her. You could see the kid was embarrassed by it. There wasn't anything wrong, though. Don't you go believing it if they hint that there was. Some of them here have dirty minds and there's no denying it."

Dalgliesh asked whether Miss Bolam had approved of Miss Priddy's friendship with Nagle.

"Oh, you're on to that, are you? Nothing to approve of, if you ask me. Nagle's a cold fish and as mean as hell. Just try getting his tea money out of him! He and Priddy play around a bit and I dare say Tigger could tell a thing or two if cats could speak. I don't think Bolam noticed though. She kept pretty much to her own office. Anyway, Nagle isn't encouraged in the general office and the medical stenogs are kept pretty busy, so there isn't much time for hanky-panky. Nagle took good care to keep in Miss B's good books. Quite the little blue-eyed boy he was. Never absent, never late, that's our Peter. Leastways, he got stuck in the Underground one Monday and wasn't he in a state about it! Spoilt his record, you see. He even came in on May first when he had the 'flu because we had a visit from the Duke and, naturally, Peter Nagle had to be here to see everything was done proper. Temperature of 103 he had. Sister took it. Miss Bolam sent him home pretty soon, I can tell you. Dr. Steiner took him in his car."

"Is it generally known that Mr. Nagle keeps his tools in the porters' duty-room?"

"Of course it is! Stands to reason. People are always wanting him to mend this or that and where else would he keep his tools? A proper old woman he is about them, too. Talk about fussy. Cully isn't allowed to touch them. Mind you they aren't clinic tools. They belong to Nagle. There wasn't half a row about six weeks ago when Dr. Steiner borrowed a screwdriver to do something to his car. Being Dr. Steiner he mucked up the job and bent the screwdriver. Talk about trouble! Nagle thought it was Cully and they had one hell of a row which brought on Cully's belly-ache again, poor old blighter. Then Nagle found out that someone had seen Dr. Steiner coming out of the porters' duty-room with the tool so he complained to Miss Bolam and she spoke to Dr. Steiner and made him buy another screwdriver. We do see life here, I can tell you. Never a dull moment. Never had a murder before, though. That's something new. Nice goings-on, I don't think."

"As you say. If you've any idea who did it, Mrs. Shorthouse, now's the time to say so."

Mrs. Shorthouse adjusted one of the curls on her forehead with a licked finger, wriggled more comfortably into her coat and got to her feet, thus indicating that, in her opinion, the interview was over.

"No fear! Catching murderers is your job, mate, and you're welcome to it. I'll say this much, though. It wasn't one of the doctors. They haven't the guts. These psychiatrists are a timid lot. Say what you like about this killer, the chap has nerve."

Dalgliesh decided to question the doctors next. He was surprised and interested by their patience, by their ready acceptance of his role. He had kept them waiting because he judged it more important to his inquiry to see other people first, even such an apparently less important witness as the domestic assistant. It looked as if they appreciated that he wasn't trying to irritate them or keep them unnecessarily in suspense. He wouldn't have hesitated to do either if it would have served his purpose, but it was his experience that useful information could most often be obtained when a witness hadn't been given time to think and could be betrayed by shock or fear into garrulity and indiscretion. The doctors had not kept themselves apart. They had waited in the front consulting-room with the others, quietly and without protest. They gave him the credit of knowing his job and let him get on with it. He wondered whether consultant surgeons or physicians would have been so accommodating and felt with the group secretary that there were worse people to deal with than psychiatrists.

Dr. Mary Ingram was seen first by request of the medical director. She had three young children at home and it was important that she get back to them as soon as possible. She had been crying spasmodically while waiting, to the embarrassment of her colleagues who had difficulty in comforting a grief which seemed to them unreasonable and ill-timed. Nurse Bolam was bearing up well, after all, and she was a relative. Dr. Ingram's tears added to the tension and provoked an irrational guilt in those whose emotions were less uncomplicated. There was a general feeling that she should be allowed to go home to her children without delay. There was little she could tell Dalgliesh. She attended the clinic only twice weekly to help with the E.C.T. sessions and had hardly known Miss Bolam. She had been in the E.C.T. room with Sister Ambrose for the whole of the crucial time from six-twenty until seven. In reply to Dalgliesh's question she admitted that Dr. Baguley may have left them for a short time after six-fifteen, but she couldn't remember when exactly or for how long. At the end of the interview she looked at Dalgliesh from reddened eyes and said:

"You will find out who did it, won't you? That poor, poor girl."

"We shall find out," replied Dalgliesh.

Dr. Etherege was interviewed next. He gave the necessary personal details without waiting to be asked and went on:

"As regards my own movements this evening, I'm afraid I can't be very helpful. I arrived at the clinic just before five and went into Miss Bolam's office to speak to her before going upstairs. We had a little general conversation. She seemed perfectly all right to me and didn't tell me that she had asked to see the group secretary. I rang the general office for Mrs. Bostock at about five-fifteen and she was with me taking dictation until about ten to six when she went downstairs with the post. She came back after ten minutes or so and we continued with the dictation, until some time before half past six, when she went next door to type material directly from a tape machine. Some of my treatment sessions are recorded and the material subsequently played back and a typescript made either for research purposes or for the medical record. I worked alone in my consulting-room except for one brief visit to the medical library—I can't remember when, but it was very shortly after Mrs. Bostock left me—until she returned to consult me on a point. That must have been just before seven because we were together when Sister rang to tell me about Miss Bolam. Miss Saxon came down from her room on the third floor to go home and caught us up on the stairs, so she and I went to the basement. You know what we found and the subsequent steps I took to ensure that no one left the clinic."

"You seem to have acted with great presence of mind, Doctor," said Dalgliesh. "As a result the field of inquiry can be considerably narrowed. It looks, doesn't it, as if the murderer is still in this building?"

"Certainly Cully has assured me that no one got past him after 5 p.m. without being entered in his register. That is our system here. The implication of that locked back door is disturbing, but I'm sure you are too experienced an officer to jump to conclusions. No building is impregnable. The . . . the person responsible could have got in at any time, even early this morning, and lain hidden in the basement."

"Can you suggest where such a person lay concealed or how he got out of the clinic?"

The medical director did not reply.

"Have you any idea who that person might be?"

Dr. Etherege slowly traced the line of his right eyebrow with his middle finger. Dalgliesh had seen him do this on television and reflected, now as then, that it served to draw attention to a fine hand and a well-shaped eyebrow even if as an indication of serious thought the gesture seemed slightly spurious.

"I have no idea at all. The whole tragedy is incomprehensible. I'm not going to claim that Miss Bolam was an altogether easy person to get on with. She sometimes aroused resentment." He smiled deprecatingly. "We're not always very easy to get on with ourselves and the most successful administrator of a psychiatric unit is probably someone far more tolerant than Miss Bolam, less obsessional perhaps. But this is murder! I can't think of anyone, patient or staff, who would want to kill her. It's very horrible to me as medical director to think that there might be someone as disturbed as that working at the Steen and I never knew."

"As disturbed or as wicked," said Dalgliesh, unable to resist the temptation. Dr. Etherege smiled again, patiently explaining a difficult point to an obtuse member of the television panel. "Wicked? I'm not competent to discuss this in theological terms."

"Nor am I, Doctor," replied Dalgliesh. "But this crime doesn't look like the work of a madman. There's an intelligence behind it."

"Some psychopaths are highly intelligent, Superintendent. Not that I am knowledgeable about psychopathy. It's a most interesting field but not mine. We have never claimed at the Steen to be able to treat the condition."

Then the Steen was in good company, thought Dalgliesh. The Mental Health Act, 1959, may have defined psychopathy as a disorder requiring or susceptible to medical treatment, but there appeared little enthusiasm on the part of doctors to treat it. The word seemed little more than a psychiatrist's term of abuse and he said as much. Dr. Etherege smiled, indulgent, unprovoked.

"I have never accepted a clinical entity because it is defined in an Act of Parliament. However, psychopathy exists. I'm not convinced at present that it is susceptible to medical treatment. What I am sure is that it is not susceptible to a prison sentence. But we have no certainty that we're looking for a psychopath."

Dalgliesh asked Dr. Etherege whether he knew where Nagle kept his tools and which key opened the door of the record-room.

"I knew about the key. If I'm working late and alone I sometimes need one of the old files and I fetch it myself. I do a certain amount of research and, of course, lecturing and writing, and it's important to have access to the medical records. I last fetched a file about ten days ago. I don't think I've ever seen the box of tools in the porters' room, but I knew that Nagle had his own set and was particular about them. I suppose if I'd wanted a chisel I should have looked in the porters' room. The tools would hardly be kept anywhere else. Obviously, too, I should expect Tippett's fetish to be in the art therapy department. It was a most curious choice of weapons! What I find interesting is the apparent care taken by the murderer to fix suspicion on the clinic staff."

"Suspicion can hardly rest elsewhere in the face of those locked doors."

"That's what I meant, Superintendent. If a member of the staff present this evening did kill Miss Bolam surely he would want to divert suspicion from the relatively few people known to be in the building at the time. The easiest way to do that would be to unlock one of the doors. He'd need to wear gloves, of course, but then, I gather that he did wear them."

"There are no prints on either of the weapons, certainly. They were wiped, but it is probable that he did wear gloves."

"And yet, those doors were kept locked, the strongest evidence that the murderer was still in the building. Why? It would be risky to unlock the back door on the ground floor. That, as you know, is between the E.C.T. room and the medical staffroom and it leads into a well-lit road. It would be difficult to unlock it without the risk of being seen and a murderer would hardly make his exit that way. But there are the two fire-escape doors on the second and third floors and the door in the basement. Why not unlock one of those? It can only be, surely, because the murderer hadn't the opportunity between the time of the crime and the finding of the body, or that he deliberately wished to throw suspicion on the clinic staff even at the inevitable cost of increasing his own danger."

"You talk about 'he', Doctor. Do you think, as a psychiatrist, that we should be looking for a man?"

"Oh, yes! I would expect this to be the work of a man."

"Although it didn't require great strength?" asked Dalgliesh.

"I wasn't thinking primarily of the strength required but of the method and the choice of weapon. I can only give my opinion, of course, and I'm not a criminologist. I would expect it to be a man's crime. But, of course, a woman could have done it. Psychologically, it's unlikely. Physically, it's perfectly possible."

It was indeed, thought Dalgliesh. It required merely knowledge and nerve. He pictured for a moment an intent, pretty face bent over Miss Bolam's body; a thin, girlish hand slipping open the sweater buttons and rolling up the fine cashmere jumper. And then, that clinical selection of exactly the right place to pierce, and the grunt of effort as the blade went home. And, last of all, the sweater drawn lightly back to conceal the chisel handle, the ugly fetish placed in position on the still twitching body in an ultimate gesture of derision and defiance. He told the medical director about Mrs. Shorthouse's evidence of the phone call.

"No one has admitted to making that call. It looks very much as if she were tricked down to the basement."

"That is mere supposition, Superintendent."

Dalgliesh pointed out mildly that it was also common sense, the basis of all sound police work. The medical director said:

"There is a card hung beside the telephone outside the record-room. Anyone, even a stranger to the clinic, could discover Miss Bolam's number."

"But what would be her reaction to an internal call from a stranger? She went downstairs without question. She must have recognized the voice."

"Then it was someone she had no reason to fear, Superintendent. That doesn't tie up with the suggestion that she was in possession of some dangerous knowledge and was killed to prevent her passing it on to Lauder. She went down to her death without fear or suspicion. I can only hope that she died quickly and without pain."

Dalgliesh said that he would know more when he got the autopsy report but that death was almost certainly instantaneous. He added:

"There must have been one dreadful moment when she looked up and saw her murderer with the fetish raised, but it happened very quickly. She would feel nothing after she was stunned. I doubt whether she even had time to cry out. If she did the sound would be muffled by the tiers of paper and I'm told that Mrs. King was being rather noisy during her treatment." He paused for a moment, then said quietly: "What made you describe to the staff just how Miss Bolam died? You did tell them?"

"Of course. I called them together in the front consulting-room—the patients were in the waiting-room—and made a brief statement. Are you suggesting that the news could have been kept from them?"

"I am suggesting that they need not have been told the

details. It would have been useful to me if you hadn't mentioned the stabbing. The murderer might have given himself away by showing more knowledge than an innocent person could have possessed."

The medical director smiled.

"I'm a psychiatrist not a detective. Strange as it may seem to you, my reaction to this crime was to assume that the rest of the staff would share my horror and distress, not to lay traps for them. I wanted to break the news to them myself, gently and honestly. They have always had my confidence and I saw no reason for withholding that confidence now."

That was all very well, thought Dalgliesh, but an intelligent man must surely have seen the importance of saying as little as possible. And the medical director was a very intelligent man. As he thanked his witness and drew the interview to its close, his mind busied itself with the problem. How carefully had Dr. Etherege considered the position before he spoke to the staff? Had his disclosure of the stabbing been as thoughtless as it appeared? It would, after all, have been impossible to deceive most of the staff. Dr. Steiner, Dr. Baguley, Nagle, Dr. Ingram and Sister Ambrose had all seen the body. Miss Priddy had seen it but had apparently fled without a second look. That left Nurse Bolam, Mrs. Bostock, Mrs. Shorthouse, Miss Saxon, Miss Kettle and Cully. Possibly Dr. Etherege was satisfied that none of these was the murderer. Cully and Shorthouse both had an alibi. Had the medical director been reluctant to lay a trap for Nurse Bolam, Mrs. Bostock or Miss Saxon? Or was he so certain in his own mind that the murderer must be a man that any subterfuge to mislead the women seemed a waste of time, likely to result only in embarrassment and resentment? The medical director had certainly been almost blatant in his hints that anyone working on the second or third floor could be eliminated since they would have had the opportunity of opening one of the fire-escape doors. But then, he himself had been in his consulting-room on the second floor. In any case, the obvious door for the killer to unlock was the one in the basement and it was hard to believe that he had lacked the opportunity. It would be a second's work only to draw back that lock and provide evidence that the murderer could have left the clinic that way. Yet the basement door had been fast bolted. Why?

Dr. Steiner came in next, short, dapper, outwardly self-composed. In the light from Miss Bolam's desk lamp his pale smooth skin looked slightly luminous. Despite his calmness he had been sweating heavily. The heavy smell hung about his clothes, about the well cut, conventional black coat of a consultant. Dalgliesh was surprised when he gave his age as forty-two. He looked older. The smooth skin, the sharp black eyes, the bouncy walk gave a superficial impression of youth but he was already thickening and his dark hair, cunningly sleeked back, could not quite conceal the tonsure-like patch on the crown of the head.

Dr. Steiner had apparently decided to treat his encounter with a policeman as a social occasion. Extending a plump, well-kept hand, he smiled a benign "how d'you do" and inquired whether he was speaking to the writer, Adam Dalgliesh.

"I have read your verse," he announced complacently. "I congratulate you. Such a deceptive simplicity. I started at the first poem and read straight through. That is my way of experiencing verse. At the tenth page I began to think that we might have a new poet."

Dalgliesh admitted to himself that Dr. Steiner had not only read the book but showed some critical insight. It was at the tenth page that he, too, sometimes felt they might have a new poet. Dr. Steiner inquired whether he had met Ernie Bales the new young playwright from Nottingham. He looked so hopeful that Dalgliesh felt positively unkind as he disclaimed acquaintance with Mr. Bales and steered the conversation from literary criticism back to the purpose of the interview. Dr. Steiner at once assumed an air of shocked gravity.

"The whole affair is dreadful, quite dreadful. I was one of the first people to see the body as you may know and it has distressed me greatly. I have always had a horror of violence. It is an appalling business. Dr. Etherege, our medical director, is due to retire at the end of the year. This is a most unfortunate thing to happen in his last months here."

He shook his head sadly, but Dalgliesh fancied that the little black eyes held something very like satisfaction.

Tippett's fetish had yielded its secrets to the fingerprint expert and Dalgliesh had stood it on the desk before him. Dr. Steiner put out his hand to touch it then drew back and said:

"I had better not handle it, I suppose, because of fingerprints." He darted a quick look at Dalgliesh and getting no response went on: "It's an interesting carving, isn't it? Quite remarkable. Have you ever noticed, Superintendent, what excellent art the mentally ill can produce, even patients without previous training or experience? It raises interesting questions on the nature of artistic achievement. As they recover their work deteriorates. The power and originality go. By the time they are well again the stuff they produce is valueless. We've got several interesting examples of patients' work in the art therapy department, but this fetish is outstanding. Tippett was very ill when he carved it and went to hospital shortly afterwards. He's a schizophrenic. The fetish has the typical facies of the chronic disease, the frog-like eyes and spreading nostrils. Tippett looked very like that himself at one time."

"Everyone knew where this thing was kept, I suppose?" said Dalgliesh.

"Oh, yes! It was kept on the shelf in the art therapy department. Tippett was very proud of it and Dr. Baguley often showed it to House Committee members when they made visits of inspection. Mrs. Baumgarden, the art therapist, likes to keep some of the best work on show. That's why she had the shelves put up. She's on sick leave at the present but you've been shown the department, I expect?"

Dalgliesh said that he had.

"Some of my colleagues feel that the art therapy is a waste of money," confided Dr. Steiner. "Certainly I never use Mrs. Baumgarden. But one must be tolerant. Dr. Baguley refers patients now and again, and it probably does them less harm to dabble about down there than to be subjected to E.C.T. But to pretend that the patients' artistic efforts can help towards a diagnosis seems very far fetched to me. Of course that claim is all part of the effort to get Mrs. Baumgarden graded as a lay psychotherapist, quite unwarrantably, I'm afraid. She has no analytical training."

"And the chisel? Did you know where that was kept, Doctor?"

"Well, not really, Superintendent. I mean, I knew that Nagle had some tools and presumably kept them in the porters' duty-room, but I didn't know exactly where."

"The toolbox is large and clearly labelled and is kept on the small table in the duty-room. It would be difficult to miss."

"Oh, I'm sure it would! But then, I have no reason to go into the porters' duty-room. That is true of all the doctors. We must get a key for that box now and see that it's kept somewhere safe. Miss Bolam was very wrong to allow Nagle to keep it unlocked. After all, we do occasionally have disturbed patients and some tools can be lethal."

"So it appears."

"This clinic wasn't intended to treat grossly psychotic patients, of course. It was founded to provide a centre for analytically orientated psychotherapy, particularly for middle class and highly intelligent patients. We treat people who would never dream of entering a mental hospital—and who would be just as out of place in the ordinary psychiatric outpatient department. In addition, of course, there is a large research element in our work."

"What were you doing between six o'clock and seven this evening, Doctor?" inquired Dalgliesh.

Dr. Steiner looked pained at this sudden intrusion of sordid curiosity into an interesting discussion but answered, meekly enough, that he had been conducting his Friday night psychotherapy session.

"I arrived at the clinic at five-thirty when my first patient was booked. Unfortunately he defaulted. His treatment has arrived at a stage when poor attendance is to be expected. Mr. Burge was booked for six-fifteen and he is usually very prompt. I waited for him in the second consulting-room on the ground floor and joined him in my own room at about ten-past six. Mr. Burge dislikes waiting with Dr. Baguley's patients in the general waiting-room and I really don't blame him. You've heard of Burge, I expect. He wrote that interesting novel *The Souls of the Righteous*, a quite brilliant exposure of the sexual conflicts concealed beneath the conventionality of a respectable English suburb. But I'm forgetting. Naturally you have interviewed Mr. Burge."

Dalgliesh had indeed. The experience had been tedious and not unenlightening. He had also heard of Mr. Burge's book, an opus of some two hundred thousand words in which the scabrous episodes are inserted with such meticulous deliberation that it only requires an exercise in simple arithmetic to calculate on what page the next will occur. Dalgliesh did not suspect Burge of any part in the murder. A writer who could produce such a hotchpotch of sex and sadism was probably impotent and certainly timid. But he was not necessarily a liar. Dalgliesh said:

"Are you quite sure of your times, Doctor? Mr. Burge says that he arrived at six-fifteen and Cully has booked him in at that time. Burge says he went straight into your own consulting-room, having checked with Cully that you weren't seeing a patient, and that it was a full ten minutes before you joined him. He was getting impatient and was thinking of going to inquire where you were."

Dr. Steiner did not appear either frightened or angry at his patient's perfidy. He did, however, look embarrassed.

"It's interesting Mr. Burge should say that. I'm afraid he may be right. I thought he seemed a little put out when we began the session. If he says that I joined him at six-twenty-five I have no doubt he's telling the truth. The poor man has had a very short and interrupted session this evening. It's very unfortunate at this particular stage in his treatment."

"So, if you weren't in the front consulting-room when your patient arrived, where were you?" persisted Dalgliesh gently.

An astonishing change came over Dr. Steiner's face. Suddenly he looked as shamefaced as a small boy who has been caught in the middle of mischief. He didn't look frightened but he did look extremely guilty. The metamorphosis from consultant psychiatrist to embarrassed delinquent was almost comical.

"But I told you, Superintendent! I was in number two consulting-room, the one between the front one and the patients' waiting-room."

"Doing what, Doctor?"

Really, it was almost laughable! What could Steiner have been up to to produce this degree of embarrassment? Dalgliesh's mind toyed with bizarre possibilities. Reading pornography? Smoking hemp? Seducing Mrs. Shorthouse? It surely couldn't be anything so conventional as planning murder. But the doctor had obviously decided that the truth must be told. He said with a burst of shamefaced candour:

"It sounds silly, I know, but . . . well . . . it was rather warm and I'd had a busy day and the couch was there." He gave a little giggle. "In fact, Superintendent, at the time Miss Bolam is thought to have died, I was, in the vulgar parlance, having a kip!"

Once this embarrassing confession was off his chest Dr. Steiner became happily voluble and it was difficult to get rid of him. But at last he was persuaded that he could help no more for the present and his place was taken by Dr. Baguley.

Dr. Baguley, like his colleagues, made no complaint of his long wait, but it had taken its toll. He was still wearing his white coat and he hugged it around himself as he drew the chair under him. He seemed to have difficulty in settling comfortably, twitching his lean shoulders and crossing and recrossing his legs. The clefts from nose to mouth looked deeper, his hair was dank, his eyes black pools in the light of the desk lamp. He lit a cigarette and, fumbling in his coat pocket, produced a slip of paper and passed it to Martin.

"I've written down my personal details. It'll save time."

"Thank you, sir," said Martin stolidly.

"I may as well say now that I haven't an alibi for the twenty minutes or so after six-fifteen. I expect you've heard that I left the E.C.T. clinic a few minutes before Sister saw Miss Bolam for the last time. I went into the medical staff cloakroom at the end of the hall and had a cigarette. The place was empty and no one came in. I didn't hurry back to the clinic so I suppose it was about twenty to seven before I rejoined Dr. Ingram and Sister. They were together for the whole of that time, of course."

"So Sister tells me."

"It's ridiculous even to consider that either of them would be involved but I'm glad they happened to stick together. The more people you can eliminate the better from your point of view, I suppose. I'm sorry not to be able to produce an alibi. I can't help in any other way either, I'm afraid. I heard and saw nothing."

Dalgliesh asked the doctor how he had spent the evening.

"It was the usual pattern, until seven o'clock that is. I arrived just before four and went into Miss Bolam's office to sign the medical attendance book. It used to be kept in the medical staff cloakroom until recently when she moved it into her office. We talked for a short time—she had some queries about the servicing arrangements for my new E.C.T. machine—and then I went to start my clinic. We were pretty busy until just after six and I also had my lysergic acid patient to visit periodically. She was being specialled by Nurse Bolam in the basement treatment-room. But I'm forgetting. You've seen Mrs. King."

Mrs. King and her husband had been sitting in the patients' waiting-room on Dalgliesh's arrival and he had taken very little time to satisfy himself that they could have had nothing to do with the murder. The woman was still weak and a little disorientated and sat holding tightly to her husband's hand. He had not arrived at the clinic to escort her home until a few minutes after Sergeant Martin and his party. Dalgliesh had questioned the woman briefly and gently and had let her go. He had not needed the assurances of the medical director to be satisfied that this patient could not have left her bed to murder anyone. But he was equally sure that she was in no state to give an alibi to anyone else. He asked Dr. Baguley when he had last visited his patient.

"I looked in on her shortly after I arrived, before I started the shock treatments actually. The drug had been given at 3.30 and the patient was beginning to react. I ought to say that LSD is given in an effort to make the patient more accessible to psychotherapy by releasing some of the more deep-seated inhibitions. It's only given under close supervision and the patient is never left. I was called down again by Nurse Bolam at five and stayed for about forty minutes. I went back upstairs and gave my last shock treatment at about twenty to six. The last E.C.T. patient actually left the clinic a few minutes after Miss Bolam was last seen. From about six-thirty I was clearing up and writing my notes."

"Was the door of the medical record-room open when you passed it at five o'clock?"

Dr. Baguley thought for a moment or two and then said:

"I think it was shut. It's difficult to be absolutely certain, but I'm pretty sure I should have noticed if it had been open or ajar."

"And at twenty to six when you left your patient?"

"The same."

Dalgliesh asked again the usual, the inevitable, the obvious questions. Had Miss Bolam any enemies? Did the doctor know of any reason why someone might wish her dead? Had she seemed worried lately? Had he any idea why she might have sent for the group secretary? Could he decipher the notes on her jotting pad? But Dr. Baguley could not help. He said:

"She was a curious woman in some ways, shy, a little aggressive, not really happy with us. But she was perfectly harmless, the last person I'd have said to invite violence. One can't go on saying how shocking it is. Words seem to lose their meaning with repetition. But I suppose we all feel the same. The whole thing is fantastic! Unbelievable!"

"You said she wasn't happy here. Is this a difficult clinic to administer? From what I've heard, Miss Bolam wasn't particularly skilled at dealing with difficult personalities."

Dr. Baguley said easily:

"Oh, you don't want to believe all you hear. We're individualists, but we get along with each other pretty well on the whole. Steiner and I scrap a bit but it's all quite amiable. He wants the place to become a psychotherapy training unit with registrars and lay professional staff running around like mice and a bit of research on the side. One of those places where time and money are spent lavishly on anything but actually treating patients—especially psychotics. There's no danger he'll get his way. The Regional Board wouldn't wear it for one thing."

"And what were Miss Bolam's views, Doctor?"

"Strictly speaking she was hardly competent to hold any, but that didn't inhibit her. She was anti-Freudian and pro-eclectic. Anti-Steiner and pro-me if you like. But that didn't mean anything. Neither Dr. Steiner nor I were likely to knock her on the head because of our doctrinal differences. As you see we haven't even taken a knife to each other yet. All this is utterly irrelevant."

"I'm inclined to agree with you," said Dalgliesh. "Miss Bolam was killed with great deliberation and considerable expertise. I think the motive was a great deal more positive and important than a mere difference of opinion or clash of personality. Did you know, by the way, which key opens the record-room?"

"Of course. If I want one of the old records I usually fetch it myself. I also know, if it's any help to you, that Nagle keeps his box of tools in the porters' rest room. Furthermore, when I arrived this afternoon, Miss Bolam told me about Tippett. But that's hardly relevant, is it? You can't seriously believe that the murderer hoped to implicate Tippett."

"Perhaps not. Tell me, Doctor. From your knowledge of Miss Bolam what would be her reaction to finding those medical records strewn about the floor?"

Dr. Baguley looked surprised for a second then gave a curt laugh.

"Bolam? That's an easy one! She was obsessionally neat. Obviously she'd start to pick them up!"

"She wouldn't be more likely to ring for a porter to do the work or to leave the records where they were as evidence until the culprit was discovered?"

Dr. Baguley thought for a moment and seemed to repent of his first categorical opinion.

"One can't possibly know for certain what she'd do. It's all conjecture. Probably you're right and she'd ring for Nagle.

She wasn't afraid of work but she was very conscious of her position as A.O. I'm sure of one thing, though. She wouldn't have left the place in a mess like that. She couldn't pass a rug or a picture without straightening it."

"And her cousin? Are they alike? I understand that Nurse Bolam works for you more than for any other consultant."

Dalgliesh noticed the quick frown of distaste that this question provoked. Dr. Baguley, however co-operative and frank about his own motives, was not disposed to comment on those of anyone else. Or was it that Nurse Bolam's gentle defencelessness had aroused his protective instincts? Dalgliesh waited for a reply. After a minute the doctor said curtly:

"I shouldn't have said the cousins were alike. You will have formed your own impression of Nurse Bolam. I can only say that I have complete trust in her, both as a nurse and a person."

"She is her cousin's heir. Or perhaps you knew that?"

The inference was too plain to be missed and Dr. Baguley too tired to resist the provocation.

"No, I didn't. But I hope for her sake that it's a bloody great sum and that she and her mother will be allowed to enjoy it in peace. And I hope, too, that you won't waste time suspecting innocent people. The sooner this murder is cleared up the better. It's a pretty intolerable position for all of us."

So Dr. Baguley knew about Nurse Bolam's mother. But, then, it was likely that most of the clinic staff knew. He asked his last question:

"You said, Doctor, that you were alone in the medical staff cloakroom from about six-fifteen until twenty to seven. What were you doing?"

"Going to the lavatory. Washing my hands. Smoking a cigarette. Thinking."

"And that was absolutely all you did during the twenty-five minutes?"

"Yes—that was all, Superintendent."

Dr. Baguley was a poor liar. The hesitation was only momentary; his face did not change colour; the fingers holding his cigarette were quite steady. But his voice was a little too nonchalant, the disinterest a little too carefully controlled. And it was with a palpable effort that he made himself meet Dalgliesh's eyes. He was too intelligent to add to his statement but his eyes held those of the detective as if willing Dalgliesh to repeat his question, and bracing himself to meet it.

"Thank you, Doctor," said Dalgliesh calmly. "That will be all for the present."

Chapter Three

And so it went on; the patient questioning; the meticulous taking of notes, the close watch of suspects' eyes and hands for the revealing flicker of fear, the tensed reaction to an unwelcome change of emphasis. Fredrica Saxon followed Dr. Baguley. As they passed each other in the doorway Dalgliesh saw that they were careful not to meet each other's eyes. She was a dark, vital, casually-dressed woman of twenty-nine who would do no more than give brief but straightforward answers to his questions and who seemed to take a perverse pleasure in pointing out that she had been alone scoring a psychological test in her own room from six until seven and could neither claim an alibi for herself nor give one to anyone else. He got little help or information from Fredrica Saxon but did not, on that account, assume that she had none to give.

She was followed by a very different witness. Miss Ruth Kettle had apparently decided that the murder was none of her affair and, although she was willing to answer Dalgliesh's questions, it was with a vague lack of interest which suggested that her thoughts were on higher things. There is only a limited number of words to express horror and surprise and the clinic staff had used most of them during the evening. Miss Kettle's reaction was less orthodox. She gave her opinion that the murder was peculiar . . . really very odd indeed, and sat blinking at Dalgliesh through her thick spectacles in gentle bewilderment as if she did indeed find it odd, but hardly sufficiently odd to be worth discussing at length. But at least two pieces of information which she was able to give were interesting. Dalgliesh could only hope that they were reliable.

She had been vague about her own movements during the evening, but Dalgliesh's persistence elicited that she had been interviewing the wife of one of the E.C.T. patients until about twenty to six when Sister had telephoned to say that the patient was ready to be taken home. Miss Kettle had walked downstairs with her client, said "good night" in the hall, and had then gone straight down to the record-room to fetch a file. She had found the room in perfect order and had locked it after her. Despite her gentle incertitude about most of the evening's activities she was positive about the time. In any case, thought Dalgliesh, it could probably be verified by Sister Ambrose. The second clue was more nebulous and Miss Kettle mentioned it with apparent indifference to its importance. Some half-hour after returning to her room on the second floor she had heard the unmistakable sound of the service lift thumping to a stop.

Dalgliesh was tired now. Despite the central heating he felt spasms of cold and recognized the familiar malaise that preceded an attack of neuralgia. The right side of his face already felt stiff and heavy, and the needling pain was beginning to stab spasmodically behind his eyeball. But his last witness was here.

Mrs. Bostock, the senior medical stenographer, had none of the doctors' tolerant acceptance of a long wait. She was angry and her anger came into the room with her like a chill wind. She seated herself without speaking, crossed a pair of long and remarkably shapely legs, and looked at Dalgliesh with frank dislike in her pale eyes. She had a striking and unusual head. Her long hair, golden as a guinea, was coiled in intricate folds above a pale, arrogant, sharp-nosed face. With her long neck, poised, colourful head and slightly protuberant eyes, she looked like some exotic bird. Dalgliesh had difficulty in concealing his shock when he saw her hands. They were as huge, red and raw-boned as the hands of a butcher and looked as if they had been incongruously grafted on to the slim wrists by some malignant fate. It was almost a deformity. She made no attempt to conceal them, but her nails were short and she wore no polish. She had a beautiful figure and was well and expensively dressed, an object lesson in the art of minimizing one's defects and emphasizing one's advantages. She probably lived her life, thought Dalgliesh, on much the same principle.

She gave details of her movements since six o'clock that evening briefly and with no apparent reluctance. She had last seen Miss Bolam at six o'clock when, as was usual, she had taken in the post for the administrative officer to sign. There were only five letters. Most of the post consisted of medical reports and letters to general practitioners from the psychiatrists and Miss Bolam was not, of course, concerned with these. All the outgoing mail was registered in the post book either by Mrs. Bostock or Miss Priddy, and was then taken across the road by Nagle to catch the six-thirty from the pillar-box. Miss Bolam had seemed her usual self at six o'clock. She had signed her own letters and Mrs. Bostock had returned to the general office, handed them with the doctors' post to Miss Priddy, and had then gone upstairs to take dictation from Dr. Etherege for the last hour of the day. It was an understood thing that she helped Dr. Etherege on Friday evenings for one hour with his research project. She and the medical director had been together except for a few short periods. Sister rang at about seven o'clock with the news of Miss Bolam's death. As she and Dr. Etherege left the consulting-room they met Miss Saxon who was just leaving. She went down to the basement with the medical director. Mrs. Bostock, at Dr. Etherege's request, had gone to join Cully at the front door to ensure that the instructions were followed about no one leaving the building. She had stayed with Cully until the party from the basement appeared and they had then all collected in the waiting-room to await the arrival of the police, except for the two porters who remained on duty in the hall.

"You said that you were with Dr. Etherege from just after six onwards except for short periods. What were you both doing?"

"We were both working, naturally." Mrs. Bostock managed to suggest that the question had been both stupid and a little vulgar. "Dr. Etherege is writing a paper on the treatment of twin schizophrenic women by psycho-analysis. As I said, it has been agreed that I shall assist him for one hour on Friday evenings. That is quite inadequate for his needs, but Miss Bolam took the view that the work wasn't strictly a clinic concern and that Dr. Etherege should do it in his own consulting-room with the help of his private secretary. Naturally that's impossible. All the material, including some on tape, is here. My part of the job is varied. For some of the time I take dictation. Sometimes I work in the little office typing directly from the tape. Sometimes I look up references in the staff library."

"And what did you do this evening?"

"I took dictation for about thirty minutes. Then I went into the adjoining office and worked from the tape. Dr. Etherege rang for me to come in at about ten to seven. We were working together when the phone rang."

"That would mean that you were with Dr. Etherege taking dictation until about six-thirty-five."

"Presumably."

"And for the whole of that time you were together?"

"I think Dr. Etherege went out for a minute or so to verify a reference."

"Why should you be uncertain, Mrs. Bostock? Either he did or he didn't."

"Naturally, Inspector. As you say, either he did or he didn't. But there is no reason why I should particularly remember. This evening was in no way remarkable. My impression is that he did go out for a short time but I really couldn't recall exactly when. I expect he may be able to help you."

Suddenly Dalgliesh changed the course of questioning. He paused for a full half-minute and then asked quietly:

"Did you like Miss Bolam, Mrs. Bostock?"

It was not a welcome question. Under the patina of make-up he saw a flush of anger or embarrassment die along her neck.

"She wasn't an easy person to like. I tried to be loyal to her."

"By loyal you mean, no doubt, that you tried to smooth down rather than exacerbate her difficulties with the medical staff and refrained from any overt criticism of her as an administrator?"

The tinge of sarcasm in his voice awoke, as was intended, all her latent hostility. Behind the mask of hauteur and detachment he glimpsed the insecure schoolgirl. He knew that she would have to justify herself even against an implied criticism. She did not like him but she could not bear to be underrated or ignored.

"Miss Bolam wasn't really a suitable administrator for a psychiatric unit. She hadn't any sympathy with what we're trying to do here."

"In what way was she unsympathetic?"

"Well, for one thing, she didn't like neurotics."

"Neither do I, God help me," thought Dalgliesh. "Neither do I." But he said nothing and Mrs. Bostock went on:

"She was difficult, for example, about paying out some of the patients' travelling expenses. They only get them if they're on National Assistance, but we help other cases from the Samaritan Fund. We have one girl, a most intelligent person, who comes here twice a week from Surrey to work in the art therapy department. Miss Bolam thought she ought to get treatment nearer home—or go without. Actually she made it pretty plain that, in her view, the patient ought to be discharged to do a job of work, as she put it."

"She didn't say this sort of thing to the patient."

"Oh, no! She was careful enough what she actually said. But I could see that the sensitive ones weren't at ease with her. Then she was very critical of intensive psychotherapy. It's a time-consuming procedure. It has to be. Miss Bolam tended to judge a psychiatrist's worth by the number of patients he saw in a session. But that was less important than her attitude to the patients. There was a reason for it, of course. Her mother was mentally ill and in analysis for years before she died. I understand that she killed herself. Miss Bolam can't have had an easy time. Naturally she couldn't allow herself to hate her mother, so she projected her resentment on to the patients here. She was subconsciously afraid of her own neurosis too. That was pretty obvious."

Dalgliesh did not feel qualified to comment on these theories. He was prepared to believe that there was truth in them but not that Mrs. Bostock had thought them out for herself. Miss Bolam may have irritated the psychiatrists by her lack of sympathy, but here at least, they had a believer.

"Do you know who treated Mrs. Bolam?" he asked.

Mrs. Bostock uncrossed her elegant legs and settled herself more comfortably in the chair before deigning to reply.

"I do, as a matter of fact. But I hardly see its relevance to this inquiry."

"Shall we leave that to me to decide? I can find out quite easily. If you don't know or aren't sure it would save time if you said so."

"It was Dr. Etherege."

"And who do you think will be appointed to succeed Miss Bolam?"

"As administrative officer? Really," said Mrs. Bostock coolly, "I've no idea."

At last the main work of the evening was over for Dalgliesh and Martin. The body had been taken away and the record-room sealed. All the clinic staff had been questioned and most of them had left for their homes. Dr. Etherege had been the last doctor to leave and had hung around uneasily for some time after Dalgliesh had said he might go. Mr. Lauder and Peter Nagle were still in the clinic and were waiting together in the hall where two uniformed policemen were on duty. The group secretary had said with quiet determination that he preferred to be on the premises while the police were still there, and Nagle could not leave until the front door had been locked and the key handed over since it was his job to open the clinic at eight o'clock on Monday morning.

Dalgliesh and Martin made their last round of the premises together. Watching them at work a casual observer might have been misled into the facile assumption that Martin was merely a foil for the younger, more successful man. Those at the Yard who knew them both judged differently. In appearance they were certainly unalike. Martin was a big man, nearly six feet and broad-shouldered and looking, with his open ruddy face, more like a successful farmer than a detective. Dalgliesh was even taller, dark, lean and easy moving. Beside him Martin seemed ponderous. No one watching Dalgliesh at work could fail to recognize his intelligence. With Martin one was less sure. He was ten years older than his chief and it was unlikely now that he would gain further promotion. But he had qualities that made him an admirable detective. He was never tormented by doubt of his own motives. Right and wrong stood for him as immutable as the two poles. He had never wandered in that twilight country where the nuances of evil and good cast their perplexing shadows. He had great determination and infinite patience. He was kind without being sentimental and meticulous for detail without losing sight of the whole. Looking at his career, no one could have called him brilliant. But if he was incapable of high intelligence he was equally incapable of stupidity. Most police work consists of the boring, repetitive and meticulous checking of detail. Most murders are sordid little crimes bred out of ignorance and despair. It was Martin's job to help solve them and, patiently and uncensoriously, that is what he did. Faced with the murder at the Steen Clinic with its frightening undertones of a trained intelligence at work, he remained unimpressed. Methodical attention to detail had solved other murders and would solve this one. And murderers, intelligent or subnormal, devious or impulsive had to be caught. He walked, as was usual, a pace or two behind Dalgliesh and said little. But when he spoke it was usually to the point.

They went through the building for the last time that evening, starting on the third floor. Here the eighteenth-century rooms had been divided to provide accommodation for psychiatric social workers, psychologists and lay therapists, together with two larger treatment-rooms for the use of psychiatrists. There was one pleasant and unconverted room at the front of the building furnished comfortably with easy chairs and a number of small tables. This, apparently, was the rendezvous of the marital problem group who could enjoy an agreeable view over the square in the intervals of analysing their domestic and sexual incompatibilities. Dalgliesh could understand the chagrin of the absent Mrs. Baumgarten. The room was admirably suited for the art therapy department.

The more important rooms were on the floor below and here there had been little alteration or adaptation so that ceilings, doors and windows could contribute their own graciousness to the atmosphere of elegance and calm. The Modigliani was out of place in the boardroom but not aggressively so. The smaller medical library next door with its antique bookcases, each bearing the name of the donor, could have been an eighteenth-century gentleman's library until one looked at the titles on the books. There were low bowls of flowers set on the bookcases and a number of armchairs which looked right together although they had obviously come originally from half a dozen different houses.

On this floor, too, the medical director had his consulting-room and it was one of the most elegant in the clinic. The treatment couch which stood against the far wall, was the same pattern as that in each of the other psychiatrists' rooms, a low single divan, covered in chintz and with a red blanket folded at its foot and one pillow. But no H.M.C. had provided the rest of the furniture. The eighteenth-century desk was uncluttered by cardboard calendars or stationery office diaries and held merely a leather-bound blotter, a silver inkstand and a tray for papers. There were two leather armchairs and a mahogany corner cupboard. It appeared that the medical director collected old prints and was particularly interested in mezzotints and eighteenth-century engravings. Dalgliesh inspected a collection of works by James McArdell and Valentine Green, arranged on each side of the chimney-piece, and noted that Dr. Etherege's patients unburdened their subconscious beneath a couple of fine lithographs by Hullmandel. He reflected that the unknown clinic thief might have been a gentleman if Cully's opinion was to be trusted, but he was certainly no connoisseur. It was more typical of the small-time professional to neglect two Hullmandels for fifteen pounds in cash. It was certainly a pleasant room, proclaiming its owner as a man with taste and the money to indulge it, the room of a man who sees no reason why his working life should be spent in less agreeable surroundings than his leisure. And yet it was not wholly successful. Somewhere there was a lack. The elegance was a little too contrived, the good taste a little too orthodox. Dalgliesh felt that a patient might well be happier in the warm, untidy, oddly-shaped cell upstairs where Fredrica Saxon worked in a litter of papers, pot-plants and the paraphernalia of tea-brewing. Despite the engravings the room lacked the nuances of personality. In that it was somehow typical of its owner. Dalgliesh was reminded of a recent conference which he had attended on mental illness and the law at which Dr. Etherege had been one of the speakers. At the time his paper had seemed a model of felicitous wisdom; afterwards Dalgliesh was unable accurately to recall a single word.

They went down to the ground floor where the group secretary and Nagle, chatting quietly to the police constables, turned to watch but made no move to join them. The four waiting figures were standing together in a sad group like mourners after a funeral, uncertain and disorganized in the hiatus that follows grief. When they talked together their voices sounded muted in the silence of the hall.

The ground-floor plan was simple. Immediately inside the front door and to the left as one entered was the glass-panelled reception kiosk. Dalgliesh noted again that it commanded a good view of the whole hall, including the great curved staircase at the end. Yet Cully's observations during the evening had been curiously selective. He was positive that everyone entering or leaving the clinic after 5 p.m. had been seen by him and entered in his book, but many of the comings and goings in the hall had passed unnoticed. He had seen Mrs. Shorthouse come out of Miss Bolam's office and into the front general office but had not seen the administrative officer passing down the hall to the basement stairs. He had seen Dr. Baguley coming out of the medical staff cloakroom but not entering it. Most of the movements of patients and their relations had not escaped him and he was able to confirm the comings and goings of Mrs. Bostock. He was certain that Dr. Etherege, Miss Saxon and Miss Kettle had not passed through the hall after 6 p.m. If they had he hadn't noticed. Dalgliesh would have felt more confidence in Cully's evidence if it were not apparent that the pathetic little man was terrified. When they arrived at the clinic he had been merely depressed and a little surly. By the time he was allowed to go home he was in a state of terror. At some stage of the investigation, thought Dalgliesh, he would have to find out why.

Behind the reception kiosk and with windows facing the square was the general office, part of which had been partitioned to form a small filing-room for the current medical records. Next to the general office was Miss Bolam's room and, beyond that, the E.C.T. suite with its treatment-room, nurses' duty-room and male and female recovery bays. This suite was separated by a hallway from the medical staff cloakroom, clerical staff lavatories and the domestic assistant's pantry. At the end of the hallway was the locked side door, seldom used except by members of the staff who had been working late and who did not want to give Nagle the trouble of undoing the more complicated locks, bolts and chains on the front door.

At the opposite side of the main hall were two consulting-rooms and the patients' waiting-room, and lavatories. The front room had been divided to form two fairly large psychotherapy-rooms which were separated from the waiting-room by a passage. Dr. Steiner could, therefore, move from one to the other without coming within Cully's view. But he could hardly move down the hall to the basement stairs without risk of being seen. Had he been seen? What was Cully keeping back and why?

Together, Dalgliesh and Martin examined the basement rooms for the last time that night. At the rear was the door which led to the area steps. Dr. Etherege had said that this door was bolted when he and Dr. Steiner had examined it after finding the body. It was still bolted. It had been tested for fingerprints, but the only decipherable ones had been Peter Nagle's. Nagle had said that he was probably the last person to touch the lock since it was his habit to check that the door was securely bolted before he locked up at night. It was rare for him or for any member of the staff to use the basement exit and the door was usually only opened when the coal or other heavy supplies were delivered. Dalgliesh shot back the bolt.

There was a short flight of iron steps leading to the rear railings. Here, again, the wrought-iron door was bolted and fitted with a lock and chain. But an intruder would have no difficulty in getting into the basement area, particularly as the mews at the back were ill lit and unoccupied. The clinic itself would be less easy of access. All the basement windows, except the small lavatory window, were barred. It was through that window the clinic thief had cut his way.

Dalgliesh bolted the door again and they went into the porters' rest room which occupied most of the back of the building. Nothing was changed since they had first examined it. Two clothes lockers stood against one wall. The centre of the floor was occupied by a heavy square table. There was a small old-fashioned gas cooker in one corner and, beside it, a cupboard containing cups and saucers and tins of tea, sugar and biscuits. Two shabby leather chairs were drawn up one on each side of the gas fire. To the left of the door was a keyboard with the hooks numbered but not named. On this board had hung, among others, the key to the basement record-room. That key was now in possession of the police.

A large striped cat was curled in a basket before the unlit gas fire. When the light was switched on it stirred and, lifting its heavy barred head, gave the intruders a stare, blank and expressionless, from immense yellow eyes. Dalgliesh knelt beside the basket and stroked the top of its head. The cat shivered then sat immobile under his touch. Suddenly it rolled on its back, and stretched out its legs, rigid as poles, to display a ridge of soft belly hair for Dalgliesh's ministrations. The superintendent stroked and talked while Martin whose preference was for dogs, looked on in tolerant patience. He said: "I've heard about him from Mrs. Shorthouse. It's Tigger, Miss Bolam's cat."

"We deduce that Miss Bolam read A. A. Milne as a child. Cats are nocturnal. Why isn't he let out at night?"

"I heard about that, too. Miss Bolam thought he'd keep the mice down if he were shut in. Nagle goes out at lunch time for a beer and a sandwich, but Cully eats his grub here and Miss B was always on to him about crumbs. The cat is shut in here every night and let out during the day. He's got his food and his scratch tin."

"So I see. Furnished with cinders from the boiler."

"Pity he can't talk, sir. He was in here for most of the evening waiting to be fed. He was probably here when the murderer came in for the record-room key."

"And for the chisel. Oh, yes, Tigger saw it all right. But what makes you think he'd tell you the truth?"

Sergeant Martin didn't reply. People who went for cats in a big way were like that, of course. Childish you might call it. Unusually talkative, he said:

"Miss B had him doctored at her own expense. Mrs. Shorthouse told P.C. Holliday that Dr. Steiner was very upset about it. He likes cats seemingly. They had words over it. Dr. Steiner told Mrs. Bostock that Miss Bolam would like everything male at the clinic doctored if she had her way. He put it rather crudely, I gather. Of course, it wasn't meant to get back to Miss Bolam but Mrs. Bostock saw that it did."

"Yes," said Dalgliesh shortly. "She would."

They continued their inspection.

It was not an uncomfortable room. It smelled of food and leather and, just perceptibly, of gas. There were a number of pictures which looked as if they had found a home with the porters when their previous owners had seen enough of them. One was of the founder of the Steen surrounded, appropriately enough, by his five sons. It was a faded sepia photograph in a gilt frame more indicative, Dalgliesh thought, of old Hyman's character than the more orthodox commemorative oil which hung upstairs in the hall.

On a smaller table against the rear wall lay Nagle's box of tools. Dalgliesh lifted the lid. The tools, meticulously cared for, lay each in its correct place. There was only one missing and that one was unlikely ever again to find its place in Nagle's toolbox.

"He could have come in through that rear door if he left it unlocked," said Martin, voicing Dalgliesh's thought.

"Of course. I admit to a perverse disposition to suspect the one person who was apparently not even in the building when the murder was committed. There's little doubt, though, that Nagle was with Miss Priddy in the general office when Mrs. Shorthouse left Miss Bolam. Cully confirms that. And Miss Priddy states that she never left the general office except momentarily to fetch a file from the next room. What did you think of Shorthouse by the way?"

"I thought she was telling the truth, sir. I wouldn't put her above a bit of lying when it suited her. She's the sort who likes things to happen and isn't averse to giving them a bit of a shove in the right direction. But she had plenty to tell us without adding any frills."

"She had, indeed," agreed Dalgliesh. "There isn't any reasonable doubt that Miss Bolam came down to the basement as a result of that call which fixes the approximate time of death for us very satisfactorily. It ties up with the police surgeon's view, too, but we shall know more about that when we get the result of the P.M. The call could have been genuine, of course. It's possible that someone phoned from the basement, spoke to Miss Bolam somewhere down here, then left her to go back to his or her own room and is now too afraid to admit making the call. As I say, it's possible, but I don't think it's likely."

"If the call was genuine it could have been someone calling her down to look at the mess in the record-room. Those files were certainly chucked about before the murder. Some of them were under the body. It looked to me as if she was struck as she crouched to pick them up."

"That's how it looked to me," said Dalgliesh. "Well, let's press on."

They passed the service lift door without comment and went next into the basement treatment-room at the front of the building. Here Nurse Bolam had sat with her patient through the early hours of the evening. Dalgliesh switched on the lights. The heavy curtains had been drawn back but the windows were hung with thin net, presumably to give privacy during the day. The room was simply furnished. There was a low stretcher bed in one corner with a hospital screen at its foot and a small armchair at its head. Against the front wall was a small table and chair, apparently for the use of the nurse in attendance.

The table held a rack of nursing report forms and blank medical record sheets. The left-hand wall was lined with cupboards where the clinic's clean linen was stored. Some attempt had been made to soundproof the fourth wall. It had been lined with acoustic panels and the door, strong and well built, was hung with a heavy curtain.

Dalgliesh said:

"If her patient were noisy I doubt whether Nurse Bolam would hear much that went on outside. Walk down the passage will you, Martin, and make a call on the telephone, the one just outside the medical record-room."

Martin closed the door behind him and Dalgliesh was alone with the heavy silence. His hearing was acute and Martin's heavy tread was just audible. He doubted whether he would have heard it against the noise of a distressed patient. He could not hear the faint ring as Martin took off the receiver nor the swing of the dial. In a few seconds he heard the footsteps again and Martin was back. He said:

"There's a card giving the internal numbers so I rang 004. That's Miss Bolam's room. Funny how eerie a telephone bell sounds when there's no one to answer. Then someone did. It gave me quite a shock when the ringing stopped. It was Mr. Lauder, of course. He sounded a bit surprised, too. I told him we wouldn't be long now."

"Nor shall we. I couldn't hear you, by the way. And yet Nurse Bolam did hear the Priddy child scream. Or so she says."

"She took her time doing anything about it, didn't she, sir? What's more she apparently heard the doctors and Sister when they came down."

"That's reasonable enough. There were four of them clattering about. She's the obvious suspect, of course. She could have telephoned her cousin from this room, saying perhaps that someone had been creating chaos in the record-room. Her patient would be far too disorientated to hear or understand. I saw her with Dr. Baguley and it was obvious that she wasn't capable of giving anyone an alibi. Nurse Bolam could have left that treatment-room and waited for her cousin in the record-room with a fair degree of safety. She had the best opportunity to kill, she has the necessary medical knowledge, she has an obvious motive. If she is the murderer the crime probably had nothing to do with the phone call to Lauder. We shall have to find out what Bolam did think was going on here, but it needn't necessarily have anything to do with her death. If Nurse Bolam knew that the group secretary was coming she might have decided to kill now with the idea of obscuring the real motive."

"She doesn't strike me as clever enough for that kind of planning, sir."

"She doesn't strike me as a murderer, Martin, but we've known less likely ones. If she is innocent then her being down here alone was very convenient for the murderer. Then there are those rubber gloves. Of course, she had an explanation for them. There are plenty of pairs about and it's perfectly reasonable for a member of the nursing staff to have a used pair in her apron pocket. But the fact remains that we haven't found any dabs on either of the weapons nor on the door key, not even old prints. Someone wiped them first and handled them with gloves. And what more suitable than thin surgical gloves. Driving that chisel in was practically a surgical operation."

"If she had the sense to use the gloves, then she'd have the sense to destroy them afterwards. The boiler was alight. What about that missing rubber apron from the art department? If the killer used that as possible protection and disposed of it in the boiler, it would be daft to hang on to the gloves."

"So daft that we're probably meant to think that no sane person would do it. I'm not sure about that apron, anyway. Apparently there's one missing and it's possible that the killer wore it. But this was a clean death and it was planned that way. Anyway, we'll know tomorrow when the boiler's cold and can be raked out. Those aprons have metal studs on the shoulder straps and, with luck, we might find them."

They closed the treatment door behind them and went upstairs. Dalgliesh began to be conscious of his tiredness and the stabbing pain behind his eye was now almost continuous. It had not been an easy week and the sherry party, which promised an agreeably relaxing finish to a busy day, had proved an unsettling preliminary to an even busier night. He wondered briefly where Deborah Riscoe had dined, and with whom. Their meeting now seemed part of a different world. Perhaps because he was tired he felt none of the confidence with which he usually began a case. He did not seriously believe that the crime would defeat him. Professionally he had never yet known the taste of failure. It was all the more irritating, therefore, to be visited by this vague sensation of inadequacy and unrest. For the first time he felt unsure of his own mastery, as if he were opposed by an intelligence actively working against him and equal to his own. And he did not think that Nurse Bolam had that intelligence.

The group secretary and Nagle were still waiting in the hall. Dalgliesh handed over the clinic keys and was promised that an additional set, now held at group headquarters, would be delivered to the police next day. Martin and he, with the two constables, waited while Nagle checked that all lights were out. Soon the whole clinic was in darkness and the six men stepped into the foggy chill of the October night and went their separate ways.

Chapter Four

Dr. Baguley knew that he couldn't in decency neglect to offer Miss Kettle a lift home. She lived in Richmond and her house was directly on the route to his Surrey village. Usually he managed to avoid her and her attendance at the clinic was so erratic that they seldom left at the same time and he could usually drive alone without compunction. He enjoyed driving. Even the frustrations of getting through the city in the rush hour were a small price to pay for those few miles of straight road before he reached home when he could feel the power of the car like a physical thrust in his back and the tensions of the day were ripped from him in the singing air. Just before he reached Stalling it was his custom to stop at a quiet pub for a pint of beer. He never drank more nor less. This nightly ritual, the formal division of day from night, had become necessary to him since he had lost Fredrica. The night brought no relief from the strain of coping with neurosis. He was accustoming himself to a life in which the greatest demands on his patience and professional skill were made in his own home. But it was good to sit alone and in peace, savouring the brief interlude between two different but essentially similar worlds.

He drove slowly at first since Miss Kettle was known to dislike speed. She sat beside him, close-wrapped in a heavy tweed coat, her grey cropped head incongruously crowned with a knitted red cap. Like many professional social workers she had little instinctive understanding of people, a lack which had gained her an undeserved reputation for insensitivity. It was, of course, different if they were her clients—and how Baguley hated that word! Once they were securely caged behind the bars of a professional relationship she gave them a dedicated and meticulous attention which left few of their privacies intact. They were understood whether they liked it or not, their weaknesses exposed and condoned, their efforts applauded and encouraged, their sins forgiven. Apart from her clients the rest of the Steen Clinic hardly existed for Miss Kettle. Baguley did not dislike her. He had long come to the melancholy conclusion that psychiatric social work held a strong attraction for those least suited to it, and Miss Kettle was better than most. The reports she provided for him were over-long and spattered with the peculiar jargon of the job, but at least she provided them. The Steen Clinic had its share of those P.S.W.s who, driven by their irresistible urge to treat patients, were restless until they had trained as lay psychotherapists and left behind such lesser excitements as the writing of social reports and the arranging of recuperative holidays. No, he did not dislike Ruth Kettle, but tonight, of all nights, he would have been happier to drive alone.

She did not speak until they had reached Knightsbridge, then her high breathy voice fluted in his ear.

"Such a very complicated murder, wasn't it? And so oddly timed. What did you think of the superintendent?"

"He's efficient, I suppose," replied Dr. Baguley. "My attitude to him is a little ambivalent, probably because I haven't an alibi. I was alone in the medical staff cloakroom when Miss Bolam is thought to have died."

He knew that he was hoping for reassurance, expecting to hear her eager protestations that, naturally, no one could think of suspecting him. Despising himself he added quickly:

"It's a nuisance, of course, but not important. I expect he'll clear the matter up pretty quickly."

"Oh, do you think so? I wonder. I thought he seemed rather puzzled by the whole thing. I was alone in my room most of the evening so I probably haven't an alibi either. But then I don't know when she's supposed to have died."

"Probably at about six-twenty," said Baguley briefly.

"Is that so? Then I most certainly haven't an alibi." Miss Kettle spoke with the liveliest satisfaction. After a moment she said: "I shall be able to arrange a country holiday from Free Money for the Worrikers now. Miss Bolam was always so difficult about spending Free Money on patients. Dr. Steiner and I feel that if the Worrikers can have a quiet fortnight together in some pleasant country hotel they may be able to sort things out. It may save the marriage."

Dr. Baguley was tempted to say that the Worriker marriage had been in jeopardy for so many years that its salvation or otherwise was hardly likely to be settled in a fortnight, however pleasant the hotel. Being precariously married was the Worrikers' main emotional preoccupation and one they were unlikely to relinquish without a struggle. He asked:

"Isn't Mr. Worriker in work then?"

"Oh, yes! He's in work," replied Miss Kettle, as if that fact could have no relevance to his ability to pay for a holiday. "But his wife is a poor manager, I'm afraid, although she does her best. They can't really afford to go away unless the clinic pays. Miss Bolam wasn't very sympathetic, I'm sorry to say. There was another matter, too. She would make appointments for me to see patients without telling me. It happened today. When I looked at my diary just before I left there was a new patient booked for ten on Monday. Mrs. Bostock had written it in, of course, but she added 'on Miss Bolam's instructions'. Mrs. Bostock would never do a thing like that herself. She's a very pleasant and efficient secretary."

Dr. Baguley thought that Mrs. Bostock was an ambitious trouble-maker, but saw no point in saying so. Instead, he asked how Miss Kettle had got on during her interview with Dalgliesh.

"I wasn't able to help him very much, I'm afraid, but he was interested to hear about the lift."

"What about the lift, Miss Kettle?"

"Someone was using it this evening. You know how it creaks when someone's using it and then bangs when it reaches the second floor? Well, I heard it bang. I don't know exactly when, of course, as it didn't seem important at the time. It wasn't very early in the evening. I suppose it could have been at about six-thirty."

"Surely Dalgliesh isn't seriously thinking that someone used the lift to get down to the basement. It's large enough, of course, but it would need two people."

"Yes, it would, wouldn't it? No one could hoist himself up in it. It would need an accomplice." She spoke the word conspiratorially as if it were part of some criminal patois, a naughty expression which she was daring to use. She went on: "I can't imagine dear Dr. Etherege squatting in the lift like a plump little Buddha while Mrs. Bostock heaved on the ropes with her strong red hands, can you?"

"No," said Dr. Baguley curtly. The description had been unexpectedly vivid. To change the image he said:

"It would be interesting to know who was last in the medical record-room. Before the murder, I mean. I can't remember when I last used the place."

"Oh, can't you! How strange! It's such a dusty claustrophobic room that I can always remember when I have to go down there. I was there at a quarter to six this evening."

Dr. Baguley nearly stopped the car in his surprise.

"At five-forty-five this evening? But that was only thirty-five minutes before the time of death!"

"Yes, it must have been, mustn't it, if she died at about six-twenty? The superintendent didn't tell me that. But he was interested to hear that I'd been in the basement. I fetched one of the old Worriker records. It must have been about five-forty-five when I went down and I didn't stay; I knew just where the record was."

"And the room was as usual? The records weren't chucked on the floor?"

"Oh, no, everything was perfectly tidy. The room was locked, of course, so I got the key from the porters' rest-room and locked the room again when I'd finished. I put the key back on the board."

"And you didn't see anyone?"

"No, I don't think so. I could hear your LSD patient, though. She seemed very noisy, I thought. Almost as if she were alone."

"She wasn't alone. She never is. As a matter of fact I was with her myself up to about five-forty. If you'd been a few minutes earlier we should have seen each other."

"Only if we'd happened to pass on the basement stairs or if you'd come into the record-room. But I don't think I saw anyone. The superintendent kept asking me. I wonder if he's a capable man. He seemed very puzzled by the whole thing, I thought."

They did not speak again about the murder although, to Dr. Baguley, the air of the car was heavy with unspoken questions. Twenty minutes later he drew up outside Miss Kettle's flat off Richmond Green and leaned over to open the car door for her with a sense of relief. As soon as she had disappeared from view he got out of the car and, in defiance of the chilly dampness, opened the roof. The next few miles fled in a gold thread of winking cats'-eyes marking the crown of the road, a rush of cold autumnal air. Outside Stalling he turned from the main road to where the dark, uninviting little pub was set well back among its surrounding elms. The bright boys of Stalling Coombe had never discovered it or had rejected it in favour of the smart pubs edging the green belt; their Jaguars were never seen parked against its black brick walls. The saloon bar was empty as usual, but there was a murmur of voices across the wooden partition which separated it from the public bar. He took his seat by the fire which burned summer and winter, evidently stoked with malodorous chunks of the publican's old furniture. It was not a welcoming room. The chimney smoked in an east wind, the stone floor was bare and the wooden benches lining the walls were too hard and narrow for comfort. But the beer was cold and good, the glasses clean, and there was a kind of peace about the place bred out of its bareness and the solitude.

George brought over his pint.

"You're late this evening, Doctor."

George had called him that since his second visit. Dr. Baguley neither knew nor cared how George had discovered what his job was.

"Yes," he replied. "I was kept late at the clinic."

He said no more and the man went back to his bar. Then he wondered whether he had been wise. It would be in all the papers tomorrow. They would probably be talking about it in the public bar. It would be natural for George to say:

"The doctor was in as usual on Friday. He didn't say anything about the murder. . . . Looked upset, though."

Was it suspicious to say nothing? Wasn't it more natural for an innocent man to want to talk about a murder case in which he was involved? Suddenly the little room became unbearably stuffy, the peace dissolved in an uprush of anxiety and pain. He had got to tell Helen somehow, and the sooner she knew the better.

But although he drove fast it was well after ten before he reached home and saw through the tall beech hedge, the light in Helen's bedroom. So she had gone up without waiting for him; that was always a bad sign. Garaging the car he braced himself for whatever lay ahead. Stalling Coombe was very quiet. It was a small private estate of architect-designed houses, built in the traditional manner, and set each in a spacious garden. It had little contact with the neighbouring village of Stalling and was, indeed, an oasis of prosperous suburbia whose inhabitants, bound by ties of common prejudices and snobberies, lived like exiles determinedly preserving the decencies of civilization in the midst of an alien culture. Baguley had bought his house fifteen years ago, soon after his marriage. He had disliked the place then and the past years had taught him the folly of disregarding first impressions. But Helen had liked it; and Helen had been pregnant then so that there was an additional reason for trying to make her happy. To Helen the house, spacious mock Tudor, had promised much. There was the huge oak in the front lawn ("just the place for the pram on hot days"), the wide entrance hall ("the children will love it for parties later on"), the quiet of the estate ("so peaceful for you, darling, after London and all those dreadful patients").

But the pregnancy had ended in a miscarriage and there had

never again been the hope of children. Would it have made any difference if there had? Would the house have been any less an expensive repository of lost hopes? Sitting quietly in the car and watching that ominous square of lighted window, Dr. Baguley reflected that all unhappy marriages were fundamentally alike. He and Helen were no different from the Worrikers. They stayed together because they expected to be less miserable together than apart. If the strain and miseries of marriage became greater than the expense, the inconvenience and the trauma of a legal separation, then they would part. No sane person continued to endure the intolerable. For him there had been only one valid and overriding need for a divorce, his hope of marrying Fredrica Saxon. Now that the hope was over for ever he might as well continue to endure a marriage which, for all its strain, at least gave him the comfortable illusion of being needed. He despised his private image, the stock predicament of the psychiatrist unable to manage his own personal relationships. But at least something remained from the marriage; a fugitive surge of tenderness and pity which for most of the time enabled him to be kind.

He locked the garage gates and crossed the wide lawn to the front door. The garden was looking unkempt. It was expensive to maintain and Helen took little interest in it. It would be better in every way if they sold and bought a smaller place. But Helen wouldn't talk of selling. She was as happy at Stalling Coombe as she could hope to be anywhere. Its narrow and undemanding social life gave her at least a semblance of security. This cocktail-and-*canapé* existence, the bright chatter of its smart, lean, acquisitive women, the gossip over the iniquities of foreign maids and *au pair* girls, the lamentations over school fees and school reports and the boorish ingratitude of the young, were preoccupations which she could sympathize with or share. Baguley had long known with pain that it was in her relationship with him that she was least at home.

He wondered how he could best break the news of Miss Bolam's murder. Helen had only met her once, that Wednesday at the clinic, and he had never learned what they had said to each other. But that brief, catalytic encounter had established some kind of intimacy between them. Or was it perhaps an offensive alliance directed against himself? But not on Bolam's part, surely? Her attitude to him had never altered. He could even believe that she approved of him more than of most psychiatrists. He had always found her co-operative, helpful and correct. It was without malice, without vindictiveness, without even disliking him particularly, that she had called Helen into her office that Wednesday afternoon and, in half an hour's conversation, destroyed the greatest happiness he had ever known. It was then that Helen appeared at the top of the stairs.

"Is that you, James?" she called.

For fifteen years he had been greeted every night with that unnecessary question.

"Yes. I'm sorry I'm late. I'm sorry, too, that I couldn't tell you more on the phone. But something pretty dreadful has happened at the Steen and Etherege thought it better to say as little as possible. Enid Bolam has been killed."

But her mind had seized on the medical director's name.

"Henry Etherege! He would, of course. He lives in Harley Street with an adequate staff and about twice our income. He might consider me a little before keeping you at the clinic until this hour. His wife isn't stuck in the country alone until he chooses to come home."

"It wasn't Henry's fault that I was kept. I told you. Enid Bolam's been killed. We've had the police at the clinic most of the evening."

This time she heard. He sensed her sharp intake of breath, saw her eyes narrow as she came down the stairs to him, clutching her dressing-gown around her.

"Miss Bolam killed?"

"Yes, murdered."

She stood motionless, seeming to consider, then asked calmly:

"How?"

As he told her she still didn't speak. Afterwards they stood facing each other. He wondered uneasily whether he ought to go to her, to make some gesture of comfort or sympathy. But why sympathy? What, after all, had Helen lost? When she spoke her voice was as cold as metal.

"You none of you liked her, did you? Not one of you!"

"That's ridiculous, Helen! Most of us hardly came into touch with her except briefly and in her capacity as A.O."

"It looks like an inside job, doesn't it?"

He winced at the crude, police-court jargon, but said curtly:

"On the face of it, yes. I don't know what the police think."

She laughed bitterly.

"Oh, I can guess what the police think!"

Again she stood silent, then suddenly asked:

"Where were you?"

"I told you. In the medical staff cloakroom."

"And Fredrica Saxon?"

It was hopeless now to wait for that spring of pity or tenderness. It was useless, even, to try to keep control. He said with a deadly calm:

"She was in her room, scoring a Rorschach. If it's any satisfaction to you, neither of us had an alibi. But if you're hoping to pin this murder on Fredrica or me you'll need more intelligence than I give you credit for. The superintendent's hardly likely to listen to a neurotic woman, acting out of spite. He's seen too many of that type. But make an effort! You might be lucky! Why not come and examine my clothes for blood?"

He threw out his hands towards her, his whole body shaking with anger. Terrified, she gave him one glance, then turned and stumbled up the stairs, tripping over her dressing-gown and crying like a child. He gazed after her, his body cold from tiredness, hunger and self-disgust. He must go to her. Somehow it must be put right. But not now, not at once. First, he must find a drink. He leaned for a moment against the banister and said with infinite tiredness:

"Oh, Fredrica. Darling Fredrica. Why did you do it? Why? Why?"

Sister Ambrose lived with an elderly nurse friend who had trained with her thirty-five years ago and who had recently retired. Together they had bought a house in Gidea Park where they had lived together for the last twenty years on their joint income, in comfort and happy accord. Neither of them had married and neither of them regretted it. In the past they had sometimes wished for children, but observation of the family life of their relations had convinced them that marriage, despite a common belief to the contrary, was designed to benefit men at the expense of women, and that even motherhood was not an unmixed blessing. Admittedly this conviction had never been put to the test since neither of them had ever received a proposal. Like any professional worker in a psychiatric clinic, Sister Ambrose was aware of the dangers of sexual repression, but it had never once occurred to her that these might apply to herself and, indeed, it would be difficult to imagine anyone less repressed. It is possible that she would have dismissed most of the psychiatrists' theories as dangerous nonsense if she had ever considered them critically. But Sister Ambrose had been trained to think of consultants as only one degree lower than God. Like God they moved in mysterious ways their wonders to perform but, like God, they were not subject to open criticism. Some, admittedly, were more mysterious in their ways than others, but it was still the privilege of a nurse to minister to these lesser deities, to encourage the patients to have confidence in their treatment, especially when its success appeared most doubtful, and to practise the cardinal professional virtue of complete loyalty.

"I've always been loyal to the doctors," was a remark frequently heard at Acacia Road, Gidea Park. Sister Ambrose often noted that the young nurses who occasionally worked at the Steen as holiday reliefs were trained in a less accommodating tradition, but she had a poor opinion of most young nurses, and an even poorer opinion of modern training.

As usual she took the Central Line to Liverpool Street, changed to an electric train on the eastern suburban line, and twenty minutes later was letting herself into the neat semi-detached house which she shared with Miss Beatrice Sharpe. Tonight, however, she fitted her key in the lock without her customary inspection of the front garden, without running a critical eye over the paintwork on the door, and even without reflecting as was her custom on the generally satisfactory appearance of the property and on the gratifying capital investment that its purchase had proved to be.

"Is that you, Dot?" called Miss Sharpe from the kitchen. "You're late."

"It's a wonder I'm not later. We've had murder at the clinic and the police have been with us for most of the evening. As far as I know they're still there. I've had my fingerprints taken and so have the rest of the staff."

Sister Ambrose deliberately kept her voice level but the effect of the news was gratifying. She had expected no less. It is not every day one has such excitement to relate and she had spent some time in the train rehearsing how most effectively to break the news. The selected sentence expressed concisely the salient details. Supper was temporarily forgotten. Murmuring that a casserole could always wait, Miss Sharpe poured her friend and herself a glass of sherry, specific against shock, and settled down with it in the sitting-room to hear the full story. Sister Ambrose, who had a reputation at the clinic for discretion and taciturnity, was a great deal more forthcoming at home, and it wasn't long before Miss Sharpe knew as much about the murder as her friend was able to tell.

"But who do you think did it, Dot?" Miss Sharpe refilled their glasses—an unprecedented extravagance—and applied her mind to analysis.

"As I see it the murder must have been done between six-twenty when you saw Miss Bolam going towards the basement stairs and seven o'clock when the body was discovered."

"Well, that's obvious! That's why the superintendent kept asking me whether I was sure about the time. I was the last person to see her alive, there's no doubt about that. Mrs. Belling had finished treatment and was ready to go home at about six-fifteen and I went across to the waiting-room to let her husband know. He's always fussed about time because he's on night duty and has to be fed and at work by eight. So I looked at my watch and saw that it was just six-twenty. As I came out of the E.C.T. room door Miss Bolam passed me and went towards the basement stairs. The superintendent asked me what she looked like and whether we spoke. Well, we didn't and, as far as I could see, she looked the same as usual."

"What's he like?" asked Miss Sharpe, visions of Maigret and Inspector Barlow crowding her mind.

"The superintendent? Perfectly polite, I must say. One of those lean, bony faces. Very dark. I didn't say a great deal. You could see he's used to smarming things out of people. Mrs. Shorthouse was with him for hours and I bet he got plenty out of her. Well, I wasn't playing that game. I've always been loyal to the clinic."

"All the same, Dot, it is murder."

"That's all very fine, Bea, but you know what the Steen is. There's enough gossip without adding to it. None of the doctors liked her and nor did anyone else as far as I know. But that's no reason for killing her. Anyway, I kept my mouth shut and if the others have any sense they'll do the same."

"Well, you're all right, anyway. You've got an alibi if you and Dr. Ingram were together in the E.T.C. room all the time."

"Oh, we're all right. So are Shorthouse and Cully and Nagle and Miss Priddy. Nagle was out with the post after six-fifteen and the others were together. I'm not sure about the doctors, though, and it's a pity that Dr. Baguley left the E.C.T. room after the Belling treatment. Mind you, no one in their senses could suspect him, but it's unfortunate all the same. While we were waiting for the police, Dr. Ingram came over to suggest that we ought not to say anything about it. A nice mess we'd get Dr. Baguley into with that kind of hanky-panky! I pretended not to understand. I just gave her one of my looks and said: 'I'm sure that if we all tell the truth, Doctor, the innocent will have nothing to fear.' That shut her up all right. And that's what I did. I told the truth. But I wasn't going any further. If the police want gossip they can go to Mrs. Shorthouse."

"What about Nurse Bolam?" inquired Miss Sharpe.

"It's Bolam I'm worried about. She was on the spot all right and you can't say an LSD patient is an alibi for anyone. The superintendent was on to her quick enough. He tried to pump me. Were she and her cousin friendly? No doubt they worked at the Steen to be together? You can tell that to the Marines, I thought, but I kept my mouth shut. He didn't get much change out of me. But you could see which way his mind was working. You can't wonder, really. We all know Miss Bolam had money and if she hasn't willed it to a cats' home it will go to her cousin. There's no one else to leave it to after all."

"I can't see her leaving it to a cats' home," said Miss Sharpe, who had a literal mind.

"I didn't mean that exactly. As a matter of fact she never took much notice of Tigger although he's supposed to be her cat. I always thought that was typical of Miss Bolam. She found Tigger practically starving in the square and took him into the clinic. Ever since then she's bought three tins of cat meat for him every week. But she never petted him or fed him or let him into any of the upstairs rooms. On the other hand, that fool Priddy is always down in the porters' room with Nagle making a fuss of Tigger, but I've never seen either of them bringing in food for him. I think Miss Bolam just bought the food out of a sense of duty. She didn't really care for animals. But she might leave her money to that church she's so keen on, or to the Guides, for that matter."

"You'd think she'd leave it to her own flesh and blood," said Miss Sharpe. She herself had a poor opinion of her own flesh and blood, and found much to criticize in the conduct of her nephews and nieces, but her small and slowly accumulated capital had been carefully willed between them. It was beyond her understanding that money should be left out of the family.

They sipped their sherry in silence. The two bars of the electric fire glowed and the synthetic coals shone and flickered as the little light behind them revolved. Sister Ambrose looked around at the sitting-room and found it good. The standard lamp threw a soft light on the fitted carpet and the comfortable sofa and chairs. In the corner a television set stood, its small twin aerials disguised as two flowers on their stems. The telephone nestled beneath the crinolined skirt of a plastic doll. On the opposite wall, above the piano, hung a cane basket from which an indoor plant, cascading streamers of green, almost concealed the wedding group of Miss Sharpe's eldest niece which had pride of place on the piano. Sister Ambrose took comfort from the unchanged homeliness of these familiar things. They at least were the same. Now that the excitement of telling her news was over she felt very tired. Planting her stout legs apart she bent to loosen the laces of her regulation black shoes, grunting a little with the effort. Usually she changed out of uniform as soon as she got home. Tonight she couldn't be bothered. Suddenly she said:

"It isn't easy to know what to do for the best. The superintendent said that anything, however small, might be important. That's all very well. But suppose it's important in the wrong way? Suppose it gives the police the wrong ideas?"

Miss Sharpe was not imaginative nor sensitive, but she had not lived in the same house as her friend for twenty years without recognizing a plea for help.

"You'd better tell me what you have in mind, Dot."

"Well, it happened on Wednesday. You know what the ladies' cloakroom is like at the Steen? There's the large outside room with the wash-basin and the lockers and two lavatories. The clinic was rather later than usual. I suppose it was well after seven when I went to wash. Well, I was in the lavatory when Miss Bolam came into the outer room. Nurse Bolam was with her. I thought they'd both gone home, but I suppose Miss Bolam must have wanted something from her locker and Nurse just followed her in. They must have been in the A.O.'s office together because they'd obviously been talking and were just carrying on with the argument. I couldn't help hearing. You know how it is. I could have coughed or flushed the pan, I suppose, to show I was there but, by the time I thought of it, it was too late."

"What were they arguing about?" inquired her friend. "Money?"

In her experience this was the most frequent cause of family dissension.

"Well, that's what it sounded like. They weren't talking loudly and I certainly didn't try to hear. I think they must have been having words about Nurse Bolam's mother—she's a D.S., you know, and more or less confined to bed now—because Miss Bolam said she was sorry, but she was doing as much as she could and that it would be wiser if Marion accepted the situation and placed her mother's name on a waiting list for a hospital bed."

"That's reasonable enough. You can't nurse these cases at home indefinitely. Not without giving up outside work and staying at home all the time."

"I don't suppose Marion Bolam could afford that. Anyway, she started arguing and saying that her mother would only end up in a geriatric ward with a lot of senile old women and Enid had a duty to help them because that's what her mother would have wanted. Then she said something about the money coming to her if Enid died and how much better to have some now when it would make such a difference to them."

"What did Miss Bolam reply to that?"

"That's what's worrying me," said Sister Ambrose. "I can't remember the actual words, but what it amounted to was that Marion shouldn't rely on getting any of the money because she was going to change her will. She said that she meant to tell her cousin quite openly as soon as she had really made up her mind. She talked about what a great responsibility the money was and how she had been praying for guidance to do the right thing."

Miss Sharpe sniffed. She found it impossible to believe that the Almighty would ever counsel leaving cash away from the family. Miss Bolam was either an ineffectual petitioner or had wilfully misinterpreted the divine instructions. Miss Sharpe was not even sure that she approved of the praying. There are some things, surely, which one ought to be able to decide on one's own. But she saw her friend's difficulty.

"It would look bad if it came out," she admitted. "No doubt about that."

"I think I know Bolam pretty well, Bea, and that child wouldn't lay hands on a fly. The idea of her murdering anyone is ridiculous. You know what I think about young nurses generally. Well, I wouldn't mind Bolam taking over when I retire next year and that's saying something. I'd trust her completely."

"Maybe, but the police wouldn't. Why should they? She's probably their first suspect already. She was on the spot; she hasn't an alibi; she has medical knowledge and would know where the skull is most vulnerable; and where to put that chisel in. She was told that Tippett wouldn't be in the clinic. And now this!"

"And it's not as if it's a small sum." Sister Ambrose leaned forward and dropped her voice. "I thought I heard Miss Bolam mention thirty thousand pounds. Thirty thousand, Bea! It would be like winning the pools!"

Miss Sharpe was impressed despite herself, but remarked merely that people who went on working when they had thirty thousand wanted their brains examined.

"What would you do, Bea? Do you think I ought to say anything?"

Sister Ambrose, sturdily independent and used to settling her own affairs, recognized that this decision was beyond her and threw half the burden on her friend. Both of them knew that the moment was unique. Never had two friends made fewer demands on each other. Miss Sharpe sat in silence for a moment or two, then said:

"No. Not yet, anyway. After all she is your colleague and you trust her. It wasn't your fault that you overheard the conversation, but it was only overhearing. It was only chance that you happened to be in the loo. I should try to forget it. The police will find out how Bolam has left her money anyway and whether the will has been changed. Either way Nurse Bolam will be suspected. And if it should come to a trial—I'm only saying 'if', remember—well, you don't want to get involved unnecessarily. Remember those nurses in the Eastbourne case, the hours they spent in the box. You wouldn't want that kind of publicity."

Indeed she wouldn't, thought Sister Ambrose. Her imagination set the scene only too vividly. Sir Somebody or Other would be prosecuting, tall, beak-nosed, bending his terrifying gaze on her, thumbs hooked in the bands of his gown.

"And now, Sister Ambrose, perhaps you will tell his Lordship and the jury what you were doing when you overheard this conversation between the accused and her cousin."

Titters in court. The judge, terrifying in scarlet and white wig, leans down from his seat.

"If there is any more of this laughter I shall clear the court."

Silence. Sir Somebody on the ball again.

"Well, Sister Ambrose . . .?"

No, she certainly wouldn't want that kind of publicity.

"I think you're right, Bea," she said. "After all, it's not as if the superintendent actually asked me whether I'd ever overheard them quarrelling." Certainly he hadn't and, with luck, he never would.

Miss Sharpe felt that it was time to change the subject.

"How did Dr. Steiner take it?" she asked. "You always said that he was working to get Bolam moved to another unit."

"That's another extraordinary thing! He was terribly upset. You know I told you that he was with us when we first saw the body? D'you know he could hardly control himself? He had to turn his back on us and I could see his shoulders shaking. He was actually crying, I think. I've never seen him so upset. Aren't people extraordinary, Bea?"

It was a vehement cry of resentment and protest. People were extraordinary! You thought you knew them. You worked with them, sometimes for years. You spent more time with them than you would with family or close friends. You knew every line of their faces. And all the time they were private. As private as Dr. Steiner who cried over the dead body of a woman he had never liked. As private as Dr. Baguley who had been having a love affair with Fredrica Saxon for years with no one knowing until Miss Bolam found out and told his wife. As private as Miss Bolam who had taken God knows what secrets to the grave. Miss Bolam, dull, ordinary, unremarkable Enid Bolam, who had inspired so much hate in someone that she had ended with a chisel in her heart. As private as that unknown member of the staff who would be at the clinic on Monday morning, dressed as usual, looking the same as usual, speaking and smiling as usual and who was a murderer.

"Damned smiling villain!" said Sister Ambrose suddenly. She thought that the phrase was a quotation from some play or other. Shakespeare probably. Most quotations were. But its terse malevolence suited her mood.

"What you need is food," said Miss Sharpe positively. "Something light and nourishing. Suppose we leave the casserole until tomorrow night and just have boiled eggs on a tray?"

She was waiting for him at the entrance to St. James's Park just as he had expected her to be. As he crossed the Mall and saw the slight figure drooping a little disconsolately by the war memorial Nagle could almost feel sorry for her. It was the hell of a raw night to be standing about. But her first words killed any impulse to pity.

"We should have met somewhere else. This is all right for you, of course. You're on the way home."

She sounded as peevish as a neglected wife.

"Come back to the flat, then," he taunted her softly. "We can get a bus down."

"No. Not the flat. Not tonight."

He smiled into the darkness and they moved together into the black shadow of the trees. They walked a little way apart and she made no move towards him. He glanced down at the calm, uplifted profile cleansed now of all traces of crying. She looked desperately tired. Suddenly she said:

"That superintendent is very good-looking, isn't he? Do you think he suspects us?"

So here it was, the grasping at reassurance, the childish need to be protected. And yet she had sounded almost uncaring. He said roughly:

"For God's sake why should he? I was out of the clinic when she died. You know that as well as I do."

"But I wasn't. I was there."

"No one's going to suspect you for long. The doctors will see to that. We've had all this out before. Nothing can go wrong if you keep your head and listen to me. Now this is what I want you to do."

She listened as meekly as a child but watching that tired, expressionless face he felt that he was in the company of a stranger. He wondered idly whether they would ever get free of each other again. And suddenly he felt that it was not she who was the victim.

As they came to the lake she stopped and gazed out over the water. Out of the darkness came the subdued cry and shuffle of ducks. He could smell the evening breeze, salt as a sea wind, and shivered. Turning to study her face, ravaged now with fatigue, he saw, in his mind's eye, another picture; a broad brow under a white nurse's cap, a swathe of yellow hair, immense grey eyes which gave nothing away. Tentatively he pondered a new idea. It might come to nothing, of course. It might easily come to nothing. But the picture would soon be finished and he could get rid of Jenny. In a month he would be in Paris, but Paris was only an hour's flight away and he would be coming back often. And with Jenny out of the way and a new life in his grasp it would be worth trying. There were worse fates than marrying the heiress to thirty thousand pounds.

Nurse Bolam let herself into the narrow terraced house at 17 Rettinger Street, N.W.1, and was met by the familiar ground-floor smell compounded of frying fat, furniture polish and stale urine. The twins' pram stood behind the door with its stained under-blanket thrown across the handle. The smell of cooking was less strong than usual. She was very late tonight and the ground-floor tenants must long have finished their evening meal. The wail of one of the babies sounded faintly from the back of the house, almost drowned by the noise of the television. She could hear the National Anthem. The B.B.C. service was closing for the day.

She mounted to the first floor. Here the smell of food was fainter and was masked by the tang of a household disinfectant. The first-floor tenant was addicted to cleanliness as the basement tenant was to drink. There was the usual note on the landing window ledge. Tonight it read: "Do not stand your dirty milk bottles here. This ledge is private. This means you." From behind the brown polished door, even at this late hour, came the roar of a vacuum cleaner in full throttle.

Up now to the third floor, to their own flat. She paused on the bottom step of the last flight and saw, as if with a stranger's eyes, the pathetic attempt she had made to improve the look of the place. The walls here were painted with white emulsion paint. The stairs were covered with a grey drugget. The door was painted a bright citrus yellow and sported a brass knocker in the shape of a frog's head. On the wall, carefully disposed one above the other, were the three flower prints she had picked up in Berwick Street market. Until tonight she had been pleased with the result of her work. It really had given the entrance quite an air. There had been times when she had felt that a visitor, Mrs. Bostock from the clinic, perhaps, or even Sister Ambrose, might safely be invited home for coffee without the need to apologize or explain. But tonight, freed, gloriously freed for ever, from the self-deceit of poverty, she could see the flat for what it was, sordid, dark, airless, smelly and pathetic. Tonight, for the first time, she could safely recognize how much she hated every brick of 17 Rettinger Street.

She trod very softly, still not ready to go in. There was so little time in which to think, in which to plan. She knew exactly what she would see when she opened the door of her mother's room. The bed stood against the window. In summer evenings Mrs. Bolam could lie and watch the sun setting behind a castellation of sloping roofs and twisting chimneys with, in the distance, the turrets of St. Pancras Station darkening against a flaming sky. Tonight the curtains would be drawn. The district nurse would have put her mother to bed, would have left the telephone and portable wireless on the bedside table, together with the handbell which could, if necessary, summon aid from the tenant of the flat below. Her mother's bedside lamp would be lit, a small pool of light in the surrounding gloom. At the other end of the room one bar of the electric fire would be burning, one bar only, the nicely calculated allocation of comfort for an October evening. As soon as she opened the door her mother's eyes would meet her, brightened by pleasure and anticipation. There would be the same intolerably bright greeting, the same minute inquiries about the doings of the day.

"Did you have a good day at the clinic, darling? Why were you late? Did anything happen?"

And how did one answer that?

"Nothing of any importance, Mummy, except that someone has stabbed Cousin Enid through the heart and we're going to be rich after all."

And what did that mean? Dear God, what didn't it mean? No more smell of polish and napkins. No more need to propitiate the second-floor harpy in case she were needed to answer that bell. No more watching the electricity meter and wondering whether it were really cold enough for that extra bar of the fire. No more thanking Cousin Enid for her generous cheque twice a year, the one in December that made such a difference to Christmas, the one late in July that paid for the hired car, the expensive hotel which catered for invalids who could afford to pay for being a nuisance. No longer any need to count the days, to watch the calendar, to wonder whether Enid were going to oblige this year. No need to take the cheque with becoming gratitude to conceal behind lowered eyes the hate and resentment that longed to tear it up and throw it in that smug, plain, condescending face. No need to climb these stairs any more. They could have the house in a suburb which her mother talked about. One of the better-class suburbs, of course, near enough to London for easy travelling to the clinic—it wouldn't be wise to give up the job before she really had to—far enough out for a small garden, perhaps, even for a country view. They might even afford a little car. She could learn to drive. And then, when it was no longer possible for her mother to be left, they could be together. It meant the end of this nagging anxiety about the future. There was no reason now to picture her mother in a chronic sick ward, cared for by overworked strangers, surrounded by the senile and incontinent, waiting hopelessly for the end. And money could buy less vital but not unimportant pleasures. She would get some clothes. It would no longer be necessary to wait for the biennial sales if she wanted a suit with some evidence of quality. It would be possible to dress well, really well, on half the amount Enid had spent on those unattractive skirts and suits. There must be wardrobes full of them in the Kensington flat. Someone would have the job of sorting them out. And who would want them? Who would want anything that had belonged to Cousin Enid? Except her money. Except her money. Except her money. And suppose she had already written to her solicitor about changing the will. Surely that wasn't possible! Nurse Bolam fought down panic and forced herself once again to consider the possibility rationally. She had thought it out so many times before. Suppose Enid had written on Wednesday night. All right, suppose she had. It would be too late to catch the post that evening so the letter would have been received only this morning. Everyone knew how long solicitors took to do anything. Even if Enid had stressed the urgency, had caught the Wednesday post, the new will couldn't possibly be ready for signature yet. And if it were ready, if it were waiting to be posted in its solid official-looking envelope, what did it matter? Cousin Enid wouldn't sign it now with that round, upright, unadult hand which had always seemed so typical of her. Cousin Enid would never sign anything again.

She thought again about the money. Not about her own share. That was hardly likely to bring her happiness now. But, even if they arrested her for murder they couldn't stop Mummy inheriting her share. No one could stop that. But somehow she must get hold of some cash urgently. Everyone knew that a will took months to prove. Would it look very suspicious or heartless if she went to Enid's solicitor to explain how poor they were and to ask what could be arranged? Or would it be wiser to approach the bank? Perhaps the solicitor would send for her. Yes, of course he would. She and her mother were the next of kin. And as soon as the will was read she could tactfully raise the question of an advance. Surely that would be natural enough? An advance of one hundred pounds wouldn't be much to ask by someone who was going to inherit a share of thirty thousand.

Suddenly she could bear it no longer. The long tension broke. She wasn't conscious of covering those last few stairs, of putting her key in the lock. At once she was in the flat and through to her mother's room. Howling with fear and misery, crying as she had not cried since childhood, she hurled herself on her mother's breast and felt around her the comfort and the unexpected strength of those brittle, shaking arms. The arms rocked her like a baby. The beloved voice cooed its reassurance. Under the cheap nightdress she smelt the soft familiar flesh.

"Hush, my darling. My baby. Hush. What is it? What's happened. Tell me, darling."

And Nurse Bolam told her.

Since his divorce two years earlier Dr. Steiner had shared a house in Hampstead with his widowed sister. He had his own sitting-room and kitchen, an arrangement which enabled Rosa and him to see little of each other, thus fostering the illusion that they got on well together. Rosa was a culture snob. Her house was the centre for a collection of resting actors, one-volume poets, aesthetes posing on the fringe of the ballet world, and writers more anxious to talk about their craft in an atmosphere of sympathetic understanding than to practise it. Dr. Steiner did not resent them. He merely ensured that they ate and drank at Rosa's expense, not his. He was aware that his profession had a certain cachet for his sister and that to introduce "my brother Paul—the famous psycho-analyst" was in some measure a compensation for the low rent which he spasmodically paid and the minor irritations of propinquity. He would hardly have been housed so economically and comfortably had he been a bank manager.

Tonight Rosa was out. It was exasperating and inconsiderate of her to be missing on the one evening when he needed her company, but that was typical of Rosa. The German maid was out, too, presumably illicitly, since Friday was not her half-day. There was soup and salad put ready for him in his kitchen, but even the effort of heating the soup seemed beyond him. The sandwiches he had eaten without relish at the clinic had taken away his appetite but left him hungry for protein, preferably hot and properly cooked. But he did not want to eat alone. Pouring himself a glass of sherry he recognized his need to talk to someone—anyone, about the murder. The need was imperative. He thought of Valda.

His marriage to Valda had been doomed from the start, as any marriage must be when husband and wife have a basic ignorance of each other's needs coupled with the illusion that they understand each other perfectly. Dr. Steiner had not been desolated by his divorce, but he had been inconvenienced and distressed, and had been harried afterwards by an irrational sense of failure and guilt. Valda, on the other hand, apparently throve on freedom. When they met he was always struck with her glow of physical well-being. They did not avoid each other, since meeting her ex-husband and discarded lovers with the greatest appearance of friendliness and good humour was what Valda meant when she talked about civilized behaviour. Dr. Steiner did not like or admire her. He liked the company of women who were well-informed, well-educated, intelligent and fundamentally serious. But these were not the kind of women he liked to go to bed with. He knew all about this inconvenient dichotomy. Its causes had occupied many expensive hours with his analyst. Unfortunately, knowing is one thing and changing is another, as some of his patients could have told him. And there had been times with Valda (christened Millicent) when he hadn't really wanted to be different.

The telephone rang for about a minute before she answered and he told her about Miss Bolam against a background noise of music and clinking glasses. The flat was apparently full of people. He wasn't even sure she had heard him.

"What is it?" he asked irritably. "Are you having a party?"

"Just a few chums. Wait while I turn down the gramophone. Now, what did you say?"

Dr. Steiner said it again. This time Valda's reaction was entirely satisfactory.

"Murdered! No! Darling, how too frightful for you! Miss Bolam. Isn't she that dreary old A.O. you hated so much? The one who kept trying to do you down over your travelling claims?"

"I didn't hate her, Valda. In some ways I respected her. She had considerable integrity. Of course, she was rather obsessional, frightened of her own subconscious aggressions, possibly sexually frigid. . . ."

"That's what I said, darling. I knew you couldn't bear her. Oh, Paulie, they won't think you did it, will they?"

"Of course not," said Dr. Steiner, beginning to regret his impulse to confide.

"But you always did say that someone should get rid of her."

The conversation was beginning to have a nightmare quality. The gramophone thudded its insistent bass to the treble cacophony of Valda's party and the pulse in Dr. Steiner's temple beat in unison. He was going to start one of his headaches.

"I meant that she should be transferred to another clinic, not bashed on the head with a blunt instrument."

The hackneyed phrase sharpened her curiosity. Violence had always fascinated her. He knew that she saw in imagination a spatter of blood and brains.

"Darling, I must hear all about it. Why not come over?"

"Well, I was thinking of it," said Dr. Steiner. He added cunningly: "There are one or two details I can't give you over the phone. But if you've got a party it's rather difficult. Frankly, Valda, I'm not capable of being sociable just now. I've got one of my heads starting. This has all been a terrible shock. After all, I did more or less discover the body."

"You poor sweet. Look, give me half an hour and I'll get rid of the chums."

The chums sounded to Dr. Steiner as if they were well entrenched and he said so.

"Not really. We were all going on to Toni's. They can manage without me. I'll give them a shove and you set off in about half an hour. All right?"

It was certainly all right. Replacing the receiver, Dr. Steiner decided that he would just have time to bath and change in comfort. He pondered on a choice of tie. The headache unaccountably seemed to have gone. Just before he left the house the telephone rang. He felt a spasm of apprehension. Perhaps Valda had changed her mind about seeing off the chums and having some time alone together. That, after all, had been a recurring pattern in his marriage. He was irritated to find that the hand reaching for the receiver was not quite steady. But the caller was only Dr. Etherege to say that he was calling an emergency meeting of the clinic Medical Committee for 8 p.m. the following evening. In his relief Dr. Steiner, momentarily forgetting Miss Bolam, just saved himself in time from the folly of asking why.

If Ralfe and Sonia Bostock had lived in Clapham their flat would have been called a basement. Since, however, it was in Hampstead, half a mile in fact from Dr. Steiner's house, a small wooden notice, lettered with impeccable taste, directed one to the garden flat. Here they paid nearly twelve pounds a week for a socially acceptable address and the privilege of seeing a green sloping lawn from the sitting-room window. They had planted this lawn with crocuses and daffodils and in spring those plants which managed to bloom in the almost complete lack of sun, at least fostered the illusion that the flat had access to a garden. In autumn, however, the view was less agreeable and dampness from the sloping soil seeped into the room. The flat was noisy. There was a nursery school two houses away and a young family in the ground-floor flat. Ralfe Bostock, dispensing drinks to their carefully selected friends and raising his voice against the wail of bath-time tantrums, would say:

"Sorry for the row. I'm afraid the intelligensia have taken to breeding but not—alas—to controlling their brats." He was given to malicious remarks, some of which were clever, but he overworked them. His wife lived in constant apprehension that he would make the same witticism twice to the same people. There were few things more fatal to a man's chances than the reputation for repeating his jokes.

Tonight he was out at a political meeting. She approved of the meeting which might be an important one for him and she did not mind being alone. She wanted time to think. She went into the bedroom and took off her suit, shaking it carefully and hanging it in the wardrobe, then put on a housecoat of brown velvet. Next she sat at her dressing-table. Binding a *crêpe* bandage about her brow she began to cream the make-up from her face. She was more tired than she had realized and needed a drink, but nothing would deter her from her evening ritual. There was much to think about, much to plan. The grey-green eyes, ringed with cream, gazed calmly back at her from the glass. Leaning forward she inspected the delicate folds of skin beneath each eye, watching for the first lines of age. She was only twenty-eight after all. There was no need to worry yet. But Ralfe was thirty this year. Time was passing. If they were to achieve anything there was no time to lose.

She considered tactics. The situation would need careful handling and there was no room for mistakes. She had made one already. The temptation to slap Nagle's face had proved irresistible, but it was still a mistake and possibly a bad one, too like vulgar exhibitionism to be safe. Aspiring administrative officers did not slap a porter's face, even when under strain, particularly if they wanted to create an impression of calm, authoritative competence. She remembered the look on Miss Saxon's face. Well, Fredrica Saxon was in no position to be censorious. It was a pity that Dr. Steiner was there, but it had all happened so quickly that she couldn't be sure that he had really seen. The Priddy child was of no importance.

Nagle would have to go, of course, once she was appointed. Here, too, she would have to be careful. He was an insolent devil, but the clinic could do much worse and the consultants knew it. An efficient porter made quite a difference to their comfort, especially when he was willing and able to carry out the many small repair jobs that were needed. It wouldn't be a popular move if they had to wait for someone to come from the group engineer's department every time a sash cord broke or a fuse needed replacing. Nagle would have to go, but she would put out feelers for a good replacement before taking any action.

The main concern at present must be to get the consultants' support for her appointment. She could be sure of Dr. Etherege and his was the most powerful voice. But it wasn't the only one. He would be retiring in six months' time and his influence would be on the wane. If she were offered an acting appointment, and all went well, the Hospital Management Committee might not be in too much of a hurry to advertise the post.

Almost certainly they would wait until the murder was either solved or the police shelved the case. It was up to her to consolidate her position in the intervening months. It wouldn't do to take anything for granted. When there had been trouble at a unit, Committees tended to make an outside appointment. There was safety in bringing in a stranger uncontaminated by the previous upset. The group secretary would be an influence there. It had been a wise move to see him last month and ask his advice about working for the diploma of the Institute of Hospital Administrators. He liked his staff to qualify and, being a man, he was flattered to be asked for advice. But he wasn't a fool. He didn't have to be. She was as suitable a candidate as the H.M.C. were likely to find, and he knew it.

She lay back, relaxed, on her single bed, her feet raised on a pillow, her mind busy with the images of success. "My wife is administrative officer of the Steen Clinic." So much more satisfactory than, "Actually, my wife is working as a secretary at present. The Steen Clinic, as a matter of fact."

And less than two miles away, in a mortuary in north London, Miss Bolam's body, tight-packed as a herring in an ice box, stiffened slowly through the autumn night.

Chapter Five

If there had to be a murder at the Steen, Friday was the most convenient day for it. The clinic did not open on Saturday so that the police were able to work in the building without the complications presented by the presence of patients and staff. The staff, presumably, were glad of two days' grace in which to recover from the shock, determine at leisure what their official reaction should be and seek the comfort and reassurance of their friends.

Dalgliesh's day began early. He had asked for a report from the local C.I.D. about the Steen burglary and this, together with typescripts of the previous day's interviews, was waiting on his desk. The burglary had puzzled the local men. There could be no doubt that someone had broken into the clinic and that the £15 was missing. It was not so certain that these two facts were related. The local sergeant thought it odd that a casual thief had picked the one drawer which held cash while neglecting the safe and leaving untouched the silver inkstand in the medical director's office. On the other hand, Cully had undoubtedly seen a man leaving the clinic and both he and Nagle had alibis for the time of entry. The local C.I.D. were inclined to suspect Nagle of having helped himself to the cash while he was alone in the building, but it had not been found on him and there was no real evidence. Besides, the porter had plenty of opportunities for dishonesty at the Steen if he were so inclined, and nothing was known against him. The whole affair was puzzling. They were still working on it but weren't very hopeful. Dalgliesh asked that any progress should be reported to him at once and set off with Sergeant Martin to examine Miss Bolam's flat.

Miss Bolam had lived on the fifth floor of a solid, red-brick block near Kensington High Street. There was no difficulty over the key. The resident caretaker handed it over with formal and perfunctory expressions of regret at Miss Bolam's death. She seemed to feel that some reference to the murder was necessary, but managed to give the impression that the company's tenants usually had the good taste to quit this life in more orthodox fashion.

"There will be no undesirable publicity, I hope," she murmured, as she escorted Dalgliesh and Sergeant Martin to the lift. "These flats are very select and the company are most particular about their tenants. We have never had trouble of this kind before."

Dalgliesh resisted the temptation to say that Miss Bolam's murderer had obviously not recognized one of the company's tenants.

"The publicity is hardly likely to affect the flats," he pointed out. "It's not as if the murder took place here." The caretaker was heard to murmur that she hoped not indeed!

They ascended to the fifth floor together in the slow, old-fashioned panelled lift. The atmosphere was heavy with disapproval.

"Did you know Miss Bolam at all?" Dalgliesh inquired. "I believe she had lived here for some years."

"I knew her to say good morning to, nothing more. She was a very quiet tenant. But then all our tenants are. She has been in residence for fifteen years, I believe. Her mother was the tenant previously and they lived here together. When Mrs. Bolam died her daughter took over the tenancy. That was before my time."

"Did her mother die here?"

The caretaker closed her lips repressively.

"Mrs. Bolam died in a nursing home in the country. There was some unpleasantness, I believe."

"You mean that she killed herself?"

"I was told so. As I said, it happened before I took this job.

Naturally I never alluded to the fact either to Miss Bolam or to any of the other tenants. It is not the kind of thing one would wish to talk about. They really do seem a most unfortunate family."

"What rent did Miss Bolam pay?"

The caretaker paused before replying. This was obviously high on her list of questions that should not properly be asked. Then, as if reluctantly admitting the authority of the police, she replied:

"Our fourth and fifth floor two-bedroom flats are from £490 excluding rates."

That was about half Miss Bolam's salary, thought Dalgliesh. It was too high a proportion for anyone without private means. He had yet to see the dead woman's solicitor, but it looked as if Nurse Bolam's assessment of her cousin's income was not far wrong.

He dismissed the caretaker at the door of the flat and he and Martin went in together.

This prying among the personal residue of a finished life was a part of his job which Dalgliesh had always found a little distasteful. It was too much like putting the dead at a disadvantage. During his career he had examined with interest and with pity so many petty leavings. The soiled underclothes pushed hurriedly into drawers, personal letters which prudence would have destroyed, half-eaten meals, unpaid bills, old photographs, pictures and books which the dead would not have chosen to represent their taste to a curious or vulgar world, family secrets, stale make-up in greasy jars, the muddle of ill-disciplined or unhappy lives. It was no longer the fashion to dread an unshriven end but most people, if they thought at all, hoped for time to clear away their debris. He remembered from childhood the voice of an old aunt exhorting him to change his vest. "Suppose you got run over, Adam. What would people think?" The question was less absurd than it had seemed to a ten-year-old. Time had taught him that it expressed one of the major preoccupations of mankind, the dread of losing face.

But Enid Bolam might have lived each day as if expecting

sudden death. He had never examined a flat so neat, so obsessively tidy. Even her few cosmetics, the brush and comb on her dressing-table were arranged with patterned precision. The heavy double bed was made. Friday was obviously her day for changing the linen. The used sheets and pillow-cases were folded into a laundry box which lay open on a chair. The bedside table held nothing but a small travelling clock, a carafe of water and a Bible with a booklet beside it appointing the passage to be read each day and expounding the moral. There was nothing in the table drawer but a bottle of aspirin and a folded handkerchief. A hotel room would have held as much individuality.

All the furniture was old and heavy. The ornate mahogany door of the wardrobe swung open soundlessly to reveal a row of tightly packed clothes. They were expensive but unexciting. Miss Bolam had bought from that store which still caters mainly for country-house dowagers. There were well-cut skirts of indeterminate colour, heavy coats tailored to last through a dozen English winters, woollen dresses which could offend no one. Once the wardrobe was closed it was impossible accurately to recall a single garment. At the back of them all, closeted from the light, were bowls of fibre, planted no doubt with bulbs whose Christmas flowering Miss Bolam would never see.

Dalgliesh and Martin had worked together for too many years to find much talking necessary and they moved about the flat almost in silence. Everywhere was the same heavy, old-fashioned furniture, the same ordered neatness. It was hard to believe that these rooms had been recently lived in, that anyone had cooked a meal in this impersonal kitchen. It was very quiet. At this height and muffled by the solid Victorian walls the clamour of traffic in Kensington High Street was a faint, distant throbbing. Only the insistent ticking of a grandfather clock in the hall stabbed the still silence. The air was cold and almost odourless except for the smell of the flowers. They were everywhere. There was a bowl of chrysanthemums on the hall table and another in the sitting-room. The bedroom mantelpiece held a small jug of anemones. On the kitchen dresser was a taller brass jug of autumn foliage, the gatherings perhaps of some recent country walk. Dalgliesh did not like autumn flowers, the chrysanthemums which obstinately refuse to die, flaunting their shaggy heads even on a rotting stem, scentless dahlias fit only to be planted in neat rows in municipal parks. His wife had died in October and he had long recognized the minor bereavements which follow the death of the heart. Autumn was no longer a good time of the year. For him the flowers in Miss Bolam's flat emphasized the general air of gloom, like wreaths at a funeral.

The sitting-room was the largest room in the flat and here was Miss Bolam's desk. Martin fingered it appreciatively.

"It's all good solid stuff, sir, isn't it? We've got a piece rather like this. The wife's mother left it to us. Mind you, they don't make furniture like it today. You get nothing for it, of course. Too big for modern rooms, I suppose. But it's got quality."

"You can certainly lean against it without collapsing," said Dalgliesh.

"That's what I mean, sir. Good solid stuff. No wonder she hung on to it. A sensible young woman on the whole, I'd say, and one who knew how to make herself comfortable." He drew a second chair up to the desk where Dalgliesh was already seated, planted his heavy thighs in it, and did indeed look comfortable and at home.

The desk was unlocked. The top rolled back without difficulty. Inside was a portable typewriter and a metal box containing files of paper, each file neatly labelled. The drawers and compartments of the desk held writing paper, envelopes, and correspondence. As they expected, everything was in perfect order. They went through the files together. Miss Bolam paid her bills as soon as they were due and kept a running account of all her household expenditure.

There was much to be gone through. Details of her investments were filed under the appropriate heading. At her mother's death the trustee securities had been redeemed and the capital reinvested in equities. The portfolio was skilfully balanced and there could be little doubt that Miss Bolam had been well advised and had increased her assets considerably during the past five years. Dalgliesh noted the name of her stockbroker and solicitor. Both would have to be seen before the investigation was complete.

The dead woman kept few of her personal letters; perhaps there had been few worth keeping. But there was one, filed under P, which was interesting. It was written in a careful hand on cheap lined paper from a Balham address, and read:

Dear Miss Bolam,

These are just a few lines to thank you for all you done for Jenny. It hasn't turned out as we wished and prayed for but we shall know in His good time what His purpose is. I still feel we did right to let them marry. It wasn't only to stop talk as I think you know. He has gone for good, he writes. Her Dad and me didn't know that things had got that bad between them. She doesn't talk much to us but we shall wait patiently and maybe, one day, she will be our girl again. She seems very quiet and won't talk about it so we don't know whether she grieves. I try not to feel bitterness against him. Dad and I think it would be a good idea if you could get Jenny a post in the health service. It is really good of you to offer and be interested after all that's happened. You know what we think about divorce so she must look to her job now for happiness. Dad and I pray every night that she'll find it.

Thanking you again for all your interest and help. If you do manage to get Jenny the post I'm sure she won't let you down. She's learnt her lesson and it's been a bitter one for us all. But His will be done.

Yours respectfully,
EMILY PRIDDY (Mrs.)

It was extraordinary, thought Dalgliesh, that people still lived who could write a letter like that, with its archaic mixture of subservience and self-respect, its unashamed yet curiously poignant emotionalism. The story it told was ordinary enough, but he felt detached from its reality. The letter could have been written fifty years ago; almost he expected to see the paper curling with age and smell the tentative scent of potpourri. It had no relevance, surely, to that pretty, ineffectual child at the Steen.

"It's unlikely to have any importance," he said to Martin. "But I'd like you to go over to Clapham and have a word with these people. We'd better know who the husband is. But, somehow, I don't think he'll prove to be Dr. Etherege's mysterious marauder. The man—or woman—who killed Miss Bolam was still in the building when we arrived. And we've talked to him."

It was then that the telephone rang, sounding ominously strident in the silence of the flat as if it were calling for the dead. Dalgliesh said:

"I'll take it. It will be Dr. Keating with the P.M. report. I asked him to ring me here if he got through with it."

He was back with Martin within two minutes. The report had been brief. Dalgliesh said:

"Nothing surprising. She was a healthy woman. Killed by a stab through the heart after being stunned, which we could see for ourselves, and *virgo intacta* which we had no reason to doubt. What have you got there?"

"It's her photograph album, sir. Pictures of Guide camps mostly. It looks as if she went away with the girls every year."

Probably making that her annual holiday, thought Dalgliesh. He had a respect bordering on simple wonder for those who voluntarily gave up their leisure to other people's children. He was not a man who liked children and he found the company of most of them insupportable after a very brief time. He took the album from Sergeant Martin. The photographs were small and technically unremarkable, taken apparently with a small box camera. But they were carefully disposed on the page, each labelled in neat white printing. There were Guides hiking, Guides cooking on primus stoves, erecting tents, blanket-swathed around the camp-fire, lining up for kit inspection. And in many of the photographs there was the figure of their captain, plump, motherly, smiling. It was difficult to connect this buxom, happy extrovert with that pathetic corpse on the record-room floor—or with the obsessional, authoritative administrator described by the staff of the Steen. The comments under some of the photographs were pathetic in their evocation of happiness remembered:

"The Swallows dish up. Shirley keeps an eye on the spotted dick."

"Valerie 'flies up' from the Brownies."

"The Kingfishers tackle the washing-up. Snap taken by Susan."

"Captain helps the tide in! Taken by Jean."

This last showed Miss Bolam's plump shoulders rising from the surf, surrounded by some half-dozen of her girls. Her hair was down and hanging in flat swaths, wet and dank as seaweed, on either side of her laughing face. Together the two detectives looked at the photograph in silence. Then Dalgliesh said:

"There haven't been many tears shed for her yet, have there? Only her cousin's and they were more shock than grief. I wonder whether the Swallows and the Kingfishers will weep for her."

They closed the album and went back to their search. It disclosed only one further item of interest, but that was very interesting indeed. It was the carbon copy of a letter from Miss Bolam to her solicitor, dated the day before her death, and making an appointment to see him "in connection with the proposed changes to my will which we discussed briefly on the telephone yesterday night."

After the visit to Ballantyne Mansions there followed a hiatus in the investigation, one of those inevitable delays which Dalgliesh had never found it easy to accept. He had always worked at speed. His reputation rested on the pace as well as the success of his cases. He did not ponder too deeply the implications of this compulsive need to get on with the job. It was enough to know that delay irritated him more than it did most men.

This hold up was, perhaps, to be expected. It was hardly likely that a London solicitor would be in his office after midday on Saturday. It was more dispiriting to learn by telephone that Mr. Babcock of Babcock and Honeywell had flown with his wife to Geneva on Friday afternoon to attend the funeral of a friend and would not be back in his City office until the following Tuesday. There was now no Mr. Honeywell in the firm, but Mr. Babcock's chief clerk would be in the office on Monday morning if he could help the superintendent. It was the caretaker speaking. Dalgliesh was not sure how far the chief clerk could help him. He much preferred to see Mr. Babcock. The solicitor was likely to be able to give a great deal of useful information about Miss Bolam's family as well as her financial affairs, but much of it would probably be given with at least a token show of resistance and obtained only by the exercise of tact. It would be folly to jeopardize success by a prior approach to the clerk.

Until the details of the will were available there was little point in seeing Nurse Bolam again. Frustrated in his immediate plans Dalgliesh drove without his sergeant to call on Peter Nagle. He had no clear aim in view but that didn't worry him. The time would be well spent. Some of his most useful work was done in these unplanned, almost casual encounters when he talked, listened, watched, studied a suspect in his own home, or gleaned the thin stalks of unwittingly dropped information about the one personality which is central to any murder investigation—that of the victim.

Nagle lived in Pimlico on the fourth floor of a large, white, stuccoed Victorian house near Eccleston Square. Dalgliesh had last visited this street three years previously when it had seemed irretrievably sunk into shabby decay. But the tide had changed. The wave of fashion and popularity which flows so inexplicably in London, sometimes missing one district while sweeping through its near neighbour, had washed the broad street bringing order and prosperity in its wake. Judging by the number of house agents' boards, the property speculators, first as always to sniff the returning tide, were reaping the usual profits. The house on the corner looked newly painted. The heavy front door stood open. Inside, a board gave the names of the tenants, but there were no bells. Dalgliesh deduced that the flats were self-contained and that, somewhere, there was a resident caretaker who would answer the front-door bell when the house was locked for the night. He could see no lift so set himself to climb the four flights to Nagle's flat.

It was a light, airy house and very quiet. There was no sign of life until the third floor where someone was playing the piano and playing well; perhaps a professional musician, practising. The treble cascade of sound fell over Dalgliesh and receded as he reached the fourth floor. Here there was a plain wooden door with a heavy brass knocker and a card pinned above it on which was lettered the one word—Nagle. He rapped and heard Nagle shout an immediate "come in".

The flat was surprising. He hardly knew what he had expected, but it was certainly not this immense, airy, impressive studio. It ran the whole length of the back of the house, the great north window, uncurtained, giving a panoramic view of twisted chimney-pots and irregular sloping roofs. Nagle was not alone. He was sitting, knees apart, on a narrow bed which stood on a raised platform at the east side of the room. Curled against him, clad only in a dressing-gown, was Jennifer Priddy. They were drinking tea from two blue mugs; a tray holding the teapot and a bottle of milk was on a small table beside them. The painting on which Nagle had recently been working stood on an easel in the middle of the room.

The girl showed no embarrassment at seeing Dalgliesh but swung her legs from the bed and gave him a smile which was frankly happy, almost welcoming, certainly without coquetry.

"Would you like some tea?" she asked.

Nagle said:

"The police never drink on duty and that includes tea. Better get your clothes on, kid. We don't want to shock the superintendent."

The girl smiled again, gathered up her clothes with one arm and the tea tray with the other and disappeared through a door at the far end of the studio. It was difficult to recognize in this confident sensual figure the tear-stained, diffident child Dalgliesh had first seen at the Steen. He watched her as she passed. She was obviously naked except for the dressing-gown of Nagle's; her hard nipples pointed the thin wool. It came to Dalgliesh that they had been making love. As she passed from view he turned to Nagle and saw in his eyes the transitory gleam of amused speculation. But neither of them spoke.

Dalgliesh moved about the studio, watched by Nagle from the bed. The room was without clutter. In its almost obsessional neatness it reminded him of Enid Bolam's flat with which it had otherwise nothing in common. The dais with its plain wooden bed, chair and small table obviously served as a bedroom. The rest of the studio was taken up with the paraphernalia of a painter, but there was none of that undisciplined muddle which the uninitiated associate with an artist's life. About a dozen large oils were stacked against the south wall and Dalgliesh was surprised by their power. Here was no amateur indulging his little talent. Miss Priddy was apparently Nagle's only model. Her heavy-busted, adolescent body gleamed at him from a diversity of poses, here foreshortened, there curiously elongated as if the painter gloried in his technical competence. The most recent picture was on the easel. It showed the girl sitting astride a stool with the childish hands hanging relaxed between her thighs, the breasts bunched forward. There was something in this flaunting of technical expertise, in the audacious use of greens and mauve and in the careful tonal relationships which caught at Dalgliesh's memory.

"Who teaches you?" he asked. "Sugg?"

"That's right." Nagle did not seem surprised. "Know his work?"

"I have one of his early oils. A nude."

"You made a good investment. Hang on to it."

"I've every intention of doing so," said Dalgliesh mildly. "I happen to like it. Have you been with him long?"

"Two years. Part time, of course. In another three years I'll be teaching him. If he's capable of learning, that is. He's getting an old dog now and too fond of his own tricks."

"You appear to have imitated some of them," said Dalgliesh.

"You think so? That's interesting." Nagle did not seem affronted. "That's why it will be good to get away. I'm off to Paris by the end of the month at the latest. I applied for the Bollinger scholarship. The old man put in a word for me and last week I had a letter to say that it's mine."

Try as he would he could not entirely keep the note of triumph from his voice. Underneath the assumption of nonchalance there was a spring of joy. And he had reason to be pleased with himself. The Bollinger was no ordinary prize. It meant, as Dalgliesh knew, two years in any European city with a generous allowance and freedom for the student to live and work as he chose. The Bollinger trust had been set up by a manufacturer of patent medicines who had died wealthy and successful, but unsatisfied. His money had come from stomach powders but his heart was in painting. His own talent was small and, to judge by the collection of paintings which he bequeathed to the embarrassed trustees of his local gallery, his taste had been on a par with his performance. But the Bollinger scholarship had ensured that artists should remember him with gratitude. Bollinger did not believe that art flourished in poverty or that artists were stimulated to their best efforts by cold garrets and empty bellies. He had been poor in his youth and had not enjoyed it. He had travelled widely in his old age and been happy abroad. The Bollinger scholarship enabled young artists of promise to enjoy the second without enduring the first and it was well worth winning. If Nagle had been awarded the Bollinger he was hardly likely to be much concerned now with the troubles of the Steen Clinic.

"When are you due to go?" Dalgliesh asked.

"When I like. By the end of the month, anyway. But I may go earlier and without notice. No sense in upsetting anyone." He jerked his head towards the far door as he spoke and added: "That's why this murder is such a nuisance. I was afraid it might hold things up. After all, it was my chisel. And that wasn't the only attempt made to implicate me. While I was in the general office waiting for the post someone phoned to ask me to go down for the laundry. It sounded like a woman. I'd got my coat on and was more or less on my way out, so I said I'd collect it when I got back."

"So that's why you went to see Nurse Bolam on your return from the post and asked her whether the laundry was ready?"

"That's right."

"Why didn't you tell her about the phone call at the time?"

"I don't know. There didn't seem any point. I wasn't anxious to hang about the LSD. room. Those patients give me the creeps with their moaning and muttering. When Bolam said the stuff wasn't ready I thought it was Miss Bolam who had phoned and it wouldn't have done to have said so. She was a bit too apt to interfere with the nursing responsibilities, or so they thought. Anyway, I didn't say anything about the call. I might have done but I didn't."

"And you didn't tell me either when you were first interviewed."

"Right again. The truth is that the whole thing struck me as a bit odd and I wanted time to think about it. Well, I've thought, and you're welcome to the story. You can believe it or not, as you like. It's all the same to me."

"You seem to be taking it pretty calmly if you really believe that someone was trying to involve you in the murder."

"I'm not worrying. They didn't succeed for one thing, and for another, I happen to believe that the chance of an innocent man getting convicted of murder in this country is practically nil. You ought to find that flattering. On the other hand—given the jury system—the chances of the guilty getting off are high. That's why I don't think you're going to solve this murder. Too many suspects. Too many possibilities."

"We shall see. Tell me more about this call. When exactly did you receive it?"

"I can't remember. About five minutes before Shorthouse came into the general office, I think. It could have been earlier. Jenny may remember."

"I'll ask her when she gets back. What exactly did the voice say?"

"Just, 'The laundry's ready if you'd fetch it now, please.' I took it that Nurse Bolam was phoning. I replied that I was just going out with the post and would see to it when I got back. Then I put down the receiver before she had a chance to argue."

"You were sure it was Nurse Bolam speaking?"

"I'm not sure at all. I naturally thought it was at the time because Nurse Bolam usually does phone about the laundry.

As a matter of fact the woman spoke softly and it could have been anyone."

"But it was a woman's voice?"

"Oh, yes. It was a woman all right."

"At any rate it was a false message because we know that, in fact, the laundry wasn't sorted."

"Yes. But what was the point of it? It doesn't add up. If the idea was to lure me down to the basement to frame me, the killer stood the risk that I'd arrive at the wrong moment. Nurse Bolam, for example, wouldn't want me on the spot inquiring for the laundry if she were planning to be in the record-room slugging her cousin. Even if Miss Bolam were dead before the call was made it still doesn't make sense. Suppose I'd nosed around and found the body? The killer couldn't have wanted it discovered that soon! Anyway, I didn't go down until I got back from the post. Lucky for me I was out with it. The box is only just across the road, but I usually go down to Beefsteak Street to buy a *Standard*. The man there probably remembers me."

Jennifer Priddy had returned during the last few words. She had changed into a plain woollen dress. Clasping a belt round her waist, she said:

"It was the row over your paper that finished poor old Cully. You might have let him have it, darling, when he asked. He only wanted to check on his horses."

Nagle said without rancour:

"Mean old devil. He'd do anything to save himself threepence. Why can't he pay for it occasionally? I'm no sooner in the door before he puts out his hand for it."

"Still, you were rather unkind to him, darling. It isn't as if you wanted it yourself. We only glanced at it downstairs then used it to wrap up Tigger's food. You know what Cully is. The least upset goes to his stomach."

Nagle expressed his opinion of Cully's stomach with force and originality. Miss Priddy glanced at Dalgliesh as if inviting his shocked admiration of the vagaries of genius and murmured:

"Peter! Really, darling, you are awful!"

She spoke with coy indulgence, the little woman administering a mild rebuke. Dalgliesh looked at Nagle to see how he bore it, but the painter seemed not to have heard. He still sat, immobile, on the bed and looked down at them. Clad now in brown linen trousers, thick blue jersey and sandals, he yet looked as formal and neat as he had in his porter's uniform, his mild eyes unworried, his long, strong arms relaxed.

Under his gaze the girl moved restlessly about the studio, touching with happy possessiveness the frame of a painting, running her fingers along the window ledge, moving a jug of dahlias from one window to the next. It was as if she sought to impose the soft nuances of femininity on this disciplined masculine workshop, to demonstrate that this was her home, her natural place. She was entirely unembarrassed by the pictures of her naked body. It was possible that she gained satisfaction from this vicarious exhibitionism. Suddenly Dalgliesh asked:

"Do you remember, Miss Priddy, whether anyone telephoned Mr. Nagle while he was in the office with you?"

The girl looked surprised but said unconcernedly to Nagle:

"Nurse Bolam phoned about the laundry, didn't she? I came in from the record-room—I'd only been gone a second—and heard you say that you were just on your way out and would go down when you came back." She laughed. "After you put the receiver down you said something much less polite about the way the nurses expect you to be at their beck and call. Remember?"

"Yes," said Nagle shortly. He turned to Dalgliesh. "Any more questions, Superintendent? Jenny'll have to be getting home soon and I usually go part of the way. Her parents don't know she sees me."

"Only one or two. Have either of you any idea why Miss Bolam should send for the group secretary?"

Miss Priddy shook her head. Nagle said:

"It was nothing to do with us, anyway. She didn't know that Jenny poses for me. Even if she found out she wouldn't send for Lauder. She wasn't a fool. She knew he wouldn't concern himself with anything the staff did in their own time. After all, she found out about Dr. Baguley's affair with Miss Saxon, but she wasn't daft enough to tell Lauder."

Dalgliesh did not ask whom Miss Bolam had told. He said: "It was obviously something concerned with the administration of the clinic. Had anything unusual happened lately?"

"Nothing but our famous burglary and the missing fifteen quid. But you know about that."

"That's nothing to do with Peter," said the girl with quick defensiveness. "He wasn't even at the clinic when the fifteen pounds arrived." She turned to Nagle. "You remember, darling? That was the morning you got stuck in the Underground. You didn't even know about the money!"

She had said something wrong. The flash of irritation in those large mud-brown eyes was momentary, but Dalgliesh did not miss it. There was a pause before Nagle spoke, but his voice was perfectly controlled.

"I knew soon enough. We all did. What with the fuss over who sent it and the row over who was to spend it, the whole damn group must have known." He looked at Dalgliesh.

"Is that all?"

"No. Do you know who killed Miss Bolam?"

"I'm glad to say I don't. I shouldn't think it was one of the psychiatrists. Those boys are the strongest reason I know for staying sane. But I can't see any of them actually killing. They haven't the nerve."

Someone very different had said much the same thing.

As he reached the door, Dalgliesh paused and looked back at Nagle. He and the girl were sitting together on the bed as he had first seen them, neither of them made any move to see him out, but Jenny gave him her happy valedictory smile.

Dalgliesh asked his last question:

"Why did you go for a drink with Cully on the night of the burglary?"

"Cully asked me."

"Wasn't that unusual?"

"So unusual that I went with him out of curiosity to see what was up."

"And what was?"

"Nothing really. Cully asked me to lend him a quid which I refused, and while the clinic was left empty someone broke in. I don't see how Cully could have foreseen that. Or maybe he did. Anyway, I can't see what it's got to do with the murder."

Nor, on the face of it, could Dalgliesh. As he passed down the stairs he was vexed by the thought of time passing, time wasted, the drag of hours before Monday morning when the clinic would reopen and his suspects reassemble in the place where they were likely to be most vulnerable. But the last forty minutes had been well spent. He was beginning to trace the dominant thread in this tangled skein. As he passed by the third-floor flat the pianist was playing Bach. Dalgliesh paused for a moment to listen. Contrapuntal music was the only kind he truly enjoyed. But the pianist stopped suddenly with a crash of discordant keys. And then nothing. Dalgliesh passed down the stairs in silence and left the quiet house unseen.

When Dr. Baguley arrived at the clinic for the Medical Committee meeting, the parking space reserved for doctors' cars was already occupied. Dr. Etherege's Bentley was there parked next to Steiner's Rolls. On the other side of it was the battered Vauxhall which proclaimed that Dr. Albertine Maddox had decided to attend.

Upstairs in the first-floor boardroom the curtains were drawn against the blue-black October sky. In the middle of the heavy mahogany table was a bowl of roses. Baguley remembered that Miss Bolam had always supplied flowers for the meetings of the Medical Committee. Someone had decided to continue the practice. The roses were the slim, hothouse buds of autumn, rigid and scentless on their thornless stems. In a couple of days they would open for their brief and barren flowering. In less than a week they would be dead. Baguley thought that so extravagant and evocative a flower was inappropriate to the mood of the meeting. But the empty bowl would have been unbearably poignant and embarrassing.

"Who supplied the roses?" he asked.

"Mrs. Bostock, I think," said Dr. Ingram. "She was up here getting the room ready when I arrived."

"Remarkable," said Dr. Etherege. He put out a finger and stroked one of the buds so gently that the stem did not even tremble. Baguley wondered whether the comment referred to the quality of the roses or to Mrs. Bostock's perspicacity in supplying them.

"Miss Bolam was very fond of flowers, very fond," said the medical director. He looked round as if challenging his colleagues to disagree.

"Well," he said. "Shall we get started?"

Dr. Baguley, as honorary secretary, seated himself on the right of Dr. Etherege. Dr. Steiner took the chair next to him. Dr. Maddox sat on Steiner's right. No other consultant was there. Dr. McBain and Dr. Mason-Giles were in the States attending a conference. The rest of the medical staff, torn between curiosity and a disinclination to interrupt their week-end break, had apparently decided to wait in patience for Monday. Dr. Etherege had thought it proper to telephone them all and let them know of the meeting. He gave their apologies formally and they were as gravely received.

Albertine Maddox had been a surgeon and a highly successful one before she qualified as a psychiatrist. It was perhaps typical of her colleagues' ambivalence towards their specialty that Dr. Maddox's double qualification enhanced her standing in their eyes. She represented the clinic on the Group Medical Advisory Committee, where she defended the Steen against the occasional snipings of physicians and surgeons with a wit and vigour which made her respected and feared. At the clinic she took no part in the Freudian versus eclectic controversy being, as Baguley observed, equally beastly to both sides. Her patients loved her, but this did not impress her colleagues. They were used to being loved by their patients and merely observed that Albertine was particularly skilful in handling a strong transference situation. Physically she was a plump, grey-haired, unremarkable woman who looked what she was, the comfortable mother of a family. She had five children, the sons intelligent and prosperous, the girls well-married. Her insignificant-looking husband and the children treated her with a tolerant, faintly amused solicitude which never failed to astonish her colleagues at the Steen to whom she was a formidable personality. She sat now with Hector, her old Pekinese, squatting malevolently on her lap looking as comfortably anticipatory as a suburban housewife at a matinée. Dr. Steiner said testily:

"Really, Albertine, need you have brought Hector? I don't want to be unkind but that animal is beginning to smell. You should have him put down."

"Thank you, Paul," replied Dr. Maddox in her deep, beautifully modulated voice. "Hector will be put down, as you so euphemistically describe it, when he ceases to find life pleasant. I judge that he has not yet reached that state. It is not my habit to kill off living creatures simply because I find certain of their physical characteristics displeasing; nor, I may say, because they have become somewhat of a nuisance."

Dr. Etherege said quickly:

"It was good of you to find time to come tonight, Albertine. I'm sorry that the notice was so short."

He spoke without irony, although he was as well aware as were his colleagues that Dr. Maddox only attended one committee meeting in four on the grounds, which she made no effort to conceal, that her contract with the Regional Board contained no clause compelling her to a monthly session of boredom laced with claptrap, and that the company of more than one psychiatrist at a time made Hector sick. The truth of this last assertion had been demonstrated too often to be safely challenged.

"I am a member of this committee, Henry," replied Dr. Maddox graciously. "Is there any reason why I should not make the effort to attend?"

Her glance at Dr. Ingram implied that not everyone present had an equal right. Mary Ingram was the wife of a suburban general practitioner and attended the Steen twice a week to give the anaesthetic at E.C.T. sessions. Not being either a psychiatrist or a consultant she was not normally present at meetings of the Medical Committee. Dr. Etherege interpreted the glance correctly and said firmly:

"Dr. Ingram has been good enough to come along tonight

at my request. The main business of the meeting is naturally concerned with Miss Bolam's murder, and Dr. Ingram was in the clinic on Friday evening."

"But is not a suspect, so I understand," replied Dr. Maddox. "I congratulate her. It is gratifying that there is one member of the medical staff who has been able to produce a satisfactory alibi."

She looked at Dr. Ingram severely, her tone implying that an alibi was, in itself, suspicious and hardly becoming to the most junior member of the staff since three senior consultants had been unable to produce one. No one asked how Dr. Maddox knew about the alibi. Presumably she had been speaking to Sister Ambrose. Dr. Steiner said pettishly:

"It's ridiculous to talk about alibis as if the police could seriously suspect one of us! It's perfectly obvious to me what happened. The murderer was lying in wait for her in the basement. We know that. He may have been hidden down there for hours, perhaps even since the previous day. He could have slipped past Cully with one of the patients or have pretended to be a relative or a hospital-car attendant. He could even have broken in during the night. That has been known, after all. Once in the basement there would be plenty of time to discover which key opened the record-room door and plenty of time to select a weapon. Neither the fetish nor the chisel were hidden."

"And how do you suggest this unknown murderer left the building?" asked Dr. Baguley. "We searched the place pretty thoroughly before the police arrived and they went over it again. The basement and first-floor doors were both bolted on the inside, remember."

"Climbed up the lift shaft by the pulley ropes and out through one of the doors leading to the fire-escape," replied Dr. Steiner, playing his trump card with a certain panache. "I've examined the lift and it's just possible. A small man—or a woman, of course—could squeeze over the top of the box and get into the shaft. The ropes are quite thick enough to support a considerable weight and the climb wouldn't be too difficult for anyone reasonably agile. They'd need to be slim, of course." He glanced at his own rounding paunch with complacency.

"It's a pleasant theory," said Baguley. "Unfortunately all the doors opening on the fire-escape were also bolted on the inside."

"There is no building in existence which a desperate and experienced man cannot break into or get out of," proclaimed Dr. Steiner, as if from a plenitude of experience. "He could have got out of a first-floor window and edged along the sill until he could get a foothold on the fire-escape. All I'm saying is that the murderer isn't necessarily one of the staff who happened to be on duty yesterday evening."

"It could be I, for example," said Dr. Maddox.

Dr. Steiner was undaunted.

"That, of course, is nonsense, Albertine. I make no accusations. I merely point out that the circle of suspects is less restricted than the police seem to think. They should direct their inquiries to Miss Bolam's private life. Obviously she has an enemy."

But Dr. Maddox was not to be diverted.

"Fortunately for me," she proclaimed, "I was at the Bach recital at the Royal Festival Hall last night with my husband and dined there before the concert. And while Alasdair's testimony on my behalf might be suspect, I was also with my brother-in-law who happens to be a bishop. A High Church bishop," she added complacently, as if incense and chasuble set a seal on episcopal virtue and veracity.

Dr. Etherege smiled gently and said:

"I should be relieved if I could produce even an evangelical curate to vouch for me between six-fifteen and seven o'clock yesterday evening. But isn't all this theorizing a waste of time? The crime is in the hands of the police and there we must leave it. Our main concern is to discuss its implications for the work of the clinic and, in particular, the suggestion of the chairman and the group secretary that Mrs. Bostock should carry on for the present as acting administrative officer. But we'd better proceed in order. Is it your pleasure that I sign the minutes of the last meeting?"

There was the unenthusiastic but acquiescent mumble which this question usually provokes and the medical director drew the minute book towards him and signed. Dr. Maddox said suddenly:

"What is he like? This superintendent, I mean."

Dr. Ingram, who hadn't so far spoken, surprisingly replied:

"He's about forty, I should think. Tall and dark. I liked his voice and he has nice hands." Then she blushed furiously, remembering that, to a psychiatrist, the most innocent remark could be embarrassingly revealing. That comment about nice hands was, perhaps, a mistake. Dr. Steiner, ignoring Dalgliesh's physical characteristics, launched into a psychological assessment of the superintendent to which his fellow psychiatrists gave the polite attention of experts interested in a colleague's theories. Dalgliesh, had he been present, would have been surprised and intrigued by the accuracy and percipience of Dr. Steiner's diagnosis. The medical director said:

"I agree that he's obsessional and also that he's intelligent. That means that his mistakes will be the mistakes of an intelligent man—always the most dangerous. We must hope for all our sakes that he makes none. The murder, and the inevitable publicity, are bound to have an effect on the patients and on the work of the clinic. And that brings us to this suggestion about Mrs. Bostock."

"I have always preferred Bolam to Bostock," said Dr. Maddox. "It would be a pity if we lost one unsuitable A.O.—however regrettably and fortuitously—only to be saddled with another."

"I agree," said Dr. Baguley. "Of the two I personally always preferred Bolam. But this would only be a temporary arrangement presumably. The job will have to be advertised. In the meantime someone's got to take over and Mrs. Bostock does at least know the work."

Dr. Etherege said:

"Lauder made it plain that the H.M.C. wouldn't favour putting in an outsider until the police have finished their investigation, even if they could find anyone willing to come. We don't want any additional upheaval. There will be enough disturbance to cope with. And that brings me to the problem of the press. Lauder suggested, and I have agreed, that all inquiries are referred to group headquarters and that no one here makes any statements. It seems much the best plan. It's important in the interests of the patients that we don't have reporters running all over the clinic. Therapy is likely to suffer enough without that. Have I this Committee's formal confirmation of the decision?"

He had. No one evinced any enthusiasm for coping with the press. Dr. Steiner did not contribute to the general murmur of consent. His thoughts were still with the problem of Miss Bolam's successor. He said querulously:

"I can't understand why Dr. Maddox and Dr. Baguley have this animus against Mrs. Bostock. I've noticed it before. It's ridiculous to compare her adversely with Miss Bolam. There's no doubt which of them is—was—is—the more suitable administrator. Mrs. Bostock is a highly intelligent woman, psychologically stable, efficient and with a real appreciation of the importance of the work we do here. No one could have said as much of Miss Bolam. Her attitude to the patients was sometimes most unfortunate."

"I didn't know that she came into contact much with the patients," said Dr. Baguley. "Anyway, none of mine complained."

"She made appointments occasionally and paid out travelling expenses. I can quite believe that your patients didn't remark on her attitude. But mine are a rather different class. They're also more sensitive to these things. Mr. Burge, for example, mentioned the matter to me."

Dr. Maddox laughed unkindly.

"Oh, Burge! Is he still coming? I see that his new opus is promised for December. It will be interesting to see, Paul, whether your efforts have improved his prose. If so, it's probably public money well spent."

Dr. Steiner burst into pained expostulation. He treated a fair number of writers and artists, some of them protégés of Rosa in search of a little free psychotherapy. Although he was sensitive to the arts his usually keen critical insight failed completely where his patients were concerned. He could not bear to hear them criticized, lived in perpetual hope that their great talents would at last be recognized, and was roused to quick defensive anger on their behalf. Dr. Baguley thought that it was one of Steiner's more endearing qualities; in many ways he was touchingly naïve. He launched now into a muddled defence both of his patient's character and his prose style, ending:

"Mr. Burge is a most talented and sensitive man, very distressed by his inability to sustain a satisfactory sexual relationship, particularly with his wives."

This unfortunate solecism seemed likely to provoke Dr. Maddox to further unkindness. It was certainly, thought Baguley, her night to be pro-eclectic.

Dr. Etherege said mildly:

"Could we forget our professional differences for a moment and concentrate on the matter in hand? Dr. Steiner, have you any objection to accepting Mrs. Bostock as a temporary administrative officer?

Dr. Steiner said grumpily:

"The question is purely academic. If the group secretary wishes her to be appointed she will be appointed. This farce of appearing to consult us is ridiculous. We have no authority either to approve or disapprove. That was made perfectly clear to me by Lauder when I approached him last month about getting Bolam transferred."

"I didn't know you had approached him," said Dr. Etherege.

"I spoke to him after the September meeting of the House Committee. It was merely a tentative suggestion."

"And was met with a pretty positive brush off, no doubt," said Baguley. "You would have been wiser to keep your mouth shut."

"Or to have brought the matter before this Committee," said Etherege.

"And with what result?" cried Steiner. "What happened last time I complained about Bolam? Nothing! You all admitted that she was an unsuitable person to hold the post of administrative officer. You all agreed—well, most of you agreed—that Bostock—or even an outsider—would be preferable. But when it came to action not one of you was prepared to put your signature to a letter to the Hospital Management Committee. And you know very well why! You were all terrified of that woman. Yes, terrified!"

Amid the murmur of outraged denial, Dr. Maddox said:

"There was something intimidating about her. It may have been that formidable and self-conscious rectitude. You were as affected by it as anyone, Paul."

"Possibly. But I did try to do something about her. I spoke to Lauder."

"I spoke to him, too," said Etherege quietly, "and possibly with more effect. I made it clear that this Committee realized that we had no control over the administrative staff, but I said that Miss Bolam appeared to me, speaking as a psychiatrist and as chairman of the Medical Committee, to be temperamentally unsuitable for her job. I suggested that a transfer would be in her own interests. There could be no criticism of her efficiency and I made none. Lauder was non-committal, of course, but he knew perfectly well that I was entitled to make the point. And I think he took it."

Dr. Maddox said:

"Allowing for his natural caution, his suspicion of psychiatrists and the usual speed of his administrative decisions, I suppose we should have been rid of Miss Bolam within the next two years. Someone has certainly speeded things up."

Suddenly Dr. Ingram spoke. Her pink, rather stupid face flushed unbecomingly. She sat stiffly upright and her hands, clasped on the table in front of her, were shaking.

"I don't think you ought to say things like that. It . . . it isn't right. Miss Bolam is dead, brutally murdered. You sit here, all of you, and talk as if you didn't care! I know she wasn't very easy to get on with but she's dead, and I don't think this is the time to be unkind about her."

Dr. Maddox looked at Dr. Ingram with interest and a kind of wonder as if she were faced by an exceptionally dull child who had somehow succeeded in making an intelligent remark. She said:

"I see that you subscribe to the superstition that one should never tell the truth about the dead. The origins of that atavistic belief have always interested me. We must have a talk about it sometime. I should like to hear your views."

Dr. Ingram, scarlet with embarrassment and close to tears, looked as if the proposed talk were a privilege she would be happy to forgo. Dr. Etherege said:

"Unkind about her? I should be sorry to think that anyone here was being unkind. There are some things, surely, which don't need saying. There can't be a member of this Committee who isn't horrified at the senseless brutality of Miss Bolam's death and who wouldn't wish her back with us no matter what her defects as an administrator."

The bathos was too blatant to be missed. As if conscious of their surprise and discomfiture, he looked up and said challengingly:

"Well, is there? Is there?"

"Of course not," said Dr. Steiner. He spoke soothingly, but the sharp little eyes slewed sideways to meet Baguley's glance. There was embarrassment in that look, but Baguley recognized also the smirk of malicious amusement. The medical director wasn't playing this too cleverly. He had allowed Albertine Maddox to get out of hand and his control over the Committee was less sure than formerly. The pathetic thing about it, thought Baguley, was that Etherege was sincere. He meant every word. He had—and so had they all, come to that—a genuine horror of violence. He was a compassionate man shocked and saddened by the thought of a defenceless woman brutally done to death. But his words sounded false. He was taking refuge in formality, deliberately trying to lower the emotional tone of the meeting to one of platitudinous convention. And he only succeeded in sounding insincere.

After Dr. Ingram's outburst the meeting seemed to lose heart. Dr. Etherege made only spasmodic attempts to control it and the conversation ranged in a tired, desultory way, from one subject to another but, always and inevitably, returned to the murder. There was a feeling that the Medical Committee should express some common view. Groping from theory to theory the meeting eventually came to accept Dr. Steiner's proposition. The killer had obviously entered the clinic earlier in the day when the system of booking people in and out was not in force. He had secreted himself in the basement, selected his weapons at leisure, and called Miss Bolam down by noting the number of her extension from the card hung beside the telephone. He had made his way to the upper floors without being observed and left by one of the windows, managing to close it behind him before edging his way on to the fire-escape. That this procedure argued considerable luck, coupled with unusual and remarkable agility, was not over-emphasized. Under Dr. Steiner's leadership the theory was elaborated. Miss Bolam's telephone call to the group secretary was dismissed as irrelevant. She had undoubtedly wished to complain about some trifling misdemeanour, real or imagined, and which was quite unconnected with her subsequent death. The suggestion that the killer had swarmed up the pulley in the lift shaft was generally discounted as somewhat fanciful although, as Dr. Maddox pointed out, a man who could shut a heavy window while balancing on the outside sill, then swing himself some five feet through space to reach the fire-escape, would hardly find the lift shaft an insuperable problem.

Dr. Baguley, wearying of his part in the fabrication of this mythical killer, half-closed his eyes and gazed from under lowered lids, at the bowl of roses. Their petals had been opening gently and almost visibly in the warmth of the room. Now the red, green and pink swam together in an amorphous pattern of colour which, as his gaze shifted, was reflected in the shining table. Suddenly he opened his eyes fully and saw Dr. Etherege looking fixedly at him. There was concern in that sharp, analytic regard; Dr. Baguley thought that there was also pity. The medical director said:

"Some of our members have had enough. So, I think, have I. If no one has any urgent business to bring forward I declare the meeting closed."

Dr. Baguley thought that it was not altogether by chance that he and the medical director found themselves alone in the room, the last to leave. As he tested the windows to check that they were locked, Dr. Etherege said:

"Well, James, have you come to a decision yet about succeeding me as medical director?"

"It's more a question of deciding whether or not to apply for the job when it's advertised, surely?" said Baguley. He asked: "What about Mason-Giles or McBain?"

"M.G. isn't interested. It's maximum sessions, of course, and he doesn't want to give up his teaching hospital connection. McBain is tied up with the new regional unit for adolescents."

It was typical of the medical director's occasional insensitivity that he didn't try to soften the fact that he had tried others first. He's scraping the bottom of the barrel, thought Baguley.

"And Steiner?" he asked. "He'll be applying, I imagine?"

The medical director smiled.

"Oh, I don't think the Regional Board will appoint Dr. Steiner. This is a multi-discipline clinic. We must have someone who can hold the place together. And there may be very great changes. You know my views. If there is to be a closer integration of psychiatry with general medicine a place like this may have to die for the greater good. We ought to have access to beds. The Steen may find its natural home in a general hospital out-patient department. I don't say it's probable. But it's possible."

So that was the way the Board was thinking? Dr. Etherege had his ear well to the ground. A small out-patient unit with no registrars, no training function and no link with a general hospital might well become anachronistic in the eyes of the planners. Dr. Baguley said:

"I don't mind where I see my patients as long as I get peace and quiet, a certain tolerance, and not too much of the hierarchical claptrap and starched linen. These proposed psychiatric units in general hospitals are all very well so long as the hospital appreciates what we're going to need in staff and space. I'm too tired to do battle."

He looked at the medical director.

"Actually, I had more or less decided not to apply. I telephoned your room yesterday evening from the medical staffroom to ask if we could chat about it after the clinic."

"Indeed? At what time?"

"At about six-twenty or six-twenty-five. There was no reply. Later, of course, we had other things to think about."

The medical director said:

"I must have been in the library. I'm very glad I was if it means that you've had time to reconsider your decision. And I hope that you will reconsider it, James."

He turned out the lights and they went downstairs together. Pausing at the foot, the medical director turned to Dr. Baguley and said:

"It was at about six-twenty that you telephoned? I find that very interesting, very interesting indeed."

"Well, about then, I suppose."

Dr. Baguley realized with irritation and surprise, that it was he, not the medical director, who sounded guilty and embarrassed. He was seized by an intense desire to get out of the clinic, to escape from the blue, speculative gaze which was so adept at putting him at a disadvantage. But there was something else which must be said. At the door he forced himself to pause and face Dr. Etherege. But despite his attempt at nonchalance his voice sounded forced, even belligerent:

"I'm wondering whether we ought to do something about Nurse Bolam."

"In what way?" asked the medical director gently. Receiving no reply, he went on: "All the staff know that they can ask to see me at any time. But I'm not inviting confidences. This is a murder investigation, James, and it's out of my hands. Out of my hands completely. I think you would be wise to take the same attitude. Good night."

Chapter Six

Early Monday morning, the anniversary of his wife's death, Dalgliesh called in at a small Catholic church behind the Strand to light a candle. His wife had been a Catholic. He had not shared her religion and she had died before he could begin to understand what it meant to her or what importance this fundamental difference between them might have for their marriage. He had lit the first candle on the day she died out of the need to formalize an intolerable grief and, perhaps, with a childish hope of somehow comforting her spirit. This was the fourteenth candle. He thought of this most private action in his detached and secretive life, not as superstition or piety, but as a habit which he could not now break even if he wished. He dreamed of his wife only seldom, but then with absolute clarity; waking he could no longer accurately recall her face. He pushed his coin through the slot and held his candle's wick to the dying flame of a moist stump. It caught immediately and the flame grew bright and clear. It had always been important to him that the wick should catch at once. He gazed through the flame for a moment feeling nothing, not even anger. Then he turned away.

The church was nearly empty, but it held for him an atmosphere of intense and silent activity which he sensed but could not share. As he walked to the door he recognized a woman, red-coated and with a dark green scarf over her head, who was pausing to dip her fingers in the water stoup. It was Fredrica Saxon, senior psychologist of the Steen Clinic. They reached the outer door together and he forced it open for her against the sudden swirl of an autumn wind. She smiled at him, friendly and unembarrassed.

"Hullo. I haven't seen you here before."

"I only come once a year," Dalgliesh replied. He gave no explanation and she asked no questions. Instead she said:

"I wanted to see you. There's something I think you ought to know. Are you off duty? If you aren't could you be unorthodox and talk to a suspect in a coffee bar? I'd rather not come to your office and it isn't easy to ask for an interview at the clinic. I need some coffee anyway. I'm cold."

"There used to be a place round the corner," said Dalgliesh. "The coffee is tolerable and it's pretty quiet."

The coffee bar had changed in a year. Dalgliesh remembered it as a clean but dull café with a row of deal tables covered with plastic cloths and a long service counter embellished with a tea urn and layers of substantial sandwiches under glass domes. It had risen in the world. The walls had been panelled with imitation old oak against which hung a formidable assortment of rapiers, ancient pistols and cutlasses of uncertain authenticity. The waitresses looked like *avant-garde* débutantes earning their pin money and the lighting was so discreet as to be positively sinister. She led the way to a table in the far corner.

"Just coffee?" asked Dalgliesh.

"Just coffee, please."

She waited until the order had been given and then said:

"It's about Dr. Baguley."

"I thought it might be."

"You were bound to hear something, I suppose. I'd rather tell you about it now than wait to be asked and I'd rather you heard it from me than from Amy Shorthouse."

She spoke without rancour or embarrassment. Dalgliesh replied:

"I haven't asked about it because it doesn't seem relevant, but if you like to tell me it may be helpful."

"I don't want you to get a wrong idea about it that's all. It would be so easy for you to imagine that we had a grudge against Miss Bolam. We didn't, you know. At one time we even felt grateful to her."

Dalgliesh had no need to ask who she meant by that "we".

The waitress, uninterested, came with their coffee, pale foam served in small transparent cups. Miss Saxon slipped her coat from her shoulders and unknotted her head scarf. Both of them wrapped their fingers round the hot cups. She heaped the sugar into her coffee then pushed the plastic bowl across the table to Dalgliesh. There was no tension about her, no awkwardness. She had the directness of a schoolchild drinking coffee with a friend. He found her curiously peaceful to be with, perhaps because he did not find her physically attractive. But he liked her. It was difficult to believe that this was only their second meeting and that the matter that had brought them together was murder. She skimmed the froth from her coffee and said, without looking up:

"James Baguley and I fell in love nearly three years ago. There wasn't any great moral struggle about it. We didn't invite love but we certainly didn't fight against it. After all, you don't voluntarily give up happiness unless you're a masochist or a saint, and we aren't either. I knew that James had a neurotic wife in the way one does get to know these things, but he didn't talk much about her. We both accepted that she needed him and that a divorce was out of the question. We convinced ourselves that we weren't doing her any harm and that she need never know. James used to say that loving me made his marriage happier for both of them. Of course, it is easier to be kind and patient when one is happy, so he may have been right. I don't know. It's a rationalization that thousands of lovers must use.

"We couldn't see each other very often, but I had my flat and we usually managed to have two evenings a week together. Once Helen—that's his wife—went to stay with her sister and we had a whole night together. We had to be careful at the clinic, of course, but we don't really see very much of each other there."

"How did Miss Bolam find out about it?" asked Dalgliesh.

"It was silly, really. We were at the theatre seeing Anouilh and she was sitting alone in the row behind. Who would suppose that Bolam would want to see Anouilh, anyway? I suppose she was sent a free ticket. It was our second anniversary and we held hands all through the play. We may have been a little drunk. Afterwards we left the theatre still hand in hand. Anyone from the clinic, anyone we knew, could have seen us. We were getting careless and someone was bound to see us sooner or later. It was just chance that it happened to be Bolam. Other people would probably have minded their own business."

"Whereas she told Mrs. Baguley? That seems an unusually officious and cruel thing to have done."

"It wasn't, really. Bolam wouldn't see it that way. She was one of those rare and fortunate people who never for one moment doubt that they know the difference between right and wrong. She wasn't imaginative so she couldn't enter into other people's feelings. If she were a wife whose husband was unfaithful I'm sure that she would want to be told about it. Nothing would be worse than not knowing. She had the kind of strength that relishes a struggle. I expect she thought it was her duty to tell. Anyway, Helen came to the Steen to see her husband unexpectedly one Wednesday afternoon and Miss Bolam invited her into the A.O.'s office and told her. I often wonder what exactly she said. I imagine that she said we were 'carrying on'. She could make practically anything sound vulgar."

"She was taking a risk, wasn't she?" said Dalgliesh. "She had very little evidence, certainly no proof."

Miss Saxon laughed.

"You're talking like a policeman. She had proof enough. Even Bolam could recognize love when she saw it. Besides, we were enjoying ourselves together without a licence and that was infidelity enough."

The words were bitter but she did not sound resentful or sarcastic. She was sipping her coffee with evident satisfaction. Dalgliesh thought that she might have been talking about one of the clinic patients, discussing with detached and mild professional interest the vagaries of human nature. Yet he did not believe that she loved easily or that her emotions were superficial. He asked what Mrs. Baguley's reaction had been.

"That's the extraordinary thing, or at least it seemed so at the time. She took it wonderfully well. Looking back I wonder whether we weren't all three mad, living in some kind of imaginary world that two minutes' rational thought would have shown us couldn't exist. Helen lives her life in a series of attitudes and the one she decided to adopt was the pose of the brave, understanding wife. She insisted on a divorce. It was going to be one of those friendly divorces. That kind is only possible, I imagine, when people have ceased to care for each other, perhaps never have cared or been capable of caring. But that was the kind we were going to have. There was a great deal of discussion. Everyone's happiness was to be safeguarded. Helen was going to open a dress shop—it's a thing she's talked about for years. We all three got interested in it and looked for suitable premises. It was pathetic really. We actually fooled ourselves that it was all going to come right. That's why I said that James and I felt grateful to Enid Bolam. People at the clinic got to know that there was to be a divorce and that Helen would name me—it was all part of the policy of frankness and honesty—but very little was said to us. Bolam never mentioned the divorce to anyone. She wasn't a gossip and she wasn't malicious, either. Somehow her part in it got about in the way these things do. I think Helen may have told someone, but Miss Bolam and I never talked about it ever.

"Then the inevitable happened. Helen began to crack. James had left her with the Surrey house and was living with me in the flat. He had to see her fairly often. He didn't say very much at first, but I knew what was happening. She was ill, of course, and we both knew it. She had played out the role of the patient, uncomplaining wife and, according to the novels and the films, her husband should, by now, have been returning to her. And James wasn't. He kept most of it from me, but I had some idea what it was doing to him, the scenes, the tears, the entreaties, the threats of suicide. One minute she was going through with the divorce, the next she would never give him his freedom. She couldn't, of course. I see that now. It wasn't hers to give. It's degrading to talk about a husband as if he's a dog chained up in the back yard. All the time that this was happening I was realizing more and more that I couldn't go on. Something that had been a slow process over years came to a head. There's no point in talking about it or trying to explain. It isn't relevant to your inquiry, is it? Nine months ago I started to receive instruction with the hope of being received into the Catholic Church. When that happened Helen withdrew her petition and James went back to her. I think he no longer cared what happened to him or where he went. But you can see, can't you, that he had no reason to hate Bolam. I was the enemy."

Dalgliesh thought that there could have been very little struggle. Her rosy, healthy face with the broad and slightly tip-tilted nose, the wide cheerful mouth, was ill-suited to tragedy. He recalled how Dr. Baguley had looked, seen in the light of Miss Bolam's desk lamp. It was stupid and presumptuous to try to assess suffering by the lines on a face or the look in the eyes. Miss Saxon's mind was probably as tough and resilient as her body. It did not mean that she felt less because she could withstand more. But he felt profoundly sorry for Baguley, rejected by his mistress at the moment of greatest trial in favour of a private happiness which he could neither share nor understand. Probably no one could fully know the magnitude of that betrayal. Dalgliesh did not pretend to understand Miss Saxon. It wasn't hard to imagine what some people at the clinic would make of it. The facile explanations came easily to mind. But he could not believe that Fredrica Saxon had taken refuge in religion from her own sexuality or had ever refused to face reality.

He thought of some of the things she had said about Enid Bolam.

"Who would suppose that Bolam would want to see Anouilh. I suppose she was sent a free ticket. . . . Even Bolam could recognize love when she saw it. . . . She could make practically anything sound vulgar." People did not automatically become kind because they had become religious. Yet there had been no real malice in her words. She spoke what she thought and would be equally detached about her own motives. She was probably the best judge of character in the clinic. Suddenly, and in defiance of orthodoxy, Dalgliesh asked:

"Who do you think killed her, Miss Saxon?"

"Judging by character and the nature of the crime and taking no account of mysterious telephone calls from the basement, creaking lifts, and apparent alibis?"

"Judging by character and the nature of the crime."

She said without hesitation and with no apparent reluctance:

"I'd have said it was Peter Nagle."

Dalgliesh felt a stab of disappointment. It was irrational to have thought that she might actually know.

"Why Nagle?" he asked.

"Partly because I think this was a masculine crime. The stabbing is significant. I can't see a woman killing in just that way. Faced with an unconscious victim I think a woman would strangle. Then there's the chisel. To use it with such expertise suggests an identification of the weapon with the killer. Why use it otherwise? He could have struck her again and again with the fetish."

"Messy, noisy and less sure," said Dalgliesh.

"But the chisel was only sure in the hands of a man who had confidence in his ability to use it, someone who is literally 'good with his hands'. I can't see Dr. Steiner killing in that way, for instance. He couldn't even knock in a nail without breaking the hammer."

Dalgliesh was inclined to agree that Dr. Steiner was innocent. His clumsiness with tools had been mentioned by more than one member of the clinic staff. Admittedly he had lied in denying that he knew where the chisel was kept, but Dalgliesh judged that he had acted from fear rather than guilt. And his shamefaced confession of falling asleep while awaiting Mr. Burge had the ring of truth.

Dalgliesh said:

"The identification of the chisel with Nagle is so certain that I think we were meant to suspect him. And you do?"

"Oh, no! I know he couldn't have done it. I only answered

the question as you posed it. I was judging by character and the nature of the crime."

They had finished their coffee now and Dalgliesh thought that she would want to go. But she seemed in no hurry. After a moment's pause, she said:

"I have one confession to make; on another person's behalf actually. It's Cully. Nothing important but something you ought to know and I promised I'd tell you about it. Poor old Cully is scared out of his wits and they aren't plentiful at the best of times."

"I knew he was lying about something," said Dalgliesh. "He saw someone passing down the hall, I suppose."

"Oh, no! Nothing as useful as that. It's about the missing rubber apron from the art therapy department. I gather you thought that the murderer might have worn it. Well, Cully borrowed it from the department last Monday to wear while he emulsion-painted his kitchen. You know what a mess paint makes. He didn't ask Miss Bolam if he could take it because he knew what the answer would be and he couldn't ask Mrs. Baumgarten because she's away sick. He meant to bring it back on Friday but when Sister was checking the inventory with your sergeant and they asked him if he'd seen it he lost his head and said 'no'. He's not very bright and he was terrified that you'd suspect him of the murder if he owned up."

Dalgliesh asked her when Cully had told her of this.

"I knew he had the apron because it just happened that I saw him take it. I guessed that he'd be in a state about it so I went round to see him yesterday morning. His stomach gets upset when he worries and I thought someone had better keep an eye on him."

"Where is the apron now?" asked Dalgliesh.

Miss Saxon laughed.

"Disposed about London in half a dozen litter baskets if they haven't been emptied. Poor old Cully daren't put it in his own dustbin in case it was searched by the police and couldn't burn it because he lives in a council flat with electric heating and no stove. So he waited until his wife was in bed, then sat up until eleven cutting it into pieces with the kitchen scissors. He put the pieces into a number of paper bags, shoved the bags into a hold-all, and took a 36 bus up the Harrow Road until he was well away from his home ground. Then he slipped one of the bags into each litter bin he came across and dropped the metal buttons down the gutter grating. It was a formidable undertaking and the poor fellow could hardly creep home what with fear, tiredness—he'd lost the last bus—and the belly-ache. He wasn't in too good a shape when I called next morning, but I did manage to convince him that it wasn't a matter of life and death—particularly death. I told him I'd let you know about it."

"Thank you," said Dalgliesh gravely. "You haven't any other confessions to pass on, I suppose? Or have you a conscientious objection to handing over an unfortunate psychopath to justice."

She laughed, pulling on her coat and tying the scarf over her dark, springing hair.

"Oh, no! If I knew who did it I'd tell you. I don't like murder and I'm quite law-abiding, really. But I didn't know we were talking about justice. That's your word. Like Portia, I feel that in the course of justice none of us would see salvation. Please, I would much rather pay for my own coffee."

She doesn't want to feel that I bought information from her, thought Dalgliesh, not even a shilling's worth. He resisted the temptation to say that the coffee could come from expenses, wondering a little at this impulse to sarcasm which she aroused in him. He liked her, but there was something about her certainty, her self-sufficiency, which he found irritating. Perhaps what he felt was envy.

As they left the café he asked her whether she was on her way to the Steen.

"Not today. I don't have a session on Monday mornings. But I shall be there tomorrow."

She thanked him formally for the coffee and they parted. He turned eastwards towards the Steen and she disappeared in the direction of the Strand. As he watched her slim, dark figure swinging out of sight he pictured Cully creeping through the night with his pathetic bundle, half petrified with fright. He was not surprised that the old porter had confided so fully in Fredrica Saxon; in Cully's place, he would probably have done the same. She had, thought Dalgliesh, given him a great deal of interesting information. But what she hadn't been able to give him was an alibi for Dr. Baguley or for herself.

Mrs. Bostock, shorthand-notebook at the ready, sat beside Dr. Etherege's chair, her elegant legs crossed at the knees and her flamingo head lifted to receive, with becoming gravity, the medical director's instructions.

"Superintendent Dalgliesh has telephoned to say that he will be here shortly. He wants to see certain members of the staff again and has asked for an interview with me before lunch."

"I don't see how you can fit him in before lunch, Doctor," said Mrs. Bostock repressively. "There's the Professional Staff Committee at two-thirty and you haven't had time to look at the agenda. Dr. Talmage from the States is booked for twelve-thirty and I was hoping for an hour's dictation from 11 a.m."

"That will have to wait. The superintendent will be taking up a great deal of your own time, I'm afraid. He has some questions about the working of the clinic."

"I'm afraid I don't quite understand, Doctor. Do you mean he's interested in the general administrative arrangements?" Mrs. Bostock's tone was a nice blend of surprise and disapproval.

"Apparently so," replied Dr. Etherege. "He mentioned the appointments diary, the diagnostic index, the arrangements for registering incoming and outgoing post, and the medical record system. You had better deal with him personally. If I want to dictate I'll send for Miss Priddy."

"I'll do what I can to help, naturally," said Mrs. Bostock. "It's unfortunate that he should have picked one of our busiest mornings. It would be simpler to arrange a programme for him if I knew what he had in mind."

"We should all like to know that, I imagine," replied the medical director. "I should just answer his questions as fully as you can. And please get Cully to ring me as soon as he wants to come up."

"Yes, Doctor," said Mrs. Bostock, recognizing defeat. And took her leave.

Downstairs, in the E.C.T. room, Dr. Baguley twitched himself into his white coat, helped by Nurse Bolam.

"Mrs. King will be here for her LSD treatment on Wednesday as usual. I think it will be best if we give it in one of the P.S.W. rooms on the third floor. Miss Kettle isn't in on Wednesday evenings, is she? Have a word with her. Alternatively we could use Mrs. Kallinski's room or one of the small interviewing rooms at the back."

Nurse Bolam said:

"It won't be so convenient for you, Doctor. It means coming up two flights when I phone."

"That isn't going to kill me. I may look in my dotage but I still have the use of my legs."

"There's the question of a bed, Doctor. I suppose we could put up one of the recovery stretchers from the E.C.T. clinic."

"Get Nagle to see to it. I don't want you alone in that basement."

"I'm not in the least frightened, really, Dr. Baguley."

Dr. Baguley lost his temper.

"For God's sake, use your brain, Nurse. Of course you're frightened! There's a murderer loose somewhere in this clinic and no one—except one person—is going to be happy about staying alone for any length of time in the basement. If you really aren't frightened then have the good sense to conceal the fact, especially from the police. Where's Sister? In the general office?"

He picked up the receiver and dialled jerkily.

"Sister? Baguley here. I've just told Nurse Bolam that I don't feel happy about using the basement room for LSD this week."

Sister Ambrose's voice came back clearly:

"Just as you like, Doctor, of course. But if the basement is more convenient and we could get a relief nurse from one of the general hospitals in the group for the E.C.T. clinic, I should be quite happy to stay downstairs with Nurse Bolam. We could special Mrs. King together."

Dr. Baguley said shortly:

"I want you in the E.C.T. clinic as usual, Sister, and the LSD patient will go upstairs. I hope that's finally understood."

In the medical director's room two hours later, Dalgliesh placed three black metal boxes on Dr. Etherege's desk. The boxes, which had small round holes punched in each of the shorter sides, were packed with buff-coloured cards. It was the clinic diagnostic index. Dalgliesh said:

"Mrs. Bostock has explained this to me. If I've understood her correctly, each of these cards represents a patient. The information on the case record is coded and the patient's code punched on the card. The cards are punched with even rows of small holes and the space between each hole is numbered. By punching any number with the hand machine I cut out the card between the two adjacent holes to form an oblong slit. If this metal rod is then inserted through say, hole number 20 on the outside of the box, and pushed right through the cards, and the box is rotated, any card which has been punched through that number will stand out. It is, in fact, one of the simplest of the many punch-card systems on the market."

"Yes. We use it principally as a diagnostic index and for research." If the medical director was surprised at Dalgliesh's interest he made no sign. The superintendent went on:

"Mrs. Bostock tells me that you don't code from the case record until the patient has completed treatment and that the system was started in 1952. That means that patients at present attending won't yet have a card—unless, of course, they were treated here earlier—and that patients who completed treatment before 1952 aren't included."

"Yes. We should like to include the earlier cases, but it's a question of staff time. The coding and punching are time-consuming and it's the kind of job that gets put on one side. At present we're coding the February 1962 discharges, so we're quite a bit behind."

"But once the patient's card is punched you can select any diagnosis or category of patient at will?"

"Yes, indeed." The medical director gave his slow sweet smile.

"I won't say that we can pick out immediately all the indigenous depressives with blue-eyed grandmothers who were born in wedlock because we haven't coded information about grandparents. But anything coded can be extracted without trouble."

Dalgliesh laid a slim manilla file on the desk.

"Mrs. Bostock has lent me the coding instructions. I see that you code sex, age, marital status, address by local authority area, diagnosis, consultant who treated the patient, dates of first and subsequent attendances and a considerable amount of detail about symptoms, treatment and progress. You also code social class. I find that interesting."

"It's unusual, certainly," replied Dr. Etherege. "Chiefly, I suppose, because it can be a purely subjective assessment. But we wanted it because it's sometimes useful in research. As you see we use the Registrar-General's classes. They're accurate enough for our purposes."

Dalgliesh ran the thin metal rod through his fingers.

"So I could select, for example, the cards of patients in class one who were treated eight to ten years ago, were married with a family, and were suffering from, say, sexual aberration, kleptomania, or any other socially unacceptable personality disorder."

"You could," admitted the medical director quietly. "But I can't see why you should want to."

"Blackmail, Doctor. It occurs to me that we have here a neatly contrived apparatus for the pre-selection of a victim. You push through the rod and out pops your card. The card bears a number on the top right-hand corner. And down in the basement record-room the medical record is filed and waiting."

The medical director said:

"This is nothing but guesswork. There isn't a shred of evidence."

"There's no proof, certainly, but it's a reasonable possibility.

Consider the facts. On Wednesday afternoon Miss Bolam saw the group secretary after the House Committee meeting and told him that all was well at the clinic. At twelve-fifteen on Friday morning she telephoned to ask for an urgent visit because 'something is going on here that he ought to know about'. It was something serious and continuing and something that started before her time here, that is more than three years ago."

"Whatever it was we've no evidence that it was the reason for her death."

"No."

"In fact, if the murderer wanted to prevent Miss Bolam seeing Lauder he left it rather late. There was nothing to stop the group secretary turning up here any time after one o'clock."

Dalgliesh said:

"She was told over the telephone that he couldn't arrive until after the J.C.C. meeting that evening. That leads us to ask who could have overheard the telephone call. Cully was officially on the board, but he was unwell most of the day and, from time to time, other members of the staff took over, sometimes only for a few minutes. Nagle, Mrs. Bostock, Miss Priddy and even Mrs. Shorthouse, all say that they helped on the board. Nagle thinks he took over for a short time at midday before he went out for his lunchtime beer, but says that he can't be sure. Nor can Cully. No one admits to having put through this particular call."

"They might not know if they had," replied Dr. Etherege. "We're insistent that the operator doesn't listen in to calls. That, after all, is important in our work. Miss Bolam may have merely asked for group offices. She must put through calls fairly often to the finance and supplies departments as well as the group secretary. The operator couldn't know there was anything special about this call. She might even have asked for an outside line and put through the call herself. That is possible, of course, with the P.A.B.X. system."

"But it could still be overheard by the person on the board."

"If he plugged in I suppose it could."

Dalgliesh said: "Miss Bolam told Cully late in the afternoon that she was expecting Mr. Lauder and she may have mentioned the visit to other people. We don't know. No one will admit to having been told except Cully. In the circumstances, that isn't perhaps surprising. We're not going to get much further with it at present. What I must do now is to find out what Miss Bolam wanted to tell Mr. Lauder. One of the first possibilities to be considered in a place like this must be blackmail. God knows that's continuing and it's serious enough."

The medical director did not speak for a moment. Dalgliesh wondered whether he was contemplating a further remonstrance, selecting appropriate words to express concern or disbelief. Then he said quietly:

"Of course it's serious. There's no point in wasting time discussing just how serious. Obviously, having thought up this theory, you have to carry through your investigation. Any other course of action would be most unfair to the members of my staff. What do you want me to do?"

"To help me select a victim. Later, perhaps, to make some telephone calls."

"You appreciate, Superintendent, that the case records are confidential?"

"I'm not asking to see a single case record. But if I did I don't think either you or the patient need worry. Shall we get started? We can take out our class 1 patients. Perhaps you would call out the codes for me."

A considerable number of the Steen patients were in class 1. "Upper-class neuroses catered for only", thought Dalgliesh. He surveyed the field for a moment and then said:

"If I were the blackmailer would I choose a man or a woman? It would depend on my own sex probably. A woman might pick on a woman. But, if it's a question of a regular income a man is probably a better bet. Let's take out the males next. I imagine our victim will live out of London. It would be risky to select an ex-patient who could too easily succumb to the temptation to pop into the clinic and let you know what was going on. I think I'd select my victim from a small town or village."

The medical director said:

"We only coded the county if it were an out-London address. London patients are coded by borough. Our best plan will be to take out all the London addresses and see what's left."

This was done. The number of cards still in the survey was now only a few dozen. Most of the Steen patients, as might be expected, came from the county of London. Dalgliesh said:

"Married or single? It's difficult to decide whether one or the other would be most vulnerable. Let's leave it open and start on the diagnosis. This is where I need your help particularly, Doctor. I realize this is highly confidential information. I suggest that you call out the codes for the diagnoses or symptoms which might interest a blackmailer. I don't want details."

Again the medical director paused. Dalgliesh waited patiently, metal rod in hand, while the doctor sat in silence, the code book opened before him. He seemed not to be seeing it. After a minute he roused himself and focused his eyes on the page. He said quietly:

"Try codes 23, 68, 69 and 71."

There were now only eleven cards remaining. Each of them bore a case record number on the top right-hand margin. Dalgliesh made a note of the numbers, and said:

"This is as far as we can go with the diagnostic index. We must now do what I think our blackmailer did, have a look at the case records, and learn more of our prospective victims. Shall we go down to the basement?"

The medical director got up without a word. As they went down the stairs they passed Miss Kettle on her way up. She nodded to the medical director and gave Dalgliesh a brief, puzzled glance as if wondering whether he were someone she had met and ought to recognize. In the hall Dr. Baguley was talking with Sister Ambrose. They broke off and turned to watch with grave, unsmiling faces as Dr. Etherege and Dalgliesh made their way to the basement stairs. At the other end of the hall the grey outline of Cully's head could be seen through the glass of the reception kiosk. The head did not turn and Dalgliesh guessed that Cully, absorbed in his contemplation of the front door, had not heard them.

The records-room was locked, but no longer sealed. In the porters' restroom Nagle was putting on his coat, evidently on his way out to an early lunch. He made no sign as the medical director took the record-room key from its hook, but the flash of interest in his mild, mud-brown eyes was not lost on Dalgliesh. They had been well observed. By early afternoon everyone in the clinic would know that he had examined the diagnostic index with the medical director and then visited the record-room. To one person that information would be of crucial interest. What Dalgliesh hoped was that the murderer would become frightened and desperate; what he feared was that he would become more dangerous.

Dr. Etherege switched on the light in the record-room and the fluorescent tubes flickered, yellowed and blazed into whiteness. The room stood revealed. Dalgliesh smelt again its characteristic smell, compounded of mustiness, old paper and the tang of hot metal. He watched without betraying any emotion while the medical director locked the door on the inside and slipped the key in his pocket.

There was no sign now that the room had been the scene of murder. The torn records had been repaired and replaced on the shelves. The chair and table placed upright in their usual position.

The records were tied together with string in bundles of ten. Some of the files had been stored for so long that they seemed to adhere to each other. The string bit into the bulging manilla covers; across their tops was a thin patina of dust. Dalgliesh said:

"It should be possible to tell which of these bundles have been untied since the records were weeded out and brought down for storage. Some of them look as if they haven't been touched for years. I realize that a bundle may have been untied to extract a record for a perfectly innocent purpose, but we may as well make a start with files from those bundles which have obviously been untied within the last year or so. The first two numbers are in the eight thousand range. These seem to be on the top shelf. Have we a ladder?"

The medical director disappeared behind the first row of

shelves and reappeared with a small step-ladder which he manœuvred with difficulty into the narrow aisle. Looking up at Dalgliesh as the detective mounted, he said:

"Tell me, Superintendent. Does this touching confidence mean that you have eliminated me from your list of suspects? If it does I should be interested to know by what process of deduction you came to that conclusion. I can't flatter myself that you believe me incapable of murder. No detective would accept that, surely, of any man."

"And no psychiatrist possibly," said Dalgliesh. "I don't ask myself whether a man is capable of murder, but whether he is capable of this particular murder. I don't think you're a petty blackmailer. I can't see how you could have known about Lauder's proposed visit. I doubt whether you've either the strength or skill to kill in that way. Lastly, I think you're probably the one person here whom Miss Bolam wouldn't have kept waiting. Even if I'm wrong you can hardly refuse to co-operate, can you?"

He was deliberately curt. The bright blue eyes were still gazing into his, inviting a confidence which he did not want to give but found it difficult to resist. The medical director went on:

"I have only met three murderers. Two of them are buried in quicklime. One of the two hardly knew what he was doing and the other couldn't have stopped himself. Are you satisfied, Superintendent, with that solution?"

Dalgliesh replied:

"No man in his senses would be. But I don't see how that affects what I'm trying to do now; catch this murderer before he—or she—kills again."

The medical director said no more. Together they found the eleven case records they sought and took them up to Dr. Etherege's room. If Dalgliesh had expected the medical director to make difficulties over the next stage of the investigation he was agreeably surprised. The hint that this killer might not stop at one victim had struck home. When Dalgliesh explained what he wanted the medical director did not protest. Dalgliesh said:

"I'm not asking for the names of these patients. I'm not

interested in what was wrong with them. All I want you to do is to telephone each of them and ask tactfully whether they rang the clinic recently, probably on Friday morning. You could explain that someone made a call which it's important to trace. If one of these patients did ring I want the name and address. Not the diagnosis. Just the name and address."

"I must ask the patient's consent before I give that information."

"If you must," said Dalgliesh. "I leave that to you. All I ask is to get that information."

The medical director's stipulation was a formality and both of them knew it. The eleven case records were on the desk and nothing but force could keep the addresses from Dalgliesh if he wanted them. He sat at some distance from Dr. Etherege in one of the large, leather-covered chairs, and prepared to watch, with professional interest, his unusual collaborator at work. The medical director picked up his receiver and asked for an outside line. The patients' telephone numbers had been noted on the case records and the first two tries at once reduced the eleven possibles to nine. In each case the patient had changed his address since his attendance. Dr. Etherege apologized for disturbing the new subscribers to the numbers concerned and dialled for the third time. The third number answered and the medical director asked if he might speak to Mr. Caldecote. There was a prolonged crackling from the other end and Dr. Etherege made the appropriate response.

"No, he hadn't heard. How very sad. Really? No, it was nothing important. Just an old acquaintance who would be driving through Wiltshire and hoped to meet Mr. Caldecote again. No, he wouldn't speak to Mrs. Caldecote. He didn't want to distress her."

"Dead?" asked Dalgliesh, as the receiver was replaced.

"Yes. Three years ago, apparently. Cancer, poor fellow. I must note that on his record."

He did so while Dalgliesh waited.

The next number was difficult to get and there was much talk with the exchange. When at last the number was rung there was no reply.

"We seem to be having no success, Superintendent. It was a clever theory of yours, but it appears, more ingenious than true."

"There are still seven more patients to try," said Dalgliesh quietly. The medical director murmured something about a Dr. Talmage whom he was expecting, but referred to the next file and dialled again. This time the patient was at home and, apparently, not in the least surprised to hear from the medical director of the Steen. He poured out a lengthy account of his present psychological condition to which Dr. Etherege listened with patient sympathy and made appropriate replies. Dalgliesh was interested and a little amused at the skill with which the call was conducted. But the patient had not recently telephoned the clinic. The medical director put down the receiver and spent some time noting what the patient had told him on the case record.

"One of our successes, apparently. He wasn't at all surprised that I telephoned. It's rather touching the way patients take it for granted that their doctors are immensely concerned for their welfare and are thinking of them personally at all times of the day and night. But he didn't phone. He wasn't lying, I assure you. This is very time-consuming, Superintendent, but I suppose we must go on."

"Yes, please. I'm sorry, but we must go on."

But the next call brought success. At first it sounded like another failure. From the conversation Dalgliesh gathered that the patient had recently been taken to hospital and that it was his wife who had answered. Then he saw the medical director's face change, and heard him say:

"You did? We knew that someone had telephoned and were trying to trace the call. I expect you've heard about the very dreadful tragedy that we've had here recently. Yes, it is in connection with that." He waited while the voice spoke at some length from the other end. Then he put down the receiver and wrote briefly on his desk jotting pad. Dalgliesh did not speak. The medical director looked up at him with an expression half puzzled, half surprised.

"That was the wife of a Colonel Fenton of Sprigg's Green in

Kent. She telephoned Miss Bolam about a very serious matter at about midday last Friday. She didn't want to talk to you on the phone about it and I thought it better not to press her. But she'd like to see you as soon as possible. I've written down the address."

"Thank you, Doctor," said Dalgliesh, and took the proffered paper. He showed neither surprise nor relief, but his heart was singing. The medical director shook his head as if the whole thing were beyond his understanding. He said:

"She sounds rather a formidable old lady and very formal. She said that she would be very glad if you would take afternoon tea with her."

Just after four o'clock Dalgliesh drove slowly into Sprigg's Green. It revealed itself as an undistinguished village lying between the Maidstone and Canterbury roads. He could not remember having passed through it before. There were few people about. The village, thought Dalgliesh, was too far from London to tempt the commuter and had no period charm to attract retired couples or artists and writers in search of country peace with a country cost of living. Most of the cottages were obviously lived in by farm workers, their front gardens clumped with cabbages and brussels sprouts, straggly and stem-scarred from recent pickings, their windows shut close against the treachery of an English autumn. Dalgliesh passed the church, its short flint-and-stone tower and clear glass windows only half visible behind the surrounding chestnut trees. The churchyard was untidy but not offensively so. The grass had been mown between the graves and some attempt made to weed the gravel paths. Separated from the churchyard by a tall laurel hedge stood the vicarage, a sombre Victorian house built to accommodate a Victorian-size family and its appendages. Next came the green itself, a small square of grass bounded by a row of weather-boarded cottages and faced by a more than usually hideous modern pub and petrol station. Outside the "King's Head" was a concrete bus shelter where a group of women waited dispiritedly. They gave Dalgliesh a brief and uninterested glance as he passed. In spring, no doubt, the surrounding cherry orchards would lend their charm even to Sprigg's Green. Now, however, there was a chill dampness in the air, the fields looked perpetually sodden, a slow mournful procession of cows being driven to the evening milking churned the road verges to mud. Dalgliesh slowed to a walking pace to pass them, keeping his watch for Sprigg's Acre. He did not want to ask the way.

He was not long in finding it. The house lay a little back from the road and was sheltered from it by a six-foot beech hedge which shone golden in the fading light. There appeared to be no drive and Dalgliesh edged his Cooper Bristol carefully on to the grass verge before letting himself in through the white gates of the garden. The house lay before him, rambling, low built and thatched, with an air of comfort and simplicity. As he turned from latching the gate behind him a woman turned the corner of the house and came down the path to meet him. She was very small. Somehow this surprised Dalgliesh. He had formed a mental picture of a stout, well-corseted colonel's wife condescending to see him, but at her own time and place. The reality was less intimidating and more interesting. There was something gallant and a little pathetic in the way she came down the path towards him. She was wearing a thick skirt and a tweed jacket and was hatless, her thick white hair lifting with the evening breeze. She wore gardening gloves, incongruously large with vast gauntlets which made the trowel she carried look like a child's toy. As they met she pulled off the right glove and held out her hand to him, looking up at him with anxious eyes which lightened, almost imperceptibly, with relief. But when she spoke her voice was unexpectedly firm.

"Good afternoon. You must be Superintendent Dalgliesh. My name is Louise Fenton. Did you come by car? I thought I heard one."

Dalgliesh explained where he had left it and said that he hoped that it would not be in anyone's way.

"Oh, no! Not at all. Such an unpleasant way to travel. You could have come by train quite easily to Marden and I would have sent the trap for you. We haven't a car. We both dislike them very much. I'm sorry you had to sit in one all the way from London."

"It was the fastest way," said Dalgliesh, wondering if he should apologize for living in the twentieth century. "And I wanted to see you as soon as possible."

He was careful to keep the urgency from his voice, but he could see the sudden tensing of her shoulders.

"Yes. Yes, of course. Would you like to see the garden before we go in? The light is fading but we might just have time."

An interest in the garden was apparently expected and Dalgliesh acquiesced. A light east wind, rising as the day died, whipped uncomfortably around his neck and ankles. But he never hurried an interview. This one promised to be difficult for Mrs. Fenton and she was entitled to take her time. He wondered at his own impatience even as he concealed it. For the last two days he had been irked by a foreboding of tragedy and failure which was the more disturbing because it was irrational. The case was young yet. His intelligence told him that he was making progress. Even at this moment he was within grasp of motive, and motive, he knew, was crucial to this case. He hadn't failed yet in his career at the Yard and this case, with its limited number of suspects and careful contriving, was an unlikely candidate for a first failure. Yet he remained worried, vexed by this unreasonable fear that time was running out. Perhaps it was the autumn. Perhaps he was tired. He turned up his coat collar and prepared himself to look interested and appreciative.

They passed together through a wrought-iron gate at the side of the house and entered the main garden. Mrs. Fenton was saying:

"I love the garden dearly, but I'm not much good at it. Things don't grow for me. My husband has the green fingers. He's in Maidstone Hospital at present having an operation for hernia. It's all been very successful I'm happy to say. Do you garden, Superintendent?"

Dalgliesh explained that he lived in a flat high above the Thames in the City and had recently sold his Essex cottage.

"I really know very little about gardening," he said.

"Then you will enjoy looking at ours," replied Mrs. Fenton, with gentle if illogical persistence.

There was, indeed, plenty to see even in the fading light of an autumn day. The colonel had given his imagination full play, compensating perhaps for the enforced regimentation of much of his life by indulgence in a picturesque and undisciplined profusion. There was a small lawn surrounding a fish pond and edged with crazy paving. There was a succession of trellis archways leading from one carefully tended plot to another. There was a rose garden with a sundial where a few last roses still gleamed white on their leafless stems. There were hedges of beech, yew and hawthorn as gold and green backcloths to the banked chrysanthemums. At the bottom of the garden ran a small stream, crossed every ten yards by wooden bridges which were a monument to the colonel's industry, if not to his taste. The appetite had grown by what it fed on. The colonel, having once successfully bridged his brook, had been unable to resist further efforts. Together they stood for a moment on one of the bridges. Dalgliesh could see the colonel's initials cut into the wood of the handrail. Beneath their feet the little stream, already half choked with the first fallen leaves, made its own sad music. Suddenly, Mrs. Fenton said:

"So somebody killed her. I know I ought to feel pity for her whatever she did. But I can't. Not yet. I should have realized that Matthew wouldn't be the only victim. These people never stop at one victim, do they? I suppose someone couldn't stand it any more and took that way out. It's a very terrible thing, but I can understand it. I read about it in the papers, you know, before the medical director telephoned. Do you know, Superintendent, for a moment I was glad. That's a terrible thing to say, but it's true. I was glad she was dead. I thought that now Matthew needn't worry any more."

Dalgliesh said gently:

"We don't think that Miss Bolam was blackmailing your husband. It's possible that she was, but not likely. We think she was killed because she had found out what was happening and meant to stop it. That's why it's so important that I talk to you."

Mrs. Fenton's knuckles whitened. The hands grasping the bridge began to shake. She said:

"I'm afraid I've been very stupid. I mustn't waste any more of your time. It's getting cold, isn't it? Shall we go indoors?"

They turned towards the house, neither of them speaking. Dalgliesh shortened his stride to the slow pace of the thin, upright figure at his side. He glanced at her anxiously. She was very pale and he thought he saw her lips moving soundlessly. But she walked firmly. She was going to be all right. He told himself that he mustn't hurry things. In half an hour, perhaps less, he would have the motive securely in his hands like a bomb that would blow the whole case wide open. But he must be patient. Once again he was touched by an indefinable unrest as if, even at this moment of imminent triumph, his heart held the sure knowledge of failure. The dusk closed in around them. Somewhere a bonfire smouldered, filling his nostrils with acrid smoke. The lawn was a wet sponge under his feet.

The house welcomed them, blessedly warm and smelling faintly of home-baked bread. Mrs. Fenton left him to put her head into a room at the far end of the hall. He guessed that tea was being ordered. Then she led him into the drawing-room to the comfort of a wood fire which threw immense shadow over the chintz-covered chairs and sofa and the faded carpet. She switched on a huge standard lamp at the side of the fireplace and tugged the curtains across the windows, shutting out desolation and decay. Tea arrived, the tray set on a low table by a stolid and aproned maid almost as old as her mistress who carefully avoided looking at Dalgliesh. It was a good tea. Dalgliesh saw with an emotion which was too like compassion to be comfortable, that trouble had been taken on his behalf. There were fresh-baked scones, two kinds of sandwiches, home-made cakes and an iced sponge. There was too much of everything, a schoolboy's tea. It was as if the two women, faced with their unknown and most unwelcome visitor, had sought relief from uncertainty in the provision of this embarrassingly liberal feast. Mrs. Fenton herself seemed surprised at the variety which faced her. She manœuvred cups on the tray like an anxious, inexperienced hostess. It was only when Dalgliesh was provided with his tea and sandwich that she spoke again about the murder.

"My husband attended the Steen Clinic for about four months, nearly ten years ago, soon after he left the army. He was living in London at the time and I was in Nairobi staying with my daughter-in-law who was expecting her first baby. I never knew about my husband's treatment until he told me a week ago."

She paused and Dalgliesh said:

"I ought to say now that we aren't, of course, interested in what was wrong with Colonel Fenton. That is a confidential medical matter and it isn't the concern of the police. I didn't ask Dr. Etherege for any information and he wouldn't have given it to me if I had. The fact that your husband was being blackmailed may have to come out—I don't think that can be avoided—but his reason for going to the clinic and the details of his treatment are no one's business but his and yours."

Mrs. Fenton replaced her cup on the tray with infinite care. She looked into the fire and said:

"I don't think it is my business, really. I wasn't upset because he didn't tell me. It's so easy to say now that I would have understood and would have tried to help, but I wonder. I think he was wise not to speak about it. People make such a fuss about absolute honesty in marriage, but it isn't very sensible to confess hurtful things unless you really mean to hurt. I wish Matthew had told me about the blackmail, though. Then he really needed help. Together I'm sure we could have thought of something."

Dalgliesh asked how it had started.

"Just two years ago, Matthew says. He had a telephone call. The voice reminded him about his treatment at the Steen and actually quoted some of the very intimate details Matthew had told the psychiatrist. Then the voice suggested that he would like to help other patients who were trying to overcome similar difficulties. There was a lot of talk about the dreadful social consequences of not getting cured. It was all very subtle and clever, but there wasn't the least doubt what the voice was after. Matthew asked what he was expected to do and was told to send fifteen pounds in notes to arrive by the first post on the first day of every month. If the first was a Saturday or Sunday, the letter was to arrive on Monday. He was to address the envelope in green ink to the administrative secretary and enclose with the money a note to say that it was a donation from a grateful patient. The voice said that he could be sure that the cash would go where it could do most good."

"It was a clever enough plan," said Dalgliesh. "Blackmail would be difficult to prove and the amount was nicely calculated. I imagine that your husband would have been forced to take a different line if the demand had been too exorbitant."

"Oh, he would! Matthew would never let us be ruined. But you see, it was such a small amount really. I don't mean that we could afford to lose fifteen pounds a month, but it was a sum which Matthew could just find by personal economies without making me suspicious. And the demand never rose. That was the extraordinary thing about it. Matthew said that he always understood a blackmailer was never satisfied but kept increasing the demand until the victim couldn't pay another penny. It wasn't like that at all. Matthew sent the money to arrive on the first day of the next month and he had another call. The voice thanked him for his kind donation and made it quite clear that no more than fifteen pounds was expected. And no more ever was. The voice said something about sharing the sacrifice equally. Matthew said he could almost persuade himself that the thing was genuine. About six months ago he decided to miss a month and see what happened. It wasn't very pleasant. There was another call and the menace was unmistakable. The voice talked about the need to save patients from social ostracism and said how distressed the people of Sprigg's Green would be to hear about his lack of generosity. My husband decided to go on. If the village really got to know, it would mean leaving this house. My family have lived here for two hundred years and we both love it. Matthew would be heartbroken to leave the garden. And then there's the village. Of course, you haven't seen it at its best, but we love it. My husband is a churchwarden. Our small son, who was killed in a road accident, is buried here. It isn't easy to pull up your roots at seventy."

No, it wouldn't be easy. Dalgliesh didn't question her assumption that discovery would mean that they must leave. A younger, tougher, more sophisticated couple would no doubt ride the publicity, ignore the innuendoes and accept the embarrassed sympathy of their friends in the sure knowledge that nothing lasts for ever and that few things in village life are as dead as last year's scandal. Pity was less easy to accept. It was probably the fear of pity that would drive most victims to retreat. He asked what had brought the matter to a head. Mrs. Fenton replied:

"Two things, really. The first is that we needed more money. My husband's younger brother died unexpectedly a month ago and left his widow rather badly off. She is an invalid and not likely to live more than a year or two, but she is very happily settled in a nursing-home near Norwich and would like to stay there. It was a question of helping with the fees. She needed about another five pounds a week and I couldn't understand why Matthew seemed so worried about it. It would mean careful planning, but I thought we ought to be able to manage it. But he knew, of course, that we couldn't if he had to go on sending the fifteen pounds to the Steen. Then there was his operation. It wasn't a very serious one I know, but any operation is a risk at seventy and he was afraid that he might die and the whole story come out without his being able to explain. So he told me. I was very glad he did. He went into hospital perfectly happy as a result and the operation went very well. Really very well indeed. Could I give you some more tea, Superintendent?"

Dalgliesh passed her his cup and asked what action she had decided to take. They were now coming to the crux of the story, but he was careful neither to hurry her nor to appear over-anxious. His comments and questions might have been those of any afternoon guest, dutifully taking a polite share in his hostess's conversation. She was an old lady who had been through a severe strain and was faced with one even greater. He guessed a little of what this revelation to a stranger must be costing her. Any formal expression of sympathy would have been a presumption, but at least he could help, with patience and understanding.

"What did I decide to do? Well, that was the problem, of course. I was determined that the blackmailing should be stopped, but I wanted to spare us both if I could. I'm not a very intelligent woman—it's no use shaking your head, if I were this murder wouldn't have happened—but I thought it out very carefully. It seemed to me that the best thing was to visit the Steen Clinic and see someone in authority. I could explain what was happening, perhaps even without mentioning my name, and ask them to make their own investigation and put a stop to the blackmail. After all, they would know about my husband, so I wouldn't be confiding his secret to anyone new and they would be just as anxious to avoid publicity as I was. It wouldn't do the clinic any good if this came out, would it? They could probably find out who was responsible without a great deal of difficulty. Psychiatrists are supposed to understand people's characters after all, and it must be someone who was at the clinic when my husband attended. And then, being a woman, would narrow the field."

"Do you mean the blackmailer was a woman?" asked Dalgliesh, surprised.

"Oh, yes! At least, the voice on the telephone was a woman's voice, my husband says."

"Is he quite sure of that?"

"He didn't express any doubt to me. It wasn't only the voice, you see. It was some of the things she said. Things like it not being only members of my husband's sex who had these illnesses, and had he ever thought what unhappiness they could cause to women, and so on. There were definite references to her being a woman. My husband remembers the telephone conversations very clearly and he will be able to tell you what the remarks were. I expect you will want to see him as soon as possible, won't you?"

Touched by the obvious anxiety in her voice, he replied:

"If his doctor thinks Colonel Fenton is well enough to have a brief talk to me I should like to see him on my way back to London tonight. There are one or two points—this matter of the blackmailer's sex is one—that only he can help with. I shan't bother him more than necessary."

"I'm sure he will be able to see you. He has a little room of his own—an amenity bed they call them—and he's doing very well. I told him that you were coming today so he won't be surprised to see you. I don't think I'll come too, if you don't mind. I think he would rather see you alone. I shall write a note for you to take."

Dalgliesh thanked her and said:

"It's interesting that your husband should say it was a woman. He could be right, of course, but it would be a clever deception on the blackmailer's part and difficult to disprove. Some men are able to mimic a woman's voice very convincingly and the casual references to establish sex would be even more effective than a disguised voice. If the colonel had decided to prosecute and the matter had come to court, it would have been very difficult to convict a man of this particular crime unless the evidence was very strong. And as far as I can see the evidence would be almost non-existent. I think we keep a very open mind on the question of the blackmailer's sex. But I'm sorry. I interrupted."

"It was rather an important point to establish, wasn't it? I hope that my husband will be able to help with it. Well, as I was saying, I decided that the best move was to visit the clinic. I went up to London last Friday morning on an early train. I had to see my chiropodist and there were one or two things Matthew needed in hospital. I decided to shop first. I should have gone direct to the clinic, of course. That was another mistake. It was cowardice, really. I wasn't looking forward to it and I tried to behave as if it were nothing so very special, just a casual visit I could fit in between the shopping and the chiropodist. In the end I didn't go at all. I telephoned instead. You see, I told you I wasn't very intelligent."

Dalgliesh asked what had led to the change of plan.

"It was Oxford Street. I know that sounds silly, but it happened that way. I hadn't been up to London alone for a very long time and I had forgotten how dreadful it is now. I used to love it when I was a girl. It seemed a gracious city then. Now the skyline has changed and the streets seem full of freaks and foreigners. One shouldn't resent them, I know—the foreigners, I mean. It's just that I felt so alien. And then there were the cars. I tried to cross Oxford Street and was stranded among them on one of the islands. Of course, they weren't killing anyone or knocking anyone down. They couldn't. They couldn't even move. But they smelt so horrible that I had to hold my handkerchief to my nose and I felt so faint and ill. When I reached the pavement I went into one of the stores to find the women's rest room. It was on the fifth floor and it took me a long time to get to the right lift. The crowds were dreadful and we were all squashed in together. When I got to the rest-room all the chairs were taken. I was standing against the wall wondering whether I could summon enough energy to queue for my lunch when I saw the row of telephone boxes. Suddenly I realized that I could telephone the clinic and save myself the journey and the ordeal of telling my story face to face. It was stupid of me, I see that now, but at the time it seemed a very good idea. It would be easier to conceal my identity on the telephone and I felt that I should be able to explain more fully. I also gained a great deal of comfort from the thought that, if the conversation became too difficult, I could always ring off. You see, I was being very cowardly and my only excuse is that I was very tired, far more tired than I imagined possible. I expect you will say that I ought to have gone straight to the police, to Scotland Yard. But Scotland Yard is a place I associate with detective stories and murders. It hardly seems possible that it actually exists and you can call there and tell your story. Besides, I was still very anxious to avoid publicity. I didn't think the police would welcome someone who wanted help, but wasn't prepared to co-operate by telling the whole story or being willing to prosecute. All I wanted, you see, was to stop the blackmailer. It wasn't very public-spirited of me, was it?"

"It was very understandable," replied Dalgliesh. "I thought

it very possible that Miss Bolam got the warning by telephone. Can you remember what you said to her?"

"Not very clearly, I'm afraid. When I had found the four pennies for the call and looked up the number in the directory I spent a few minutes deciding what I would say. A man's voice answered and I asked to speak to the administrative secretary. Then there was a woman's voice which said, 'Administrative officer speaking.' I hadn't expected to hear a woman and I suddenly got it into my mind that I was speaking to the blackmailer. After all, why not? So I said that someone from the clinic, and probably she, had been blackmailing my husband and that I was telephoning to say that she wouldn't get another penny from now on and that if we received any more telephone calls we should go straight to the police. It all came out in a rush. I was shaking rather badly and had to lean against the wall of the telephone box for support. I must have sounded a little hysterical. When she could get a word in she asked me whether I was a patient and who was treating me and said something about asking one of the doctors to have a word with me. I suppose she thought I was out of my mind. I replied that I had never attended the clinic and that, if ever I needed treatment, which God forbid, I should know better than to go to a place where a patient's indiscretions and unhappiness were made an opportunity for blackmail. I think I ended up by saying that there was a woman involved, that she must have been at the clinic for nearly ten years, and that, if the administrative officer wasn't the person concerned, I hoped that she would make it her duty to discover who was. She tried to get me to leave my name or to come to see her, but I rang off."

"Did you give her any details about how the blackmail was organized?"

"I told her that my husband had sent fifteen pounds a month in an envelope addressed in green ink. That's when she became suddenly very anxious that I should visit the clinic or at least leave my name. It was rude of me to ring off without ending the conversation, but I suddenly became frightened. I don't know why. And I had said all that I meant to say. One of the chairs in the restroom was vacant by then, so I sat down for half an hour until I felt better. Then I went straight to Charing Cross and had some coffee and sandwiches in the buffet there and waited for my train home. I read about the murder in the paper on Saturday and I'm afraid I took it for granted that one of the other victims—for there must have been others, surely—had taken that way out. I didn't connect the crime with my telephone call, at least, not at first. Then I began to wonder whether it might not be my duty to let the police know what had been going on at that dreadful place. Yesterday I talked to my husband about it and we decided to do nothing in a hurry. We thought it might be best to wait and see whether we received any further calls from the blackmailer. I wasn't very happy about our silence. There haven't been many details of the murder in the papers, so I don't know what exactly happened. But I did realize that the blackmail might be in some way connected with the crime and that the police would wish to know about it. While I was still worrying about what to do, Dr. Etherege telephoned. You know the rest. I'm still wondering how you managed to trace me."

"We found you in the same way as the blackmailer picked out Colonel Fenton, from the clinic diagnostic index and the medical record. You mustn't think that they don't look after their confidential papers at the Steen. They do. Dr. Etherege is very distressed indeed about the blackmail. But no system is completely proof against clever and deliberate wickedness."

"You will find him, won't you?" she asked. "You will find him?"

"Thanks to you, I think we shall," Dalgliesh replied. As he held out his hand to say good-bye, she suddenly asked:

"What was she like, Superintendent? I mean the woman who was murdered. Tell me about Miss Bolam."

Dalgliesh said:

"She was forty-one years old. Not married. I never saw her alive, but she had light brown hair and blue-grey eyes. She was rather stout, wide browed, thin mouthed. She was an only child and both her parents were dead. She lived rather a lonely life, but her church meant a great deal to her and she was a Guide captain. She liked children and flowers. She was conscientious and efficient, but not very good at understanding people. She was kind when they were in trouble but they thought her rigid, humourless and censorious. I think they were probably right. She had a great sense of duty."

"I am responsible for her death. I have to accept that."

Dalgliesh said gently:

"That's nonsense, you know. Only one person is responsible and, thanks to you, we shall get him.

She shook her head.

"If I had come to you in the first place or even had the courage to turn up at the clinic instead of telephoning she would be alive today."

Dalgliesh thought that Louise Fenton deserved better than to be pacified with easy lies. And they would have brought no comfort. Instead he replied:

"I suppose that could be true. There are so many 'ifs'. She would be alive today if her group secretary had cancelled a meeting and hurried to the clinic, if she herself had gone at once to see him, if an old porter hadn't had stomach-ache. You did what you thought right and no one can do more."

"So did she, poor woman," replied Mrs. Fenton. "And look where it led her."

She patted Dalgliesh briefly on the shoulder, as if it were he who needed the comfort and reassurance.

"I didn't mean to bore you. Please forgive me. You've been very patient and kind. Might I ask one more question? You said that, thanks to me, you would get this murderer. Do you know now who it is?"

"Yes," said Dalgliesh. "I think I now know who it is."

Chapter Six

Back in his office at the Yard just over two hours later, Dalgliesh talked over the case with Sergeant Martin. The file lay open on the desk before him.

"You got corroboration of Mrs. Fenton's story all right, sir?"

"Oh, yes. The colonel was quite forthcoming. Now that he's recovered from the twin ordeals of his operation and the confession to his wife, he's inclined to take both experiences rather lightly. He even suggested that the request for money could have been genuine and that it was reasonable to assume that it was. I had to point out that a woman has been murdered before he faced the realities of the situation. Then he gave me the full story. It agreed with what Mrs. Fenton had told me except for one interesting addition. I give you three guesses."

"Would it be about that burglary? It was Fenton I suppose?"

"Damn you Martin, you might make an effort sometimes to look surprised. Yes, it was our colonel. But he didn't take the fifteen pounds. I wouldn't have blamed him if he had. The money was his after all. He admits himself that he would have taken it back if he'd seen it, but, of course, he didn't. He was there for quite another purpose, to get hold of that medical record. He was a bit out of his depth in most things but he did realize that the medical record was the only real evidence of what happened when he was a patient at the Steen. He mucked up his burglary attempt of course despite having practised glass-cutting in his greenhouse, and made an undignified exit when he heard Nagle and Cully arriving. He got nowhere near the record he wanted.

He assumed it was in one of the files in the general office and managed to prise those open. When he saw that the records were filed numerically he knew he couldn't succeed. He had long forgotten his clinic number. I expect he put it firmly out of his mind when he felt he was cured."

"Well, the clinic did that for him, anyway."

"He doesn't admit it I can tell you. I believe that's not uncommon with psychiatric patients. It must be rather disheartening for psychiatrists. After all, you don't get surgical patients claiming that they could have performed their own operation given half a chance. No, the colonel isn't feeling particularly grateful to the Steen, nor inclined to give the clinic much credit for keeping him out of trouble. I suppose he could be right. I don't imagine that Dr. Etherege would claim that you can do a great deal for a psychiatric patient in four months which was the length of time Fenton attended. His cure—if you can call it that—probably had something to do with leaving the army. It's difficult to judge whether he welcomed that or dreaded it. Anyway, we'd better resist the temptation to be amateur psychologists."

"What sort of a man is the colonel, sir?"

"Small. Probably looks smaller because of his illness. Sandy hair; bushy eyebrows. Rather like a small fierce animal glaring out from its hole. A much weaker personality than his wife, I'd say, despite Mrs. Fenton's apparent frailty. Admittedly it's difficult to be at one's best lying in a hospital bed wearing a striped bedjacket and with a formidable Sister warning one to be a good boy and not talk too long. He wasn't very helpful about the telephone voice. He says that it sounded like a woman and it never occurred to him that it mightn't be. On the other hand he wasn't surprised when I suggested that the voice could have been disguised. But he's honest, and, obviously, he can't go further than that. He just doesn't know. Still, we've got the motive. This is one of those rare cases in which knowing why is knowing who."

"Are you applying for a warrant?"

"Not yet. We're not ready. If we don't go carefully now the whole case could come apart in our hands."

Again he was visited by the chilling presentiment of disaster. He found himself analysing the case as if he had already failed. Where had it gone wrong? He had shown his hand to the murderer when he had taken the clinic diagnostic index so openly into the medical director's room. That fact would be round the clinic quickly enough. He had meant it to be. There came a time when it was useful to frighten your man. But was this killer the kind who could be frightened into betraying himself? Had it been an error of judgment to move so openly? Suddenly Martin's plain, honest face looked irritatingly bovine as he stood there unhelpfully waiting for instructions. Dalgliesh said:

"You went to the Priddys' place, I suppose. Well, let's have the dirt about that. The girl is married, I suppose?"

"There's no doubt about that, sir. I was there earlier this evening and I had a chat with the parents. Luckily Miss Priddy was out, fetching fish and chips for supper. They're in quite poor circumstances."

"That's a *non sequitur*. However, go on."

"There isn't much to report. They live in one of those terrace houses leading down to the southern railway line in Clapham. Everything's very comfortable and neat but there's no television or anything like that. I suppose their religion's against it. Both the Priddys are over sixty I reckon. Jennifer's the only child and her mother must have been more than forty when she was born. It's the usual story about the marriage. I was surprised they told me but they did. The husband's a warehouseman; used to work with the girl at her last job. Then there was a baby on the way so they had to get married."

"It's almost pitiably common. You'd think that her generation, who think they know all the answers about sex, would make themselves familiar with a few basic facts. However, we're told these little mishaps don't worry anyone these days."

Dalgliesh was shocked by the bitterness in his own voice. Was it really necessary, he wondered, to protest quite so vehemently about so common a little tragedy. What was happening to him? Martin said stolidly:

"They worry people like the Priddys. These kids get themselves into trouble but it's usually the despised older generation who have to cope. The Priddys did their best. They made the kids marry of course. There isn't much room in the house but they gave up the first floor and made it into a small flat for the young couple. Very nicely done it was too. They showed me."

Dalgliesh thought how much he disliked the expression "young couple" with its cosy undertones of dewy-eyed domesticity, its echo of disillusion.

"You seem to have made a hit in your brief visit," he said.

"I liked them, sir. They're good people. The marriage didn't last of course, and I think that they wonder now whether they did the right thing in forcing it. The chap left Clapham over two years ago and they don't know where he is now. They told me his name and I saw his photograph. He's got nothing to do with the Steen Clinic, sir."

"I didn't think he had. We hardly expected to discover that Jennifer Priddy was Mrs. Henry Etherege. Neither her parents nor her husband have anything to do with this crime."

Nor had they, except that their lives, like flying tangents, had made brief contact with the circle of death. Every murder case produced such people. Dalgliesh had sat more times than he could remember in sitting-rooms, bedrooms, pubs and police stations talking to people who had come, however briefly, in touch with murder. Violent death was a great releaser of inhibitions, the convulsive kick which spun open the top of so many ant hills. His job, in which he could deceive himself that non-involvement was a duty, had given him glimpses into the secret lives of men and women whom he might never see again except as half-recognized faces in a London crowd. Sometimes he despised his private image, the patient, uninvolved, uncensorious inquisitor of other people's misery and guilt. How long could you stay detached, he wondered, before you lost your own soul.

"What happened to the child?" he asked suddenly.

"She had a miscarriage, sir," answered Martin.

"Of course," thought Dalgliesh. "She would." Nothing could go right for such as the Priddys. Tonight he felt that he, too, was tainted with their ill luck. He asked what Martin had learned about Miss Bolam.

"Not much that we didn't know already. They went to the same church and Jennifer Priddy used to be a girl guide in Bolam's company. The old people spoke of her with a great deal of respect. She was helpful to them when the baby was on the way—I got the impression that she paid to have the house converted—and when the marriage failed she suggested that the Priddy child should work at the Steen. I think the old people were glad to think that someone was keeping an eye on Jenny. They couldn't tell me much about Miss Bolam's private life, at least, nothing that we don't know. There was one odd thing though. It happened when the girl got back with the supper. Mrs. Priddy asked me to stay and have a meal with them but I said I'd better be getting back. You know what it is with fish and chips. You just buy the right number of pieces and it isn't easy to fit in an extra. Anyway, they called the girl in to say 'good-bye' and she came in from the kitchen looking like death. She only stayed a second or two and the old people didn't seem to notice anything. But I did. Something had scared the kid properly."

"Finding you there, perhaps. She may have thought that you'd mentioned her friendship with Nagle."

"I don't think it was that, sir. She looked into the sitting-room when she first got back from the shop and said 'good evening' without turning a hair. I explained that I was just having a chat with her parents because they were friends of Miss Bolam and might be able to tell us something useful about her private life. It didn't seem to worry her. It was about five minutes later that she came back looking so odd."

"No one arrived at the house or telephoned during that time?"

"No. I heard no one anyway. They aren't on the phone. I suppose it was something that occurred to her while she was alone in the kitchen. I couldn't very well ask her. I was on my way out and there wasn't anything you could put tongue to. I just told them all that if they thought of anything that might help they should let us know at once."

"We've got to see her again, of course, and the sooner the better. That alibi's got to be broken and she's the only one who can do it. I don't think the girl was consciously lying, or even deliberately withholding evidence. The truth simply never occurred to her."

"Nor to me, sir, until we got the motive. What do you want to do now? Let him sweat a bit?"

"I daren't, Martin. It's too dangerous. We've got to press on. I think we'll go now and have a little chat with Nagle."

But when they reached the Pimlico house twenty minutes later they found the flat locked and a folded scrap of paper wedged under the knocker. Dalgliesh smoothed it out and read aloud. "Darling. Sorry I missed you. I must speak to you. If I don't see you tonight I'll be at the clinic early. Love, Jenny."

"Any point in waiting for him, sir?"

"I doubt it. I think I can guess where he is. Cully was on the board when we did our phoning this morning but I made sure that Nagle, and probably everyone else at the Steen, knew that I was interesting myself in the medical records. I asked Dr. Etherege to put them back after I left. Nagle goes into the Steen on one or two evenings in the week to see to the boiler and turn off the art therapy department kiln. I imagine that he's there tonight, taking the opportunity of seeing which records have been moved. We'll look in anyway."

As the car moved northwards towards the river, Martin said:

"It's easy to see that he needed the cash. You couldn't rent a flat like that on a porter's pay. And then there would be his painting gear."

"Yes. The studio is pretty impressive. I should like you to have seen it. And there were the lessons from Sugg. Nagle may have got those on the cheap but Sugg doesn't teach for nothing. I don't think the blackmailing was particularly lucrative. That's where he was clever. There was probably more than one victim and the amounts were nicely calculated. But even if he only made fifteen to thirty pounds a month, tax free, it would be enough to carry him over until he won the Bollinger or made his name."

"Is he any good?" asked Sergeant Martin. There were subjects on which he never expressed an opinion but took it for granted that his Super was an expert.

"The trustees of the Bollinger Trust think so apparently."

"There's not much doubt is there, sir?" And Martin was not referring to Nagle's talent for painting. Dalgliesh said irritably:

"Of course there's doubt. There always is at this stage of an investigation. But consider what we know. The blackmailer instructed that the cash should be sent in a distinctively addressed envelope, presumably so that he could pick it out before the post was opened. Nagle gets to the clinic first and is responsible for sorting and distributing the post. Colonel Fenton was asked to send the money so that it arrived on the first of each month. Nagle came to the clinic on 1st May although he was ill and had to be taken home later. I don't think it was anxiety about the Duke's visit that brought him in. The only time he didn't manage to get first to work was the day he got stuck in the tube and that was the day Miss Bolam received fifteen pounds from an unknown grateful patient.

"And now we come to the murder and theory replaces fact. Nagle was helping on the switchboard that morning because of Cully's belly-ache. He listens to Mrs. Fenton's call. He knows what Miss Bolam's reaction will be and, sure enough, he is asked to put through a call to the group offices. He listens again and learns that Mr. Lauder will be at the Steen after the J.C.C. meeting. Sometime before then Miss Bolam has got to die. But how? He can't hope to entice her away from the Steen. What excuse could he use and how could he provide himself with an alibi? No, it must be done in the clinic. And perhaps that isn't such a bad plan after all. The A.O. isn't popular. With luck there will be plenty of suspects to keep the police occupied, some of them with pretty good reasons for wishing Miss Bolam dead.

So he makes his plans. It was obvious, of course, that the phone call to Miss Bolam wasn't necessarily made from the basement. Nearly all the rooms have telephones. But if the murderer wasn't in the record-room waiting for her how could he ensure that she would stay there until he could get down? That's why Nagle chucked the records about. He knew Miss Bolam well enough to be fairly sure that she couldn't bear not to pick them up. Dr. Baguley thought that her first reaction might be to phone for Nagle to help. She didn't, of course, because she was expecting him to appear any minute. Instead she made a start on the job herself, giving him the two or three minutes that he needed.

"This is what I think happened. At about ten past six he goes down to the porters' rest room to put on his outdoor coat. It's then that he unlocks the record-room door and throws the files on the floor. He leaves the light on and shuts the door but doesn't bolt it. Then he unlocks the back door. Next he goes into the general office to collect the outgoing post. Miss Priddy is there but periodically visits the adjoining filing-room. He only needs half a minute to telephone Miss Bolam and to ask her to come down to the record-room as he has something serious to show her. We know how she reacted to that message. Before Nagle has a chance to replace the receiver Jennifer Priddy is back. He keeps his head, depresses the receiver rest, and pretends to be speaking to Nurse Bolam about the laundry. Then, without wasting any more time, he leaves with the post. He has only to take it to the box across the road. Then he darts down the mews, enters the basement by the unlocked back door, slips the chisel in his pocket, collects Tippett's fetish and enters the record-room. Miss Bolam is there as he expects, kneeling to pick up the torn and scattered files. She looks up at him, ready no doubt to ask where he's been. But, before she has time to speak he strikes. Once she's unconscious he can take his time over the stabbing. There mustn't be any mistake, and there isn't. Nagle paints from the nude and his knowledge of anatomy is probably as good as that of most psychiatrists. And he was handy with that chisel. For this most important job he chose a tool he had confidence in and knew how to use."

Martin said:

"He couldn't have got down to the basement in time if he'd walked to the corner of Beefsteak Street for his *Standard*. But the newsboy there couldn't swear that he'd seen him. He was carrying a paper when he returned to the Steen but he could have got that in his lunch hour and kept it in his pocket."

"I think he did," said Dalgliesh. "That's why he wouldn't let Cully see it to check the racing results. Cully would have seen at once that it was the midday edition. Instead Nagle takes it downstairs and later uses it to wrap up the cat's food before burning it in the boiler. He wasn't in the basement alone for long, of course. Jenny Priddy was hard on his heels. But he had time to bolt the back door again and visit Nurse Bolam to ask if the clean laundry was ready to be carried upstairs. If Priddy hadn't come down Nagle would have joined her in the general office. He would take care not to be alone in the basement for more than a minute. The killing had to be fixed for the time when he was out with the post." Martin said:

"I wondered why he didn't unbolt the basement door after the killing but like as not he couldn't bring himself to draw attention to it. After all, if an outsider could have gained access that way it wouldn't take long for people to start thinking 'and so could Nagle'. He took that fifteen quid no doubt after Colonel Fenton's break-in. The local boys always did think it odd that the thief knew where to find it. Nagle thought he had a right to it I suppose."

"More likely he wanted to obscure the reason for the break-in, to make it look like a common burglary. It wouldn't do for the police to start wondering why an unknown intruder should want to get his hands on the medical records. Pinching that fifteen pounds—which only Nagle had the chance to do—confused the issue. So did that business with the lift, of course. That was a nice touch. It would only take a minute to wind it up to the second floor before he slipped out of the basement door and there was a reasonable chance that someone would hear it and remember."

Sergeant Martin thought that it all hung together very well but that it was going to be the devil to prove and said so.

"That's why I showed my hand at the clinic yesterday. We've got to get him rattled. That's why it's worth looking in at the Steen tonight. If he's there we'll put on the pressure a bit. At least we know now where we're going."

Half an hour before Dalgliesh and Martin called at the Pimlico flat, Peter Nagle let himself into the Steen by the front door and locked it behind him. He did not put on the lights but made his way to the basement with the aid of his heavy torch. There wasn't much to be done; just the kiln to be turned off, the boiler inspected. Then there was a little matter of his own to be attended to. It would mean entering the record-room but that warm, echoing place of death had no terror for him. The dead were dead, finished, powerless, silenced for ever. In a world of increasing uncertainty that much was certain. A man with the nerve to kill had much that he might reasonably fear. But he had nothing to fear from the dead.

It was then that he heard the front-door bell. It was a hesitant, tentative ring but it sounded unnaturally loud in the silence of the clinic. When he opened the door the figure of Jenny slid through so quickly that she seemed to pass by him like a wraith, a slim ghost born of the darkness and mist of the night. She said breathlessly:

"I'm sorry darling, I had to see you. When you weren't at the studio I thought you might be here."

"Did anyone see you at the studio?" he asked. He felt that the question was important without knowing why.

She looked up at him surprised.

"No. The house seemed empty. I didn't meet anyone. Why?"

"Nothing. It doesn't matter. Come on downstairs. I'll light the gas stove. You're shivering."

They went down to the basement together, their footsteps echoing in the eerie, presageful calm of a house which, with tomorrow, will awaken to voices, movement and the ceaseless hum of purposeful activity. She began walking on tiptoe and when she spoke it was in whispers. At the top of the stairs she reached for his hand and he could feel hers trembling. Halfway down there was a sudden faint noise and she started.

"What is it? What's that noise?"

"Nothing. Tigger in his scratch tin I imagine."

When they were in the rest room and the fire was lit he threw himself into one of the armchairs and smiled up at her. It was the devil of a nuisance that she should turn up now but somehow he must hide his irritation. With any luck he could get rid of her fairly quickly. She would be out of the clinic well before ten.

"Well?" he asked.

Suddenly she was on the rug at his feet and clasping his thighs. Her pale eyes searched his in passionate entreaty.

"Darling I've got to know! I don't mind what you've done as long as I know. I love you and I want to help. Darling, you must tell me if you're in any trouble."

It was worse than he feared. Somehow she had got hold of something. But how, and what? Keeping his voice light he asked:

"What sort of trouble for God's sake? You'll be saying next that I killed her."

"Oh, Peter, please don't joke! I've been so worried. There is something wrong, I know there is. It's the money isn't it? You took that fifteen pounds."

He could have laughed aloud with relief. In a surge of emotion he put his arms round her and drew her down upon him, his voice muffled in her hair.

"You silly kid. I could have helped myself to the petty cash any time if I wanted to steal. What the hell started you off on this nonsense?"

"That's what I've been telling myself. Why should you take it? Oh, darling, don't be angry with me. I've been so worried. You see, it was the paper."

"What paper, for God's sake." It was all he could do not to shake her into coherence. He was glad that she could not see his face. So long as he need not meet her eyes he could fight his anger and the fatal, insidious panic. What in God's name was she trying to say?

"The *Standard*. That sergeant came to see us this evening. I'd been to fetch the fish and chips. When I was unwrapping them in the kitchen I looked at the paper they were wrapped in. It was Friday's *Standard* and it had a large picture of that air crash, all over the front page. Then I remembered that we had used your *Standard* to wrap up Tigger's food and the front page was different. I hadn't seen that picture before."

He tightened his hold on her and said very quietly:

"Did you say anything about this to the police?"

"Darling, of course I didn't! Suppose it made them suspect you! I didn't say anything to anyone; but I needed to see you. I don't care about the fifteen pounds. I don't care if you did meet her in the basement. I know you didn't kill her. All I want is for you to trust me. I love you and I want to help. I can't bear it if you keep things from me."

That's what they all said but there wasn't one in a million who really wanted to know the truth about a man. For a second he was tempted to tell her, spit the whole brutal story into her silly pleading face and watch the sudden draining away of pity and love. She could probably bear to know about Bolam. What she couldn't bear would be the knowledge that he hadn't blackmailed for her sake, that he hadn't acted to preserve their love, that there wasn't any love to preserve and never had been. He would have to marry her, of course. He had always known that it might be necessary. Only she could effectively witness against him and there was one sure way to stop her tongue. But time was short. He planned to be in Paris by the end of the week. Now it looked as if he wouldn't be travelling alone. He thought quickly. Shifting her weight to the arm of the chair but still keeping his arms around her, his face resting against her cheek he said softly:

"Listen darling. There's something you've got to know. I didn't tell you before because I didn't want to worry you. I did take the fifteen quid. It was a bloody stupid thing to do but there's no sense in worrying about that now. I suppose Miss Bolam might have guessed. I don't know. She didn't say anything to me and it wasn't I who phoned her. But I was in the basement after she was killed. I left the back door open and came back that way. I get sick of that old fool Cully booking me in and out as if I were as nutty as a patient and asking for the paper as soon as I appear. Why can't he buy his own, the mean old devil. I thought I'd fool him for once. When I came in at the basement door I saw that there was a light in the record-room and the door was ajar, so I went to look. I found her body. I knew that I daren't be found there, particularly if they ever discovered about the fifteen quid, so I said nothing and left again by the back door and came in as usual by the front. I've kept quiet ever since. I must darling. I've got to take up the Bollinger by the end of this week and the police wouldn't let me go if they started suspecting me. If I don't get away now I'll never have the chance again as long as I live."

That at least was true. He had to get away now. It had become an obsession. It wasn't only the money, the freedom, the sun and the colours. It was the final vindication of the lean, pallid years of struggle and humiliation. He had to take up the Bollinger. Other painters could fail here and still succeed in the end. But not him.

And, even now, he might fail. It was a thin story. He was struck, as he spoke, by the inconsistencies, the improbabilities. But it hung together—just. He couldn't see how she could prove it false. And she wouldn't want to try. But he was surprised by her reaction.

"By the end of this week! You mean, you're going to Paris almost at once. What about the clinic . . . your job?"

"For God's sake, Jenny, what the hell does that matter? I shall leave without notice and they'll find someone else. They'll have to do without me."

"And me?"

"You're coming with me of course. I always meant that you should. Surely you knew that?"

"No," she said, and it seemed to him that her voice held a great sadness. "No, I never knew that."

He tried to assume a tone of confidence tinged with slight reproach.

"I never discussed it because I thought there were some things we didn't need to say. I know the time's short but it'll be easier if you don't have to stick around too long at home waiting. They'd only get suspicious. You've got a passport, haven't you? Didn't you go to France with the guides that Easter? What I suggest is that we marry by special licence as soon as possible—after all we've got the money now—and write to your parents when we get to Paris. You do want to come, don't you, Jenny?"

Suddenly she was shaking in his arms and he felt the warm wetness of her tears stinging his face.

"I thought you meant to go without me. The days went by and you never said anything. Of course, I want to come. I don't care what happens as long as we're together. But we can't get married. I never told you because I was afraid you'd be angry and you've never asked me anything about myself. I can't get married because I'm married already."

The car had turned into Vauxhall Bridge Road but traffic was heavy and they were making poor time. Dalgliesh sat back in his seat as if all day were before him, but inwardly he was fidgeting with anxiety. He could discover no rational cause for this impatience. The call at the Steen was merely speculative. The chances were that Nagle, if indeed he had called at the clinic, would have left before they arrived. Probably he was even now putting down his evening pint in some Pimlico pub. At the next corner the traffic lights were against them and the car slowed to a halt for the third time in a hundred yards. Suddenly Martin said:

"He couldn't have got away with it for long, even by killing Bolam. Sooner or later Mrs. Fenton—or another victim maybe—would have turned up at the Steen."

Dalgliesh replied:

"But he might well have got away with it for long enough to take up the Bollinger. And even if the blackmailing came to light before he got away—what could we prove? What can we prove now, come to that? With Bolam dead what jury could be sure beyond reasonable doubt that she wasn't the blackmailer? Nagle's only got to say that he remembers seeing the odd envelope addressed in green ink and that he placed it with the A.O.'s post. Fenton will confirm that he thought the telephone calls came from a woman. And blackmailers do occasionally come to a violent end. Nagle wouldn't go on with it after Mrs. Fenton's call. Even that would help his case. Bolam dies and the blackmailing stops. Oh, I know all the arguments against it! But what can anyone prove?"

Martin said stolidly:

"He'll try to be too clever. They always do. The girl's under his thumb of course, poor little devil. If she sticks to her story that he wasn't alone long enough to make that call. . . ."

"She'll stick all right, Sergeant."

"I'm pretty sure he doesn't know about the husband. If she looks dangerous he probably thinks that he can stop her tongue by marrying her."

Dalgliesh said quietly:

"What we've got to do is to pull him in before he finds out that he can't."

In the porters' room at the Steen, Nagle was writing a letter. He wrote easily. The glib and lying phrases flowed with unexpected ease. He would have died rather than send such a letter. It would have been unbearable to think that any eyes could see this spate of emotional clap-trap and recognize it as his. But the letter never would be read except by Jenny. Within thirty minutes it would be thrust into the boiler, its purpose served and the oily phrases only an uncomfortable memory. In the meantime he might as well make it convincing. It was easy enough to guess what Jenny would want him to say. He turned over the paper and wrote:

"By the time you read this we shall be in France together. I know that this will cause you very great unhappiness, but please believe me when I say that we can't live without each other. I know that one day we shall be free to marry. Until then Jenny will be safe with me and I shall spend my life trying to make her happy. Please try to understand and to forgive."

It was a good ending, he thought. It would appeal to Jenny, anyway, and no one else was going to see it. He called to her and pushed the paper across the table.

"Will this do?"

She read it in silence.

"I suppose so."

"Damn it all kid, what's wrong with it?" He felt a surge of anger that his careful effort should be found inadequate. He had expected and had braced himself to meet, her astonished gratitude. She said quietly:

"Nothing's wrong with it."

"You'd better write your bit then. Not on the end. Take a fresh sheet."

He slid the paper across the table at her, not meeting her eyes. This was taking time, and he could not be sure how much time there was.

"Better make it short," he said.

She took up the pen but made no effort to write.

"I don't know what to say."

"There isn't much you need say. I've said it all."

"Yes," she said with great sadness. "You've said it all."

He kept the rising irritation from his voice and told her:

"Just write that you're sorry to cause them unhappiness, but you can't help yourself. Something like that. Damn it all, you're not going to the end of the world. It's up to them. If they want to see you I shan't stop them. Don't pile the agony on too much. I'm going upstairs to mend that lock in Miss Saxon's room. When I come down we're going to celebrate. There's only beer, but tonight you'll drink beer my darling and like it."

He took a screwdriver from the tool box and went out quickly before she had time to protest. His last glimpse was of her frightened face staring after him. But she didn't call him back.

Upstairs it was a moment's work only to slip on a pair of rubber gloves and prise open the door of the dangerous-drugs cupboard. It gave with a terrifyingly loud crack so that he stood rooted for a moment half expecting to hear her call. But there was no sound. He remembered clearly that scene some six months ago when one of Dr. Baguley's patients had become violent and disorientated. Nagle had helped to control him while Baguley had called to Sister for paraldehyde. Nagle recalled the words:

"We'll give it in beer. It's pretty filthy stuff but they can hardly taste it in beer. Odd that. Two drams, Sister, to 2 cc."

And Jenny, who disliked beer, would taste it even less.

Quickly he put the screwdriver and the small blue bottle of paraldehyde in his jacket pocket and slipped out, lighting his way with the torch. All the clinic curtains were drawn, but it was important to show as little light as possible. He needed at least another undisturbed half-hour.

She looked up in surprise at his quick reappearance. He went over to her and kissed the back of her neck.

"I'm sorry sweetie, I shouldn't have left you. I'd forgotten that you might be nervous. The lock can wait, anyway. How's the letter going?"

She pushed it over to him. He turned his back on her to read the few carefully penned lines deliberately, taking his time. But his luck had held. It was as neat and convincing a suicide note as was ever read in a Coroner's court. He couldn't have dictated anything better. He felt a surge of confidence and excitement as he did when a painting was going well. Nothing could spoil it now. Jenny had written:

"I can't say I'm sorry for what I've done. I haven't any choice. I feel so happy and it would all be perfect if I didn't know that I'm making you miserable. But it's the only and best thing for me. Please try to understand. I love you very much. Jenny."

He put the letter back on the table and went to pour out the beer, his actions hidden by the open door of the cupboard. God, the stuff did stink! Quickly he added the foaming light ale and called to her.

"Are you happy?"

"You know I am."

"Then let's drink to it. To us, darling."

"To us."

She grimaced as the liquid met her lips. He laughed.

"You look as if you're drinking poison. Knock it back, girl. Like this!"

He opened his throat and drained his own glass. Laughing, she shuddered slightly and gulped down her ale. He took the empty glass from her and folded her in his arms. She clung to him, her hands like a cold compress on the back of his neck. Releasing himself he drew her down beside him on to the armchair. Then, clasped together they slid to the floor and lay together on the rug in front of the gas fire. He had turned off the light and her face shone in the fierce red glow of the fire as if she lay in the full sun. The hiss of the gas was the only sound in the silence.

He pulled a cushion from one of the armchairs and pushed it under her head. Only one cushion; he had a use for the other. It could rest on the bottom of the gas stove. She would be less likely to wake if he made her comfortable on that last brief slide from unconsciousness to death. He put his left arm around her and they lay tight clasped without speaking. Suddenly she turned her face to his and he felt her tongue, wet and slippery as a fish, infiltrating between his teeth. Her eyes, their pupils black in the gaslight, were heavy with desire. "Darling," she whispered. "Darling." Christ, he thought, not that. He couldn't make love to her now. It would keep her quiet but it wasn't possible. There wasn't time. And surely the police pathologist could tell how recently that had happened to a woman. He thought for the first time with relief of her obsession with safety and whispered. "We can't darling. I haven't got anything with me. We can't risk it now."

She gave a little murmur of acquiescence and nuzzled against him, moving her left leg over his thighs. It lay there, heavy and inert, but he dare not move nor speak in case he broke that insidious drop into unconsciousness. She was breathing more deeply now, hotly and irritatingly into his left ear. God, how much longer was it going to take! Holding his own breath he listened. Suddenly she gave a little snort like a contented animal. Under his arm he sensed a change in the rhythm of her breathing. There was an almost physical release of tension as her body relaxed. She was asleep.

Better give her a few minutes, he thought. There wasn't much time to spare, but he dare not hurry. It was important that there were no bruises on her body and he knew he couldn't face a struggle. But there could be no turning back now. If she woke and resisted it would still have to be done.

So he waited, lying so still that they might both have been dead bodies stiffening together into a final stylized embrace. After a little time he raised himself cautiously on his right elbow and looked at her. Her face was flushed, her mouth with its short upper lip curved against the white childish teeth was half open. He could smell the paraldehyde on her breath. He watched her for a moment, noting the length of the pale lashes against her cheeks, the upward slant of the eyebrows and the shadows under the broad cheek bones. Strange that he had never got round to drawing her face. But it was too late to think of that now.

He murmured to her as he lifted her gently across the room to the black mouth of the gas oven.

"It's all right, Jenny darling. It's only me. I'm making you comfortable. It's all right, darling."

But it was himself that he was reassuring.

There was plenty of room in the large, old-fashioned oven, even with the cushion. The bottom of the oven was only a few inches from the ground. Feeling for her shoulder blades he edged her gently forward. As the cushion took the weight of her head he looked to make sure that the gas jets were still unimpeded. Her head rolled gently sideways so that the half-open mouth, moist and vulnerable as a baby's, hung just above them, poised and ready to suck up death. As he slid his hands from under her body she gave a little sigh as if she were comfortable at last.

He gave one last look at her, satisfied with his handiwork.

And now it was time to hurry. Feeling in his pocket for the rubber gloves, he moved with fantastic speed, treading lightly, his breath coming in shallow gasps as if he could no longer bear the sound of his own breathing. The suicide note was on the table. He took the chisel and wrapped her right hand gently round it, pressing the palm around the shining handle, the right finger-tip against the base of the blade. Was that how she would have held it? Near enough. He placed the chisel on top of the suicide note.

Next he washed up his own glass and put it back in the cupboard, holding the dish-cloth in front of the gas fire for a second until the damp stain had evaporated. He turned off the fire. No need to worry about prints here. There was nothing to show when last it had been lit. He wondered briefly about the paraldehyde bottle and Jenny's glass, but decided to leave them on the table with the note and the chisel. The natural thing would surely be for her to drink sitting at the table and then to move to the stove when she felt the first signs of drowsiness. He wiped his own prints from the bottle and clasped her left hand around it, her right-hand index finger and thumb on the stopper. He was almost afraid to touch her, but she was now deeply asleep. Her hand was very warm to his touch and so relaxed that it felt boneless. He was repelled by its limp flaccidity, by this touch which was without communication, without desire. He was glad when he had dealt similarly with the drinking glass and the bottle of beer. It would only be necessary now to touch her once again.

Last of all he took his own letter to the Priddys and the pair of gloves and threw them into the boiler. There was only the gas tap to turn on. It was on the right of the stove and within easy reach of her limp right arm. He lifted the arm, pressed her index finger and thumb against the tap, and turned it on. There was the soft hiss of escaping gas. How long, he wondered, was it likely to take. Not long surely? Perhaps only a matter of minutes. He put out the light and backed out, closing the door behind him.

It was then that he remembered the front-door keys. They must be found on her. His heart struck cold as he realized how fatal that one mistake could have been. He edged into the room again by the light of his torch. Taking the keys from his pocket and holding his breath against the gas, he placed them in her left hand. He had reached the door before he heard Tigger's mew. The cat must have been sleeping under the cupboard. It was moving slowly round the body now, putting out a tentative paw towards the girl's right foot. Nagle found that he could not bear to go near her again.

"Come here Tigger," he whispered. "Come here boy."

The cat turned its great amber eyes on him and seemed to be considering, but without emotion and without haste. Then it came slowly across to the door. Nagle hooked his left foot under the soft belly and lifted the cat through the door in one swift movement.

"Come out of it, you bloody fool. D'you want to lose all nine lives at one go? That stuff's lethal."

He closed the door, and the cat, suddenly active, shot away into the dark.

Nagle made his way without lights to the back door, felt for the bolts, and let himself out. He paused for a moment, back against the door, to check that the mews was empty. Now that it was over he had time to note the signs of strain. His forehead and hands were wet with sweat and he had difficulty with his breathing. He drew in deep gasps of the damp and blessedly cool night air. The fog wasn't thick, hardly more than a heavy mist, through which the street lamp which marked the end of the mews gleamed like a yellow smudge in the darkness. That gleam, only forty yards away, represented safety. Yet all at once it seemed unattainable. Like an animal in its lair he gazed in horrified fascination at the dangerous beacon and willed his legs to move. But their power had gone. Crouching in the darkness and shelter of the doorway, his back pressed against the wood, he fought off panic. After all, there was no great hurry. In a moment he would leave this spurious sanctuary and put the mews behind him. Then it was only a matter of re-entering the square from the other side and waiting until there was a casual passer-by to witness his vain hammering at the front door. Even the words he would speak were ready. "It's my girl. I think she's in there, but she won't open up. She was with me earlier this evening and when she'd gone I found the keys were missing. She was in a queer state. Better get a copper. I'm going to smash this window."

Then the crash of broken glass, the dash to the basement and the chance to lock the back door again before the hurrying footsteps were at his heels. The worst was over. From now on it was all so easy. By ten o'clock the body would have been removed, the clinic empty. In a moment he would move on to the final act. But not yet. Not quite yet.

Along the Embankment the traffic was almost stationary. There seemed to be some kind of function on at the Savoy. Suddenly Dalgliesh said:

"There's no guard at the clinic now, of course?"

"No, sir. You remember I asked you this morning if we need keep a man there and you said no."

"I remember."

"After all, sir, it hardly seemed necessary. We'd examined the place thoroughly and there aren't all those men to spare."

"I know, Martin," replied Dalgliesh testily. "Surprisingly enough those were the reasons for my decision." The car came to a stop once more. Dalgliesh put his head out of the window. "What the hell does he think he's doing?"

"I think he's doing his best, sir."

"That's what I find so depressing. Come on, Sergeant. Get out! We'll do the rest on foot. I'm probably being a bloody fool, but when we get to the clinic, we'll cover both exits. You go round to the back."

If Martin felt surprise it was not his nature to show it. Something seemed to have got into the old man. As like as not Nagle was back in his flat and the clinic locked and deserted. A couple of fools they'd look creeping up on an empty building. Still, they'd know soon enough. He bent his energies to keeping up with the superintendent.

Nagle never knew how long he waited in the doorway, bent almost double and panting like an animal. But after a time, calmness returned and with it the use of his legs. He moved stealthily forward, hoisted himself over the rear railings and set off down the mews. He walked like an automaton, hands stiffly by his sides, his eyes closed. Suddenly he heard the footfall. Opening his eyes, he saw silhouetted against the street lamp, a familiar bulky figure. Slowly, inexorably, it moved towards him through the mist. His heart leapt in his chest then settled into a regular tumultuous throbbing that shook his whole body. His legs felt heavy and cold as death, checking that first fatal impulse to flight. But at least his mind worked. While he could think there was hope. He was cleverer than they. With luck they wouldn't even think of entering the clinic. Why should they? And surely she would be dead by now! With Jenny dead they could suspect what they liked. They'd never prove a thing.

The torch shone full on his face. The slow unemphatic voice spoke:

"Good evening, lad. We were hoping to meet you. Going in or coming out?"

Nagle did not reply. He stretched his mouth into the semblance of a smile. He could only guess how he looked in that fierce light; a death's head, the mouth agape with fright, the eyes staring.

It was then that he felt the tentative rub against his legs. The policeman bent and scooped up the cat, holding it between them. Immediately it began to purr, throbbing its contentment at the warmth of that huge hand.

"So here's Tigger. You let him out, did you? You and the cat came out together."

Then, instantaneously, they were both aware of it and their eyes met. From the warmth of the cat's fur there rose between them, faint but unmistakable, the smell of gas.

The next half-hour passed for Nagle in a confused whirl of noise and blinding lights out of which a few vivid tableaux sprang into focus with unnatural clarity and stayed fixed in his mind for the rest of his life. He had no memory of the sergeant dragging him back over the iron railings, only of the grip, firm as a tourniquet, numbing his arm and the hot rasp of Martin's breath in his ear. There was a smash and the sad, delayed tinkle of broken glass as someone kicked out the windows of the porters' room, the shrill screech of a whistle, a confusion of running feet on the clinic stairs, a blaze of lights hurting his eyes. In one of the tableaux Dalgliesh was crouched over the girl's body, his mouth wide-stretched as a gargoyle's, clamped over her mouth as he forced his breath into her lungs. The two bodies seemed to be fighting, locked in an obscene embrace like the rape of the dead. Nagle didn't speak. He was almost beyond thought, but instinct warned him that he must say nothing. Pinned against the wall by strong arms and watching fascinated the feverish heave of Dalgliesh's shoulders, he felt tears start in his eyes. Enid Bolam was dead, and Jenny was dead, and he was tired now, desperately tired.

He hadn't wanted to kill her. It was Bolam who had forced him into all the trouble and danger of murder. She and Jenny between them had left him no choice. And he had lost Jenny. Jenny was dead. Faced with the enormity, the unfairness of what they had made him do, he felt without surprise the tears of self-pity flow in a warm stream down his face.

The room was suddenly full. There were more uniformed men, one of them burly as a Holbein, pig-eyed, slow-moving. There was the hiss of oxygen, a murmur of consulting voices. Then they were edging something on to a stretcher with gentle, experienced hands, a red-blanketed shape which rolled sideways as the poles were lifted. Why were they carrying it so carefully? It couldn't feel jolting any more.

Dalgliesh didn't speak until Jenny had been taken away. Then, without looking at Nagle, he said:

"Right, Sergeant. Get him down to the station. We can hear his story there."

Nagle moved his mouth. His lips were so dry that he heard them crack. But it was some seconds before the words would come and then there was no stopping them. The carefully rehearsed story tumbled out in a spate, bald and unconvincing:

"There's nothing to tell. She came to see me at my flat and we spent the evening together. I had to tell her that I was going away without her. She took it pretty badly, and after she'd left I found that the clinic keys were missing. I knew she was in a bit of a state so I thought I'd better come along. There's a note on the table. She's left a note. I could see she was dead and I couldn't help, so I came away. I didn't want to be mixed up in it. I've got the Bollinger to think of. It wouldn't look good getting mixed up with a suicide."

Dalgliesh said:

"You'd better not say anything else for the present. But you'll have to do better than that. You see, it isn't quite what she has told us. That note on the table isn't the only one she left."

With slow deliberation he took from his breast pocket a small folded sheet of paper and held it an inch from Nagle's fascinated, fear-glazed eyes:

"If you were together this evening in your flat, how do you explain this note which we found under your door knocker?"

It was then that Nagle realized with sick despair that the dead, so impotent and so despised, could bear witness against him after all. Instinctively he put out his hand for the note, then dropped his arm. Dalgliesh replaced the note in his pocket. Watching Nagle closely, he said:

"So you rushed here tonight because you were concerned for her safety? Very touching! In that case let me put your mind at rest. She's going to live."

"She's dead," said Nagle dully. "She killed herself."

"She was breathing when we'd finished with her. Tomorrow, if all goes well, she'll be able to tell us what happened. And not only what happened here tonight. We shall have some questions about Miss Bolam's murder."

Nagle gave a shout of harsh laughter:

"Bolam's murder! You'll never get me for that! And I'll tell you why, you poor boobs. Because I didn't kill her! If you want to make fools of yourselves, go ahead. Don't let me stop you. But I warn you. If I'm arrested for Bolam's murder I'll make your names stink in every newspaper in the country."

He held out his wrists to Dalgliesh.

"Come on, Superintendent! Go ahead and charge me. What's stopping you? You've worked it all out very cleverly, haven't you? You've been too clever by half, you bloody supercilious copper!"

"I'm not charging you," said Dalgliesh. "I'm inviting you to come to headquarters to answer some questions and to make a statement. If you want a solicitor present you're entitled to have one."

"I'll have one all right. But not just at the moment. I'm in no hurry, Superintendent. You see, I'm expecting a visitor. We arranged to meet here at ten and it's nearly that now. I must say we'd planned to have the place to ourselves and I don't think my visitor will be particularly pleased to see you. But if you want to meet Miss Bolam's killer you'd better stick around. It won't be long. The person I'm expecting has been trained to be on time."

Suddenly all his fear seemed to have left him. The large brown eyes were expressionless again, muddy pools in which only the black iris burned with life. Martin, still clasping Nagle's arms could feel the muscles bracing, could sense the physical return of confidence. But before anyone had time to speak their ears caught simultaneously the sound of footsteps. Someone had come in by the basement door and was moving quietly down the passage.

Dalgliesh moved to the door in one silent stride and braced himself against it. The footsteps, timid, hesitant, stopped outside. Three pairs of eyes watched as the door-knob turned, first right, then left. A voice called softly:

"Nagle! Are you there, Nagle! Open the door."

With a single movement Dalgliesh stepped to one side and crashed open the door. The slight figure moved forward involuntarily under the blaze of the fluorescent lights. The immense grey eyes widened and slewed from face to face, the eyes of an uncomprehending child. Whimpering, she clutched a handbag to her breast in a sudden protective gesture as if she were shielding a baby. Wrenching himself from Martin's grip Nagle snatched it from her and tossed it to Dalgliesh. It fell plumply into the detective's hands, the cheap plastic sticking warmly to his fingers. Nagle tried to keep his voice level, but it cracked with excitement and triumph.

"Take a look inside, Superintendent. It's all there. I'll tell you what you'll find. A signed confession of Enid Bolam's murder and one hundred pounds in notes, a first payment on account to keep my mouth shut."

He turned to his visitor.

"Sorry, kid. I didn't plan it this way. I was willing enough to keep quiet about what I'd seen, but things have changed since Friday night. I've got troubles of my own to worry about now and no one's going to pin a murder charge on me. Our little arrangement's off."

But Marion Bolam had fainted.

Two months later a Magistrate's court committed Marion Grace Bolam for trial on a charge of her cousin's murder. A capricious autumn had hardened into winter and Dalgliesh walked back alone to headquarters under a grey blanket of sky which sagged with its weight of snow. The first moist flakes were already falling, melting gently against his face. In his chief's office the lights were lit and the curtains drawn, shutting out the glittering river, the necklace of light along the Embankment and all the cold inertia of a winter afternoon. Dalgliesh made his report briefly. The A.C. listened in silence, then said:

"They'll try for diminished responsibility, I suppose. How did the girl seem?"

"Perfectly calm, like a child who knows she's been naughty and is on her best behaviour in the hope that the grown-ups will overlook it. She feels no particular guilt, I suspect, except the usual female guilt at being found out."

"It was a perfectly straightforward case," said the A.C. "The obvious suspect, the obvious motive."

"Too obvious for me, apparently," said Dalgliesh bitterly. "If this case doesn't cure me of conceit, nothing will. If I'd paid more attention to the obvious I might have questioned why she didn't get back to Rettinger Street until after eleven when the television service was closing down. She'd been with Nagle, of course, arranging the blackmail payments. They met in St. James's Park, apparently. He saw his chance all right when he went into that record-room and found her bending over her cousin's body. He must have been on her before she heard a sound. He took over from there with his usual efficiency. It was he who put the fetish so carefully on the body, of course. Even that detail misled me. Somehow I couldn't see Marion Bolam making that final contemptuous gesture. But it was an obvious crime, all right. She hardly made an attempt at concealment. The rubber gloves she wore were stuffed back in her uniform pocket. The weapons she chose were the ones nearest to hand. She wasn't trying to incriminate anyone else. She wasn't even trying to be clever. At about six-twelve she telephoned the general office and asked Nagle not to come down yet for the laundry; he couldn't resist lying about that call, incidentally which gave me another opportunity for being over-subtle. Then she rang for her cousin. She couldn't be absolutely sure that Enid would come alone and the excuse had to be valid so she threw the medical records on the floor. Then she waited in the record-room for her victim, fetish in hand and chisel in her uniform pocket. It was unfortunate for her that Nagle returned secretly to the clinic when he was out with the post. He'd overheard Miss Bolam's call to the group secretary and wanted to get his hands on the Fenton record. It seemed safer to chuck it in the basement furnace. Coming upon the murder forced him to change his plan and he didn't get another chance once the body was discovered and the record-room sealed. Nurse Bolam, of course, had no choice of time. She discovered on Wednesday night that Enid intended to alter her will. Friday was the earliest evening when there was a lysergic acid session and she would have the basement to herself. She couldn't act earlier: she daren't act later."

"The murder was highly convenient for Nagle," said his chief. "You can't blame yourself for concentrating on him. But if you insist on indulging in self-pity don't let me spoil your fun."

"Convenient, perhaps, but not necessary," Dalgliesh replied. "And why should he have killed Bolam? His one aim, apart from making easy money, was to take up the Bollinger and get away to Europe without fuss. He must have known that it would be difficult to pin the Fenton blackmail on him even if the group secretary decided to call in the police. And, in fact, we still haven't enough evidence to charge him. But murder is different. Anyone connected with murder is likely to have his private plans disorganized. Even the innocent can't so easily shake off that contaminating dust. To kill Bolam only increased his danger. But to kill Priddy was a different matter. At one stroke he could safeguard his alibi, get rid of an encumbrance and give himself the hope of marrying the heiress of nearly thirty thousand. He knew he'd have little chance with Marion Bolam if she learned that Priddy had been his mistress. She wasn't Enid Bolam's cousin for nothing."

The A.C. said:

"At least we've got him as an accessory after the fact and that should put him away for quite a time. I'm not sorry that the Fentons will be spared the ordeal of giving evidence. But I doubt whether the charge of attempted murder will stick—not unless Priddy changes her mind. If she persists in supporting his story we'll get nowhere."

"She won't change her mind, sir," said Dalgliesh bitterly. "Nagle doesn't want to see her, of course, but nothing makes any difference. All she thinks about is planning their life together when he comes out. And God help her when he does."

The A.C. shifted his immense bulk irritably in his chair, closed the file and pushed it across the table to Dalgliesh. He said:

"There's nothing that you or anyone else can do about that. She's the kind of woman who pursues her own destruction. I've had that artist, Sugg, on to me by the way. Extraordinary ideas about judicial procedure these people have! I told him that it's out of our hands now and referred him to the proper quarter. He wants to pay for Nagle's defence, if you please! Said that if we've made a mistake the world will lose a remarkable talent."

"It will be lost, anyway," replied Dalgliesh. Thinking aloud, added: "I wonder just how good an artist would have to be before one let him get away with a crime like Nagle's. Michelangelo? Velazquez? Rembrandt?"

"Oh, well," said the A.C. easily. "If we had to ask ourselves that question we wouldn't be policemen."

Back in Dalgliesh's office Sergeant Martin was putting away papers. He took one look at his super's face, pronounced a stolid "Good night, sir," and left. There were some situations which his uncomplicated nature found it prudent to avoid. The door had hardly closed behind him when the telephone rang. It was Mrs. Shorthouse.

"Hullo!" she yelled. "Is that you? I had the devil of a job getting through to you. Saw you in court today. Don't suppose you noticed me, though. How are you?"

"Well, thank you, Mrs. Shorthouse."

"Don't suppose we'll be meeting again, so I thought I'd give you a ring to say cheerio and tell you the news. Things have been happening at the clinic, I can tell you. Miss Saxon's leaving for one thing. She's going to work in a home for subnormal kids up north. Run by the R.C.s it is. Fancy going off to work in a convent! No one at the Steen ever did that before."

Dalgliesh said he could well believe it.

"Miss Priddy's been transferred to one of the group's chest clinics. Mr. Lauder thought the change would do her good. She's had a terrible row with her people and she's living alone now in a bed-sitter in Kilburn. But you know all about that, no doubt. Mrs. Bolam's gone to an expensive nursing-home near Worthing. All on her share of Cousin Enid's money, of course. Poor sod. I'm surprised she could bring herself to touch a penny of it."

Dalgliesh wasn't surprised, but did not say so. Mrs. Shorthouse went on:

"And then there's Dr. Steiner. He's getting married to his wife."

"What did you say, Mrs. Shorthouse?"

"Well, re-married. Fixed it up very sudden they did. They got divorced and now they're getting married again. What d'you think of that?"

Dalgliesh said that it was a question of what Dr. Steiner thought of it.

"Oh, he's as pleased as a dog with a new collar. And a collar is just about what he's getting, if you ask me. There's a rumour that the Regional Board may close the clinic and move everyone to a hospital out-patient department. Well, you can't wonder! First a stabbing and then a gassing, and now a murder trial. Not nice really. Dr. Etherege says it's upsetting for the patients, but I haven't noticed it to speak of. The numbers haven't half gone up since last October. That would have pleased Miss Bolam. Always worrying about the numbers she was. Mind you there are those who say we wouldn't have had that trouble with Nagle and Priddy if you'd picked on the right one first go. It was a near thing all right. But what I say is, you did your best and there's no harm done to speak of."

No harm to speak of! So these, thought Dalgliesh bitterly,

as he replaced the receiver, were the concomitants of failure. It was enough to taste this sour, corroding self-pity without enduring the A.C.'s moralizing, Martin's tact, Emily Shorthouse's condolences. If he were to break free from this pervasive gloom he needed a respite from crime and death, needed to walk for one brief evening out of the shadow of blackmail and murder. It came to him that what he wanted was to dine with Deborah Riscoe. At least, he told himself wryly, it would be a change of trouble. He put his hand on the receiver and then paused, checked by the old caution, the old uncertainties. He was not even sure that she would wish to take a call at the office, what exactly her place was at Hearne and Illingworth. Then he remembered how she had looked when last they met and he lifted the receiver. He could surely dine with an attractive woman without this preparatory morbid self-analysis. The invitation would commit him to nothing more crucial than seeing that she had a pleasant evening and paying the bill. And a man was surely entitled to call his own publishers.

SHROUD FOR A NIGHTINGALE

FOR
J.M.C.

Contents

Chapter One

Demonstration of Death

I

On the morning of the first murder Miss Muriel Beale, Inspector of Nurse Training Schools to the General Nursing Council, stirred into wakefulness soon after 6 o'clock and into a sluggish early morning awareness that it was Monday, 12th January, and the day of the John Carpendar Hospital inspection. Already she had half-registered the first familiar sounds of a new day: Angela's alarm silenced almost before she was conscious of hearing it; Angela herself padding and snuffling about the flat like a clumsy but benevolent animal; the agreeably anticipatory tinklings of early tea in preparation. She forced open her eyelids, resisting an insidious urge to wriggle down into the enveloping warmth of the bed and let her mind drift again into blessed unconsciousness. What on earth had prompted her to tell Matron Taylor that she would arrive shortly after 9 a.m. in time to join the third-year students' first teaching session of the day? It was ridiculously, unnecessarily early. The hospital was in Heatheringfield on the Sussex/Hampshire border, a drive of nearly fifty miles, some of which would have to be done before daybreak. And it was raining, as it had rained with dreary insistence for the past week. She could hear the faint hiss of car tyres on the Cromwell Road and an occasional spatter against the window-pane. Thank God she had taken the trouble to check the map of Heatheringfield to find out exactly where the hospital lay. A developing market town, particularly if it were unfamiliar, could be a time-wasting maze to the motorist in the snarl of commuter traffic on a wet Monday morning. She felt instinctively that it was going to be a difficult day and stretched out under the bedclothes as if bracing herself to meet it. Extending her cramped fingers, she half-relished the sharp momentary ache of her stretched joints. A touch of arthritis there. Well, it was to be expected. She was forty-nine after all. It was time she took life a little more gently. What on earth had led her to think she could get to Heatheringfield before half past nine?

The door opened, letting in a shaft of light from the passage. Miss Angela Burrows jerked back the curtains, surveyed the black January sky and the rain-spattered window and jerked them together again. "It's raining," she said with the gloomy relish of one who has prophesied rain and who cannot be held responsible for the ignoring of her warning. Miss Beale propped herself on her elbow, turned on the bedside lamp, and waited. In a few seconds her friend returned and set down the early morning tray. The tray cloth was of starched embroidered linen, the flowered cups were arranged with their handles aligned, the four biscuits on the matching plate were precisely placed, two of a kind, the teapot gave forth a delicate smell of freshly made Indian tea. The two women had a strong love of comfort and an addiction to tidiness and order. The standards which they had once enforced in the private ward of their teaching hospital were applied to their own comfort, so that life in the flat was not unlike that in an expensive and permissive nursing home.

Miss Beale had shared a flat with her friend since they had both left the same training school twenty-five years ago. Miss Angela Burrows was the Principal Tutor at a London teaching hospital. Miss Beale had thought her the paradigm of nurse tutors and, in all her inspections, subconsciously set her standard by her friend's frequent pronouncements on the principles of sound nurse teaching. Miss Burrows, for her part, wondered how the General Nursing Council would manage when the time came for Miss Beale to retire. The happiest marriages are sustained by such comforting illusions and Miss Beale's and Miss Burrows's very different, but essentially innocent, relationship was similarly founded. Except in this capacity for mutual but unstated admiration they were very different. Miss Burrows was sturdy, thick-set and formidable, hiding a vulnerable sensitivity under an air of blunt common sense. Miss Beale was small and birdlike, precise in speech and movement and threatened with an out-of-date gentility which sometimes brought her close to being thought ridiculous. Even their physiological habits were different. The heavy Miss Burrows awoke to instantaneous life at the first sound of her alarm, was positively energetic until teatime, then sank into sleepy lethargy as the evening advanced. Miss Beale daily opened her gummed eyelids with reluctance, had to force herself into early morning activity and became more brightly cheerful as the day wore on. They had managed to reconcile even this incompatibility. Miss Burrows was happy to brew the early morning tea and prepare breakfast and Miss Beale washed up after dinner and made the nightly cocoa.

Miss Burrows poured out both cups of tea, dropped two lumps of sugar in her friend's cup and took her own to the chair by the window. Early training forbade Miss Burrows to sit on the bed. She said: "You need to be off early. I'd better run your bath. When does it start?"

Miss Beale muttered feebly that she had told Matron that she would arrive as soon as possible after nine o'clock. The tea was blessedly sweet and reviving. The promise to start out so early was a mistake but she began to think that she might after all make it by 9.15.

"That's Mary Taylor, isn't it? She's got quite a reputation considering she's only a provincial matron. Extraordinary that she's never come to London. She didn't even apply for our job when Miss Montrose retired." Miss Beale muttered incomprehensibly which, since they had had this conversation before, her friend correctly interpreted as a protest that London wasn't everybody's choice and that people were too apt to assume that nothing remarkable ever came out of the provinces.

"There's that, of course," conceded her friend. "And the John Carpendar's in a very pleasant part of the world. I like that country on the Hampshire border. It's a pity you're not visiting it in summer. Still, it's not as if she's matron of a major teaching hospital. With her ability she easily could be; she might have become one of the Great Matrons." In their student days she and Miss Beale had suffered at the hands of one of the Great Matrons but they never ceased to lament the passing of that terrifying breed.

"By the way, you'd better start in good time. The road's up just before you strike the Guildford by-pass."

Miss Beale did not inquire how she knew that the road was up. It was the sort of thing Miss Burrows invariably did know. The hearty voice went on:

"I saw Hilda Rolfe, their Principal Tutor, in the Westminster Library this week. Extraordinary woman! Intelligent, of course, and reputedly a first-class teacher, but I imagine she terrifies the students."

Miss Burrows frequently terrified her own students, not to mention most of her colleagues on the teaching staff, but would have been amazed to be told it. Miss Beale asked:

"Did she say anything about the inspection?"

"Just mentioned it. She was only returning a book and was in a hurry so we didn't talk long. Apparently they've got a bad attack of influenza in the school and half her staff are off with it."

Miss Beale thought it odd that the Principal Tutor should find time to visit London to return a library book if staffing problems were so difficult, but she didn't say so. Before breakfast Miss Beale reserved her energy for thought rather than speech. Miss Burrows came round the bed to pour out the second cups. She said:

"What with this weather and with half the training staff off sick, it looks as if you're in for a pretty dull day."

As the two friends were to tell each other for years to come, with that cosy predilection for re-stating the obvious which is one of the pleasures of long intimacy, she could hardly have been more wrong. Miss Beale, expecting nothing worse of the day than a tedious drive, an arduous inspection, and a possible tussle with those members of the Hospital Nurse Education Committee who took the trouble to attend, dragged her dressing-gown around her shoulders, stubbed her feet into her bedroom slippers and shuffled off to the bathroom. She had taken the first steps on her way to witness a murder.

II

Despite the rain, the drive was less difficult than Miss Beale had feared. She made good time and was in Heatheringfield just before

9 o'clock in time to meet the last surge of the morning rush to work. The wide Georgian high street was blocked with vehicles. Women were driving their commuter husbands to the station or their children to school, vans were delivering goods, buses were discharging and loading their passengers. At the three sets of traffic lights the pedestrians streamed across the road, umbrellas slanted against the soft drizzle. The young had the spruce, over-uniformed look of the private-school child; the men were mostly bowler-hatted and carrying briefcases; the women were casually dressed with that nice compromise between town smartness and country informality, typical of their kind. Watching for the lights, the pedestrian crossings and the signpost to the hospital, Miss Beale had only a brief chance to notice the elegant eighteenth-century guildhall, the carefully preserved row of timber-fronted houses and the splendid crocketed spire of Holy Trinity church, but she gained an impression of a prosperous community which cared about preserving its architectural heritage even if the row of modern chain stores at the end of the high street suggested that the caring might well have begun thirty years earlier.

But here at last was the signpost. The road to the John Carpendar Hospital led upward from the High Street between a broad avenue of trees. To the left was a high stone wall which bounded the hospital grounds.

Miss Beale had done her homework. Her briefcase, plump on the back seat of the car, contained a comprehensive note on the hospital's history as well as a copy of the last General Nursing Council Inspector's report and the comments of the Hospital Management Committee on how far it had been possible to implement the inspector's optimistic recommendations. As she knew from her researches, the hospital had a long history. It had been founded in 1791 by a wealthy merchant who had been born in the town, had left it in youthful penury to seek his fortune in London, and had returned there in his retirement to enjoy patronizing and impressing his neighbours. He could have purchased fame and ensured his salvation by succouring the widows and fatherless or by re-building the church. But the age of science and reason was succeeding the age of faith and it had become fashionable to endow a hospital for the sick poor. And so, with the almost obligatory meeting in a local coffee house, the John Carpendar Hospital was born. The original house, of some architectural interest, had long since been replaced, first by a solid Victorian monument to ostentatious piety and then by the more functional gracelessness of the twentieth century.

The hospital had always flourished. The local community was predominantly middle-class and prosperous, with a well-developed charitable sense and too few objects on which to indulge it. Just before the Second World War a well-equipped private patients' wing had been added. Both before and after the advent of the National Health Service it had attracted wealthy patients, and consequently eminent consultants, from London and further afield. Miss Beale reflected that it was all very well for Angela to talk about the prestige of a London teaching hospital, but the John Carpendar had its own reputation. A woman might well think there were worse jobs than being Matron of a developing district general hospital, well thought of by the community it served, agreeably placed and fortified by its own local traditions.

She was at the main gates now. There was a porter's lodge on the left, an ornate doll's house in tessellated brick, a relic of the Victorian hospital, and—on the right—the doctors' car park. Already a third of the marked plots were occupied by the Daimlers and the Rolls. It had stopped raining and the dawn had given way to the grey normality of a January day. The lights were full on in the hospital. It lay before her like a great ship at anchor, brightly lit, latent with activity and power. To the left stretched the low glass-fronted buildings of the new out-patient department. Already a thin stream of patients was making its dispirited way to the entrance.

Miss Beale drew up alongside the inquiry hatch of the lodge, wound down the car window, and announced herself. The porter, ponderous and uniformed in self-importance, deigned to come out to present himself.

"You'll be the General Nursing Council, Miss," he stated grandiloquently. "What a pity you decided to come in this gate. The Nurse Training School is in Nightingale House, only a 100 yards or so from the Winchester Road entrance. We always use the back entrance for Nightingale House."

He spoke with reproachful resignation, as if deploring a singular lack of judgement which would cost him dear in extra work.

"But presumably I can get to the school this way?"

Miss Beale had no stomach for a return to the confusion of the High Street or intention of circling the hospital grounds in search of an elusive back entrance.

"Well you can, Miss." The porter's tone implied that only the wilfully obstinate would try, and he settled himself against the car door as if to deliver confidential and complicated directions. They proved, however, remarkably simple. Nightingale House was in the hospital grounds at the rear of the new out-patient department.

"Just take this road to the left, Miss, and keep straight on past the mortuary till you get to the resident medical quarters. Then turn to the right. There's a signpost where the road forks. You can't miss it."

For once this notoriously unpropitious assertion seemed justified. The grounds of the hospital were extensive and well wooded, a mixture of formal garden, grass, and clumped unkempt trees which reminded Miss Beale of the grounds of an old mental hospital. It was rare to find a general hospital so well endowed with space. But the several roads were well signposted and only one led to the left of the new out-patient department. The mortuary was easily identified, a squat, ugly little building tactfully sited among the trees and made more sinister by its strategic isolation. The medical officers' residence was new and unmistakable. Miss Beale had time to indulge her usual, frequently quite unjustified, resentment that Hospital Management Committees were always more ready to rehouse their doctors than to provide adequate accommodation for the nurse training school, before noting the promised sign. A white painted board pointed to the right and read "Nightingale House, Nurse Training School".

She changed gear and turned carefully. The new road was narrow and winding, banked high on each side with sodden leaves so that there was barely room for the single car. Everywhere was dampness and desolation. The trees grew close to the path and knitted themselves above it, ribbing the dark tunnel with their strong black boughs. From time to time a gust of wind brought down a spatter of raindrops on the car roof or flattened a falling leaf against the windscreen. The grass verge was scarred with flower beds, regular and oblong as graves and spiked with stunted bushes. It was so dark under the trees that Miss Beale switched on her side lamps. The road shone before her like an oiled ribbon. She had left the car window down and could smell, even above the inevitable car smell of petrol and warm vinyl, a sweet fungoid stench of decay. She felt strangely isolated in the dim quietness and suddenly she was touched with an irrational unease, a bizarre sensation of journeying out of time into some new dimension, borne onwards towards an uncomprehended and inescapable horror. It was only a second's folly and she quickly shook it off, reminding herself of the cheerful bustle of the High Street less than a mile away and the nearness of life and activity. But it had been an odd and disconcerting experience. Angry at herself at this lapse into morbid folly, she wound up the car window and stepped on the accelerator. The little car leaped forward.

Suddenly she found she had turned the last corner and Nightingale House was before her. She nearly stood on the brakes in surprise. It was an extraordinary house, an immense Victorian edifice of red brick, castellated and ornate to the point of fancy, and crowned with four immense turrets. It was brightly lit in the dark January morning and after the gloom of the road it blazed at her like the castle from some childhood mythology. An immense conservatory was grafted onto the right side of the house, looking, thought Miss Beale, more appropriate to Kew Gardens than to what had obviously once been a private residence. It was less brightly lit than the house but through the faintly luminous glass she could discern the sleek green leaves of aspidistras, the harsh red of poinsettias and the yellow and bronze blobs of chrysanthemums.

Miss Beale's recent moment of panic under the trees was completely forgotten in her amazement at Nightingale House. Despite her normal confidence in her own taste, she was not entirely immune to the vagaries of fashion and she wondered uneasily whether in certain company it might not be proper to admire it. But it had become a habit with her to look at every building with an eye to its suitability as a nurse training school—she had once, on a Paris holiday, found herself to her horror rejecting the Elysée Palace as unworthy of further notice—and as a nurse training school Nightingale House was obviously quite impossible. She had only to look at it for the objections to spring to mind. Most of the rooms would be far too large. Where, for instance, would one find cosy offices for the principal tutor, clinical instructor or school secretary? Then the building would be extremely difficult to heat adequately and those oriel windows, picturesque no doubt if one liked that sort of thing, would keep out a great deal of light. Worse still, there was something forbidding, even frightening, about the house. When the Profession (Miss Beale, in defiance of an unfortunate comparison, always thought of it with a capital P) was climbing so painfully into the twentieth century, kicking away the stones of outworn attitudes and methods—Miss Beale was frequently required to make speeches and certain pet phrases tended to stick in her mind—it really was a pity to house young students in this Victorian pile. It would do no harm to incorporate a strong comment about the need for a new school in her report. Nightingale House was rejected even before she set foot in it.

But there was nothing to criticize in her welcome. As she reached the top step, the heavy door swung open letting out a gust of warm air and a smell of fresh coffee. A uniformed maid stood deferentially aside and behind her down the wide oak staircase, gleaming against the dark panelling like a Renaissance portrait in grey and gold, came the figure of Matron Mary Taylor, hand outstretched. Miss Beale assumed her bright professional smile, compounded of happy expectation and general reassurance, and stepped forward to meet her. The ill-fated inspection of the John Carpendar Training School had begun.

III

Fifteen minutes later, four people made their way down the main staircase to the demonstration room on the ground floor where they were to watch the first teaching session of the day. Coffee had been served in Matron's sitting-room in one of the turret blocks where

Miss Beale had been introduced to the principal tutor, Miss Hilda Rolfe, and to a senior consultant surgeon, Mr. Stephen Courtney-Briggs. She knew both by reputation. Miss Rolfe's presence was necessary and expected, but Miss Beale was a little surprised that Mr. Courtney-Briggs was prepared to devote so much of his morning to the inspection. He had been introduced as Vice-Chairman of the Hospital Nurse Education Committee and she would normally have expected to meet him with other members of the committee for the summing-up discussion at the end of the day. It was unusual for a senior surgeon to sit in at a teaching session and it was gratifying that he took such a personal interest in the school.

There was room for three to walk abreast in the wide wood-panelled corridors and Miss Beale found herself escorted by the tall figures of Matron and Mr. Courtney-Briggs rather, she felt, like a diminutive delinquent. Mr. Courtney-Briggs, stoutly impressive in the formal striped trousers of a consultant, walked on her left. He smelt of after-shave lotion. Miss Beale could discern it even above the pervading smell of disinfectant, coffee and furniture cream. She thought it surprising but not disagreeable. The Matron, tallest of the three, walked in serene silence. Her formal dress of grey gaberdine was buttoned high to the neck with a thin band of white linen around the throat and cuffs. Her corn-gold hair, almost indistinguishable in colour from her skin, was combed back from the high forehead and bound tight by an immense triangle of muslin, its apex reaching nearly to the small of her back. The cap reminded Miss Beale of those worn during the last war by Sisters of the Army Nursing Service. She had seldom seen it since. But its simplicity suited Miss Taylor. That face, with its high cheekbones and large, slightly protuberant eyes—they reminded Miss Beale irreverently of pale veined gooseberries—could have looked grotesque under the fripperies of a more orthodox head-dress. Behind the three of them Miss Beale could sense the disturbing presence of Sister Rolfe, uncomfortably close on their heels.

Mr. Courtney-Briggs was talking:

"This influenza epidemic has been a thorough nuisance. We've had to defer taking the next set off the wards and we thought at one time that this set would have to go back. It was a close thing."

"It would be," thought Miss Beale. Whenever there was a crisis in the hospital the first people to be sacrificed were the student nurses. Their training programme could always be interrupted. It was a sore point with her, but now was hardly the time to protest. She made a vaguely acquiescent noise. They started down the last staircase. Mr. Courtney-Briggs continued his monologue:

"Some of the training staff have gone down with it too. The demonstration this morning is being taken by our clinical instructor, Mavis Gearing. We've had to recall her to the school. Normally, of course, she would be doing nothing but ward teaching. It's a comparatively new idea that there should be a trained instructor to teach the girls on the wards, using the patients as clinical material. Ward sisters just haven't the time these days. Of course the whole idea of the block system of training is relatively new. When I was a medical student the probationers, as we called them then, were taught entirely on the wards with occasional lectures in their own free time from the medical staff. There was little formal teaching and certainly no taking them off the wards each year for a period in the nurse training school. The whole concept of nurse training has altered."

Miss Beale was the last person to require an explanation of the function and duties of a clinical instructor or the development of nurse training methods. She wondered whether Mr. Courtney-Briggs had forgotten who she was. This elementary instruction was more suitable for new members of a Hospital Management Committee, who were generally as ignorant of nurse training as they were of anything else to do with hospitals. She had the feeling that the surgeon had something on his mind. Or was this merely the aimless chatter, unrelated to its hearer, of an egotist who could not tolerate even a moment without the comforting resonance of his own voice? If so, the sooner he got back to his out-patient session or ward round and let the inspection proceed without the benefit of his presence, the better for all concerned.

The little procession passed across the tessellated hall to a room at the front of the building. Miss Rolfe slipped forward to open the door and stood aside as the others entered. Mr. Courtney-Briggs ushered Miss Beale in before him. Immediately she was at home.

Despite the anomalies of the room itself—the two great windows with their spatter of coloured panes, the immense fireplace of carved marble with its draped figures supporting the chimney-piece, the high moulded ceiling desecrated with the three tubes of fluorescent light—it was happily evocative of her own student days, an utterly acceptable and familiar world. Here was all the paraphernalia of her profession; the rows of glass-fronted cabinets, with their instruments placed in shining precision; the wall charts showing in lurid diagram the circulation of the blood and the improbable processes of digestion; the wall-mounted blackboard smeared with the dust of past lecture notes imperfectly erased; the demonstration trolleys with their linen-covered trays; the two demonstration beds, one containing a life-sized doll propped among the pillows; the inevitable skeleton hanging from its gibbet in forlorn decrepitude. Pervading all was the astringent and potent smell of disinfectant. Miss Beale breathed it in like an addict. Whatever faults she might later find with the room itself, the adequacy of the teaching equipment, the lighting or the furniture, she never felt other than at home in this intimidating atmosphere.

She bestowed on students and teacher her brief smile of reassurance and encouragement and perched herself on one of the four chairs placed ready at the side of the room. Matron Taylor and Miss Rolfe seated themselves on each side of her as quietly and unobtrusively as possible in the face of Mr. Courtney-Briggs's determination to be fussily gallant over pulling out the ladies' chairs. The arrival of the little party, however tactfully arranged, seemed temporarily to have disconcerted the nurse tutor. An inspection was hardly a natural teaching situation, but it was always interesting to see how long it took a tutor to re-establish *rapport* with her class. A first-class teacher, as Miss Beale knew from personal experience, could hold a class's interest even through a heavy bombing raid let alone the visit of a General Nursing Council Inspector; but she did not feel that Mavis Gearing was likely to prove one of that rare and dedicated band. The girl—or woman rather—lacked authority. She had a propitiatory air; she looked as though she might easily simper. And she was a great deal too heavily made up for a woman who should have her mind on less ephemeral arts.

But she was, after all, merely the clinical instructor, not a qualified nurse tutor. She was taking the session at short notice and under difficulties. Miss Beale made a mental resolution not to judge her too harshly.

The class, she saw, were to practise feeding a patient by intragastric tube. The student who was to act as patient was already in one of the demonstration beds, her check dress protected by a mackintosh bib, her head supported by the back rest and a bank of pillows. She was a plain girl with a strong, obstinate and oddly mature face, her dull hair drawn back unbecomingly from a high nobbly forehead. She lay there immobile under the harsh strip lighting, looking a little ridiculous but strangely dignified as if concentrating on some private world and dissociating herself from the whole procedure by an effort of will. Suddenly it occurred to Miss Beale that the girl might be frightened. The thought was ridiculous but it persisted. She found herself suddenly unwilling to watch that resolute face. Irritated by her own unreasonable sensitivity, she turned her attention to the nurse tutor.

Sister Gearing cast an apprehensive and interrogative glance at the Matron, received a confirmatory nod and resumed her lesson.

"Nurse Pearce is acting the part of our patient this morning. We have just been going through her history. She is Mrs. Stokes, the fifty-year-old mother of four children, wife of a council refuse collector. She has had a larynectomy for the treatment of cancer." She turned to a student sitting on her right.

"Nurse Dakers, will you please describe Mrs. Stokes's treatment so far."

Nurse Dakers dutifully began. She was a pale, thin girl who blushed unbecomingly as she spoke. It was difficult to hear her but she knew her facts and presented them well. A conscientious little thing, thought Miss Beale, not outstandingly intelligent, perhaps, but hard working and reliable. It was a pity that no one had done anything about her acne. She retained her air of bright professional interest whilst Nurse Dakers propounded the fictional medical history of Mrs. Stokes and took the opportunity of a close look at the remaining students in the class, making her customary private assessment of their characters and ability.

The influenza epidemic had certainly taken its toll. There was a total of seven girls only in the demonstration room. The two who were standing one on each side of the demonstration bed made an immediate impression. They were obviously identical twins, strong, ruddy-faced girls, with copper-coloured hair clumped in a thick fringe above remarkable blue eyes. Their caps, the pleated crowns as small as saucers, were perched well forward, the two immense wings of white linen jutting behind. Miss Beale, who knew from her own student days what could be done with a couple of white-tipped hat pins, was nevertheless intrigued by the art which could so firmly attach such a bizarre and unsubstantial edifice on such a springing bush of hair. The John Carpendar uniform struck her as interestingly out of date. Nearly every hospital she visited had replaced these old-fashioned winged caps with the smaller American-type which were easier to wear, quicker to make up, and cheaper to buy and launder. Some hospitals, to Miss Beale's regret, were even issuing disposable paper caps. But a hospital's nurse uniform was always jealously defended and changed with reluctance and the John Carpendar was obviously wedded to tradition. Even the uniform dresses were slightly old fashioned. The twins' plump and speckled arms bulged from sleeves of check pink gingham which reminded Miss Beale of her own student days. Their skirt lengths paid no concession to modern fashion and their sturdy feet were planted in low-heeled black lace-up shoes.

She glanced quickly at the remaining students. There was a calm, bespectacled girl with a plain intelligent face. Miss Beale's immediate reaction was that she would be glad to have her on any ward. Next to her sat a dark, sulky-looking girl, rather over-made-up and assuming an air of careful disinterest in the demonstration. Rather common, thought Miss Beale. Miss Beale, to her superiors' occasional embarrassment, was fond of such unfashionable adjectives, used them unashamedly and knew precisely what she meant by them. Her dictum "Matron recruits a very nice type of girl" meant that they came of respectable middle-class families, had received the benefit of grammar school education, wore their skirts knee length or longer, and were properly aware of the privilege and responsibilities of being a student nurse. The last student in the class was a very pretty girl, her blonde hair worn in a fringe as low as her eyebrows above a pert, contemporary face. She was attractive enough for a recruiting poster, thought Miss Beale, but somehow it was the last face one would choose. While she was wondering why, Nurse Dakers came to the end of her recital.

"Right, Nurse," said Sister Gearing. "So we are faced with the problem of a post-operative patient, already seriously undernourished and now unable to take food by mouth. That means what? Yes, Nurse?"

"Intra-gastric or rectal feeding, Sister."

It was the dark sulky-looking girl who answered, her voice carefully repressing any note of enthusiasm or even interest. Certainly not an agreeable girl, thought Miss Beale.

There was a murmur from the class. Sister Gearing raised an interrogative eyebrow. The spectacled student said:

"Not rectal feeding, Sister. The rectum can't absorb sufficient nourishment. Intra-gastric feeding by the mouth or nose."

"Right, Nurse Goodale, and that's what the surgeon has ordered for Mrs. Stokes. Will you carry on please, Nurse. Explain what you are doing at each step."

One of the twins drew the trolley forward and demonstrated her tray of requirements: the gallipot containing sodium bicarbonate mixture for cleaning mouth or nostrils; the polythene funnel and eight inches of tubing to fit it; the connector; the lubricant; the kidney bowl with the tongue spatula, tongue forceps and gag. She held up the Jacques oesophageal tube. It dangled from her freckled hand obscenely like a yellow snake.

"Right, Nurse," encouraged Sister Gearing. "Now the feed. What are you giving her?"

"Actually, it's just warm milk, Sister."

"But if we were dealing with a real patient?"

The twin hesitated. The spectacled student said with calm authority: "We could add soluble protein, eggs, vitamin preparations and sugar."

"Right. If tube feeding is to continue for more than forty-eight hours we must ensure that the diet is adequate in calories, protein and vitamins. At what temperature are you giving the feed, Nurse?"

"Body temperature, Sister, 38° C."

"Correct. And as our patient is conscious and able to swallow we are giving her this feed by mouth. Don't forget to reassure your patient, Nurse. Explain simply to her what you are going to do and why. Remember this, girls, never begin any nursing procedure without telling your patient what is to happen."

They were third-year students, thought Miss Beale. They should know this by now. But the twin, who no doubt would have coped easily enough with a real patient, found it embarrassingly difficult to explain her procedure to a fellow student. Suppressing a giggle she muttered a few words at the rigid figure in the bed and almost thrust the oesophageal tube at her. Nurse Pearce, still gazing fixedly ahead, felt for the tube with her left hand and guided it into her mouth. Then shutting her eyes she swallowed. There was a convulsive spasm of the throat muscles. She paused to take breath, and then swallowed again. The tube shortened. It was very silent in the demonstration room. Miss Beale was aware that she felt unhappy but was unsure why. It was a little unusual perhaps for gastric feeding to be practised on a student in this way but it was not unknown. In a hospital it might be more usual for a doctor to pass the tube but a nurse might well have to take the responsibility; it was better to learn on each other than on a seriously ill patient and the demonstration doll wasn't really a satisfactory substitute for a living subject. She had once acted as the patient in her own training school and had found swallowing the tube unexpectedly easy. Watching the convulsive movements of Nurse Pearce's throat and swallowing in an unconscious sympathy she could almost recall, after thirty years, the sudden chill as the tube slid over the soft palate and the faint shock of surprise at the ease of it all. But there was something pathetic and disturbing about that rigid white-faced figure on the bed, eyes tight closed, bibbed like a baby, the thin tube dragging and wriggling like a worm from the corner of her mouth. Miss Beale felt that she was watching gratuitous suffering, that the whole demonstration was an outrage. For a second she had to fight an urge to protest.

One of the twins was now attaching a 20-ml. syringe to the end of the tube, ready to aspirate some of the gastric juices to test that the end of the tube had reached the stomach. The girl's hands were quite steady. Perhaps it was just Miss Beale's imagination that the room was preternaturally silent. She glanced across at Miss Taylor. The Matron had her eyes fixed on Nurse Pearce. She was frowning slightly. Her lips moved and she shifted in her seat. Miss Beale wondered if she were about to expostulate. But the Matron made no sound. Mr. Courtney-Briggs was leaning forward in his chair, his hands clasping his knees. He was gazing intently, not at Nurse Pearce, but at the drip as if mesmerized by the gentle swing of the tubing. Miss Beale could hear the heavy rasp of his breathing. Miss Rolfe sat bolt upright, her hands folded loosely in her lap, her black eyes expressionless. But Miss Beale saw that they were fixed, not on the girl in the bed, but on the fair pretty student. And for a fleeting second the girl looked back at her, equally expressionless.

The twin who was administering the feed, obviously satisfied that the end of the oesophageal tube was safely in the stomach, lifted the funnel high over Nurse Pearce's head and began slowly to pour the milky mixture down the tube. The class seemed to be holding its breath. And then it happened. There was a squeal, high-pitched, horribly inhuman, and Nurse Pearce precipitated herself from the bed as if propelled by an irresistible force. One second she was lying, immobile, propped against her mound of pillows, the next she was out of bed, teetering forward on arched feet in a parody of a ballet dancer, and clutching ineffectually at the air as if in frantic search of the tubing. And all the time she screamed, perpetually screamed, like a stuck whistle. Miss Beale, aghast, had hardly time to register the contorted face, the foaming lips, before the girl thudded to the floor and writhed there, doubled like a hoop, her forehead touching the ground, her whole body twitching in agony.

One of the students screamed. For a second no one moved. Then there was a rush forward. Sister Gearing tugged at the tube and tore it from the girl's mouth. Mr. Courtney-Briggs moved resolutely into the mêlée, his arms wide. Matron and Sister Rolfe bent over the twitching figure hiding her from view. Then Miss Taylor rose and looked round at Miss Beale.

"The students . . . could you look after them please? There's an empty room next door. Keep them together."

She was trying to keep calm but urgency made her voice sharp. "Quickly please."

Miss Beale nodded. The Matron bent again over the convulsed figure. The screaming had stopped now. It was succeeded by a piteous moaning and a dreadful staccato drumming of heels on the wooden floor. Mr. Courtney-Briggs took off his coat, threw it to one side, and began to roll up his sleeves.

IV

Muttering gentle encouragement, Miss Beale shepherded the little group of students across the hall. One of them, she was not sure which, said in a high-pitched voice: "What happened to her? What happened? What went wrong?" But no one replied. They moved in a shocked daze into the room next door. It was at the back of the house, a small, odd-shaped room which had obviously been partitioned from the original high-ceilinged drawing-room and which now served as the Principal Tutor's office. Miss Beale's first glance took in a business-like desk, a bank of green steel filing cabinets, a crowded notice board, a small pegboard fitted with hooks from which hung a variety of keys, and a chart along the whole of one wall showing the teaching programme and the progress of each individual student. The partition wall cut the mullioned window in half so that the office, unpleasing in its proportions, was also inconveniently dark. One of the students clicked down the switch and the central bar of fluorescence began to flicker into light. Really, thought Miss Beale, her mind clutching desperately at the comfort of its normal preoccupations, it was a most unsuitable room for a Principal Tutor, or for any other tutor, come to that.

This brief remembrance of the purpose of her visit brought a second's comfort. But almost immediately the awful reality of the moment reasserted itself. The students—a pathetic and disorganized little bunch—had crowded together in the middle of the room as if incapable of action. Glancing quickly around, Miss Beale saw that there were only three chairs. For a moment she felt as embarrassed and nonplussed as a hostess who is not sure how she is going to seat all her guests. The concern wasn't altogether irrelevant. She would have to get the girls comfortable and relaxed if there were to be any chance of keeping their minds off what was happening next door; and they might be incarcerated for a long time.

"Come along," she said brightly. "Let's move Sister's desk back against the wall, then four of you can perch there. I'll take the desk chair and two of you can have the easy chairs."

At least it was activity. Miss Beale saw that the thin, fair student was shaking. She helped her into one of the easy chairs and the dark, sulky-looking girl promptly took the other. Trust her to look after number one, thought Miss Beale. She busied herself helping the other students to clear the desk and push it back against the wall. If only she could send one of them to make some tea! Despite her intellectual assent to more modern methods of combating shock, Miss Beale still put her faith in warm strong sweet tea. But there wasn't a chance of any. It wouldn't do to upset and alert the kitchen staff.

"Now suppose we introduce ourselves," she said encouragingly. "My name is Miss Muriel Beale. There's no need to tell you I'm a G.N.C. Inspector. I know some of your names but I am not really sure who is who."

Five pairs of eyes gazed at her with startled incomprehension. But the efficient student—as Miss Beale still thought of her—quictly identified them.

"The twins are Maureen and Shirley Burt. Maureen is the elder by about two minutes and has the most freckles. Otherwise we don't find it easy to tell them apart. Next to Maureen is Julia Pardoe. Christine Dakers is in one armchair and Diane Harper in the other. I'm Madeleine Goodale."

Miss Beale, never good at remembering names, made her customary mental recapitulation. The Burt twins. Bonny and bouncing. It would be easy enough to remember their name, although impossible to decide which was which. Julia Pardoe. An attractive name for an attractive girl. Very attractive if one liked that blonde, rather feline prettiness. Smiling into the unresponsive violet-blue eyes, Miss Beale decided that some people, and not all of them men, might like it very much indeed. Madeleine Goodale. A good sensible name for a good sensible girl. She thought she would have no difficulty in remembering Goodale. Christine Dakers. Something very wrong there. The girl had looked ill throughout the brief demonstration and now seemed close to collapse. She had a poor skin, unusually so for a nurse. It was now drained of colour so that the spots around the mouth and over the forehead stood out in an angry rash. She was huddled deep into the armchair, her thin hands alternately smoothing and plucking at her apron. Nurse Dakers was certainly the most affected of all the group. Perhaps she had been a particular friend of Nurse Pearce. Miss Beale superstitiously made a quick mental amendment of tense. Perhaps she was a particular friend. If only they could get the girl some hot reviving tea!

Nurse Harper, her lipstick and eye shadow garish on the whitened face said suddenly: "There must have been something in the feed."

The Burt twins turned to her simultaneously. Maureen said:

"Of course there was! Milk."

"I mean something beside the milk." She hesitated. "Poison."

"But there couldn't be! Shirley and I took a fresh bottle of milk out of the kitchen fridge first thing this morning. Miss Collins was there and saw us. We left it in the demo room and didn't pour it into the measuring jug until just before the demonstration, did we, Shirley?"

"That's right. It was a fresh bottle. We took it at about 7 o'clock."

"And you didn't add anything by mistake?"

"Like what? Of course we didn't."

The twins spoke in unison, sounding sturdily confident, almost unworried. They knew exactly what they had done and when, and no one, Miss Beale saw, was likely to shake them. They weren't the type to be tormented by unnecessary guilt or fretted by those irrational doubts which afflict less stolid, more imaginative personalities. Miss Beale thought that she understood them very well.

Julia Pardoe said: "Perhaps someone else mucked about with the feed."

She looked round at her fellow students from under lowered lids, provocative, a little amused.

Madeleine Goodale said calmly: "Why should they?"

Nurse Pardoe shrugged and pursed her lips into a little secret smile. She said: "By accident. Or it might have been a practical joke. Or perhaps it was done on purpose."

"But that would be attempted murder!" It was Diane Harper who spoke. She sounded incredulous. Maureen Burt laughed.

"Don't be daft, Julia. Who would want to murder Pearce?"

No one replied. The logic was apparently unassailable. It was impossible to imagine anyone wanting to murder Pearce. Pearce, Miss Beale realized, was either of the company of the naturally inoffensive or was too negative a personality to inspire the tormenting hatred which can lead to murder. Then Nurse Goodale said drily: "Pearce wasn't everyone's cup of tea."

Miss Beale glanced at the girl, surprised. It was an odd remark to come from Nurse Goodale, a little insensitive in the circumstances, disconcertingly out of character. She noted, too, the use of the past tense. Here was one student who didn't expect to see Nurse Pearce alive again.

Nurse Harper reiterated stoutly: "It's daft to talk about murder. No one would want to kill Pearce."

Nurse Pardoe shrugged: "Perhaps it wasn't meant for Pearce. Jo Fallon was supposed to act as patient today, wasn't she? It was Fallon's name next on the list. If she hadn't been taken ill last night, it would have been Fallon in that bed this morning."

They were silent. Nurse Goodale turned to Miss Beale.

"She's right. We take it in strict turn to act as patient; it wasn't really Pearce's turn this morning. But Josephine Fallon was taken into the sick bay last night—you've probably heard that we have an influenza epidemic—and Pearce was next on the list. Pearce was taking Fallon's place."

Miss Beale was momentarily at a loss. She felt that she ought to put a stop to the conversation, that it was her responsibility to keep their minds off the accident, and surely it could only have been an accident. But she didn't know how. Besides, there was a dreadful fascination in getting at the facts. For her, there always had been. Perhaps, too, it was better that the girls should indulge this detached, investigatory interest, rather than sit there making unnatural and ineffective conversation. Already she saw that shock was giving way to that half-ashamed excitement which can follow tragedy, so long, of course, as it is someone else's tragedy.

Julia Pardoe's composed, rather childish voice went on: "So if the victim was really meant to be Fallon, it couldn't have been one of us, could it? We all knew that Fallon wouldn't be acting the patient this morning."

Madeleine Goodale said: "I should think that everyone knew. Everyone at Nightingale House anyway. There was enough talk about it at breakfast."

They were silent again, considering this new development. Miss Beale noted with interest that there were no protestations that no one would want to murder Fallon. Then Maureen Burt said:

"Fallon can't be all that sick. She was back here in Nightingale House this morning, just after eight-forty. Shirley and I saw her slipping out of the side door just before we went into the demo room after breakfast."

Nurse Goodale asked sharply: "What was she wearing?" Maureen was unsurprised at this apparently irrelevant question.

"Slacks. Her top coat. That red headscarf she wears. Why?"

Nurse Goodale, obviously shaken and surprised, made an attempt to conceal it. She said:

"She slipped those on before we took her to the sick bay last night. I suppose she came back to fetch something she wanted from her room. But she shouldn't have left the ward. It was stupid. She had a temperature of 103·8 when she was warded. Lucky for her that Sister Brumfett didn't see her."

Nurse Pardoe said maliciously: "Funny though, isn't it?" No one replied. It was indeed funny, thought Miss Beale. She recalled her long damp drive from the hospital to the nurse training school. The road was a winding one; obviously there would be a short cut through the trees. But it was a strange journey for a sick girl to make on an early January morning. There must have been some compelling reason to bring her back to Nightingale House. After all, if she did want something from her room there was nothing to prevent her asking for it. Any of the students would gladly have taken it across to the sick bay. And this was the girl who should have played the patient that morning, who should, logically, be lying next door among the tangle of tubes and linen.

Nurse Pardoe said: "Well, there's one person who knew that Fallon wouldn't be acting patient this morning. Fallon herself."

Nurse Goodale, white-faced, looked across at her.

"If you want to be stupid and malicious I suppose I can't stop you. But, if I were you, I would stop short of slander."

Nurse Pardoe looked unconcerned, even a little pleased. Catching sight of her sly, gratified smile, Miss Beale decided that it was time this talking stopped. She was searching for a change of topic when Nurse Dakers said faintly from the depths of her chair: "I feel sick."

There was immediate concern. Only Nurse Harper made no move to help. The rest gathered around the girl, glad of the chance to be doing something. Nurse Goodale said: "I'll take her to the downstairs cloakroom."

She supported the girl out of the room. To Miss Beale's surprise Nurse Pardoe went with her, their recent antagonism apparently forgotten as they supported Nurse Dakers between them. Miss Beale was left with the Burt twins and Nurse Harper. Another silence fell. But Miss Beale had learned her lesson. She had been unforgivably irresponsible. There was to be no more talk of death or murder. While they were here and in her charge they might as well work. She gazed sternly at Nurse Harper and invited her to describe the signs, symptoms and treatment of pulmonary collapse.

Ten minutes later the absent three returned. Nurse Dakers still looked pale but was composed. It was Nurse Goodale who looked worried. As if unable to keep it to herself, she said:

"The bottle of disinfectant is missing from the lavatory. You know the one I mean. It's always kept there on the little shelf. Pardoe and I couldn't find it."

Nurse Harper interrupted her bored but surprisingly competent recital and said:

"You mean that bottle of milky-looking mixture? It was there after supper last night."

"That's a long time ago. Has anyone been in that loo this morning?"

Apparently no one had. They looked at each other in silence.

It was then that the door opened. Matron came quietly in and shut it behind her. There was a creak of starched linen as the twins slipped from the desk and stood to attention. Nurse Harper rose gracelessly from her chair. All of them turned towards Miss Taylor.

"Children," she said, and the unexpected and gentle word told them the truth before she spoke.

"Children, Nurse Pearce died a few minutes ago. We don't yet know how or why, but when something inexplicable like this happens we have to call the police. The Hospital Secretary is doing that now. I want you to be brave and sensible as I know you will be. Until the police arrive, I think it would be better if we don't talk about what has happened. You will collect your textbooks and Nurse Goodale will take you to wait in my sitting-room. I shall be ordering some strong hot coffee and it will be brought up to you soon. Is that understood?"

There was a subdued murmur of, "Yes, Matron."

Miss Taylor turned to Miss Beale.

"I'm so very sorry, but it will mean your waiting here too."

"Of course, Matron, I quite understand."

Across the heads of the students their eyes met in bewildered speculation and wordless sympathy.

But Miss Beale was a little horrified to remember afterwards the banality and irrelevance of her first conscious thought.

"This must be the shortest inspection on record. What on earth will I say to the General Nursing Council?"

V

A few minutes earlier the four people in the demonstration room had straightened up and looked at each other, white-faced, utterly exhausted. Heather Pearce was dead. She was dead by any criteria, legal or medical. They had known it for the last five minutes but had worked on, doggedly and without speaking, as if there were still a chance that the flabby heart would pulse again into life. Mr. Courtney-Briggs had taken off his coat to work on the girl and the front of his waistcoat was heavily stained with blood. He stared at the thickening stain, brow creased, nose fastidiously wrinkled, almost as if blood were an alien substance to him. The heart massage had been messy as well as ineffectual. Surprisingly messy for Mr. Courtney-Briggs, the Matron thought. But surely the attempt had been justified? There hadn't been time to get her over to the theatre. It was a pity that Sister Gearing had pulled out the oesophageal tube. It had, perhaps, been a natural reaction but it might have cost Pearce her only chance. While the tube was in place they could at least have tried an immediate stomach wash-out. But an attempt to pass another tube by the nostril had been frustrated by the girl's agonized spasms and, by the time these had ceased, it was too late and Mr. Courtney-Briggs had been forced to open the chest wall and try the only measure left to him. Mr. Courtney-Briggs's heroic efforts were well known. It was only a pity that they left the body looking so pathetically mangled and the demonstration room stinking like an abattoir. These things were better conducted in an operating theatre, shrouded and dignified by the paraphernalia of ritual surgery.

He was the first to speak.

"This wasn't a natural death. There was something other than milk in that feed. Well, that's obvious to all of us I should have thought. We'd better call the police. I'll get on to the Yard. I know someone there, as it happens. One of the Assistant Commissioners."

He always did know someone, thought the Matron. She felt the need to oppose him. Shock had left an aftermath of irritation and, irrationally, it focused on him. She said calmly:

"The local police are the ones to call and I think that the Hospital Secretary should do it. I'll get Mr. Hudson on the house telephone now. They'll call in the Yard if they think it necessary. I can't think why it should be. But that decision is for the Chief Constable, not for us."

She moved over to the wall telephone, carefully walking round the crouched figure of Miss Rolfe. The Principal Tutor was still on her knees. She looked, thought the Matron, rather like a character from a Victorian melodrama with her smouldering eyes in a deathly white face, her black hair a little dishevelled under the frilly cap, and those reeking hands. She was turning them over slowly and studying the red mass with a detached, speculative interest as if she, too, found it difficult to believe that the blood was real. She said:

"If there's a suspicion of foul play ought we to move the body?" Mr. Courtney-Briggs said sharply: "I have no intention of moving the body."

"But we can't leave her here, not like this!" Miss Gearing was almost weeping in protest. The surgeon glared at her.

"My dear woman, the girl's dead! Dead! What does it matter where we leave the body? She can't feel. She can't know. For God's sake don't start being sentimental about death. The indignity is that we die at all, not what happens to our bodies."

He turned brusquely and went over to the window. Sister Gearing made a movement as if to follow him, and then sank into the nearest chair and began to cry softly like a snuffling animal. No one took any notice of her. Sister Rolfe got stiffly to her feet. Holding her hands raised in front of her in the ritual gesture of an operating theatre nurse she walked over to a sink in the corner, nudged on the tap with her elbow, and began to wash her hands. At the wall-mounted telephone the Matron was dialling a five-digit number. They heard her calm voice.

"Is that the Hospital Secretary's office? Is Mr. Hudson there? It's Matron." There was a pause. "Good morning, Mr. Hudson. I am speaking from the ground floor demonstration room in Nightingale House. Could you please come over immediately? Yes. Very urgent. I'm afraid something tragic and horrible has happened and it will be necessary for you to telephone the police. No, I'd rather not tell you on the telephone. Thank you." She replaced the receiver and said quietly: "He's coming at once. He'll have to put the Vice-Chairman in the picture, too—it's unfortunate that Sir Marcus is in Israel—but the first thing is to get the police. And now I had better tell the other students."

Sister Gearing was making an attempt to control herself. She blew loudly into her handkerchief, replaced it in her uniform pocket, and raised a blotched face.

"I'm sorry. It's the shock, I suppose. It's just that it was all so horrible. Such an appalling thing to happen. And the first time

I've taken a class too! And everyone sitting and watching it like that. The other students as well. Such a horrible accident."

"Accident, Sister?" Mr. Courtney-Briggs turned from the window. He strode over to her and bent his bull-like head close to hers. His voice was harsh, contemptuous as he almost spat the words into her face. "Accident? Are you suggesting that a corrosive poison found its way into that feed by accident? Or that a girl in her right mind would choose to kill herself in that particularly horrible way? Come, come, Sister, why not be honest for once? What we've just witnessed was murder!"

Chapter Two

Cease Upon the Midnight

I

It was late in the evening of Wednesday, 28th January, sixteen days after the death of Nurse Pearce and, in the students' sitting-room on the first floor of Nightingale House, Nurse Dakers was writing her mid-week letter to her mother. It was usual for her to finish it in time for the Wednesday evening post but, this week, she had lacked the energy and inclination to settle down to the task. Already the waste-paper basket at her feet held the screwed-up copies of the first two rejected drafts. And now she was trying again.

She was sitting at one of the twin writing-desks in front of the window, her left elbow almost brushing the heavy curtains which shut out the dank blackness of the night, her forearm curled protectively around the writing-pad. Opposite to her, the desk lamp shone on the bent head of Madeleine Goodale, so close that Nurse Dakers could see the clean white scalp at the hair parting and smell the almost imperceptible antiseptic tang of shampoo. Two text-books were open before Goodale and she was making notes. Nothing, thought Nurse Dakers with resentful envy, was worrying her; nothing in the room or beyond it could disturb her quiet concentration. The admirable and secure Goodale was making sure that the John Carpendar Gold Medal for top marks in the final examination would eventually be pinned on her immaculate apron.

Frightened by the strength of this sudden and shaming antagonism, which she felt must communicate itself to Goodale, Nurse Dakers slid her eyes from the bent head so disconcertingly close to hers and gazed around the room. It was so familiar to her after nearly three years of training that normally she hardly noticed the details of architecture or furnishing. But tonight she saw it with an unexpected clarity, as if it had nothing to do with her or with her life. It was too large to be cosy and was furnished as if it had acquired odd items over the years and taken them to itself. It must once have been an elegant drawing-room, but the walls had long since lost their paper and were now painted and scruffy, due—it was rumoured—for redecoration when money allowed. The ornate fireplace of carved marble and surrounding oak was fitted with a large gas stove, old and ugly in design but still remarkably efficient, hissing a strong heat even into the dark corners of the room. The elegant mahogany table against the far wall with its jumble of magazines might have been bequeathed by John Carpendar himself. But it was scratched and dull now, dusted regularly but rarely polished, its surface scarred and ringed. To the left of the fireplace, in incongruous contrast, stood a large, modern television set, the gift of the Hospital League of Friends. In front of it was an immense cretonne-covered sofa with sagging springs, and a single matching armchair. The rest of the chairs were similar to those in the hospital out-patient department but were now too old and shabby to be tolerated for the use of patients. The arm-rests of pale wood were grubby; the coloured vinyl seats were stretched and dented and now smelt unpleasantly in the heat from the fire. One of the chairs was empty. It was the red-seated one which Nurse Pearce had invariably used. Scorning the intimacy of the sofa, she would sit there, a little apart from the huddle of students around the television set, watching the screen with careful disinterest as if it were a pleasure she could easily forgo. Occasionally she would drop her eyes to a book in her lap as if the folly presented for her entertainment had become too much to bear. Her presence, thought Nurse Dakers, had always been a little unwelcome and oppressive. The atmosphere of the students' sitting-room had always been lighter, more relaxed without that upright and censorious figure. But the empty chair, the dented seat, was almost worse. Nurse Dakers wished that she had the courage to walk over to it, to swing it into line with the other chairs around the television set and settle herself nonchalantly into its sagging curves, exorcizing once and for all that oppressive ghost. She wondered if the other students felt the same. It was impossible to ask. Were the Burt twins, bunched together in the depths of the sofa, really as absorbed as they appeared by the old gangster film they were watching? They were each knitting one of the heavy sweaters which they invariably wore in winter, their fingers clicking away, their eyes never leaving the screen. Beside them Nurse Fallon lolled in the armchair, one trousered leg swung casually over the arm. It was her first day back in the school after her sick leave and she still looked pale and drawn. Was her mind really on the sleek-haired hero with his tall wide-ribboned and ridiculous trilby, his over-padded shoulders, whose raucous voice, punctuated with gunshots, filled the room? Or was she, too, morbidly conscious of that empty red chair, the dented seat, the rounded ends of the arm-rests polished by Pearce's hand?

Nurse Dakers shivered. The wall clock showed that it was already after nine-thirty. Outside the wind was rising. It was going to be a wild night. In the rare intervals of quiet from the television set she could hear the creaking and sighing of the trees and could picture the last leaves falling softly on grass and path, isolating Nightingale House in a sludge of silence and decay. She forced herself to pick up her pen. She really must get on! Soon it would be time for bed and, one by one, the students would say their good nights and disappear, leaving her to brave alone the poorly-lit staircase and the dark corridor beyond. Jo Fallon would still be here of course. She never went to bed until the television programme closed for the night. Then she would make her lonely way upstairs to prepare her nightly hot whisky and lemon. Everyone knew Fallon's invariable habit. But Nurse Dakers felt that she could not face being left alone with Fallon. Hers was the last company she would choose, even in that lonely, frightening walk from the sitting-room to bed.

She began writing again.

"Now please, Mummy, don't keep on worrying about the murder."

The impossibility of the sentence struck her as soon as she saw the words on the paper. Somehow she must avoid the use of that emotive, blood-stained word. She tried again. "Now please,

Mummy, don't start worrying about the things you read in the papers. There really isn't any need. I'm perfectly safe and happy and no one really believes that Pearce was deliberately killed."

It wasn't true of course. Some people must think that Pearce had been deliberately killed or why would the police be here? And it was ridiculous to suppose that the poison could have got into the feed by accident or that Pearce, the god-fearing, conscientious and essentially dull Pearce, would have chosen to kill herself in that agonizing and spectacular way. She wrote on:

"We still have the local C.I.D. here, but they don't come in so often now. They have been very kind to us students and I don't think they suspect anyone. Poor Pearce wasn't very popular, but it's ridiculous to think that anyone here would want to harm her."

Had the police really been kind, she wondered? They had certainly been very correct, very polite. They had produced all the usual reassuring platitudes about the importance of co-operating with them in solving this terrible tragedy, telling the truth at all times, keeping nothing back however trivial and unimportant it might seem. Not one of them had raised his voice; not one had been aggressive or intimidating. And all of them had been frightening. Their very presence in Nightingale House, masculine and confident, had been, like the locked door of the demonstration room, a constant reminder of tragedy and fear. Nurse Dakers had found Inspector Bailey the most frightening of them all. He was a huge, ruddy, moon-faced man whose encouraging and avuncular voice and manner were in unnerving contrast to his cold pig-like eyes. The questioning had gone on and on. She could still recall the interminable sessions, the effort of will necessary to meet that probing gaze.

"Now I'm told that you were the most upset of them all when Nurse Pearce died. She was a particular friend of yours perhaps?"

"No. Not really. Not a particular friend. I hardly knew her."

"Well, there's a surprise! After nearly three years of training with her? Living and working so closely together, I should have thought that you all got to know each other pretty well."

She had struggled to explain.

"In some ways we do. We know each other's habits. But I

didn't really know what she was like; as a person, I mean." A silly reply. How else could you know anyone except as a person? And it wasn't true. She had known Pearce. She had known her very well.

"But you got on well together? There hadn't been a quarrel or anything like that? No unpleasantness?"

An odd word. Unpleasantness. She had seen again that grotesque figure, teetering forward in agony, fingers scrabbling at the ineffectual air, the thin tubing stretching the mouth like a wound. No, there had been no unpleasantness.

"And the other students? They got on well with Nurse Pearce, too? There had been no bad blood as far as you know?"

Bad blood. A stupid expression. What was the opposite she wondered? Good blood? There was only good blood between us. Pearce's good blood. She had answered:

"She hadn't any enemies as far as I know. And if anyone did dislike her, they wouldn't kill her."

"So you all tell me. But someone did kill her, didn't they? Unless the poison wasn't intended for Nurse Pearce. She only played the part of the patient by chance. Did you know that Nurse Fallon had been taken ill that night?"

And so it had gone on. Questions about every minute of that last terrible demonstration. Questions about the lavatory disinfectant. The empty bottle, wiped clean of finger-prints, had been quickly found by the police lying among the bushes at the back of the house. Anyone could have thrown it from a bedroom window or bathroom window in the concealing darkness of that January morning. Questions about her movements from the moment of first awakening. The constant reiteration in that minatory voice that nothing should be held back, nothing concealed.

She wondered whether the other students had been as frightened. The Burt twins had seemed merely bored and resigned, obeying the Inspector's sporadic summons with a shrug of the shoulders and a weary, "Oh, God, not again!" Nurse Goodale had said nothing when she was called for questioning and nothing afterwards. Nurse Fallon had been equally reticent. It was known that Inspector Bailey had interviewed her in the sick bay as soon as she was well enough to be seen. No one knew what had happened at that interview. It was rumoured that Fallon had admitted returning to Nightingale House early in the morning of the crime but had refused to say why. That would be very like Fallon. And now she had returned to Nightingale House to rejoin her set. So far she hadn't even mentioned Pearce's death. Nurse Dakers wondered if and when she would; and, morbidly sensitive to the hidden meaning in every word, struggled on with her letter:

"We haven't used the demonstration room since Nurse Pearce's death but otherwise the set is continuing to work according to plan. Only one of the students, Diane Harper, has left the school. Her father came to fetch her two days after Nurse Pearce died and the police didn't seem to mind her leaving. We all thought it was silly of her to give up so near to her finals but her father has never been keen on her training as a nurse and she is engaged to be married anyway, so I suppose she thought it didn't matter. No one else is thinking of leaving and there really isn't the slightest danger. So please, darling, do stop worrying about me. Now I must tell you about tomorrow's programme."

There was no need to go on drafting now. The rest of the letter would be easy. She read over what she had written and decided that it would do. Taking a fresh sheet of paper from the pad she began to write the final letter. With any luck she would just get it finished before the film ended and the twins put away their knitting and went to bed.

She scribbled quickly on and, half an hour later, her letter finished, saw with relief that the film had come to the last holocaust and the final embrace. At the same moment Nurse Goodale removed her reading spectacles, looked up from her work, and closed her book. The door opened and Julia Pardoe appeared.

"I'm back," she announced, and yawned. "It was a lousy film. Anyone making tea?" No one answered but the twins stubbed their knitting-needles into the balls of wool and joined her at the door, switching off the television on their way. Pardoe would never bother to make tea if she could find someone else to do it and the twins usually obliged. As she followed them out of the sitting-room Nurse Dakers looked back at the silent, immobile figure of Fallon alone now with Madeleine Goodale. She had a sudden impulse to speak to Fallon, to welcome her back to the school, to ask after her health, or simply to say good night. But the words seemed to stick in her throat, the moment passed, and the last thing she saw as she closed the door behind her was Fallon's pale and individual face, blank eyes still fixed on the television set as if unaware that the screen was dead.

II

In a hospital, time itself is documented, seconds measured in a pulse beat, the drip of blood or plasma; minutes in the stopping of a heart; hours in the rise and fall of a temperature chart, the length of an operation. When the events of the night of 28th–29th January came to be documented there were few of the protagonists at the John Carpendar Hospital who were unaware what they had been doing or where they were at any particular moment of their waking hours. They might not choose to tell the truth, but at least they knew where the truth lay.

It was a night of violent but erratic storm, the wind varying in intensity and even in direction from hour to hour. At ten o'clock it was little more than a sobbing *obbligato* among the elms. An hour later it suddenly reached a crescendo of fury. The great elms around Nightingale House cracked and groaned under the onslaught, while the wind screamed among them like the cachinnation of devils. Along the deserted paths, the banks of dead leaves, still heavy with rain, shifted sluggishly then broke apart into drifts and rose in wild swirls like demented insects, to glue themselves against the black barks of the trees. In the operating theatre at the top of the hospital Mr. Courtney-Briggs demonstrated his imperturbability in the face of crisis by muttering to his attendant registrar that it was a wild night before bending his head again to the satisfying contemplation of the intriguing surgical problem which throbbed between the retracted lips of the wound. Below him in the silent and dimly lit wards the patients muttered and turned in their sleep as if conscious of the tumult outside. The radiographer, who had been called from home to take urgent X-rays of Mr. Courtney-Briggs's patient, replaced the covers on the apparatus, switched out the lights and wondered whether her small car would hold the road. The night nurses moved silently among their patients testing the windows, drawing the curtains more closely as if to keep out some threatening and alien force. The porter on duty in the main gate lodge shifted uneasily in his chair then rose cramped to his feet and put a couple more chunks of coal on the fire. He felt in need of warmth and comfort in his isolation. The little house seemed to shake with every gust of the wind.

But shortly before midnight the storm abated, as if sensing the approach of the witching hour, the dead of night when the pulse of man beats slowest and the dying patient slips most easily into the last oblivion. There was an eerie silence for about five minutes, succeeded by a soft rhythmic moaning as the wind swooped and sighed among the trees as if exhausted by its own fury. Mr. Courtney-Briggs, the operation completed, peeled off his gloves and made his way into the surgeons' changing room. As soon as he was disrobed he made a telephone call from the wall instrument to the Sisters' floor at Nightingale House and asked Sister Brumfett, the Sister in charge of the private ward, to return to the ward to supervise the care of his patient for the first critical hour. He noted with satisfaction that the wind had dropped. She could make her own way through the grounds as she had done at his bidding countless times before. He need feel under no obligation to fetch her in his car.

Less than five minutes later Sister Brumfett plodded resolutely through the trees, her cloak folded around her like a flag whipped close to a flag pole, her hood drawn down over the frilly Sister's cap. It was curiously peaceful in this brief interlude of the storm. She moved silently over the sodden grass, feeling the pull of the rain-soaked earth through the thick soles of her shoes while, from time to time, a thin branch, torn by the storm, broke loose from its last thread of bark and thudded with gentle inadvertence at her feet. By the time she had gained the peace of the private ward and was helping the third-year student make up the post-operative bed and prepare the stand ready for the blood drip, the wind was rising again. But Sister Brumfett, absorbed in her task, no longer noticed it.

Shortly after half past twelve Albert Colgate, the porter on night duty in the main lodge, who was nodding over his evening paper, was jerked into consciousness by a band of light sweeping across the lodge window and the purr of an approaching car. It must, he thought, be Mr. Courtney-Briggs's Daimler. So the operation was over. He expected the car to sweep out of the main gate but unexpectedly it stopped. There were two peremptory hoots on the horn. Muttering, the porter thrust his arms into his overcoat and made his way out of the lodge door. Mr. Courtney-Briggs wound down the window and shouted at him through the wind.

"I tried to get out of the Winchester gate but there's a tree down across the path. I thought I'd better report it. Get it seen to as soon as you can."

The porter thrust his head through the car window encountering an immediate and luxurious smell of cigar smoke, after-shave lotion and leather. Mr. Courtney-Briggs recoiled slightly from his nearness. The porter said:

"That'll be one of those old elms no doubt, sir. I'll report it first thing in the morning. There's nothing I can do tonight, sir, not in this storm."

Mr. Courtney-Briggs began to wind up the window. Colgate's head made a sudden withdrawal.

The surgeon said: "There's no need to do anything tonight. I've tied my white scarf on one of the boughs. I doubt whether anyone else will use that road until the morning. If they do, they'll see the scarf. But you might warn anyone who drives in this way. Good night, Colgate."

The large car purred out of the front gate and Colgate made his way back into the lodge. Meticulously he noted the time by the wall clock over the fireplace and made a record in his book. "12.32 Mr. Courtney-Briggs reports fallen tree across the Winchester Road path."

He had settled again into his chair and taken up his paper before the thought struck him that it was odd that Mr. Courtney-Briggs should have tried to drive out through the Winchester gate. It wasn't on his quickest route home and it was a road he seldom used.

Mr. Courtney-Briggs invariably used the front entrance. Presumably, thought Colgate, he had a key to the Winchester Road gate. Mr. Courtney-Briggs had a key to most parts of the hospital. But it was odd all the same.

Just before 2 o'clock on the silent second floor of Nightingale House, Maureen Burt stirred in her sleep, muttered incoherently through her moist pursed lips and awoke to the disagreeable awareness that three cups of tea before bed had been two too many. She lay still for a moment, sleepily aware of the groaning of the storm, wondered whether she might not after all manage to get to sleep again, realized that her discomfort was too great to be reasonably borne and felt for the switch of her bedside lamp. The light was instantaneous and blinding, shocking her into full consciousness. She wriggled her feet into her bedroom slippers, threw her dressing-gown around her shoulders and padded out into the corridor. As she quietly closed her bedroom door behind her a sudden gust of wind billowed out the curtains at the far corridor window. She went across to shut it. Through the agitated tracery of boughs and their leaping shadows on the window-pane she could see the hospital riding the storm like a great ship at anchor, the ward windows only faintly luminous in comparison with the vertical line of brightly lit eyes marking the Sisters' offices and ward kitchens. She shut down the window carefully and, reeling slightly with sleep, felt her way down the passage to the cloakroom. Less than a minute later she came out again into the corridor, pausing momentarily to accustom her eyes to the gloom. From the confusion of shadows at the top of the stairs a deeper shadow detached itself, moved forward and was revealed as a cloaked and hooded figure. Maureen was not a nervous girl and in her somnolent state was conscious only of surprise that someone else should be awake and about. She saw at once that it was Sister Brumfett. Two piercing bespectacled eyes peered at her through the gloom. The Sister's voice was unexpectedly sharp.

"It's one of the Burt twins, isn't it? What are you doing here? Is anyone else up?"

"No, Sister. At least I don't think so. I've just been to the lavatory."

"Oh I see. Well, as long as everyone's all right. I thought that the storm might have disturbed you all. I've just come back from my ward. One of Mr. Courtney-Briggs's patients had a relapse and he had to operate urgently."

"Yes, Sister," said Nurse Burt, uncertain what else was expected of her. She was surprised that Sister Brumfett should bother to explain her presence to a mere student nurse, and she watched a little uncertainly as the Sister drew her long cloak more firmly around her and stumped briskly down the corridor towards the far stairs. Her own room was on the floor above, immediately next to Matron's flat. When she reached the bottom of the stairs, Sister Brumfett turned and seemed about to speak. It was at that moment that Shirley Burt's door opened slowly, and a tousled red head appeared.

"What's up?" it inquired sleepily.

Sister Brumfett walked towards them.

"Nothing, Nurse. I'm just on my way back to bed. I've come from my ward. And Maureen had to get up to go to the lavatory. There's nothing to worry about."

Shirley gave no impression that she was or ever had been worried. She now trotted out on to the landing, pulling her dressing-gown around her. Resigned and a little complacent, she said:

"When Maureen wakes up I do too. We've always been like that ever since we were babies. You ask Mum!" A little unsteady with sleep but not ungratified that the family theurgy still worked, she closed her bedroom door behind her with the finality of one who, being up, intends to stay up.

"No use trying to get off again in this wind. I'm going to brew some cocoa. Can we bring you up a mug, Sister. It'd help you to sleep?"

"No thank you, Nurse. I don't think I shall have any trouble in sleeping. Be as quiet as you can. You don't want to disturb the others. And don't get cold." She turned again towards the stairs. Maureen said: "Fallon's awake. At least her bedside lamp's still on."

The three of them looked down the corridor to where an eye of light from Nurse Fallon's keyhole pierced the darkness and threw a small luminous shadow on the linenfold panelling opposite.

Shirley said: "We'll take her a mug then. She's probably awake and reading. Come on, Maureen! Good night, Sister."

They shuffled off together down the corridor to the small utility room at the end. After a second's pause Sister Brumfett, who had been looking steadily after them, her face rigid and expressionless, turned finally towards the stairs and made her way up to bed.

Exactly one hour later but unheard and unrecorded by anyone in Nightingale House, a weakened pane of glass in the conservatory which had rattled spasmodically throughout the night, fell inwards to explode into splinters on the tessellated floor. The wind rushed in through the aperture like a questing animal. Its cold breath rustled the magazines on the wicker tables, lifted the fronds of the palms and sent the fern leaves gently waving. Finally it found the long white cupboard centred under the plant shelves. Early in the evening, the door had been left ajar by the desperate and hurried visitor who had last thrust a hand into the cupboard depths. All night the door had stayed open, motionless on its hinges. But now the wind set it gently swinging to and fro, then as if wearying of the game, finally closed it with a soft, decisive thud.

And everything living under the roof of Nightingale House, slept.

III

Nurse Dakers was awoken by the whirr of the bedside alarm clock. The faintly luminous dial showed the time as 6.15. Even with the curtains drawn back the room was still completely dark. The square of faint light came, as she knew, not from the door but from the distant lights of the hospital where already the night staff would be taking round the first morning cups of tea. She lay still for a moment, adjusting to her own wakefulness, putting out tentative feelers to the day. She had slept well despite the storm of which she had been only briefly aware. She realized with a spring of joy that she could actually face the day with confidence. The misery and apprehension of the previous evening, of the previous weeks, seemed to have lifted. It seemed now no more than the effect of tiredness and temporary depression. She had passed down a tunnel of misery and insecurity since Pearce's death but this morning, miraculously, she had come out into daylight again. It was like Christmas morning in childhood. It was the beginning of a summer holiday from school. It was waking refreshed at the end of a febrile illness with the comfortable knowledge that Mummy was there and that all the solaces of convalescence lay ahead. It was familiar life restored.

The day shone before her. She catalogued its promises and pleasures. In the morning there would be the materia-medica lecture. This was important. She had always been weak on drugs and dosages. Then, after the coffee break, Mr. Courtney-Briggs would give his third year surgery seminar. It was a privilege that a surgeon of his eminence should take so much trouble with the student nurse training. She was a little afraid of him, particularly of his sharp staccato questions. But this morning she would be brave and speak up confidently. Then in the afternoon the hospital bus would take the set to the local maternity and child welfare clinic to watch the local authority staff at work. This, too, was important to someone who hoped in time to become a district nurse. She lay for a few moments contemplating this gratifying programme then she got out of bed, shuffled her feet into her slippers, struggled into her cheap dressing-gown and made her way along the passage to the students' utility room.

The Nightingale nurses were called promptly at seven each morning by one of the maids, but most students, accustomed to early waking when on the wards, set their alarm clocks at 6.30 to give themselves time for tea-making and gossip. The early arrivals were already there. The little room was brightly lit, cheerfully domestic, smelling, as always, of tea, boiled milk and detergent. The scene was reassuringly normal. The Burt twins were there, faces still puffy from sleep, each twin stoutly cocooned into a bright red dressing-gown. Maureen was carrying her portable wireless tuned to Radio 2 and was gently jerking hips and shoulders to the rhythm of the B.B.C.'s early morning syncopation. Her twin was setting their two immense mugs on a tray and rummaging in a tin for biscuits. The only other student present was Madeleine Goodale who, clad in an ancient plaid dressing-gown, was watching, teapot in hand, for the first spurt of steam from the kettle. In her mood of optimism and relief, Nurse Dakers could have hugged them all.

"Where's Fallon this morning?" asked Maureen Burt with no great interest.

Nurse Fallon was a notoriously late riser, but she was usually one of the first to make tea. It was her habit to carry it back to enjoy at leisure in bed, where she would stay until the last possible moment consistent with presenting herself at breakfast on time. But this morning her personal teapot and the matching cup and saucer were still on the cupboard shelf beside the canister of china tea which Fallon preferred to the strong brown brew which the rest of the set considered necessary before they could face the day.

"I'll give her a call," suggested Nurse Dakers, happy to be of use and longing to celebrate her release from the strain of the last few weeks by general benevolence.

"Wait a moment, then you can take her a cuppa out of my pot," suggested Maureen.

"She won't like Indian tea. I'll see if she's awake and just let her know the kettle's on the boil."

For a moment it occurred to Nurse Dakers to make Fallon's tea for her. But the impulse faded. It was not that Fallon was particularly temperamental or unpredictable, but somehow people did not interfere with her personal things nor expect her to share them. She had few possessions but they were expensive, elegant, carefully chosen and so much part of her *persona* that they seemed sacrosanct.

Nurse Dakers almost ran along the passage to Fallon's room. The door was unlocked. That did not surprise her. Ever since one of the students had been taken ill in the night some years ago and had been too weak to creep across the room to unlock the door, there had been a rule forbidding girls to lock themselves in at night. Since Pearce's death one or two had taken to turning their keys, and if the Sisters suspected it they said nothing. Perhaps they, too, slept more soundly behind locked doors. But Fallon had not been afraid.

The curtains were closely drawn. The bedside lamp was on but with the adjustable shade tilted so that it threw a pale moon on the far wall and left the bed in shadow. There was a tangle of black hair on the pillow. Nurse Dakers felt along the wall for the light switch and paused before clicking it on. Then she pressed it down very gently as if it were possible softly and gradually to illuminate the room and spare Fallon that first fierce wakening. The room blazed into light. She blinked in the unexpected glare. Then she moved very quietly across to the bed. She didn't scream or faint. She stood absolutely still for a moment looking down at Fallon's body, and smiling a little as if surprised. She had no doubt that Fallon was dead. The eyes were still wide open but they were cold and opaque, like the eyes of dead fish. Nurse Dakers bent down and stared into them as if willing them into brightness or seeking in vain some trace of her own reflection. Then she slowly turned and left the room, switching off the light and closing the door behind her. She swayed like a sleep-walker along the passage, steadying her hands against the wall.

At first the students didn't notice her return. Then three pairs of eyes were suddenly fixed on her, three figures stood frozen in a tableau of puzzled inquiry. Nurse Dakers leaned against the door post and opened her mouth soundlessly. The words wouldn't come. Something seemed to have happened to her throat. Her whole jaw was trembling uncontrollably and her tongue was stuck to the roof of her mouth. Her eyes pleaded with them. It seemed minutes while they watched her struggle. When the words did come she sounded calm, gently surprised.

"It's Fallon. She's dead."

She smiled like someone waking from a dream, patiently explaining: "Someone's murdered Fallon."

The room emptied. She wasn't aware of their concerted dash down the corridor. She was alone. The kettle was screeching now, the lid rattling under the force of the steam. Carefully she turned down the gas, frowning with concentration. Very slowly, like a child entrusted with a precious task, she took down the canister, the elegant teapot, the matching cup and saucer, and humming gently to herself, made Fallon's early morning tea.

Chapter Three

Strangers in the House

I

"The pathologist is here, sir."

A detective constable put his cropped head round the bedroom door and raised an interrogative eyebrow.

Chief Superintendent Adam Dalgliesh turned from his examination of the dead girl's clothes, his six feet two inches uncomfortably trapped between the foot of the bed and the wardrobe door. He looked at his watch. It was eight minutes past ten. Sir Miles Honeyman, as always, had made good time.

"Right, Fenning. Ask him to be good enough to wait for a moment, will you? We'll be finished in here in a minute. Then some of us can clear out and make room for him."

The head disappeared. Dalgliesh closed the wardrobe door and managed to squeeze himself between it and the foot of the bed. Certainly there was no room for a fourth person at present. The huge bulk of the finger-print man occupied the space between the bedside table and the window as, bent almost double, he brushed charcoal carefully on to the surface of the whisky bottle, turning it by its cork. Beside the bottle stood a glass plate bearing the dead girl's prints, the whorls and composites plainly visible.

"Anything there?" asked Dalgliesh.

The print man paused and peered more closely.

"A nice set of prints coming up, sir. They're hers all right. Nothing else, though. It looks as if the chap who sold it gave the bottle the usual wipe over before wrapping. It'll be interesting to see what we get from the beaker."

He cast a jealously possessive glance at it as it lay where it had fallen from the girl's hand, lightly poised in a curve of the counterpane. Not until the last photograph had been taken would it be yielded up for his examination.

He bent again to his task on the bottle. Behind him the Yard photographer manœuvred his tripod and camera—a new Cambo monorail, Dalgliesh noticed—to the right-hand foot of the bed. There was a click, an explosion of light, and the image of the dead girl leapt up at them and lay suspended in air, burning itself on Dalgliesh's retina. Colour and shape were intensified and distorted in that cruel, momentary glare. The long black hair was a tangled wig against the whiteness of the pillows; the glazed eyes were exophthalmic marbles, as if rigor mortis were squeezing them out of their sockets; the skin was very white and smooth, looking repulsive to the touch, an artificial membrane, tough and impermeable as vinyl. Dalgliesh blinked, erasing the image of a witch's plaything, a grotesque puppet casually tossed against the pillow. When he next looked at her she was again a dead girl on a bed; no more and no less. Twice more the distorted image leapt up at him and lay petrified in air as the photographer took two pictures with the Polaroid Land camera to give Dalgliesh the immediate prints for which he always asked. Then it was over. "That was the last. I'm through, sir," said the photographer. "I'll let Sir Miles in now." He put his head around the door while the print man, grunting with satisfaction, lovingly lifted the drinking beaker from the counterpane with a pair of forceps and set it alongside the whisky bottle.

Sir Miles must have been waiting on the landing for he trotted in immediately, a familiar rotund figure with his immense head of black curling hair and eager beady eyes. He brought with him an air of music hall *bonhommie* and, as always, a faint smell of sour sweat. He was unfretted by the delay. But then Sir Miles, God's gift to forensic pathology or an amateur mountebank as you chose to take him, did not easily take offence. He had gained much of his reputation and also, possibly, his recent knighthood by adhering to the principle that you should never willingly offend anyone, however humble. He greeted the departing photographer and the finger-print officer as if they were old friends, and Dalgliesh by his Christian name. But the socialities were perfunctory; his preoccupation preceded him like a miasma as he wriggled up close to the bed.

Dalgliesh despised him as a ghoul; hardly, he admitted, a rational cause for dislike. In a perfectly organized world, foot fetishists would, no doubt, become chiropodists; hair fetishists, hairdressers; and ghouls, morbid anatomists. It was surprising that so few of them did. But Sir Miles laid himself open to the implication. He approached each new corpse with eagerness, almost with glee; his macabre jokes had been heard at half the dining clubs in London; he was an expert in death who obviously enjoyed his work. Dalgliesh felt inhibited in his company by the consciousness of his dislike for the man. Antipathy seemed to crackle from him. But Sir Miles was oblivious of it. He liked himself too well to conceive that other men might find him less lovable, and this endearing naïvety gave him a kind of charm. Even those colleagues who most deplored his conceit, his publicity seeking, and the irresponsibility of most of his public utterances, found it hard to dislike him as much as they felt they should. Women were said to find him attractive. Perhaps he had a morbid fascination for them. Certainly his was the infectious good nature of a man who necessarily finds the world an agreeable place since it contains himself.

He always tut-tutted over a body. He did so now, plucking back the sheet with a curiously mincing gesture of his pudgy fingers. Dalgliesh walked over to the window and gazed out at the tracery of boughs through which the distant hospital, still lit up, gleamed like an insubstantial palace suspended in air. He could hear the faint rustling of bed linen. Sir Miles would only be making a preliminary examination, but even to think of those pudgy fingers insinuating themselves into the body's tender orifices was enough to make one hope for a peaceful death in one's own bed. The real job would be done later on the mortuary table, that aluminium sink with its grim accessories of drains and sprays on which Josephine Fallon's body would be systematically dismembered in the cause of justice, or science, or curiosity, or what you will. And afterwards, Sir Miles's mortuary attendant would earn his guinea by stitching it up again into a decent semblance of humanity so that the family could view it without trauma. If there were a family. He wondered who, if anyone, would be Fallon's official mourners. Superficially there was nothing in her room—no photographs, no letters—to suggest that she had close ties with any living soul.

While Sir Miles sweated and muttered, Dalgliesh made a second tour of the room, carefully avoiding watching the pathologist. He knew this squeamishness to be irrational and was half ashamed of it. Post mortem examinations did not upset him. It was this impersonal examination of the still warm female body which he couldn't stomach. A few short hours ago she would have been entitled to some modesty, to her own choice of doctor, free to reject those unnaturally white and eagerly probing fingers. A few hours ago she was a human being. Now she was dead flesh.

It was the room of a woman who preferred to be unencumbered. It contained the necessary basic comforts and one or two carefully chosen embellishments. It was as if she had itemized her needs and provided for them expensively but precisely and without extravagance. The thick rug by the bed was not, he thought, the kind provided by the Hospital Management Committee. There was only one picture but that was an original water colour, a charming landscape by Robert Hills, hung where the light from the window lit it most effectively. On the window-sill stood the only ornament, a Staffordshire pottery figure of John Wesley preaching from his pulpit. Dalgliesh turned it in his hands. It was perfect; a collector's piece. But there were none of the small trivial impedimenta which those living in institutions often dispose about them to provide comfort or reassurance.

He walked over to the bookcase beside the bed and again examined the books. They, too, seemed chosen to minister to predictable moods. A collection of modern poetry, his own last volume included; a complete set of Jane Austen, well worn but in a leather binding and printed on India paper; a few books on philosophy nicely balanced between scholarship and popular appeal; about two dozen paper-backs of modern novels, Greene, Waugh, Compton Burnett, Hartley, Powell, Cary. But most of the books were poetry. Looking at them, he thought, we shared the same tastes. If we had met we should at least have had something to say to each other. "Everyman's death diminishes me." But, of course, Doctor Donne. The over-exploited dictum had become a fashionable catch phrase in a crowded world where non-involvement was practically a social necessity. But some deaths still held their power to diminish more than others. For the first time in years he was conscious of a sense of waste, of a personal irrational loss.

He moved on. At the foot of the bed was a wardrobe with a chest of drawers attached, a bastard contraption in pale wood, designed, if anyone had consciously designed an object so ugly, to provide the maximum of space in the minimum of room. The top of the chest was meant to serve as a dressing-table and held a small looking-glass. In front of it were her brush and comb. Nothing else.

He opened the small left-hand drawer. It held her make-up, the jars and tubes neatly arranged on a small papiermâché tray. There was a great deal more than he had expected to find: cleansing cream, a box of tissues, foundation cream, pressed powder, eye shadow, mascara. She had obviously made up with care. But there was only one of each item. No experiments, no impulse buying, no half used and discarded tubes with the make-up congealed round the stopper. The collection said: "This is what suits me. This is what I need. No more and no less."

He opened the right-hand drawer. It held nothing but a concertina file, each compartment indexed. He thumbed through the contents. A birth certificate. A certificate of baptism. A post office savings account book. The name and address of her solicitor. There were no personal letters. He tucked the file under his arm.

He moved on to the wardrobe and examined again the collection of clothes. Three pairs of slacks. Cashmere jumpers. A winter coat in bright red tweed. Four well-cut dresses in fine wool. They all spoke of quality. It was an expensive wardrobe for a student nurse.

He heard a final satisfied grunt from Sir Miles and turned round. The pathologist was straightening himself and peeling off his rubber gloves. They were so thin that it looked as if he were shedding his epidermis. He said:

"Dead, I should say, about ten hours. I'm judging mainly by rectal temperature and the degree of rigor in the lower limbs. But it's no more than a guess, my dear fellow. These things are chancy, as you know. We'll have a look at the stomach contents; that may give us a clue. At present, and on the clinical signs, I should say she died about midnight give or take an hour. Taking a common sense view, of course, she died when she drank that nightcap."

The finger-print officer had left the whisky bottle and beaker on the table and was working now on the door handle. Sir Miles trotted round to them and without touching the beaker bent his head and placed his nose close to the rim.

"Whisky. But what else? That's what we're asking ourselves, my dear fellow. That's what we're asking ourselves. One thing, it wasn't a corrosive. No carbolic acid this time. I didn't do the P.M. on that other girl by the way. Rikki Blake did that little job. A bad business. I suppose you're looking for a connection between the two deaths?"

Dagliesh said: "It's possible."

"Could be. Could be. This isn't likely to be a natural death. But we'll have to wait for the toxicology. Then we may learn something. There's no evidence of strangulation or suffocation. No external marks of violence come to that. By the way, she was pregnant. About three months gone, I'd say. I got a nice little *ballottement* there. Haven't found that sign since I was a student. The P.M. will confirm it of course."

His little bright eyes searched the room. "No container for the poison apparently. If it were poison, of course. And no suicide note?"

"That's not conclusive evidence," said Dalgliesh.

"I know. I know. But most of them leave a little *billet doux*. They like to tell the tale, my dear fellow. They like to tell the tale. The mortuary van's here by the way. I'll take her away if you're finished with her."

"I've finished," said Dalgliesh.

He waited and watched while the porters manœuvred their stretcher into the room and with brisk efficiency dumped the dead weight onto it. Sir Miles fretted around them with the nervous anxiety of an expert who has found a particularly good specimen and must carefully supervise its safe transport. It was odd that the removal of that inert mass of bone and tightening muscle, to which each in his different way had been ministering, should have left the room so empty, so desolate. Dalgliesh had noticed it before when the body was taken away; this sense of an empty stage, of props casually disposed and bereft of meaning, of a drained air. The recently dead had their own mysterious *charisma*; not without reason did men talk in whispers in their presence. But now she was gone, and there was nothing further for him to do in the room. He left the finger-print man annotating and photographing his finds, and went out into the passage.

II

It was now after eleven o'clock but the corridor was still very dark, the one clear window at the far end discernible only as a square haze behind the drawn curtains. Dalgliesh could at first just make out the shape and colour of the three red fire buckets filled with sand and the cone of a fire extinguisher gleaming against the carved oak panelling of the walls. The iron staples, driven brutally into the woodwork, on which they were supported, were in incongruous contrast to the row of elegant light fittings in convoluted brass which sprang from the centres of the quatrefoil carvings. The fittings had obviously originally been designed for gas, but had been crudely adapted without imagination or skill to the use of electricity. The brass was unpolished and most of the delicate glass shades, curved in a semblance of flower petals, were missing or broken. In each of the deflowered clusters a single socket was now monstrously budded with one grubby and low-powered bulb whose faint and diffused light threw shadows across the floor and served only to accentuate the general gloom. Apart from the one small window at the end of the corridor there was little other natural light. The huge window over the well of the staircase, a pre-Raphaelite representation in lurid glass of the expulsion from Eden, was hardly functional.

He looked into the rooms adjacent to that of the dead girl. One was unoccupied, with the bed stripped, the wardrobe door ajar and the drawers, lined with fresh newspaper, all pulled out as if to demonstrate the room's essential emptiness. The other was in use but looked as if it had been hurriedly left; the bedclothes were carelessly thrown back and the bedside rug was rumpled. There was a little pile of textbooks on the bedside table and he opened the flyleaf of the first to hand and read the inscription, "Christine Dakers". So this was the room of the girl who had found the body. He inspected the wall between the two rooms. It was thin, a light partition of painted hardboard which trembled and let out a soft boom as he struck it. He wondered whether Nurse Dakers had heard anything in the night. Unless Josephine Fallon had died instantly and almost soundlessly some indication of her distress must surely have penetrated this insubstantial partition. He was anxious to interview Nurse Christine Dakers. At present she was in the nurses' sick bay suffering, so he was told, from shock. The shock was probably genuine enough, but even if it were not, there was nothing he could do about it. Nurse Dakers was for the moment effectively protected by her doctors from any questioning by the police.

He explored a little further. Opposite the row of nurses' bedrooms was a suite of bathroom cubicles and lavatories leading out of a large square cloakroom fitted with four wash-basins, each surrounded by a shower curtain. Each of the bath cubicles had a small sash window fitted with opaque glass, inconveniently placed but not difficult to open. They gave a view of the back of the house and of the two short wings, each built above a brick cloister, which were incongruously grafted on to the main building. It was as if the architect, having exhausted the possibilities of Gothic revival and baroque, had decided to introduce a more contemplative and ecclesiastical influence. The ground between the cloisters was an overgrown jungle of laurel bushes and untended trees which grew so close to the house that some of the branches seemed to scrape the downstairs windows. Dalgliesh could see dim figures searching among the bushes and could hear the faint mutter of voices. The discarded bottle of disinfectant which had killed Heather Pearce had been found among these bushes and it was possible that a second container, its contents equally lethal, might also have been hurled in the dark hours from the same window. There was a nail brush on the bath rack and, reaching for it, Dalgliesh hurled it in a wide arc through the window and into the bushes. He could neither see nor hear its fall but a cheerful face appeared among the parted leaves, a hand was waved in salute and the two searching constables moved back deeper into the undergrowth.

He next made his way along the passage to the nurses' utility room at the far end. Detective Sergeant Masterson was there with Sister Rolfe. Together they were surveying a motley collection of objects laid out before them on the working surface rather as if they were engaging in a private Kim's game. There were two squeezed lemons; a bowl of granulated sugar; an assortment of mugs containing cold tea, the surface of the liquid mottled and puckered; and a delicate Worcester teapot with matching cup and saucer and milk jug. There was also a crumpled square of thin white wrapping paper bearing the words "Scunthorpe's Wine Stores, 149, High Street, Heatheringfield" and a scribbled receipt smoothed out and held flat by a couple of tea canisters.

"She bought the whisky yesterday morning, sir," Masterson said. "Luckily for us, Mr. Scunthorpe is punctilious about receipts. That's the bill and that's the wrapping paper. So it looks as if she first opened the bottle when she went to bed yesterday."

Dalgliesh asked: "Where was it kept?"

It was Sister Rolfe who replied. "Fallon always kept her whisky in her bedroom."

Masterson laughed.

"Not surprising with the stuff costing nearly three quid a bottle."

Sister Rolfe looked at him with contempt.

"I doubt whether that would worry Fallon. She wasn't the type to mark the bottle."

"She was generous?" asked Dalgliesh.

"No, merely unconcerned. She kept her whisky in her room because Matron asked her to."

But brought it in here yesterday to prepare her late night drink, thought Dalgliesh. He stirred the sugar gently with his finger.

Sister Rolfe said: "That's innocent. The students tell me that they all used it when they made their morning tea. And the Burt twins, at least, drank some of theirs."

"But we'll send it and the lemon to the lab just the same," said Dalgliesh.

He lifted the lid from the little teapot and looked inside. Answering his unspoken question, Sister Rolfe said:

"Apparently Nurse Dakers made early tea in it. The pot is Fallon's of course. No one else has early tea in antique Worcester."

"Nurse Dakers made tea for Nurse Fallon before she knew that the girl was dead?"

"No, afterwards. It was a purely automatic reaction, I imagine. She must have been in shock. After all, she had just seen Fallon's body. She could hardly expect to cure rigor mortis with hot tea, even with the best China blend. I suppose you'll want to see Dakers, but you'll have to wait. She's in the sick bay at the moment. I think they told you. It's part of the private wing and Sister Brumfett is looking after her. That's why I'm here now. Like the police, we're a hierarchical profession and when Matron isn't in Nightingale House, Brumfett is next in the pecking order. Normally she would be dancing attendance on you, not I. You've been told, of course, that Miss Taylor is on her way back from a conference in Amsterdam. She had to deputise unexpectedly for the Chairman of the Area Nurse Training Committee, luckily for her. So at least there's one senior member of the staff with an alibi."

Dalgliesh had been told, and more than once. The absence of the Matron seemed to be a fact which everyone he had met, however briefly, had found it necessary to mention, explain or regret. But Sister Rolfe was the first to make a snide reference to the fact that it gave Miss Taylor an alibi, at least for the time of Fallon's death.

"And the rest of the students?"

"They're in the small lecture room on the floor below. Sister Gearing, our clinical instructor, is taking them for a private study period. I don't suppose they're doing much reading. It would have been better to set them something more active but it's not easy at a moment's notice. Will you see them there?"

"No, later. And in the demonstration room where Nurse Pearce died."

She glanced at him and then turned her eyes away quickly, but not so quickly that he missed the look of surprise and, he thought, disapproval. She had expected him to show more sensitivity, more consideration. The demonstration room had not been used since Nurse Pearce's death. To interview the students there so soon after this second tragedy would reinforce memory with fresh horror. If any of them were ready to be unnerved, this might do it and he had never considered using any other room. Sister Rolfe, he thought, was like all the rest of them. They wanted their murderers caught but only by the most gentlemanly means. They wanted them punished, but only if the punishment did not outrage their own sensibility.

Dalgliesh asked: "How is this place locked at night?"

"Sister Brumfett, Sister Gearing, and myself take responsibility for a week at a time. It's Gearing's turn this week. We're the only three Sisters who are resident here. We lock and bolt the front door and the kitchen door at eleven o'clock promptly. There's a small side door with a Yale lock and an inside bolt. If any student or member of the staff has a late pass she is issued with a key to that door and bolts it when she comes in. Sisters have a key in their possession permanently. There's only one other door and that leads from Matron's flat on the third floor. She has a private staircase and, of course, her own key. Apart from that, there are the fire escape doors but they are all kept locked on the inside. The place wouldn't be difficult to break into. I imagine that few institutions are. But we've never had a burglar so far as I know. Incidentally, there's a pane of glass out in the conservatory. Alderman Kealey, the Vice-Chairman, seems to think that Fallon's murderer got in that way. He's a great man for finding comfortable explanations for all life's embarrassing problems. It looks to me as if the pane blew in with the wind, but you'll no doubt form your own opinion."

She's talking too much, he thought. Loquacity was one of the commonest reactions to shock or nervousness and one which any interrogating officer made the most of. Tomorrow she would despise herself for it, and become that much more difficult, that much less co-operative. In the meantime she was telling him more than she realized.

The broken pane would, of course, have to be looked at, the woodwork examined for marks of entry. But he thought it unlikely that Nurse Fallon's death had been the work of any intruder. He asked: "How many people slept here last night?"

"Brumfett, Gearing and myself. Brumfett was out for part of the night. I understand she was recalled to the ward by Mr. Courtney-Briggs. Miss Collins was here. She's the housekeeper. And there were five student nurses: Nurse Dakers, the Burt twins, Nurse Goodale, and Nurse Pardoe. And Fallon slept here of course. That is, if Fallon had time to sleep! Incidentally, her bedside light was on all night. The Burt twins were up brewing cocoa shortly after two and nearly took a cup in to Fallon. If they'd done so you might have got a clearer idea of the time of death. But it occurred to them that she might have fallen asleep with the light on and wouldn't exactly welcome being woken, even to the sight and smell of cocoa. The twins' invariable solace is food and drink, but at least they've lived long enough to realize that not everyone shares their pre-occupation and that Fallon, in particular, might prefer sleep and privacy to cocoa and their company."

"I shall be seeing the Burt twins. What about the hospital grounds? Are they left open at night?"

"There's always a porter on duty at the front lodge. The main gates aren't locked because of the accident ambulances but he keeps an eye on anyone else who comes in or leaves. Nightingale House is much closer to the rear entrance to the grounds, but we don't usually go that way by foot because the path is ill-lit and rather frightening. Besides, it leads into the Winchester Road which is almost two miles from the main part of the town. The back gate is locked at dusk summer and winter by one of the porters but all the Sisters and Matron have keys."

"And the nurses with late passes?"

"They're expected to use the front gate and walk along the main path which skirts the hospital. There's a much shorter cut through the trees which we use in the daytime—it's only about two hundred yards—but not many people choose to come that way at night. I daresay Mr. Hudson, he's the Hospital Secretary, can let you have a plan of the grounds and of Nightingale House. Incidentally, he and the Vice-Chairman are waiting for you now in the library. The Chairman, Sir Marcus Cohen, is in Israel. Even so, it's quite a reception committee. Even Mr. Courtney-Briggs has deferred his out-patient session to welcome the Yard to Nightingale House."

"Then," said Dalgliesh, "perhaps you'll be good enough to let them know that I'll be with them shortly."

It was a dismissal. Sergeant Masterson, as if to soften it, said suddenly and loudly: "Sister Rolfe has been very helpful."

The woman gave a guttural snort of derision.

"Helping the police! Isn't there a sinister connotation about that phrase? Anyway, I don't think I can be particularly helpful. I didn't kill either of them. And last night I was at a film at the new arts cinema here. They're showing an Antonioni series. This week it's *L'Avventura.* I didn't get in until just before eleven and went straight to bed. I didn't even see Fallon."

Dalgliesh asked: "Did you go to the cinema alone?"

Sister Rolfe hesitated for a second and said curtly: "Yes."

Dalgliesh recognized with weary resignation the first lie and wondered how many more, important and unimportant, would be spoken before the investigation was complete. But this wasn't the time to interrogate Sister Rolfe. She wasn't going to be an easy witness. She had answered his questions fully but with undisguised resentment. He wasn't sure whether it was he or his job which she disliked, or whether any man would have provoked this tone of angry contempt. Her face matched her personality, rebarbative and defensive. It was strong and intelligent but without softness or feminity. The deep-set and very dark eyes might have been attractive but they were set under a pair of perfectly straight black eyebrows, so dark and bushy that they gave to the face a faint suggestion of deformity. Her nose was large and open pored, her lips a thin uncompromising line. It was the face of a woman who had never learnt to come to terms with life, and had, perhaps, given up trying. He thought suddenly that, if she proved to be a murderess and her photograph were at last published, other women, avidly searching that uncompromising mask for the marks of depravity, would profess themselves unsurprised. Suddenly he felt sorry for her with a mixture of irritation and compassion one might feel for the inadequate or the physically deformed. He turned quickly away so that she should not catch that sudden spasm of pity. To her it would, he knew, be the ultimate insult. And when he turned again to thank her formally for her help, he saw that she had gone.

III

Sergeant Charles Masterson was six feet three inches tall and broad shouldered. He carried his bulk easily and all his movements were surprisingly controlled and precise for such an assertively masculine and heavy man. He was generally considered handsome, particularly by himself, and with his strong face, sensual lips and hooded eyes looked remarkably like a well-known American film actor of the guts-and-guns school. Dalgliesh occasionally suspected that the sergeant, aware, as he could hardly fail to be, of the resemblance, was helping it along by assuming a trace of an American accent.

"All right, Sergeant. You've had a chance to look at the place, you've talked to some of the people. Tell me about it."

This invitation had been known to strike terror into the hearts of Dalgliesh's subordinates. It meant that the Superintendent now expected to hear a brief, succinct, accurate, elegantly phrased but comprehensive account of the crime which would give all the salient facts so far known to someone who came to it freshly. The ability to know what you want to say and to say it in the minimum of appropriate words is as uncommon in policemen as in other members of the community. Dalgliesh's subordinates were apt to complain that they hadn't realized that a degree in English was the new qualification for joining the C.I.D. But Sergeant Masterson was less intimidated than most. He had his weaknesses, but lack of confidence was not one of them. He was glad to be working on the case. It was well known at the Yard that Superintendent Dalgliesh couldn't tolerate a fool and that his definition of folly was individual and precise. Masterson respected him because Dalgliesh was one of the Yard's most successful detectives and for Masterson success was the only real criteria. He thought him very able, which is not to say that he thought Adam Dalgliesh as able as Charles Masterson. Most of the time, and for reasons which it seemed to him unprofitable to explore, he disliked him heartily. He suspected that the antipathy was mutual, but this didn't particularly worry him. Dalgliesh wasn't a man to prejudice a subordinate's career because he disliked him and was known to be meticulous, if judicious, in ascribing credit where it was due. But the situation would need watching, and Masterson intended to watch it. An ambitious man on his carefully planned climb to senior rank was a fool if he didn't early recognize that it was bloody daft to antagonize a senior officer. Masterson had no intention of being that kind of a fool. But a little co-operation from the Super in this campaign of mutual goodwill wouldn't be unwelcome. And he wasn't sure he was going to get it. He said:

"I'll deal with the two deaths separately, sir. The first victim. . . ."

"Why talk like a crime reporter, Sergeant? Let's be sure we have a victim before we use that word."

Masterton began: "The first deceased . . . the first girl to die was a twenty-one-year-old student nurse, Heather Pearce." He went on to recite the facts of both girls' deaths, as far as they were known, taking care to avoid the more blatant examples of police jargon, to which he knew his Super to be morbidly sensitive, and resisting the temptation to display his recently acquired knowledge of intragastric feeding about which he had taken trouble to extract from Sister Rolfe a comprehensive, if grudging, explanation. He ended: "So we have, sir, the possibilities that one or both of the deaths was suicide, that one or both was accidental, that the first was murder but that the wrong victim was killed, or that there were two murders with two intended victims. An intriguing choice, sir."

Dalgliesh said: "Or that Fallon's death was due to natural causes. Until we get the toxicology report we're theorizing in advance of the facts. But for the present we treat both deaths as murder. Well, let's go to the library and see what the Vice-Chairman of the Hospital Management Committee has to say to us."

IV

The library, easily identified by a large painted sign above the door, was a pleasant high-ceilinged room on the first floor, next to the student nurses' sitting-room. One wall was entirely taken up with three ornate oriel windows, but the other three were book-lined to the ceiling, leaving the centre of the room bare. It was furnished with four tables ranged in front of the windows and two shabby sofas, one on each side of the stone fireplace, where now an ancient gas fire hissed its sinister welcome. In front of it, under the two strips of fluorescent lighting, a group of four men, muttering together conspiratorially, turned in one movement at the entrance of Dalgliesh and Masterson and watched them with wary curiosity. It was a familiar moment to Dalgliesh, compounded as always of interest, apprehension and hope—this first confrontation of the protagonists in a murder case with the outsider, the alien expert in violent death who has come among them, an unwelcome guest, to demonstrate his invidious talents.

Then the silence broke, the rigid figures relaxed. The two men Dalgliesh had already met—Stephen Courtney-Briggs and Paul Hudson, the Hospital Secretary—moved forward with formal welcoming smiles. Mr. Courtney-Briggs, who apparently took charge of any situation dignified by his presence, made the introductions. The Group Secretary, Raymond Grout, shook hands damply. He had a gently lugubrious face, puckered now with distress like that of the child on the verge of crying. His hair lay in strands of silver silk over a high-domed forehead. He was probably younger than he appeared, thought Dalgliesh, but even so, he must be very near retirement.

Beside the tall, stooped figure of Grout, Alderman Kealey looked as perky as a terrier. He was a ginger-haired, foxy little man, bandy as a jockey and wearing a plaid suit, the awfulness of its pattern emphasized by the excellence of its cut. It gave him an anthropomorphic appearance, like an animal in a child's comic; and Dalgliesh almost expected to find himself shaking a paw.

"It was good of you to come, Superintendent, and so promptly," he said.

The folly of the remark apparently struck him as soon as he had made it, for he darted a keen glance from under spiky ginger eyebrows at his companions, as if defying them to smirk. No one did, but the Group Secretary looked as humiliated as if the solecism had been his, and Paul Hudson turned his face away to hide an embarrassed grin. He was a personable young man who, on Dalgliesh's first arrival at the hospital, had shown himself as both efficient and authoritative. Now, however, the presence of his Vice-Chairman and the Group Secretary seemed to have inhibited his speech and he had the apologetic air of a man present on sufferance. Mr. Courtney-Briggs said:

"It's too much to hope for any news yet, I suppose? We saw the mortuary van leaving, and I had a few words with Miles Honeyman. He couldn't commit himself at this stage, of course, but he'll be surprised if this was a natural death. The girl killed herself. Well, I should have thought that was obvious to anyone."

Dalgliesh said: "Nothing is obvious yet."

There was a silence. The Vice-Chairman seemed to find it embarrassing for he cleared his throat noisily and said:

"You'll want an office, of course. The local C.I.D. worked from the police station here. They were really very little trouble to us. We hardly knew they were in the place." He looked with faint optimism at Dalgliesh, as if hardly sanguine that the flying squad would be equally accommodating. Dalgliesh replied shortly:

"We shall want a room. Is it possible to make one available in Nightingale House? That would be the most convenient."

The request seemed to disconcert them. The Group Secretary said tentatively: "If Matron were here... it's difficult for us to know what's free. She shouldn't be long now."

Alderman Kealey grunted. "We can't let everything wait for Matron. The Superintendent wants a room. Find him one."

"Well there's Miss Rolfe's office on the ground floor, just next to the demonstration room." The Group Secretary bent his sad eyes on Dalgliesh. "You've met Miss Rolfe, our Principal Tutor, of course. Now if Miss Rolfe can move temporarily into her secretary's room . . . Miss Buckfield is off with flu, so it's free. It's rather cramped, only a cupboard really, but if Matron . . ."

"Get Miss Rolfe to move out any of her things she'll need. The porters can shift the filing cabinets." Alderman Kealey turned and barked at Dalgliesh: "Will that do?"

"If it's private, reasonably soundproof, has a lock on the door, is large enough to take three men and has a direct telephone to the exchange, it will do. If it also has running water, so much the better."

The Vice-Chairman, chastened by this formidable list of requirements, said tentatively: "There's a small cloakroom and lavatory on the ground floor opposite Miss Rolfe's room. That could be put at your disposal."

Mr. Grout's misery deepened. He glanced across at Mr. Courtney-Briggs as if seeking an ally but the surgeon had been unaccountably silent for the last few minutes and seemed reluctant to meet his eyes. Then the telephone rang. Mr. Hudson, apparently glad of a chance of activity, sprang to answer it. He turned to his Vice-Chairman.

"It's the *Clarion*, sir. They're asking for you personally."

Alderman Kealey grasped the receiver resolutely. Having decided to assert himself he was apparently ready to take command of any situation, and this one was well within his capabilities. Murder might be outside his normal preoccupations but dealing tactfully with the local Press was something he understood.

"Alderman Kealey here. The Vice-Chairman of the Management Committee. Yes, we've got the Yard here. The victim? Oh, I don't think we want to talk about a victim. Not yet anyway. Fallon. Josephine Fallon. Age?" He placed his hand over the mouthpiece and turned to the Group Secretary. Oddly enough, it was Mr. Courtney-Briggs who replied.

"She was thirty-one years, ten months," he said. "She was precisely twenty years younger than me to the day."

Alderman Kealey, unsurprised by the gratuitous information, returned to his listener.

"She was thirty-one. No, we don't know yet how she died. No one knows. We are awaiting the post mortem report. Yes, Chief Superintendent Dalgliesh. He's here now but he's too busy to talk. I hope to issue a Press statement this evening. We ought to have the autopsy report by then. No, there's no reason to suspect murder. The Chief Constable has called in the Yard as a precautionary measure. No, as far as we're aware, the two deaths aren't connected in any way. Very sad. Yes, very. If you care to telephone about six I may have some more information. All we know at present is that

Nurse Fallon was found dead in her bed this morning shortly after seven. It could very well have been a heart attack. She was just recovering from flu. No, there wasn't a note. Nothing like that."

He listened for a moment then again placed his hand over the mouthpiece and turned to Grout.

"They're asking about relatives. What do we know about them?"

"She hadn't any. Fallon was an orphan." Again it was Mr. Courtney-Briggs who replied.

Alderman Kealey passed on this information and replaced the receiver. Smiling grimly he gave Dalgliesh a look of mingled self-satisfaction and warning. Dalgliesh was interested to hear that the Yard had been called in as a precautionary measure. It was a new conception of the flying squad's responsibilities and one which he felt was unlikely to deceive the local Press boys, still less the London reporters who would soon be on the scent. He wondered how the hospital was going to cope with the publicity. Alderman Kealey was going to need some advice if the inquiry were not to be hampered. But there was plenty of time for that. Now all he wanted was to get rid of them, to get started with the investigation. These social preliminaries were always a time-consuming nuisance. And soon there would be a Matron to propitiate, to consult, possibly even to antagonize. From the Group Secretary's unwillingness to move a step without her consent, it looked as if she were a strong personality. He didn't relish the prospect of making it clear to her, tactfully, that there would be room for only one strong personality in this investigation.

Mr. Courtney-Briggs, who had been standing at the window, staring out at the storm-wrecked garden, turned, shook himself free of his preoccupations and said:

"I'm afraid I can't spare any more time now. I have a patient to see in the private wing and then a ward round. I was due to lecture to the students here later this morning but that'll have to be cancelled now. You'll let me know, Kealey, if there's anything I can do."

He ignored Dalgliesh. The impression given, and no doubt intended, was that he was a busy man who had already wasted too much time on a triviality. Dalgliesh resisted the temptation to delay him. Agreeable as it would be to tame Mr. Courtney-Briggs's arrogance, it was an indulgence which he couldn't afford at present. There were more pressing matters.

It was then that they heard the sound of a car. Mr. Courtney-Briggs returned to the window and looked out, but did not speak. The rest of the little group stiffened and turned as if pulled by a common force to face the door. A car door slammed. Then there was silence for a few seconds followed by the clip of hurried footsteps on a tessellated floor. The door opened and Matron came in.

Dalgliesh's first impression was of a highly individual yet casual elegance and a confidence that was almost palpable. He saw a tall slender woman, hatless, with pale honey-gold skin and hair of almost the same colour, drawn back from a high forehead and swathed into an intricate coil at the nape of her neck. She was wearing a grey tweed coat with a bright green scarf knotted at her neck and carrying a black handbag and a small travelling case. She came into the room quietly and, placing her case on the table, drew off her gloves and surveyed the little party silently. Almost instinctively, as if watching a witness, Dalgliesh noticed her hands. The fingers were very white, long and tapering but with unusually bony joints. The nails were clipped short. On the third finger of the right hand an immense sapphire ring in an ornate setting gleamed against the knuckle. He wondered irrelevantly whether she took it off when she was on duty and, if so, how she forced it over those nodular joints.

Mr. Courtney-Briggs, after a brief, "Good morning, Matron," made his way to the door and stood there like a bored guest, demonstrating his anxiety to make a quick get-away. But the others crowded around her. There was an immediate sense of relief. Muttered introductions were made.

"Good morning, Superintendent." Her voice was deep, a little husky, a voice as individual as herself. She seemed hardly aware of him, yet he was conscious of a swift appraisal from the green exophthalmic eyes. Her handshake was firm and cool, but so momentary that it seemed a fleeting meeting of palms, nothing more.

The Vice-Chairman said: "The police will want a room. We thought perhaps Miss Rolfe's office?"

"Too small, I think, and not private enough, so close to the main hall. It would be better if Mr. Dalgliesh had the use of the visitors' sitting-room on the first floor and the cloakroom next door to it. The room has a key. There's a desk with lockable drawers in the general office and that can be moved up. That way the police will get some privacy and there'll be a minimum of interference with the work of the school."

There was a murmur of assent. The men looked relieved. The Matron said to Dalgliesh: "Will you need a bedroom? Do you want to sleep in the hospital?"

"That won't be necessary. We shall be staying in the town. But I would prefer to work from here. We shall probably be here late every night so that it would be helpful if we could have keys."

"For how long?" asked the Vice-Chairman suddenly. It was on the face of it, a stupid question, but Dalgliesh noticed that all their faces turned to him as if it were one he could be expected to answer. He knew his reputation for speed. Did they perhaps know it too?

"About a week," he said. Even if the case dragged on for longer, he would learn all he needed from Nightingale House and its occupants within seven days. If Nurse Fallon had been murdered—and he believed she had—the circle of suspects would be small. If the case didn't break within a week it might never break. He thought there was a small sigh of relief.

Matron said: "Where is she?"

"They took the body to the mortuary, Matron."

"I didn't mean Fallon. Where is Nurse Dakers? I understood it was she who found the body."

Alderman Kealey replied. "She's being nursed in the private ward. She was pretty shaken up so we asked Dr. Snelling to take a look at her. He's given her a sedative and Sister Brumfett's looking after her."

He added: "Sister Brumfett was a little concerned about her. On top of that she's got rather a sick ward. Otherwise she would have met you at the airport. We all felt rather badly about your arriving with no one to meet you, but the best thing seemed to be to telephone a message for you, asking you to ring us here as soon as you landed. Sister Brumfett thought that the shock would be less if you learnt it in that way. On the other hand it seemed wrong not to have someone there. I wanted to send Grout but. . . ."

The husky voice broke in with its quiet reproof: "I should have thought that sparing me shock was the least of your worries." She turned to Dalgliesh:

"I shall be in my sitting-room here on the third floor in about forty-five minutes' time. If it's convenient for you, I should be glad to have a word with you then."

Dalgliesh, resisting the impulse to reply with a docile, "Yes, Matron," said that it would. Miss Taylor turned to Alderman Kealey.

"I'm going to see Nurse Dakers now. Afterwards the Superintendent will want to interview me and then I shall be in my main office in the hospital if you or Mr. Grout want me. I shall, of course, be available all day."

Without a further word or look she gathered up her travelling case and handbag and went out of the room. Mr. Courtney-Briggs perfunctorily opened the door for her, then prepared to follow. Standing in the open doorway, he said with jovial belligerence:

"Well, now that Matron's back and the important matter of accommodation for the police has been settled, perhaps the work of the hospital can be permitted to continue. I shouldn't be late for your interview if I were you, Dalgliesh. Miss Taylor isn't accustomed to insubordination."

He shut the door behind him. Alderman Kealey looked for a moment perplexed, then he said:

"He's upset, of course. Well, naturally. Wasn't there some kind of rumour. . . ."

Then his eyes lit on Dalgliesh. He checked himself suddenly, and turned to Paul Hudson:

"Well, Mr. Hudson, you heard what Matron said. The police are to use the visitors' sitting-room on this floor. Get on with it, my dear fellow. Get on with it!"

V

Miss Taylor changed into uniform before she went over to the private ward. At the time it seemed an instinctive thing to do, but, wrapping her cloak tightly around her as she walked briskly along the small footpath leading from Nightingale House to the hospital, she realized that the instinct had been prompted by reason. It was important to the hospital that Matron was back, and important that she should be seen to be back.

The quickest way to the private wing was through the outpatients' hall. The department was already buzzing with activity. The circles of comfortable chairs, carefully disposed to give an illusion of informality and relaxed comfort, were filling quickly. Volunteers from the ladies' committee of the League of Friends were already presiding at the steaming urn, serving tea to those regular patients who preferred to attend an hour before their appointments for the pleasure of sitting in the warmth, reading the magazines and chatting to their fellow habitués. As Matron passed she was aware of heads turning to watch her. There was a brief silence, followed by the customary murmur of deferential greeting. She was conscious of the white-coated junior medical staff standing briefly to one side as she passed, of the student nurses pressing themselves back against the wall.

The private ward was on the second floor of what still was called the new building, although it had been completed in 1945. Miss Taylor went up by the lift, sharing it with two radiographers and a young houseman. They murmured their formal, "Good morning, Matron," and stood in unnatural silence until the lift stopped, then stood back while she went out before them.

The private ward consisted of a suite of twenty single rooms, opening each side of a wide central corridor. The Sister's office, the kitchen, and the utility room were just inside the door. As Miss Taylor entered, a young first-year student nurse appeared from the kitchen. She flushed when she saw Matron and muttered something about fetching Sister.

"Where is Sister, Nurse?"

"In room 7 with Mr. Courtney-Briggs, Matron. His patient isn't too well."

"Don't disturb them: just tell Sister when she appears that I've come to see Nurse Dakers. Where is she?"

"In room 3, Matron." She hesitated.

"It's all right, Nurse, I'll find my own way. Get on with what you are doing."

Room 3 was at the far end of the corridor, one of six single rooms, usually reserved for sick nurses. Only when these rooms were all occupied were the staff nursed in the side rooms of the wards. It was not, Miss Taylor noted, the room in which Josephine Fallon had been nursed. Room 3 was the sunniest and most pleasant of the six rooms reserved for nurses. A week ago it had been occupied by a nurse with pneumonia, a complication of influenza. Miss Taylor, who visited every ward in the hospital once a day and who received daily reports on every sick nurse, thought it unlikely that Nurse Wilkins was fit enough yet to be discharged. Sister Brumfett must have moved her to make room 3 available for Nurse Dakers. Miss Taylor could guess why. The one window gave a view of the lawns and smoothly forked flower beds at the front of the hospital; from this side of the ward it was impossible to glimpse Nightingale House even through the bare tracery of the winter trees. Dear old Brumfett! So unprepossessingly rigid in her views, but so imaginative when it came to the welfare and comfort of her patients. Brumfett, who talked embarrassingly of duty, obedience, loyalty, but who knew exactly what she meant by those unpopular terms and lived by what she knew. She was one of the best ward sisters that the John Carpendar had, or ever would have. But Miss Taylor was glad that devotion to duty had kept Sister Brumfett from meeting the plane at Heathrow. It was bad enough to come home to this further tragedy without the added burden of Brumfett's doglike devotion and concern.

She drew the stool from under the bed and seated herself beside the girl. Despite Dr. Snelling's sedative, Nurse Dakers was not asleep. She was lying very still on her back gazing at the ceiling. Now her eyes turned to look at Matron. They were blank with misery. On the bedside locker there was a copy of a textbook, *Materia Medica for Nurses*. The Matron picked it up.

"This is very conscientious of you, Nurse, but just for the short time you are in here, why not have a novel from the Red Cross trolley or a frivolous magazine? Shall I bring one in for you?"

She was answered by a flood of tears. The slim figure twisted convulsively in the bed, buried her head in the pillow and clasped it with shaking hands. The bed shook with the paroxysm of grief. The Matron got up, moved over to the door and clicked across the board which covered the nurses' peephole. She returned quickly to her seat and waited without speaking, making no move except to place her hand on the girl's head. After a few minutes the dreadful shaking ceased and Nurse Dakers grew calmer. She began to mutter, her voice hiccuping with sobs, half muffled by the pillow:

"I'm so miserable, so ashamed."

The Matron bent her head to catch the words. A chill of horror swept over her. Surely she couldn't be listening to a confession of murder? She found herself praying under her breath.

"Dear God, please not. Not this child! Surely not this child?"

She waited, not daring to question. Nurse Dakers twisted herself round and gazed up at her, her eyes reddened and swollen like two amorphous moons in a face blotched and formless with misery.

"I'm wicked, Matron, wicked. I was glad when she died."

"Nurse Fallon?"

"Oh no, not Fallon! I was sorry about Fallon. Nurse Pearce."

The Matron placed her hands on each of the girl's shoulders, pressing her back against the bed. She held the trembling body firmly and looked down into the drowned eyes.

"I want you to tell me the truth, Nurse. Did you kill Nurse Pearce?"

"No, Matron."

"Or Nurse Fallon?"

"No, Matron."

"Or have anything at all to do with their deaths?"

"No, Matron."

Miss Taylor let out her breath. She relaxed her hold on the girl and sat back.

"I think you'd better tell me all about it."

So, calmly now, the pathetic story came out. It hadn't seemed like stealing at the time. It had seemed like a miracle. Mummy had so needed a warm winter coat and Nurse Dakers had been saving thirty shillings from her monthly salary cheque. Only the money had taken so long to save and the weather was getting colder; and Mummy, who never complained, and never asked her for anything, had to wait nearly fifteen minutes for the bus some mornings and caught cold so easily. And if she did catch cold she couldn't stay away from work because Miss Arkwright, the buyer in the department store, was only waiting for an opportunity to get her sacked. Serving in a store wasn't really the right job for Mummy, but it wasn't easy to find a job when you were over fifty and unqualified, and the young assistants in the department weren't very kind. They kept hinting that Mummy wasn't pulling her weight, which wasn't true. Mummy might not be as quick as they were but she really took trouble with the customers.

Then Nurse Harper had dropped the two crisp new £5 notes almost at her feet. Nurse Harper who had so much pocket money from her father that she could lose £10 without really worrying about it. It had happened about four weeks ago. Nurse Harper had been walking with Nurse Pearce from the Nurses' Home to the hospital dining-room for breakfast, and Nurse Dakers had been following a few feet behind. The two notes had fallen out of Nurse Harper's cape pocket and had lain there fluttering gently. Her first instinct had been to call after the other two students, but something about the sight of the money had stopped her. The notes had been so unexpected, so unbelievable, so beautiful in their pristine crispness. She had just stood looking at them for a second, and then she had realized that she was really looking at Mummy's new coat. And, by then, the other two students had passed almost out of sight, the notes were folded in her hand, and it was too late.

The Matron asked: "How did Nurse Pearce know that you had the notes?"

"She said that she'd seen me. She just happened to glance round when I was bending to pick up the notes. It meant nothing to her at the time, but when Nurse Harper told everyone that she'd lost the money and that the notes must have fallen out of her cape pocket on the way over to breakfast, Nurse Pearce guessed what had happened. She and the twins went with Nurse Harper to search the path to see if they could find the money. I expect that was when she remembered about my stooping down."

"When did she first talk to you about it?"

"A week later, Matron, a fortnight before our set came into block. I expect she couldn't bring herself to believe it before then. She must have been trying to make up her mind to speak to me."

So Nurse Pearce had waited. The Matron wondered why. It couldn't have taken her a whole week to clarify her suspicions. She must have recalled seeing Dakers stoop to pick up the notes as soon as she heard that they were missing. So why hadn't she tackled the girl at once? Had it perhaps been more satisfying to her twisted ego to wait until the money was spent and the culprit safely in her power?

"Was she blackmailing you?" she demanded.

"Oh no, Matron!" The girl was shocked.

"She only took back five shillings a week, and that wasn't blackmail. She sent the money every week to a society for discharged prisoners. She showed me the receipts."

"And did she, incidentally, explain why she wasn't re-paying it to Nurse Harper?"

"She thought it would be difficult to explain without involving me and I begged her not to do that. It would have been the end of everything, Matron. I want to take a district nurse training after I'm qualified so that I can look after Mummy. If I could get a country district we could have a cottage together and perhaps even a car. Mummy will be able to give up the store. I told Nurse Pearce about that. Besides, she said that Harper was so careless about money that it wouldn't hurt her to learn a lesson. She sent the payments to the society for discharged prisoners because it seemed appropriate. After all, I might have gone to prison if she hadn't shielded me."

The Matron said drily: "That, of course, is nonsense and you should have known it was nonsense. Nurse Pearce seems to have been a very stupid and arrogant young woman. Are you sure that she wasn't making any other demands on you? There is more than one kind of blackmail."

"But she wouldn't do that, Matron!" Nurse Dakers struggled to lift her head from the pillow. "Pearce was . . . well, she was good." She seemed to find the word inadequate and puckered her brow as if desperately anxious to explain.

"She used to talk to me quite a lot and she gave me a card with a passage out of the Bible which I had to read every day. Once a week she used to ask me about it."

The Matron was swept by a sense of moral outrage so acute that she had to find relief in action. She got up from the stool and walked over to the window, cooling her flaring face against the pane. She could feel her heart bumping and noticed with almost clinical interest that her hands were shaking. After a moment she came back again to the bedside.

"Don't talk about her being good. Dutiful, conscientious, and well-meaning if you like, but not good. If ever you meet real goodness you will know the difference. And I shouldn't worry about being glad that she is dead. In the circumstances you wouldn't be normal if you felt differently. In time you may be able to pity her and forgive her."

"But Matron, it's me who ought to be forgiven. I'm a thief." Was there a suggestion of masochism in the whine of the voice, the perverse self-denigration of the born victim? Miss Taylor said briskly:

"You're not a thief. You stole once; that's a very different thing. Every one of us has some incident in our lives that we're ashamed and sorry about. You've recently learned something about yourself, about what you're capable of doing, which has shaken your confidence. Now you have to live with that knowledge. We can only begin to understand and forgive other people when we have learned to understand and forgive ourselves. You won't steal again. I know that, and so do you. But you did once. You are capable of stealing. That knowledge will save you from being too pleased with yourself, from being too self-satisfied. It can make you a much more tolerant and understanding person and a better nurse. But not if you go on indulging in guilt and remorse and bitterness. Those insidious emotions may be very enjoyable but they aren't going to help you or anyone else."

The girl looked up at her.

"Will the police have to know?"

That, of course, was the question. And there could be only one answer.

"Yes. And you will have to tell them, just as you've told me. But I shall have a word first with the Superintendent. He's a new detective, from Scotland Yard this time, and I think he's an intelligent and understanding man."

Was he? How could she possibly tell? That first meeting had been so brief, merely a glance and a touching of hands. Was she merely comforting herself with a fleeting impression that here was a man with authority and imagination who might be able to solve the mystery of both deaths with a minimum of harm to the innocent and guilty alike. She had felt this instinctively. But was the feeling rational? She believed Nurse Dakers's story; but then she was disposed to believe it. How would it strike a police officer faced with a multiplicity of suspects but no other discernible motive? And the motive was there all right. It was Nurse Dakers's whole future, and that of her mother. And Dakers had behaved rather oddly. True she had been most distressed of all the students when Pearce had died, but she had pulled herself together remarkably quickly. Even under intense police questioning she had kept her secret safe. What then had precipitated this disintegration into confession and remorse? Was it only the shock of finding Fallon's body? And why should Fallon's death be so cataclysmic if she had had no hand in it?

Miss Taylor thought again about Pearce. How little one really knew about any of the students. Pearce, if one thought about her at all, had typified the dull, conscientious, unattractive student who was probably using nursing to compensate for the lack of more orthodox satisfactions. There was usually one such in every nurse training school. It was difficult to reject them when they applied for training since they offered more than adequate educational qualifications and impeccable references. And they didn't on the whole make bad nurses. It was just that they seldom made the best. But now she began to wonder. If Pearce had possessed such a secret craving for power that she could use this child's guilt and distress as fodder for her own ego, then she had been far from ordinary or ineffective. She had been a dangerous young woman.

And she had worked it all out very cleverly. By waiting a week until she could be reasonably certain that the money had been spent, she had left Dakers no option. The child could hardly claim then that she had yielded to a sudden impulse but intended to return the money. And even if Dakers had decided to confess, perhaps to the Matron, Nurse Harper would have had to be told: Pearce would have seen to that. And only Harper could decide whether or not to prosecute. It might have been possible to influence her, to persuade her to mercy. But suppose it had not been possible? Nurse Harper would almost certainly have confided in her father, and the Matron couldn't see Mr. Ronald Harper showing mercy to anyone who had helped herself to his money. Miss Taylor's acquaintance with him had been brief but revealing. He had arrived at the hospital two days after Pearce's death, a large, opulent-looking and aggressive man, top heavy in his fur-lined motoring coat. Without preliminaries or explanation he had launched into his prepared tirade, addressing Matron as if she were one of his garage hands. He wasn't going to let his girl stay another minute in a house with a murderer at large, police or no police. This nurse training had been a damn fool idea in the first place, and now it was going to stop. His Diane didn't need a career anyway. She was engaged, wasn't she? A bloody good match too! His partner's son. They could put the marriage forward instead of waiting until the summer and, in the meantime, Diane could stay at home and help in the office. He was taking her away with him now, and he'd like to see anyone try to stop him.

No one had stopped him. The girl had made no objection. She had stood meekly in the Matron's office overtly demure, but smiling a little as if gratified by all the fuss, by her father's assertive masculinity. The police could not prevent her leaving, nor had they seemed concerned to try. It was odd, thought the Matron, that no one had seriously suspected Harper; and if the two deaths were the work of one hand, their instinct had been right. She had last seen the girl stepping into her father's immense and ugly car, legs spindly beneath the new fur coat he had bought her to compensate for her disappointment at cutting short her training, and turning to wave good-bye to the rest of the set like a film star condescending to her assembled fans. No, not a particularly attractive family: Miss Taylor would be sorry for anyone who was in their power. And yet, such were the vagaries of personality, Diane Harper had been an efficient nurse, a better nurse in many ways than Pearce.

But there was one more question which had to be asked, and it took her a second to summon the courage to ask it.

"Did Nurse Fallon know about this business?"

The girl answered at once, confident, a little surprised.

"Oh no, Matron! At least I don't think so. Pearce swore that she wouldn't tell a soul, and it wasn't as if she was particularly friendly with Fallon. I'm sure she wouldn't have told Fallon."

"No," said the Matron. "I don't suppose she would."

Gently she lifted Nurse Dakers's head and smoothed the pillows.

"Now I want you to try and get some sleep. You'll feel a great deal better when you wake up. And try not to worry."

The girl's face relaxed. She smiled up at the Matron and, putting out her hand, briefly touched Miss Taylor's face. Then she snuggled down into the sheets as if resolute for sleep. So that was all right. But of course it was. It always worked. How easy and how insidiously satisfying was this doling out of advice and comfort, each portion individually flavoured to personal taste! She might be a Victorian vicar's wife presiding over a soup kitchen. To each according to her need. It happened in the hospital every day. A ward Sister's brightly professional voice. "Here's Matron to see you, Mrs. Cox. I'm afraid Mrs. Cox isn't feeling quite so well this morning, Matron." A tired pain-racked face smiling bravely up from the pillow, mouth avid for its morsel of affection and reassurance. The Sisters bringing their problems, the perpetual unsolvable problems over work and incompatible personalities.

"Are you feeling happier about it now, Sister?"

"Yes, thank you, Matron. Much happier."

The Group Secretary, desperately coping with his own inadequacies.

"I should feel better if we could have just a word about the problem, Matron." Of course he would! They all wanted to have just a word about the problem. They all went away feeling better. Hear what comfortable words our Matron saith. Her whole working life seemed a blasphemous liturgy of reassurance and absolution. And how much easier both to give and to accept was this bland milk of human kindness than the acid of truth. She could imagine the blank incomprehension, the resentment with which they would greet her private credo.

"I haven't anything to offer. There isn't any help. We are all alone, all of us from the moment of birth until we die. Our past is our present and our future. We have to live with ourselves until there isn't any more time left. If you want salvation look to yourself. There's nowhere else to look."

She sat for a few more minutes and then quietly left the room. Nurse Dakers gave a brief valedictory smile. As she entered the corridor she saw Sister Brumfett and Mr. Courtney-Briggs coming out of his patient's room. Sister Brumfett bustled up.

"I'm sorry, Matron. I didn't know you were on the ward."

She always used the formal title. They might spend the whole of their off-duty together driving or golfing; they might visit a London show once a month with the cosy, boring regularity of an old married couple; they might drink their early morning tea and late night hot milk together in indissoluble tedium. But in the hospital Brumfett always called her Matron. The shrewd eyes searched hers.

"You've seen the new detective, the man from the Yard?"

"Only briefly. I'm due for a session with him as soon as I get back."

Mr. Courtney-Briggs said: "I know him as a matter of fact; not well but we have met. You'll find him reasonable and intelligent. He's got quite a reputation of course. He's said to work very quickly. As far as I'm concerned, that's a considerable asset. The hospital can stand only so much disruption. He'll want to see me I suppose, but he'll have to wait. Let him know that I'll pop across to Nightingale House when I've finished my ward round, will you Matron?"

"I'll tell him if he asks me," replied Miss Taylor calmly. She turned to Sister Brumfett.

"Nurse Dakers is calmer now, but I think it would be better if she were not disturbed by visitors. She'll probably manage to get some sleep. I'll send over some magazines for her and some fresh flowers. When is Dr. Snelling due to see her?"

"He said he would come in before lunch, Matron."

"Perhaps you would ask him to be good enough to have a word with me. I shall be in the hospital all day."

Sister Brumfett said: "I suppose that Scotland Yard detective will want to see me too. I hope he isn't going to take too long about it. I've got a very sick ward."

The Matron hoped that Brum wasn't going to be too difficult. It would be unfortunate if she thought she could treat a Chief Superintendent of the Metropolitan Police as if he were a recalcitrant House Surgeon. Mr. Courtney-Briggs, no doubt, would be his usual arrogant self, but she had a feeling that Superintendent Dalgliesh would be able to cope with Mr. Courtney-Briggs.

They walked to the door of the ward together. Miss Taylor's mind was already busy with fresh problems. Something would have to be done about Nurse Dakers's mother. It would be some years before the child was fully qualified as a district nurse. In the meantime she must be relieved of the constant anxiety about her mother. It might be helpful to have a word with Raymond Grout. There might be a clerical job somewhere in the hospital which would suit her. But would that be fair? One couldn't indulge one's own urge to help at someone else's expense. Whatever problems of staff recruitment the hospital service might have in London, Grout had no difficulty in filling his clerical jobs. He had a right to expect efficiency; and the Mrs. Dakers of this world, dogged by their own inadequacy as much as by ill-luck, could seldom offer that. She supposed she would have to telephone the woman; the parents of the other students too. The important thing was to get the girls out of Nightingale House. The training schedule couldn't be disrupted; it was tight enough as it was. She had better arrange with the House Warden for them to sleep in the Nurses' Home—there would be room enough with so many nurses in the sick bay—and they could come over each day to use the library and lecture room. And then there would be the Vice-Chairman of the Hospital Management

Committee to consult and the Press to cope with, the inquest to attend and the funeral arrangements to be discussed. People would be wanting to get in touch with her continually. But first, and most important, she must see Superintendent Dalgliesh.

Chapter Four

Questions and Answers

I

The Matron and the Sisters had their living-quarters on the third floor of Nightingale House. When he reached the top of the staircase Dalgliesh saw that the south-west wing had been cut off from the rest of the landing by a specially constructed partition in white-painted wood in which a door, meanly proportioned and insubstantial in contrast to the high ceiling and oak-lined walls, bore the legend 'Matron's Flat'. There was a push bell, but before pressing it he briefly explored the corridor. It was similar to the one below but fitted with a red carpet which, although faded and scuffed, gave an illusion of comfort to the emptiness of this upper floor.

Dalgliesh moved silently from door to door. Each bore a hand-written name card slotted into the brass holder. He saw that Sister Brumfett occupied the room immediately adjacent to Matron's flat. Next was a bathroom, functionally divided into three mean cubicles, each with its bath and lavatory. The slot on the next door bore Sister Gearing's name; the next two rooms were empty. Sister Rolfe was at the north end of the corridor immediately next to the kitchen and utility room. Dalgliesh had no authority to enter any of the bedrooms but he tentatively turned the handles on each of the doors. As he expected, they were locked.

The Matron herself opened the door of her flat to him within seconds of his ring, and he followed her into the sitting-room. Its size and magnificence caught the breath. It occupied the whole of the south-west turret, an immense white-painted octagonal room, the ceiling starred in patterns of gold and pale blue, and with two huge windows facing out towards the hospital. One of the walls was lined from ceiling to floor with white bookcases. Dalgliesh resisted the impertinence of walking casually towards them in the hope of assessing Mary Taylor's character by her taste in literature. But he could see from where he stood that there were no textbooks, no bound official reports or sloping banks of files. This was a living-room, not an office.

An open fire burnt in the grate, the wood still crackling with its recent kindling. It had as yet made no impression on the air of the room which was cold and very still. Matron was wearing a short scarlet cape over her grey dress. She had taken off her head-dress and the huge coil of yellow hair lay like a burden on the frail, etiolated neck.

She was fortunate, he thought, to have been born in an age which could appreciate individuality of feature and form, owing everything to bone structure and nothing to the gentle nuances of femininity. A century ago she would have been called ugly, even grotesque. But today most men would think her interesting, and some might even describe her as beautiful. For Dalgliesh she was one of the most beautiful women he had ever met.

Placed precisely in the middle of the three windows was a sturdy oak table bearing a large black-and-white telescope. Dalgliesh saw that this was no amateur's toy but an expensive and sophisticated instrument. It dominated the room. The Matron saw his eyes upon it and said:

"Are you interested in astronomy?"

"Not particularly."

She smiled. "'Le silence éternel de ces espaces infinis m'affraie'?"

"Discomforts rather than terrifies. It's probably my vanity. I can't interest myself in anything which I not only don't understand but know that I have no prospect of ever understanding."

"That for me is the attraction. It's a form of escapism, even of voyeurism, I suppose—this absorption in an impersonal universe which I can't do anything to influence or control and, better still, which no one expects me to. It's an abdication of responsibility. It restores personal problems to their proper proportion."

She motioned Dalgliesh towards the black leather sofa in front of the fire. Before it, a low table held a tray with a coffee percolator, hot milk, crystal sugar and two cups.

As he seated himself, he smiled and said: "If I want to indulge in humility or speculate on the incomprehensible, I prefer to look at a primrose. The expense is nugatory, the pleasure is more immediate, and the moral just as valid."

The mobile mouth mocked him.

"And at least you restrict your indulgence in these dangerous philosophical speculations to a few short weeks in the spring."

This conversation is, he thought, a verbal pavane. If I'm not careful I shall begin to enjoy it. I wonder when she will get down to business. Or is she expecting me to make the first move? And why not? It is I who am the suppliant, the intruder.

As if reading his thoughts, she said suddenly:

"It's odd that they should both have been such friendless girls, both orphans. It makes my task less onerous. There aren't any desolated parents to be comforted, thank God. Nurse Pearce only had the grandparents who brought her up. He's a retired miner and they live in some poverty in a cottage just outside Nottingham. They belong to a very puritanical religious sect and their only reaction to the child's death was to say, 'God's Will be Done.' It seemed an odd response to a tragedy which was so obviously the will of man."

"So you think Nurse Pearce's death was murder then?"

"Not necessarily. But I don't accuse God of tampering with the intra-gastric drip."

"And Nurse Fallon's relatives?"

"None, as far as I know. She was asked for her next of kin when she first became a student and told us she was an orphan with no blood relations living. There was no reason to question it. It was probably true. But her death will be in the papers tomorrow and if there are any relatives or friends no doubt we shall be hearing from them. You've spoken to the students, I expect?"

"I've just had a preliminary talk with them as a group. I saw them in the demonstration room. It's been useful in giving me a background to the case. They've all agreed to be finger-printed and that's being done now. I shall need the prints of everyone who was in Nightingale House last night and this morning, if only for elimination purposes. And I shall, of course, need to interview everyone separately. But I'm glad of this chance to see you first. After all, you were in Amsterdam when Nurse Fallon died. That means there's one less suspect for me to worry about."

He saw with surprise her knuckles whiten around the handle of the coffee pot. Her face flushed. She closed her eyes and he thought he heard her sigh. He watched her a little disconcerted. What he had said must surely be obvious to a woman of her intelligence. He hardly knew why he had bothered to say it. If this second death were murder, then anyone with an alibi covering the whole of yesterday evening and night must be free of suspicion. As if sensing his surprise, she said:

"I'm sorry. I must seem obtuse. I know it's foolish to feel such relief at not being under suspicion when one knows anyway that one is innocent. Perhaps it's because none of us is innocent in any real sense. A psychologist could explain it, I'm sure. But ought you to be so confident? Couldn't the poison—if it were poison—have been put into Fallon's whisky bottle any time after she bought it, or another and poisoned bottle substituted for the one she purchased? That could have been done before I left for Amsterdam on Tuesday evening."

"I'm afraid you must resign yourself to innocence. Miss Fallon bought this particular bottle of whisky from Scunthorpe's wine shop in the High Street yesterday afternoon, and took her first and only drink from it on the night she died. The bottle is still almost full, the whisky remaining is perfectly good whisky as far as we know, and the only prints on the bottle are Miss Fallon's own."

"You've worked very fast. So the poison was put either into the glass after she'd poured her hot drink or into the sugar?"

"If she were poisoned. We can't be sure of anything till we get the P.M. report and perhaps not even then. The sugar is being tested but that is really only a formality. Most of the students helped themselves from that bowl when they had their early morning tea and at least two of the girls drank theirs. So that leaves us with the beaker of whisky and hot lemon. Miss Fallon made it very easy for a murderer. Apparently the whole of Nightingale House knew that, if she didn't go out in the evening, she watched the television until the programme closed down. She was a poor sleeper and never went to bed early. When the television ended she would go to her room and undress. Then in her bedroom slippers and dressing-gown she would go to the little pantry on the second floor and make her nightcap. She kept the whisky in her room but she couldn't make the drink there because there's no water laid on and no means of heating it. So it was her habit to take the insulated tumbler with the whisky poured out ready and add the hot lemon in the pantry. A supply of lemons was kept there in the cupboard with the cocoa, coffee, chocolate and other items with which the nurses used to make their late night drinks. Then she would take the tumbler back to her room and leave it on the bedside locker while she had her bath. She always bathed quickly and she liked to get into bed immediately afterwards while she was still warm. I expect that's why she made her drink before she went into the bathroom. By the time she got back to her room and into bed, the drink was at precisely the right temperature. And apparently the routine never varied."

The Matron said: "It's rather frightening how much people get to know about each other's habits in a small closed community like this. But, of course, it's inevitable. There's no real privacy. How can there be? I knew about the whisky, of course, but it hardly seemed my business. The girl certainly wasn't an incipient alcoholic and she wasn't handing it out to the younger students. At her age she was entitled to her own choice of nightcap."

Dalgliesh asked how the Matron had learned about the whisky.

"Nurse Pearce told me. She asked to see me and gave me the information in a spirit of 'I don't want to tell tales but I think you ought to know'. Drink and the devil were one and the same to Nurse Pearce. But I don't think Fallon made any secret of the whisky drinking. How could she? As I said, we know about each other's little habits. But there are some things, of course, that we don't know. Josephine Fallon was a very private person. I can't give you any information about her life outside the hospital and I doubt whether anyone here can."

"Who was her friend here? She must have had someone she confided in, surely? Isn't that necessary for any woman in this kind of closed community?"

She looked at him a little strangely.

"Yes. We all need someone. But I think Fallon needed a friend less than most. She was remarkably self-sufficient. If she confided in anyone it would be Madeleine Goodale."

"The plain one with the round face and large spectacles?"

Dalgliesh recalled her. It was not an unattractive face, mainly because of the good skin and the intelligence of those large grey eyes behind the thick horn rims. But Nurse Goodale could never be other than plain. He thought he could picture her future; the years of training willingly endured, the success in examinations; the gradually increasing responsibility until, at last, she too was a Matron. It was not unusual for such a girl to be friendly with a more attractive woman. It was one way of gaining at least a vicarious share in a more romantic, less dedicated life. As if reading his thoughts, Miss Taylor said:

"Nurse Goodale is one of our most efficient nurses. I was hoping that she would stay on after her training to take a post as staff nurse. But that is hardly likely. She's engaged to our local vicar and they want to marry next Easter."

She glanced across at Dalgliesh a little maliciously.

"He is considered a most eligible young man. You seem surprised, Superintendent."

Dalgliesh laughed: "After over twenty years as a policeman I should have learnt not to make superficial judgements. I think I had better see Nurse Goodale first. I understand the room you're making available isn't ready yet. I suppose we could go on using the demonstration room. Or are you likely to be needing it?"

"I would prefer you to see the girls somewhere else if you would. That room has very unhappy and dramatic memories for them. We're not even using it yet for teaching demonstrations. Until the small visitors' room on the first floor is ready I'd be happy for you to interview the students here."

Dalgliesh thanked her. He replaced his coffee cup on the table. She hesitated, then said:

"Mr. Dalgliesh, there's one thing I want to say. I feel—I am—*in loco parentis* to my students. If ever any question . . . if you should begin to suspect that any one of them is involved, I can rely on you to let me know? They would then need protection. There would surely be the question of getting a solicitor." She hesitated again:

"Please forgive me if I'm being offensive. One has so little experience in these matters. It's just that I shouldn't like them . . ."

"To be trapped?"

"To be rushed into saying things which might quite wrongly incriminate them or other members of the staff."

Dalgliesh found himself unreasonably irritated.

"There are rules laid down, you know," he said.

"Oh, rules! I know there are rules. But I'm sure you are both too experienced and too intelligent to let them hinder you over much. I'm just reminding you that these girls are less intelligent and in such matters not experienced at all."

Fighting his irritation, Dalgliesh said formally:

"I can only tell you that the rules are there and that it's in our interests to keep them. Can't you imagine what a gift to the defending counsel any infringement would be? A young unprotected girl, a student nurse, bullied by a senior police officer with years of experience in trapping the unwary. Enough difficulties are placed in the path of the police in this country; we don't voluntarily add to them."

She flushed and he was interested to see the wave of colour sweep from her neck over the pale honey glowing skin making her look momentarily as if the veins ran with fire. Then, instantaneously, it passed. The change was so sudden that he couldn't be sure that he had actually seen that tell-tale metamorphosis. She said composedly:

"We both have our responsibilities. We must hope that they don't conflict. In the meantime you must expect me to be as concerned with mine as you are with yours. And that brings me to some information which I have to give you. It concerns Christine Dakers, the student who discovered Nurse Fallon's body."

She described briefly and succinctly what had happened during her visit to the private ward. Dalgliesh noted with interest that she made no comment, offered no opinion, and attempted no justification of the girl. He didn't ask her whether she believed the story. She was a highly intelligent woman. She must know that what she had handed him was the first motive. He asked when he would be able to interview Nurse Dakers.

"She's sleeping now. Dr. Snelling, who is in charge of the nurses' health, is to see her later this morning. He will then report to me. If he agrees, it should be possible for you to see her this afternoon. And now I'll send for Nurse Goodale. That is, if there is nothing more I can tell you?"

"I shall need a great deal of information about people's ages, backgrounds and the time they've been at the hospital. Won't that be on their personal records? It would be helpful if I could have those."

The Matron thought. Dalgliesh noticed that when she did so her face fell into absolute repose. After a moment she said:

"All the staff here have personal dossiers, of course. Legally these are the property of the Hospital Management Committee. The Chairman won't be back from Israel until tomorrow evening but I'll consult the Vice-Chairman. I imagine that he will ask me to look through the records, and if they contain nothing private which is irrelevant to your inquiry, to pass them over."

Dalgliesh decided that it would be prudent not to press for the moment the question of who should decide what was irrelevant to his inquiry.

He said: "There are personal questions I shall have to ask, of course. But it would be a great deal more convenient and would save time if I could get the routine information from the records."

It was strange that her voice could be so agreeable and yet so obstinate.

"I can see that it would be a great deal more convenient; it would also be a check on the truth of what you are told. But the records can only be handed over under the conditions I have just stated."

So she was confident that the Vice-Chairman would accept and endorse her view of what was right. And undoubtedly he would. Here was a formidable woman. Faced with a tricky problem she had given the matter thought, come to a decision and had stated it firmly without apology or wavering. An admirable woman. She would be easy to deal with as long, of course, as all her decisions were as acceptable as this.

He asked if he might use the telephone; recalled Sergeant Masterson from his supervision of the preparation of the small visitors' room to serve as an office; and prepared himself for the long tedium of the individual interviews.

II

Nurse Goodale was summoned by telephone and arrived within two minutes looking unhurried and composed. Miss Taylor seemed to think that neither explanation nor reassurance was necessary to this self-possessed young woman but simply said:

"Sit down, Nurse. Superintendent Dalgliesh wants to talk to you."

Then she took up her cloak from the chair, swung it over her shoulders, and went out without another glance at either of them. Sergeant Masterson opened his notebook. Nurse Goodale seated herself in an upright chair at the table but when Dalgliesh motioned her to an armchair before the fire, moved without demur. She sat stiffly on the very edge of the chair, her back straight, her surprisingly shapely and elegant legs planted modestly side by side. But the hands lying in her lap were perfectly relaxed and Dalgliesh, seated opposite, found himself confronting a pair of disconcertingly intelligent eyes. He said:

"You were probably closer to Miss Fallon than anyone else in the hospital. Tell me about her."

She showed no surprise at the form of his first question, but paused for a few seconds before replying as if marshalling her thoughts. Then she said:

"I liked her. She tolerated me better than she did most of the other students but I don't think her feeling for me was much stronger than that. She was thirty-one after all, and we must all have seemed rather immature to her. She had a rather sarcastic tongue which didn't help, and I think some of the girls were rather afraid of her.

"She seldom spoke to me about her past but she did tell me that both her parents were killed in 1944 in a bombing raid on London. She was brought up by an elderly aunt and educated at one of those boarding-schools where they take children from an early age and keep them until they're ready to leave. Provided the fees are paid of course, but I got the impression that there wasn't any difficulty about that. She always wanted to be a nurse but she got tuberculosis after she left school and had to spend two years in a sanatorium. I don't know where. After that, two hospitals turned her down on grounds of health, so she took a number of temporary jobs. She told me soon after we began our training that she had once been engaged but that it didn't work out."

"You never asked her why?"

"I never asked her anything. If she had wanted to tell me she would have done so."

"Did she tell you that she was pregnant?"

"Yes. She told me two days before she went sick. She must have suspected before then but the confirming report came that morning. I asked her what she intended doing about it and she said that she would get rid of the baby."

"Did you point out that this was probably illegal?"

"No. She didn't care about legality. I told her that it was wrong."

"But she still intended to go ahead with the abortion?"

"Yes, she said that she knew a doctor who would do it and that there wouldn't be any real risk. I asked her if she needed money and she said that she would be all right, that money was the least of her problems. She never told me who she was going to, and I didn't ask."

"But you were prepared to help her with money had she needed it, even though you disapproved of getting rid of the baby?"

"My disapproval wasn't important. What was important was that it was wrong. But when I knew that she had made up her mind I had to decide whether to help her. I was afraid that she might go to some unqualified back street abortionist and risk her life and health. I know that the law has changed, that it's easier now to get a medical recommendation, but I didn't think she would qualify. I had to make a moral decision. If you are proposing to commit a sin it is as well to commit it with intelligence. Otherwise you are insulting God as well as defying Him, don't you think?"

Dalgliesh said gravely: "It's an interesting theological point which I'm not competent to argue. Did she tell you who was the father of the child?"

"Not directly. I think it may have been a young writer she was friendly with. I don't know his name or where you can find him but I do know that Jo spent a week with him in the Isle of Wight last October. She had seven days' holiday due and she told me that she'd decided to walk in the island with a friend. I imagine he was the friend. It certainly wasn't anyone from here. They went during the first week and she told me that they'd stayed in a small inn about five miles south of Ventnor. That's all she did tell me. I suppose it's possible that she became pregnant during that week?"

Dalgliesh said: "The dates would fit. And she never confided in you about the father of the child?"

"No. I asked her why she wouldn't marry the father and she said that it would be unfair to the child to burden it with two irresponsible parents. I remember her saying: 'He would be horrified at the idea, anyway, unless he had a sudden urge to experience fatherhood just to see what it was like. And he might like to see the baby born so that he could write a lurid account of childbirth some day. But he really isn't committed to anyone but himself.' "

"But did she care for him?"

The girl paused a full minute before replying. Then she said:

"I think she did. I think that may have been why she killed herself."

"What makes you think that she did?"

"I suppose because the alternative is even more unlikely. I never thought that Jo was the type to kill herself—if there is a type. But I really didn't know her. One never does really know another human being. Anything is possible for anyone. I've always believed that. And it's surely more likely that she killed herself than that someone murdered her. That seems absolutely incredible. Why should they?"

"I was hoping you might be able to tell me."

"Well, I can't. She hadn't any enemies at the John Carpendar as far as I know. She wasn't popular. She was too reserved, too solitary. But people didn't dislike her. And even if they did, murder surely suggests something more than ordinary dislike. It seems so much more probable that she came back to duty too soon after influenza, was overcome by psychological depression, felt she couldn't cope with getting rid of the baby, and yet couldn't face up to having an illegitimate child and killed herself on impulse."

"You said when I questioned you all in the demonstration room that you were probably the last person to see her alive. What exactly happened while you were together last night? Did she give you any idea that she might be thinking of suicide?"

"If she had, I should hardly have left her to go to bed alone. She said nothing. I don't think we exchanged more than half a dozen words. I asked her how she felt and she replied that she was all right. She obviously wasn't in the mood to chat so I didn't make myself a nuisance. After about twenty minutes I went up to bed. I never saw her again."

"And she didn't mention her pregnancy?"

"She mentioned nothing. She looked tired, I thought, and rather pale. But then, Jo always was rather pale. It's distressing for me to think that she might have needed help and that I left her without speaking the words that might have saved her. But she wasn't a woman to invite confidences. I stayed behind when the others left because I thought she might want to talk. When it was plain that she wanted to be alone, I left."

She talked about being distressed, thought Dalgliesh, but she neither looked nor sounded it. She felt no self-reproach. Why indeed should she? He doubted whether she felt particular grief. She had been closer to Josephine Fallon than any of the students. But she had not really cared. Was there anyone in the world who had? He asked:

"And Nurse Pearce's death?"

"I think that was essentially an accident. Someone put the poison in the feed as a joke or out of vague malice without realizing that the result would be fatal."

"Which would be odd in a third-year student nurse whose programme of lectures presumably included basic information on corrosive poisons."

"I wasn't suggesting that it was a nurse. I don't know who it was.

I don't think you'll ever find out now. But I can't believe that it was wilful murder."

That was all very well, thought Dalgliesh, but surely it was a little disingenuous in a girl as intelligent as Nurse Goodale. It was, of course, the popular, almost the official view. It exonerated everyone from the worst crime and indicted no one of anything more than malice and carelessness. It was a comforting theory, and unless he were lucky it might never be disproved. But he didn't believe it himself, and he couldn't accept that Nurse Goodale did. But it was even harder to accept that here was a girl to comfort herself with false theories or deliberately to shut her eyes to unpalatable facts.

Dalgliesh then asked her about her movements on the morning of Pearce's death. He already knew them from Inspector Bailey's notes and her previous statement and was not surprised when Nurse Goodale confirmed them without hesitation. She had got up at 6.45 and had drunk early morning tea with the rest of the set in the utility room. She had told them about Fallon's influenza since it was to her room that Nurse Fallon had come when she was taken ill in the night. None of the students had expressed particular concern but they had wondered how the demonstration would go now that the set was so decimated and had speculated, not without malice, how Sister Gearing would acquit herself in the face of a G.N.C. inspection. Nurse Pearce had drunk her tea with the rest of the set and Nurse Goodale thought that she remembered Pearce saying:

"With Fallon ill, I suppose I shall have to act the patient." Nurse Goodale couldn't recall any comment or discussion about this. It was well accepted that the next student on the list substituted for anyone who was ill.

After she had drunk her tea, Nurse Goodale had dressed and had then made her way to the library to revise the treatment of laryngectomy in preparation for the morning's session. It was important that there should be a quick and lively response to questions if the seminar were to be a success. She had settled herself to work at about 7.15 and Nurse Dakers had joined her shortly afterwards, sharing a devotion to study which, thought Dalgliesh, had at least been rewarded by an alibi for most of the time before breakfast.

She and Dakers had said nothing of interest to each other while they had been working and had left the library at the same time and gone into breakfast together. That had been at about ten minutes to eight. She had sat with Dakers and the Burt twins, but had left the breakfast room before them. That was at 8.15. She had returned to her bedroom to make the bed, and then gone to the library to write a couple of letters. That done, she had paid a brief visit to the cloakroom and had made her way to the demonstration room just before a quarter to nine. Only Sister Gearing and the Burt twins were already there, but the rest of the set had joined them shortly afterwards; she couldn't remember in what order. She thought that Pearce had been one of the last to arrive.

Dalgliesh asked: "How did Nurse Pearce seem?"

"I noticed nothing unusual about her, but then I wouldn't expect to. Pearce was Pearce. She made a negligible impression."

"Did she say anything before the demonstration began?"

"Yes, she did as a matter of fact. It's odd that you should ask that. I haven't mentioned it before, I suppose because Inspector Bailey didn't ask. But she did speak. She looked round at us—the set had all assembled by then—and asked if anyone had taken anything from her bedroom."

"Did she say what?"

"No. She just stood there with that accusing rather belligerent look she occasionally had and said: 'Has anyone been to my room this morning or taken anything from it?' "

"No one replied. I think we just all shook our heads. It wasn't a question we took particularly seriously. Pearce was apt to make a great fuss about trifles. Anyway, the Burt twins were busy with their preparations and the rest of us were chatting. Pearce didn't get a great deal of attention paid to her question. I doubt whether half of us heard her even."

"Did you notice how she reacted? Was she worried or angry or distressed?"

"None of those things. It was odd really. I remember now. She looked satisfied, almost triumphant, as if something she suspected had been confirmed. I don't know why I noticed that, but I did. Sister Gearing then called us to order and the demonstration began."

Dalgliesh did not immediately speak at the end of this recital and, after a little time, she took his silence for dismissal and rose to go. She got out of the chair with the same controlled grace as she had seated herself, smoothed her apron with a scarcely discernible gesture, gave him a last interrogatory glance and walked to the door. Then she turned as if yielding to an impulse.

"You asked me if anyone had a reason to kill Jo. I said I knew of no one. That is true. But I suppose a legal motive is something different. I ought to tell you that some people might think I had a motive."

Dalgliesh said: "Had you?"

"I expect you'll think so. I am Jo's heir, at least I think I am. She told me about three months ago that she had made her will and that she was leaving me all she had. She gave me the name and address of her solicitor. I can let you have the information. They haven't yet written to me but I expect they will, that is if Jo really made her will. But I expect she did. She wasn't a girl to make promises she didn't fulfil. Perhaps you would prefer to get in touch with the solicitors now? These things take time, don't they?"

"Did she say why she was making you her legatee?"

"She said that she had to leave her money to someone and that I would probably do most good with it. I didn't take the matter very seriously and neither, I think, did she. After all she was only thirty-one. She wasn't expecting to die. And she warned me that she'd probably change her mind long before she got old enough to make the legacy a serious prospect for me. After all she'd probably marry. But she felt she ought to make a will and I was the only person at the time who she cared to remember. I thought that it was only a formality. It never occurred to me that she might have much to leave. It was only when we had our talk about the cost of an abortion that she told me how much she was worth."

"And was it—is it—much?"

The girl answered calmly: "About £16,000 I believe. It came from her parents' insurances."

She smiled a little wryly.

"Quite worth having you see, Superintendent. I should think it would rank as a perfectly respectable motive, wouldn't you? We shall be able to put central heating in the vicarage now. And if you saw my fiancé's vicarage—twelve rooms, nearly all of them facing north or east—you would think I had quite a motive for murder."

III

Sister Rolfe and Sister Gearing were waiting with the students in the library; they had moved from the nurses' sitting-room in order to occupy the waiting time with reading and revision. How much the girls were really taking in was problematic but the scene certainly looked peaceful and studious enough. The students had seated themselves at the desks in front of the window and sat, books open before them, in apparent absorption. Sister Rolfe and Sister Gearing, as if to emphasize their seniority and solidarity, had withdrawn to the sofa in front of the fire and were seated side by side. Sister Rolfe was marking with green biro a pile of first-year students' exercises, picking up each notebook from a stack on the floor at her feet, and adding it, when dealt with, to the growing pile which rested against the back of the sofa. Sister Gearing was ostensibly making notes for her next lecture, but seemed unable to keep her eyes from her colleague's decisive hieroglyphics.

The door opened and Madeleine Goodale returned. Without a word she went back to her desk, took up her pen and resumed work.

Sister Gearing whispered: "Goodale seems calm enough. Odd, considering she was supposed to be Fallon's best friend."

Sister Rolfe did not raise her eyes. She said drily:

"She didn't really care about Fallon. Goodale has only a limited emotional capital and I imagine she expends it all on that extraordinarily dull parson she's decided to marry."

"He's good-looking, though. Goodale's lucky to get him, if you ask me."

But the subject was of a secondary interest to Sister Gearing and she didn't pursue it. After a minute she said peevishly:

"Why haven't the police sent for someone else?"

"They will." Sister Rolfe added another exercise book, liberally embellished in green, to a completed pile by her side. "They're probably still discussing Goodale's contribution."

"They ought to have seen us first. After all, we're Sisters. Matron should have explained. And why isn't Brumfett here? I don't see why she should be treated any differently from us."

Sister Rolfe said: "Too busy. Apparently a couple of the second-year students on the ward have now gone down with flu. She sent over some sort of note to Mr. Dalgliesh by a porter, presumably giving information about her movements last night. I met him bringing it in. He asked me where he could find the gentlemen from Scotland Yard."

Sister Gearing's voice became petulant:

"That's all very well, but she ought to be here. God knows, we're busy too! Brumfett lives in Nightingale House; she had as much opportunity to kill Fallon as anyone."

Sister Rolfe said quietly: "She had more chance."

"What do you mean, more chance?"

Sister Gearing's sharp voice cut into the silence and one of the Burt twins lifted her head.

"She's had Fallon in her power in the sick bay for the last ten days."

"But surely you don't mean. . . ? Brumfett wouldn't!"

"Precisely," said Sister Rolfe coldly. "So why make stupid and irresponsible remarks?"

There was a silence broken only by the rustle of paper and the hiss of the gas fire. Sister Gearing fidgeted.

"I suppose if Brumfett's lost another two nurses with flu she'll be pressing Matron to recall some of this block. She's got her eyes on the Burt twins, I know."

"Then she'll be unlucky. This set have had their training disrupted enough already. After all, it's their last block before their finals. Matron won't let it be cut short."

"I shouldn't be too sure. It's Brumfett, remember. Matron doesn't usually say no to her. Funny though, I did hear a rumour that they aren't going on holiday together this year. One of the pharmacists' assistants had it from Matron's secretary that Matron plans to motor in Ireland on her own."

My God, thought Sister Rolfe. Isn't there any privacy in this place? But she said nothing, only shifting a few inches from the restless figure at her side.

It was then that the wall telephone rang. Sister Gearing leapt up and went across to answer it. She turned to the rest of the group, her face creased with disappointment.

"That was Sergeant Masterson. Superintendent Dalgliesh would like to see the Burt twins next please. He's moved to the visitors' sitting-room on this floor."

Without a word and with no signs of nervousness, the Burt twins closed their books and made for the door.

IV

It was half an hour later and Sergeant Masterson was making coffee. The visitors' sitting-room had been provided with a miniature kitchen, a large recess fitted with a sink and Formica covered cupboard, on which stood a double gas-ring. The cupboard had been cleared of all its paraphernalia except for four large beakers, a canister of sugar and one of tea, a tin of biscuits, a large earthenware jug and strainer, and three transparent air-tight packets of fresh-ground coffee. By the side of the sink were two bottles of milk. The cream-line was easily discernible, but Sergeant Masterson prised the cap away from one of the bottles and sniffed at the milk suspiciously before heating a quantity in a saucepan. He warmed the earthenware jug with hot water from the tap, dried it carefully in the tea towel which hung by the side of the sink, spooned in a generous quantity of coffee and stood waiting for the kettle's first burst of steam. He approved of the arrangements that had been made. If the police had to work in Nightingale House this room was as convenient and comfortable as any and the coffee was an unexpected bonus which mentally, he credited to Paul Hudson. The Hospital Secretary had struck him as an efficient and imaginative man. His couldn't be an easy job. The poor devil probably had one hell of a life, sandwiched between those two old fools, Kealey and Grout, and that high-handed bitch of a Matron.

He strained the coffee with meticulous care and carried a beaker over to his chief. They sat and drank companionably together, eyes straying to the storm-wrecked garden. Both of them had a strong dislike of badly cooked food or synthetic coffee and Masterson thought that they never got closer to liking each other than when they were eating and drinking together, deploring the inadequacies of the meals at the inn, or as now, rejoicing in good coffee. Dalgliesh comforted his hands around the beaker and thought that it was typical of Mary Taylor's efficiency and imagination to ensure that they had real coffee available. Hers couldn't be an easy job. That ineffectual couple, Kealey and Grout, wouldn't be much help to anyone, and Paul Hudson was too young to give much support.

After a moment of appreciative sipping, Masterson said:

"That was a disappointing interview, sir."

"The Burt twins? Yes, I must say I had hoped for something more interesting. After all, they were at the centre of the mystery; they administered the fatal drip; they glimpsed the mysterious Nurse Fallon on her way out of Nightingale House; they met Sister Brumfett on her perambulations in the early hours. But we knew all that already. And we don't know any more now."

Dalgliesh thought about the two girls. Masterson had drawn up a second chair on their entrance and they had sat there side by side, freckled hands ritualistically disposed in their laps, legs modestly crossed, each girl a mirror image of her twin. Their polite antiphonal answers to his questions, spoken in a West Country burr, were as agreeable to the ear as their shining good health to the eye. He had rather taken to the Burt twins. He might, of course, have been facing a couple of experienced accomplices in evil. Anything was possible. Certainly they had had the best opportunity to poison the drip and as good a chance as anyone in Nightingale House to doctor Fallon's nightcap. Yet they had seemed perfectly at ease with him, a little bored perhaps at having to repeat much of their story, but neither frightened nor particularly worried. From time to time they had gazed at him with a gentle speculative concern rather as if he were a difficult patient whose condition was beginning to give rise to some anxiety. He had noticed this intent and compassionate regard on the faces of the other nurses during their first encounter in the demonstration room and had found it disconcerting.

"And you noticed nothing odd about the milk?"

They had answered almost in unison, rebuking him in the calm voice of common sense.

"Oh no! Well, we wouldn't have gone ahead with the drip if we had, would we?"

"Can you remember taking the cap off the bottle; was it loose?"

Two pairs of blue eyes looked at each other, almost as if in signal. Then Maureen replied:

"We don't remember that it was. But even if it had been, we wouldn't have suspected that someone had been at the milk. We would just have thought that the dairy put it on like that."

Then Shirley spoke on her own:

"I don't think we would have noticed anything wrong with the milk anyway. You see, we were concentrating on the procedures for giving the drip, making sure that we had all the instruments and equipment we needed. We knew that Miss Beale and Matron would arrive at any minute."

That, of course, was the explanation. They were girls who had been trained to observe, but their observation was specific and limited. If they were watching a patient they would miss nothing of his signs or symptoms, not a flicker of the eyelids or a change of pulse; anything else happening in the room, however dramatic, would probably be unnoticed. Their attention had been on the demonstration, the apparatus, the equipment, the patient. The bottle of milk presented no problems. They had taken it for granted. And yet they were farmer's daughters. One of them—it had been Maureen—had actually poured the stuff from the bottle. Could they really have mistaken the colour, the texture, the smell of milk?

As if reading his thoughts Maureen said:

"It wasn't as if we could smell the carbolic. The whole demo room stinks of disinfectant. Miss Collins throws the stuff around as if we're all lepers."

Shirley laughed: "Carbolic isn't effective against leprosy!"

They looked at each other, smiling in happy complicity.

And so the interview had gone on. They had no theories to propound, no suggestions to offer. They knew no one who could wish Pearce or Fallon dead, and yet both deaths—since they had occurred—seemed to cause them no particular surprise. They could recall every word of the conversation between Sister Brumfett and themselves in the small hours of that morning, yet the encounter apparently had made little impression on them. When Dalgliesh asked if the Sister had seemed unusually worried or distressed, they gazed at him simultaneously, brows creased in perplexity, before replying that Sister had seemed just the same as usual.

As if following his chief's thoughts, Masterson said:

"Short of asking them outright if Sister Brumfett looked as if she'd just come straight from murdering Fallon you couldn't have put it much plainer. They're an odd uncommunicative couple."

"At least they're sure of the time. They took that milk shortly after seven o'clock and went straight into the demonstration room with it. They stood the bottle unopened on the instrument trolley while they made preliminary preparations for the demonstration. They left the demonstration room at seven twenty-five for breakfast and the bottle was still on the trolley when they returned at about twenty-to-nine to complete their preparations. They then stood it, still unopened, in a jug of hot water to bring it to blood heat and it remained there until they poured the milk from the bottle into a measuring jug about two minutes before Miss Beale and Matron's party arrived. Most of the suspects were at breakfast together from eight until eight twenty-five, so that the mischief was either done between seven twenty-five and eight o'clock or in the short period between the end of breakfast and the twins' return to the demonstration room."

Masterson said: "I still find it strange that they noticed nothing odd about that milk."

"They may have noticed more than they realize at present. After all, this is the umpteenth time they've told their story. During the weeks since Pearce's death, their first statements have become fixed in their minds as the immutable truth. That's why I haven't asked them the crucial question about the milk bottle. If they gave me the wrong answer now they'd never change it. They need to be shocked into total recall. They're not seeing anything that happened with fresh eyes. I dislike reconstructions of the crime; they always make me feel like a fictional detective. But I think there may be a case for reconstruction here. I shall have to be in London early tomorrow, but you and Greeson can see to it. Greeson will probably enjoy himself."

He told Masterson briefly what he proposed and ended:

"You needn't bother to include the Sisters. I expect you can get a supply of the disinfectant from Miss Collins. But for God's sake keep an eye on the stuff and chuck it away afterwards. We don't want another tragedy."

Sergeant Masterson took up the two beakers and carried them over to the sink. He said:

"Nightingale House does seem to be touched with ill-luck, but I can't see the killer having another go while we're around."

It was to prove a singularly unprophetic remark.

V

Since her encounter with Dalgliesh in the nurses' utility room earlier that morning Sister Rolfe had had time to recover from shock and to consider her position. As Dalgliesh had expected she was now far less forthcoming. She had already given to Inspector Bailey a clear and unambiguous statement about the arrangements for the demonstration and the intra-gastric feeding and about her own movements on the morning that Nurse Pearce died. She confirmed the statement accurately and without fuss. She agreed that she had known that Nurse Pearce was to act the part of the patient and pointed out sarcastically that there would be little point in denying the knowledge since it was she whom Madeleine Goodale had called when Fallon was taken ill.

Dalgliesh asked: "Did you have any doubt of the genuineness of her illness?"

"At the time?"

"Then or now."

"I suppose you're suggesting that Fallon could have feigned influenza to ensure that Pearce took her place, and then sneaked back to Nightingale House before breakfast to doctor the drip? I don't know why she did come back, but you can put any idea that she was pretending to be ill out of your head. Even Fallon couldn't simulate a temperature of 103·8, a minor rigor and a racing pulse. She was a very sick girl that night, and she remained sick for nearly ten days."

Dalgliesh pointed out that it was all the more odd that she should have been well enough to make her way back to Nightingale House next morning. Sister Rolfe replied that it was so odd that she could only assume that Fallon had had an imperative need to return. Invited to speculate on what that need could have been she replied that it wasn't her job to propound theories. Then, as if under a compulsion, she added:

"But it wasn't to murder Pearce. Fallon was highly intelligent, easily the most intelligent of her year. If Fallon came back to put the corrosive in the feed she would know perfectly well that there was a considerable risk of her being seen in Nightingale House even if she weren't missed on the ward, and she'd have taken good care to have a story ready. It wouldn't have been difficult to think of something. As it is, I gather she merely declined to give Inspector Bailey any explanation."

"Perhaps she was clever enough to realize that this extraordinary reticence would strike another intelligent woman in exactly that way."

"A kind of double bluff? I don't think so. It would be banking too heavily on the intelligence of the police."

She admitted calmly that she had no alibi for any of the time from seven o'clock when the twins had collected the bottle of milk from the kitchen until ten minutes to nine when she had joined the Matron and Mr. Courtney-Briggs in Miss Taylor's sitting-room to await the arrival of Miss Beale, except for the period from eight to eight twenty-five when she had breakfasted at the same table as Sister Brumfett and Sister Gearing. Sister Brumfett had left the table first and she had followed at about eight twenty-five. She had gone first to her office next door to the demonstration room, but finding Mr. Courtney-Briggs in occupation, had made her way at once to her bed-sitting-room on the third floor.

When Dalgliesh asked whether Sister Gearing and Sister Brumfett had appeared their usual selves at breakfast she replied drily that they exhibited no signs of impending homicidal mania if that was what he meant. Gearing had read the *Daily Mirror* and Brumfett the *Nursing Times*, if that were of any significance, and the conversation had been minimal. She regretted she could offer no witnesses to her own movements before or after the meal but that was surely understandable; for some years now she had preferred to wash and go to the lavatory in private. Apart from that, she valued the free time before the day's work and preferred to spend it alone.

Dalgliesh asked: "Were you surprised to find Mr. Courtney-Briggs in your office when you went there after breakfast?"

"Not particularly. I took it for granted that he had spent the night in the medical officers' quarters and had come over early to Nightingale House to meet the G.N.C. Inspector. He probably wanted somewhere to write a letter. Mr. Courtney-Briggs assumes the right to use any room in the John Carpendar as his private office if the fancy takes him."

Dalgliesh asked her about her movements the previous night. She repeated that she had been to the cinema alone but added this time that she had met Julia Pardoe on the way out and that they had walked back to the hospital together. They had come in through the Winchester Road gate to which she had a key and had got back to Nightingale House shortly after eleven. She had gone immediately to her room and had seen no one. Nurse Pardoe, she assumed, had either gone straight to bed or had joined the rest of the set in the student nurses' sitting-room.

"So you have nothing to tell me, Sister? Nothing that can help?"

"Nothing."

"Not even why, unnecessary surely, you lied about going to the cinema alone?"

"Nothing. And I shouldn't have thought my private affairs were any concern of yours."

Dalgliesh said calmly: "Miss Rolfe, two of your students are dead. I'm here to find out how and why they died. If you don't want to co-operate, say so. You don't have to answer my questions. But don't try to tell me what questions I am to ask. I'm in charge of this investigation. I do it my way."

"I see. You make up the rules as you go along. All we can do is say when we don't want to play. Yours is a dangerous game, Mr. Dalgliesh."

"Tell me something about these students. You're the Principal Nurse Tutor; you must have a good many girls through your hands. I think you're a good judge of character. We'll start with Nurse Goodale."

If she felt surprise or relief at his choice she concealed it.

"Madeleine Goodale is confidently expected to take the Gold Medal as the best nurse of her year. She is less intelligent than Fallon—than Fallon was—but she's hard working and extremely conscientious. She's a local girl. Her father is well known in the town, an extremely successful estate agent who inherited a long established family business. He's a member of the Town Council and was on the Hospital Management Committee for a number of years. Madeleine went to the local grammar school and then came to us. I don't think she ever considered any other nurse training school. The whole family has a strong local loyalty. She is engaged to the young vicar of Holy Trinity and I understand they plan to marry as soon as she completes her training. Another good career lost to the profession, but she knows her own priorities I suppose."

"The Burt twins?"

"Good sensible kindly girls, with more imagination and sensitivity than they are usually credited with. Their people are farmers near Gloucester. I'm not sure why they chose this hospital. I have an idea a cousin trained here and was happy enough. They are the kind of girls who would choose a training school on that kind of family basis. They aren't particularly intelligent but they aren't stupid. We don't have to take stupid girls here, thank God. Each of them has a steady boy friend and Maureen is engaged. I don't think either of them looks on nursing as a permanent job."

Dalgliesh said: "You're going to have trouble finding leaders for the profession if this automatic resignation on marriage becomes the rule."

She said drily: "We're having trouble now. Who else are you interested in?"

"Nurse Dakers."

"Poor kid! Another local girl, but with a very different background from Goodale. Father was a minor local government officer who died of cancer when she was twelve. Mother has been struggling on ever since with a small pension. The girl was educated at the same school as Goodale but they were never friendly as far as I know. Dakers is a conscientious hard-working student with a great deal of ambition. She'll do all right but she won't do better than all right. She tires easily, isn't really robust. People think of her as timid and highly strung, whatever that euphemism means. But Dakers is tough enough. She's a third-year student, remember. A girl doesn't get this far with her training if she's fundamentally weak, physically or mentally."

"Julia Pardoe?"

Sister Rolfe had herself well under control now and there was no change in her voice as she went on.

"The only child of divorced parents. Mother is one of those pretty but selfish women who find it impossible to stay long with one husband. She's on her third now, I believe. I'm not sure that the girl really knows which is her father. She hasn't been often at home. Mother sent her off to a prep. school when she was five. She had a stormy school career and came here straight from the sixth form of one of those independent girls' boarding-schools, where the girls are taught nothing but manage to learn a great deal. She first applied to one of the London teaching hospitals. She didn't quite measure up to their standard of acceptance either socially or academically but the Matron referred her here. Schools like ours have this kind of arrangement with the teaching hospitals. They get a dozen applications for every place. It's mostly snobbery and the hope of catching a husband. We're quite happy to take a number of their rejects; I suspect that they often make better nurses than the girls they accept. Pardoe was one of them. An intelligent but untrained mind. A gentle and considerate nurse."

"You know a great deal about your students."

"I make it my business to. But I take it I'm not expected to give an opinion of my colleagues."

"Sister Gearing and Sister Brumfett? No. But I'd be glad of your opinion of Nurse Fallon and Nurse Pearce."

"I can't tell you much about Fallon. She was a reserved, almost a secretive girl. Intelligent, of course, and more mature than the majority of students. I think I only had one personal conversation with her. That was at the end of her first year when I called her for an interview and asked her for her impressions of nursing. I was interested to know how our methods here struck a girl who was so different from the ordinary run of the straight-from-school student. She said that it wasn't fair to judge while one was still an apprentice and treated as if one were a sub-normal kitchen maid but that she still thought nursing was her job. I asked her what had attracted her to the profession and she said that she wanted to acquire a skill which would make her independent anywhere in the world, a qualification which would always be in demand. I don't think she had any particular ambition to get on in the profession. Her training was just a means to an end. But I could be wrong. As I said, I never really knew her."

"So you can't say whether she had enemies?"

"I can't say why anyone should want to kill her, if that's what you mean. I should have thought that Pearce was a much more likely victim."

Dalgliesh asked her why.

"I didn't take to Pearce. I didn't kill her, but then I'm not given to murdering people merely because I dislike them. But she was a strange girl, a mischief maker and a hypocrite. It's no use asking me how I know. I haven't any real evidence and, if I had, I doubt whether I should give it to you."

"So you didn't find it surprising that she should have been murdered?"

"I found it astonishing. But I never for one moment thought her death was suicide or an accident."

"And who do you suppose killed her?"

Sister Rolfe looked at him with a kind of grim satisfaction.

"You tell me, Superintendent. You tell me!"

VI

"So you went to the cinema last night and on your own?"

"Yes, I told you."

"To see a revival of *L'Avventura*. Perhaps you felt that the subtleties of Antonioni could best be experienced without a companion? Or perhaps you couldn't find anyone willing to go with you?"

She couldn't, of course, resist that.

"There are plenty of people to take me to the movies if I want them to."

The movies. It had been the flicks when Dalgliesh was her age. But the generation chasm was deeper than a matter of mere semantics, the alienation more complete. He simply didn't understand her. He hadn't the slightest clue to what was going on behind that smooth and childish forehead. The remarkable violet blue eyes, set wide apart under curved brows, gazed at him, wary but unconcerned. The cat's face with its small rounded chin and wide cheek bones expressed nothing but a vague distaste for the matter in hand. It was difficult, Dalgliesh thought, to imagine finding a prettier or more agreeable figure than Julia Pardoe beside one's sick bed; unless, of course, one happened to be in real pain or distress when the Burt twins' sturdy common sense or Madeleine Goodale's calm efficiency would be a great deal more acceptable. It might be a personal prejudice, but he couldn't imagine any man willingly exposing his weakness or physical distress to this pert and self-absorbed young woman. And what precisely, he wondered, was she getting out of nursing? If the John Carpendar had been a teaching hospital he could have understood it. That trick of widening the eyes when she spoke so that the hearer was treated to a sudden blaze of blue, of slightly parting moist lips above the neat eburnean teeth would go down very well with a gaggle of medical students. It was not, he noticed, without its effect on Sergeant Masterson.

But what was it that Sister Rolfe had said of her?

"An intelligent but untrained mind; a gentle and considerate nurse."

Well, it could be. But Hilda Rolfe was prejudiced. And so, in his own way, was Dalgliesh.

He pressed on with his interrogation, resisting the impulse to sarcasm, to the cheap jibes of antipathy.

"Did you enjoy the film?"

"It was all right."

"And you returned to Nightingale House from this all right film when?"

"I don't know. Just before eleven, I suppose. I met Sister Rolfe outside the cinema and we walked back together. I expect she's told you."

So they must have talked since this morning. This was their story and the girl was repeating it without even the pretence that she cared whether she were believed. It could be checked of course. The girl in the cinema box office might remember whether they had arrived together. But it was hardly worth the trouble of inquiry. Why indeed should it matter, unless they had spent the evening concocting murder as well as imbibing culture? And if they had, here was one partner in iniquity who wasn't apparently worried.

Dalgliesh asked: "What happened when you got back?"

"Nothing. I went to the nurses' sitting-room and they were all watching the telly. Well, actually they switched it off as I came in. The Burt twins came to make tea in the nurses' kitchen and we took it into Maureen's room to drink it. Dakers came with us. Madeleine Goodale was left with Fallon. I don't know what time they came up. I went to bed as soon as I'd had my tea. I was asleep before twelve."

So she might have been. But this had been a very simple murder. There had been nothing to prevent her waiting, perhaps in one of the lavatory cubicles, until she heard Fallon running her bath. Once Fallon was in the bathroom, Nurse Pardoe would know what all the other students knew; that a beaker of whisky and lemon would be waiting on Fallon's bedside table. How simple to slip into her room and add something to the drink. Add what? It was maddening, this working in the dark with its inevitable tendency to theorize in advance of the facts. Until the autopsy was completed and the toxicology result available he couldn't even be sure that he was investigating a murder.

He suddenly changed tack, reverting to a previous course of questioning.

"Are you sorry about Nurse Pearce's death?"

Again the wide opened eyes, the little *moue* of consideration, the suggestion that it was really rather a silly question.

"Of course." A little pause. "She never did me any harm."

"Did she do anyone any harm?"

"You'd better ask them." Another pause. Perhaps she felt that she had been imprudently foolish and rude. "What harm could Pearce do to anyone?"

It was spoken with no tinge of contempt, almost with disinterest, a mere statement of fact.

"Someone killed her. That doesn't suggest that she was innocuous. Someone must have hated her enough to want her out of the way."

"She could have killed herself. When she swallowed that tube she knew what was coming to her all right. She was terrified. Anyone watching her could see that."

Julia Pardoe was the first student to have mentioned Nurse Pearce's fear. The only other person present to have noticed it had been the General Nursing Council Inspector who, in her statement, had stressed the girl's look of apprehension, almost of endurance. It was interesting and surprising that Nurse Pardoe should have been so perceptive. Dalgliesh said:

"But do you really believe that she put a corrosive poison into the feed herself?"

The blue eyes met his. She gave her little secret smile.

"No. Pearce was always terrified when she had to act as patient. She hated it. She never said anything, but anyone could see what she was feeling. Swallowing that tube must have been particularly bad for her. She told me once that she couldn't bear the thought of a throat examination or operation. She'd had her tonsils out as a child and the surgeon—or it may have been a nurse—was rough with her and hurt her badly. Anyway, it had been a horrible experience and had left her with this phobia about her throat. Of course, she could have explained to Sister Gearing and one of us would have taken her place. She didn't have to act the patient. No one was forcing her. But I suppose Pearce thought it was her duty to go through with it. She was a great one for duty."

So anyone present could have seen what Pearce was feeling. But in fact, only two of them had seen. And one of them had been this apparently insensitive young woman.

Dalgliesh was intrigued, but not particularly surprised, that Nurse Pearce should have chosen to confide in Julia Pardoe. He had met it before, this perverse attraction which the pretty and popular often held for the plain and despised. Sometimes it was even reciprocated; an odd mutual fascination which, he suspected, formed the basis of many friendships and marriages that the world found inexplicable. But if Heather Pearce had been making a pathetic bid for friendship or sympathy by a recital of childhood woes she had been unlucky. Julia Pardoe respected strength, not weakness. She would be impervious to a plea for pity. And yet—who knew?—Pearce might have got something from her. Not friendship, or sympathy, or pity even; but a modicum of understanding.

He said on a sudden impulse:

"I think you probably knew more about Nurse Pearce than anyone else here, probably understood her better. I don't believe her death was suicide, neither do you. I want you to tell me everything about her which would help me to a motive."

There was a second's pause. Was it his imagination or was she really making up her mind to something? Then she said in her high, unemphatic, childish voice:

"I expect she was blackmailing someone. She tried it with me once."

"Tell me about it."

She looked up at him speculatively as if assessing his reliability or wondering whether the story was worth the trouble of telling. Then her lips curved in a little reminiscent smile. She said calmly:

"My boy friend spent a night with me about a year ago. Not here; in the main nurses' home. I unlocked one of the fire escape doors and let him in. We did it for a lark really."

"Was he someone from the John Carpendar?"

"Um, um. One of the surgical registrars."

"And how did Heather Pearce find out about it?"

"It was the night before our preliminary—the first examination for State Registration. Pearce always got a stomach-ache before exams. I suppose she was prowling down the corridor to the loo and saw me letting Nigel in. Or she may have been on her way back to bed and listened at the door. Perhaps she heard us giggling or something. I expect she listened as long as she could. I wonder what she made of it. No one has ever wanted to make love to Pearce so I suppose she got a thrill just out of listening to someone else in bed with a man. Anyway, she tackled me about it next morning and then threatened to tell Matron and have me chucked out of the nurse training school."

She spoke without resentment, almost with a touch of amusement. It hadn't bothered her at the time. It didn't bother her now.

Dalgliesh asked: "And what price was she asking for her silence?"

He had no doubt that, whatever the price, it hadn't been paid.

"She said she hadn't made up her mind about that; she would have to think about it. It would have to be appropriate. You should have seen her face. It was all mottled and red like a disgusted turkey cock. I don't know how I kept a straight face. I pretended to be terribly worried and contrite and asked if we should talk about it that night. That was just to give me time to get in touch with Nigel. He lived with his widowed mother just outside the town. She adores him and I knew she wouldn't make any difficulty about swearing that he spent the night at home. She wouldn't even mind that we'd been together. She thinks that her precious Nigel's entitled to take just what he likes. But I didn't want Pearce to talk before I got that fixed up. When I saw her that evening I told her that both of us would deny the story absolutely and that Nigel would back it up with an alibi. She'd forgotten about his mother. There was something else she'd forgotten too. Nigel is Mr. Courtney-Briggs's nephew. So if she talked, all that would happen would be that Mr. Courtney-Briggs would get her chucked out, not me. Pearce was terribly stupid, really."

"You seem to have coped with admirable efficiency and composure. So you never learned what punishment Pearce had in store for you?"

"Oh yes I did! I let her talk about that before I told her. It was more amusing that way. It wasn't a question of punishment; it was more like blackmail. She wanted to come in with us, be one of my crowd."

"Your crowd?"

"Well, me, Jennifer Blain and Diane Harper really. I was going with Nigel at the time and Diane and Jennifer had his friends. You haven't met Blain; she's one of the students who are off with flu. Pearce wanted us to fix her up a man for her so that she could make up a fourth."

"Didn't you find that surprising? From what I've heard of her, Heather Pearce wasn't exactly the type to be interested in sex."

"Everyone is interested in sex, in their own way. But Pearce didn't put it like that. She made out that the three of us weren't to be trusted and that we ought to have someone reliable to keep an eye on us. No prizes for guessing who! But I knew what she really wanted. She wanted Tom Mannix. He was the paediatric registrar at the time. He was spotty and rather a drip really, but Pearce fancied him. They both belonged to the hospital Christian Fellowship and Tom was going to be a missionary or something after his two years here were up. He'd have suited Pearce all right, and I daresay I could have made him go out with her once or twice if I'd pressed him. But it wouldn't have done her any good. He didn't want Pearce; he wanted me. Well, you know how it is."

Dalgliesh did know. This, after all, was the commonest, the most banal of personal tragedies. You loved someone. They didn't love you. Worse still, in defiance of their own best interests and to the destruction of your peace, they loved another. What would half the world's poets and novelists do without this universal tragicomedy? But Julia Pardoe was untouched by it. If only, thought Dalgliesh, her voice had held a trace of pity, or even interest! But Pearce's desperate need, the longing for love which had led her to this pathetic attempt at blackmail, provoked in her victim nothing, not even an amused contempt. She couldn't even be bothered to ask him to keep the story a secret. And then, as if reading his thoughts, she told him why.

"I don't mind your knowing about it now. Why should I? After all, Pearce is dead. Fallon too. I mean, with two murders in the place, Matron and the Hospital Management Committee have something more important to worry about than Nigel and me in bed together. But when I think of that night! Honestly, it was hilarious. The bed was far too narrow and it kept creaking and

Nigel and I were giggling so much we could hardly. . . . And then to think of Pearce with one eye to the keyhole!"

And then she laughed. It was a peal of spontaneous and reminiscent joy, innocent and infectious. Looking up at her, Masterson's heavy face coruscated into a wide indulgent grin and, for one extraordinary second, he and Dalgliesh had to restrain themselves from laughing aloud with her.

VII

Dalgliesh hadn't summoned the members of the little group in the library in any particular order and it wasn't with malice aforethought that he had left Sister Gearing to the last. But the long wait had been unkind to her. She had obviously found time, earlier in the morning, to make up her face with lavish care; an instinctive preparation, no doubt, for whatever traumatic encounters the day might bring. But the make-up had worn badly. The mascara had run and was now smudged into the eye shadow, there were beads of sweat along the forehead and a trace of lipstick in the cleft of the chin. Perhaps she had been unconsciously fiddling with her face. Certainly, she was finding it difficult now to keep her hands still. She sat twisting her handkerchief through her fingers and crossing and recrossing her legs in fidgety discomfort. Without waiting for Dalgliesh to speak she broke into a high frenetic chatter.

"You and your sergeant are staying with the Maycrofts at the Falconer's Arms, aren't you? I hope they're making you comfortable. Sheila's a bit of a drag but Bob's good value when you get him on his own."

Dalgliesh had taken very good care not to get Bob on his own. He had chosen the Falconer's Arms because it was small, convenient, quiet, and half empty; it had not taken long to understand why. Group Captain Robert Maycroft and his wife were more concerned to impress visitors with their own gentility than to minister to the comfort of their guests, and Dalgliesh fervently hoped to be out of the place by the end of the week. In the meantime he had no intention of discussing the Maycrofts with Sister Gearing and he guided her politely but firmly towards more relevant subjects.

Unlike the other suspects she found it necessary to waste the first five minutes in expressing her horror at the deaths of the two girls. It had been all too horrible, tragic, awful, ghastly, beastly, unforgettable, inexplicable. The emotion, thought Dalgliesh, was real enough even if its expression wasn't original. The woman was genuinely distressed. He suspected that she was also very frightened.

He took her through the events of Monday, 12th January. She had little new of interest to say and her account tallied with that already on the file. She had woken very late, dressed in a hurry, and had only just managed to get down to the dining-room by eight o'clock. There she had joined Sister Brumfett and Sister Rolfe for breakfast and had first heard from them that Nurse Fallon had been taken ill in the night. Dalgliesh asked her if she remembered which of the Sisters had given her the news.

"Well, I can't say I do really. I think it was Rolfe but I can't be sure. I was in a bit of a tizzy that morning what with one thing and another. It hadn't helped oversleeping like that, and I was naturally a bit nervous about the General Nursing Council inspection. After all, I'm not a qualified Sister Tutor. I was only deputizing for Sister Manning. And it's bad enough taking the first demonstration of a set without Matron and the G.N.C. Inspector, Mr. Courtney-Briggs and Sister Rolfe all sitting there with their beady eyes on every move you make. It struck me that with Fallon absent, there would only be about seven students left in the set. Well, that suited me all right; the fewer the better as far as I was concerned. I only hoped the little beasts would answer up and show some intelligence."

Dalgliesh asked her who had left the dining-room first.

"Brumfett did. Dead keen as usual to get back to her ward, I suppose. I left next. I took my papers through into the conservatory with a cup of coffee and sat down for ten minutes' read. Christine Dakers, Diane Harper and Julia Pardoe were there. Harper and Pardoe were chatting together and Dakers was sitting on her own reading a magazine. I didn't stay long and they were still there when I left. I went up to my room at about half past eight, collecting my post on the way, and then came down again and went straight into the demonstration room just before quarter to nine.

The Burt twins were already there finishing their preparations and Goodale arrived almost immediately. The rest of the set came in together at about ten to nine, except Pearce, who didn't arrive until last. There was the usual girlish chatter before we got down to work but I can't remember any of it. The rest you know."

Dalgliesh did know. But although he thought it unlikely that there was anything new to learn from Sister Gearing he took her again through the events of that traumatic demonstration. But she had nothing fresh to reveal. It had all been too awful, terrible, ghastly, frightful, unbelievable. She would never forget it as long as she lived.

Dalgliesh then turned to the death of Fallon. But here Sister Gearing had a surprise for him. She was the first suspect to produce an alibi, or what she obviously hoped was one, and she put it forward with understandable satisfaction. From eight o'clock until after midnight she had been entertaining a friend in her room. She gave Dalgliesh his name with coy reluctance. He was Leonard Morris, the chief pharmacist of the hospital. She had invited him to dinner, had produced a simple meal of spaghetti bolognaise in the Sisters' kitchen on the third floor and had served it in her sitting-room at eight o'clock, shortly after his arrival. They had been together for the whole of the four hours except for the few minutes when she had fetched the supper dish from the kitchen, and for a couple of minutes at about midnight when he had visited the lavatory, and a similar period earlier in the evening when she had left him for the same purpose. Apart from that they had never been out of each other's sight. She added eagerly that Len—Mr. Morris that was—would be only too happy to confirm her story. Len would remember the times perfectly well. Being a pharmacist he was precise and accurate about details. The only difficulty was that he wasn't in the hospital this morning. He had telephoned the pharmacy just before nine to say that he was sick. But he would be back at work tomorrow, she was sure of it. Len hated taking time off.

Dalgliesh asked at what hour he had actually left Nightingale House.

"Well, it couldn't have been long after midnight. I remember that when my clock struck twelve Len said that it was really time he was off. We went out about five minutes later, down the back staircase, the one leading from Matron's flat. I left the door open: Len collected his bicycle from where he'd left it and I walked with him to the first turn in the path. It wasn't exactly a night for a stroll but we'd still one or two matters about the hospital to discuss —Len lectures in pharmacology to the second-year students—and I thought I could do with a breath of air. Len didn't like to leave me to walk back alone so he came back as far as the door. I suppose it was about twelve fifteen when we finally parted. I came in through Matron's door and locked it behind me. I went straight back to my room, took the supper things into the kitchen to wash them up, went to the bathroom, and was in bed by a quarter to one. I didn't see Fallon all the evening. The next thing I knew was Sister Rolfe dashing in to wake me up with the news that Dakers had found Fallon dead in bed."

"So you went out and returned through Miss Taylor's flat. Was her door left unlocked then?"

"Oh, yes! Matron usually leaves it open when she's away. She knows we find it convenient and more private to use her staircase. After all we're grown women. We're not exactly forbidden to entertain friends in our rooms and it isn't particularly nice to have to show them out through the main house with every little student watching with her eyes out on stalks. Matron's awfully good like that. I think she even leaves her sitting-room unlocked when she's not in Nightingale House. I suppose that's so that Sister Brumfett can use it if she feels inclined. Brumfett, in case you hadn't heard, is Matron's spaniel. Most Matrons keep a little dog you know. Mary Taylor has Brumfett."

The note of bitter cynicism was so unexpected that Masterson's head came up from his note-taking with a jerk and he looked at Sister Gearing as if she were an unpromising candidate who had suddenly revealed unexpected potentialities. But Dalgliesh let it pass. He asked:

"Was Sister Brumfett using Miss Taylor's flat last night?"

"At midnight! Not Brumfett! She goes to bed early unless she's in town gallivanting with Matron. She's usually brewing her last cuppa by ten-fifteen. Anyway, she was called out last night. Mr.

Courtney-Briggs rang her to go over to the private ward and receive one of his patients back from the theatre. I thought everyone knew. That was just before twelve."

Dalgliesh asked if Sister Gearing had seen her.

"No, but my friend did. Len, I mean. He popped his head out of the door to see if the coast was clear to go to the loo before we left and saw Brumfett wrapped in her cloak, carrying that old bag of hers, disappearing down the staircase. It was obvious that she was going out, and I guessed that she had been called back to the ward. That's always happening to Brumfett. Mind you, it's partly her own fault. There's such a thing as being too conscientious."

It was not, thought Dalgliesh, a fault to which Sister Gearing was likely to be prone. It was difficult to imagine her tramping through the grounds at midnight in the depth of winter at the casual summons of any surgeon, however eminent. But he felt rather sorry for her. She had given him a depressing glimpse into the stultifying lack of privacy, and of the small pettinesses and subterfuges with which people living in unwelcome proximity try to preserve their own privacy or invade that of others. The thought of a grown man peeping surreptitiously around the door before coming out, of two adult lovers creeping furtively down a back staircase to avoid detection, was grotesque and humiliating. He remembered the Matron's words. "We do get to know things here; there's no real privacy." Even poor Brumfett's choice of nightcap and her usual hour for bed were common knowledge. Small wonder that Nightingale House bred its own brand of neurosis, that Sister Gearing felt it necessary to justify a walk with her lover in the grounds, their obvious and natural wish to prolong the final good night, with unconvincing twaddle about the need to discuss hospital business. He found it all profoundly depressing and he wasn't sorry when it was time to let her go.

VIII

Dalgliesh rather enjoyed his half hour with the housekeeper, Miss Martha Collins. She was a thin, brown-skinned woman, brittle and nobbly as a dead branch who looked as if the sap had long since dried in her bones. She gave the appearance of having gradually shrunk in her clothes without having noticed it. Her working overall of thick fawn cotton hung in long creases from her narrow shoulders to mid-calf and was bunched around her waist by a schoolboy's belt of red and blue stripes clasped with a snake buckle. Her stockings were a concertina around her ankles, and either she preferred to wear shoes at least two sizes too large, or her feet were curiously disproportionate to the rest of her body. She had appeared as soon as summoned, had plonked herself down opposite Dalgliesh, her immense feet planted firmly astride, and had eyed him with anticipatory malevolence as if about to interview a particularly recalcitrant housemaid. Throughout the interview she didn't once smile. Admittedly there was nothing in the situation to provoke amusement but she seemed incapable of raising even the briefest smile of formal recognition. But despite these inauspicious beginnings the interview hadn't gone badly. Dalgliesh wondered whether her acidulated tone and perversely unattractive appearance were part of a calculated *persona*. Perhaps some forty years earlier she had decided to become a hospital character, the beloved tyrant of fiction, treating everyone from the matron to the junior maid with equal irreverence, and had found the characterization so successful and satisfying that she had never managed to drop it. She grumbled incessantly but it was without malice, a matter of form. He suspected that, in fact, she enjoyed her work and was neither as unhappy nor discontented as she chose to appear. She would hardly have stayed in the job for forty years if it were as intolerable as she made it sound.

"Milk! Don't talk to me about milk. There's more trouble about milk in this house than about the rest of the catering put together and that's saying something. Fifteen pints a day we're getting through even with half the house down with the flu. Don't ask me where it's all going. I've stopped being responsible for it and so I told Matron. There's a couple of bottles go up first thing each morning to the Sisters' floor so that they can make their own early tea. Two bottles between three I send up. You'd think that'd be enough for everyonc. Matron's is separate, of course. She gets a pint and not a drop grudged. But the trouble that milk causes! The first Sister to get at it takes all the cream, I suppose. Not very considerate, and so I told Matron. They're lucky to get a bottle or two of Channel Island milk; no one else in the house does. There's nothing but complaints. Sister Gearing going on because it's too watery for her and Sister Brumfett because it's not all Channel Island and Sister Rolfe wanting it sent up in half-pint bottles which she knows as well as I do you can't get any more. Then there's the milk for the students' early tea and that cocoa and stuff they brew themselves at night. They're supposed to sign for the bottles which they take from the fridge. The stuff isn't grudged, but that's the rule. Well, you take a look at the record book yourself! Nine times out of ten they can't be troubled. And then there are the empties. They're supposed to rinse them out and return them to the kitchen. You wouldn't think that would be too much bother. Instead they leave the bottles about the house, in their rooms, in the cupboards, and in the utility room—half-rinsed too—until the place stinks. My girls have got enough to do without running around after the students and their empties, and so I told Matron.

"What do you mean, was I in the kitchen when the Burt twins took their pint? You know I was. I said so to the other policeman. Where else would I be at that hour of the day? I'm always in my kitchen by quarter to seven and it was nearly three minutes past when the Burt twins came in. No, I didn't hand the bottle to them. They helped themselves from the fridge. It's not my job to wait hand and foot on the students and so I told Matron. But there was nothing wrong with that milk when it left my kitchen. It wasn't delivered until six thirty and I've got enough to do before breakfast without messing about putting disinfectant into the milk. Besides, I've got an alibi. I was with Mrs. Muncie from six forty-five onwards. She's the daily woman who comes in from the town to lend a hand when I'm short. You can see her any time you like but I don't suppose you'll get much out of her. The poor soul hasn't got much between the ears. Come to think of it, I doubt whether she'd notice if I spent the whole morning poisoning the milk. But she was with me for what it's worth. And I was with her all the time. No popping out every other minute to the lavatory for me, thank you. I do all that sort of thing at the proper time.

"The lavatory disinfectant? I thought you'd be asking about that. I fill up the bottles myself from the big tin they send over once a week from the main hospital store. It's not really my job but I don't like to leave it to the housemaids. They're so careless. They'd only get the stuff slopped all over the lavatory floors. I refilled that bottle in the downstairs W.C. the day before Nurse Pearce died so it must have been nearly full. Some of the students bother to put a little down the bowl when they've finished with the lavatory but most of them don't. You'd think student nurses would be particular about little things like that, but they're no better than other young people. The stuff is mostly used by the maids when they've cleaned the W.C. bowl. All the lavatories get cleaned once a day. I'm very particular about having clean lavatories. The downstairs one was due to be cleaned by Morag Smith after lunch, but Nurse Goodale and Nurse Pardoe noticed that the bottle was missing before then. I'm told that the other policeman found it empty among the bushes at the back of the house. And who put it there, I'd like to know?

"No, you can't see Morag Smith. Didn't they tell you? She's on a day's leave. She went off after tea yesterday, lucky for her. They can't pin this latest spot of bother on Morag. No. I don't know whether she went home. I didn't inquire. The maids are enough responsibility when they're under my nose in Nightingale House. I don't concern myself with what they do on their days off. Just as well from some of the things I hear. She'll be back late tonight more than likely and Matron has left instructions that she's to move to the Resident Staff Hostel. This place is too dangerous for us now apparently. Well, no one's shifting me. I don't know how I'm supposed to manage in the mornings if Morag doesn't show her face until just before breakfast. I can't control my staff if they're not under my eyes and so I told Matron. Not that Morag's much bother. She's as obstinate as they come but she's not a bad worker once you get her started. And if they try to tell you that Morag Smith interfered with the dripfeed, don't you believe them. The girl may be a bit dense but she's not a raving lunatic. I'll not have my staff slandered without cause.

"And now I'll tell you something, Mr. Detective." She raised her thin rump from her chair, leaned forward across the desk and fixed Dalgliesh with her beady eyes. He willed himself to meet them without blinking and they stared at each other like a couple of wrestlers before a bout.

"Yes, Miss Collins?"

She stuck out a lean nodular finger and prodded him sharply in the chest. Dalgliesh winced.

"No one had any right to take that bottle out of the lavatory without my permission or to use it for any other purpose except for cleaning the lavatory bowl. Nobody!"

It was apparent where in Miss Collins's eyes the full enormity of the crime had lain.

IX

At twenty minutes to one, Mr. Courtney-Briggs appeared. He knocked briskly at the door, came in without waiting for an invitation, and said curtly:

"I can give you a quarter of an hour now, Dalgliesh, if it's convenient."

His tone assumed that it would be. Dalgliesh assented and indicated the chair. The surgeon looked across at Sergeant Masterson sitting impassively with his notebook at the ready, hesitated, then turned the chair so that its back was to the sergeant. Then he seated himself and slipped his hand into his waistcoat pocket. The cigarette case he drew out was of finely tooled gold and so slim that it looked hardly functional. He offered a cigarette to Dalgliesh but not to Masterson and seemed neither surprised nor particularly interested at the Superintendent's refusal. He lit his own. The hands cupped around the lighter were large, square-fingered; not the sensitive hands of a fictional surgeon, but strong carpenter's hands, beautifully cared for.

Dalgliesh, overtly busy with his papers, observed the man. He was big but not yet fat. The formal suit fitted him almost too well, containing a sleek well-fed body and enhancing the effect of latent power only imperfectly controlled. He could still be called handsome. His long hair brushed straight back from a high forehead was strong and dark, except for one single white strand. Dalgliesh wondered whether it were bleached. His eyes were too small for the large, rather florid face, but were well shaped and set wide apart. They gave nothing away.

Dalgliesh knew that it had been Mr. Courtney-Briggs who had been mainly responsible for the Chief Constable calling in the Yard. From Inspector Bailey's somewhat bitter account during their brief colloquy when Dalgliesh had taken over the case, it was easy to understand why. The surgeon had made himself a nuisance from the beginning and his motives, if they were capable of rational explanation, raised interesting speculations. At first he had asserted vigorously that Nurse Pearce had obviously been murdered, that it was unthinkable that anyone connected with the hospital could have been concerned with the crime, and that the local police had a duty to proceed on this assumption and to find and arrest the killer with a minimum of delay. When their investigations yielded no immediate results, he became restive. He was a man used to exercising power and he was certainly not without it. There were eminent people in London who owed their lives to him and some of them had considerable nuisance value. Telephone calls, some tactful and half-apologetic, others frankly critical, were made both to the Chief Constable and to the Yard. As the Inspector in charge of the investigation became more convinced that Nurse Pearce's death was the result of a practical joke which had tragically misfired, so Mr. Courtney-Briggs and his co-agitators proclaimed more loudly that she had been murdered, and pressed more strongly for the case to be handed over to the Yard. And then Nurse Fallon had been found dead. It could be expected that the local C.I.D. would be galvanized into fresh activity, that the diffuse light which had played over the first crime would sharpen and focus on this second death. And it was at this moment that Mr. Courtney-Briggs had chosen to telephone the Chief Constable to announce that no further activity was necessary, that it was obvious to him that Nurse Fallon had committed suicide, that this could only have been in remorse at the tragic result of the practical joke which had killed her colleague, and that it was now in the hospital's interest to close the case with the minimum of fuss before nurse recruitment and indeed the whole future of the hospital was jeopardized. The police are not unused to these sudden quirks of temperament, which is not to say that they welcome them. Dalgliesh thought that it must have been with considerable satisfaction that the Chief Constable decided that, in all the circumstances, it would be prudent to call in the Yard to investigate both the deaths.

During the week following Nurse Pearce's death, Courtney-Briggs had even rung up Dalgliesh, who had been his patient three years earlier. It had been a case of uncomplicated appendicitis, and although Dalgliesh's vanity was gratified by the smallness and neatness of the resultant scar, he felt that the surgeon's expertise had been adequately rewarded at the time. He had certainly no wish to be used for Courtney-Briggs's private ends. The telephone call had been embarrassing and he had resented it. He was interested to see that the surgeon had apparently decided that this was an incident it would be advisable for both of them to forget.

Without lifting his eyes from his papers, Dalgliesh said:

"I understand that you take the view that Miss Fallon killed herself?"

"Of course. It's the obvious explanation. You're not suggesting that someone else put stuff into her whisky? Why should they?"

"There's the problem, isn't there, of the missing container? That is, if it were poison. We shan't know until we get the autopsy report."

"What problem? There's no problem. The beaker was opaque, heat insulated. She could have put the stuff into it earlier that evening. No one would have noticed. Or she could have carried a powder in a slip of paper and flushed it down the lavatory. The container's no problem. Incidentally, it wasn't a corrosive this time. That much was evident when I saw the body."

"Were you the first doctor on the scene?"

"No. I wasn't in the hospital when they found her. Dr. Snelling saw her. He's the general physician who looks after the nurses here. He realized at once that there was nothing to be done. I went across to have a look at the body as soon as I heard the news. I arrived at the hospital just before nine. By then the police had arrived, of course. The local people, I mean. I can't think why they weren't left to get on with it. I rang the Chief Constable to make my views known. Incidentally, Miles Honeyman tells me that she died about midnight. I saw him just as he was leaving. We were at medical school together."

"So I understand."

"You were wise to call him in. I gather that he's generally considered to be the best."

He spoke complacently, success condescending to recognize success. His criteria were hardly subtle, thought Dalgliesh. Money, prestige, public recognition, power. Yes, Courtney-Briggs would always demand the best for himself, confident of his ability to pay for it.

Dalgliesh said: "She was pregnant. Did you know?"

"So Honeyman told me. No, I didn't know. These things happen, even today when birth control is reliable and easily obtained. But I should have expected a girl of her intelligence to be on the Pill."

Dalgliesh remembered the scene that morning in the library when Mr. Courtney-Briggs had known the girl's age to a day. He asked his next question without apology.

"Did you know her well?"

The implication was plain and the surgeon did not reply for a moment. Dalgliesh had not expected him to bluster or threaten and he did neither. There was an increased respect in the sharp look which he gave his interrogator.

"For a time, yes." He paused. "You could say I knew her intimately."

"Was she your mistress?"

Courtney-Briggs looked at him, impassive, considering. Then he said:

"That's putting it rather formally. We slept together fairly regularly during her first six months here. Are you objecting?"

"It's hardly for me to object if she didn't. Presumably she was willing?"

"You could say that."

"When did it end?"

"I thought I told you. It lasted until the end of her first year. That's a year and a half ago."

"Did you quarrel?"

"No. She decided she'd, shall we say, exhausted the possibilities. Some women like variety. I do myself. I wouldn't have taken her on if I'd thought she was the type to make trouble. And don't get me wrong. I don't make it a practice to sleep with student nurses. I'm reasonably fastidious."

"Wasn't it difficult to keep the affair secret? There's very little privacy in a hospital."

"You have romantic ideas, Superintendent. We didn't kiss and cuddle in the sluice room. When I said I slept with her I meant just that. I don't use euphemisms for sex. She came to my Wimpole Street flat when she had a night off and we slept there. I haven't a resident man there and my house is near Selborne. The porter at Wimpole Street must have known, but he can keep his mouth shut. There wouldn't be many tenants left in the building if he couldn't. There wasn't any risk, provided that she didn't talk, and she wasn't a talker. Not that I would have minded particularly. There are certain areas of private behaviour in which I do as I like. You too no doubt."

"So it wasn't your child?"

"No. I'm not careless. Besides the affair was over. But if it hadn't been I should hardly have killed her. That kind of solution causes more embarrassment than it prevents."

Dalgliesh asked: "What would you have done?"

"That would have depended on the circumstances. I should have had to be sure it was my child. But this particular problem is hardly uncommon and not insoluble if the woman is reasonable."

"I've been told that Miss Fallon planned to get an abortion. Did she approach you?"

"No."

"She might have done?"

"Certainly she might have done. But she didn't."

"Would you have helped her if she had?"

The surgeon looked at him.

"That question is hardly within your terms of reference, I should have thought."

Dalgliesh said: "That's for me to judge. The girl was pregnant;

she apparently intended to get an abortion; she told a friend that she knew someone who would help her. I'm naturally interested to know who she had in mind."

"You know the law. I'm a surgeon not a gynaecologist. I prefer to stick to my own speciality and to practice it legally."

"But there are other kinds of help. Referring her to an appropriate consultant, helping with the fees."

A girl with £16,000 to bequeath was hardly likely to want help with the fees for an abortion. But Miss Goodale's legacy was not being made public and Dalgliesh was interested to learn whether Courtney-Briggs knew about Fallon's capital. But the surgeon gave no sign.

"Well, she didn't come to me. She may have had me in mind but she didn't come. And if she had, I wouldn't have helped. I make it my business to assume my own responsibilities; but I don't take on other people's. If she chose to look elsewhere for her satisfaction she could look elsewhere for her help. I didn't impregnate her. Someone did. Let him look after her."

"That would have been your response?"

"Certainly it would. And rightly."

His voice held a note of grim satisfaction. Looking at him, Dalgliesh saw that his face was flushed. The man was controlling his emotion with difficulty. And Dalgliesh had little doubt of the nature of that emotion. It was hate. He went on with his interrogation.

"Were you in the hospital last night?"

"Yes. I was called to operate on an emergency. One of my patients relapsed. It wasn't altogether unexpected, but very serious. I finished operating at eleven forty-five p.m. The time will be noted in the theatre register. Then I rang Sister Brumfett at Nightingale House to ask her to be good enough to return to her ward for an hour or so. My patient was a private patient. After that I rang my home to say that I would be returning that night instead of sleeping here in the medical officers' quarters as I do occasionally after a late operation. I left the main building shortly after twelve. I intended driving out by the Winchester Road gate. I have my own key. However, it was a wild night, as you probably noticed, and I discovered that there was an elm down over the path. I was lucky not to drive into it. I got out of the car and knotted my white silk scarf round one of the branches to warn anyone else who might be driving that way. It wasn't likely that anyone would, but the tree was an obvious danger and there was no chance of getting it moved before daylight. I reversed the car and left by the main entrance, reporting the fallen tree to the gate porter on my way out."

"Did you notice the time then?"

"I didn't. He may have done. But, at a guess, it was probably about twelve fifteen, maybe later. I wasted a bit of time at the tree."

"You would have had to drive past Nightingale House to reach the back gate. You didn't go in?"

"I had no reason to go in and I didn't go in, either to poison Nurse Fallon or for any other reason."

"And you saw no one in the grounds?"

"After midnight and in the middle of a storm? No, I saw no one."

Dalgliesh switched his questioning.

"You saw Nurse Pearce die, of course. I suppose there was never a real chance of saving her?"

"Never, I should say. I took pretty vigorous measures, but it isn't easy when you don't know what you're treating."

"But you knew it was poison?"

"Pretty soon. Yes. But I didn't know what. Not that it would have made any difference. You've seen the post-mortem report. You knew what that stuff did to her."

Dalgliesh asked: "You were in Nightingale House from eight o'clock onwards on the morning that she died?"

"You know perfectly well that I was if, as I assume, you've taken the trouble to read my original statement. I arrived in Nightingale House shortly after eight. My contract here is for six notional half-days a week; I'm in the hospital all day on Monday, Thursday and Friday; but it's not uncommon for me to be called in to operate on an emergency, particularly if it's a private patient, and I occasionally do a Saturday morning session in the theatre if the lists are long. I'd been called out shortly after eleven o'clock on Sunday night for an emergency appendicectomy—one of my private patients—and it was convenient to spend the night in the medical officers' quarters."

"Which are where?"

"In that deplorably designed new building near the out-patients' department. They serve breakfast at the ungodly hour of seven thirty."

"You were here rather early surely. The demonstration wasn't due to begin until nine."

"I wasn't here merely for the demonstration, Superintendent. You're really rather ignorant of hospitals, aren't you? The Senior Consultant Surgeon doesn't normally attend nurse training sessions unless he's actually lecturing the students. I only attended on January 12th because the G.N.C. Inspector was to be there and I'm Vice-Chairman of the Nurse Education Committee. It was a courtesy to Miss Beale to be here to meet her. I came in early because I wanted to work on some clinical notes which I had left in Sister Rolfe's office after a previous lecture. I also wanted to have a chat with Matron before the inspection began and to be sure that I was there in time to receive Miss Beale. I went up to Matron's flat at eight thirty-five and found her finishing breakfast. And, if you're thinking that I could have put the corrosive in the milk bottle any time between eight and eight thirty-five, you're perfectly right. As it happens, I didn't."

He looked at his watch.

"And now if there's nothing else you need to ask I must get my lunch. I've another out-patients' session this afternoon and time's pressing. If it's really necessary, I can probably give you a few more minutes before I leave but I hope it won't be. I've already signed one statement about Pearce's death and I've nothing to add or to alter. I didn't see Fallon yesterday. I didn't even know she was discharged from the sick-bay. She wasn't carrying my child, and even if she had been, I shouldn't have been foolish enough to kill her. Incidentally, what I told you about our previous relationship was naturally in confidence."

He looked across meaningly at Sergeant Masterson.

"Not that I care whether it's made public. But, after all, the girl is dead. We may as well try to protect her reputation."

Dalgliesh found it difficult to believe that Mr. Courtney-Briggs was interested in anyone's reputation but his own. But, gravely, he gave the necessary assurance. He saw the surgeon leave without regret. An egotistical bastard whom it was agreeable, if childish, to provoke. But a murderer? He had the hubris, the nerve and the egotism of a killer. More to the point, he had had the opportunity. And the motive? Hadn't it been a little disingenuous of him to have confessed so readily to his relationship with Josephine Fallon? Admittedly he couldn't have hoped to keep his secret for long; a hospital was hardly the most discreet of institutions. Had he been making a virtue of necessity, ensuring that Dalgliesh heard the version of the affair before the inevitable gossip reached his ears? Or had it been merely the candour of conceit, the sexual vanity of a man who wouldn't trouble to conceal any exploit which proclaimed his attraction and virility?

Putting his papers together, Dalgliesh became aware that he was hungry. He had made an early start to the day and it had been a long morning. It was time to turn his mind from Stephen Courtney-Briggs and for him and Masterson to think about luncheon.

Chapter Five

Table Talk

I

The resident Sisters and students from Nightingale House took only their breakfast and afternoon tea in the dining-room at the school. For their main midday and evening meal they joined the rest of the staff in the hospital cafeteria where all but the consultants ate in institutionalized and noisy proximity. The food was invariably nourishing, adequately cooked, and as varied as was compatible with the need to satisfy the differing tastes of several hundred people, avoid outraging their religious or dietary susceptibilities, and keep within the catering officer's budget. The principles governing the menu planning were invariable. Liver and kidneys were never served on the days when the urinary surgeon operated, and the nurses were not faced with the same menu as that which they had just served to the patients.

The cafeteria system had been introduced at the John Carpendar hospital against strong opposition from all grades of staff. Eight years ago there had been separate dining-rooms for the Sisters and nurses, one for the administrative and lay professional staff, and a canteen for the porters and artisans. The arrangements had suited everyone as making a proper distinction between grades and ensuring that people are in reasonable quietness and in the company of those with whom they preferred to spend their lunch break. But now only the senior medical staff enjoyed the peace and privacy of their own dining-room. This privilege, jealously defended, was under perpetual attack from Ministry auditors, Government catering advisers and work study experts who, armed with costing statistics, had no difficulty in proving that the system was uneconomical. But so far the doctors had won. Their strongest argument was their need to discuss the patients in privacy. This suggestion that they never stopped working, even for meals, was greeted with some scepticism but was difficult to refute. The need to keep the patients' affairs confidential touched on that area of patient-doctor relationship which the doctors were always quick to exploit. Before this mystique even the Treasury auditors were powerless to prevail. Furthermore, they had had the support of Matron. Miss Taylor had made it known that she considered it eminently reasonable that the senior medical staff should continue to have their own dining-room. And Miss Taylor's influence over the Chairman of the Hospital Management Committee was so obvious and of such long standing that it had almost ceased to excite comment. Sir Marcus Cohen was a wealthy and personable widower and the only surprise now was that he and Matron hadn't married. This, it was generally accepted, was either because Sir Marcus, an acknowledged leader of the country's Jewish community, chose not to marry outside his faith or because Miss Taylor, wedded to her vocation, chose not to marry at all.

But the extent of Miss Taylor's influence over the Chairman and thus over the Hospital Management Committee was beyond speculation. It was known to be particularly irritating to Mr. Courtney-Briggs since it considerably diminished his own. But in the matter of the consultants' dining-room it has been exercised in his favour and had proved decisive.

But if the rest of the staff had been forced into proximity they had not been forced into intimacy. The hierarchy was still apparent. The immense dining-room had been divided into smaller dining areas separated from each other by screens of lattice work and troughs of plants, and in each of these alcoves the atmosphere of a private dining-room was re-created.

Sister Rolfe helped herself to plaice and chips, carried her tray to the table which, for the past eight years, she had shared with Sister Brumfett and Sister Gearing, and looked around at the denizens of this strange world. In the alcove nearest the door were the laboratory technicians in their stained overalls, noisily animated. Next to them was old Fleming, the out-patient pharmacist, rolling bread pellets like pills in his nicotine-stained fingers. At the next table were four of the medical stenographers in their blue working overalls. Miss Wright, the senior secretary, who had been at the John Carpendar for twenty years, was eating with furtive speed as she always did, avid to get back to her typewriter. Behind the adjacent screen was a little clutch of the lay professional staff—Miss Bunyon the head radiographer, Mrs. Nethern, the head medical social worker and two of the physiotherapists, carefully preserving their status by an air of calm unhurried efficiency, an apparent total disinterest in the food they were eating and the choice of a table as far removed as possible from that of the junior clerical staff.

And what were they all thinking about? Fallon probably. There couldn't be anyone in the hospital from the consultants to the ward maids who didn't know by now that a second Nightingale student had died in mysterious circumstances and that Scotland Yard had been called in. Fallon's death was probably the subject of gossip at most of the tables this morning. But it didn't prevent people from eating their lunch or from getting on with their job. There was so much to do; there were so many other pressing concerns; there was even so much fresh gossip. It wasn't just that life had to go on; in hospital that cliché had particular relevance. Life did go on, carried forward by the imperative momentum of birth and death. New booked admissions came in; ambulances daily disgorged the emergencies; operation lists were posted; the dead were laid out and the healed discharged. Death, even sudden and unexpected death, was more familiar to these young fresh-faced students than it was to even the most experienced senior detective. And there was a limit to its power to shock. You either came to terms with death in your first year, or you gave up being a nurse. But murder? That was different. Even in this violent world, murder still held its macabre and primitive power to shock. But how many people in Nightingale House really believed that Pearce and Fallon had been murdered? It would take more than the presence of the Yard's wonder boy and his retinue to give credence to such an extraordinary idea. There were too many other possible explanations, all of them simpler and more believable than murder. Dalgliesh might believe as he chose; proving it would be another matter.

Sister Rolfe bent her head and began unenthusiastically to dissect her plaice. She felt no particular hunger. The strong smell of food was heavy on the air, stifling appetite. The noise of the cafeteria beat against her ears. It was ceaseless and inescapable, a confused continuum of discord in which individual sounds were scarcely distinguishable.

Next to her, her cloak folded neatly at the back of her chair and the shapeless tapestry bag which accompanied her everywhere dumped at her feet, Sister Brumfett was eating steamed cod and parsley sauce with belligerent intensity as if she resented the need to eat and was venting her irritation on the food. Sister Brumfett invariably chose steamed fish; and Sister Rolfe felt suddenly that she couldn't face another lunch hour of watching Brumfett eat cod.

She reminded herself that there was no reason why she should. There was nothing to prevent her sitting somewhere else, nothing except this petrification of the will which made the simple act of carrying her tray three feet to a different table seem impossibly cataclysmic and irrevocable. On her left, Sister Gearing toyed with her braised beef, and chopped her wedge of cabbage into neat squares. When she actually began to eat she would shove the food in avidly like a greedy schoolgirl. But always there were these finicky and salivatory preliminaries. Sister Rolfe wondered how many times she had resisted the urge to say, "For God's sake Gearing, stop messing about and eat it!" One day, no doubt, she would say it. And another middle-aged and unlikeable Sister would be pronounced "getting very difficult. It's probably her age".

She had considered living out of the hospital. It was permissible and she could afford it. The purchase of a flat or small house would be the best investment for her retirement. But Julia Pardoe had disposed of that idea in a few half-interested, destructive comments dropped like cold pebbles into the deep pool of her hopes and plans. Sister Rolfe could still hear that high, childish voice.

"Live out. Why should you want to do that? We shouldn't see so much of each other."

"But we should, Julia. And in much greater privacy and without all this risk and deceit. It would be a comfortable and agreeable little house. You'd like it."

"It wouldn't be as easy as slipping upstairs to see you when I feel like it."

When she felt like it? Felt like what? Sister Rolfe had desperately fought off the question she never dared to let herself ask.

She knew the nature of her dilemma. It wasn't, after all, peculiar to herself. In any relationship there was one who loved and one who permitted himself or herself to be loved. This was merely to state the brutal economics of desire; from each according to his ability, to each according to his need. But was it selfish or presumptuous to hope that the one who took knew the value of the gift; that she wasn't wasting love on a promiscuous and perfidious little cheat who took her pleasure wherever she chose to find it? She had said:

"You could probably come twice or three times a week, perhaps more often. I wouldn't move far."

"Oh, I don't see how I could manage that. I don't see why you want the work and bother of a house. You're all right here."

Sister Rolfe thought: "But I'm not all right here. This place is souring me. It isn't only the long-stay patients who become institutionalized. It's happening to me. I dislike and despise most of the people I'm required to work with. Even the job is losing its hold. The students get more stupid and worse educated with every intake. I'm not even sure any more of the value of what I'm supposed to be doing."

There was a crash near the counter. One of the maids had dropped a tray of used crockery. Looking instinctively across, Sister Rolfe saw that the detective had just come in and taken up his tray at the end of the line. She watched the tall figure, disregarded by the chattering queue of nurses, as he began to move slowly down the line between a white-coated houseman and a pupil midwife, helping himself to roll and butter, waiting for the girl to hand out his choice of main course. She was surprised to see him there. It had never occurred to her that he would eat in the hospital dining-hall or that he would be on his own. Her eyes followed him as he reached the end of the line, handed over his meal ticket and turned to look for a vacant seat. He seemed utterly at ease and almost oblivious of the alien world around him. She thought that he was probably a man who could never imagine himself at a disadvantage in any company since he was secure in his private world, possessed of that core of inner self-esteem which is the basis of happiness. She wondered what kind of a world his was, then bent her head to her plate irritated at this unusual interest he aroused in her. Probably he would be thought handsome by most women, with that lean bony face, at once arrogant and sensitive. It was probably one of his professional assets, and being a man he would make the most of it. No doubt it was one of the reasons why he had been given this case. If dull Bill Bailey could make nothing of it, let the Yard's wonder boy take over. With a house full of women and three middle-aged spinsters as his chief suspects, no doubt he fancied his chances. Well, good luck to him!

But she was not the only one at the table to notice his arrival. She felt rather than saw Sister Gearing stiffen and a second later heard her say:

"Well, well. The handsome sleuth! He'd better feed with us or he may find himself in a gaggle of students. Someone should have told the poor man how the system works."

And now, thought Sister Rolfe, she'll give him one of her street corner come-hither looks and we shall be burdened with him for the rest of the meal. The look was given and the invitation not refused. Dalgliesh, carrying his tray nonchalantly and apparently completely at ease, threaded his way across the room and came up to their table. Sister Gearing said:

"What have you done with that handsome sergeant of yours? I thought policemen went about in pairs like nuns."

"My handsome sergeant is studying reports and lunching on sandwiches and beer in the office while I enjoy the fruits of seniority with you. Is this chair taken?"

Sister Gearing moved her own chair closer to Sister Brumfett and smiled up at him:

"It is now."

II

Dalgliesh sat down, well aware that Sister Gearing wanted him, that Sister Rolfe didn't, and that Sister Brumfett, who had acknowledged his arrival with a brief nod, didn't care whether he joined them or not. Sister Rolfe looked across at him unsmilingly and said to Sister Gearing:

"Don't imagine Mr. Dalgliesh is sharing our table for the sake of your *beaux yeux*. The Superintendent plans to take in information with his braised beef."

Sister Gearing giggled: "My dear, it's no use warning me! I couldn't keep a thing to myself if a really attractive man set his mind to wangle it out of me. It would be quite useless for me to commit a murder. I haven't the brain for it. Not that I think for one moment that anyone has—committed murder I mean. Anyway, let's leave the grisly subject during lunch. I've had my grilling, haven't I, Superintendent?"

Dalgliesh disposed his cutlery around the plate of braised beef and tilting back his chair to save himself the trouble of rising, added his used tray to the stack on the nearby stand. He said:

"People here seem to be taking Nurse Fallon's death calmly enough."

Sister Rolfe shrugged: "Did you expect them to be wearing black arm bands, talking in whispers, and refusing their lunch? The job goes on. Anyway, only a few will have known her personally, and still fewer knew Pearce."

"Or liked her apparently," said Dalgliesh.

"No, I don't think they did on the whole. She was too self-righteous, too religious."

"If you can call it religious," said Sister Gearing.

"It wasn't my idea of religion. *Nil nisi* and all that, but the girl was just a prig. She always seemed to be a damn sight more concerned with other people's shortcomings than she was with her own. That's why the other kids didn't like her. They respect genuine religious conviction. Most people do, I find. But they didn't like being spied on."

"Did she spy on them?" asked Dalgliesh.

Sister Gearing seemed half to regret what she had said.

"Perhaps that's putting it a bit strongly. But if anything went wrong in the set you can bet Nurse Pearce knew all about it. And she usually managed to bring it to the notice of authority. Always with the best motives, no doubt."

Sister Rolfe said drily: "She had an unfortunate habit of interfering with other people for their own good. It doesn't make for popularity."

Sister Gearing pushed her plate to one side, drew a bowl of plums and custard towards her and began to extract the stones from the fruit as carefully as if it were a surgical operation. She said:

"She wasn't a bad nurse, though. You could rely on Pearce. And the patients seemed to like her. I suppose they found that holier than thou attitude reassuring."

Sister Brumfett looked up from her plate and spoke for the first time.

"You're not in a position to give an opinion on whether she was a good nurse. Nor is Rolfe. You only see the girls in the training school. I see them on the wards."

"I see them on the wards too. I'm the clinical instructor remember. It's my job to teach them on the ward."

Sister Brumfett was unrepentant.

"Any student teaching that's done on my ward is done by me, as you know very well. Other ward Sisters can welcome the clinical instructor if they like. But on the private ward I do the teaching. And I prefer it that way when I see some of the extraordinary ideas you seem to put into their heads. And, by the way, I happen to know—Pearce told me, as a matter of fact—that you visited my ward when I was off duty on 7th January and conducted a teaching session. In future, please consult me before using my patients as clinical material."

Sister Gearing flushed. She tried to laugh but her amusement sounded artificial. She glanced across at Sister Rolfe as if enlisting her aid but Sister Rolfe kept her eyes firmly on her plate. Then, belligerently and rather like a child determined to have the last word, she said with apparent irrelevance:

"Something happened to upset Pearce while she was on your ward."

Sister Brumfett's sharp little eyes glared up at her.

"On my ward? Nothing upset her on my ward!"

The sturdy assertion conveyed unmistakedly that no nurse worthy of the name could be upset by anything that happened on the private ward; that upsetting things just weren't permitted when Sister Brumfett was in charge.

Sister Gearing shrugged.

"Well, something upset her. It could have been something totally unconnected with the hospital, I suppose, but one never quite believes that poor Pearce had any real life outside these walls. It was the Wednesday of the week before this block went into school. I visited the chapel just after five o'clock to do the flowers—that's how I remember which day it was—and she was sitting there alone. Not kneeling or praying, just sitting. Well, I did what I had to do and then went out without speaking to her. After all, the chapel's open for rest and meditation and if one of the students wants to meditate that's all right by me. But when I went back nearly three hours later because I'd left my scissors in the sacristy she was still there, sitting perfectly still and in the same seat. Well, meditation's all very well, but four hours is a bit excessive. I don't think that the kid could have had any supper. She looked pretty pale too, so I went up to her and asked her if she was all right, if there was anything I could do for her. She didn't even look at me as she replied. She said: 'No thank you, Sister. There was something troubling me which I had to think over very carefully. I did come here for help but not from you.'"

For the first time during the meal Sister Rolfe sounded amused. She said: "Caustic little beast! Meaning, I suppose, that she'd come to consult a higher power than the clinical instructor."

"Meaning mind your own business. So I did."

Sister Brumfett said, as if feeling that her colleague's presence at a place of worship needed some explanation:

"Sister Gearing is very good at arranging flowers. That's why Matron asked her to look after the chapel. She sees to the flowers every Wednesday and Saturday. And she does very charming arrangements for the Annual Sisters' Dinner." Sister Gearing stared at her for a second and then laughed.

"Oh, little Mavis isn't just a pretty face. But thanks for the compliment."

A silence fell. Dalglicsh addressed himself to his braised beef. He wasn't disconcerted by the lack of conversation and had no intention of helping them out by introducing a fresh subject. But Sister Gearing seemed to feel that silence was reprehensible in the presence of a stranger. She said brightly:

"I see from the minutes that the Hospital Management Committee have agreed to introduce the Salmon Committee proposals. Better late than never. I suppose that means that Matron will be head of the nursing services over all the hospitals in the group. Chief Nursing Officer! It'll be a big thing for her, but I wonder how C.B. will take it. If he had his way, Matron would be given less authority not more. She's a big enough thorn in his flesh as it is."

Sister Brumfett said: "It's time something was done to wake up the psychiatric hospital and the geriatric units. But I don't know why they want to change the title. If Matron was good enough for Florence Nightingale it's good enough for Mary Taylor. I don't suppose she particularly wants to be called Chief Nursing Officer. It sounds like an army rank. Ridiculous."

Sister Rolfe shrugged her thin shoulders.

"Don't expect me to get enthusiastic about the Salmon Report. I'm beginning to wonder what's happening to nursing. Every report and recommendation seems to take us further away from the bedside. We have dieticians to see to the feeding, physiotherapists to exercise the patients, medical social workers to listen to their troubles, ward orderlies to make the beds, laboratory technicians to take blood, ward receptionists to arrange the flowers and interview the relatives, operating theatre technicians to hand the surgeon the instruments. If we're not careful nursing will become a residual skill, the job which is left when all the technicians have had their turn. And now we have the Salmon Report with all its talk of first, second and third tiers of management. Management for what? There's too much technical jargon. Ask yourself what is the function of the nurse today. What exactly are we trying to teach these girls?"

Sister Brumfett said: "To obey orders implicitly and be loyal to their superiors. Obedience and loyalty. Teach the students those and you've got a good nurse."

She sliced a potato in two with such viciousness that the knife rasped the plate. Sister Gearing laughed.

"You're twenty years out of date, Brumfett. That was good enough for our generation, but these kids ask whether the orders are reasonable before they start obeying and what their superiors have done to deserve their respect. A good thing too on the whole. How on earth do you expect to attract intelligent girls into nursing if you treat them like morons? We ought to encourage them to question established procedures, even to answer back occasionally."

Sister Brumfett looked as if she, for one, would willingly dispense with intelligence if its manifestations were so disagreeable.

"Intelligence isn't the only thing. That's the trouble nowadays. People think it is."

Sister Rolfe said: "Give me an intelligent girl and I'll make a good nurse of her whether she thinks she has a vocation or not. You can have the stupid ones. They may minister to your ego but they'll never make good professional women." She looked at Sister Brumfett as she spoke and the undertone of contempt was unmistakable. Dalgliesh dropped his eyes to his plate and pretended more interest than he could feel in the careful separation of meat from fat and gristle. Sister Brumfett reacted predictably:

"Professional women! We're talking about nurses. A good nurse thinks of herself as a nurse first and last. Of course she's a professional woman! I thought we'd all accepted that by now. But there's too much thinking and talking of status nowadays. The important thing is to get on with the job."

"But what job exactly? Isn't that precisely what we're asking ourselves?"

"You may be. I'm perfectly clear what I'm doing. Which, at the moment, is coping with a very sick ward."

She pushed her plate to one side, flicked her cloak around her shoulders with brisk expertise, gave them a valedictory nod which was as much a warning as a good-bye, and strutted out of the dining-room with her brisk ploughman's waddle, the tapestry bag swinging at her side. Sister Gearing laughed and watched her go.

"Poor old Brum! According to her, she's always got a very sick ward."

Sister Rolfe said drily: "She invariably has."

III

They finished the meal almost in silence. Then Sister Gearing left, first murmuring something about a clinical teaching session on the E.N.T. ward. Dalgliesh found himself walking back to Nightingale House with Sister Rolfe. They left the dining-room together and he retrieved his coat from the rack. They then passed down a long corridor and through the out-patients' department. It had obviously only recently been opened and the furniture and decoration were still bright and new. The large waiting-hall with its groups of formica-topped tables and easy chairs, its troughs of pot plants and unremarkable pictures was cheerful enough, but Dalgliesh had no wish to linger. He had the healthy man's dislike and disgust of hospitals, founded partly on fear and partly on repugnance, and he found this atmosphere of determined cheerfulness and spurious normality unconvincing and frightening. The smell of disinfectant, which to Miss Beale was the elixir of life, infected him with the gloomier intimations of mortality. He did not think that he feared death. He had come close to it once or twice in his career and it had not unduly dismayed him. But he did grievously fear old age, mortal illness and disablement. He dreaded the loss of independence, the indignities of senility, the yielding up of privacy, the abomination of pain, the glimpses of patient compassion in the faces of friends who knew that their indulgences would not be claimed for long. These things might have to be faced in time unless death took him quickly and easily. Well, he would face them. He was not arrogant enough to suppose himself secure from the lot of other men. But in the meantime, he preferred not to be reminded.

The out-patients' department was next to the casualty department entrance and as they passed it a stretcher was wheeled in. The patient was an emaciated old man; his moist lips spewed feebly above the rim of a vomit bowl, his immense eyes rolled uncomprehendingly in the skull-like head. Dalgliesh became aware that Sister Rolfe was looking at him. He turned his head in time to catch her glance of speculation and, he thought, contempt.

"You don't like this place, do you?" she asked.

"I'm not very happy in it, certainly."

"Neither am I at present, but I suspect for very different reasons."

They walked on for a minute in silence. Then Dalgliesh asked if Leonard Morris lunched in the staff dining-room when he was in the hospital.

"Not often. I believe he brings sandwiches and eats them in the pharmacy office. He prefers his own company."

"Or that of Sister Gearing?"

She laughed contemptuously.

"Oh, you've got on to that have you? But of course! She was entertaining him last night, I hear. Either the food or the subsequent activity seems to have been rather more than the little man could take. What thorough little scavengers the police are! It must be a strange job, sniffing around for evil like a dog round trees."

"Isn't evil a strong word for Leonard Morris's sexual preoccupations?"

"Of course. I was just being clever. But I shouldn't let the Morris-Gearing affair worry you. It's been hiccuping on for so long now that it's become almost respectable. It isn't even good for a gossip. She's the kind of woman who must have someone in tow, and he likes someone to confide in about the awfulness of his family and the beastliness of the hospital medical staff. They don't exactly take him at his own evaluation as an equal professional man. He's got four children, by the way. I imagine that if his wife decided to divorce him and he and Gearing were free to marry nothing would disconcert them more. Gearing would like a husband no doubt, but I don't think she's cast poor little Morris for the role. It's more likely . . ."

She broke off. Dalgliesh asked:

"You think she has a more eligible candidate in mind?"

"Why not try asking her? She doesn't confide in me."

"But you are responsible for her work? The clinical instructor comes under the senior nurse tutor?"

"I'm responsible for her work not her morals."

They had reached the far door of the casualty department and as Sister Rolfe put out her hand to push it open Mr. Courtney-Briggs swept in. He was followed by a half-dozen chattering junior staff, white-coated and with stethoscopes slung round their necks. The two on each side of him were nodding in deferential attention as the great man spoke. Dalgliesh thought that he had the conceit, the patina of vulgarity and the slightly coarse *savoir-faire* which he associated with one type of successful professional man. As if reading his thoughts, Miss Rolfe said:

"They're not all alike, you know. Take Mr. Molravey, our ophthalmic surgeon. He reminds me of a dormouse. Every Tuesday morning he patters in and stands for five hours in the theatre without speaking an unnecessary word, whiskers twitching and picking away with fastidious little paws at a succession of patients' eyes. Then he thanks everyone formally down to the most junior theatre nurse, peels off his gloves and patters away again to play with his collection of butterflies."

"A modest little man, in fact."

She turned towards him and he detected again in her eyes that uncomfortable elliptical flicker of contempt.

"Oh no! Not modest! He gives a different performance, that's all. Mr. Molravey is just as convinced as is Mr. Courtney-Briggs that he's a very remarkable surgeon. They are both vain in a professional sense. Vanity, Mr. Dalgliesh, is a surgeon's besetting sin as subservience is a nurse's. I've never yet met a successful surgeon who wasn't convinced that he ranked only one degree lower than Almighty God. They're all infected with hubris." She paused:

"Isn't that supposed to be true also of murderers?"

"Of one type of murderer. You must remember that murder is a highly individual crime."

"Is it? I should have thought that the motives and the means would be monotonously familiar to you. But you, of course, are the expert."

Dalgliesh said: "You have little respect for men apparently, Sister?"

"A great deal of respect. I just don't happen to like them. But you have to respect a sex that has brought selfishness to such an art. That's what gives you your strength, this ability to devote yourselves entirely to your own interest."

Dalgliesh said, a little maliciously, that he was surprised that Miss Rolfe, since she obviously resented the subservience of her job, hadn't chosen a more masculine occupation. Medicine perhaps? She laughed bitterly.

"I wanted to do medicine but I had a father who didn't believe in educating women. I'm forty-six, remember. When I was at school we didn't have universal free grammar school education. Father earned too much for me to get a free place, so he had to pay. He stopped paying as soon as he decently could, when I was sixteen."

Dalgliesh found nothing appropriate to say. The confidence surprised him. She was hardly the woman, he would have thought, to expose a personal grievance to a stranger and he didn't flatter himself that she found him sympathetic. She would find no man sympathetic. The outburst was probably a spontaneous release of pent up bitterness, but whether against her father, men in general or the limitations and subservience of her job it was hard to say.

They had left the hospital now and were passing along the narrow path which led to Nightingale House. Neither of them spoke another word until the house was reached. Sister Rolfe wrapped her long cloak tightly around her and pulled up her hood as if it could protect her from more than the bite of the wind. Dalgliesh was immersed in his private thoughts. And thus, with the width of the path between them, they paced together in silence under the trees.

IV

In the office Detective Sergeant Masterson was typing a report. Dalgliesh said:

"Immediately before she came into the school, Nurse Pearce was working on the private ward under Sister Brumfett. I want to know if anything significant happened there. And I want a detailed account of her last week's duty and an hour-by-hour account of what she did on her last day. Find out who the other nursing staff were, what her duties were, when she was off duty, how she appeared to the other staff. I want the names of the patients who were on the ward while she was nursing there and what happened to them. Your best plan is to talk to the other nurses and to work from the nursing reports. They're bound to keep a book which is written up daily."

"Shall I get it from Matron?"

"No. Ask Sister Brumfett for it. We deal directly with her, and for God's sake be tactful. Have you those reports ready yet?"

"Yes, sir. They've been typed. Do you want to read them now?"

"No. Tell me if there's anything I ought to know. I'll look at them tonight. I suppose it's too much to expect that any of our suspects has a police record?"

"If they have, sir, it isn't noted on the personal dossiers. There's remarkable little information in most of them. Julia Pardoe was expelled from school, though. She seems to be the only delinquent among them."

"Good God! What for?"

"Her dossier doesn't say. Apparently it was something to do with a visiting maths master. Her headmistress felt it right to mention it when she sent Matron a reference before the girl started here. It isn't very specific. She writes that Julia was more sinned against than sinning and that she hoped the hospital would give her the chance of training for the only career she has ever shown any interest in, or signs of being suited for."

"A nice double edged comment. So that's why the London teaching hospitals wouldn't take her. I thought Sister Rolfe was being a little disingenuous about the reasons. Anything about the others? Any previous connections between them?"

"Matron and Sister Brumfett trained together in the north at Nethercastle Royal Infirmary, did their midwifery training at the Municipal Maternity Hospital there and came here fifteen years ago, both as ward Sisters. Mr. Courtney-Briggs was in Cairo during 1946–7 and so was Sister Gearing. He was a major in the R.A.M.C. and she was a nursing sister in the Q.A.R.N.S. There's no suggestion that they knew each other there."

"If they did, you'd hardly expect to find the fact recorded on their personal records. But they probably did. Cairo in '46 was a chummy place, so my army friends tell me. I wonder if Miss Taylor served in the Q.A.R.N.S. That's an army nursing service cap which she wears."

"If she did, sir, it isn't on her dossier. The earliest document is her reference from her training school when she came here as a Sister. They thought very highly of her at Nethercastle."

"They think very highly of her here. Have you checked on Courtney-Briggs?"

"Yes, sir. The lodge porter makes a note of every car in and out after midnight. Mr. Courtney-Briggs left at twelve thirty-two a.m."

"Later than he led us to believe. I want a check on his schedule. The precise time he finished the operation will be in the operating theatre book. The junior doctor assisting him will probably know when he left—Mr. Courtney-Briggs is the kind of man who gets escorted to his car. Then drive over the route and time him. They will have moved the tree by now but it should be possible to see where it came down. He can't have wasted more than a few minutes at the most tying on his scarf. Find out what happened to that. He'd hardly lie about something so easily disproved, but he's arrogant enough to think he can get away with anything, including murder."

"Constable Greeson can do the checking, sir. He likes these reconstruction jobs."

"Tell him to curb his urge for verisimilitude. There's no need for him to don an operating gown and go into the theatre. Not that they'd let him. Is there any news yet from Sir Miles or the lab?"

"No, sir, but we've got the name and address of the man Nurse Fallon spent that week in the Isle of Wight with. He's a G.P.O. night telephonist and lives in North Kensington. The local people got on to them almost at once. Fallon made it very easy for them. She booked in her own name and they had two single rooms."

"She was a woman who valued her privacy. Still, she hardly got pregnant by staying in her own room. I'll see the man tomorrow morning after I've visited Miss Fallon's solicitor. Is Leonard Morris in the hospital yet, do you know?"

"Not yet, sir. I checked at the pharmacy that he telephoned this morning and said he wasn't well. Apparently he suffers from a duodenal ulcer. They assume that it's playing him up again."

"It will play him up a great deal worse if he doesn't come back soon and get the interview over. I don't want to embarrass him by visiting his house, but we can't wait indefinitely to get Sister Gearing's story verified. Both these murders, if they were murders, hinge on the question of timing. We must know everyone's movements, if possible, to the minute. Time is crucial."

Masterson said: "That's what surprises me about the poisoned drip. The carbolic couldn't have been added to the milk without a great deal of care, particularly in replacing the bottle seal and making sure that the concentration was right and that the stuff had the texture and colour of milk. It couldn't have been done in a hurry."

"I've no doubt a great deal of care and time were taken. But I think I know how it was done."

He described his theory. Sergeant Masterson, cross with himself for having missed the obvious, said:

"Of course. It must have been done that way."

"Not must, Sergeant. It was probably done that way."

But Sergeant Masterson had seen an objection and voiced it.

Dalgliesh replied: "But that wouldn't apply to a woman. A woman could do it easily and one woman in particular. But I admit it would be more difficult for a man."

"So the assumption is that the milk was doctored by a woman?"

"The probability is that both girls were murdered by a woman. But it's still only a probability. Have you heard yet whether Nurse Dakers is well enough to be interviewed? Dr. Snelling was supposed to be seeing her this morning."

"Matron rang just before lunch to say that the girl is still asleep, but that she'll probably be fit enough once she wakes up. She's under sedation, so God knows when that'll be. Shall I take a look at her while I'm in the private wing?"

"No. I'll see her later. But you might check on this story that Fallon returned to Nightingale House on the morning of 12th January. Someone might have seen her leave. And where were her clothes kept while she was warded? Could anyone have got hold of them and impersonated her? It seems unlikely but it ought to be checked."

"Inspector Bailey did check, sir. No one saw Fallon leave but they admit that she could have got out of the ward undetected. They were very busy and she had a private room. If it were found empty they would probably have assumed that she'd gone to the bathroom. Her clothes were hung in the wardrobe in her room. Anyone who had a right to be in the ward could have got at them, provided, of course, that Fallon was asleep or out of the room. But no one thinks it likely that anyone did."

"Nor do I. I think I know why Fallon came back to Nightingale House. Nurse Goodale told us that Fallon had received the pregnancy confirmation only two days before she went sick. It's possible that she didn't destroy it. If so, it's the one possession in her room which she wouldn't want to leave for someone else to find. It certainly isn't among her papers. My guess is that she came back to retrieve it, tore it up, and flushed it down the lavatory."

"Couldn't she have telephoned Nurse Goodale and asked her to destroy it?"

"Not without exciting suspicion. She couldn't be sure that she'd get Goodale herself when she rang and she wouldn't want to give anyone else a message. This insistence to speak to one particular nurse and the reluctance to accept help from anyone else would look rather odd. But it's no more than a theory. Is the search of Nightingale House completed?"

"Yes, sir. They've found nothing. No trace of poison and no container. Most of the rooms contain bottles of aspirin and Sister Gearing, Sister Brumfett and Miss Taylor all have a small supply of sleeping tablets. But surely Fallon didn't die of hypnotic or soporific poisoning?"

"No. It was quicker than that. We shall just have to possess ourselves in patience until we get the laboratory report."

V

At two thirty-four p.m. precisely, in the largest and most luxurious of the private rooms, Sister Brumfett lost a patient. She always thought of death in that way. The patient was lost; the battle was over; she, Sister Brumfett, had been personally defeated.

The fact that so many of her battles were foredoomed to failure, that the enemy even if repulsed in the present skirmish, was always assured of final victory, never mitigated her sense of failure. Patients did not come into Sister Brumfett's ward to die; they came in to get better, and with Sister's indomitable will to fortify them, they usually did get better, often to their own surprise and occasionally despite their own wishes.

She had hardly expected to win this particular battle but it was only when Mr. Courtney-Briggs lifted his hand to turn off the blood drip that she accepted failure. The patient had certainly fought well; a difficult patient, a demanding patient, but a good fighter. He had been a wealthy business man whose meticulous plans for his future certainly didn't include dying at forty-two. She recalled the look of wild surprise, almost of outrage, with which he had greeted the realization that death was something neither he nor his accountant could fix. Sister Brumfett had seen too much of his young widow on that lady's daily visits to suppose that she would suffer much grief or inconvenience. The patient was the only one who would have been furious at the failure of Mr. Courtney-Briggs's heroic and expensive efforts to save him, and happily for the surgeon, the patient was the one person in no position to demand either explanation or excuse.

Mr. Courtney-Briggs would see the widow and offer her his customary carefully phrased condolences, his assurance that everything humanly possible had been done. In this case, the size of the bill would be a guarantee of that and a powerful antidote, no doubt, to the inevitable guilt of bereavement. Courtney-Briggs was really very good with the widows; and to do him justice, the poor as well as the rich received the consolation of his hand on their shoulder, of the stereotyped phrases of comfort and regret.

She drew the fold of the sheet up over the suddenly vacant face. Closing the dead eyes with practised fingers, she felt the eyeballs still warm under the wrinkled lids. She was conscious neither of grief nor anger. There was only, as always, this dragging weight of failure tugging like a physical load at the tired muscles of her stomach and back.

They turned away from the bed together. Glancing at the surgeon's face, Sister Brumfett was struck by his look of weariness. For the first time he, too, appeared threatened with failure and with age. It was, of course, unusual for a patient to die when he was there to see it happen. Still less frequently did they die on the operating table, even if the scramble from the theatre to the ward was sometimes a little undignified. But, unlike Sister Brumfett, Mr. Courtney-Briggs did not have to watch over his patients to the last gasp. All the same, she did not believe that this particular death had depressed him. It was, after all, not unexpected. He had nothing with which to reproach himself even if he had been given to self-criticism. She felt that he was stressed by some subtler worry, and she wondered whether it was something to do with Fallon's death. He's lost some of his bounce, thought Sister Brumfett. He looks suddenly ten years older.

He preceded her down the passage to her office. As they neared the ward kitchen there was the sound of voices. The door was open. A student nurse was setting a trolley with the afternoon tea trays. Sergeant Masterson was leaning against the sink and watching her with the air of a man completely at home. As the Sister and Mr. Courtney-Briggs appeared in the doorway the girl flushed, muttered a low "good afternoon, sir" and pushed her trolley past them into the corridor with clumsy haste. Sergeant Masterson gazed after her with tolerant condescension, then transferred his level gaze to the Sister. He appeared not to notice Mr. Courtney-Briggs.

"Good afternoon, Sister, could I have a word with you?"

Baulked of the initiative, Sister Brumfett said repressively:

"In my office if you please, Sergeant. That is where you should have waited in the first place. People do not wander in and out of my ward just as they please, and that includes the police."

Sergeant Masterson, unchastened, looked slightly gratified at this speech as if it confirmed something to his satisfaction. Sister Brumfett bustled into her office, tight-lipped and ready for battle. Rather to her surprise Mr. Courtney-Briggs followed.

Sergeant Masterson said: "I wonder, Sister, if I could see the ward report book covering the period when Nurse Pearce was on this ward? I'm particularly interested in her last week here."

Mr. Courtney-Briggs broke in roughly:

"Aren't they confidential medical records, Sister? Surely the police will have to apply for a subpoena before they can make you produce them?"

"Oh, I don't think so, sir." Sergeant Masterson's voice, quiet, almost too respectful, yet held a tinge of amusement which wasn't lost on his hearer. "Ward nursing records surely aren't medical documents in the proper sense. I merely want to see who was being nursed here during that period and whether anything happened which might be of interest to the Superintendent. It's been suggested that something occurred to upset Nurse Pearce while she was nursing on your ward. She went from here straight to the school, remember."

Sister Brumfett, mottled and shaking with an anger which left small room for fear, found her voice.

"Nothing happened on my ward. Nothing! It's all stupid, malicious gossip. If a nurse does her job properly and obeys orders there's no need for her to be upset. The Superintendent is here to investigate a murder not to interfere with my ward."

Mr. Courtney-Briggs broke in blandly:

"And even if she were—upset is the word I think you used, Sergeant—I don't see what relevance that has to her death."

Sergeant Masterson smiled at him as if humouring a wilfully obstinate child.

"Anything that happened to Nurse Pearce in the week immediately before she was killed may have relevance, sir. That's why I'm asking to see the ward report book."

As neither Sister Brumfett nor the surgeon made any move to comply, he added:

"It's only a matter of confirming information we already have. I know what she was doing on the ward during that week. I'm told she was devoting all her time to nursing one particular patient. A Mr. Martin Dettinger. 'Specializing' him, I think you call it. My information is that she seldom left his room while she was on duty here during the last week of her life."

So, thought Sister Brumfett, he had been gossiping with the student nurses. But of course! That was how the police worked. It was pointless to try to keep anything private from them. Everything, even the medical secrets of her ward, the nursing care of her own patients, would be nosed out by this impertinent young man and reported to his superior officer. There was nothing in the ward report book which he couldn't find out by more devious means; discover, magnify, misinterpret and use to make mischief. Inarticulate with anger and something close to panic she heard Mr. Courtney-Briggs's bland and reassuring voice.

"Then you'd better hand the book over, Sister. If the police insist on wasting their own time there's no need for us to encourage them to waste ours."

Without another word, Sister Brumfett went to her desk and, bending down, opened the deep right-hand drawer and took out a large, hard-backed book. Silently and without looking at him, she handed it to Sergeant Masterson. The Sergeant thanked her profusely and turned to Mr. Courtney-Briggs:

"And now, sir, if the patient's still with you, I'd like to have a word with Mr. Dettinger."

Mr. Courtney-Briggs made no attempt to keep the satisfaction out of his voice.

"I think that is likely to challenge even your ingenuity, Sergeant. Mr. Martin Dettinger died on the day Nurse Pearce left this ward. If I remember rightly, she was with him when he died. So both of them are safely out of reach of your inquisition. And now, if you'd be good enough to excuse us, Sister and I have work to do."

He held open the door and Sister Brumfett strutted out before him. Sergeant Masterson was left alone, holding the ward record book in his hand.

"Bloody bastard," he said aloud.

He stood for a moment, thinking. Then he went in search of the medical record department.

VI

Ten minutes later he was back in the office. Under his arm was the ward report book and a buff-coloured file, stamped with a warning in black capital letters that it was not to be handed to the patient, and bearing the name of the hospital and Martin Dettinger's medical record number. He placed the book on the table and handed the file to Dalgliesh.

"Thank you. You got it without trouble?"

"Yes, sir," said Masterson. He saw no reason to explain that the Medical Records Officer had been out of his department and that he had half persuaded, half bullied the junior clerk on duty into handing over the file on the grounds, which he didn't for a moment believe, that the rules about the confidentiality of medical records no longer applied when the patient was dead and that when a Superintendent of the Yard asked for a thing he was entitled to get it without fuss and without delay. They studied the file together. Dalgliesh said:

"Martin Dettinger. Aged forty-six. Gave his address as his London Club. C. of E. Divorced. Next-of-kin, Mrs. Louise Dettinger, 23 Saville Mansions, Marylebone. Mother. You had better see the lady, Masterson. Make an appointment for tomorrow evening. I shall need you here during the day while I'm in town. And take trouble with her. She must have visited her son pretty frequently when he was in hospital. Nurse Pearce was specializing him. The two women probably saw quite a lot of each other. Something happened to upset Pearce while she was working on the private ward during the last week of her life and I want to know what it was."

He turned back to the medical record.

"There's a lot of paper here. The poor chap seems to have had a stormy medical history. He suffered from colitis for the past ten years, and before that there's a record of long spells of undiagnosed ill health, perhaps a forerunner of the condition which killed him. He was in hospital for three periods during his army service, including a spell of two months in an army hospital in Cairo in 1947. He was invalided out of the army in 1952 and emigrated to South Africa. That doesn't seem to have done him much good. There are notes here from a hospital in Johannesburg. Courtney-Briggs wrote for them; he certainly takes trouble. His own notes are pretty copious. He took over the case a couple of years ago and seems to have been acting as a kind of general practitioner to Dettinger as well as his surgeon. The colitis became acute about a month ago, and Courtney-Briggs operated to remove a large part of the bowel on Friday, 2nd January. Dettinger survived the operation, although he was in a pretty bad state by then, and made some progress until the early morning of Monday, 5th January, when he relapsed. After that he was seldom conscious for long, and he died at five thirty p.m. on Friday, 9th January."

Masterson said: "Nurse Pearce was with him when he died."

"And apparently she nursed him almost single-handed for the last week of his life. I wonder what the nursing record tells us."

But the nursing record was far less informative than the medical file. Nurse Pearce had entered in her careful schoolgirl's hand the details of her patient's temperature, respiration and pulse, his restlessness and brief hours of sleep, his medication and food. It could not be faulted as a meticulous record of nursing care. Beyond that it told them nothing.

Dalgliesh closed the book.

"You'd better return this to the ward and the medical folder to the proper department. We've learnt all we can from them. But I feel in my bones that Martin Dettinger's death has something to do with this case."

Masterson did not reply. Like all detectives who had worked with Dalgliesh, he had a healthy respect for the old man's hunches. Inconvenient, perverse and far-fetched they might seem, but they had been proved right too often to be safely ignored. And he had no objection to an evening trip to London. Tomorrow was Friday. The time-table on the hall notice-board showed that the students' sessions ended early on Friday. They would be free soon after five. He wondered whether Julia Pardoe would fancy a drive to town. After all, why not? Dalgliesh wouldn't be back by the time he was due to set out. It could be arranged with care. And there were some suspects it would be a positive pleasure to interview on their own.

VII

Just before half past four Dalgliesh, in defiance of convention and prudence, took tea alone with Sister Gearing in her bed-sitting-room. She had met him casually passing across the ground floor hall as the students were filing out of the lecture room after the last seminar of the day. She had given the invitation spontaneously and without coyness, although Dalgliesh noted that Sergeant Masterson was not included. He would have accepted the invitation even had it been delivered on highly scented and pink writing-paper and accompanied by the most blatant of sexual innuendoes. What he wanted after the formal interrogation of the morning was to sit in comfort and listen to a flow of artless, candid and slightly malicious gossip; to listen with the surface of his mind soothed, uninvolved, even a little cynically amused, but with the sharp claws of the intelligence sharpened for their pickings. He had learned more about the Nightingale House Sisters from their conversation at luncheon than he had in all his formal interviews, but he couldn't spend all his time tagging along behind the nursing staff, picking up scraps of gossip like so many dropped handkerchiefs. He wondered whether Sister Gearing had something to tell or something to ask. Either way he didn't expect an hour in her company to be wasted.

Dalgliesh hadn't yet been in any of the rooms on the third floor except Matron's flat and he was struck by the size and pleasant proportions of Sister Gearing's room. From here, even in winter, the hospital couldn't be seen, and the room had a calm of its own, remote from the frenetic life of wards and departments. Dalgliesh thought that in summer it must be very pleasant with nothing but a curdle of tree tops breaking the view of the far hills. Even now, with the curtains drawn against the fading light and the gas fire giving out a merry hiss, it was welcoming and warm. Presumably the divan bed in the corner with its cretonne cover and carefully arranged bank of cushions had been provided by the Hospital Management Committee, as had the two comfortable armchairs similarly covered and the rest of the uninteresting but functional furniture. But Sister Gearing had imposed her own personality on the room. There was a long shelf along the far wall on which she had arranged a collection of dolls in different national costumes. On another wall was a smaller shelf holding an assortment of china cats of different sizes and breeds. There was one particularly repulsive specimen in spotted blue, bulging of eye and adorned with a bow of blue ribbon; and propped beside it was a greetings card. It showed a female robin, the sex denoted by a frilly apron and flowered bonnet, perched on a twig. At her feet, a male robin was spelling out the words "Good luck" in worms. Dalgliesh hastily averted his eyes from this abomination and continued his tactful examination of the room.

The table in front of the window was presumably intended as a desk but about half a dozen photographs in silver frames effectively took up most of the working space. There was a record player in a corner with a cabinet of records beside it and a poster of a recent pop idol pinned on the wall above. There was a large number of cushions of all sizes and colours, three pouffes of unattractive design, an imitation tiger rug in brown-and-white nylon, and a coffee table on which Sister Gearing had set out the tea. But the most remarkable object in the room, in Dalgliesh's eyes, was a tall vase of winter foliage and chrysanthemums, beautifully arranged, standing on a side table. Sister Gearing was reputably good with flowers, and this arrangement had a simplicity of colour and line which was wholly pleasing. It was odd, he thought, that a woman with such an instinctive taste in flower arrangement should be content to live in this vulgarly over-furnished room. It suggested that Sister Gearing might be a more complex person than one would at first suppose. On the face of it, her character was easily read. She was a middle-aged, uncomfortably passionate spinster, not particularly well educated or intelligent, and concealing her frustrations with a slightly spurious gaiety. But twenty-five years as a policeman had taught him that no character was without its complications, its inconsistencies. Only the young or the very arrogant imagined that there was an identikit to the human mind.

Here in her own place Sister Gearing was less overtly flirtatious than she was in company. Admittedly she had chosen to pour the tea while curled on a large cushion at his feet, but he guessed from the number and variety of these cushions plumped around the room that this was her usual comfortable habit, rather than a kittenish invitation for him to join her. The tea was excellent. It was hot and freshly brewed, and accompanied by lavishly buttered crumpets with anchovy paste. There was an admirable absence of doilys and sticky cakes, and the cup handle could be comfortably held without dislocating one's fingers. She looked after him with quiet efficiency. Dalgliesh thought that Sister Gearing was one of those women who, when alone with a man, consider it their duty to devote themselves entirely to his comfort and the flattering of his ego. This may arouse fury in other less dedicated women, but it is unreasonable to expect a man to object.

Relaxed by the warmth and comfort of her room and stimulated by tea, Sister Gearing was obviously in a mood for talk. Dalgliesh let her chatter on, only occasionally throwing in a question. Neither of them mentioned Leonard Morris. The artless confidences for which Dalgliesh hoped would hardly spring from embarrassment or restraint.

"Of course, what happened to that poor kid Pearce is absolutely appalling, however it was caused. And with the whole set looking on like that! I'm surprised that it hadn't upset their work completely, but the young are pretty tough these days. And it isn't as if they liked her. But I can't believe any one of them put that corrosive into the feed. After all, these are third-year students. They know that carbolic acid taken straight into the stomach in that concentration is lethal. Damn it all, they had a lecture about poisons in their previous block. So it couldn't have been a practical joke that misfired."

"All the same, that seems to be the general view."

"Well, it's natural, isn't it? No one wants to believe that Pearce's death was murder. And if this were a first-year block I might believe it. One of the students might have tampered with the feed on impulse, perhaps with the idea that lysol is an emetic and that the demonstration might be enlivened by Pearce sicking up all over the G.N.C. Inspector. An odd idea of humour, but the young can be pretty crude. But these kids must have known what that stuff would do to the stomach."

"And what about Nurse Fallon's death?"

"Oh, suicide I should think. After all, the poor girl was pregnant. She probably had a moment of intense depression and didn't see the point of going on. Three years of training wasted and no family to turn to. Poor old Fallon! I don't think she was really the suicidal type, but it probably happened on impulse. There has been a certain amount of criticism about Dr. Snelling—he looks after the students' health—letting her come back to the block so soon after her influenza. But she hates being off and it isn't as if she were on the wards. This is hardly the time of the year to send people away for convalescence. She was as well off in school as anywhere. Still, the flu couldn't have helped. It probably left her feeling pretty low. This epidemic is having some pretty nasty after-effects. If only she'd confided in someone. It's awful to think of her putting an end to herself like that with a houseful of people who would have been glad to help if only she'd asked. Here, let me give you another cup. And try one of those shortbreads. They're home made. My married sister sends me them from time to time."

Dalgliesh helped himself to a piece of shortbread from the proffered tin and observed that there were those who thought that Nurse Fallon might have had another reason for suicide, apart from her pregnancy. She could have put the corrosive in the feed. She had certainly been seen in Nightingale House at the crucial time.

He put forward the suggestion slyly, awaiting her reaction. It wouldn't, of course, be new to her; it must have occurred to everyone in Nightingale House. But she was too simple to be surprised that a senior detective should be discussing his case so frankly with her, and too stupid to ask herself why.

She dismissed this theory with a snort.

"Not Fallon! It would have been a foolish trick and she was no fool. I told you, any third-year nurse would know that the stuff was lethal. And if you're suggesting that Fallon intended to kill Pearce —and why on earth should she?—I'd say that she was the last person to suffer remorse. If Fallon decided to do murder she wouldn't waste time repenting afterwards, let alone kill herself in remorse. No, Fallon's death is understandable enough. She had post-flu depression and she felt she couldn't cope with the baby."

"So you think they both committed suicide?"

"Well, I'm not so sure about Pearce. You'd have to be pretty crazy to choose that agonizing way of dying, and Pearce seemed sane enough to me. But it's a possible explanation, isn't it? And I can't see you proving anything else however long you stay."

He thought he detected a note of smug complacency in her voice and glanced at her abruptly. But the thin face showed nothing but its usual look of vague dissatisfaction. She was eating shortbread, nibbling at it with sharp, very white teeth. He could hear them rasping against the biscuits. She said:

"When one explanation is impossible, the improbable must be true. Someone said something like that. G. K. Chesterton wasn't it? Nurses don't murder each other. Or anyone else for that matter."

"There was Nurse Waddingham," said Dalgliesh.

"Who was she?"

"An unprepossessing and unpleasant woman who poisoned with morphine one of her patients, a Miss Baguley. Miss Baguley had been so ill advised as to leave Nurse Waddingham her money and property in turn for life-long treatment in the latter's nursing home. She struck a poor bargain. Nurse Waddingham was hanged."

Sister Gearing gave a frisson of simulated distaste.

"What awful people you do get yourself mixed up with! Anyway, she was probably one of those unqualified nurses. You can't tell me that Waddingham was on the General Nursing Council's Register."

"Come to think of it, I don't believe she was. And I wasn't mixed up with it. It happened in 1935."

"Well, there you are then," Sister Gearing said as if vindicated.

She stretched across to pour him a second cup of tea, then wriggled herself more comfortably into her cushion and leaned back against the arm of his chair, so that her hair brushed his knee. Dalgliesh found himself examining with mild interest the narrow band of darker hair each side of the parting where the dye had grown out. Viewed from above, her foreshortened face looked older, the nose sharper. He could see the latent pouch of skin under the bottom eyelashes and a spatter of broken veins high on the cheekbones, the purple threads only half disguised by make-up. She was no longer a young woman; that he knew. And there was a great deal more about her that he had gleaned from her dossier. She had trained at a hospital in the East End of London after a variety of unsuccessful and unprofitable office jobs. Her nursing career had been chequered and her references were suspiciously non-committal. There had been doubt about the wisdom of seconding her for training as a clinical instructor, a suggestion that she had been motivated less by a desire to teach than by the hope of an easier job than that of ward Sister. He knew that she was having difficulty with the menopause. He knew more about her than she realized, more than she would think he had any right to know. But he didn't yet know whether she was a murderess. Intent for a moment on his private thoughts, he hardly caught her next words.

"It's odd your being a poet. Fallon had your last volume of verse in her room, didn't she? Rolfe told me. Isn't it difficult to reconcile poetry with being a policeman?"

"I've never thought of poetry and police work as needing to be reconciled in that ecumenical way."

She laughed coyly.

"You know very well what I mean. After all it is a little unusual. One doesn't think of policemen as poets."

He did, of course, know what she meant. But it wasn't a subject he was prepared to discuss. He said:

"Policemen are individuals like people in any other job. After all, you three nursing Sisters haven't much in common have you? You and Sister Brumfett could hardly be more different personalities. I can't see Sister Brumfett feeding me on anchovy crumpets and home-made shortbread."

She reacted at once, as he had known she would.

"Oh, Brumfett's all right when you get to know her. Of course she's twenty years out of date. As I said at lunch, the kids today aren't prepared to listen to all that guff about obedience and duty and a sense of vocation. But she's a marvellous nurse. I won't hear a word against Brum. I had an appendicectomy here about four years ago. It went a bit wrong and the wound burst. Then I got an infection which was resistant to antibiotics. The whole thing was a mess. Not one of our Courtney-Briggs's most successful efforts. Anyway I felt like death. One night I was in ghastly pain and couldn't sleep and I felt absolutely sure I wouldn't see the morning. I was terrified. It was sheer funk. Talk about the fear of death! I knew what it meant that night. Then Brumfett came round. She was looking after me herself; she wouldn't let the students do a thing for me when she was on duty. I said to her: 'I'm not going to die, am I?' She looked down at me. She didn't tell me not to be a fool or give me any of the usual comforting lies. She just said in that gruff voice of hers: 'Not if I can help it you aren't.' And immediately the panic stopped. I knew that if Brumfett was fighting on my side I'd win through. It sounds a bit daft and sentimental put like that, but that's what I thought. She's like that with all the really sick patients. Talk about confidence! Brumfett makes you feel that she'd drag you back from the edge of the grave by sheer will-power, even if all the devils in hell were tugging the other way; which in my case they probably were. They don't make them like that any more."

Dalgliesh made appropriately assenting noises and paused briefly before picking up the references to Mr. Courtney-Briggs. He asked rather naïvely whether many of the surgeon's operations went so spectacularly wrong. Sister Gearing laughed:

"Lord, no! Courtney-Briggs's operations usually go the way he wants. That's not to say they go the way the patient would choose if he knew the whole of it. C.B. is what they call a heroic surgeon. If you ask me, most of the heroism has to be shown by the patients. But he does an extraordinary good job of work. He's one of the last remaining great general surgeons. You know, take anything on, the more hopeless the better. I suppose a surgeon is rather like a lawyer. There's no glory to be had in getting someone off if he's obviously innocent. The greater the guilt the greater the glory."

"What is Mrs. Courtney-Briggs like? I presume he's married. Does she show herself at the hospital?"

"Not very often, although she's supposed to be a member of the League of Friends. She gave the prizes away last year when the Princess couldn't come at the last moment. Blonde, very smart. Younger than C.B. but beginning to wear a bit now. Why do you ask? You don't suspect Muriel Courtney-Briggs surely? She wasn't even in the hospital the night Fallon died. Probably tucked up in bed in their very nice little place near Selborne. And she certainly hadn't any motive for killing poor Pearce."

So she did have a motive for getting rid of Fallon. Mr. Courtney-Briggs's liaison had probably been more noticed than he had realized. Dalgliesh wasn't surprised that Sister Gearing should know about it. Her sharp nose would be adept at smelling out sexual scandal.

He said: "I wondered if she were jealous."

Sister Gearing, unaware of what she had told, rambled happily on.

"I don't suppose she knew. Wives don't usually. Anyway, C.B. wasn't going to break up his marriage to wed Fallon. Not him! Mrs. C.B. has plenty of money of her own. She's the only child of Price of Price and Maxwell, the building firm—and what with C.B.'s earnings and Daddy's ill-gotten gains, they're very comfortable. I don't think Muriel worries much what he does as long as he behaves himself properly to her and the money keeps rolling in. I know I wouldn't. Besides, if rumour's correct, our Muriel doesn't exactly qualify for the League of Purity."

"Anyone here?" asked Dalgliesh.

"Oh no, nothing like that. It's just that she goes around with quite a smart set. She usually gets her picture in every third issue of the social glossies. And they're in with the theatrical crowd too. C.B. had a brother who was an actor, Peter Courtney. He hanged himself about three years ago. You must have read about it."

Dalgliesh's job gave him few opportunities to see a play and theatre going was one of the pleasures he missed most. He had seen Peter Courtney act only once but it had been a performance not easily forgotten. He had been a very young Macbeth, as introspective and sensitive as Hamlet, in thrall sexually to a much older wife, and whose physical courage was compounded of violence and hysteria. It had been a perverse but interesting interpretation, and it had very nearly succeeded. Thinking of the performance now, Dalgliesh imagined that he could detect a likeness between the brothers, something to do with the set of the eyes perhaps. But Peter must have been the younger by nearly twenty years. He wished he knew what the two men, so widely separated in age and talent, had made of each other.

Suddenly and irrelevantly Dalgliesh asked:

"How did Pearce and Fallon get on together?"

"They didn't. Fallon despised Pearce. I don't mean she hated her or would have harmed her; she just despised her."

"Was there any particular reason?"

"Pearce took it upon herself to tell Matron about Fallon's little tipple of whisky at nights. Self-righteous little beast. Oh, I know she's dead and I ought not to have said that. But really, Pearce could be insufferably self-righteous. Apparently what happened was that Diane Harper—she's left the training school now—had a bad cold about a fortnight before the set came into the block, and Fallon fixed her a hot whisky and lemon. Pearce could smell the stuff half-way along the corridor and concluded that Fallon was now attempting to seduce her juniors with the demon drink. So she appeared in the utility room—they were in the main nurses' home then, of course—in her dressing-gown, sniffing the air like an avenging angel, and threatened to report Fallon to Matron unless she promised more or less on her knees never to touch the stuff again. Fallon told her where to go and what to do with herself when she got there. She had a picturesque turn of phrase when roused, had Fallon. Nurse Dakers burst into tears, Harper lost her temper and the general noise brought the House Sister on to the scene. Pearce reported it to Matron all right, but no one knows with what result, except that Fallon started keeping her whisky in her own room. But the whole thing caused a great deal of feeling in the third year. Fallon was never popular with the set, she was too reserved and sarcastic. But they liked Pearce a damn sight less."

"And did Pearce dislike Fallon?"

"Well, it's difficult to say. Pearce never seemed to concern herself with what other people thought of her. She was an odd girl, pretty insensitive too. For example, she might disapprove of Fallon and her whisky-drinking but that didn't prevent her from borrowing Fallon's library ticket."

"When did this happen?"

Dalgliesh leaned across and replaced his teacup on the tray. His voice was level, unconcerned. But he felt again that spring of excitement and anticipation, the intuitive sense that something important had been said. It was more than a hunch; it was, as always, a certainty. It might happen several times during a case if he were lucky, or not at all. He couldn't will it to happen and he was afraid to examine its roots too closely since he suspected that it was a plant easily withered by logic.

"Just before she came into block, I think. It must have been the week before Pearce died. The Thursday, I think. Anyway, they hadn't yet moved into Nightingale House. It was just after supper time in the main dining-room. Fallon and Pearce were walking out of the door together and I was just behind them with Goodale. Then Fallon turned to Pearce and said: 'Here's the library token I promised you. I'd better give it to you now as I don't suppose we'll see each other in the morning. You'd better take the reader's ticket too, or they may not let you have the book.' Pearce mumbled something and grabbed the token rather ungraciously I thought, and that was that. Why? It isn't important, is it?"

"I can't think why it should be," said Dalgliesh.

VIII

He sat through the next fifteen minutes in exemplary patience. Sister Gearing couldn't have guessed from his courteous attention to her chattering and the leisurely way in which he drank his third and last cup of tea, that every moment was now grudged. When the meal was over, he carried the tray for her into the small Sisters' kitchen at the end of the corridor while she fretted at his heels, bleating her protests. Then he said, "Thank you," and left.

He went at once to the cell-like bedroom which still held nearly all the possessions Nurse Pearce had owned at the John Carpendar. It took him a moment to select the correct key from the heavy bunch in his pocket. The room had been locked after her death and was still locked. He went in, switching on the light. The bed was stripped and the whole room was very tidy and clean as if it, too, had been laid out for burial. The curtains were drawn back so that, from outside, the room would look no different from any other. The window was open but the air held a faint tang of disinfectant as if someone had tried to obliterate the memory of Pearce's death by a ritual purification.

He had no need to refresh his memory. The detritus of this particular life was pathetically meagre. But he went through her leavings again, turning them in careful hands as if the feel of cloth and leather could transmit their own clues. It didn't take long. Nothing had altered since his first inspection. The hospital wardrobe, identical to that in Nurse Fallon's room, was more than adequate for the few woollen dresses, unexciting in colour and design, which, under his questing hands, swung from their padded hangers and gave out a faint smell of cleaning fluid and mothballs. The thick winter coat in fawn was of good quality but obviously old. He sought once more in the pockets. There was nothing except the handkerchief which had been there on his first examination, a crumpled ball of white cotton smelling of sour breath.

He moved to the chest of drawers. Here again the space provided had been more than sufficient. The two top drawers were filled with underclothes, strong sensible vests and knickers, comfortably warm no doubt for an English winter but with no concessions to glamour or fashion. The drawers were lined with newspaper. The sheets had been taken out once already, but he ran his hand under them and felt nothing but the gritty surface of bare unpolished wood. The remaining three drawers held skirts, jumpers and cardigans; a leather handbag, carefully wrapped in tissue paper; a pair of best shoes in a string bag; an embroidered handkerchief sachet with a dozen handkerchiefs carefully folded; an assortment of scarves; three pairs of identical nylon stockings still in their wrappers.

He turned again to the bedside locker and the small shelf fixed above it. The locker held a bedside lamp, a small alarm clock in a leather case which had long since run down, a packet of paper handkerchiefs with one crumpled tissue half-pulled through the slit, and an empty water carafe. There was also a leather-bound Bible and a writing-case. Dalgliesh opened the Bible at the flyleaf and read again the inscription in careful copper plate. "Awarded to Heather Pearce for attendance and diligence. St. Mark's Sunday School." Diligence. An unfashionable, intimidating word, but one, he felt, of which Nurse Pearce would have approved.

He opened the writing-case, but with little hope of finding what he sought. Nothing had changed since his first examination. Here still was the half-finished letter to her grandmother, a dull recital of the week's doings written as impersonally as a ward report, and a quarto-sized envelope, posted to her on the day of her death and obviously slipped into the writing-case by someone who, having opened it, couldn't think of what else to do with it. It was an illustrated brochure on the work of a home in Suffolk for German war refugees apparently sent in the hope of a donation.

He turned his attention to the small collection of books on the wall shelf. He had seen them before. Then, as now, he was struck by the conventionality of her choice and by the meagreness of this personal library. A school prize for needlework. *Lamb's Tales from Shakespeare.* Dalgliesh had never believed that any child read them and there was no evidence that Nurse Pearce had done so. There were two travel books, *In the Steps of St. Paul* and *In the Steps of the Master*. In both the girl had carefully inscribed her name. There was a well-known but out-of-date edition of a nursing textbook. The date on the flyleaf was nearly four years old. He wondered whether she had bought it in anticipation of her training, only to find that its advice on applying leeches and administering enemas had become out of date. There was a copy of Palgrave's *Golden Treasury*, also a school prize, but this time inappropriately for deportment. This, too, showed little sign of having been read. Lastly there were three paper-backs—novels by a popular woman writer, each advertised as "The Book of the Film"—and a fictional and highly sentimental account of the wanderings across Europe of a lost dog and cat which Dalgliesh remembered had been a best-seller some five years previously. This was inscribed, "To Heather, with love from Auntie Edie, Christmas 1964." The whole collection told him little about the dead girl, except that her reading had apparently been as restricted as her life. And nowhere he found what he was seeking.

He didn't go again to look in Nurse Fallon's room. The scene-of-crime officer had searched every inch of it, and he himself could have described the room in minute detail and given an accurate inventory of all its contents. Wherever the library ticket and the token were, he could be sure that they weren't there. Instead he ran lightly up the wide staircase to the floor above where he had noticed a wall-mounted telephone when carrying Sister Gearing's tea tray to the utility room. A card listing the internal extensions hung beside it and, after a moment's thought, he rang the nurses' sitting-room. Maureen Burt answered. Yes, Nurse Goodale was still there. Almost immediately Dalgliesh heard her voice and he asked her to come up to see him in Nurse Pearce's room.

She came so promptly that he had hardly reached the door before he saw the self-assured, uniformed figure at the top of the stairs. He stood aside and she moved into the room before him and silently surveyed the stripped bed, the silent bedside clock, the closed Bible, letting her gaze rest briefly on each object with gentle uninquisitive interest. Dalgliesh moved to the window and, both standing, they regarded each other wordlessly across the bed. Then he said:

"I'm told that Nurse Fallon lent a library ticket to Nurse Pearce sometime during the week before she died. You were leaving the dining-room with Sister Gearing at the time. Can you remember what happened?"

Nurse Goodale was not given to showing surprise.

"Yes, I think so. Fallon had told me earlier that day that Pearce wanted to visit one of the London libraries and had asked to borrow her reader's ticket and the token. Fallon was a member of the Westminster library. They've got a number of branches in the City but you aren't really supposed to belong unless you either live or work in Westminster. Fallon had a flat in London before she became a student here and had kept her reader's card and token. It's an excellent library, much better than we've got here, and it's useful to be able to borrow books. I think Sister Rolfe is a member too. Fallon took her reader's ticket and one of the tokens across to lunch and handed them to Pearce as we were leaving the dining-room."

"Did Nurse Pearce say why she wanted them?"

"Not to me. She may have told Fallon. I don't know. Any of us could borrow one of Fallon's tokens if we wanted to. Fallon didn't require an explanation."

"What precisely are these tokens like?"

"They're small oblongs of pale blue plastic with the City Arms stamped on them. The library usually gives four to every reader and you hand one in every time you take out a book, but Jo only had three. She may have lost the fourth. There's also the reader's ticket. That's the usual small piece of cardboard with the name, address and date of expiry. Sometimes the assistant asks to see the reader's ticket and I suppose that's why Jo handed it over with the token."

"Do you know where the other two are?"

"Yes, in my room. I borrowed them about a fortnight ago when I went up to town with my fiancé to attend a special service in the Abbey. I thought we might have time to visit the Great Smith Street branch to see whether they had the new Iris Murdoch. However, we met some friends from Mark's theological college after the service and never got to the library. I meant to return the tokens to Jo but I slipped them in my writing-case and forgot about them. She didn't remind me. I can show them to you if it would be helpful."

"I think it would. Did Heather Pearce use her token, do you know?"

"Well, I assume she did. I saw her waiting for the Green Line bus to town that afternoon. We were both off duty so it must have been the Thursday. I imagine that she had it in mind to visit the library."

She looked puzzled.

"Somehow I feel quite sure that she did take out a library book but I can't think why I should be so certain."

"Can't you? Think very hard."

Nurse Goodale stood silently, her hands folded composedly as if in prayer over the white stiffness of her apron. He did not hurry her. She gazed fixedly ahead then turned her eyes to the bed and said quietly:

"I know now. I saw her reading a library book. It was the night when Jo was taken ill, the night before Pearce herself died. I went into her bedroom just after half past eleven to ask her to go and look after Jo while I fetched Sister. She was sitting up in bed with her hair in two plaits and she was reading. I remember now. It was a large book, bound in a dark colour, dark blue I think, and with a reference number stamped in gold at the foot of the spine. It looked an old and rather heavy book. I don't think it was fiction. She was holding it propped up against her knees I remember. When I appeared she closed it quickly and slipped it under her pillow. It was a strange thing to do but it didn't mean anything to me at the time. Pearce was always oddly secretive. Besides, I was too concerned about Jo. But I remember it now."

She stood again in silence for a few moments. Dalgliesh waited. Then she said quietly:

"I know what's worrying you. Where's that book now? It wasn't among her things when Sister Rolfe and I tidied her room and made a list of her belongings after her death. The police were with us and we didn't find a book anything like it. And what happened to the ticket? It wasn't among Fallon's things either."

Dalgliesh asked:

"What exactly happened that night? You said you went in to Nurse Fallon shortly after eleven thirty. I thought she didn't go to bed before midnight."

"She did that night. I suppose it was because she wasn't feeling well and hoped that an early bed would put her right. She didn't tell anyone she was ill. Jo wouldn't. And I didn't go in to her. She came into me. Shortly after eleven thirty she woke me up. She looked ghastly. She was obviously in a high fever and she could hardly stand. I helped her back to her bed, went in to ask Pearce to stay with her, and then rang Sister Rolfe. She's generally responsible for us when we're in Nightingale House. Sister came to look at Jo and then telephoned the private wing and asked for an ambulance to come over for her. Then she rang Sister Brumfett to let her know what had happened. Sister Brumfett likes to know what's happening on her ward even when she's off duty. She wouldn't have been pleased to arrive in the hospital next morning and find that Jo had been warded without her being told. She came down to have a look at Jo but didn't go over in the ambulance with her. It wasn't really necessary."

"Who did accompany her?"

"I did. Sister Rolfe and Sister Brumfett went back to their rooms and Pearce returned to hers."

So the book could hardly have been removed that night, thought Dalgliesh. Pearce would certainly have noticed its absence. Even if she had decided not to continue reading it, she would hardly settle to sleep with a heavy book under her pillow. So the probability was that someone had taken it after her death. One thing was certain. A particular book had been in her possession late on the night before she died yet was not in her room when the police, Miss Rolfe and Nurse Goodale examined it for the first time at about ten past ten the next morning. Whether or not that book had come from Westminster library, it was missing, and if the book wasn't from the library, then what had happened to the token and the reader's ticket? Neither was among her things. And if she had decided not to use them and handed them back to Fallon, why weren't they among Fallon's possessions?

He asked Nurse Goodale what had happened immediately after Nurse Pearce's death.

"Matron sent us students up to her sitting-room and asked us to wait there. Sister Gearing joined us after about half an hour and then some coffee came and we drank that. We stayed there together talking and trying to read until Inspector Bailey and Matron arrived. That must have been about eleven o'clock, perhaps a little earlier."

"And were you all together in that room for the whole of that time?"

"Not all the time. I went out to the library to fetch a book I wanted and was away about three minutes. Nurse Dakers left the room too. I'm not sure why but I think she muttered something about going to the lavatory. Otherwise, as far as I can remember, we all stayed together. Miss Beale, the G.N.C. Inspector, was with us."

She paused.

"You think that this missing library book has something to do with Pearce's death, don't you? You think it's important."

"I think that it may be. That's why I want you to say nothing about our conversation."

"Of course, if that's what you want." She paused.

"But couldn't I try to find out what has happened to the book?

I could ask the other students quite casually if they had the ticket and token. I could pretend that I wanted to use them."

Dalgliesh smiled: "Leave the detecting to me. I'd much prefer you to say nothing."

He saw no reason to suggest to her that in a murder investigation too much knowledge could be dangerous. She was a sensible girl. She would think it out for herself soon enough. Taking his silence for dismissal she turned to go. When she reached the door she hesitated and turned:

"Superintendent Dalgliesh, forgive me if I'm interfering. I can't believe that Pearce was murdered. But if she was, then surely the library book could have been taken from her room any time after five to nine when Pearce went into the demo room. The murderer would know that she wouldn't come out of that room alive and that it would be safe for him, or her, to remove it. If the book were taken after Pearce's death it could have been taken by anyone and for a perfectly innocent reason. But if it were taken before she died then it was taken by her killer. That would be true even if the book itself had nothing to do with the reason why she was killed. And Pearce's question to us all about something missing from her room suggests that the book was taken before she died. And why should the murderer bother to remove it if it wasn't in some way connected with the crime?"

"Exactly," said Dalgliesh. "You're a very intelligent young woman."

For the first time he saw Nurse Goodale disconcerted. She blushed, looking at once as pink and pretty as a young bride, then smiled at him, turned quickly and was gone. Dalgliesh, intrigued by the metamorphosis, decided that the local vicar had shown much sense and discernment in choosing his wife. What the parochial church council would make of her uncompromising intelligence was another matter. And he hoped that he wouldn't have to arrest her for murder before they had a chance to make up their minds.

He followed her into the corridor. As usual it was gloomily obscure, lit only by the two bulbs high in a cluster of entwined brass. He had reached the top of the staircase when instinct made him pause and then retrace his steps. Switching on his torch he bent low and moved the beam slowly over the surface of sand in the two fire buckets. The nearer one was caked and grey with dust; it had obviously not been disturbed since it was filled. But the surface of the second one bore a fresher look. Dalgliesh put on his thin cotton searching gloves, fetched from Nurse Pearce's bedroom a sheet of newspaper from one of the drawers, spread it on the corridor floor and slowly tipped out the sand in a rising pyramid. He found no hidden library ticket. But there tumbled out a squat, screw-topped tin, with a stained label. Dalgliesh brushed off the grains of sand to reveal the black print of a skull and the word POISON in capitals. Underneath were the words: "Plant Spray. Death to Insects, Harmless to Plants. Use carefully in accordance with instructions."

He did not need to read the instructions to know what he had found. This stuff was almost pure nicotine. The poison which had killed Nurse Fallon was at last in his hands.

Chapter Six

Long Day's Ending

I

Five minutes later Dalgliesh, having spoken to the forensic science laboratory director and to Sir Miles Honeyman, looked up at a sulkily defensive Sergeant Masterson.

"I'm beginning to see why the Force is so keen on training civilian searchers. I told the scene-of-crime officer to stick to the bedroom, that we'd see to the rest of the house. I thought for some reason that policemen could use their eyes."

Sergeant Masterson, the more furious because he knew the rebuke to be justified, controlled himself with difficulty. He found any criticism difficult to take; from Dalgliesh it was almost impossible. He stiffened to attention like an old soldier on a charge, knowing full well that Dalgliesh would be exasperated rather than mollified by this punctilio, and contrived to sound at the same time both aggrieved and contrite.

"Greeson is a good searcher. I haven't known Greeson miss anything before. He can use his eyes all right, sir."

"Greeson has excellent eyesight. The trouble is that there's no connection between his eyes and his brain. And that's where you come in. The damage is done now. There's no point in holding a post mortem. We don't know whether this tin was in the bucket or not when Fallon's body was discovered this morning. But at least we've found it now. The laboratory has the viscera by the way. Sir Miles called in with it about an hour ago. They're already putting some of the stuff through the gas chromatograph. Now that they know what they're looking for it should speed things. We'd better get this tin off to them as soon as possible. But we'll have a look at it first."

He went over to his murder bag for the finger-print powder, insufflator and lens. The squat little tin became sooty under his careful hands. But there were no prints, only a few amorphous smudges on the faded label.

"Right," he said. "Find the three Sisters, will you Sergeant? They're the ones most likely to know where this tin came from. They live here. Sister Gearing is in her sitting-room. The others should be somewhere around. And if Sister Brumfett is still on her ward she'll have to leave it. Anyone who dies in the next hour must do so without her assistance."

"Do you want to see them separately or together?"

"Either. It doesn't matter. Just get them. Gearing's the one most likely to help. She looks after the flowers."

Sister Gearing arrived first. She came in jauntily, her face perked with curiosity and flushed with the lingering euphoria of a successful hostess. Then her eyes lit on the tin. The transformation was so immediate and startling that it was almost comic. She gasped, "Oh, no!", shot her hand to her mouth and sank into the chair opposite Dalgliesh, deadly pale.

"Where did you. . . ? Oh my God! You're not telling me that Fallon took nicotine?"

"Took, or was given. You recognize this tin, Sister?"

Sister Gearing's voice was almost inaudible.

"Of course. It's my . . . isn't it the tin of rose spray? Where did you find it?"

"Somewhere about the place. Where and when did you see it last?"

"It's kept in that white cupboard under the shelf in the conservatory, just to the left of the door. All my gardening stuff is there. I can't remember when I saw it last."

She was on the edge of tears; happy confidence completely dissolved.

"Honestly, it's just too awful! It's frightful! I feel dreadful about it. I really do. But how was I to tell that Fallon would know the stuff was there and use it? I didn't even remember about it myself. If I had, I'd have gone to check that it was still there. I suppose there's no doubt about it? She did die of nicotine poisoning?"

"There's a great deal of doubt until we get the toxicology report. But taking the common-sense view, it looks as if this stuff killed her. You bought it when?"

"Honestly, I can't remember. Sometime early last summer, just before the roses were due. One of the other Sisters might remember. I'm responsible for most of the plants in the conservatory here. At least, I'm not really responsible; it's never been an official arrangement. But I like flowers and there's no one else to bother so I do what I can. I was trying to establish a small rose bed outside the dining-room, too, and I needed the stuff to kill pests. I bought it from Bloxham's Nurseries on the Winchester Road. Look, you can see the address stamped on the label. And I kept it with my other gardening things, gloves and string and the watering cans and trowels and so on, in the corner cupboard in the conservatory."

"Can you remember when you last saw it?"

"Not really. But I went to the cupboard for my gloves last Saturday morning. We had a special service at the chapel on Sunday and I wanted to do the flowers. I thought I might be able to find some interesting boughs, bits of autumn foliage or seed pods in the garden to help the decoration. I don't remember seeing the tin there on Saturday but I think I might have noticed if it were actually missing. But I'm not sure. I haven't used it for months."

"Who else knew that it was there?"

"Well, anyone could have known. I mean, the cupboard isn't locked and there was nothing to stop people looking inside. I suppose I ought to have locked it but one doesn't expect . . . I mean if people are going to kill themselves they'll find a way somehow. I feel absolutely awful but I won't be made to feel responsible. I won't! It isn't fair! She could have used anything. Anything!"

"Who could?"

"Well, Fallon. If Fallon did kill herself. Oh, I don't know what I'm saying."

"Did Nurse Fallon know about the nicotine?"

"Not unless she looked in the cupboard and found it. The only people I can say for certain who did know are Brumfett and Rolfe. I remember that they were sitting in the conservatory when I put the tin into the cupboard. I held it up and said something daft about having enough poison there to kill the lot of them, and Brumfett told me that I ought to lock it up."

"But you didn't?"

"Well, I put it straight away in the cupboard. There isn't a lock so I couldn't do anything about it. Anyway, the tin's labelled clearly enough. Anyone can see that it's poison. And one doesn't expect people to kill themselves. Besides, why the nicotine? Nurses have plenty of opportunity to get hold of drugs. It's not fair to blame me. After all, the disinfectant which killed Pearce was just as lethal. No one complained because that was left in the lavatory. You can't run a nurse training school like a psychiatric unit. I'm not going to be blamed. People here are supposed to be sane, not homicidal maniacs. I won't be made to feel guilty. I won't!"

"If you didn't use the stuff on Nurse Fallon there's no reason why you should feel guilty. Did Sister Rolfe say anything when you brought in the tin?"

"I don't think so. Just looked up from her book. But I can't really remember. I can't even tell you exactly when it was. But it was a warm sunny day. I do remember that. I think it was probably in late May or early June. Rolfe may remember, and Brumfett certainly will."

"We'll ask them. In the meantime I'd better have a look at this cupboard."

He left the tin of nicotine for Masterson to pack for despatch to the laboratory, told him to send Sister Brumfett and Sister Rolfe to the conservatory, and followed Sister Gearing out of the room. She led him down to the ground floor, still muttering her indignant protests. They passed into the empty dining-room. The discovery that the door into the conservatory was locked shook Sister Gearing from her mood of frightened resentment.

"Damn! I'd forgotten. Matron thought we'd better keep it locked after dark because some of the glass isn't too secure. You remember that a pane fell out during the storm? She's afraid someone could get in this way. Usually we don't bother to lock it until we do the final locking up last thing at night. The key will be on the board in Rolfe's office. Wait here. I won't be a jiffy."

She returned almost immediately and fitted the large old-fashioned key into the lock. They passed into the warm fungoid smell of the conservatory. Sister Gearing unerringly reached for the switch, and the two long tubes of fluorescent light, suspended from the high concave ceiling, flickered erratically, then burst into brilliance, revealing the arboreal jungle in all its lushness. The conservatory was a remarkable sight. Dalgliesh had thought so on his first tour of the house, but now, dazzled by the fierce glare on leaves and glass, he blinked in wonder. Around him a minor forest of greenery twined, sprouted, crept and burst in menacing profusion while, outside, its pale reflection hung in the evening air and stretched, motionless and insubstantial, into a green infinity.

Some of the plants looked as if they had flourished in the conservatory since the day it was built. They sprang like mature if miniature palm trees from ornate urns, spreading a canopy of glistening leaves under the glass. Others, more exotic, sprouted bursts of foliage from their scarred and dentate stalks or, like giant cacti, lifted rubber lips, spongy and obscene, to suck the humid air. Between them the ferns sprayed a green shadow, their fragile fronds moving in the draught from the door. Around the sides of the great room were white shelves on which stood pots of the more domestic and agreeable plants which were Sister Gearing's care—red, pink and white chrysanthemums, and African violets. The conservatory should have evoked a tender scene of Victorian domesticity, of fluttering fans and whispered confidences behind the palms. But for Dalgliesh, no corner of Nightingale House was free of the oppressive atmosphere of evil; the very plants seemed to be sucking their manna from a tainted air.

Mavis Gearing went straight over to a low, four-foot-long cupboard in white-painted wood, fitted underneath the wall shelf to the left of the door and hardly visible behind the curtain of waving ferns. It had one inadequate door fitted with a small knob and no lock. Together they crouched to look in it. Although the overhead fluorescent lights were unpleasantly garish, the recesses of the cupboard were dim and their view obstructed by the shadow of their heads. Dalgliesh switched on his torch. Its beam revealed the usual paraphernalia of the indoor gardener. He made a mental inventory. There were balls of green twine, a couple of watering cans, a small spray, packets of seed, some opened and half-used with their tops pressed back, a small plastic bag of potting compost and one of fertilizer, about two dozen flower pots of varying sizes, a small stack of seed trays, pruning shears, a trowel and small fork, a disorderly pile of seedmen's catalogues, three clothbound books on gardening, their covers stained and dirty, an assortment of flower vases, and bundles of tangled wire.

Mavis Gearing pointed to a space in the far corner.

"That's where it was. I put it well back. It couldn't have been a temptation to anyone. You wouldn't even notice it, just opening the door. It was quite hidden really. Look, that's the space—you can see where it was."

She spoke with urgent self-justification, as if the empty space acquitted her of all responsibility. Then her voice changed. It dropped a tone and became huskily pleading like an amateur actress playing a seduction scene.

"I know it looks bad. First, I was in charge of the demonstration when Pearce died. And now this. But I haven't touched the stuff since I used it last summer. I swear I haven't! I know some of them won't believe me. They'll be glad—yes glad—and relieved if suspicion falls on me and Len. It'll let them out. Besides they're jealous. They've always been jealous. It's because I've got a man and they haven't. But you believe me don't you? You've got to believe me!"

It was pathetic and humiliating. She pressed her shoulder against his, as they knelt huddled together in a ridiculous parody of prayer. He could feel her breath against his cheek. Her right hand, the fingers twitching nervously, crept across the floor towards his hand.

Then her mood broke. They heard Sister Rolfe's cold voice from the door.

"The Sergeant told me to meet you here. Am I interrupting anything?"

Dalgliesh felt the pressure on his shoulder immediately released, and Sister Gearing scrambled gracelessly to her feet. He got up more slowly. He neither felt nor looked embarrassed, but he was not sorry that Miss Rolfe had chosen that moment to appear.

Sister Gearing broke into explanation:

"It's the rose spray. That stuff containing nicotine. Fallon must have taken it. I feel absolutely ghastly about it, but how was I to know? The Superintendent has found the tin."

She turned to Dalgliesh.

"You didn't say where?"

"No," Dalgliesh said. "I didn't say where." He spoke to Miss Rolfe.

"Did you know the stuff was kept in this cupboard?"

"Yes, I saw Gearing put it there. Some time last summer wasn't it?"

"You didn't mention this to me."

"I didn't think of it until now. It never occurred to me that Fallon might have taken nicotine. And, presumably, we don't yet know that she did."

Dalgliesh said: "Not until we get the toxicology report."

"And even then, Superintendent, can you be sure that the drug came from this tin? There are other sources of nicotine at the hospital surely? This could be a blind."

"Of course, although it seems to me highly unlikely. But the forensic science laboratory should be able to tell us that. This nicotine is mixed with a proportion of concentrated detergent. It will be identifiable by gas chromatography."

She shrugged.

"Well, that should settle it then."

Mavis Gearing cried out: "What do you mean, other sources of supply? Who are you getting at? Nicotine isn't kept in the pharmacy, as far as I know. And anyway Len had left Nightingale House before Fallon died."

"I wasn't accusing Leonard Morris. But he was on the spot when both of them died, remember, and he was here in this room when you put the nicotine in the cupboard. He's a suspect like the rest of us."

"Was Mr. Morris with you when you bought the nicotine?"

"Well, he was as a matter of fact. I'd forgotten it or I would have told you. We'd been out together that afternoon and he came back here to tea."

She turned angrily to Sister Rolfe.

"It's nothing to do with Len, I tell you! He hardly knew Pearce or Fallon. Pearce hadn't anything on Len."

Hilda Rolfe said calmly: "I wasn't aware that she had anything on anyone. I don't know whether you're trying to put ideas into Mr. Dalgliesh's head, but you're certainly putting them into mine."

Sister Gearing's face disintegrated into misery. Moaning, she jerked her head from side to side as if desperately seeking help or asylum. Her face, sickly and surrealist, was suffused with the green light of the conservatory.

Sister Rolfe gave Dalgliesh one sharp look, then ignoring him, moved over to her colleague and said with unexpected gentleness:

"Look Gearing, I'm sorry. Of course I'm not accusing Leonard Morris or you. But the fact that he was here would have come out anyway. Don't let the police fluster you. It's how they work. I don't suppose the Superintendent cares a damn whether you or I or Brumfett killed Pearce and Fallon so long as he can prove someone did. Well, let him get on with it. Just answer his questions and keep calm. Why not get on with your job and let the police get on with theirs?"

Mavis Gearing wailed like a child seeking reassurance:

"But it's all so awful!"

"Of course it is! But it won't last for ever. And in the meantime, if you must confide in a man, find yourself a solicitor, a psychiatrist or a priest. At least you can be reasonably sure that they'll be on your side."

Mavis Gearing's worried eyes moved from Dalgliesh to Rolfe. She looked like a child hesitating to decide where her allegiance lay. Then the two women moved imperceptibly together and gazed at Dalgliesh, Sister Gearing in puzzled reproach and Sister Rolfe with the tight satisfied smile of a woman who has just brought off a successful piece of mischief.

II

At that moment Dalgliesh caught the sound of approaching footsteps. Someone was moving across the dining-room. He turned to the door, expecting to find that Sister Brumfett had at last come to be interviewed. The conservatory door opened but, instead of her squat figure, he saw a tall bare-headed man wearing a belted raincoat and with a gauze patch taped across his left eye. A peevish voice spoke from the doorway:

"What's happened to everyone? This place is like a morgue."

Before anyone could reply, Miss Gearing had darted forward and seized his arm. Dalgliesh saw with interest his frown and twitch of involuntary recoil.

"Len, what is it? You're hurt! You never told me! I thought it was your ulcer. You never said anything about hurting your head!"

"It was my ulcer. But this didn't help it."

He spoke directly to Dalgliesh:

"You must be Chief Superintendent Dalgliesh of New Scotland Yard. Miss Gearing told me that you wanted to see me. I'm on my way to my general practitioner's surgery but I'm at your disposal for half an hour."

But Sister Gearing was not to be diverted from her concern.

"But you never said anything about an accident! How did it happen? Why didn't you tell me about it when I rang?"

"Because we had other things to discuss and because I didn't want you to fuss."

He shook off her detaining arm and sat himself down in a wicker chair. The two women and Dalgliesh moved in close to him. There was a silence. Dalgliesh revised his unreasonably preconceived notions of Miss Gearing's lover. He should have looked ridiculous, sitting there in his cheap raincoat with his patched eye and bruised face and speaking in that grating sarcastic voice. But he was curiously impressive. Sister Rolfe had somehow conveyed the impression of a little man, nervous, ineffectual and easily intimidated. This man had force. It might be only the manifestation of pent-up nervous energy; it might be the obsessive resentment born of failure or unpopularity. But his was certainly not a comfortable or negligible personality.

Dalgliesh asked: "When did you learn that Josphine Fallon was dead?"

"When I rang my pharmacy office just after nine thirty this

morning to say that I wouldn't be in. My assistant told me. I suppose the news was all over the hospital by then."

"How did you react to the news?"

"React? I didn't react. I hardly knew the girl. I was surprised, I suppose. Two deaths in the same house and so close together in time; well, it's unusual to say the least of it. It's shocking really. You could say I was shocked."

He spoke like a successful politician condescending to express an attributable opinion to a cub reporter.

"But you didn't connect the two deaths?"

"Not at the time. My assistant just said that another Nightingale—we call the students Nightingales when they are in block—that another Nightingale student, Jo Fallon, had been found dead. I asked how and he said something about a heart attack following influenza. I thought it was a natural death. I suppose that's what everyone thought at first."

"When did you think otherwise?"

"I suppose when Miss Gearing rang me about an hour later to say that you were here."

So Sister Gearing had telephoned Morris at his home. She must have wanted to reach him urgently to have risked that. Was it perhaps to warn him, to agree their story? While Dalgliesh was wondering what excuse, if any, she had given to Mrs. Morris, the pharmacist answered the unspoken question.

"Miss Gearing doesn't usually ring me at home. She knows that I like to keep my professional and my private life absolutely separate. But she was naturally anxious about my health when she rang the laboratory after breakfast and was told that I wasn't in. I suffer from a duodenal ulcer."

"Your wife, no doubt, was able to reassure her."

He replied calmly but with a sharp glance at Sister Rolfe, who had moved to the periphery of the group:

"My wife takes the children to her mother's all day on Fridays."

As Mavis Gearing would no doubt have known. So they had, after all, had a chance to consult each other, to decide on their story. But if they were concocting an alibi, why fix it for midnight? Because they knew for the best or worse of reasons that Fallon had died at that hour? Or because, knowing her habits, they judged that midnight was the most likely time? Only the killer, and perhaps not even he, could know precisely when Fallon had died. It could have been before midnight. It could have been as late as two thirty. Even Miles Honeyman with his thirty years' experience couldn't time the death precisely from clinical signs alone. The only certain thing was that Fallon was dead and that she had died almost immediately after drinking her whisky. But when exactly had that been? It was her usual habit to prepare her late night drink as soon as she went upstairs to bed. But no one admitted to having seen her after she left the nurses' sitting-room. Fallon could, just possibly, have been alive when Sister Brumfett and the Burt twins saw her light shining through the keyhole just after two a.m. And if she had been alive then what had she been doing between midnight and two o'clock? Dalgliesh had been concentrating on those people who had access to the school. But suppose Fallon had left Nightingale House that night, perhaps to keep an assignation. Or suppose she had deferred making her nightly drink of whisky and lemon because she was expecting a visitor. The front and back doors of Nightingale House had been found bolted in the morning, but Fallon could have let her visitor out any time during the night and bolted the door behind him.

But Mavis Gearing was still preoccupied with her lover's damaged head and bruised face.

"What happened to you, Len? You've got to tell me. Did you come off your bicycle?"

Sister Rolfe laughed unkindly. Leonard Morris bestowed on her a measured glance of intimidating contempt, then turned to Sister Gearing.

"If you must know Mavis, yes I did. It happened after I left you last night. There was one of the big elms down across the path and I cycled right into it."

Sister Rolfe spoke for the first time.

"Surely you could see it in the light of your bicycle lamp?"

"My bicycle lamp, Sister, not unreasonably, is fixed to shine on the road. I saw the tree trunk. What I didn't see in time was one of the high jutting boughs. I was lucky not to lose an eye."

Sister Gearing, predictably, gave an anguished yelp.

Dalgliesh asked: "What time did this happen?"

"I've just told you. Last night after I had left Nightingale House. Oh, I see! You're asking what time precisely? As it happens I can answer that. I came off my bicycle under the impact and was afraid that my watch had been broken. Fortunately it hadn't. The hands stood at twelve seventeen a.m. precisely."

"Wasn't there some warning—a white scarf—tied to the branch?"

"Of course not, Superintendent. If there had been I should hardly have ridden straight into it."

"If it were tied high up on a bough you might not have noticed it."

"It wasn't there to notice. After I'd picked up my bicycle and recovered a little from the shock I inspected the tree carefully. My first thought was that I might be able to shift it at least slightly and leave part of the road clear. That was obviously impossible. The job was going to need a tractor and tackle. But there was no scarf on any part of that tree at twelve seventeen a.m."

"Mr. Morris," said Dalgliesh, "I think it's time you and I had a little talk."

But Sister Brumfett was waiting for him outside the interview room. Before Dalgliesh could speak she said accusingly:

"I was summoned to see you in this room. I came promptly at some inconvenience to my ward. When I arrive I'm told that you're not in your room and will I please go down to the conservatory. I don't propose to chase around Nightingale House for you. If you want to see me I can spare you half an hour now."

"Miss Brumfett," said Dalgliesh, "you seem determined by your behaviour to give me the impression that you killed these girls. It's possible you did. I shall come to a conclusion about that as soon as I reasonably can. In the meantime, please curb your enthusiasm for antagonizing the police and wait until I can see you. That will be when I've finished talking to Mr. Morris. You can wait here outside the office or go to your own room, whichever suits you. But I shall want you in about thirty minutes and I, too, have no intention of chasing over the house to find you."

He had no idea how she would take this rebuke. Her reaction was surprising. The eyes behind the thick spectacles softened and twinkled. Her face broke into a momentary grin and she gave a satisfied little nod as if she had at least succeeded in provoking a particularly docile student into showing a flash of spirit.

"I'll wait here." She plonked herself down on the chair outside the office door then, nodded towards Morris.

"And I shouldn't let him do all the talking or you'll be lucky to be through in half an hour."

III

But the interview took less than thirty minutes. The first couple were spent by Morris in making himself comfortable. He took off his shabby raincoat, shaking it and smoothing down the folds as if it had somehow become contaminated in Nightingale House, then folded it with fussy precision over the back of his chair. Then he seated himself opposite Dalgliesh and took the initiative.

"Please don't fire questions at me, Superintendent. I don't like being interrogated. I prefer to tell my story in my own way. You needn't worry about it being accurate. I'd hardly be chief pharmacist of an important hospital if I hadn't the head for detail and a good memory for facts."

Dalgliesh said mildly: "Then could I have some facts please, starting perhaps with your movements last night."

Morris continued as if he hadn't heard this eminently reasonable request.

"Miss Gearing has given me the privilege of her friendship for the past six years. I've no doubt that certain people here, certain women living in Nightingale House, have placed their own interpretation on that friendship. That is to be expected. When you get a community of middle-aged spinsters living together you're bound to get sexual jealousy."

"Mr. Morris," said Dalgliesh gently. "I'm not here to investigate your relationship with Miss Gearing or hers with her colleagues. If those relationships have anything to do with the deaths of these two girls, then tell me about them. Otherwise let's leave out the amateur psychology and get down to the material facts."

"My relationship with Miss Gearing is germane to your inquiry in that it has brought me into this house at about the time Nurse Pearce and Nurse Fallon died."

"All right. Then tell me about those two occasions."

"The first was the morning when Nurse Pearce died. You are, no doubt, aware of the details. Naturally I reported my visit to Inspector Bailey since he caused a notice to be appended to all the hospital notice-boards inquiring the names of people who had visited Nightingale House on the morning on which Nurse Pearce died. But I have no objection to repeating the information. I called in here on my way to the pharmacy to leave Miss Gearing a note. It was in fact a card, one of those 'good luck' cards which it is customary to send friends before some important event. I knew that Miss Gearing would have to take the first demonstration of the day, indeed the first demonstration of this school, as Sister Manning, who is Miss Rolfe's first assistant, is sick with flu. Miss Gearing was naturally nervous, particularly as the General Nursing Council Inspector was to be present. Unfortunately I missed the previous evening's post. I was anxious for her to get my card before she went into the demonstration so I decided to slip it into her cubby hole myself. I came to work especially early, arrived at Nightingale House shortly after eight, and left almost immediately. I saw no one. Presumably the staff and students were at breakfast. I certainly didn't enter the demonstration room. I wasn't particularly keen to draw attention to myself. I merely inserted the card in its envelope into Miss Gearing's cubby hole and withdrew. It was rather an amusing card. It showed two robins, the male bird forming the words 'good luck' in worms at the feet of the female. Miss Gearing may well have kept the card; she has a fancy for such trifles. No doubt she would show it to you on request. It would corroborate my story of what I was doing in Nightingale House."

Dalgliesh said gravely: "I have already seen the card. Did you know what the demonstration would be about?"

"I knew that it was on intra-gastric feeding but I didn't know that Nurse Fallon had been taken ill in the night or who was to act the part of the patient."

"Have you any idea at all how the corrosive poison got into the drip?"

"If you would just let me take my own time. I was about to tell you. I have none. The most likely explanation is that someone was playing a stupid joke and didn't realize that the result would be fatal. That, or an accident. There are precedents. A new-born baby was killed in the maternity wing of a hospital—not happily one of ours—only three years ago when a bottle of disinfectant was mistaken for milk. I can't explain how the accident here could have occurred or who in Nightingale House could have been so ignorant and stupid as to think that the result of putting a corrosive poison in the milk feed would entertain anyone."

He paused as if defying Dalgliesh to interrupt with another question. Meeting only a bland interrogatory gaze, he went on:

"So much for Nurse Pearce's death. I can't help you further there. It's rather a different matter with Nurse Fallon."

"Something that happened last night; someone you saw?"

The irritation snapped out: "Nothing to do with last night, Superintendent, Miss Gearing has already told you about last night. We saw no one. We left her room immediately after twelve o'clock and went out down the back stairs through Miss Taylor's flat. I retrieved my bicycle from the bushes at the rear of the house —I see no reason why my visits here should be advertised to every mean-minded female in the neighbourhood—and we walked together to the first turn in the path. Then we paused to talk and I escorted Miss Gearing back to Nightingale House and watched her in through the back door. She had left it open. I finally rode off and, as I have told you, got to the fallen elm at twelve seventeen a.m. If anyone passed that way after me and fixed a white scarf to a branch, I can only say that I didn't see him. If he came by car it must have been parked at the other side of Nightingale House. I saw no car."

Another pause. Dalgliesh made no sign, but Masterson permitted himself a sigh of weary resignation as he rustled over a page of his note pad.

"No, Superintendent, the event which I am about to relate took place last spring when this present set of students, including Nurse Fallon, were in their second-year block. As was customary, I gave them a lecture on poisons. At the end of my talk all the students except Nurse Fallon had gathered up their books and left. She came up to the desk and asked me for the name of a poison which could kill painlessly and instantaneously and which an ordinary person might be able to obtain. I thought it an unusual question but saw no reason why I should refuse to answer it. It never occurred to me for one moment that the question had any personal application and, in any case, it was information she could have obtained from any book in the hospital library on materia medica or forensic medicine."

Dalgliesh said: "And what exactly did you tell her, Mr. Morris?"

"I told her that one such poison was nicotine and that it could be obtained from an ordinary rose spray."

Truth or a lie? Who could tell? Dalgliesh fancied that he could usually detect lying in a suspect; but not this suspect. And if Morris stuck to his story, how could it ever be disproved? And if it were a lie, its purpose was plain—to suggest that Josephine Fallon had killed herself. And the obvious reason why he should wish to do that was to protect Sister Gearing. He loved her. This slightly ridiculous, pedantic man; that silly, flirtatious, ageing woman—they loved each other. And why not? Love wasn't the prerogative of the young and desirable. But it was a complication in any investigation—pitiable, tragic or ludicrous, as the case might be, but never negligible. Inspector Bailey, as he knew from the notes on the first crime, had never fully believed in the story of the greetings card. It was in his opinion a foolish and childish gesture for a grown man, and particularly out of character for Morris; therefore he distrusted it. But Dalgliesh thought differently. It was one with Morris's lonely, unromantic cycle rides to visit his mistress; the machine hidden ignominiously in the bushes behind Nightingale House; the slow walk together through the cold of a January midnight prolonging those last precious minutes; his clumsy but strangely dignified defence of the woman he loved. And this last statement, true or false, was inconvenient to say the least. If he stuck to it it would be a powerful argument for those who preferred to believe that Fallon had died by her own hand. And he would stick to it. He looked at Dalgliesh now with the steadfast, exalted gaze of a prospective martyr, holding his adversary's eyes, daring him to disbelieve. Dalgliesh sighed:

"All right," he said. "We won't waste time in speculation. Let's go once again over the timing of your movements last night."

IV

Sister Brumfett, true to her promise, was waiting outside the door when Masterson let Leonard Morris out. But her previous mood of cheerful acquiescence had vanished and she settled herself down opposite Dalgliesh as if to do battle. Before that matriarchal glare he felt something of the inadequacy of a junior student nurse newly arrived on the private ward; and something stronger and horribly familiar. His mind traced the surprising fear unerringly to its source. Just so had the Matron of his prep. school once looked at him, producing in the homesick eight-year-old the same inadequacy, the same fear. And for one second he had to force himself to meet her gaze.

It was the first opportunity he had had to observe her closely and on her own. It was an unattractive and yet an ordinary face. The small shrewd eyes glared into his through steel spectacles, their bridge half embedded in the deep fleshy cleft above the mottled nose. Her iron grey hair was cut short, framing in ribbed waves the plump marsupial cheeks and the obstinate line of the jaw. The elegant gophered cap which on Mavis Gearing looked as delicate as a meringue of spun lace and which flattered even Hilda Rolfe's androgynous features was bound low on Sister Brumfett's brow like a pie frill circling a particularly unappetizing crust. Take that symbol of authority away and replace it by an undistinguished felt hat, cover the uniform with a shapeless fawn coat, and you would have the prototype of a middle-aged suburban housewife strutting through the supermarket, shapeless bag in hand, eyes shrewd for this week's bargain. Yet here, apparently, was one of the best ward Sisters John Carpendar had ever had. Here, more surprisingly, was Mary Taylor's chosen friend.

Before he could begin to question her, she said:

"Nurse Fallon committed suicide. First she killed Pearce and then herself. Fallon murdered Pearce. I happen to know that she did. So why don't you stop worrying Matron and let the work of the hospital go on? There's nothing you can do to help either of them now. They're both dead."

Spoken in that authoritative and disconcertingly evocative tone the statement had the force of a command. Dalgliesh's reply was unreasonably sharp. Damn the woman! He wouldn't be intimidated.

"If you know that for certain, you must have some proof. And anything you know ought to be told. I'm investigating murder, Sister, not the theft of a bedpan. You have a duty not to withhold evidence."

She laughed; a sharp, derisive hoot like an animal coughing.

"Evidence! You wouldn't call it evidence. But I know!"

"Did Nurse Fallon speak to you when she was being nursed on your ward? Was she delirious?"

It was no more than a guess. She snorted her derision.

"If she did, it wouldn't be my duty to tell you. What a patient lets out in delirium isn't gossip to be bandied about. Not on my ward anyway. It isn't evidence either. Just accept what I tell you and stop fussing. Fallon killed Pearce. Why do you think she came back to Nightingale House that morning, with a temperature of 103? Why do you think she refused to give the police a reason? Fallon killed Pearce. You men like to make things so complicated. But it's all so simple really. Fallon killed Pearce, and there's no doubt she had her reasons."

"There are no valid reasons for murder. And even if Fallon did kill Pearce, I doubt whether she killed herself. I've no doubt your colleagues have told you about the rose spray. Remember that Fallon hadn't been in Nightingale House since that tin of nicotine was placed in the conservatory cupboard. Her set haven't been in Nightingale House since the spring of last year and Sister Gearing bought the rose spray in the summer. Nurse Fallon was taken ill on the night that this block began and didn't return to Nightingale House until the evening before she died. How do you account for the fact that she knew where to find the nicotine?"

Sister Brumfett looked surprisingly disconcerted. There was a moment's silence and then she muttered something unintelligible. Dalgliesh waited. Then she said defensively:

"I don't know how she got hold of it. That's for you to discover. But it's obvious that she did."

"Did you know where the nicotine had been put?"

"No. I don't have anything to do with the garden or the conservatory. I like to get out of the hospital on my free days. I usually play golf with Matron or we go for a drive. We try to arrange our off duty together."

Her tone was smug with satisfaction. She made no attempt to hide her complacency. What was she trying to convey, he wondered. Was this reference to the Matron her way of telling him that she was teacher's pet, to be treated with deference?

He said: "Weren't you in the conservatory that evening last summer when Miss Gearing came in with the stuff?"

"I don't remember."

"I think you'd better try to remember, Sister. It shouldn't be difficult. Other people remember perfectly well."

"If they say I was there, I probably was."

"Miss Gearing says that she showed you all the bottle and made a facetious remark about being able to poison the whole school with a few drops. You told her not to be childish and to make sure the tin was locked away. Do you remember now?"

"It's the sort of silly remark Mavis Gearing would make and I daresay I did tell her to be careful. It's a pity she didn't take notice of me."

"You take these deaths very calmly, Sister."

"I take every death very calmly. If I didn't I couldn't do my job. Death is happening all the time in a hospital. It's probably happening now on my ward as it did this afternoon to one of my patients!"

She spoke with sudden and passionate protest, stiffening as if in outrage that the dread finger could touch anyone for whom she was responsible. Dalgliesh found the sudden change of mood disconcerting. It was as if this thickening, unattractive body housed the temperament of a *prima donna*, passionate and irrational. At one moment the eyes, small and unremarkable behind their thick lenses, met his in dull resentment, the obstinate little mouth snapped out its grievances. And then, suddenly, there was this metamorphosis. She blazed at him, her face flaming with indignation so that it came fiercely alive. He had a glimpse of that fervent and possessive love with which she encompassed those in her care. Here was a woman, outwardly unremarkable, who had dedicated her life to a single aim with formidable determination. If something —or someone—got in the way of what she regarded as the greater good, how far would that determination carry her? She seemed to Dalgliesh a fundamentally unintelligent woman. But murder was frequently the last resort of the unintelligent. And were these murders, for all their complexity, the work of a clever woman? A bottle of disinfectant quickly seized; a tin of nicotine readily available. Didn't both these deaths speak of a sudden uncontrolled impulse, an unthinking reliance on the easiest means? Surely in a hospital there were more subtle methods of disposal?

The shrewd eyes were regarding him with watchful dislike. The whole interrogation was an outrage to her. It was hopeless to try to propitiate such a witness and he had no stomach to try. He said:

"I want to go through your movements on the morning Nurse Pearce died, and last night."

"I've already told Inspector Bailey about the morning Pearce died. And I've sent you a note."

"I know. Thank you for it. Now I want you to tell me yourself."

She made no further protest but recited the sequence of her movements and actions as if they were a railway time-table.

Her account of her movements on the morning of Heather Pearce's death agreed almost exactly with the written statement she had already given to Inspector Bailey. She described only her own actions, put forward no theories, gave no opinion. After that first revealing outburst she had apparently decided to stick to facts.

She had woken at six thirty on the Monday the twelfth of January, and had then joined the Matron for early morning tea which it was their habit to drink together in Miss Taylor's flat. She had left Matron at seven fifteen and had then bathed and dressed. She had stayed in her own room until about ten minutes to eight when she had collected her paper from the rack in the hall and had gone in to breakfast. She had seen no one on the stairs or in the hall. Sister Gearing and Sister Rolfe had joined her in the dining-room and they had breakfasted together. She had finished her breakfast and had left the room first; she was unable to say precisely when but it was probably not later than twenty-past eight, had returned briefly to her sittingroom on the third floor, and had then walked over to the hospital where she had arrived on her ward shortly before nine o'clock. She had known about the General Nursing Council Inspection since, obviously, Matron had talked to her about it. She had known about the demonstration since details of the nurse training programme were on the hall notice-board. She had known about Josephine Fallon's illness since Sister Rolfe had telephoned her during the night. She had not, however, known that Nurse Pearce was to take Fallon's place. She agreed that she could have discovered this easily by a glance at the notice-board, but she had not troubled to look. There was no reason why she should be concerned. Taking an interest in the general nurse training programme was one thing, bothering to check on who was to act as the patient was quite another.

She had not known that Nurse Fallon had returned to Nightingale House that morning. Had she done so, she would have reprimanded the girl severely. By the time she had reached the ward Nurse Fallon was in her room and in bed. No one in the ward had noticed her absence. Apparently the Staff Nurse had thought she was in the bathroom or the lavatory. It was reprehensible of the Staff Nurse not to have checked, but the ward was particularly busy and one did not expect patients, particularly student nurses, to behave like idiots. Nurse Fallon had probably only left the ward for about twenty minutes. Her walk through the dark morning had apparently done her no harm. She had made a quick recovery from the influenza and there had been no complications. She had not seemed particularly depressed while she was in the ward, and if there was anything worrying her, she had not confided in Sister Brumfett. In Sister Brumfett's opinion, the girl had been perfectly well enough on discharge from the ward to rejoin her set in Nightingale House.

Next she went through her movements on the previous night, in the same dull, unemphatic voice. Matron had been in Amsterdam at the International Conference so she had spent the evening alone watching television in the Sisters' sitting-room. She had gone to bed at ten p.m. and had been awakened at about quarter to twelve by Mr. Courtney-Briggs's telephone call. She had made her way across to the hospital by a short cut through the trees and had helped the student nurse on duty to prepare the bed for the patient's return. She had stayed with her patient until satisfied that the oxygen and drip were being satisfactorily administered and that his general condition was as good as could be expected. She had returned to Nightingale House shortly after two a.m. and on her way up to her room had seen Maureen Burt coming out of the lavatory. The other twin had appeared almost immediately and she had had a brief conversation with them. She had declined their offer to make her cocoa and had gone straight up to her room. Yes, there was a light shining through Fallon's keyhole at that time. She had not gone into Fallon's room and had no way of knowing whether the girl was alive or dead. She had slept well and had awoken just after seven o'clock when Sister Rolfe had come rushing in with the news that Fallon's body had been discovered. She hadn't seen Fallon since the girl was discharged from her ward after supper on the Tuesday.

At the end of the recital there was a silence, then Dalgliesh asked:

"Did you like Nurse Pearce, Sister? Or Nurse Fallon?"

"No. I didn't dislike them either. I don't believe in having personal relationships with the student nurses. Like and dislike don't come into it. They're either good nurses or they aren't."

"And were they good nurses?"

"Fallon was better than Pearce. She had more intelligence and more imagination. She wasn't an easy colleague but the patients liked her. Some people thought her callous but you wouldn't find a patient who said so. Pearce tried too hard. She went about looking like a young Florence Nightingale, or so she thought. Always thinking of the impression she was making. A silly girl fundamentally. But you could rely on her. She always did what was correct. Fallon did what was right. That takes instinct as well as training. Wait until you're dying, my good man. You'll know the difference."

So Josephine Fallon had been both intelligent and imaginative. He could believe it. But these were the last two qualities he would have expected Sister Brumfett to praise. He recalled the conversation at luncheon, her insistence on the need for unquestioning obedience. He said carefully:

"I'm surprised that you should rank imagination among the virtues of a student nurse. I thought that you valued absolute obedience above all. It's difficult to reconcile imagination, which is surely individual, even iconoclastic, with the submission to authority of the good subordinate. I'm sorry if I sound presumptuous. This conversation hasn't much to do with my business here, I know. But I'm curious."

It had a great deal to do with his business there; his curiosity wasn't irrelevant. But she wasn't to know that. She said gruffly:

"Obedience to rightful authority comes first. You're in a disciplined service; you shouldn't need telling. It's only when the obedience is automatic, when the discipline is accepted and even welcomed, that one learns the wisdom and courage that can safely step outside the rules when the moment comes. Imagination and intelligence are dangerous in nursing if they aren't founded on discipline."

So she wasn't as simple or as obstinately conformist as she appeared, or chose to appear to her colleagues. And she, too, had imagination. Was this the Brumfett, he wondered, that Mary Taylor knew and valued. And yet, he was convinced that his first impressions hadn't been wrong. Fundamentally, she wasn't an intelligent woman. Was she, even now, voicing the theory, the very words perhaps, of another? "The wisdom and courage to step outside the rules." Well, someone in Nightingale House had stepped outside them, someone hadn't lacked the courage. They looked at each other. He was beginning to wonder if Nightingale House had put some kind of spell on him, if its threatening atmosphere had begun to affect his judgement. For behind the thick spectacles he thought he saw the eyes change, thought he detected an urgency to communicate, to be understood, even a plea for help. And then the illusion passed. He was facing again the most ordinary, the most uncompromising, the least complex of all his suspects. And the interview was at an end.

V

It was now after nine o'clock but Dalgliesh and Masterson were still together in the office. There were at least a couple of hours' work ahead before they could break for the night, checking and comparing statements, searching for the tell-tale discrepancy, planning tomorrow's activity. Dalgliesh decided to let Masterson get on with it and dialling the internal number of Matron's flat, he asked if she could give him twenty minutes of her time. Courtesy and policy both dictated that he should keep her informed, but there was another reason for seeing her before he left Nightingale House.

She had left the door of the flat open for him and he passed straight down the corridor to the sitting-room, knocked and entered. He walked into peace, quietness, light. And coldness. The room was surprisingly chilly. A bright fire was burning in the grate but its warmth hardly reached the far corners of the room. As he went across to her he saw that she was appropriately dressed, her long legs encased in brown velvet slacks topped by a high necked cashmere sweater in pale fawn, the sleeves pushed back from brittle wrists. A silk scarf in bright green was knotted around her throat.

They sat down together on the sofa. Dalgliesh saw that she had been working. There was an open briefcase propped against the leg of the coffee table and a spread of papers across its surface. A coffee pot stood in the grate, and the comforting scent of warm wood and coffee pervaded the room.

She offered him coffee or whisky; nothing else. He accepted the coffee and she rose to fetch a second cup. When she had returned, the coffee poured, he said:

"They've told you, I expect, that we've found the poison."

"Yes. Gearing and Rolfe both came to see me after you'd finished questioning them. I suppose this means that it must be murder?"

"I think so, unless Nurse Fallon hid the tin herself. But somehow that seems unlikely. To make a deliberate mystery of suicide with the object of causing the maximum of trouble would be the action of an exhibitionist or a neurotic. This girl seems to me to have been neither, but I wanted your view."

"I agree with you. Fallon, I would have said, was essentially a rational person. If she decided to kill herself it would be for reasons which seemed good to her at the time and I would expect her to leave a brief but lucid note explaining them. A great many suicides kill themselves to make trouble for other people. But not Fallon."

"That would be my assessment, but I wanted to ask someone who had actually known her."

She asked: "What does Madeleine Goodale say?"

"Nurse Goodale thinks that her friend killed herself; but that was before we found the nicotine."

He didn't say where and she didn't ask. He had no intention of telling anyone in Nightingale House where the tin had been found. But one person would know where it had been hidden and with luck might inadvertently reveal their guilty knowledge.

He went on: "There is another matter. Miss Gearing tells me she entertained a friend in her room last night; she says that she let him out through your door. Does that surprise you?"

"No. I leave the flat open when I'm not here so that the Sisters can use the back staircase. It gives them at least the illusion of privacy."

"At the cost, surely, of your own?"

"Oh, I think it's understood that they don't come into the flat. I trust my colleagues. Even if I didn't, there's nothing here to interest them. I keep all official papers in my office over at the hospital."

She was right of course. There was nothing here to interest anyone except him. The sitting-room for all its individuality was almost as plain as his own flat high above the Thames at Queenhithe. Perhaps that was one reason why he felt so at home. Here were no photographs to invite speculation; no bureau bursting with its accumulated hoard of trivia; no pictures to betray a private taste; no invitations to advertise the diversity, the existence even, of a social life. He held his own flat inviolate; it would have been intolerable to him to think that people could walk in and out at will.

But here was an even greater reticence; the self-sufficiency of a woman so private that even her personal surroundings were permitted to give nothing away.

He said: "Mr. Courtney-Briggs tells me that he was Josephine Fallon's lover for a short period during her first year. Did you know that?"

"Yes. I knew it in the same way that I know Mavis Gearing's visitor yesterday was almost certainly Leonard Morris. In a hospital, gossip spreads by a kind of osmosis. One can't always remember being told the latest scandal; one just gets to know."

"And is there much to know?"

"More perhaps than in less sensational institutions. Is that so very surprising? Men and women who have to watch daily what the body can suffer in agony and degradation aren't likely to be too scrupulous about availing themselves of its solace."

When, and with whom, he wondered, did she find her consolation? In her job; in the power which that job undoubtedly gave her? In astronomy, tracing through long nights the paths of the movable stars? With Brumfett? Surely to God not with Brumfett!

She said: "If you're thinking that Stephen Courtney-Briggs might have killed to protect his reputation, well, I don't believe it. I got to know about the affair. So did half the hospital, I've no doubt. Courtney-Briggs isn't particularly discreet. Besides, such a motive would only apply to a man vulnerable to public opinion."

"Every man is vulnerable in some way to public opinion."

She gave him a sudden keen glance from those extraordinary exophthalmic eyes.

"Of course. No doubt Stephen Courtney-Briggs is as capable of killing to prevent personal disaster or public disgrace as any of us. But not, I think, to prevent people knowing that a young and attractive woman was willing to go to bed with him; or that, middle-aged as he may be, he is still able to take his sexual pleasure where he finds it."

Was there a trace of contempt, of resentment almost, in her voice? For a moment he caught an echo of Sister Rolfe.

"And Hilda Rolfe's friendship with Julia Pardoe? You knew about that?"

She smiled a little bitterly.

"Friendship? Yes, I know, and I think that I understand. But I'm not sure that you do. The orthodox reaction, if the affair became known, would be that Rolfe is corrupting Pardoe. But if that young woman has been corrupted, I suspect that it happened before she came to the John Carpendar. I don't propose to interfere. The affair will settle itself. Julia Pardoe should qualify as a State Registered Nurse in a few months' time. I happen to know that she has plans for her future and they certainly don't include staying on here. I'm afraid there is a great deal of unhappiness ahead for Sister Rolfe. But we must meet that when it comes."

Her voice told him that she knew, that she was watching, that she had the situation under control. And that it was not a matter for further discussion.

He finished his coffee in silence, then rose to go. There was nothing else he needed to ask at present and he found himself disagreeably sensitive to every nuance in her voice, every silence which might imply that his presence was irksome. It could hardly be welcome, he knew that. He was used to being the harbinger, at best of ill news, at worst of disaster. But at least he could avoid forcing his company on her a minute more than was necessary.

As she rose to accompany him to the door he made a casual reference to the architecture of the house and asked how long it had been in the possession of the hospital. She said:

"It's a tragic and rather horrible story. The place was built in 1880 by a Thomas Nightingale, a local string and rope manufacturer who had come up in the world and wanted a house to dignify his new position. The name is fortuitously appropriate; it has nothing to do with Florence or with the bird. Nightingale lived here with his wife, they had no children, until 1886. In the January of that year the body of one of the maidservants, a nineteen-year-old girl called Nancy Gorringe, who had been taken by Mrs. Nightingale from an orphanage, was found hanging from one of the trees in the grounds. When the body was cut down it was apparent that she had been systematically ill-treated, beaten, tortured even, over a period of months. It had been calculated sadism. One of the most horrible features of the case was that the other members of the staff must have had some idea what was going on, but did nothing. They were apparently well treated; they paid touching tribute at the trial to Nightingale as a just and considerate master. It must have been similar to some of these modern cases of child cruelty where only one member of the family is singled out for violence and neglect and the others acquiesce in the ill treatment. A taste for vicarious sadism, I suppose, or just the desperate hope of preserving their own safety. And yet it's odd. Not one of them turned against Nightingale, not even when local feeling was at its height in the weeks following the trial. He and his wife were both convicted and spent many years in prison. I have an idea that they died there. Anyway, they never returned to Nightingale House. It was sold to a retired boot manufacturer who lived here for only two years before deciding that he didn't like it. He sold it to one of the governors of the hospital who spent the last twelve years of his life here and bequeathed it to the John Carpendar. It has always been something of an embarrassment to the hospital; no one has been quite sure what to do with it. It's not really suitable as a nurse training school, but it's difficult to see what exactly it would be suitable for. There's a story that Nancy Gorringe's ghost can be heard weeping in the grounds after dark at this time of year. I've never heard her and it's a tale we try to keep from the students. But it's never been a happy house."

And it was less happy than ever now, thought Dalgliesh, as he made his way back to the office. Now there were two murders to add to the history of the violence and hate.

He told Masterson that he could go off duty, then settled down for a last solitary study of the papers. Hardly had the Sergeant left when the outside telephone rang. It was the director of the forensic science laboratory to say that the tests were complete. Josephine Fallon had died of nicotine poisoning and the nicotine had come from the tin of rose spray.

VI

It was two hours before he finally locked the side door of Nightingale House behind him and set out to walk back to the Falconer's Arms.

The path was lit by the old-fashioned type of street lamp, but the lamps were widely spaced and dim so that for most of the time he walked in darkness. He met no one and could well believe that this lonely path was unpopular with the students once night had fallen. The rain had stopped but the wind was rising, shaking down the last drops from the interlocking branches of the elms. He could feel them spitting against his face and seeping under the collar of his coat, and felt a momentary regret that he had decided that morning not to use his car. The trees grew very close to the path, separated from it by a narrow verge of sodden turf. It was a warm night despite the rising wind, and a light mist moved among the trees and coiled around the lamps. The pathway was about ten feet wide. It must have been once a main drive to Nightingale House, but it wound inconsequently among the clumps of elms and birch as if the original owner of the house had hoped to increase his self-importance by the length of his drive.

As he walked he thought about Christine Dakers. He had seen the girl at three forty-five p.m. The private ward had been very quiet at that time and, if Sister Brumfett were about, she had taken care to keep out of his way. The Staff Nurse had received him and had shown him into Nurse Dakers's room. The girl had been sitting up against the pillows looking as flushed and triumphant as a newly-delivered mother and had welcomed him as if she expected congratulations and an offering of flowers. Someone had already supplied her with a vase of daffodils and there were two pots of chrysanthemums beside the tea tray on the overbed table, and a spatter of magazines strewn over the bed cover.

She had tried to appear unconcerned and contrite as she told her story but the acting had been unconvincing. In truth she had been radiant with happiness and relief. And why not? Matron had visited her. She had confessed and had been forgiven. She was filled now with the sweet euphoria of absolution. More to the point, he thought, the two girls who might have menaced her had gone for good. Diane Harper had left the hospital. And Heather Pearce was dead.

And to what exactly had Nurse Dakers confessed? Why this extraordinary liberation of spirit? He wished he knew. But he had come out of her room little wiser than when he went in. But at least, he thought, she had confirmed Madeleine Goodale's evidence of their study time together in the library. Unless there was collusion, which seemed unlikely, they had given each other an alibi for the time before breakfast. And, after breakfast, she had taken her final cup of coffee into the conservatory where she had sat reading the *Nursing Mirror* until it was time to join the demonstration. Nurse Pardoe and Nurse Harper had been with her. The three girls had left the conservatory at the same time, had paid a brief visit to the bathroom and lavatories on the second floor, and had then made their way straight to the demonstration room. It was very difficult to see how Christine Dakers could have poisoned the feed.

Dalgliesh had covered about fifty yards when he stopped in mid-stride, frozen into immobility by what, for one unbelievable second, he thought was the sound of a woman crying. He stood still, straining to distinguish that desperate alien voice. For a moment all was silent, even the wind seemed to have dropped. Then he heard it again, this time unmistakably. This wasn't the night cry of an animal or the figment of a tired but over-stimulated brain. Somewhere in the cluster of trees to his left a woman was howling in misery.

He was not superstitious, but he had the imaginative man's sensitivity to atmosphere. Standing alone in the darkness and hearing that human voice wailing in descant to the rising wind he felt a frisson of awe. The terror and helplessness of that nineteenth-century maidservant touched him briefly as if with her own cold finger. He entered for one appalling second into her misery and hopelessness. The past fused with the present. The terror was eternal. The last desperate act was here and now. Then the moment passed. This was a real voice, a living woman. Pressing on his torch, he turned from the path into the utter darkness of the trees.

About twenty yards from the edge of the turf he could see a wooden hut about twelve feet square, its one dimly lit window casting a square of light on the bark of the nearest elm. He strode over to it, his feet soundless on the sodden earth, and pushed open the door. The warm, rich smell of wood and of paraffin wafted out to meet him. And there was something else. The smell of human life. Sitting huddled in a broken wicker chair, with a storm lantern on the upturned box beside her, was a woman.

The impression of an animal trapped in its lair was immediate and inevitable. They gazed at each other soundlessly. Despite her wild crying, cut off instantaneously at his entrance as if it had been simulated, the eyes which peered keenly into his were unclouded and bright with menace. This animal might be in distress but it was on its own ground and all its senses were alert. When she spoke she sounded gloomily belligerent but with no trace of curiosity or fear.

"Who are yer?"

"My name's Adam Dalgliesh. What's yours?"

"Morag Smith."

"I've heard about you, Morag. You must have got back to the hospital this evening."

"That's right. And told by Miss Collins to report to the resident staff hostel if yer please. I asked to go back to the medical officers' quarters if I couldn't stay in Nightingale House. But oh no! No bloody fear! Got on too well with the doctors I did. So it's off to the 'ostel. They bugger you about properly in this place, they do. I asked to see Matron but Sister Brumfett said she wasn't to be worried."

She paused in her recital of woes to fiddle with the wick of the lantern. The light increased. She screwed up her eyes at him.

"Adam Dalgliesh. Funny name. You're new around 'ere, aren't yer?"

"I only arrived this morning. I expect they've told you about Nurse Fallon. I'm a detective. I'm here to find out how she and Nurse Pearce died."

At first he thought that the news was going to precipitate another bout of wailing. She opened her mouth wide but then, thinking better of it, gave a little gasp and closed it sharply again. She said gruffly:

"I never killed 'er."

"Nurse Pearce? Of course not. Why should you?"

"That's not what the other one thought."

"What other one?"

"That Inspector, Inspector bloody Bill Bailey. I could see what 'e was thinking. Asking all them questions, and his eyes fixed on yer all the bleeding time. What were yer doing from the moment you got up? What the 'ell did he think I was doing? Working! That's what I was doing. Did you like Nurse Pearce? Was she ever unkind to you? I'd 'ave like to see 'er try. Anyway, I never even knew 'er. Well, I 'adn't been over Nightingale 'ouse for more than a week. But I could see what 'e was after. It's always the same. Blame the poor bloody maid."

Dalgliesh moved into the hut and seated himself on a bench against the wall. He would have to question Morag Smith and this seemed as good a time as any. He said:

"I think you're wrong, you know. Inspector Bailey didn't suspect you. He told me so."

She gave a derisive snort.

"Yer don't want to believe everything the police tell yer. Blimey, didn't yer dad tell yer that? 'e suspected me all right. Bloody Bugger Bailey. My God, my dad could tell you some things about the police."

No doubt the police could tell a lot about dad, thought Dalgliesh, but rejected that line of conversation as unlikely to be profitable. The inspector's name lent itself to alliterative abuse and Morag was in the mood to relish it. Dalgliesh hastened to defend his colleague.

"Inspector Bailey was only doing his job. He didn't mean to upset you. I'm a policeman too, and I shall have to ask questions. We all do. I shan't get anywhere unless you help. If Nurse Pearce and Nurse Fallon were killed, then I'm going to find out who did it. They were young, you know. Nurse Pearce was about your age. I don't suppose they wanted to die."

He was not sure how Morag would react to this nicely judged appeal to justice and sentiment but he could see the sharp little eyes probing through the semi-darkness.

" 'elp yer!" Her voice was full of scorn. "Don't kid me. Your sort don't need 'elp. Yer know 'ow the milk got into the coconut all right."

Dalgliesh considered this startling metaphor and decided, in the absence of contrary evidence, that it was intended as a compliment. He balanced his torch upright on the bench so that it threw one bright pool of light on the roof, wriggled his thighs more firmly against the wall, and cushioned his head against a thick bundle of raffia which hung from a nail above him. He was surprisingly comfortable. He asked conversationally:

"Do you come here often?"

"Only when I'm upset." Her tone suggested that this was an eventuality for which any reasonable woman would make provision. "It's private 'ere." She added defensively: "It used to be private, anyway."

Dalgliesh felt rebuked.

"I'm sorry. I won't come here again."

"Oh, I don't mind you. You can come again if you like."

The voice might be ungracious but the compliment was unmistakable. They sat for a moment in curiously companionable silence.

The stout walls of the hut enclosed them, insulating them in an unnatural silence from the moaning of the wind. Inside, the air was cold but musty, smelling pungently of wood, paraffin and humus. Dalgliesh looked around him. The place was not uncomfortable. There was a bale of straw in the corner, a second old cane chair similar to that in which Morag was curled, and an upturned packing-case covered with oilcloth which served as a table. On it he could just make out the shape of a primus oil stove. One of the wall shelves held a white aluminium teapot and a couple of mugs. He guessed that the gardener had once used the place as a comfortable retreat from the ardours of work as well as a potting and storage shed. In spring and summer, isolated in the quiet of the trees and surrounded by bird song, it must, Dalgliesh thought, be an agreeable hiding place. But this was mid-winter. He said:

"Forgive my asking, but wouldn't it be more comfortable to be upset in your own room? And more private?"

"It isn't cosy over in Nightingale 'ouse. And it isn't cosy in the resident staff 'ostel either. I like it 'ere. It smells like my dad's shed on the allotment. And nobody comes after dark. They're all afraid of the ghost."

"And you aren't?"

"I don't believe in 'em."

It was, thought Dalgliesh, the ultimate vindication of sturdy scepticism. You didn't believe in a thing, therefore it didn't exist. Untortured by imagination, you could enjoy the reward of your own certainty even if it were only the undisputed possession of a garden shed when you were feeling upset. He found this admirable. He wondered whether he ought to inquire the cause of her grief, suggest perhaps that she should confide in Matron. Had that wild crying really been caused by nothing more than Bill Bailey's passionately resented attentions? Bailey was a good detective, but not particularly subtle with people. One couldn't afford to be critical. Every detective, however competent, knew what it was unwittingly to antagonize a witness. Once this happened it was the devil to get anything useful out of her—and it usually was a woman—even if the antipathy were partly subconscious. Success in a murder investigation depended largely on making people want to help you, getting them to talk. Bill Bailey had singularly failed with Morag Smith. Adam Dalgliesh, too, had failed in his time.

He remembered what Inspector Bailey, in that brief hour's colloquy when the case had been handed over, had told him about the two maids.

"They're out of it. The old one, Miss Martha Collins, has been at the hospital for forty years and if she had homicidal tendencies would have shown them before now. She's mainly concerned about the theft of the lavatory disinfectant. Seems to regard it as a personal affront. Probably takes the view that the lavatory is her responsibility and the murder isn't. The young girl, Morag Smith, is half dotty if you ask me, and as obstinate as an army mule. She might have done it, I suppose, but I can't for the life of me see why. Heather Pearce hadn't done anything to upset her as far as I know. And in any case she hardly had the time. Morag was only transferred from the doctors' residence to Nightingale House on the day before Pearce died. I gather that she wasn't too pleased about the change, but that's scarcely a motive for starting to kill off the student nurses. Besides, the girl isn't frightened. Obstinate, but not frightened. If she did it, I doubt whether you'll ever prove it."

They sat on in silence. He wasn't anxious to probe into her grief and suspected that she had been indulging an irrational need for a good cry. She had chosen her secret place for it and was entitled to emotional privacy even if her physical privacy had been invaded. He was too reticent himself to have any stomach for the emotional prying which gives so many people the comforting illusion that they care. He seldom did care. Human beings were perpetually interesting to him, and nothing about them surprised him any more. But he didn't involve himself. He wasn't surprised that she should like the shed, smelling as it did of home.

He became aware of a confused background mumbling. She had returned to a recital of her grievance.

"Kept looking at me all the time 'e did. And asking the same old thing over and over again. Stuck up too. You could see that he fancied himself."

Suddenly she turned to Dalgliesh.

"You feeling sexy?"

Dalgliesh gave the question serious attention.

"No. I'm too old to feel sexy when I'm cold and tired. At my age you need the creature comforts if you're to perform with any pleasure to your partner or credit to yourself."

She gave him a look in which disbelief struggled with commiseration.

"You're not that old. Thanks for the 'anky anyway."

She gave one last convulsive blow before handing it back. Dalgliesh slipped it quickly into his pocket, resisting the temptation to drop it unobtrusively behind the bench. Stretching his legs ready to move, he only half heard her next words.

"What did you say?" he asked, careful to keep his voice level, uninquisitorial.

She answered sulkily.

"I said that 'e never found out about me drinking the milk anyway, bugger 'im. I never told 'im."

"Was that the milk used for the demonstration feed? When did you drink it?"

He tried to sound conversational, only mildly interested. But he was aware of the silence in the hut and the two sharp eyes staring at him. Could she really be unaware of what she was telling him?

"It was at eight o'clock, maybe a minute before. I went into the demo room to see if I'd left my tin of polish there. And there was this bottle of milk on the trolley and I drank some of it. Just a bit off the top."

"Just out of the bottle?"

"Well, there wasn't any cup 'andy was there? I was thirsty and I saw the milk and I just fancied a bit. So I took a swig."

He asked the crucial question.

"You just had the cream off the top?"

"There wasn't no cream. It wasn't that kind of milk."

His heart leapt.

"And what did you do then?"

"I didn't do nothing."

"But weren't you afraid that Sister Tutor would notice that the bottle wasn't full?"

"The bottle was full. I filled it up with water from the tap. Anyway, I only took a couple of gulps."

"And replaced the seal on top of the bottle?"

"That's right. Careful like so as they wouldn't notice."

"And you never told anyone?"

"No one asked me. That Inspector asked me if I'd been in the demo room and I said only before seven o'clock when I did a bit of cleaning. I wasn't going to tell 'im nothing. It wasn't 'is bloody milk anyway; 'e never paid for it."

"Morag, are you quite, quite sure of the time?"

"Eight o'clock. The demo clock said eight anyway. I looked at it because I was supposed to help serve the breakfasts, the dining-room maids being off with flu. Some people think you can be in three places at once. Anyway, I went into the dining-room where the Sisters and the students had all started eating. Then Miss Collins gave me one of 'er looks. Late again Morag! So it must 'ave been eight. The students always start breakfast at eight."

"And were they all there?"

"Of course they was all there! I told yer! They was at their breakfast."

But he knew that they had been there. The twenty-five minutes from eight until eight twenty-five was the only time in which all the female suspects had been together, eating under the eye of Miss Collins and full in each other's gaze. If Morag's story were true, and he didn't for one moment doubt it, then the scope of the inquiry had been dramatically narrowed. There were only six people who had no firm alibi for the whole of the period from eight o'clock until the class assembled at eight forty. He would have to check the statements of course, but he knew what he would find. This was the sort of information he had been trained to recall at will and the names came obediently to mind. Sister Rolfe, Sister Gearing, Sister Brumfett, Nurse Goodale, Leonard Morris and Stephen Courtney-Briggs.

He pulled the girl gently to her feet.

"Come on, Morag, I'm going to see you back to the hostel. You're a very important witness and I don't want you to get pneumonia before I've had a chance to take your statement."

"I don't want to write nothing down. I'm no scholar."

"Someone will write it down for you. You'll only have to sign it."

"I don't mind doing that. I'm not daft. I can sign my name I 'ope."

And he would have to be there to see that she did. He had a feeling that Sergeant Masterson would be no more successful than Inspector Bailey in dealing with Morag. It would be safer to take her statement himself even if it meant a later start than he had planned for his journey to London.

But it would be time well spent. As he turned to pull the shed door firmly closed behind them—it had no lock—he felt happier than at any time since the finding of the nicotine. Now he was making progress. On the whole, it hadn't been too bad a day.

Chapter Seven

Danse Macabre

I

It was five minutes to seven the next morning. Sergeant Masterson and Detective Constable Greeson were in the kitchen at Nightingale House with Miss Collins and Mrs. Muncie. It seemed like the middle of the night to Masterson, dark and cold. The kitchen smelt agreeably of new baked bread, a country smell, nostalgic and comforting. But Miss Collins was no prototype of the buxom and welcoming country cook. She watched, lips tight and arms akimbo, as Greeson placed a filled milk bottle in the front of the middle shelf of the refrigerator, and said:

"Which one are they supposed to take?"

"The first bottle to hand. That's what they did before, didn't they?"

"So they say. I had something better to do than sit and watch them. I've got something better to do now."

"That's okay by us. We'll do the watching."

Four minutes later the Burt twins came in together. No one spoke. Shirley opened the refrigerator door and Maureen took out the first bottle to hand. Followed by Masterson and Greeson the twins made their way to the demonstration room through the silent and echoing hall. The room was empty and the curtains drawn. The two fluorescent lights blazed down on a semicircle of vacant chairs and on the high narrow bed where a grotesque demonstration doll, round mouthed, nostrils two black and gaping apertures, was propped against the pillows. The twins set about their preparations in silence. Maureen set down the bottle on the trolley, then dragged out the drip-feed apparatus and positioned it by the side of the bed.

Shirley collected instruments and bowls from the various cupboards and set them out on the trolley. The two policemen watched. After twenty minutes Maureen said:

"That's as much as we did before breakfast. We left the room just like it is now."

Masterson said: "Okay. Then we'll put forward our watches to eight forty when you came back here. There's no point in hanging about. We can call the rest of the students in now."

Obediently the twins adjusted their pocket watches while Greeson rang the library where the remaining students were waiting. They came almost immediately and in the order of their original appearance. Madeleine Goodale first, followed by Julia Pardoe and Christine Dakers who arrived together. No one made any attempt to talk and they took their places silently on the semicircle of chairs, shivering a little as if the room were cold. Masterson noticed that they kept their eyes averted from the grotesque doll in the bed. When they had settled themselves he said:

"Right, Nurse. You can go ahead with the demonstration now. Start heating the milk."

Maureen looked at him puzzled.

"The milk?But no one's had a chance to . . ." Her voice died away.

Masterson said: "No one's had a chance to poison it? Never mind. Just go ahead. I want you to do precisely what you did last time."

She filled a large jug with hot water from the tap then stood the unopened bottle in it for a few seconds to warm the milk. Receiving Masterson's impatient nod to get on with it, she prised the cap off the bottle and poured the liquid into a glass measuring jug. Then she took a glass thermometer from the instrument trolley and checked the temperature of the liquid. The class watched in fascinated silence. Maureen glanced at Masterson. Receiving no sign, she took up the oesophageal tube and inserted it into the rigid mouth of the doll. Her hand was perfectly steady. Lastly she lifted a glass funnel high over her head and paused. Masterson said:

"Go ahead, Nurse. It isn't going to hurt the doll to get a bit damp. That's what it's made for. A few ounces of warm milk isn't going to rot its guts."

Maureen paused. This time the fluid was visible and all their eyes were on the white curving stream. Then suddenly the girl paused, arm still poised high, and stood motionless, like a model awkwardly posed.

"Well," said Masterson: "Is it or isn't it?"

Maureen lowered the jug to her nostrils, then without a word passed it to her twin. Shirley sniffed and looked at Masterson.

"This isn't milk, is it? It's disinfectant. You wanted to test whether we really could tell!"

Maureen said: "Are you telling us that it was disinfectant last time; that the milk was poisoned before we took the bottle out of the fridge?"

"No. Last time the milk was all right when you took it out of the fridge. What did you do with the bottle once the milk had been poured into the measuring jug?"

Shirley said: "I took it over to the sink in the corner and rinsed it out. I'm sorry I forgot. I should have done that earlier."

"Never mind. Do it now."

Maureen had placed the bottle on the table by the side of the sink, its crumpled cap at its side. Shirley picked it up. Then she paused. Masterson said very quietly:

"Well?"

The girl turned to him, perplexed.

"There's something different, something wrong. It wasn't like this."

"Wasn't it? Then think. Don't worry yourself. Relax. Just relax and think."

The room was preternaturally silent. Then Shirley swung round to her twin.

"I know now, Maureen! It's the bottle top. Last time we took one of the homogenized bottles from the fridge, the kind with the silver cap. But when we came back into the demonstration room after breakfast it was different. Don't you remember? The cap was gold. It was Channel Island milk."

Nurse Goodale said quietly from her chair: "Yes. I remember too. The only cap I saw was gold."

Maureen looked across at Masterson in puzzled inquiry.

"So someone must have changed the cap?"

Before he had a chance to reply they heard Madeleine Goodale's calm voice.

"Not necessarily the cap. Somebody changed the whole bottle."

Masterson did not reply. So the old man had been right! The solution of disinfectant had been made up carefully and at leisure and the lethal bottle substituted for the one from which Morag Smith had drunk. And what had happened to the original bottle? Almost certainly it had been left in the small kitchen on the Sisters' floor. Wasn't it Sister Gearing who had complained to Miss Collins that the milk was watery?

II

Dalgliesh's business at the Yard was quickly completed and by eleven o'clock he was in North Kensington.

Number 49 Millington Square, W.10, was a large dilapidated Italianate house fronted with crumbling stucco. There was nothing remarkable about it. It was typical of hundreds in this part of London. It was obviously divided into bed-sitting-rooms since every window showed a different set of curtains, or none, and it exuded that curious atmosphere of secretive and lonely over-occupation which hung over the whole district. Dalgliesh saw that there was no bank of bell pushes in the porch and no neat list of the tenants. The front door was open. He pushed through the glass panelled door which led to the hall and was met at once by a smell of sour cooking, floor polish and unwashed clothes. The walls of the hall had been papered with a thick encrusted paper, now painted dark brown, and glistening as if it exuded grease and perspiration. The floor and staircase were laid with a patterned linoleum, patched with a brighter newer design where the tears would have been dangerous, but otherwise torn and unmended. The paintwork was an institutional green. There was no sign of life but, even at this time of the day, he felt its presence behind the tightly closed and numbered doors as he made his way unchallenged to the upper floors.

Number 14 was on the top floor at the back. As he approached the door he heard the sharp staccato clatter of typing. He knocked loudly and the sound stopped. There was a wait of more than a minute before the door half opened and he found himself facing a pair of suspicious and unwelcoming eyes.

"Who are you? I'm working. My friends know not to call in the mornings."

"But I'm not a friend. May I come in?"

"I suppose so. But I can't spare you much time. And I don't think it'll be worth your while. I don't want to join anything; I haven't the time. And I don't want to buy anything because I haven't the money. Anyway, I've got everything I need." Dalgliesh showed his card.

"I'm not buying or selling; not even information which is what I'm here for. It's about Josephine Fallon. I'm a police officer and I'm investigating her death. You, I take it, are Arnold Dowson."

The door was opened wider.

"You'd better come in." No sign of fear but perhaps a certain wariness in the grey eyes.

It was an extraordinary room, a small attic with a sloping roof and a dormer window, furnished almost entirely with crude and unpainted wooden boxes, some still stencilled with the name of the original grocer or wine merchant. They had been ingeniously fitted together so that the walls were honeycombed from floor to ceiling with pale wooden cells, irregular in size and shape and containing all the impedimenta of daily living. Some were stacked close with hard-backed books; others with orange paperbacks. Another framed a small two-bar electric fire, perfectly adequate to heat so small a room. In another box was a neat pile of clean but unironed clothes. Another held blue-banded mugs and other crockery, and yet another displayed a group of *objets trouvés*, sea-shells, a Staffordshire dog, a small jam jar or bird feathers. The single bed, blanket-covered, was under the window. Another upturned box served as a table and desk. The only two chairs were the folding canvas type sold for picnicking. Dalgliesh was reminded of an article once seen in a Sunday colour supplement on how to furnish your bed-sitting-room for under £50. Arnold Dowson had probably done it for half the price. But the room was not unpleasing. Everything was functional and simple. It was perhaps too claustrophobic for some tastes and there was something obsessional in the meticulous tidiness and the way in which every inch of space had been used to the full which prevented it from being restful. It was the room of a self-sufficient, well-organized man who, as he had told Dalgliesh, plainly had everything he wanted.

The tenant suited the room. He looked almost excessively tidy. He was a young man, probably not much over twenty, Dalgliesh thought. His fawn polo-neck sweater was clean, with each cuff neatly turned back to match its fellow, and the collar of a very white shirt visible at the neck. His blue jeans were faded but unstained and had been carefully washed and ironed. There was a crease down the centre of each leg and the ends had been turned up and stitched carefully into place. It gave an oddly incongruous effect to such an informal outfit. He wore leather sandals of the buckled style normally seen on children, and no socks. His hair was very fair and was brushed into a helmet which framed his face in the manner of a medieval page. The face beneath the sleek fringe was bony and sensitive, the nose crooked and too large, the mouth small and well shaped with a hint of petulance. But his most remarkable feature were his ears. They were the smallest Dalgliesh had ever seen on a man, and were without colour even at the tips. They looked as if they were made of wax. Sitting on an upturned orange box with his hands held loosely between his knees and his watchful eyes on Dalgliesh, he looked like the centrepiece of a surrealist painting; singular and precise against the multi-cellular background. Dalgliesh pulled out one of the boxes and seated himself opposite the boy. He said:

"You knew that she was dead, of course?"

"Yes. I read about it in this morning's papers."

"Did you know that she was pregnant?"

This at least produced emotion. The boy's tight face whitened. His head jerked up and he stared at Dalgliesh silently for a moment before replying.

"No. I didn't know. She didn't tell me."

"She was nearly three months' pregnant. Could it have been your child?"

Dowson looked down at his hands.

"It could have been, I suppose. I didn't take any precautions, if that's what you mean. She told me not to worry, that she'd see to that. After all, she was a nurse. I thought she knew how to take care of herself."

"That was something I suspect she never did know. Hadn't you better tell me about it?"

"Do I have to?"

"No. You don't have to say anything. You can demand to see a solicitor and make any amount of fuss and trouble and cause a great deal of delay. But is there any point? No one is accusing you of murdering her. But someone did. You knew her and presumably you liked her. For some of the time, anyway. If you want to help you can best do it by telling me everything you knew about her."

Dowson got slowly to his feet. He seemed as slow-moving and clumsy as an old man. He looked round as if disoriented. Then he said:

"I'll make some tea."

He shuffled over to a double gas ring, fitted to the right of the meagre and unused fireplace, lifted the kettle as if testing by weight that it held sufficient water, and lit the gas. He took down two of the mugs from one of the boxes and set them out on a further box which he dragged between himself and Dalgliesh. It held a number of neatly folded newspapers which looked as if they hadn't been read. He spread one over the top of the box and set out the blue mugs and a bottle of milk as formally as if they were about to drink from Crown Derby. He didn't speak again until the tea was made and poured. Then he said:

"I wasn't her only lover."

"Did she tell you about the others?"

"No, but I think one of them was a doctor. Perhaps more than one. That wouldn't be surprising in the circumstances. We were talking once about sex and she said that a man's nature and character were always completely revealed when he made love. That if he were selfish or insensitive or brutal he couldn't conceal it in bed whatever he might do with his clothes on. Then she said that she had once slept with a surgeon and it was only too apparent that most of the bodies he came into contact with had been anaesthetized first; that he was so busy admiring his own technique that it never occurred to him that he was in bed with a conscious woman. She laughed about it. I don't think she minded very much. She laughed about a great many things."

"But you don't think she was happy?"

He appeared to be considering. Dalgliesh thought: And for God's sake don't answer, "who is?"

"No, not really happy. Not for most of the time. But she did know how to be happy. That was the important thing."

"How did you meet her?"

"I'm learning to be a writer. That's what I want to be and I've never wanted to be anything else. I have to earn some money to live while I get my first novel finished and published, so I work at night as a continental telephone operator. I know enough French to make it possible. The pay isn't bad. I don't have many friends because there isn't time and I never went to bed with any woman until I met Jo. Women don't seem to like me. I met her last summer in St. James's Park. She was there on one of her off-duty days and I was there to watch the ducks and see what the park looked like. I wanted to set one of the scenes in my book in St. James's Park in July, and I went there to make some notes. She was lying on her back on the grass staring at the sky. She was quite alone. One of the pages of my notebook got detached and blew across the grass into her face. I went after it and apologized, and we chased it together."

He was holding the mug of tea looking at it as if staring again into the summer surface of the lake.

"It was an odd day—very hot, sunless and blustery. The wind blew in warm gusts. The lake looked heavy like oil."

He paused for a moment, and when Dalgliesh didn't speak, went on:

"So we met and talked, and I asked her to come back for tea. I don't know what I expected. After tea we talked more and she made love to me. She told me weeks later that she didn't have that in mind when she came here but I don't know. I don't even know why she came back. Perhaps she was bored."

"Did you have it in mind?"

"I don't know that either. Perhaps. I know that I wanted to make love to a woman. I wanted to know what it was like. That's one experience you can't write about until you know."

"And sometimes not even then. And how long did she continue to provide you with copy?"

The boy seemed unaware of the irony. He said:

"She used to come here about once a fortnight on her day off. We never went out together except to a pub occasionally. She would bring in some food and cook a meal and afterwards we would talk and go to bed."

"What did you talk about?"

"I suppose I did most of the talking. She didn't tell me much about herself, only that both her parents had been killed while she was a child and that she had been brought up in Cumberland by an elderly aunt. The aunt is dead now. I don't think Jo had a very happy childhood. She always wanted to be a nurse but she got T.B. when she was seventeen. It wasn't very bad and she spent eighteen months in a sanitorium in Switzerland and was cured. But the doctors advised her not to train as a nurse. So she did a number of other jobs. She was an actress for about three years; but that wasn't much of a success. Then she was a waitress and a shop assistant for a time. Then she became engaged but nothing came of it. She broke it off."

"Did she say why?"

"No, except that she found something out about the man which made it impossible to marry him."

"Did she say what it was or who the man was?"

"No, and I didn't ask. But I think he may have been some kind of sexual pervert."

Seeing Dalgliesh's face he added quickly:

"I don't really know. She never told me. Most of the things I know about Jo just came up casually in conversation. She never really talked about herself for long. It's just an idea I have. There was a kind of bitter hopelessness about the way she spoke of her engagement."

"And after that?"

"Well, apparently she decided that she might as well go back to her original idea of being a nurse. She thought she could get through the medical examination with luck. She chose the John Carpendar Hospital because she wanted to be near London but not actually in it, and thought that a small hospital would be less arduous. She didn't want her health to break down, I suppose."

"Did she talk about the hospital?"

"Not much. She seemed happy enough there. But she spared me the intimate details of the bedpan rounds."

"Do you know whether she had an enemy?"

"She must have had, mustn't she, if somebody killed her? But she never told me about it. Perhaps she didn't know."

"Do these names mean anything to you?"

He went through the names of all the people, students, sisters, surgeon, pharmacist, who had been in Nightingale House the night Josephine Fallon had died.

"I think she mentioned Madeleine Goodale to me. I've a feeling they were friendly. And the Courtney-Briggs name seems familiar. But I can't remember any details."

"When did you last see her?"

"About three weeks ago. She came on her night off and cooked supper."

"How did she seem then?"

"She was restless and she wanted to make love rather badly. Then just before she left she said that she wouldn't see me again. A few days later I got a letter. It merely said, 'I meant what I said. Please don't try to get in touch. It's nothing you've done so don't worry. Good-bye and thank you. Jo.' "

Dalgliesh asked if he had kept the letter.

"No. I only keep important papers. I mean, there isn't room here to hoard letters."

"And did you try to get in touch with her again?"

"No. She'd asked me not to and there didn't seem much point in it. I suppose if I'd known about the child I might have done. But I'm not sure. There's nothing I could have done. I couldn't have had a child here. Well, you can see that. How could I? She wouldn't want to marry me and I never considered marrying her.

I don't want to marry anyone. But I don't think she killed herself because of the baby. Not Jo."

"All right. You don't think she killed herself. Tell me why."

"She wasn't the type."

"Oh, come now! You can do better than that."

The boy said belligerently: "It's true enough. I've known two people in my life who killed themselves. One was a boy in my last year at school when we were sitting for our G.C.E. The other was a manager of a dry cleaning firm I worked for. I drove the delivery van. Well, in both cases, everyone said all the usual things about how dreadful and how surprising it was. But I wasn't really surprised. I don't mean that I was expecting it or anything like that. I just wasn't really surprised. When I thought about both deaths I could believe that they had actually done it."

"Your sample is too small."

"Jo wouldn't kill herself. Why should she?"

"I can think of reasons. She hadn't made much success of her life so far. She hadn't any relatives to care about her, and very few friends. She didn't sleep easily at night, wasn't really happy. She had at last succeeded in training to be a nurse and was within a few months of her final examination. And then she finds herself pregnant. She knows that her lover won't want the child, that it's no use looking to him for comfort or support."

Dowson cried out in vehement protest.

"She never looked to anyone for comfort or support! That's what I'm trying to tell you! She slept with me because she wanted to. I'm not responsible for her. I'm not responsible for anyone. Anyone! I'm only responsible for myself. She knew what she was doing. It wasn't as if she were a young, inexperienced girl who needed kindness and protection."

"If you believe that only the young and innocent need comfort and protection you're thinking in clichés. And if you begin by thinking in clichés you end by writing them."

The boy said sullenly: "Maybe. But that's what I believe."

Suddenly he got up and went over to the wall. When he came back to the centre box Dalgliesh saw that he held a large smooth stone. It fitted snugly into his curved palm, a perfect ovoid. It was a pale grey, flecked like an egg. Dowson let it slide from his hand on to the table where it rocked gently into stillness. Then he sat down again and bent forward, his head in his hands. Together they looked at the stone. Dalgliesh did not speak. Suddenly the boy said:

"She gave it to me. We found it together on the beach at Ventnor, in the Isle of Wight. We went there together last October. But of course you know. That must have been how you traced me. Lift it. It's surprisingly heavy."

Dalgliesh took the stone in his hands. It was satisfying to touch, smooth and cool. He took pleasure in the sea-washed perfection of its shape, in the hard unyielding roundness of it which yet fitted with such gentleness into the palm of his hand.

"I never had a holiday by the sea when I was a boy. Dad died before I was six and the old woman hadn't the money. So I missed out on the seaside. Jo thought it would be fun to go there together. It was very warm last October. Remember? We took the ferry from Portsmouth and there were only half a dozen people on it besides ourselves. The island was empty too. We could walk from Ventnor to St. Catherine's Lighthouse without meeting a soul. It was warm enough and deserted enough to bathe naked. Jo found this stone. She thought it would do as a paper-weight. I wasn't going to tear my pocket carrying that weight home but she did. Then, when we got back here, she gave it to me as a keepsake. I wanted her to have it but she said that I'd forget the holiday long before she did. Don't you see? She knew how to be happy. I'm not sure that I do. But Jo did. If you're like that you don't kill yourself. Not when you know how marvellous living can be. Colette knew about that. She wrote about 'a compelling fierce and secret *rapport* with the earth and everything that gushes from its breasts'." He looked at Dalgliesh.

"Colette was a French writer."

"I know. And you believe that Josephine Fallon could feel that?"

"I know she could. Not for long. Not often. But when she was happy she was marvellous. If you once know that kind of happiness you don't kill yourself. While you live there's a hope it could happen again. So why cut yourself off from the hope of it for ever?"

Dalgliesh said: "You cut yourself off from the misery too. That might seem more important. But I think you're right. I don't believe Josephine Fallon killed herself. I believe she was murdered. That's why I'm asking if there's anything else you can tell me."

"No. I was on duty at the Exchange the night she died. I had better give you the address. I suppose you'll want to check."

"There are reasons why it's extremely unlikely to have been anyone who wasn't familiar with Nightingale House. But we shall check."

"Here's the address then."

He tore a corner from the newspaper covering the table and taking a pencil from his trouser pocket, wrote down the address in a crabbed hand, his head nearly touching the paper. Then he folded it as if the message were secret, and pushed it across the table.

"Take the stone too. I'd like you to have it. No, take it. Please take it. You think I'm heartless, that I'm not grieving for her. But I am. I want you to find out who killed her. It won't do any good to her or to the man, but I want you to find out. And I am sorry. It's just that I can't let myself feel too much. I can't let myself get involved. You understand?"

Dalgliesh took the stone in his hand and rose to go.

"Yes," he said: "I understand."

III

Mr. Henry Urquhart of Messrs. Urquhart, Wimbush and Portway was Josephine Fallon's solicitor. Dalgliesh's appointment with him was for twelve twenty-five p.m., a time disobligingly chosen, he felt, to intimate that every minute of the solicitor's time was valuable and that he was prepared to spare the police no more than half an hour before lunch. Dalgliesh was admitted immediately. He doubted whether a detective sergeant would have been received so promptly. This was one of the minor advantages for his passion of doing the job himself, for resisting the pressures to make him into a desk detective, controlling the investigation from his office with a small army of detective constables, scenes-of-crime men, photographers, finger-print experts and scientists ministering to his ego and effectively cutting him off from all but the main protagonists of the crime. He knew that he had a reputation for solving his cases very fast, but he never grudged time on jobs which some of his colleagues thought more appropriate to a detective constable. As a result he was sometimes given information which a less experienced interrogator would have missed. He hardly expected this happy bonus from Mr. Henry Urquhart. This interview was likely to be little more than the formal and punctilious exchange of relevant facts. But it had been necessary for him to visit London. There were matters which he had to attend to at the Yard. And it was always a pleasure to visit on foot and in the fitful sunlight of a winter morning these secluded corners of the City.

Messrs. Urquhart, Wimbush and Portway were one of the most respected and successful of the City's firms of solicitors. Dalgliesh felt that few of Mr. Urquhart's clients could have been mixed up in a murder investigation. They might have their little difficulties from time to time with the Queen's proctor; they might, against all advice, indulge in imprudent litigation or obstinately persist in devising unwise wills; they might require their solicitor's services to devise technical defences to the drink and driving laws; it might indeed be necessary to extricate them from all manner of folly and imprudence. But their killing would be done legally.

The room into which he was shown could have served as a stage set for a successful solicitor's office. The coal fire was banked high in the grate. From above the mantel shelf the portrait of the founder gazed down in approval on his great grandson. The desk at which the great grandson sat was of the same period as the portrait and displayed the same qualities of durability, fitness for the task in hand, and a sturdy opulence which stopped just short of ostentation. On the other wall there was a small oil. Dalgliesh thought that it looked very like a Jan Steen. It proclaimed to the world that the firm knew a good picture when it saw one and could afford to display it on the wall.

Mr. Urquhart, tall, ascetic, discreetly grey at the temples and with the air of a reserved dominie, was well cast for the role of a successful solicitor. He was wearing an exceedingly well-cut suit, but in lovat tweed as if the more orthodox pin stripe would have verged on caricature. He received Dalgliesh without apparent curiosity or concern but the Superintendent noted with interest that Miss Fallon's box was already on the table before him. Dalgliesh stated his business briefly and ended:

"Can you tell me anything about her? In a murder inquiry anything we can learn about the past life and personality of the victim is helpful."

"And this, you are now confident, is murder?"

"She was killed by taking nicotine in her late night beaker of whisky. As far as we know, she wasn't aware that the tin or rose spray was in the conservatory cupboard, and if she knew and it occurred to her to use it, I doubt whether she would subsequently have hidden the tin."

"I see. And there is, too, the suggestion that the poison administered to the first victim—Heather Pearce wasn't it—was intended for my client?"

Mr. Urquhart sat for a moment finger to finger with his head slightly bent as if consulting either his own subconscious, a higher power, or the ghost of his former client before divulging what he knew. Dalgliesh thought that he could have saved the time. Urquhart was a man who knew perfectly well how far he was prepared to go, professionally or otherwise. The pantomime was unconvincing. And his story, when it came, did nothing to clothe the dry bones of Josephine Fallon's life. The facts were there. He consulted the papers in front of him, and presented them logically, unemotionally, lucidly. The time and place of her birth; the circumstances of her parents' death; her subsequent upbringing by an elderly aunt, who together with him had been a trustee until Miss Fallon's majority; the date and circumstance of that aunt's death from cancer of the uterus; the money left to Josephine Fallon and the exact way in which it had been invested; the girl's movements after her twenty-first birthday in so far, as he pointed out dryly, she had troubled to inform him of them.

Dalgliesh said: "She was pregnant. Did you know?"

It could not be said that this news disconcerted the solicitor although his face creased into the vaguely pained look of a man who can never quite reconcile himself to the messiness of the world.

"No. She didn't tell me. But then I would not expect her to do so, unless, of course, she was thinking of applying for an affiliation order. I gather that was not in question."

"She told her friend, Madeleine Goodale, that she intended to have an abortion."

"Indeed. An expensive and to my mind, despite the recent legislation, a dubious business. I speak morally, of course, not legally. The recent legislation . . ."

Dalgliesh said: "I am aware of the recent legislation. So there is nothing else you can tell me?"

The solicitor's tone held a tinge of reproof.

"I have already told you a great deal about her background and financial position in so far as they were known to me. I am afraid I can't supply you with any more recent or intimate information. Miss Fallon consulted me seldom. Indeed she had no reason to do so. The last time was about her will. You are, I believe, already appraised of its terms. Miss Madeleine Goodale is the sole legatee. The estate is likely to amount to approximately twenty thousand pounds."

"Was there a previous will?"

Was it Dalgliesh's imagination, or did he detect the slight stiffening of facial muscles, the almost imperceptible frown which greeted an unwelcome question.

"There were two, but the second of these was never signed. The first, made soon after her majority, left everything to medical charities, including cancer research. The second she proposed to execute on the occasion of her marriage. I have the letter here."

He handed this across to Dalgliesh. It was addressed from a flat in Westminster and was written in a confident upright and unfeminine hand.

"Dear Mr. Urquhart, This is to let you know that I shall be married on 14th March at St. Marylebone Registry Office to Peter Courtney. He is an actor; you may have heard of him. Will you please draw up a will for me to sign on that date. I shall leave everything to my husband. His full name incidentally is Peter Albert Courtney Briggs. No hyphen. I expect you'll need to know that to draw up the will. We shall be living at this address.

"I shall also need some money. Could you please ask Warranders to make two thousand pounds available to me by the end of the month? Thank you. I hope that you and Mr. Surtees are keeping well. Yours sincerely, Josephine Fallon."

A cool letter, thought Dalgliesh. No explanations. No justification. No expressions of happiness or hope. And come to that, no invitation to the wedding.

Henry Urquhart said: "Warranders were her stockbrokers. She always dealt with them through us, and we kept all her official papers. She preferred us to do so. She said she preferred to travel unencumbered."

He repeated the phrase, smiling complacently as if he found it in some way remarkable, and glanced at Dalgliesh as if expecting him to comment.

He went on: "Surtees is my clerk. She always asked after Surtees."

He seemed to find that fact more puzzling than the terms of the letter itself.

Dalgliesh said: "And Peter Courtney subsequently hanged himself."

"That is so, three days before the wedding. He left a note for the coroner. It wasn't read out at the inquest, I'm thankful to say. It was quite explicit. Courtney wrote that he had planned to marry to extricate himself from certain financial and personal difficulties, but at the last moment had found he couldn't face it. He was a compulsive gambler apparently. I am informed that uncontrolled gambling is, in fact, a disease akin to alcoholism. I know little of the syndrome but can appreciate that it could be tragic in its consequences, particularly for an actor whose earnings, although large, are erratic. Peter Courtney was very heavily in debt and totally unable to extricate himself from a compulsion which daily made that debt worse."

"And the personal difficulties? I believe he was a homosexual. There was gossip about it at the time. Do you know whether your client knew?"

"I have no information. It seems unlikely that she should not have known since she committed herself so far as to become engaged. She may, of course, have been so sanguine or so unwise as to suppose that she could help to cure him. I should have advised her against the marriage had she consulted me, but as I have said she did not consult me."

And shortly afterwards, thought Dalgliesh, a matter of months only, she had begun her training at the John Carpendar and was sleeping with Peter Courtney's brother. Why? Loneliness? Boredom? A desperate need to forget? Payment for services rendered? What services? Simple sexual attraction, if physical need were ever simple, for a man who physically was a coarse edition of the fiancé she had lost? The need to reassure herself that she could attract heterosexual desire? Courtney-Briggs himself had suggested that it was she who had taken the initiative. It was certainly she who had brought the affair to an end. There had been no mistaking the surgeon's bitter resentment of a woman who had had the temerity to reject him before he had chosen to reject her.

As he rose to go Dalgliesh said: "Peter Courtney's brother is a consultant surgeon at the John Carpendar Hospital. But perhaps you knew?"

Henry Urquhart smiled his tight, unamused smile.

"Oh yes, I know. Stephen Courtney-Briggs is a client of mine. Unlike his brother, he has acquired a hyphen to his name and a more permanent success." He added with apparent irrelevance:

"He was holidaying in a friend's yacht in the Mediterranean when his brother died. He came home immediately. It was, of course, a great shock as well as being a considerable embarrassment."

It must have been, thought Dalgliesh. But Peter dead was decidedly less embarrassing than Peter living. It would no doubt have suited Stephen Courtney-Briggs to have had a well-known actor in the family, a younger brother who, without competing in his own field, would have added his lustre to the patina of success and given Courtney-Briggs an entrée to the extravagantly egotistical world of the stage. But the asset had become a liability; the hero an object of derision or, at best, of pity. It was a failure his brother would find hard to forgive.

Five minutes later Dalgliesh shook hands with Urquhart and left. As he passed through the hall the girl at the switchboard, hearing his footsteps, glanced round, flushed, and paused in momentary confusion, plug in hand. She had been well trained but not quite well enough. Unwilling to embarrass her further, Dalgliesh smiled and passed swiftly out of the building. He had no doubt that, on Henry Urquhart's instructions, she was ringing Stephen Courtney-Briggs.

IV

Saville Mansions was a block of late Victorian flats close to Marylebone Road, respectable, prosperous but neither ostentatious nor opulent. Masterson had the expected trouble in finding a vacant lot to park his car and it was after seven thirty before he entered the building. The entrance hall was dominated by a grille-encased lift of ornate design and a reception desk presided over by a uniformed porter. Masterson, who had no intention of stating his business, nodded to him casually and ran lightly up the stairs. Number 23 was on the second floor. He pressed the bell and prepared for a brief wait.

But the door opened immediately and he found himself almost embraced by an extraordinary apparition, painted like the caricature of a stage whore and wearing a short evening dress of flame-coloured chiffon which would have looked incongruous on a woman half her age. The bodice was so low that he could glimpse the fold between the sagging breasts bunched high into the cups of her brassière, and could see where the powder lay caked in the cracks of dry yellow skin. Her lashes were weighted with mascara; the brittle hair, dyed an improbable blonde, was dressed in lacquered swathes around the raddled face; her carmine-painted mouth hung open in incredulous dismay. Their surprise was mutual. They stared at each other as if unable to believe their eyes. The change in her face from relief to disappointment was almost comic.

Masterson recovered first and announced himself:

"You remember", he said, "I telephoned early this morning and made an appointment?"

"I can't see you now. I'm just going out. I thought you were my dancing partner. You said you'd come early in the evening."

A shrill nagging voice made sharper by disappointment. She

looked as if she might close the door in his face. Quickly he slid one foot across the threshold.

"I was unavoidably detained. I'm sorry."

Unavoidably detained. Too right, he had been. That frantic but ultimately satisfying interlude in the back of the car had occupied more of the evening than he had anticipated. It had taken longer, too, to find a sufficiently secluded spot even on a dark winter's evening. The Guildford Road had offered few promising turnings into open country with its prospect of grass verges and unfrequented lanes. Julia Pardoe had been fussy too. Every time he slowed the car at a likely spot he had been met with her quiet, "not here". He had first seen her as she was about to step off the pavement on to the pedestrian crossing which led to the entrance of Heatheringfield station. He had slowed the car for her but, instead of waving her on, had leaned over and opened the passenger door. She had paused for only a second before walking over to him, coat swinging above the knee-length boots, and had slipped into the seat beside him without a word or glance. He had said:

"Coming up to town?"

She had nodded and had smiled secretively, eyes fixed on the windscreen. It had been as simple as that. She had hardly spoken a dozen words throughout the drive. The tentative or more overt preliminaries which he felt the game demanded of him had met with no response. He might have been a chauffeur with whom she was driving in unwelcome proximity. In the end, pricked by anger and humiliation, he had begun to wonder whether he could have been mistaken. But there had been the reassurance of that concentrated stillness, the eyes which, for minutes at a time, had watched with blue intensity his hands stroking the wheel or busy with the gears. She had wanted it all right. She had wanted it as much as he. But you could hardly call it a quick lay. One thing, surprisingly, she had told him. She was on her way to meet Hilda Rolfe; they were going to a theatre together after an early dinner. Well, either they would have to go without dinner or miss the first act; she was apparently unconcerned either way.

Amused and only slightly curious he had asked:

"How are you going to explain your lateness to Sister Rolfe? Or won't you bother now to turn up?"

She had shrugged.

"I shall tell her the truth. It might be good for her." Seeing his sudden frown she had added with contempt:

"Oh, don't worry! She won't sneak to Mr. Dalgliesh. Hilda isn't like that."

Masterson hoped she was right. This was something Dalgliesh wouldn't forgive.

"What will she do?" he had asked.

"If I tell? Chuck in her job I imagine; leave the John Carpendar. She's pretty fed up with the place. She only stays on because of me."

Wrenching his mind from the memory of that high, merciless voice into the present, Masterson forced himself to smile at the very different woman now confronting him and said in a propitiatory tone:

"The traffic you know. . . . I had to drive from Hampshire. But I shan't keep you long."

Holding out his warrant card with that slightly furtive air inseparable from the gesture he edged himself into the flat. She didn't try to stop him. But her eyes were blank, her mind obviously elsewhere. As she closed the door, the telephone rang. Without a murmur she left him standing in the hall and almost ran into a room to the left. He could hear her voice rising in protest. It seemed to be expostulating, then pleading. Then there was a silence. He moved quietly up the hall and strained his ears to hear. He thought he detected the clicking of the dial. Then she was speaking again. He couldn't hear the words. This time the conversation was over in seconds. Then came another click of the dial. Another wail. In all she rang four numbers before she reappeared in the hall.

"Is anything wrong?" he asked. "Can I help?"

She screwed up her eyes and regarded him intently for a second like a housewife assessing the quality and price of a piece of beef. Her reply when it came was peremptory and astonishing.

"Can you dance?"

"I was the Met. police champion for three years running," he lied. The Force, not surprisingly, held no dancing championships but he thought it unlikely that she would know this and the lie, like most of his lies, came easily and spontaneously.

Again that speculative, intent gaze.

"You'll need a dinner-jacket. I've still got Martin's things here. I'm going to sell them but the man hasn't come yet. He promised he'd come this afternoon but he didn't. You can't rely on anyone these days. You look about the same size. He was quite broad before his illness."

Masterson resisted the temptation to laugh aloud. He said gravely:

"I'd like to help you out if you're in a difficulty. But I'm a policeman. I'm here to get information not to spend the night dancing."

"It isn't the whole night. The ball stops at eleven thirty. It's the Delaroux Dancing Medal Ball at the Athenaeum Ballroom off the Strand. We could talk there."

"It would be easier to talk here." Her sullen face set in obstinacy.

"I don't want to talk here."

She spoke with the peevish insistence of a whining child. Then her voice hardened for the ultimatum.

"It's the ball or nothing."

They faced one another in silence. Masterson considered. The idea was grotesque, of course, but he wasn't going to get anything out of her tonight unless he agreed. Dalgliesh had sent him to London for information and his pride wouldn't let him return to Nightingale House without it. But would his pride permit him to spend the rest of the evening escorting this painted hag in public? There was no difficulty about the dancing. That was one of the skills, although not the most important, that Sylvia had taught him. She had been a randy blonde, ten years older than himself, with a dull bank manager husband whom it had been a positive duty to cuckold. Sylvia had been crazy on ballroom dancing and they had progressed together through a series of bronze, silver and gold medal competitions before the husband had become inconveniently menacing, Sylvia had begun to hint about divorce, and Masterson had prudently decided that the relationship had outlasted its usefulness, not to say his capacity for indoor exercise, and that the police service offered a reasonable career for an ambitious man who was looking for an excuse for a period of comparative rectitude. Now his taste in women and dancing had changed and he had less time for either. But Sylvia had had her uses. As they told you at Detective Training School, no skill is ever wasted in police work.

No, there would be no difficulty about the dancing. Whether she was equally expert was another matter. The evening would probably be a fiasco and whether he went with her or not she would probably talk in time. But when would that be? Dalgliesh liked to work fast. This was one of those cases where the number of suspects was limited to a small, closed community and he didn't normally expect to spend more than a week on them. He wouldn't exactly thank his subordinate for a wasted evening. And then there was that time in the car to be accounted for somehow. It wouldn't be a good night to return empty-handed. And what the hell! It would make a good story for the boys. And if the evening became too impossible he could always ditch her. He'd better remember to take his own clothes in the car in case he needed to make a quick escape.

"All right," he said. "But it's got to be worth my while."

"It will be."

Martin Dettinger's dinner-jacket fitted him better than he had feared. It was strange, this ritual of dressing up in another man's clothes. He found himself searching in the pockets as if they too could hold some kind of clue. But he found nothing. The shoes were too small and he made no effort to force them on his feet. Luckily he was wearing black shoes with leather soles. They were too heavy for dancing and looked incongruous with the dinner-jacket but they would have to do. He bundled his own suit in a cardboard box reluctantly provided by Mrs. Dettinger and they set off.

He knew that there would be little chance of finding a space for the car in or near the Strand so drove over the South Bank and parked next to County Hall. Then they walked to Waterloo Station and hired a taxi. That part of the evening wasn't too bad. She had wrapped herself in a voluminous, old-fashioned fur coat. It smelt strong and sour as if a cat had got at it, but at least it was concealing. For the whole of the journey neither of them spoke a word.

The dance had already started when they arrived shortly after eight and the great hall was unpleasantly full. They made their way to one of the few remaining empty tables under the balcony. Masterson noticed that each of the male instructors sported a red carnation; the women a white one. There was a great deal of promiscuous kissing and caressing pats of shoulders and arms. One of the men minced up to Mrs. Dettinger with little bleats of welcome and congratulation.

"You're looking marvellous Mrs. D. Sorry to hear that Tony's ill. But I'm glad you found a partner."

The glance at Masterson was perfunctorily curious. Mrs. Dettinger received this greeting with a clumsy jerk of the head and a slight leer of gratification. She made no attempt to introduce Masterson.

They sat out the next two dances and Masterson contented himself with looking round the hall. The whole atmosphere was drearily respectable. A huge bunch of balloons hung from the ceiling, ready no doubt to descend for some orgiastic climax to tonight's festivities. The band wore red jackets with gold epaulettes and had the gloomily resigned look of men who have seen it all before. Masterson looked forward to an evening of cynical uninvolvement, the gratification of observing the folly of others, the insidious pleasure of disgust. He recalled the description of a French diplomat of the English dancing "avec les visages si tristes, les derrières si gais". Here the bottoms were positively staid, but the faces were fixed in grins of stimulated delight so unnatural that he wondered whether the school had taught the approved facial expression with the correct steps. Away from the dance floor all the women looked worried, their expressions ranging from slight apprehension to almost frantic anxiety. They greatly outnumbered the men and some of them were dancing together. The majority were middle-aged or older and the style of dress was uniformly old-fashioned, the bodices tight and low cut, the immense circular skirts studded with sequins.

The third dance was a quick step. She turned to him suddenly and said, "We'll dance this." Unprotesting, he led her on to the floor and clasped her rigid body with his left arm. He resigned himself to a long and exhausting evening. If this old harpy had anything useful to tell—and the old man seemed to think she had—then, by God, she would tell it even if he had to jangle her round this bloody floor until she dropped. The notion was pleasing and he indulged it. He could picture her, disjointed as a puppet loosed from its cords, the brittle legs sprawled awkwardly, the arms swinging into the final exhaustion. Except that he would probably drop first. That half-hour with Julia Pardoe hadn't been the best possible preparation for a night on the dance floor. But the old bitch had plenty of life in her. He could taste and feel the beads of sweat tickling the corners of his mouth, but she was hardly breathing faster and her hands were cool and dry. The face close to his was intent, the eyes glazed, the lower lip sagging open. It was like dancing with an animated bag of bones.

The music crashed to a stop. The conductor swung round and flashed his artificial smile over the floor. The players relaxed, permitting themselves a brief smile. The kaleidoscope of colour in the middle of the floor coalesced then flowed into new patterns as the dancers disengaged and minced back to their tables. A waiter was hovering for orders. Masterson crooked his finger.

"What will you have?"

He sounded as ungracious as a miser forced into standing his round. She asked for a gin and tonic and when it came accepted it without thanks or apparent gratification. He settled for a double whisky. It was to be the first of many. Spreading the flame-coloured skirt around her chair, she began to survey the hall with that look of disagreeable intensity which he was beginning to know so well. He might not have been there. Careful, he thought, don't get impatient. She wants to keep you here. Let her.

"Tell me about your son," he said quietly, careful to keep his voice even and unemphatic.

"Not now. Some other evening. There's no hurry."

He nearly shouted aloud with exasperation. Did she really think that he planned to see her again? Did she expect him to dance with her for ever on the half promise of a titbit of information? He pictured them, capering grotesquely through the years, involuntary participants in a surrealist charade. He put down his glass.

"There won't be another time. Not unless you can help me. The Superintendent isn't keen on spending public money when there's nothing to be learned. I have to justify every minute of my time."

He instilled into his voice the right degrees of resentment and self-righteousness. She looked at him for the first time since they had sat down.

"There might be something to be learned. I never said there wasn't. What about the drinks?"

"The drinks?" He was momentarily nonplussed.

"Who pays for the drinks?"

"Well, normally they are on expenses. But when it's a question of entertaining friends, like tonight for example, naturally I pay myself."

He lied easily. It was one of the talents which he thought helped most in his job.

She nodded as if satisfied. But she didn't speak. He was wondering whether to try again when the band crashed into a cha-cha. Without a word she rose and turned towards him. They took the floor again.

The cha-cha was succeeded by a mamba, the mamba by a waltz, the waltz by a slow fox-trot. And still he had learned nothing. Then there was a change in the evening's programme. The lights suddenly dimmed and a sleek man, glistening from head to toe as if he had bathed in hair oil, appeared in front of the microphone and adjusted it for his height. He was accompanied by a languid blonde, her hair elaborately dressed in a style already five years out of date. The spotlight played upon them. She dangled a chiffon scarf negligently from her right hand and surveyed the emptying dance floor with a proprietorial air. There was an anticipatory hush. The man consulted a list in his hand.

"And now, ladies and gentlemen, the moment we have all been waiting for. The exhibition dances. Our medalists for the year will demonstrate for our delight the dances which won them their awards. We begin with our silver medallist, Mrs. Dettinger, dancing"—he consulted the list—"dancing the tango."

He swept a chubby hand around the floor. The band crashed into a discordant fanfare. Mrs. Dettinger rose, dragging Masterson with her. Her claw was like a vice round his wrist. The spotlight swung round and settled on them. There was a little burst of applause. The sleek man continued:

"Mrs. Dettinger is dancing with—could we have the name of your new partner Mrs. Dettinger?" Masterson called out loudly:

"Mr. Edward Heath."

The sleek man paused, then decided to take it at its face value. Forcing enthusiasm into his voice, he proclaimed:

"Mrs. Dettinger, silver medallist, dancing the tango with Mr. Edward Heath."

The cymbals clashed, there was a further spatter of applause. Masterson led his partner on to the floor with exaggerated courtesy. He was aware that he was slightly drunk and was glad of it. He was going to enjoy himself.

He clasped his hand to the small of her back and assumed an expression of lecherous expectancy. It won an immediate giggle from the nearest table. She frowned and he watched fascinated while an unbecoming crimson flowed over her face and neck. He realized with delight that she was intensely nervous, that this pathetic charade actually mattered to her. It was for this moment that she had dressed so carefully, painted her raddled face. The Delaroux Medal Ball. The demonstration tango. And then her partner had failed her. Lost courage probably, the poor sap. But fate had provided her with a personable and competent substitute. It must have seemed like a miracle. It was for this moment that he had been enticed to the Athenaeum Hall, kept dancing here hour after tedious hour. The knowledge was exhilarating. By God, he had her now. This was to be her big moment. He would see that she didn't forget it in a hurry.

The slow rhythm began. He noted with irritation that it was the same old tune for this dance that they had played most of the evening. He hummed the words in her ear. She whispered:

"We're supposed to be dancing the Delaroux tango."

"We're dancing the Charles Masterson tango, sweetheart."

Clasping her tightly he marched her belligerently across the floor in a strutting parody of the dance, swung her viciously around so that her laquered hair nearly brushed the floor and he heard her bones cracking, and held her in the pose while he bestowed a smile of surprised gratification on the party at the nearest table. The giggle was louder now, more prolonged. As he jerked her upright and waited for the next beat she hissed:

"What do you want to know?"

"He recognized someone, didn't he? Your son. When he was in the John Carpendar Hospital. He saw someone he knew?"

"Will you behave yourself and dance properly?"

"Perhaps."

They were moving again in an orthodox tango. He could feel her relaxing a little in his arms, but he still kept a firm hold on her.

"It was one of the Sisters. He'd seen her before."

"Which Sister?"

"I don't know, he didn't tell me."

"What did he tell you?"

"After the dance."

"Tell me now if you don't want to end on the floor. Where had he seen her before?"

"In Germany. She was in the dock. It was a war trial. She got off but everybody knew she was guilty."

"Where in Germany?"

He mouthed the words through lips stretched into the fatuous smile of a professional dancing partner.

"Felsenheim. It was a place called Felsenheim."

"Say it again. Say that name again!"

"Felsenheim."

The name meant nothing to him but he knew he would remember it. With luck he would get the details later but the salient facts must be torn from her now while he had her in his power. It might not be true, of course. None of it might be true. And if true it might not be relevant. But this was the information he had been sent to get. He felt a surge of confidence and good humour. He was even in danger of enjoying the dance. He decided that it was time for something spectacular and led her into a complicated routine beginning with a progressive link and ending with a close promenade that took them diagonally across the hall. It was faultlessly executed and the applause was loud and sustained. He asked:

"What was her name?"

"Irmgard Grobel. She was only a young girl then, of course. Martin said that was why she got off. He never had any doubt she was guilty."

"Are you sure he didn't tell you which Sister it was?"

"No. He was very ill. He told me about the trial when he came home from Europe, so I already knew about it. But he was unconscious most of the time in hospital. And when he wasn't he was mostly delirious."

So he could have made a mistake, thought Masterson. It was an unlikely enough story. And surely it would be hard to recognize a face after over twenty-five years; except that he must have watched that particular face with fascinated intensity all through the trial. It must have made an impression on a young and probably sensitive man. Enough, perhaps, for him to relive it in his delirium and delude himself that one of the faces bending over him in those few moments of consciousness and lucidity was the face of Irmgard Grobel. But supposing, just supposing, he had been right. If he had told his mother he might well have told his special nurse or blurted it out in his delirium. And what use had Heather Pearce made of her knowledge?

He whispered softly into her ear: "Who else have you told?"

"Nobody. I haven't told anybody. Why should I?"

Another rock swing. Then an over swing. Very nice. More applause. He tightened his hold on her and made his voice husky with menace beneath the fixed grin.

"Who else? You must have told someone."

"Why should I?"

"Because you're a woman."

It was a lucky reply. The mulish obstinacy on her face softened. She glanced up at him for a second, then fluttered her sparse mascara-coated eyelashes in a travesty of flirtation. Oh God, he thought, she's going to be coy.

"Oh well . . . perhaps I did tell just one person."

"I know bloody well you did. I'm asking who?"

Again the deprecatory glance, the little moo of submission. She had decided to enjoy this masterful man. For some reason, perhaps the gin, perhaps the euphoria of the dance, her resistance had crumbled. It was going to be hunky-dory from now on.

"I told Mr. Courtney-Briggs, Martin's surgeon. Well, it seemed only right."

"When?"

"Last Wednesday. The Wednesday of last week, I mean. At his consulting rooms in Wimpole Street. He had just left the hospital on the Friday when Martin died so I couldn't see him earlier. He's only at the John Carpendar on Monday, Thursday and Friday."

"Did he ask to see you?"

"Oh no! The staff nurse who was taking Sister's place said that he would be very glad to have a talk with me if I thought it would be helpful and that I could phone Wimpole Street to make an appointment. I didn't then. What was the use? Martin was dead. But then I got his bill. Not very nice, I thought, so soon after Martin had passed away. Two hundred guineas! I thought it was monstrous. After all, it's not as if he did any good. So I thought I'd just pop into Wimpole Street and see him and mention what I knew. It wasn't right for the hospital to employ a woman like that. A murderess really. And then to charge all that money. There was a second bill from the hospital for his maintenance you know, but it wasn't anything like Mr. Courtney-Briggs's two hundred guineas."

The sentences were disjointed. She spoke them close into his ear as opportunity offered. But she was neither breathless nor incoherent. She had plenty of energy for both the dance and the talk. And it was Masterson who was feeling the strain. Another progressive link leading into the *doré* and ending with a close promenade. She didn't put a foot wrong. The old girl had been well taught even if they couldn't give her grace or *élan*.

"So you trotted along to tell him what you knew and suggested that he took a slice off his profits?"

"He didn't believe me. He said that Martin was delirious and mistaken and that he could personally vouch for all the Sisters. But he took £50 off the bill."

She spoke with grim satisfaction. Masterson was surprised. Even if Courtney-Briggs had believed the story there was no reason why he should deduct a not inconsiderable amount from his bill. He wasn't responsible for recruiting or appointing the nursing staff. He had nothing to worry about. Masterson wondered whether he had believed the story. He had obviously said nothing, either to the Chairman of the Hospital Management Committee or to the Matron. Perhaps it was true that he could vouch personally for all the Sisters and the £50 deduction had merely been a gesture to keep a tiresome woman quiet. But Courtney-Briggs hadn't struck Masterson as the kind of man to submit himself to blackmail or to relinquish a penny of what he thought was due to him.

It was at that moment that the music crashed to a finish. Masterson smiled benevolently on Mrs. Dettinger, and led her back to their table. The applause lasted until they reached it and then was cut off abruptly as the sleek man announced the next dance. Masterson looked around for the waiter and beckoned.

"Well, now," he said to his partner, "that wasn't so bad, was it? If you behave yourself nicely for the rest of the evening I might even take you home."

He did take her home. They left early but it was well past midnight before he finally left the Baker Street flat. By then he knew that he had as much of the story as she could tell him. She had grown maudlin after their return, a reaction, he felt, to triumph and gin. He had kept her supplied with the latter through the rest of the evening, not enough to make her unmanageably drunk but sufficient to keep her talkative and pliable. But the journey home had been a nightmare, not made easier by the cab driver's glances of mingled amusement and contempt as he drove them from the hall to the South Bank car park, and by the disapproving superciliousness of the hall porter when they arrived at Saville Mansions. Once in the flat he had coaxed, comforted and bullied her into coherence, making black coffee for them both in the unbelievably squalid kitchen—a slut's kitchen he thought, glad of one more reason to despise her—and giving it to her with promises that, of course, he wouldn't leave her, that he would call for her again the following Saturday, that they would be permanent dancing partners. By midnight he had got out of her all he wanted to know about Martin

Dettinger's career and his stay in the John Carpendar Hospital. There wasn't a great deal to be learned about the hospital. She hadn't visited often during the week he was there. Well, what was the point of it? There wasn't anything she could do for him. He was unconscious most of the time and didn't really know her even when he woke. Except that once, of course. She had hoped then for a little word of comfort and appreciation, but all she had got was that odd laugh and the talk about Irmgard Grobel. He had told her that story years before. She was tired of hearing it. A boy ought to be thinking of his mother when he was dying. It had been a terrible effort to sit there watching. She was a sensitive person. Hospitals upset her. The late Mr. Dettinger hadn't understood how sensitive she was.

There was apparently a great deal that the late Mr. Dettinger hadn't understood, his wife's sexual needs among them. Masterson listened to the story of her marriage without interest. It was the usual story of an unsatisfied wife, a henpecked husband and an unhappy and sensitive child. Masterson heard it without pity. He wasn't particularly interested in people. He divided them into two broad groups, the law-abiding and the villains and the ceaseless war which he waged against the latter fulfilled, as he knew, some inarticulated need of his own nature. But he was interested in facts. He knew that, when anybody visited the scene of a crime, some evidence was left behind or some was taken away. It was the detective's job to find that evidence. He knew that finger-prints hadn't yet been known to lie and that human beings did frequently, irrationally, whether they were innocent or guilty. He knew that facts stood up in court and people let you down. He knew that motive was unpredictable although he had honesty enough sometimes to recognize his own. It had struck him at the very moment of entering Julia Pardoe that his act, in its anger and exaltation, was in some way directed against Dalgliesh. But it never occurred to him to ask why. That would have seemed profitless speculation. Nor did he wonder whether, for the girl also, it had been an act of malice and private retribution.

"You'd think a boy would want his mother when he was dying. It was terrible to sit there and hear that dreadful breathing, first soft and then dreadfully loud. Of course he had a private room. That's why the hospital was able to charge. He wasn't National Health. But the other patients must have heard the noise all over the ward."

"Cheyne-Stoke's breathing," said Masterson. "It comes before the death rattle."

"They should have done something about it. It upset me dreadfully. That special nurse he had should have done something about it. The plain one. I suppose she was doing her duty, but she never gave a thought to me. After all, the living need some attention. There wasn't anything else she could do for Martin."

"That was Nurse Pearce. The one who died."

"Yes, I remember you told me. So she's dead too. I hear of nothing but death. It's all around me. What did you call that breathing?"

"Cheyne Stoke's. It means that you're going to die."

"They should have done something about it. That girl should have done something about it. Did she breathe like that before she died?"

"No, she screamed. Someone poured disinfectant into her stomach and burned it out."

"I don't want to hear about it! I don't want to hear about it any more! Tell me about the dance. You will come back next Saturday, won't you?"

And so it had gone on. It had been tedious and exhausting and, in the end, almost frightening. The triumphant glow of getting what he wanted had faded before midnight and he was aware only of hatred and disgust. While he listened to her babblings he toyed with imagined violence. It was easy to see how these things happened. A handy poker. The silly face smashed into pulp. Blow on blow on blow. The bones splintering. A gush of blood. An orgasm of hatred. Imagining it, he found it hard to keep his breathing even. He took her hand gently.

"Yes," he said. "Yes, I'll come again. Yes. Yes."

The flesh was dry and hot now. She might have been in a fever. The painted nails were ridged. On the back of the hand the veins stood out like purple cords. He traced with a caressing finger the brown stains of age.

Shortly after midnight her voice burbled into incoherency, her head sank forward, and he saw that she was asleep. He waited for a moment, then disengaged his hand and tiptoed into the bedroom. It took him only a couple of minutes to change his clothes. Then he tiptoed into the bathroom and washed his face and the hand which had touched hers, washed them over and over again. Finally he left the flat, shutting the door quietly behind him as if afraid to wake her, and went out into the night.

V

Fifteen minutes later, Masterson's car passed the flat where Miss Beale and Miss Burrows, cosily dressing-gowned, were sipping their late night cocoa before the dying fire. They heard it as one brief crescendo in the intermittent flow of traffic, and broke off their chatter to speculate with desultory interest on what brought people out in the small hours of the morning. It was certainly unusual for them to be still up at this hour, but tomorrow was Saturday and they could indulge their fondness for late-night conversation in the comforting knowledge that they could lie in next morning.

They had been discussing the visit that afternoon of Chief Superintendent Dalgliesh. Really, they agreed, it had been a success, almost a pleasure. He had seemed to enjoy his tea. He had sat there, deep in their most comfortable armchair, and the three of them had talked together as if he were as harmless and familiar as the local vicar.

He had said to Miss Beale: "I want to see Nurse Pearce's death through your eyes. Tell me about it. Tell me everything you saw and felt from the moment you drove through the hospital gates."

And Miss Beale had told him, taking a shameful pleasure in her half-hour of importance, in his obvious appreciation that she had observed so carefully and could describe with such clarity. He was a good listener, they conceded. Well, that was part of his job. He was clever, too, at making people talk. Even Angela, who had sat in watchful silence for most of the time, couldn't explain why she had felt drawn to mention her recent encounter with Sister Rolfe in the Westminster library. And his eyes had flickered with interest, interest which had faded into disappointment when she told him the date. The friends agreed that they couldn't have been mistaken. He had been disappointed. Sister Rolfe had been seen in the library on the wrong day.

VI

It was after eleven o'clock when Dalgliesh turned the key in his desk drawer, locked the office behind him and let himself out of the side door of Nightingale House to walk back to the Falconer's Arms. At the turn of the path where it narrowed before losing itself in the dark shadows of the trees, he looked back at the gaunt pile of the house, enormous and sinister, with its four turrets black against the night sky. The house was in almost total darkness. There was only one lighted window and it took him a minute to identify the room. So Mary Taylor was in her bedroom but not yet asleep. The light was merely a faint glow, perhaps from a bedside lamp, and as he watched it went out.

He made his way towards the Winchester Gate. The trees here were very close to the path. Their black boughs arched over his head shutting out the faint light from the nearest lamp. For about fifty yards he walked in absolute darkness, treading swiftly and silently over the mush of dead leaves. He was in that state of physical tiredness when the mind and body seem detached, the body, conditioned to reality, moving half consciously in the familiar physical world, while the liberated mind swings into uncontrolled orbit in which fantasy and fact show an equally ambiguous face. Dalgliesh was surprised that he was so tired. This job was no more arduous than any other. He was working long hours, but then a sixteen-hour day was normal for him when he was on a case. And this extraordinary weariness wasn't the exhaustion of frustration or failure. The case would break by tomorrow morning. Later tonight Masterson would be back with another piece of the jigsaw and the picture would be complete. In two days at the latest he would have left Nightingale House. In two days' time he would have seen the last of that gold and white room in the south-west turret.

Moving like an automaton he heard, too late, the sudden muted footfall at his back. Instinctively, he threw himself round to face his adversary and felt the blow glance from his left temple to his shoulder. There was no pain, only a crack as if his whole cranium had split, a numbness of his left arm, and after a second which seemed an eternity, the warm, almost comforting, gush of blood. He gave one gasp and crumpled forward. But he was still conscious. Blinded by blood and fighting against nausea, he tried to rise, feeling for the earth with both hands, willing himself to get up and fight. But his feet scrabbled ineffectively in the moist earth and there was no strength in his arms. His eyes were blinded by his own blood. The suffocating smell of damp humus pressed against his nose and mouth, pungent as an anaesthetic. He lay there, helplessly retching, waking pain with every spasm, and waited in angry impotence for the final annihilating blow.

But nothing happened. He sank, unresisting, into unconsciousness. A few seconds later he was recalled to reality by a hand gently shaking his shoulder. Someone was bending over him. He heard a woman's voice.

"It's me. What's 'appened? Somebody cosh yer?"

It was Morag Smith. He struggled to answer, to warn her to get away quickly. The two of them would be no match for a determined killer. But his voice seemed incapable of forming words. He was aware that somewhere very close a man was groaning, then realized with bitter humour, that the voice was his. He seemed to have no control over it. He was aware of hands moving around his head. Then she shuddered like a child.

"Ugh! Yer all over blood!"

Again he tried to talk. She bent her head nearer. He could see the dark strands of hair and the white face hovering in front of him. He struggled to rise and this time managed to get to his knees.

"Did you see him?"

"Not really—'e 'eard me coming through. Made off towards Nightingale 'ouse. Blimey, you don't 'alf look a bloody mess. 'ere, lean on me."

"No. Leave me and get help. He may be back."

"Not 'im. Anyway, we're better together. I don't fancy going it alone. Ghosts is one thing, bloody murderers is another. Come on, I'll give yer a 'and."

He could feel the sharp bones in her thin shoulders, but the fragile body was remarkably wiry and she stood his weight well. He forced himself to his feet and stood there swaying. He asked:

"Man or woman?"

"Didn't see. Could've been either. Never mind about that now. Think yer can make it to Nightingale 'ouse? That'd be the nearest."

Dalgliesh felt remarkably better now that he was on his legs. He could scarcely see the path but he took a few tentative steps forward, his hand supported by her shoulder.

"I think so. The back door would be the nearest. It can't be more than fifty yards. Ring the bell of Matron's flat. I know she's there."

Together they shuffled slowly along the path obliterating, as Dalgliesh realized bitterly, any footprints as he might have otherwise have hoped to find next morning. Not that these sodden leaves would yield many clues. He wondered what had happened to the weapon. But this was pointless speculation. He could do nothing until it was light. He felt a wave of gratitude and affection for the tough little person whose brittle arm lay weightless as a child's around his hip. We must look an odd pair, he thought. He said:

"You probably saved my life, Morag. He only ran off because he heard you coming."

He, or was it she? If only Morag had been in time to glimpse whether it were a man or a woman. He could scarcely catch her reply.

"Don't talk bloody daft."

He heard, without surprise, that she was crying. She made no attempt to suppress or check her sobbing and it didn't impede their progress. Perhaps, to Morag, crying was almost as natural as walking. He made no effort to comfort her except to press on her shoulders. She took that as a plea for more support and tightened her arm around his hips, leaning against him, helping him on his way. And thus incongruously entwined they passed under the shadows of the trees.

VII

The light in the demonstration room was bright, too bright. It pierced even his gummed eyelids and he moved his head restlessly from side to side to escape the shaft of pain. Then his head was being steadied by cool hands. Mary Taylor's hands. He heard her speaking to him, telling him that Courtney-Briggs was in the hospital. She had sent for Courtney-Briggs. Then the same hands were taking off his tie, undoing the buttons of his shirt, slipping his arms out of his jacket with practised skill.

"What happened?"

It was Courtney-Briggs's voice, harsh and masculine. So the surgeon had arrived. What had he been doing in the hospital? Another emergency operation? Courtney-Briggs's patients seemed curiously prone to relapse. What alibi had he for the last half-hour? Dalgliesh said:

"Someone was lying in wait for me. I've got to check who's in Nightingale House."

A firm grip was on his arm. Courtney-Briggs was pressing him back into his chair. Two swinging blobs of grey hovered over him. Her voice again.

"Not now. You can hardly stand. One of us will go."

"Go now."

"In a minute. We've locked all the doors. We shall know if anyone returns. Rely on us. Just relax."

So reasonable. Rely on us. Relax. He gripped metal arms on the chair, taking hold on reality.

"I want to check for myself."

Half blinded by blood, he sensed rather than saw their mutual glance of concern. He knew that he sounded like a petulant child, beating his insistence against the implacable calm of the grown-ups. Maddened with frustration, he tried to rise from the chair. But the floor tipped sickeningly, then rose up to meet him through whorls of screaming colour. It was no good. He couldn't stand.

"My eyes," he said. Courtney-Briggs's voice, annoyingly reasonable:

"In one moment. I must look first at your head."

"But I want to see!"

His blindness infuriated him. Were they doing this to him deliberately? He put up a hand and began to pick at the caked eyelids. He could hear them talking together, low voiced, in the muttered idiom of their craft from which he, the patient, was excluded. He was conscious of new sounds, the hiss of a sterilizer, a jingle of instruments, the closing of a metal lid. Then the smell of disinfectant sharpened. Now she was cleaning his eyes. A pad, deliciously cool, was wiped across each lid, and he opened them blinking to see more clearly the sheen of her dressing-gown and the long plait of hair falling over her left shoulder. He spoke to her directly.

"I must know who's in Nightingale House. Could you check now, please?"

Without another word or a further glance at Courtney-Briggs, she slipped out of the room. As soon as the door was closed, Dalgliesh said:

"You didn't tell me that your brother was once engaged to Josephine Fallon."

"You didn't ask me."

The surgeon's voice was deliberate, uninterested, the response of a man with his mind on his job. There was a snip of scissors, a momentary chill of steel against the skull. The surgeon was clipping Dalgliesh's hair around the wound.

"You must have known that I should be interested."

"Oh, interested! You'd be interested all right. Your kind have an infinite capacity for taking an interest in other people's affairs. But I confined myself to satisfying your curiosity only so far as the deaths of these two girls were concerned. You can't complain that I've held anything relevant back. Peter's death isn't relevant—merely a private tragedy."

Not so much a private tragedy thought Dalgliesh as a public embarrassment. Peter Courtney had violated his brother's first principle, the necessity of being successful. Dalgliesh said:

"He hanged himself."

"As you say, he hanged himself. Not a very dignified or pleasant way to go, but the poor boy hadn't my resources. The day when they make my final diagnosis I shall have more appropriate measures available than doing myself to death on the end of a rope."

His egotism, thought Dalgliesh, was astounding. Even his brother's death had to be seen in relationship to himself. He stood complacently secure at the hub of his private universe while other people—brother, mistress, patient—revolved round that central sun existing by virtue of its warmth and light, obedient to its centripetal force. But wasn't that how most people saw themselves? Was Mary Taylor less self-absorbed? Was he himself? Wasn't it merely that she and he pandered more subtly to their essential egotism?

The surgeon moved over to his black instrument case and took out a mirror mounted on a metal band which he clipped around his head. He came back to Dalgliesh, ophthalmoscope in hand and settled himself into a chair opposite his patient. They sat confronting each other, foreheads almost touching. Dalgliesh could sense the metal of the instrument against his right eye. Courtney-Briggs commanded:

"Look straight ahead."

Dalgliesh stared obediently at the pinpoint of light. He said:

"You left the main hospital building at about midnight. You spoke to the porter at the main gate at twelve thirty-eight a.m. Where were you between those times?"

"I told you. There was a fallen elm blocking the back path. I spent some minutes examining the scene and making sure that other people didn't injure themselves on it."

"One person did precisely that. That was at twelve seventeen a.m. There was no warning scarf tied on the branches at that time."

The ophthalmoscope moved to the other eye. The surgeon's breathing was perfectly regular.

"He was mistaken."

"He doesn't think so."

"So you deduce that I arrived at the fallen tree later than twelve seventeen a.m. It may have been so. As I wasn't concocting an alibi, I didn't check the time every two minutes."

"But you're not suggesting that it took you over seventeen

minutes to drive from the main hospital to that particular place."

"Oh, I think I could make out quite a case for the delay, don't you know. I could claim that I needed, in your deplorable police jargon, to obey a call of nature and left my car to meditate among the trees."

"And did you?"

"I may have done. When I've dealt with your head, which incidentally is going to need about a dozen stitches, I'll give some thought to the matter. You'll forgive me if I concentrate now on my own job."

The matron had quietly returned. She took up her stance next to Courtney-Briggs like an acolyte waiting for orders. Her face was very white. Without waiting for her to speak the surgeon handed her the ophthalmoscope. She said:

"Everyone who should be in Nightingale House is in her room."

Courtney-Briggs was running his hands over Dalgliesh's left shoulder causing pain with every thrust of the strong probing fingers. He said:

"The collar-bone seems all right. Badly bruised but not fractured. Your attacker must have been a tall woman. You're over six feet yourself."

"If it were a woman. Or she may have had a long weapon, a golf club perhaps."

"A golf club. Matron, what about your clubs? Where do you keep them?"

She answered dully: "In the hall at the bottom of my staircase. The bag is usually left just inside the door."

"Then you'd better check them now."

She was gone for less than two minutes and they waited her return in silence. When she came back she spoke directly to Dalgliesh.

"One of the irons is missing."

The news seemed to hearten Courtney-Briggs. He said almost jovially:

"Well, there's your weapon for you! But there's not much point in searching for it tonight. It'll be lying about somewhere in the grounds. Your men can find it and do everything necessary to it tomorrow; test it for finger-prints, look for blood and hair, all the usual tricks. You're not in any fit state to bother yourself tonight. We've got to get this wound sutured. I shall have to get you over to the out-patient theatre. You'll need an anaesthetic."

"I don't want an anaesthetic."

"Then I can give you a local. That just means a few injections around the wound. We could do this here, Matron."

"I don't want any anaesthetic. I just want it stitched."

Courtney-Briggs explained patiently as if to a child.

"It's a very deep cut and it's got to be sutured. It's going to hurt badly if you won't accept an anaesthetic."

"I tell you I don't want one. And I don't want a prophylactic injection of penicillin or anti-tetanus. I just want it sutured."

He felt them look at each other. He knew that he was being obstinately unreasonable but he didn't care. Why couldn't they get on with it? Then Courtney-Briggs spoke, curiously formal:

"If you'd prefer another surgeon. . . ."

"No, I just want you to get on with it."

There was a moment's silence. Then the surgeon spoke:

"All right. I'll be as quick as I can."

He was aware that Mary Taylor had moved behind him. She drew his head back against her breast, supported it between cold, firm hands. He shut his eyes like a child. The needle felt immense, an iron rod simultaneously ice cold and red hot which pierced his skull time and time again. The pain was an abomination, made bearable only by anger and by his obstinate determination not to betray weakness. He set his features into a rigid mask. But it was infuriating to feel the involuntary tears seeping under his eyelids.

After an eternity he realized that it was over. He heard himself say:

"Thank you. And now I'd like to get back to my office. Sergeant Masterson has instructions to come on here if I'm not in the hotel. He can drive me home."

Mary Taylor was winding a crêpe bandage around his head. She didn't speak. Courtney-Briggs said:

"I'd prefer you to go straight to bed. We can let you have a room in the Medical Officers' quarters for tonight. I'll arrange for an X-ray first thing in the morning. Then I'd like to see you again."

"You can arrange what you like for tomorrow. Just now I'd like to be left alone."

He got up from the chair. She put a hand on his arm, supporting him. But he must have made some kind of gesture for she dropped her arm. He felt surprisingly light on his feet. It was odd that such an insubstantial body could support the weight of so heavy a head. He put up an exploring hand and felt the scrape of the bandage; it seemed an immense distance from his skull. Then, focusing his eyes carefully, he walked unhindered across the room to the door. As he reached it, he heard Courtney-Briggs's voice.

"You will want to know where I was at the time of the attack. I was in my room in the Medical Officers' quarters. I'm staying there for tonight ready for an early operating session. I'm sorry I can't oblige you with an alibi. I can only hope that you realize that, if I want to put anyone out of the way, I have subtler methods at my disposal than a golf iron."

Dalgliesh didn't reply. Without looking round and without a further word he left them and closed the door of the demonstration room quietly behind him. The stairs looked a formidable climb and, at first, he was afraid that he wouldn't be able to make it. But he grasped the banister resolutely and, step by careful step, made his way back to the office and settled down to wait for Masterson.

Chapter Eight

A Circle of Burnt Earth

I

It was nearly two in the morning when the gate porter waved Masterson through the main entrance of the hospital. The wind was rising steadily as he drove along the twisting path to Nightingale House between an avenue of black rumbustious trees. The house was in darkness except for the one lit window where Dalgliesh was still working. Masterson scowled at it. It had been irritating and disconcerting to discover that Dalgliesh was still at Nightingale House. He expected to have to give his report on the day's activities; the prospect wasn't unpleasing since he was fortified by success. But it had been a long day. He hoped that they weren't in for one of the Superintendent's all-night sessions.

Masterson let himself in at the side door, double locking it behind him. The silence of the vast entrance hall received him, eerie and portentous. The house seemed to be holding its breath. He smelt again the alien but now familiar amalgam of disinfectant and floor polish, unwelcoming and faintly sinister. As if afraid to stir the sleeping house—half empty as it was—he did not switch on the light but made his way across the hall by the beam of his electric torch. The notices on the hall board gleamed white reminding him of mourning cards in the vestibule of some foreign cathedral. Of your charity pray for the soul of Josephine Fallon. He found himself tiptoeing up the stairs as if afraid to wake the dead.

In the first-floor office Dalgliesh was sitting at his desk with the file open before him. Masterson stood stock-still in the doorway, concealing his surprise. The Superintendent's face was drawn and grey under an immense cocoon of white crêpe bandage. He was sitting bolt upright, forearms resting on the desk, palms spread lightly each side of the page. The pose was familiar. Masterson reflected, not for the first time, that the Superintendent had remarkable hands and knew how to display them to advantage. He had long decided that Dalgliesh was one of the proudest men he knew. This essential conceit was too carefully guarded to be generally recognized, but it was gratifying to catch him out in one of the lesser vanities. Dalgliesh looked up without smiling.

"I expected you back two hours ago, Sergeant. What were you doing?"

"Extracting information by unorthodox means, sir."

"You look as if the unorthodox means have been used on you."

Masterson bit back the obvious retort. If the old man chose to be mysterious about his injury he wasn't going to give him the gratification of showing curiosity.

"I was dancing until nearly midnight, sir."

"At your age that shouldn't be too exhausting. Tell me about the lady. She seems to have made an impression on you. You had an agreeable evening?"

Masterson could have retorted with reason that he had had one hell of an evening. He contented himself with an account of what he had learned. The exhibition tango was prudently forgotten. Instinct warned him that Dalgliesh might think it neither funny nor clever. But he gave an otherwise accurate account of the evening. He tried to keep it factual and unemotional but became aware that he was enjoying some of the telling. His description of Mrs. Dettinger was concise but caustic. Towards the end he hardly troubled to conceal his contempt and disgust of her. He felt that he was making rather a good job of it.

Dalgliesh listened in silence. His cocooned head was still bent over the file and Masterson got no hint of what he was feeling. At the end of the recital Dalgliesh looked up:

"Do you enjoy your work, Sergeant?"

"Yes sir, for most of the time."

"I thought you might say that."

"Was the question intended as a rebuke, sir?"

Masterson was aware that he was entering on dangerous ground but was unable to resist this first tentative step.

Dalgliesh didn't answer the question. Instead he said:

"I don't think it's possible to be a detective and remain always kind. But if you ever find that cruelty is becoming pleasurable in itself, then it's probably time to stop being a detective."

Masterson flushed and was silent. This from Dalgliesh! Dalgliesh who was so uncaring about his subordinates' private life as to seem unaware that they had any; whose caustic wit could be as devastating as another man's bludgeon. Kindness! And how kind exactly was he himself? How many of his notable successes had been won with kindness? He would never be brutal, of course. He was too proud, too fastidious, too controlled, too bloody inhuman in fact for anything so understandable as a little down-to-earth brutality. His reaction to evil was a wrinkle of the nose not a stamp of the foot. But kindness! Tell that to the boys, thought Masterson.

Dalgliesh went on talking as if he said nothing remarkable.

"We'll have to see Mrs. Dettinger again, of course. And we'll want a statement. Did you think she was telling the truth?"

"It's difficult to tell. I can't think why she should lie. But she's a strange woman and she wasn't feeling too pleased with me at the time. It might give her some kind of perverse satisfaction to mislead us. She might have substituted Grobel's name for one of the other defendants, for example."

"So that the person her son recognized on the ward could have been any one of the Felsenheim defendants, those who are still alive and unaccounted for. What exactly did her son tell her?"

"That's the problem, sir. Apparently he gave her to understand that this German woman, Irmgard Grobel, was employed at the John Carpendar but she can't recall his exact words. She thinks he said something like:

" 'This is a funny kind of hospital, ma, they've got Grobel here, working as one of the Sisters.' "

Dalgliesh said: "Suggesting that it wasn't the Sister who was actually nursing him, otherwise he'd presumably have said so. Except, of course, that he was unconscious most of the time and may not have seen Sister Brumfett previously or appreciated that she was in charge of the ward. He wasn't in any state to recognize the niceties of the hospital hierarchy. According to his medical record he was either delirious or unconscious most of the time, which would make his evidence suspect even if he hadn't inconveniently died. Anyway, his mother at first didn't apparently take the story too seriously. She didn't mention it to anyone at the hospital? Nurse Pearce, for example?"

"She says not. I think at the time Mrs. Dettinger's main concern was to collect her son's belongings and the death certificate and claim on the insurance."

"Bitter, Sergeant?"

"Well, she's paying nearly £2,000 a year for dancing lessons and she'd come to the end of her capital. These Delaroux people like payment in advance. I heard all about her finances when I took her home. Mrs. Dettinger wasn't out to make trouble. But then she received Mr. Courtney-Briggs's bill, and it occurred to her that she might use her son's story to get a reduction. And she got one too. Fifty quid."

"Which suggests that Mr. Courtney-Briggs is either more charitable than we had supposed or thought that the information was worth the money. Did he pay it over at once?"

"She says not. She first visited him at his Wimpole Street consulting rooms on the evening of Wednesday, January twenty-first. She didn't get much joy on that occasion so she rang him up last Saturday morning. The receptionist told her that Mr. Courtney-Briggs was out of the country. She intended to ring again on the Monday but the cheque for fifty pounds came by the first post. There was no letter and no explanation, merely his compliment slip. But she got the message all right."

"So he was out of the country last Saturday. Where, I wonder? Germany? That's something to check, anyway."

Masterson said, "It all sounds so unlikely, sir. And it doesn't really fit."

"No. We're pretty certain who killed both those girls. Logically all the facts point to one person. And as you say, this new evidence doesn't really fit in. It's disconcerting when you scramble around in the dirt for a missing piece of the jigsaw and then find it's part of a different puzzle."

"So you don't think it's relevant, sir? I should hate to think that my evening's exertions with Mrs. Dettinger were in vain."

"Oh, it's relevant. It's exceedingly relevant. And we've found some corroboration. We've traced the missing library book. Westminster City Library were very helpful. Miss Pearce went to the Marylebone Branch on the afternoon of Thursday, 8th January, when she was off duty and asked if they had a book dealing with German war trials. She said she was interested in a trial at Felsenheim in November 1945. They couldn't find anything in stock but they said they would make inquiries of other London libraries and suggested that she should come back or telephone them in a day or two. She telephoned on the Saturday morning. They told her that they'd been able to trace a book which dealt with the Felsenheim trial among others, and she called in for it that afternoon. On each visit she gave her name as Josephine Fallon and presented Fallon's ticket and the blue token. Normally, of course, they wouldn't have noticed the name and address. They did so because the book had to be specially obtained from another library."

"Was the book returned, sir?"

"Yes, but anonymously, and they can't say exactly when. It was probably on the Wednesday after Pearce died. Someone left it on the non-fiction trolley. When the assistant went to fill up the trolley with recently returned books she recognized it and took it back to the counter to be registered and put on one side ready for return to its parent library. No one saw who returned it. The library is particularly busy and people come in and out at will. Not everyone has a book to return or calls at the counter. It would be easy enough to bring in a book in a basket or a pocket and slip it among the others on the trolley. The assistant who found it had been on counter duty for most of the morning and afternoon and one of the junior staff had been replenishing the trolley. The girl was getting behind with the work so her senior went to give a hand. She noticed the book at once. That was at four thirty approximately. But it could have been put there at any time."

"Any prints, sir?"

"Nothing helpful. A few smudges. It had been handled by quite a number of the library staff and God knows how many of the public. And why not? They weren't to know that it was part of the evidence in a murder inquiry. But there's something interesting about it. Have a look."

He opened one of the desk drawers and brought out a stout book bound with a dark blue cloth and embossed with a library catalogue number on the spine. Masterson took it and laid it on the table. He seated himself and opened it carefully, taking his time. It was an account of various war trials held in Germany from 1945 onwards, apparently carefully documented, unsensational in treatment and written by a Queen's Counsel who had once been on the staff of the Judge Advocate General. There were only a few plates and of these only two related to the Felsenheim trial. One showed a general view of the Court with an indistinct glimpse of the doctor in the dock, and the other was a photograph of the camp commandant. Dalgliesh said:

"Martin Dettinger is mentioned, but only briefly. During the war he served in the King's Wiltshire Light Infantry and in November 1945 he was appointed as a member of a military Court set up in West Germany to try four men and one woman accused of war crimes. These Courts were established under a Special Army Order of June 1945 and this one consisted of a President who was a Brigadier of the Grenadier Guards, four army officers of whom Dettinger was one, and the Judge Advocate appointed by the Judge Advocate General to the Forces. As I said, they had the job of trying five people who, it was alleged—you'll find the indictment on page 127—'acting jointly and in pursuance of a common intent and acting for and on behalf of the then German Reich did on or about 3rd September 1944 wilfully, deliberately and wrongfully aid, abet and participate in the killing of 31 human beings of Polish and Russian nationality'."

Masterson was not surprised that Dalgliesh should be able to quote the indictment word for word. This was an administrator's trick, this ability to memorize and present facts with accuracy and precision. Dalgliesh could do it better than most, and if he wanted to exercise his technique it was hardly for his Sergeant to interrupt. He said nothing. He noticed that the Superintendent had taken up a large grey stone, a perfect ovoid, and was rolling it slowly between his fingers. It was something that had caught his eye in the grounds, presumably, and which he had picked up to serve as a paper-weight. It certainly hadn't been on the office desk that morning. The tired, strained voice went on.

"These 31 men, women and children were Jewish slave workers in Germany and were said to have been suffering from tuberculosis. They were sent to an institution in Western Germany which was originally designed to care for the mentally sick but which since the summer of 1944 had been dedicated, not to curing, but to the business of killing. There is no evidence to how many German mentally ill patients were done to death there. The staff had been sworn to secrecy about what went on, but there were plenty of rumours in the neighbouring districts. On the 3rd September 1944, a transport of Polish and Russian nationals were sent to the institution. They were told they were to receive treatment for tuberculosis. That night they were given lethal injections—men, women and children—and by the morning they were dead and buried. It was for this crime, not for the murder of the German nationals, that the five accused were on trial. One was the head doctor Max Klein, one a young pharmacist Ernst Gumbmann, one the chief male nurse Adolf Straub, and one a young, untrained female nurse aged 18, Irmgard Grobel. The head doctor and the chief male nurse were found guilty. The doctor was condemned to death and the male nurse to twenty-three years' imprisonment. The pharmacist and the woman were acquitted. You can find what her council said on page 140. You had better read it out."

Surprised, Masterson took up the book in silence and turned to page 140. He began reading. His voice sounded unnaturally loud.

"This court is not trying the defendant Irmgard Grobel for participation in the death of German nationals. We know now what was happening at Steinhoff Institution. We know, too, that it was in accordance with German law as proclaimed by Adolf Hitler alone. In accordance with orders handed down from the highest authority, many thousands of insane German people were put to death with perfect legality from 1940 onward. On moral grounds one can judge this action as one pleases. The question is not whether the staff at Steinhoff thought it wrong or whether they thought it merciful. The question is whether they thought it was lawful. It has been proved by witnesses that there was such a law in existence. Irmgard Grobel, if she were concerned with the deaths of these people, acted in accordance with this law.

"But we are not concerned with the mentally ill. From July 1944 this same law was extended to cover incurably tubercular foreign workers. It might be contended that the accused would be in no doubt of the legality of such killings when she had seen German nationals put out of their misery in the interests of the State. But that is not my contention. We are not in a position to judge what the accused thought. She was not implicated in the only killings which are the concern of this Court. The transport of Russians and Poles arrived at Steinhoff on 3rd September 1944 at half past six in the evening. On that day Irmgard Grobel was returning from her leave. The Court has heard how she entered the nurses' quarters at half past seven and changed into her uniform. She was on duty from nine o'clock. Between the time of entering the Institution and arriving in the nurses' duty room in E Block she spoke only to two other nurses, witnesses Willig and Rohde. Both these women have testified that they did not tell Grobel of the arrival of the transport. So Grobel enters the duty room. She had had a difficult journey and is tired and sick. She is hesitating whether or not to seek permission to go off duty. It is then that the telephone rings and Doctor Klein speaks to her. The Court has heard the evidence of witnesses to this conversation. Klein asks Grobel to look in the drug store and tell him how much evipan and phenol there is in stock. You have heard how the evipan was delivered in cartons, each carton containing 25 injections and each injection consisting of one capsule of evipan in powder form and one container of sterile water. The evipan and phenol, together with other dangerous drugs, were kept in the nurses' duty room. Grobel checks the amounts and reports to Klein that there are two cartons of evipan and about 150 c.c. of liquid phenol in stock. Klein then orders her to have all the available evipan and phenol ready to hand over to male nurse Straub who will fetch it. He also orders her to hand over twelve 10 c.c. syringes and a quantity of strong needles. The accused claimed that at no time did he state for what purpose these drugs were required and you have heard from the accused Straub that he, also, did not enlighten her.

"Irmgard Grobel did not leave the duty room until she was carried back to her quarters at nine twenty that night. The Court has heard how Nurse Rohde coming late on duty found her in a faint on the floor. For five days she was confined to her bed with acute vomiting and fever. She did not see the Russians and Poles enter E Block, she did not see their bodies carried out in the early hours of 4th September. When she returned to duty the corpses had been buried.

"Mr. President, this Court has heard witnesses who have testified to the kindness of Irmgard Grobel, to her gentleness with the child patients, to her skill as a nurse; I would remind the Court that she is young, hardly more than a child herself. But I do not ask for an acquittal on the grounds of her youth nor her sex but because she, alone of the accused, is manifestly innocent of this charge. She had no hand in the deaths of these 31 Russians and Poles. She did not even know that they existed. The Defence has nothing further to add."

Dalgliesh's bitter voice broke in on the silence.

"The usual Teutonic plea of legality you note, Sergeant. They didn't waste much time with their killings did they? Admitted at seven thirty and injected soon after nine. And why evipan? They couldn't be sure that death would be instantaneous unless they injected a heavy dose. I doubt whether less than 20 c.c. would kill immediately. Not that it would worry them. What saved Grobel was being on leave until late that evening. The Defence claimed that she was never told that the foreign prisoners had arrived, that no one knew until the morning of the fourth. That same plea gave the pharmacist his freedom. Technically they were both innocent, if you can use that word of anyone who worked at Steinhoff."

Masterson was silent. It was all so long ago. Grobel had been a girl. Ten years younger than he was now. The war was old history. It had no more relevance to his life than had the Wars of the Roses, less since it did not even evoke the faintly romantic and chivalrous overtones of the history learned in his boyhood. He had no particular feelings about the Germans, or indeed about any race other than the few he regarded as culturally and intellectually inferior. The Germans were not among these. Germany to him meant clean hotels and good roads, *rippchen* eaten with the local wine at the Apfel Wine Struben Inn, the Rhine curving below him like a silver ribbon, the excellence of the camping ground at Koblenz.

And if any of the accused from Felsenheim were alive they would be well into middle age now. Irmgard Grobel herself would be forty-three. It was all such old history. It had relevance only because it touched this present case. He said:

"It happened so long ago. Is a secret like that worth killing to preserve? Who really cares now? Isn't the official policy to forgive and forget?"

"We English are good at forgiving our enemies; it releases us from the obligation of liking our friends. Take a look at this book, Masterson. What do you notice?"

Masterson let the pages fall apart, shook them gently, lifted the book to eye level and examined the binding. Then he replaced it on the table and pressed back the middle pages. There, embedded deep in the folds were a few grains of sand.

Dalgliesh said: "We've sent a sample to the lab for analysis, but the result isn't much in doubt. It's almost certainly from one of the fire buckets in Nightingale House."

"So that's where it was hidden until he, or she, could return it to the library. The same person hid the book and the tin of rose spray. It all hangs together very neatly, sir."

"A little too neatly, don't you think?" said Dalgliesh.

But Sergeant Masterson had remembered something else.

"That brochure, the one we found in Pearce's room! Wasn't it about the work of a Suffolk Refuge for Fascist War Victims? Suppose Pearce sent for it? Is this another example of making the punishment fit the crime?"

"I think so. We'll get in touch with the place in the morning and find out what, if anything, she promised them. And we'll talk again to Courtney-Briggs. He was in Nightingale House at about the time Fallon died. When we know who he came to see and why, we shall be close to solving this case. But all that must wait for tomorrow."

Masterson stifled a yawn. He said: "It's been tomorrow, sir, for nearly three hours."

II

If the night porter of the Falconer's Arms was surprised at the return of the two guests in the small hours of the morning, one obviously ill and with his head ostentatiously bandaged, he was trained not to show it. His inquiry whether there was anything he could get for the gentlemen was perfunctory; Masterson's reply barely civil. They climbed the three flights of stairs to their floor since the old-fashioned lift was erratic and noisy. Dalgliesh, obstinately determined not to betray his weakness to his Sergeant, made himself take each step without grasping the banister. He knew it to be a foolish vanity and by the time he had gained his room he was paying for it. He was so weak that he had to lean against the closed door for a minute before weaving his unsteady way over to the wash-basin. Grasping the taps for support, he retched painfully and ineffectually, his forehead resting on his forearms. Without lifting his head he twisted on the right-hand tap. There was a gush of ice-cold water. He swilled it over his face and gulped it down from cupped hands. Immediately he felt better.

He slept fitfully. It was difficult to rest his cocooned head comfortably on the pillows, and loss of blood seemed to have left his mind preternaturally active and lucid, militating against sleep. When he did doze it was only to dream. He was walking in the grounds of the hospital with Mavis Gearing. She was skipping girlishly between the trees, brandishing her garden shears and saying kittenishly:

"It's wonderful what you can find to make a show even in this dead time of the year."

It didn't strike him as incongruous that she was snipping full blown red roses from the dead branches, or that neither of them remarked on the body of Mary Taylor, white neck encircled by the hangman's noose, as she swung gently from one of the boughs.

Towards morning he slept more deeply. Even so, the harsh incessant ring of the telephone woke him to instant consciousness.

The illuminated dial of his travelling clock showed 5.49 a.m. He shifted his head with difficulty from the hollowed pillow and felt for the receiver. The voice was instantly recognizable. But then he knew that he could have distinguished it from any other woman's voice in the world.

"Mr. Dalgliesh? This is Mary Taylor. I'm sorry to disturb you but I thought you'd prefer me to ring. We have a fire here. Nothing dangerous; it's only in the grounds. It seems to have started in a disused gardener's hut about fifty yards from Nightingale House. The house itself isn't in any danger but the fire spread very quickly among the trees."

He was surprised how clearly he could think. His wound no longer ached. He felt literally light-headed and it was necessary to touch the rough gauze of the bandage to reassure himself that it was still there. He said:

"Morag Smith. Is she all right? She used that hut as a kind of refuge."

"I know. She told me so this evening after she'd brought you in. I gave her a bed here for the night. Morag is safe. That was the first thing I checked."

"And the others in Nightingale House?"

There was a silence. Then she spoke, her voice sharper.

"I'll check now. It never occurred to me. . . ."

"Of course not. Why should it? I'll come over."

"Is that necessary? Mr. Courtney-Briggs was insistent that you should rest. The fire brigade have things under control. At first they were afraid that Nightingale House was threatened but they've axed some of the nearer trees. The blaze should be out in half an hour. Couldn't you wait till morning?"

"I'm coming over now," he said.

Masterson was lying flat on his back, drugged with tiredness, his heavy face vacant with sleep, his mouth half-open. It took nearly a minute to rouse him. Dalgliesh would have preferred to leave him there in his stupor, but he knew that, in his present weakened state, it wouldn't be safe for him to drive. Masterson, shaken at last into wakefulness, listened to his Superintendent's instructions without comment, then pulled on his clothes in resentful silence.

He was too prudent to question Dalgliesh's decision to return to Nightingale House, but it was obvious by his sullen manner that he thought the excursion unnecessary, and the short drive to the hospital was spent in silence.

The fire was visible as a red glow on the night sky long before they came in sight of the hospital, and as they drove through the open Winchester Road gate they could hear the staccato crackle of burning trees and could smell the rich evocative scent of smouldering wood, strong and sweet on the cold air. It broke Masterson's mood of sullen resentment. He breathed it in with noisy enjoyment and said in happy candour:

"I like that smell, sir. It reminds me of boyhood, I suppose. Summer camps with the Boy Scouts. Huddled in a blanket around the camp fire with the sparks soaring off into the night. Bloody marvellous when you're thirteen and being patrol leader is more power and glory than you're ever likely to feel again. You know, sir."

Dalgliesh didn't know. His solitary and lonely boyhood had been devoid of these tribal delights. But it was an interesting and curiously touching glimpse into Masterson's character. Patrol leader in the Boy Scouts! Well, why not? Given a different heritage, a different twist of fate and he could have easily been a leader in a street gang, his essential ambition and ruthlessness channelled into less conformist paths.

Masterson drove the car under the trees at a safe distance and they walked towards the blaze. As if by unspoken consent, they halted and stood together in the shadow of the trees watching in silence. No one appeared to notice them and no one approached. The firemen were getting on with their job. There was only one appliance and they were apparently running the hose from Nightingale House. The fire was by now well under control but it was still spectacular. The shed had gone completely with nothing but a ring of black earth to show where it had once stood, and the surrounding trees were blackened gibbets, stunted and twisted as if with the agony of their burning. On the periphery a few saplings still burned fiercely, crackling and spluttering in the jets from the fire hose. A single flame, writhing and twisting in the stiff breeze, leapt from tree top to tree top and burned there with the clear incandescent light of a candle before it was scotched by one unerring jet from the hose. As they watched a tall conifer burst into instantaneous fire and exploded in a shower of golden needles. There was a soft gasp of appreciation, and Dalgliesh saw that a little group of black-cloaked students who had been watching at a distance had crept imperceptibly forward into the light of the fire. It shone momentarily on their faces and he thought he recognized Madeleine Goodale and Julia Pardoe. Then he saw the tall unmistakable figure of Matron move across to them. She spoke a few words and the little group turned and reluctantly melted into the trees. It was then that she saw Dalgliesh. For a moment she stood absolutely still. Wrapped in her long black cloak, the hood thrown back, she stood against a single sapling like a victim at the stake, the fire glow dancing behind her and the light flaming her pale skin. Then she walked slowly across to him. He saw then that her face was very white. She said:

"You were right. She wasn't in her room. She's left me a letter."

Dalgliesh didn't reply. His mind was so clear that it seemed to be operating outside his own volition, not so much ranging over all the clues of the crime, but seeing it as if from a great height; a landscape without shadows spread out beneath him, comprehensible, familiar, unambiguous. He knew it all now. Not just how the two girls had been murdered; not just when and why; not just by whom. He knew the essential truth of the whole crime, for it was one crime. He might never be able to prove it; but he knew.

Half an hour later the fire was out. The spent hoses crept and thudded on the blackened earth as they were wound in, sending up little spurts of acrid smoke. The last of the onlookers had melted away and the cacophony of fire and wind was replaced by a gentle background hiss broken only by the orders of the fire officer and the blurred voices of his men. Even the wind had died a little and its touch on Dalgliesh's face was gentle and warm as it passed over the steaming earth. Everywhere there hung the reek of charred wood. The headlights of the fire engine were turned on the smoking circle where the hut had stood. Dalgliesh walked over to it, Masterson on his left, Mary Taylor on his right. The heat struck uncomfortably through the soles of his shoes. There was little to be seen; a grotesquely twisted piece of metal which might once have been part of a stove; the charred shape of a metal teapot—one kick would disintegrate it beyond recognition. And there was something else, a shape, nothing more, which even in death's extreme desecration, was still horribly human. They stood looking down in silence. It took them a few minutes to identify the few details; the pelvic girdle ridiculously small when denuded of its animate wrapping of muscle and flesh; the skull upturned and innocent as a chalice; the stain where the brain had burst away.

Dalgliesh said: "Get a screen around this place and see that it's kept guarded, then ring Sir Miles Honeyman."

Masterson said: "There's a pretty problem of identification for him here, sir."

"Yes," replied Dalgliesh, "if we didn't know already who it was."

III

They went by tacit consent and without exchanging a word through the quiet house to the Matron's flat. No one followed them. As they entered the sitting-room the carriage clock on the mantelpiece struck half past six. It was still very dark and in contrast to the fire-warmed air of the grounds the room was bitterly cold. The curtains had been drawn back and the casement window left open. Matron went quickly across to close it, drew the curtains together with a swift defensive sweep of her arms and turned to look at Dalgliesh steadily and compassionately, as if seeing him for the first time.

"You look desperately tired and cold. Come over to the fire and sit down."

He walked over and leaned against the fireplace, fearing that if he once sat down he might never be able to get up again. But the mantelpiece felt unstable, the marble slippery as ice. He let himself down into the armchair and watched while she knelt on the hearth rug and added the dry sticks of kindling to the still warm ashes of the previous evening's fire. The sticks blazed into life. She added a few nuggets of coal, holding out her hands to the blaze. Then without getting up she reached into the pocket of her cloak and handed him a letter.

A pale blue envelope unsealed and addressed in a round, childish but firm hand "to whom it may concern". He took out the letter. Cheap, blue paper, perfectly ordinary, unruled, but with the lines of writing so straight that she must have used the ruled sheet as a guide.

"I killed Heather Pearce and Josephine Fallon. They had discovered something about my past, something which was no concern of theirs, and were threatening to blackmail me. When Sister Gearing rang to tell me Fallon had been taken ill and was warded I knew that Nurse Pearce would act the patient in her place. I collected the bottle of disinfectant very early that morning and filled one of the empty milk bottles from the Sisters' utility room. I replaced the cap carefully and took the bottle with me to breakfast in my tapestry bag. All I had to do was to slip into the demonstration room after I had finished breakfast and substitute the bottle of poison for the bottle of milk on the trolley. If anyone had been in the room I should have made an excuse and tried another time and in another way. But the room was empty. I took the bottle of milk upstairs to the Sisters' utility room and threw the empty bottle of disinfectant out of one of the bathroom windows.

"I was in the conservatory when Sister Gearing produced her tin of nicotine rose spray and I thought of it when it came to killing Fallon. I knew where the key to the conservatory was kept and I wore surgical gloves so that there would be no finger-prints. It was an easy matter to pour the poison into Fallon's beaker of lemon and whisky while she was in the bathroom and the drink was cooling on her bedside table. Her nightly routine never varied. I intended to keep the tin, then place it on her bedside table later that night so that it would look as if she had killed herself. I knew it would be important to impress her finger-prints on the tin but that wouldn't be difficult. I had to change my plan because Mr. Courtney-Briggs telephoned shortly before twelve to call me back to my ward. I couldn't keep the tin in my possession since it wouldn't be possible to have my bag always with me on the ward and I didn't think it would be safe to leave it in my room. So I hid it in the sand bucket opposite Nurse Fallon's room with the intention of retrieving it and placing it on her bedside table when I returned to Nightingale House. That plan, too, proved impossible. As I got to the top of the stairs the Burt twins came out of their rooms. There was a light shining through Nurse Fallon's keyhole and they said they would take her some cocoa. I expected the body to be discovered that night. There was nothing I could do but to go upstairs to bed. I lay there waiting, expecting every minute to hear the alarm raised. I wondered if the twins had changed their plan and if Fallon had fallen asleep before drinking her whisky and lemon. But I didn't dare to go down and see. If I had been able to place the tin of nicotine by Fallon's bed no one would ever have suspected that she was murdered and I should have committed two perfect crimes.

"There is nothing else to say except that no one knew what I intended to do and no one helped me.

Ethel Brumfett."

Mary Taylor said: "It's her handwriting, of course. I found it on her mantelshelf when I came back after I had telephoned you to check that everyone was safe. But is it true?"

"Oh yes, it's true. She killed both of them. Only the murderess could have known where the tin of nicotine was hidden. It was obvious that the second death was meant to look like suicide. Why then wasn't the tin left on the bedside table? It could only have been because the killer was interrupted in her plan. Sister Brumfett was the one person in Nightingale House who was called out that night and who was prevented on her return from going into Fallon's room. But she was always the first suspect. The bottle of poison must have been prepared at leisure and by someone who had access to milk bottles and to the disinfectant and who could carry the lethal bottle about with her undetected. Sister Brumfett went nowhere without that large tapestry bag. It was bad luck for her that she happened to choose a bottle with the wrong coloured cap. I wonder if she even noticed. Even if she did, there wouldn't be time to change it. The whole plan depended on a substitution which would take merely a second. She would have to hope that no one noticed. And, in fact, no one did. And there is one way in which she was unique among the suspects. She was the only one who wasn't present to witness either of the deaths. She couldn't lift a hand against Fallon while the girl was her patient. That would have been impossible for her. And she preferred to watch neither murder. It takes a psychopathic killer or a professional willingly to watch their victim die."

She said: "We know that Heather Pearce was a potential blackmailer. I wonder what pathetic incident from poor Brumfett's dreary past she'd raked up for her entertainment?"

"I think you know that, just as I know. Heather Pearce had found out about Felsenheim."

She seemed to freeze into silence. She was curled on the edge of the armchair at his feet, her face turned away from him. After a moment she turned and looked at him.

"She wasn't guilty, you know. Brumfett was conforming, authoritarian, trained to think of unquestioning obedience as a nurse's first duty. But she didn't kill her patients. The verdict of that court at Felsenheim was just. And even if it wasn't, it was the verdict of a properly constituted court of law. She is officially innocent."

Dalgliesh said: "I'm not here to question the verdict at Felsenheim."

As if he had not spoken she went on eagerly, as if willing him to believe.

"She told me about it when we were both students together at Nethercastle General Infirmary. She lived in Germany most of her childhood but her grandmother was English. After the trial she naturally went free and eventually in 1944 married an English sergeant, Ernest Brumfett. She had money and it was a marriage of convenience only, a way of getting out of Germany and into England. Her grandmother was dead by now but she still had some ties with this country. She went to Nethercastle as ward orderly and was so efficient that, after eighteen months, there was no difficulty in getting the Matron to take her on as a student. It was a clever choice of hospital. They weren't likely to delve too carefully into anyone's past, particularly into the past of a woman who had proved her worth. The hospital is a large Victorian building, always busy, chronically understaffed. Brumfett and I finished our training together, went together to the local maternity hospital to train as midwives, came south together to the John Carpendar. I've known Ethel Brumfett for nearly twenty years. I've watched her pay over and over again for anything that happened at the Steinhoff Institution. She was a girl then. We can't know what happened to her during those childhood years in Germany. We can only know what the grown woman did for this hospital and for her patients. The past has no relevance."

Dalgliesh said: "Until the thing which she must always have subconsciously dreaded happened at last. Until someone from that past recognized her."

She said: "Then all the years of work and striving would come to nothing. I can understand that she felt it necessary to kill Pearce. But why Fallon?"

"For four reasons. Nurse Pearce wanted some proof of Martin Dettinger's story before she spoke to Sister Brumfett. The obvious way to get it seemed to be to consult a record of the trial. So she asked Fallon to lend her a library ticket. She went up to the Westminster library on the Thursday and again on the Saturday when the book was produced. She must have shown it to Sister Brumfett when she spoke to her, must have mentioned where she got the ticket. Sooner or later Fallon would want that ticket back. It was essential that no one ever found out why Nurse Pearce had wanted it or the name of the book she had borrowed from the library. That was one of several significant facts which Sister Brumfett chose to omit from her confession. After she had substituted the bottle of poison for the one of milk, she came upstairs, took the library book from Nurse Pearce's room, and hid it in one of the fire buckets until she had an opportunity to return it anonymously to the library. She knew only too well that Pearce would never come out of that demonstration room alive. It was typical of her to choose the same hiding place later for the tin of nicotine. Sister Brumfett wasn't an imaginative woman.

"But the problem of the library book wasn't the main reason for killing Nurse Fallon. There were three others. She wanted to confuse the motives, to make it look as if Fallon were the intended victim. If Fallon died there would always be the probability that

Pearce had been killed by mistake. It was Fallon who was listed to act as patient on the morning of the inspection. Fallon was a more likely victim. She was pregnant; that alone might provide a motive. Sister Brumfett had nursed her and could have known or guessed about the pregnancy. I don't think there were many signs or symptoms that Sister Brumfett missed in her patients. Then there was the possibility that Fallon would be held responsible for Pearce's death. After all, she had admitted returning to Nightingale House on the morning of the murder and had refused to give any explanation. She could have put the poison in the drip. Then afterwards, tormented by remorse perhaps, she killed herself. That explanation would dispose very neatly of both mysteries. It's an attractive theory from the hospital's point of view and quite a number of people preferred to believe it."

"And the last reason? You said there were four. She wanted to avoid inquiries about the library ticket; she wanted to suggest that Fallon had been the intended victim; alternatively she wanted to implicate Fallon in Pearce's death. What was the fourth motive?"

"She wanted to protect you. She always wanted that. It wasn't easy with the first murder. You were in Nightingale House; you had as much opportunity as anyone to interfere with the drip feed. But at least she could ensure that you had an alibi for the time of Fallon's death. You were safely in Amsterdam. You couldn't possibly have killed the second victim. Why, therefore, should you have killed the first? From the beginning of this investigation I decided that the two murders were connected. It was too much of a coincidence to postulate two killers in the same house at the same time. And that automatically excluded you from the list of suspects."

"But why should anyone suspect me of killing either girl?"

"Because the motive we've imputed to Ethel Brumfett doesn't make sense. Think about it. A dying man came momentarily out of unconsciousness and saw a face bending over him. He opened his eyes and through his pain and delirium he recognized a woman. Sister Brumfett? Would you recognize Ethel Brumfett's face after twenty-five years? Plain, ordinary, inconspicuous Brumfett? There's only one woman in a million who has a face so beautiful and so individual that it can be recognized even in a fleeting glance across twenty-five years of memory. Your face. It was you and not Sister Brumfett who was Irmgard Grobel."

She said quietly: "Irmgard Grobel is dead."

He went on as if she had not spoken.

"It's not surprising that Nurse Pearce never suspected for one moment that Grobel could be you. You're the Matron, protected by a quasi-religious awe from the taint of human weakness, let alone human sin. It must have been psychologically impossible for her to think of you as a killer. And then, there were the words used by Martin Dettinger. He said it was one of the Sisters. I think I know how he made that mistake. You visit every ward in the hospital once a day, speak to nearly all the patients. The face he saw bending over him was not only clearly the face of Irmgard Grobel. He saw a woman wearing what to him was a Sister's uniform, the short cape and wide triangular cap of the army nursing service. To his drug-muddled mind that uniform meant a Sister. It still means a Sister to anyone who has been nursed in an army hospital, and he had spent months in them."

She said again quietly: "Irmgard Grobel is dead."

"So he told Nurse Pearce much the same as he told his own mother. Mrs. Dettinger wasn't particularly interested. Why should she be? And then she received a hospital account and thought that there might be a way of saving herself a few pounds. If Mr. Courtney-Briggs hadn't been greedy I doubt whether she would have taken it any further. But she did, and Courtney-Briggs was given an intriguing piece of information which he thought it worth taking some time and trouble to verify. We can guess what Heather Pearce thought. She must have experienced much the same triumph and sense of power as when she saw Nurse Dakers stooping to pick up those pound notes fluttering on the path in front of her. Only this time someone a great deal more important and interesting than a fellow student would be in her power. It never occurred to her that the patient could be referring to a woman other than the Sister nursing him. But she knew she had to get proof, or at least assure herself that Dettinger, who after all was a dying man, wasn't deluded or hallucinated. So she spent her half-day on Thursday visiting the Westminster library and asked them for a book about the Felsenheim trial. They had to borrow it for her from another branch and she returned for it on Saturday. I think she learned enough from that book to convince herself that Martin Dettinger knew what he was talking about. I think that she spoke to Sister Brumfett on the Saturday night and that the Sister didn't deny the charge. I wonder what price Pearce was asking? Nothing as commonplace or understandable or as reprehensible as direct payment for her silence. Pearce liked to exercise power; but even more she enjoyed indulging in moral rectitude. It must have been on Sunday morning that she wrote to the Secretary of the League for the Assistance of Fascist Victims. Sister Brumfett would be made to pay, but the money would go in regular instalments to the League. Pearce was a great one for making the punishment fit the crime."

This time she was silent, sitting there with her hands folded gently in her lap and looking expressionless into some unfathomable past. He said gently:

"It can all be checked, you know. We haven't much of her body left but we don't need it while we have your face. There will be records of the trial, photographs, the record of your marriage to a Sergeant Taylor.

She spoke so quietly that he had to bend his head to hear:

"He opened his eyes very wide and looked at me. He didn't speak. There was a wildness, a desperation about that look. I thought that he was becoming delirious, or perhaps that he was afraid. I think he knew in that moment that he was going to die. I spoke to him a little and then his eyes closed. I didn't recognize him. Why should I?

"I'm not the same person as that child in Steinhoff. I don't mean I think of Steinhoff as if it happened to someone else. It did happen to someone else. I can't even remember now what exactly happened in that court at Felsenheim; I can't recall a single face."

But she had had to tell someone. That must have been part of becoming another person, of putting Steinhoff out of her thoughts. So she had told Ethel Brumfett. They had both been young student nurses at Nethercastle and Dalgliesh supposed that Brumfett represented something to her: kindness, reliability, devotion. Otherwise, why Brumfett? Why on earth choose her as a confidante? He must have been speaking his words aloud because she said eagerly as if it were important to make him understand:

"I told her because she was so ordinary. There was a security about her ordinariness. I felt that, if Brumfett could listen and believe me and still like me, then nothing that had happened was so very terrible after all. You wouldn't understand that."

But he did understand. There had been a boy in his prep. school like that, so ordinary, so safe, that he was a kind of talisman against death and disaster. Dalgliesh remembered the boy. Funny, but he hadn't thought of him now for over thirty years. Sproat Minor with his round, pleasant, spectacled face, his ordinary conventional family, his unremarkable background, his blessed normality. Sproat Minor, protected by mediocrity and insensitivity from the terrors of the world. Life could not be wholly frightening while it held a Sproat Minor. Dalgliesh wondered briefly where he was now.

He said: "And Brumfett had stuck to you ever since. When you came here she followed. That impulse to confide, the need to have at least one friend who knew all about you, put you in her power. Brumfett, the protector, adviser, confidante. Theatres with Brumfett; morning golf with Brumfett; holidays with Brumfett; country drives with Brumfett; early morning tea and last night drinks with Brumfett. Her devotion must have been real enough. After all, she was willing to kill for you. But it was blackmail all the same. A more orthodox blackmailer, merely demanding a regular tax-free income, would have been infinitely preferable to Brumfett's intolerable devotion."

She said sadly: "It's true. It's all true. How can you possibly know?"

"Because she was essentially a stupid and dull woman and you are not."

He could have added: "Because I know myself."

She cried out in vehement protest.

"And who am I to despise stupidity and dullness? What right had I to be so particular? Oh, she wasn't clever! She couldn't even kill for me without making a mess of it. She wasn't clever enough to deceive Adam Dalgliesh, but when is that to be the criteria for intelligence? Have you ever seen her doing her job? Seen her with a dying patient or a sick child? Have you ever watched this stupid and dull woman, whose devotion and company it is apparently proper for me to despise, working all night to save a life?"

"I've seen the body of one of her victims and read the autopsy report on the other. I'll take your word for her kindness to children."

"Those weren't her victims. They were mine."

"Oh no," he said. "There has only been one victim of yours in Nightingale House and she was Ethel Brumfett."

She rose to her feet in one swift movement and stood facing him, those astonishing green eyes, speculative and unwavering, gazed into his. Part of his mind knew that there were words he ought to speak. What were they, those over-familiar phrases of statutory warning, the professional spiel which came almost unbidden to the lips at the moment of confrontation? They had slipped away, a meaningless irrelevancy, into some limbo of his mind. He knew that he was a sick man, still weak from loss of blood, and that he ought to stop now, to hand over the investigation to Masterson, and get to his bed. He, the most punctilious of detectives, had already spoken as if none of the rules had been formulated, as if he were facing a private adversary. But he had to go on. Even if he could never prove it, he had to hear her admit what he knew to be the truth. As if it were the most natural question in the world he asked quietly:

"Was she dead when you put her into the fire?"

IV

It was at that moment that someone rang the doorbell of the flat. Without a word Mary Taylor swung her cape around her shoulders and went to open it. There was a brief murmur of voices; then Stephen Courtney-Briggs followed her into the sitting-room. Glancing at the clock, Dalgliesh saw that the hands stood at 7.24 a.m. The working day had almost begun.

Courtney-Briggs was already dressed. He showed no surprise at

Dalgliesh's presence and no particular concern at his obvious weakness. He spoke to them both impartially:

"I'm told there was a fire in the night. I didn't hear the engines."

Mary Taylor, her face so white that Dalgliesh thought she might faint, said calmly:

"They came in at the Winchester Road entrance and kept the bells silent so as not to wake the patients."

"And what's this rumour that they found a burnt body in the ashes of the garden shed? Whose body?"

Dalgliesh said: "Sister Brumfett's. She left a note confessing to the murders of Nurse Pearce and Nurse Fallon."

"Brumfett killed them! Brumfett!"

Courtney-Briggs looked at Dalgliesh belligerently, his large handsome features seeming to disintegrate into irritated disbelief.

"Did she say why? Was the woman mad?"

Mary Taylor said: "Brumfett wasn't mad and no doubt she believed that she had a motive."

"But what's going to happen to my ward today? I start operating at nine o'clock. You know that, Matron. And I've got a very long list. Both the staff nurses are off with flu. I can't trust dangerously sick patients to first and second-year students."

The Matron said calmly: "I'll see to it at once. Most of the day nurses should be up by now. It isn't going to be easy but, if necessary, we'll have to withdraw someone from the school."

She turned to Dalgliesh: "I prefer to do my telephoning from one of the Sisters' sitting-rooms. But don't worry. I realize the importance of our conversation. I shall be back to complete it."

Both men looked after her as she went out of the door and closed it quietly behind her. For the first time Courtney-Briggs seemed to notice Dalgliesh. He said brusquely:

"Don't forget to go over to the radiography department and get that head X-rayed. You've no right to be out of bed. I'll examine you as soon as I've finished my list this morning." He made it sound like a tedious chore which he might find time to attend to.

Dalgliesh asked: "Who did you come to visit in Nightingale House the night Josephine Fallon was murdered?"

"I told you. No one. I never entered Nightingale House."

"There are at least ten minutes unaccounted for, ten minutes when the back door leading to the Matron's flat was unlocked. Sister Gearing had let her friend out that way and was walking with him in the grounds. So you thought that the Matron must be in despite the absence of lights and made your way up the stairs to her flat. You must have spent some time there. Why, I wonder? Curiosity? Or were you searching for something?"

"Why should I visit the Matron? She wasn't there. Mary Taylor was in Amsterdam that night."

"But you didn't know that at the time, did you? Miss Taylor wasn't accustomed to attending International Conferences. For reasons we can guess she didn't want her face to be too widely known. This reluctance to undertake public duties was thought becomingly modest in a woman so able and so intelligent. She was only asked late on Tuesday to go to Amsterdam to deputize for the Chairman of the Area Nurse Training Committee. Your sessions are on Mondays, Thursdays and Fridays. Then, on Wednesday night, you were called to operate on a private patient. I don't suppose that the operating-theatre staff, busy with an emergency, thought to mention that the Matron wasn't in the hospital. Why should they?" He paused.

Courtney-Briggs said: "And why am I supposed to have planned to visit the Matron at midnight? You're not supposing that I would have been a welcome visitor? You're not suggesting that she was expecting me?"

"You came to see Irmgard Grobel."

There was a moment's silence. Then Courtney-Briggs said:

"How do you know about Irmgard Grobel?"

"From the same person who told you, Mrs. Dettinger."

Another silence. Then he said with the obstinate finality of a man who knows he won't be believed:

"Irmgard Grobel is dead."

"Is she?" asked Dalgliesh. "Didn't you expect to find her in the Matron's flat? Wasn't this your first opportunity to confront her with what you knew? And you must have been looking forward to it. The exercise of power is always pleasurable, isn't it?"

Courtney-Briggs said calmly: "You should know that."

They stood looking at each other in silence. Dalgliesh asked: "What had you in mind?"

"Nothing. I didn't connect Grobel with the deaths of Pearce or Fallon. Even if I had, I doubt whether I should have spoken. This hospital needs Mary Taylor. As far as I'm concerned Irmgard Grobel doesn't exist. She was tried once and found not guilty. That was good enough for me. I'm a surgeon, not a moral theologian. I should have kept her secret."

Of course he would, thought Dalgliesh. Its value would be lost to him once the truth were known. This was very special, very important information, gained at some cost, and he would use it in his own way. It put Mary Taylor for ever in his power. The Matron who so frequently and irritatingly opposed him; whose power was increasing; who was about to be appointed Director of Nursing Services over all the hospitals in the Group; who influenced the Chairman of the Hospital Management Committee against him. Sir Marcus Cohen. How much influence would she retain with that dedicated Jew once he learned about the Steinhoff Institution? It had become fashionable to forget these things. But would Sir Marcus Cohen forgive?

He thought of Mary Taylor's words. There are more ways than one of blackmail. Heather Pearce and Ethel Brumfett both knew that. And perhaps the most subtly pleasurable was the blackmail which made no financial demands but enjoyed its secret knowledge under the cloak of generosity, kindness, complicity or moral superiority. Sister Brumfett hadn't asked much after all, only a room next to her idol; the prestige of being known as the Matron's friend; a companion for her off-duty hours. Poor stupid Pearce had asked only a few shillings a week and a verse or two of scripture. But how they must have relished their power. And how infinitely more gratifying would Courtney-Briggs have found his. No wonder that he had been determined to keep the secret to himself, that he hadn't welcomed the thought of the Yard descending on Nightingale House.

Dalgliesh said: "We can prove that you flew to Germany last Friday night. And I think I can guess why. It was a quicker and surer way of getting the information you wanted than pestering the Judge Advocate's Department. You probably consulted the newspaper files and the record of the trial. That's what I would have done. And, no doubt, you have useful contacts. But we can find out where you went and what you did. You can't slip in and out of the country anonymously, you know."

Courtney-Briggs said: "I admit that I knew. I admit, too, that I came to Nightingale House to see Mary Taylor on the night Fallon died. But I've done nothing illegal, nothing which could put me in jeopardy."

"I can believe that."

"Even if I'd spoken earlier I should have been too late to save Pearce. She was dead before Mrs. Dettinger came to see me. I've nothing with which to reproach myself."

He was beginning to defend himself clumsily like a schoolboy. Then they heard the soft footfall and looked round. Mary Taylor had returned. She spoke directly to the surgeon.

"I can let you have the Burt twins. I'm afraid it means the end of this block but there's no choice. They'll have to be recalled to the wards."

Courtney-Briggs said grudgingly: "They'll do. They're sensible girls. But what about a Sister?"

"I thought that Sister Rolfe might take over temporarily. But I'm afraid that's impossible. She's leaving the John Carpendar."

"Leaving! But she can't do that!"

"I don't see how I can prevent her. But I don't think I shall be given the opportunity to try."

"But why is she leaving? What's happened?"

"She won't say. I think something about the police investigation has upset her."

Courtney-Briggs swung round at Dalgliesh.

"You see! Dalgliesh, I realize that you're only doing your job, that you were sent here to clear up these girls' deaths. But, for God's sake, doesn't it ever occur to you that your interference makes things a bloody sight worse?"

"Yes," said Dalgliesh. "And in your job? Does it ever occur to you?"

V

She went with Courtney-Briggs to the front door. They didn't linger. She was back in less than a minute, and walking briskly over to the fire, she slipped her cloak from her shoulders and laid it tidily over the back of the sofa. Then, kneeling, she took up a pair of brass tongs and began to build up the fire, coal carefully disposed on coal, each licking flame fed with its gleaming nugget. Without looking up at Dalgliesh, she said:

"We were interrupted in our conversation, Superintendent. You were accusing me of murder. I have faced that charge once before, but at least the court at Felsenheim produced some evidence. What evidence have you?"

"None."

"Nor will you ever find any."

She spoke without anger or complacency but with an intensity, a quiet finality that had nothing to do with innocence. Looking down at the gleaming head burnished by the firelight Dalgliesh said:

"But you haven't denied it. You haven't lied to me yet and I don't suppose you'll trouble to begin now. Why should she have killed herself in that way? She liked her comfort. Why be uncomfortable in death? Suicides seldom are unless they're too psychotic to care. She had access to plenty of pain-killing drugs. Why not use one of them? Why trouble to creep away to a cold dark garden shed to immolate herself in lonely agony? She wasn't even fortified by the gratifications of a public show."

"There are precedents."

"Not many in this country."

"Perhaps she was too psychotic to care."

"That will be said of course."

"She may have realized that it was important not to leave an identifiable body if she wanted to convince you that she was Grobel. Faced with a written confession and a heap of charred bones, why should you bother any further? There was no point in killing herself to protect me if you could confirm her real identity without trouble."

"A clever and far-sighted woman might argue like that. She was neither. But you are. It must have seemed just worth a try. And even if we never found out about Irmgard Grobel and Felsenheim, it had become important to get rid of Brumfett. As you've said, she couldn't even kill without making a mess of it. She had already panicked once when she tried to murder me. She might easily panic again. She had been an encumbrance for years; now she had become a dangerous liability. You hadn't asked her to kill for you. It wasn't even a reasonable way out of the difficulty. Pearce's threats could have been dealt with if Sister Brumfett had only kept her head and reported the matter to you. But she had to demonstrate her devotion in the most spectacular way she knew. She killed to protect you. And those two deaths bound you and she together indissolubly for life. How could you ever be free or secure while Brumfett lived?"

"Aren't you going to tell me how I did it?"

They might, Dalgliesh thought, be two colleagues talking over a case together. Even through his weakness he knew that this bizarre conversation was dangerously unorthodox, that the woman kneeling at his feet was an enemy, that the intelligence opposed to his was inviolate. She had no hope now of saving her reputation, but she was fighting for freedom, perhaps even for her life. He said:

"I can tell you how I would have done it. It wasn't difficult. Her bedroom was the one nearest the door of your flat. I suppose she asked for that room, and nothing Sister Brumfett wanted could be denied. Because she knew about the Steinhoff Institution? Because she had a hold over you? Or merely because she had lumbered you with the weight of her devotion and you hadn't the ruthlessness to break free? So she slept close to you.

"I don't know how she died. It could have been a tablet, an injection, something you administered on the pretence that it would help her to sleep. She had already, at your request, written the confession. I wonder how you persuaded her to do that? I don't suppose she thought for one moment that it was going to be used. It isn't addressed to me or to any particular person. I imagine you told her that there ought to be something in writing just in case anything happened to her or to you and it was necessary sometime in the future to have a record of what really happened, proof that would protect you. So she wrote that plain note, probably at your dictation. It has a directness and lucidity that has little, I imagine, to do with Sister Brumfett.

"And so she dies. You have only to carry her body two yards to gain the safety of your door. Even so, this is the most risky part of your plan. Suppose Sister Gearing or Sister Rolfe should appear? So you prop open Sister Brumfett's door and the door of your flat and listen carefully to make sure that the corridor is clear. Then you hoist the body over your shoulder and move swiftly into your flat. You lay the body on the bed and go back to shut her bedroom door and to shut and lock your own front door. She was a plump but short woman. You are tall and strong and have been trained to lift helpless patients. That part wasn't so difficult.

"But now you must move her to your car. It's convenient having access to your garage from the downstairs hall and a private stairway. With both the outside and inside doors of the flat locked you can work without fear of interruption. The body is hoisted into the back of your car and covered with a travelling rug. Then you drive out through the grounds and reverse the car under the trees, as close as possible to the garden shed. You keep the engine running. It is important to make a quick getaway, be back in your flat before the fire is seen. This part of the plan is a little risky but the Winchester Road path is seldom used after dark. The ghost of Nancy Gorringe sees to that. It would be inconvenient but not catastrophic if you were seen. After all, you are the Matron, there is nothing to prevent you taking a night drive. If anyone passes, you will have to drive on and choose another place or another time. But no one does pass. The car is deep under the trees; the lights are out. You carry the body to the shed. Then there is a second journey with the can of petrol. And after that there is nothing to do but souse the body and the surrounding furniture and piles of wood and throw in a lighted match from the open doorway.

"It takes only a moment to restart the car and to drive straight back through the garage doors. Once they are closed behind you, you are safe. Certainly you know that the fire will burn with such fierceness that it will be seen almost at once. But by then you are back in your own flat, ready to receive the telephone call which tells you that the fire engine is on its way, ready to ring me. And the suicide note which she left in your charge, perhaps never to be used, is ready to be handed over."

She asked quietly: "And how will you prove it?"

"Probably never. But I know that is how it happened."

She said: "But you will try to prove it, won't you? After all, failure would be intolerable for Adam Dalgliesh. You will try to prove it no matter what the cost to yourself or anyone else. And after all, there is a chance. There isn't much hope of finding tyre marks under the trees of course. The effects of the fire, the wheels of the fire engine, the trampling of the men, will have obliterated any clues on the ground. But then you will examine the inside of the car surely, particularly the rug. Don't neglect the car rug, Superintendent. There may be fibres from the clothes, even a few hairs, perhaps. But that wouldn't be surprising. Miss Brumfett often drove with me; the car rug actually belongs to her; it's probably covered with her hairs. But what about clues in my flat? If I carried her body down that narrow back staircase surely there will be marks on the walls where they were grazed by her shoes? Unless, of course, the woman who killed Brumfett had sufficient sense to remove her victim's shoes and carry them separately, perhaps slung by the laces around her neck. They couldn't be left in the flat. You might check on the number of pairs that Brumfett owned. After all, someone in Nightingale House could tell you. We have so little privacy from each other. And no woman would walk through the woods barefoot to her death.

"And the other clues in the flat? If I killed her, ought there not to be a syringe, a bottle of pills, something to indicate how I did it? But her medicine cupboard and mine both contain a supply of aspirin and sleeping tablets. Suppose I gave her those? Or simply stunned or suffocated her? Any method would be as good as another provided it didn't make a mess. How can you possibly prove how she died when all you have for the autopsy are a few charred bones? And there's the suicide note, a note in her own handwriting and containing facts which only the killer of Pearce and Fallon could have known. Whatever you may choose to believe, Superintendent, are you going to tell me that the Coroner won't be satisfied that Ethel Brumfett intended that note as a confession before burning herself to death?"

Dalgliesh knew that he could no longer stay upright. He was fighting sickness now as well as weakness. The hand which grasped the mantelshelf for support was colder than the marble and slippery with sweat, and the marble itself was soft and yielding as putty. His wound was beginning to throb painfully, and the dull headache which up to now had been little more than vague discomfort was sharpening and localizing into needles of pain behind his left eye. To drop in a faint at her feet would be unforgettably humiliating. He reached out his arm and found the back of the nearest chair. Then gently he lowered himself into it. Her voice seemed to be coming from a long way off, but at least he could hear the words and knew that his own voice was still steady.

She said: "Suppose I told you that I could manage Stephen Courtney-Briggs, that no one but the three of us need ever know about Felsenheim? Would you be willing to leave my past out of your report so that at least those girls need not have died entirely in vain? It is important for this hospital that I stay on as Matron. I'm not asking you for mercy. I'm not concerned for myself. You will never prove that I killed Ethel Brumfett. Aren't you going to make yourself look ridiculous if you try? Isn't the most courageous and sensible course to forget that this conversation ever took place, to accept Brumfett's confession for the truth which it is, and to close the case?"

He said: "That's not possible. Your past is part of the evidence. I can't suppress evidence or omit relevant facts from my report because I don't choose to like them. If I once did that I should have to give up my job. Not just this particular case, my job. And for always."

"And you couldn't do that, of course. What would a man like you be without his job, this particular job? Vulnerable like the rest of us. You might even have to begin living and feeling like a human being."

"You can't touch me like that. Why humiliate yourself trying? There are regulations, orders, and an oath. Without them no one could safely do police work. Without them Ethel Brumfett wouldn't be safe, you wouldn't be safe, an Irmgard Grobel wouldn't be safe."

"Is that why you won't help me?"

"Not altogether. I don't choose to."

She said sadly: "That's honest, anyway. And you haven't any doubts?"

"Of course I have. I'm not as arrogant as that. There are always doubts." And so there were. But they were intellectual and philosophical doubts, untormenting and uninsistent. It had been many years since they had kept him awake at night.

"But there are the regulations, aren't there? And the orders. An oath even. They're very convenient shields to shelter behind if the doubts become troublesome. I know. I sheltered behind them once myself. You and I are not so very different after all, Adam Dalgliesh."

She took up her cloak from the back of the chair and threw it around her shoulders. She came over and stood in front of him smiling. Then, seeing his weakness, she held out both her hands and grasping his, helped him to his feet. They stood there facing each other. Suddenly there was the ring of her front door and almost simultaneously the harsh insistent burr of the telephone. For both of them the day had begun.

Chapter Nine

Summer Epilogue

I

It was shortly after nine o'clock when the call came through to him, and Dalgliesh walked out of the Yard and across Victoria Street through an early morning haze, a sure harbinger of yet another hot August day. He found the address without difficulty. It was a large red brick building between Victoria Street and Horseferry Road, not particularly sordid but depressingly dull, a functional oblong with the front punctuated with meanly proportioned windows. There was no lift and he walked unchallenged up the three linoleum-covered flights of stairs to the top floor.

The landing smelt of sour sweat. Outside the flat a grossly fat middle-aged woman in a flowered apron was expostulating to the police constable on duty in an adenoidal whine. As Dalgliesh approached she turned on him, spieling forth a flood of protest and recrimination. What was Mr. Goldstein going to say? She wasn't really allowed to sub-let a room. She had only done it to oblige the lady. And now this. People had no consideration.

He passed her without speaking and went into the room. It was a square box, stuffy and smelling of furniture polish, and overfurnished with the heavy prestige symbols of an earlier decade. The window was open and the lace curtains drawn back but there was little air. The police surgeon and the attendant constable, both large men, seemed to have used all there was.

One corpse more to be viewed; only this one wasn't his responsibility. He need only glance, as if verifying a memory, at the stiffening body on the bed, noting with detached interest that the left arm hung loosely over the side, long fingers curled, and that the hypodermic syringe was still attached to the underarm, a metallic insect with its fang deep embedded in the soft flesh. Death hadn't robbed her of individuality, not yet anyway. That would come soon enough with all the grotesque indignities of decay.

The police surgeon, shirt-sleeved and sweating, was apologetic as if concerned that he might have done the wrong thing. As he turned from the bed Dalgliesh was aware that he was speaking:

"And as New Scotland Yard is so close and the second note was addressed personally to you" . . . he paused uncertainly.

"She injected herself with evipan. The first note is quite explicit. It's a clear case of suicide. That's why the constable didn't want to ring you. He thought it wasn't worth your trouble to come. There's really nothing here of interest."

Dalgliesh said: "I'm glad you did ring. And it isn't any trouble."

There were two white envelopes, one sealed and addressed to himself; the other unsealed and bearing the words, "To anyone whom it may concern." He wondered if she had smiled when she wrote that phrase. Watched by the police surgeon and the constable, Dalgliesh opened the letter. The writing was perfectly firm, black and spiky. He realized with a kind of shock that it was the first time he had seen her handwriting.

"They wouldn't believe you but you were right. I killed Ethel Brumfett. It was the first time I had ever killed; it seems important that you should know that. I injected her with evipan, just as I shall shortly do myself. She thought I was giving her a sedative. Poor trusting Brumfett! She would have easily taken nicotine from my hand and it would have been as appropriate.

"I thought it might be possible for me to make some kind of a useful life. It hasn't been, and I haven't the temperament to live with failure. I don't regret what I did. It was best for the hospital, best for her, best for me. I wasn't likely to be deterred because Adam Dalgliesh sees his job as the embodiment of the moral law."

She was wrong, he thought. They hadn't disbelieved him, they had just demanded, reasonably enough, that he find some proof. He had found none, either at the time or later, although he had pursued the case as if it were a personal vendetta, hating himself and her. And she had admitted nothing; not for one moment had she been in any danger of panicking.

There had been very little left unexplained at the resumed inquest on Heather Pearce and the inquest on Josephine Fallon and Ethel Brumfett. Perhaps the Coroner felt that there had been enough rumours and speculation. He had sat with a jury and had made no attempt to inhibit their questions to witnesses, or even to control the proceedings. The story of Irmgard Grobel and the Steinhoff Institution had come out, and Sir Marcus Cohen had sat with Dalgliesh at the back of the Court and listened with a face rigid with pain. After the inquest Mary Taylor walked across the room to him, handed him her letter of resignation, and turned away without a word. She had left the hospital the same day. And that, for the John Carpendar, had been the end. Nothing else had come out. Mary Taylor had gone free; free to find this room, this death.

Dalgliesh walked over to the fireplace. The small grate, tiled in bilious green, was filled with a dusty fan and a jam jar of dried leaves. Carefully he moved them out of the way. He was aware of the police surgeon and the uniformed constable watching him expressionlessly. What did they think he was doing? Destroying evidence? Why should they worry? They had their piece of paper ready to be docketed, produced as evidence, filed away for oblivion. This concerned only him.

He shook the note open in the chimney recess and, striking a match, set light to one of the corners. But there was little draught and the paper was tough. He had to hold it, shaking it gently, until the tips of his fingers scorched before the blackened sheet drifted from his grasp, disappeared into the darkness of the chimney recess and was wafted upwards towards the summer sky.

II

Ten minutes later on the same day Miss Beale drove through the front entrance gate of the John Carpendar Hospital and drew up at the porter's lodge. She was greeted by an unfamiliar face, a new youngish porter, shirt-sleeved in his summer uniform.

"The General Nursing Council Inspector? Good morning, miss. I'm afraid this entrance isn't very convenient for the new school of nursing. It's just a temporary building at present, miss, built on a cleared part of the grounds where we had the fire. It's quite close to where the old school was. If you just take this first turn. . . ."

"It's all right, thank you," said Miss Beale. "I know the way."

There was an ambulance standing at the entrance to the Casualty Department. As Miss Beale drove slowly past, Nurse Dakers, wearing the lace-trimmed cap and blue belt of a staff nurse, came out of the hospital, conferred briefly with the attendants, and stood supervising the transfer of the patient. She seemed to Miss Beale's eyes to have grown in stature and authority. There was no trace of the terrified student nurse about this confident figure. So Nurse Dakers had qualified. Well, that was to be expected. Presumably the Burt twins, equally elevated, were working somewhere in the hospital. But there had been changes. Nurse Goodale had married; Miss Beale had seen the notice in the national Press. And Hilda Rolfe, so Angela reported, was nursing somewhere in Central Africa. There would be a new Principal Tutor to meet this morning. And a new Matron. Miss Beale wondered briefly about Mary Taylor. She would be earning a good living somewhere if not in nursing. The Mary Taylors of the world were natural survivors.

She drove down the familiar path between the parched summer lawns, the flower beds blotched with overblown roses, and turned into the green tunnel of the trees. The air was still and warm, the narrow road chequered with the first bright sunlight of the day. And here was the last remembered corner. Nightingale House, or what was left of it, was before her.

Once again she stopped the car and gazed. The house looked as if it had been clumsily cut in two by a giant's cleaver, a living thing wantonly mutilated, with its shame and its nakedness exposed to every gaze. A staircase, bereft of its banister and brutally hacked, reeled into nothingness; on the second landing a delicate light filament hung by a thread of flex against the cracked panelling; downstairs the front arched windows, empty of glass, were an elegant arcade of carved stone giving a view of faded wallpaper with lighter patches where pictures and mirrors had once hung. From the remaining ceilings, naked wires sprouted like the bristles of a brush. Propped against a tree at the front of the house was a motley collection of fireplaces, mantelshelves, and sections of carved panelling, obviously selected for preservation. On top of what remained of the rear wall, a figure silhouetted against the sky was picking in a desultory way at the loose bricks. They tumbled one by one into the rubble of the interior of the house, sending up small spurts of dust.

In front of the building another workman, naked to the waist and burnt bronze, was operating a tractor mounted with a crane from which hung an immense iron ball and chain. As Miss Beale watched, hands taut on the steering-wheel as if bracing herself against an instinctive recoil of protest, the ball swung forward and crashed against all that remained of the front wall. For a moment there was nothing but the reverberation of hideous noise. Then the wall buckled gently and collapsed inwards with a roar of cascading bricks and mortar, sending up a monstrous cloud of yellow dust through which the lonely figure on the skyline could be seen dimly like some supervising demon.

Miss Beale paused for a moment, then gently let in the clutch and steered the car to the right to where the low, functional, clean-looking lines of the new temporary school could be glimpsed between the trees. Here was normality, sanity, a world she recognized and knew. This emotion, suspiciously like regret, at witnessing the violent destruction of Nightingale House was really too ridiculous. She fought against it resolutely. It was a horrible house; an evil house. It should have been pulled down fifty years ago. And it had never been in the least suitable as a nurse training school.